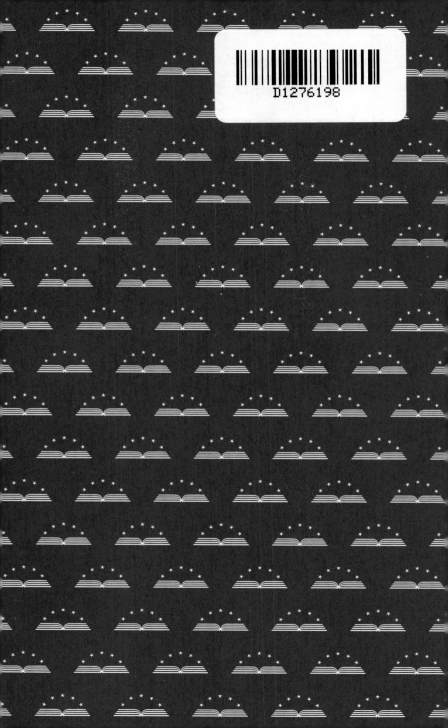

THORNTON WILDER

THORNTON WILDER

THE EIGHTH DAY
THEOPHILUS NORTH
AUTOBIOGRAPHICAL WRITINGS

J. D. McClatchy, *editor*

THE LIBRARY OF AMERICA

Contents

THE EIGHTH DAY

For Isabel Wilder

Contents

Prologue

IN THE early summer of 1902 John Barrington Ashley of Coaltown, a small mining center in southern Illinois, was tried for the murder of Breckenridge Lansing, also of Coaltown. He was found guilty and sentenced to death. Five days later, at one in the morning of Tuesday, July 22, he escaped from his guards on the train that was carrying him to his execution.

That was the "Ashley Case" that aroused considerable interest, indignation, and derision throughout the Middle West. No one doubted that Ashley shot Lansing, willfully or accidentally; but the trial was felt to have been bungled by a senile judge, an inept defense, and a prejudiced jury—the "Coalhole Case," the "Coalbin Case." When, to top it all, the convicted murderer escaped from a guard of five men and vanished into thin air—handcuffed, in prison garb, and with shaved head—the very State of Illinois was held up to ridicule. About five years later, the State's Attorney's office in Springfield announced that fresh evidence had been uncovered fully establishing Ashley's innocence.

So: there had been a miscarriage of justice in an unimportant case in a small Middlewestern town.

Ashley shot Lansing in the back of the head while the two men were engaged in their customary Sunday afternoon rifle practice on the lawn behind the Lansing house. Even the defense did not claim that the tragedy was the result of a mechanical accident. The rifle was repeatedly fired for the benefit of the jurors and was found to be in excellent condition. Ashley was known to have been a superior marksman. The victim was five yards to the front and left of Ashley. It was a little surprising that the bullet entered Lansing's skull above his left ear, but it was assumed that he had turned his head to catch the sounds issuing from a young people's picnic in the Memorial Park across the hedge. Ashley never wavered in his assurance that he was innocent in both intention and deed, laughable though the assertion was. The only witnesses were the wives of the accused and the victim. They were sitting under the butternut trees nearby making lemonade. Both testified that only one

5

shot had been fired. The trial was unduly prolonged because of illness among members of the court, and even death among the jurors and their alternates. Reporters called attention to the delay occasioned by laughter, for a demon of contrariety hovered over the hall. There were frequent slips of the tongue. Witness followed witness in a confusion of names. Judge Crittenden's gavel broke. A St. Louis reporter called it the "Hyena Trial."

It was the failure to establish a motive for the crime that aroused wide indignation. The prosecution advanced too many motives and no one of them convincing. Coaltown, however, was convinced that it knew why Ashley had killed Lansing and most of the members of the court were from Coaltown. Everyone knew it and no one mentioned it. Coaltown folk of the better sort do not talk to strangers. Ashley killed Lansing because Ashley was in love with Lansing's wife, and the jury sent him to his death, firmly and unanimously, with what a Chicago paper called "shameless calm." Old Judge Crittenden's admonition to the jury on this point was particularly weighty; he enjoined them—with something approaching a wink of connivance—to perform their solemn duty, and they did. To out-of-town reporters the trial was a farce and it soon became a scandal in the upper Mississippi Valley. The defense raged, the newspapers sneered, telegrams rained upon the Governor's mansion in Springfield, but Coaltown knew what it knew. This silence about the guilty relations between John Ashley and Eustacia Lansing did not proceed from any chivalrous desire to protect a lady's good name; there was a solider foundation for silence than that. No witness ventured to voice the charge because no witness was in possession of the smallest evidence. Gossip had solidified into conviction as prejudice solidifies into self-evident truth.

Just at the moment when public outrage was at its height John Ashley escaped from his guards. Flight tends to be interpreted as an acknowledgment of guilt and questions concerning motive became irrelevant.

It is possible that the verdict might have been less severe if Ashley had behaved differently in court. He showed no signs of fear. He afforded no fascinating spectacle of mounting terror and remorse. He sat through the long trial listening serenely as though he expected the proceedings to satisfy his moderate curiosity as to who killed Breckenridge Lansing. But then, for Coaltown, he was an odd man. He was practically a foreigner—that is, he came from New York State and spoke in the way they speak there. His wife was German and spoke with a slight accent of her own. He seemed to have no ambition. He had worked for almost twenty years in the mines' office on a very small salary—as small as the second-best-paid clergyman's in town—in apparent contentment. He was odd through a very lack of striking characteristics. He was neither dark nor light, tall nor short, fat nor thin, bright nor dull. He had an agreeable enough presence, but one that seldom attracted a second glance. A Chicago reporter, at the beginning of the trial, repeatedly alluded to him as "our uninteresting hero." (He changed his mind later—a man on trial for his life who exhibits no anxiety arouses interest.) Women liked Ashley, because he liked them and because he was an attentive listener; men—except for the foremen in the mine—paid him little attention, though something in his self-effacing silence aroused in them a constant attempt to impress him.

Breckenridge Lansing was big and blond. He crushed everyone's hand in genial friendship. He laughed loudly; he did not restrain himself when he was in a rage. He was gregarious; he belonged to every lodge, fraternal order, and association that the town afforded. He loved the rituals: tears came to his eyes —manly tears; he wasn't ashamed of them—when he swore for the hundredth time to "maintain friendship with the brothers until death" and "to live under God in virtue and to be prepared to lay down his life for his country." It's vows like that, by golly, that give meaning to a man's life. He had his little weaknesses. He spent many an evening at those taverns up the River Road, not returning home until morning. This was not the behavior of an exemplary family man and Mrs. Lansing might have had some reason to resent it. But in public places—at the volunteer firemen's picnic, at the school's graduation exercises—he showered her with attentions, he broadly displayed his pride in her. It was generally known that he was incompetent as resident manager at the mines and that he seldom showed up there before eleven. As a father he had certainly failed in the rearing of two of his three children. George was held to be a "rowdy" and a "terror." Anne was a winning child who won by tantrums and rudeness. But these little failings were understandable. Several of them were shared by the most esteemed citizens in town. Lansing was a likable man and good company. What a splendid trial it would have been if Lansing had shot Ashley! What a performance he would have put on! The town would have seen to it that he was first thoroughly frightened—cowering—and then acquitted him.

This unimportant case in a small town in southern Illinois might have been forgotten even sooner had it not been for the mysterious circumstances surrounding the convict's escape. He did not raise a finger. He was rescued. Six men—dressed as railway porters, their faces blackened with burnt cork—entered the locked car. They smashed the hanging lanterns; without firing a shot or uttering a word they overcame the guards and carried the prisoner out of the train. Two of the guards fired once, but dared not continue for fear of killing one of their own number in the darkness. Who were these men who risked their lives to save John Ashley's? Paid hirelings? Mrs. Ashley declared repeatedly to the representatives of the State's Attorney's office—the furious, humiliated police—that she had no idea who they were. Everything about the rescue was awe-inspiring—the strength, the skill, the precision, but above all the silence and the fact that the rescuers were unarmed. It was eerie; it was unearthly.

John Ashley's trial and escape brought ridicule on the State of Illinois. Up to the time of the First World War—which started Americans moving about all over the country and changing their residences on a whim—every man, woman, and child believed that he or she lived in the best town in the best state in the best country in the world. This conviction filled them with a certain strength. It was reinforced by an unremitting depreciation of any neighboring town, state, or country. This pride in place was inculcated in children and the prides and humiliations of childhood are tenacious. Children applied the principle to the very streets on which they lived. You could hear them as they returned from school: "If I had to live on Oak Street, I'd die!" "Well, everybody knows that anybody who lives on Elm Street is craze-e-e, so there!" Colonel Stotz, the State's Attorney for Illinois, was a leading citizen of the greatest state in the world's greatest country. The dome of the State House (Abraham Lincoln's State House) in which he held office was the visible symbol of justice, dignity, and order. The contempt poured upon Illinois as a result of the Ashley Case during his fourth and last term of office darkened his day at noon and opened a crack in the ground beneath his feet. He hated the name of Ashley and resolved to pursue the convict to the farthest corners of the earth.

From the Monday morning after Lansing's death the Ashley children were withdrawn from school, much to the disappointment of their classmates. Only Sophia circulated in town, doing the shopping for her mother. Ella Gates spat in her face on the post office steps. Ashley forbade his daughters to attend the trial. Day after day, Roger—seventeen and a half—sat beside his mother in court, also frustrating his fellow townsmen of any spectacle of fear. As Roger said later, "Mama's at her best when things are going badly." She sat a few yards from the prisoner's bench. It distressed her to realize that sleeplessness was robbing her cheeks of color. At eight-thirty every morning she scrubbed them long and roughly to induce a semblance of well-being and of unshakable confidence.

An additional odd fact about the Ashleys came to light during the trial: no relative of either John or Beata arrived in town to aid or comfort them.

In time the story entered legend and was retold more and more incorrectly. It was said that some thugs from New York had held up the train; they had been paid a thousand dollars each by Ashley's lady love, the widow of the man he murdered. Or that Ashley, with the help of his son Roger, had shot his way out of a posse of eleven men. Even after the State's Attorney's office had exonerated John Ashley, there were many people to be found who would narrow their eyes and say knowingly: "There was a lot *behind* that affair that never came to light." The Ashley children and the Lansing children left Coaltown, one by one. Then first Mrs. Ashley, then Mrs. Lansing, moved to the Pacific Coast. It seemed as though time were gradually expunging the whole unhappy story as it had expunged so many others. But no!

About nine years later people began talking about the Ashley Case again. Newspapermen, ordinary citizens, even scientists took to visiting the periodical rooms in libraries to read the yellowing files of old newspapers. People were more and more interested in the "Ashley children"—each so distinguished in a different life-work. Everyone was interested in the "Ashley children" except the "Ashley children" themselves. They were the object of that particularly clamorous form of celebrity that surrounds those who are both ridiculed and admired, adored and hated. They were rendered increasingly conspicuous because they had called attention to themselves at so early an age and because they were vaguely associated with a background of tragedy and disgrace. It was generally recognized that they possessed a number of traits in common. Though only those who had known them in their early Coaltown years—Dr. Gillies, Eustacia Lansing, Olga Doubkov—knew the extent to which these were inherited from their parents, particularly from their father. They were without any competitive sense with its concomitants of envy and retaliation, though Lily and Roger were engaged in dog-eat-dog professions. They were without self-consciousness, had no deference whatever toward the opinion of others, and were without fear—though Constance spent over two years in jail, in six arrests in four countries, and Roger was burned in effigy at home and abroad. Lily and Constance had no vanity though they were among the most beautiful women of their time. All were without a sense of humor, though with the years they acquired a trenchancy of speech that resembled wit and were widely quoted. They were not self-regarding. Some who knew them best described them as being "abstract." No wonder they puzzled their contemporaries and were variously charged with being ruthless, self-seeking, stony-hearted, hypocritical, and athirst for publicity. They would perhaps have aroused an even stronger antagonism had there not been something absurd about them, too—naïve, didactic, "small town." All had big protruding ears ("swinging barn doors") and big feet—Heaven's gifts to caricaturists. When Constance—on her endless crusades, "Votes for Women," "Refuges for Destitute Children," "Rights of Married Women"—climbed the steps of a platform (she was particularly loved in India and Japan) gales of laughter would sweep the multitude; she never could understand why.

So it was that as early as 1910 and 1911 people began to study the records of the Ashley Case and to ask questions—frivolous or thoughtful questions—about John and Beata Ashley and their children, about Coaltown, about those old teasers Heredity and Environment, about gifts and talents, and destiny and chance.

This John Ashley—what was there in *him* (as in some hero in those old plays of the Greeks) that brought down upon him so mixed a portion of fate: unmerited punishment, a "miraculous" rescue, exile, and an illustrious progeny?

What was there in the ancestry and later in the home life of the Ashleys that fostered this energy of mind and spirit?

What was there in this Kangaheela Valley as geographical matrix, as spiritual climate, to shape such exceptional men and women?

Was there a connection between the catastrophe that befell both houses and these later developments? Are humiliation, injustice, suffering, destitution, and ostracism—are they blessings?

Nothing is more interesting than the inquiry as to how creativity operates in anyone, in everyone: mind, propelled by passion, imposing itself, building and unbuilding; mind—the latest-appearing manifestation of life—expressing itself in statesman and criminal, in poet and banker, in street cleaner and housewife, in father and mother—establishing order or spreading havoc; mind—condensing its energy in groups and nations, rising to an incandescence and then ebbing away exhausted; mind—enslaving and massacring or diffusing justice and beauty:

Pallas Athene's Athens, like a lighthouse on a hill, sending forth beams that still illuminate men in council;

Palestine, for a thousand years, like a geyser in the sand, producing genius after genius, and soon there will be no one on earth who has not been affected by them.

Is there more and more of it, or less and less?

Is the brain neutral between destruction and beneficence?

Is it possible that there will someday be a "spiritualization" of the human animal?

It is absurd to compare our children of the Kangaheela Valley to the august examples of good and evil action I have referred to above (already in the middle of this century they are largely forgotten), but:

They are near,
They are accessible to our indiscreet observation.

The central portion of Coaltown is long and narrow, lying between two steep bluffs. Since its main street runs north to southeast, it receives little direct sunlight. Many of the citizens seldom see a sunrise or a sunset or more than a fragment of a constellation. At the northern end are the depot, the town hall, the courthouse, the Illinois Tavern, and the Ashley house, built long ago by Airlee MacGregor and called "The Elms"; at the southern end are the Memorial Park with its statue of a Union soldier, the cemetery, and the Breckenridge Lansing house, "St. Kitts"—named after the island in the Caribbean on which Eustacia Lansing was born. These two houses are the only ones in Coaltown possessing sufficient level space about them to be described as having "grounds." An unhappy stream, the Kangaheela, flows through the valley on the eastern side of the main street; it widens into ponds behind both "The Elms" and "St. Kitts." The town is larger than it appears to be. Since its center is confined within a narrow valley, the homes of many of its citizens are perched on the surrounding hills or line the roads that lead north and south. The miners live in communities of their own on Bluebell Ridge and Grimble Mountain. They have their company stores, their schools, and their churches. They seldom descend into town. Coaltown had expanded and shrunk several times during the nineteenth century. The mines had once given employment to as many as three thousand men and several hundred children. Waves of immigrants had settled briefly in the region and moved on— hunters and trappers, religious sects, miners from Silesia, and entire farming communities in search of good land. There were not a few abandoned churches and schoolhouses and cemeteries in the nearby hills and along the River Road. Dr. Gillies estimated that a hundred thousand persons had lived in the two counties; learning of the great Indian burial grounds near Goshen and Penniwick, he raised his figure.

There must have been a great shallow lake here to have produced all that sandstone, but the land rose and most of the water flowed off into the Ohio and the Mississippi. There must have been great forests to have produced all that coal and centuries of earthquakes to have lifted the hills and folded them over the forests like pancakes over jelly. The great cumbersome reptiles were unable to waddle away in time and left their imprints in stone—you can see them in the museum at Fort Barry. What stretches of time are required to complete the procession of a marsh to a forest. The professors have drawn up the time plan: so much for the grasses to furnish humus for the bushes; so much for the bushes to accommodate the trees; so much for the young of the oak family to take root under the grateful shade of the wild cherry and the maple, and to supplant them; so much for the white oak to replace the red; so much for the majestic entrance of the beech family, which has been waiting for its propitious hour—the war of the saplings, so to speak. The internecine warfare of the plants was joined by that of the animals. The blat of the deer struck terror in the forest as the great cats sank their teeth in the jugular vein; the hawk bore skyward the snake that held a fieldmouse in its jaws.

Then man came.

One of the finest "turtle mounds" in all the Algonquin region is near Coaltown, in Goshen, and there are three superb "snake mounds" to the north. In our time any boy with spirit in him had his collection of Indian arrowheads, pestles, and axes. The professors disagree as to the reason for the several massacres, for these were notably peace-loving tribes. One scholar attributes them to the custom of exogamic marriage—raids on the tribes of other totems in order to steal brides for their young braves. Another, however, holds that these aggressions were prompted by economic needs; the Bleu Barrés had depleted the game within their territory and were driven to encroach upon the Kangaheelas' land. Whatever the reason, an examination of the skeletons in the various necropolises reveals an appalling amount of mayhem.

In 1907, long after these tribes were thought to be extinct, a wandering ethnologist came upon a small community of Kangaheelas living and coughing in shanties at Gilchrist's Ferry on the Mississippi, sixty miles west of Coaltown. It was hard to understand how they lived; a few sold ill-made moccasins, pipes, arrows, and beadwork from roadside stands. One night, for whiskey, an old man told the story of his people. They were the envy of the other nations for the elegance of their dress, the splendor of their dances (Kangaheela means "sacred dance floor"), their wisdom, and for their proficiency in divination. Every male from his eighteenth year could repeat without mistake the Book of Beginnings and Endings, a recital that filled two nights and days interrupted by dances. The Kangaheelas were famous for their hospitality; places were reserved for guests from the other nations who may have understood a portion of the text. The council fire lit up the faces of thousands seated about the sacred dance floor. Glorious was the first night—the story of creation with its exhausting account of the warfare between the sun and darkness. This was followed by an account of the birth of the first man from the All-Father's nostrils—the first Kangaheela. A morning was given over to a catalogue of the laws and tabus he had instituted—matter so old that at times the words were unintelligible and the intention unclear. By noon the reciter entered upon the chronicle and genealogy of heroes and traitors—eight hours long. Just before the second midnight there was delivered the Book of Hard Prophecies given to us by the All-Father, three hours of humiliation and bitterness. The sins of men had turned the beauty of the earth into a midden. Brother had slain brother. The sacred duty of generation had been made a sport of the unthinking. The All-Father carries in His heart all the nations of the forest, but they will creep like the snake; their numbers will be reduced; the rejoicing at the birth of a child will be feigned.

There followed a long silence, broken at last by drumbeats and shouting. This was the Dance of the Kangaheela, the heart of the flint, dear to the All-Father as His eye. This is the dance which has been so widely copied. Even the Saysays of Michigan have been invited to perform it in their debased and trumpery version at world's fairs—admission: fifty cents; children a quarter. At the conclusion of the dance there was another silence—but all expectation, all held breath. The sachem seemed to descend into the furthest reaches of his body; he collected himself; he rose. This was the Book of Promises. Who can describe the consolation of that great song? The aged forgot their incommodities; to boys and girls it made clear why they were born and why the universe was set in motion. There are many peoples on the earth—more men than there are leaves in the forest—but He has singled out the Kangaheelas from among them. He will return. Let them BLAZE THE TRAIL against that day. The race of men will be saved by a few.

So much for the Indians. The professors estimate that there were never more than three thousand Kangaheelas alive at one time.

The white men came. They brought their account of the creation, their name for the All-Father, their laws and tabus, their catalogue of heroes and traitors, their burden of reproach, their hopes of a golden age. There was very little dancing, but a good deal of music, sacred and profane. They brought, too, a speculative turn of mind, unknown to the red man; its product was loosely referred to as philosophy. All the citizens, young and old, occasionally troubled their heads with questions about why are human beings alive and what's the sense of living and dying —what Dr. Gillies called "the four-o'clock-in-the-morning questions." Dr. Gillies was Coaltown's most articulate and exasperating philosopher. In flat contradiction to the Bible he believed that the earth had been millions of years in the making and that Man was descended from you-know-what. Moreover, he talked of serious things in a way that left his listeners puzzled as to whether he was joking or not. A choice selection of the town's citizens was to remember for a long time an occasion when Dr. Gillies's speculative turn of mind was given a free rein.

It was on a New Year's Eve, but not just an ordinary New Year's Eve: it was December 31, 1899—the eve of a new century. A large group was gathered in front of the courthouse waiting for the clock to strike. There was a mood of exaltation in the crowd, as though it expected the heavens to open. The twentieth century was to be the greatest century the world had ever known. Man would fly; tuberculosis, diphtheria, and cancer would be eradicated; there would be no more wars. The country, the state, and the very town in which they lived were to play large and solemn roles in this new era. When the clock struck all the women and some of the men were weeping. Suddenly, they burst out singing, not "Auld Lang Syne," but "O God, Our Help in Ages Past." Soon they were throwing their arms about one another; they were kissing—an unheard-of demonstration. Breckenridge Lansing and Olga Sergeievna

Doubkov—who hated one another—kissed; John Ashley and Eustacia Lansing—who loved one another—kissed, for the only time in their lives, and evasively. (Beata Ashley avoided gatherings; she was sitting beside the tall grandfather's clock at "The Elms," surrounded by her three daughters, Lily, Sophia, and Constance.) Roger Ashley, fourteen years and fifty-one weeks old, kissed Félicité Lansing, to whom he would be married nine years later. George Lansing, fifteen, the town's "holy terror," stricken dumb with awe at the portentousness of the occasion and by the behavior of the grownups, hid behind his mother. (Great artists tend to be ebullient in gloomy company and subdued in the midst of elation.) Finally the crowd dispersed; about twenty lingered under the great clock, seeking some further expression of an emotion that was giving place to reflection and questioning. They went into the Tavern in order —as they said—to drink something hot. The young girls were sent to their homes. The group entered the bar wherein no woman had ever been admitted and presumably would not be admitted again for a hundred years. They went into the back room. Mugs of hot milk, hot grog, and "Sally Croker" (spiced crabapples floating in hot cider) were passed around by the great Mr. Sorbey himself.

Breckenridge Lansing—always at his best in company, the perfect host, and, as resident manager of the mines, the first citizen in town—spoke up for the company.

"Dr. Gillies, what will the new century be like?"

The ladies murmured, "Yes! . . . Yes! . . . Tell us what you think." The men cleared their throats.

Dr. Gillies made no deprecatory noises, but began:

"Nature never sleeps. The process of life never stands still. The creation has not come to an end. The Bible says that God created man on the sixth day and rested, but each of those days was many millions of years long. That day of rest must have been a short one. Man is not an end but a beginning. We are at the beginning of the second week. We are children of the eighth day."

He described the earth before the appearance of life—millions of years of steam arising from the boiling waters . . . The noise, the terrible winds, the waves . . . the noise. Then tiny floating organisms choking the seas. Passive . . . then, here and there, one and other, acquiring the ability to propel themselves toward light, toward food. A nervous system began to take shape in the Pre-Cambrian age; fins and feet began to afford sufficient strength to walk on dry land in the Upper Devonian; blood grew warmer in the Mesozoic.

It was somewhere in the Mesozoic age that Mr. Goodhue, Coaltown's banker, exchanged an outraged glance with his wife. They rose and left the room, head high, gazing straight before them. *Evolution!* Godless evolution! Dr. Gillies went on. Having divided the plants from the animals he sent them off on their long journeys. The birds and fishes, after some hesitation, parted company. The insects multiplied. The arrival of the mammals and that breathtaking moment when they stood on their rear feet releasing their front feet for a varied activity.

"Life! Why life? What for? To what end? Something came out of the ooze. Where was it going?"

He paused. His gaze rested with such inquiry on the boys that they felt impelled to answer. They murmured. "To man."

"Yes," said Dr. Gillies, "to all kinds of men."

A pained uneasiness had descended on the company. Breckenridge Lansing, an experienced chairman, again spoke up for the group. "You haven't answered our question, Dr. Gillies."

"I have laid down the ground plan for my answer to your question. In this new century we shall be able to see that mankind is entering a new stage of development—the Man of the Eighth Day."

Dr. Gillies was lying for all he was worth. He had no doubt that the coming century would be too direful to contemplate—that is to say, like all the other centuries.

Dr. Gillies was the only member of the group to have felt no elation. He had had no part in the congratulations and embraces. At a quarter before twelve he had slipped into the Tavern and paid a call on old Mrs. Billings, his long-time patient. His soul (a word he used only in jest) was filled with bitterness. Twenty-three months ago his son had died in a sledding accident at Williams College in Massachusetts—Hector Gillies who should be entering tonight into the twentieth century—his other self, his extended self, his lengthened shadow. Dr. Gillies had no faith in progress, in the future of mankind. He knew more about Coaltown than any of its citizens. (As he had known much about Terre Haute, Indiana, during his first ten years of practice.) Coaltown was no worse and no better than any other town. Any community is a portion of the vast body of the human race. You may cut into Breckenridge Lansing or the Emperor of China; you will find the same viscera. Like the devil in the old story, you may lift the roofs of Coaltown or Vladivostok; you will hear the same phrases. His midnight reading of the great historians confirmed his sense that Coaltown is everywhere—though even the greatest historians fall victim to the distortion induced by elapsed time; they elevate and abase at will. There are no Golden Ages and no Dark Ages. There is the oceanlike monotony of the generations of men under the alternations of fair and foul weather.

What would the twentieth century and its successors be like?

He lied roundly because his eyes rested on Roger Ashley and George Lansing. He spoke as he would have spoken if Hector had been there. It is the duty of old men to lie to the young. Let these encounter their own disillusions. We strengthen our souls, when young, on hope; the strength we acquire enables us later to endure despair as a Roman should.

"The New Man is emerging. Nature never sleeps. Hitherto the sporadic great man, the lone genius, has carried the children of fear and inertia on his coattails. Henceforth, the whole mass will emerge from the cave-dwelling condition . . ."

Oh, it was splendid!

". . . emerge from the cave-dwelling condition where most men cower still—terrified of encroachment, hugging their possessions, in bondage to fears of the Thunder God, fears of the vengeful dead, fears of the untamable beast in themselves."

It was splendid.

"Mind and Spirit will be the next climate of the human. The race is undergoing its education. What is education, Roger? What is education, George? It is the bridge man crosses from the self-enclosed, self-favoring life into a consciousness of the entire community of mankind."

A number of his listeners had soon fallen asleep in the beatific

air of the twentieth century—not John Ashley and his son, not
Eustacia Lansing and her son.

Olga Doubkov walked home with Wilhelmina Thoms, Lansing's secretary at the mines.

"Dr. Gillies didn't believe a word of it," she said. "I did. I
believed every word of it. And so did my father. I couldn't
walk straight if I didn't."

It has never been satisfactorily explained why the early settlers
of Coaltown (or Maple Bluffs, as it was first called) chose to
center and expand their agglomeration in a sunless gorge when
they might have built their homes, their first church, and their
first school in the open meadows to the north and south. The
town lay on a moderately important trade route. The itinerant
vendors are still with us. Coaltown has always been a favorite
with commercial travelers—fortunately for Beata Ashley and
her children when the time came—even when Fort Barry, thirty
miles to the north, and Summerville, forty miles to the south,
offered larger returns. The Illinois Tavern of the Sorbeys, builder,
son, and grandson, suited them. They assigned two nights to it
in their itineraries. Its rooms were spacious; its thirty-five-cent
dinners generous. The woodwork and brass fixtures in the saloon were installed in expectation of an ever greater prosperity.
The genial smell of sawdust, spilt beer, and mash whiskey
welcomed the tired wanderer. There were nightly games in the
back room. Free transportation was available to a number of
establishments a few miles south on the River Road—Hattie's
Hitching Post and Nicky's We Have It. Business representatives (agricultural implements and wholesale pharmaceuticals)
arrived by train; drummers (sewing machines, jewelry, patent
medicines, and kitchenware) by horse and buggy. Pedlars drew
up by the side of the road and slept under their carts.

With the discovery of coal came black, gray, yellow, and
white dust; came turbid water into the Kangaheela; came the
town's first and last rich man, Airlee MacGregor; came more
foreigners—the Silesians and West Virginians, Miss Doubkov's
father (an exiled Russian prince, some said), John and Beata
Ashley from New York, speaking the "New York dialect."
Many birds, beasts, fishes, and plants retreated from the region.

It became customary to say that the soil was "sour." Above all came poverty and unrest and the threat of violence. Many of the men who worked ten hours a day underground seemed unable to feed and clothe a twelve- or fourteen-headed family, even when, of a Saturday afternoon, their dear offspring laid their week's wages in the father's hand. Shoes played an important role. They haunted the dreamer. Even horses had shoes. A father could feed his family on beans, bran, greens, apples, and occasionally fatback; but it was generally understood that worshipers did not go to church unshod. One's children went turn and turn about. A number of times in the last half of the nineteenth century there had been revolt in the wind. There are few things more dispiriting than half-hearted strikes. They were ill led and ill supported. The windows of the miners' store were broken, the company offices wrecked. A group of roaming men was dispersed after it had torn up the picket fence surrounding Airlee MacGregor's house and hurled his croquet balls at his front door. (Through all that din and splintering wood Old MacGregor sat in his front room, his rifle by his side, righteous as Moses.) Holidays were looked forward to with apprehension. In 1897 the Mayor prudently canceled the Fourth of July parade and oration in Memorial Park. The quadrennial election days were particularly dreaded. The miners swarmed down the hills and gave vent to their long frustration and rage. The administration strictly deducted fines from their wages for nonappearance in the shafts the following day. The men drank and shouted through the night and started lurching up the slopes at dawn; their wives collected them from the ditches beside the road. Many children were born the following August, resignedly welcomed. People in Coaltown had locked their doors at night from as long ago as anyone could remember and the better-off had installed various reinforcements and barricades. Breckenridge Lansing was not the first to train his family in the use of firearms, though it was to be expected of him as managing director of the mines. It astonished the out-of-town reporters at the trial, but not the citizens of Coaltown, to learn that he was murdered during his customary Sunday afternoon rifle practice.

Five years after that notorious trial the mines near Coaltown closed down—the "Bluebell Mine" and the "Henrietta B.

MacGregor." The quality of the coal had been deteriorating for a long time and now the quantity was diminishing. The town dwindled in size. The families of the convict and the murdered man moved away. Their houses changed hands a number of times. They bore signs that said ROOMS and FOR SALE, but finally the signs became illegible and fell from the walls. Their broken windows admitted rain and snow; birds built nests upstairs and down; their picket fences leaned across the sidewalks like breaking waves. The summerhouse behind "The Elms" slid into the pond. In the autumn children were sent by their mothers to gather the butternuts at "St. Kitts," the chestnuts at "The Elms."

With the cessation of activity in the mines the quality of the air improved. No housewife ventured to hang white window curtains, but the girls at the high school's graduation exercises first wore white dresses in 1910. There were fewer hunters; deer, foxes, and quail increased. Caperfish and checkerbelly and Mulligan trout found their way up the Kangaheela in large numbers. The redbud and goldenrod and poneytail which had long bypassed the region began advancing upon it from all directions.

Often in the spring after heavy rains a strange roar filled the air. The hills were honeycombed with abandoned mines; the earth's surface above them caved in with a noise that sounded more like an earthquake than a landslide. The townspeople would drive out to peer into these earthworks. They seemed more to resemble the ruins of some past greatness than the prisons where so many had labored twelve hours—later, ten hours—a day and where so many had coughed and spat their lungs away. Even small boys were hushed by the view of those long galleries and arcades, rotundas and throne rooms. By the following year squawbush and wild vines were covering the entrances to the underworld. The population of bats increased, emerging at first dark in whirling clouds above the valley.

As Dr. Gillies was so fond of saying, "Nature never sleeps."

Coaltown no longer has a post office building. The mail is distributed in a corner of Mr. Bostwick's grocery store. The county seat has been transferred to Fort Barry.

I. "The Elms"

1885–1905

"THE ELMS" was the second-handsomest house in Coaltown. It had been built by Airlee MacGregor in the days when the mines were less dependent on the administration in Pittsburgh and the resident supervisors could make money for themselves. He had sunk the shafts of the "Bluebell" and the "Henrietta B. MacGregor" and had become a very rich man. John Ashley could never have afforded to buy it outright. He had been called to Coaltown as mere maintenance engineer when the mines were already in decline. It was his duty on a straitened budget to repair and shore up a dilapidating fabric. The owners could not have foreseen that his gifts lay, precisely, in ingenuity and improvisation. He was delighted with the work, though his salary was little over a third that of Breckenridge Lansing, the managing director. Ashley was a poor man and would have acknowledged it with a smile. He had everything he wanted and more. His wife was an accomplished housekeeper, and both he and Beata were extremely resourceful at supplying necessities and devising amenities that require little or no outlay of money. He gradually came into ownership of the house through half-yearly payments. The house had long stood vacant. The people of lower Illinois are not given to superstition; they did not say the house was haunted, but it was known that "The Elms" had been built in spite, maintained in hatred, and abandoned in tragedy. Every town of some size had one or two such houses. John Ashley was more superstitious than his neighbors; he believed that no misfortune could befall him. He and Beata lived there in happiness for almost seventeen years.

When, in 1885, Ashley first saw the house his eyes opened wide. As he mounted the steps and entered the hall his lips parted, his breathing was arrested, as it is when we try to hear a distant music. He seemed to have seen it before or to have dreamt it. A large verandah surrounded the ground floor on three sides; another verandah overhung the front door; above it rose a cupola in which a telescope had been installed. Within, a wide staircase ascended from the front hall; the newel post supported an iridescent crystal globe. At the right a large living room extended the length of the house. Newspapers, already ten years old, had been spread over the tables and chairs, over the well-worn sofas, over the old square piano. Behind the house stretched an untended lawn; rains and snows had discolored the croquet balls half-hidden in the weeds. At the bottom of the lawn was a pond with a summerhouse beside it. In the grove of elms at the right stood a large shed which the children were to call the "Rainy Day House" and which was to serve also as workshop for their father's "inventions" and "experiments." He knew before he saw them that there were some chicken-houses, now collapsed on one side and open to the rain, a small orchard, blackberry bushes, and some chestnut trees. A sort of awe filled him. Who could be richer?

But it was Airlie MacGregor's dream into which he had entered. MacGregor had built it in expectation of a large family. There were to have been croquet parties on the lawn until the fading light drove the young people into the summerhouse, where there would be singing to the accompaniment of a banjo. There would be fireflies. In bad weather there would be taffy pulls in the kitchen, and clamorous games of slapjack and who's-got-the-thimble in the living room. The rugs would be rolled back against the walls and there would be dancing— Virginia reels and "Melissa, make your bow." On clear nights the children would be taken up to the cupola; each in turn would be lifted up to look through the telescope. Nothing dull would ever be reflected on that lens, but red Mars and the hoops of Saturn and the solemnizing craters on the moon.

All came true, but not for Airlie MacGregor. On Sunday nights, when the hired girl had gone to visit her sister, Beata Ashley and Eustacia Lansing would prepare the supper. "Come in, children. Come to supper." Hector Gillies, the doctor's son, taught Roger Ashley to play the banjo. All of them could sing, but none like Lily Ashley. She sang so beautifully that at fifteen she was invited to sing in church before all the people. At sixteen she sang "Home, Sweet Home," at the volunteer fire department's picnic; strong men sobbed. Mrs. Lansing forbade the children to play slapjack and muggins because her two younger children, George and Anne (it was their Creole blood), became overexcited and boisterous. After supper Ashley and Lansing went off to the "Rainy Day House" to work on their inventions of locks and firearms. At the end of the evening there was reading aloud—Ulysses and the Cyclops, Robinson Crusoe and his man Friday, Gulliver's shipwrecks, and the Arabian Nights. On other Sunday afternoons, the same children and the same elders gathered at "St. Kitts." Targets were set up for rifle practice—Breckenridge Lansing was a great huntsman—and the men and boys fired away and set the town's dogs barking. After supper Eustacia Lansing would tell some of her native Caribbean stories. Her children and the Ashley children spoke French, but she deftly inserted a translation for the visitors. She was a vivid narrator and the company listened spellbound to the adventures of Père-Père Tortue and Dédenni Iguanou.

At "The Elms" it all came true, but not for Airlee MacGregor. If he had planned the staircase to exhibit the grace and distinction of his wife's carriage, it had failed of its purpose. The unhappy Mrs. MacGregor soon developed the obesity which so often accompanies a life of enforced leisure and unremitting anxiety. She was incapable of descending a staircase without clutching its railing. No brides hurled their bouquets to the uplifted hands below. It admirably facilitated the descent of a succession of coffins. But Beata Ashley came down these stairs like that Queen of Prussia who had been the lifelong admiration of her mother, *geborene* Clotilde von Diehlen of Hamburg and Hoboken, New Jersey. There were to be no Ashley weddings at "The Elms," but Lily, Sophia, and Constance were taught to go up and down the stairs balancing an atlas on their heads. The iridescent crystal ball reflected the fulfillment of another's dream.

Both Breckenridge Lansing and John Ashley found their way to Coaltown because they had failed in their previous situations. They did not know this, though their wives had an inkling of it. Lansing thought he had been promoted to a better position; Ashley knew he had been transferred to a happier one. John Ashley had become increasingly discontented in an office in Toledo, Ohio, where he had been set to designing machine tools for nine hours a day, and felt that the invitation to Coaltown was a stroke of good fortune—poor though the pay was. As the most brilliant student in his class at the engineering school, he had been free to choose among the opportunities offered to him. He chose that from Toledo because both he and his bride were eager to leave the East behind them and because the position seemed to afford outlet to his inventive gift. Great was his disappointment when he discovered that he was expected to sit the entire day on one stool before one drawing board, designing bits of machinery that he described derisively as "cookie molds." We shall see later how the supposedly dynamic young Lansing was gently shunted out of the important offices in Pittsburgh and sent—in 1880, at the age of twenty-six—to the Kangaheela Valley. He was not a mining engineer; his work was to be administrative. He was the resident manager.

In the board's offices at Pittsburgh the mines at Coaltown were referred to as "Poor John" mines. The phrase in the Middle West denoted a catchall for the superannuated and the incompetent. A prosperous farmer, owning several farms, set aside one to which he sent aging hands, aging horses, and aging machinery. Every four or five years the board took up the question of closing them down altogether. They still showed a small profit, however; they bore famous names; and they were convenient as a "Poor John" enterprise. They were kept running on the condition that no improvements were made, no wages raised, and few operatives replaced. Lansing's predecessor, Cayley Debevoise—brother of a director's wife—had been a discard also. Like Lansing, he had been enthusiastically engaged in the Pittsburgh area—"Best young man we've seen in a long time," "bright as a penny," "full of ideas," "charming wife." The board could have terminated their contracts at any moment, but—perhaps reluctant to acknowledge their bad judgment—they sent the no longer promising young men to Coaltown instead.

Who did run the mines? The office on the hill was staffed with presumably competent mining engineers, but these, too, were "Poor John" rejects, aging and subject to the inertia inherent in such institutions. The mines were running down like a tired clock, but somehow they managed to stumble and jerk along by themselves. Miss Thoms, assistant to the successive resident managers, met the foremen of the various departments at seven o'clock in the morning before they descended into the earth; together they arrived at various decisions in an improvisatory way. The measures they adopted were presented to the resident manager—at nine o'clock or at ten—in such a way that they appeared to him as brilliant ideas that had just occurred to him. For years Miss Thoms received sixteen dollars a week. If she had fallen ill, the mines would have been thrown into a chaos, and she would have found her way, early or late, to the poorhouse in Goshen.

When Breckenridge Lansing succeeded Cayley Debevoise, Miss Thoms picked up hope; it appeared that the burden was to be lifted from her shoulders. Breckenridge Lansing never failed to make a good impression at the start of everything he started. He examined the books dynamically; dynamically he descended, once, into the bowels of the earth. He teemed with ideas. He managed simultaneously to be shocked at what he saw and to commend everyone for the splendid work that was being carried on. But presently the truth came to light: Lansing could not remember a fact from one day to the next. Memory is the servant of our interests and Lansing's primary interest was the impression he made on others. Numerals, charts, carloads do not applaud. Miss Thoms was soon back in harness.

"Mr. Lansing, the Forbush gallery has run into pan cobble."

"Is that so!"

"You remember that you thought pretty well of Number Seven-B. Don't you think it would be a good idea to direct Jeremiah to put all their effort over there?"

"Very good idea, Wilhelmina! Let's do that!"

"Mr. Lansing, Conrad has been having the tumbles."

Men who have worked ten hours a day for years at the lower levels are subject to falling asleep suddenly; they tumble to the ground in a stupor. They are more terrified of these manifestations than they are of accidents or of tuberculosis itself. When a man starts to tumble four times a day he is on his way to Goshen.

"Hmm," said Lansing, narrowing his eyes judiciously.

"Now I remember your saying you thought the second Bragg boy looked like a good worker. We'll need a new rolling jacker in 'Bluebell.'"

"Just the ticket, Wilhelmina! We'll put it on the bulletin board. You draw it up and I'll sign it."

The bulletin boards were Lansing's signal contribution to the mines. He was soon signing his name to them fifteen times a day. When there were no more bulletins to sign he took a little nap on the horsehair sofa or went hunting in the hills.

Ashley was called to the mines, for a short term, to patch and bolster this vast collapsing skeleton. For two months he held his tongue; he observed and listened. He spent half his time underground, a lamp on his forehead. The flying cages descended and rose by old-fashioned rope, drum, and pulley. The foremen were not unintelligent, but living so long like moles they had lost the faculty of making a choice between evils. As they laid their problems before Ashley this faculty revived; they saw which seams were running into pan cobble or noggers; they were ready to risk new probes. Everywhere Ashley saw danger. The men, stupefied by the conditions under which they lived, had come to assume that the hazards of mining were an expression of God's will. When Ashley finally began to speak—in an "Eastern" accent all but unintelligible to them— his first suggestions were in the direction of ventilation. He "wasted" hands and hours in opening "gangs"; he devised a crude clattering system of fans and the rate of tumbling decreased. There was some shifting about of operatives, though that was not in his province; the almost blind, the tubercular, the unredeemable tumblers were sent to a "Poor John" shaft. He reconditioned the forge; cars, cages, frames, rackets, tracks, stomps were rendered more serviceable. The skeleton began to twitch and right itself. It was a deplorable mine, but it was no longer a moribund one. Ashley's salary was never increased, though he saw to it that Miss Thoms, in return for her instructions, received an additional five dollars a week. Lansing was delighted with all the brilliant ideas that sprang to his mind daily; they were posted on the bulletin board. He felt free to go hunting oftener. As he was frequently out late at night in the taverns on the River Road there was a good deal of napping on the horsehair sofa. Ashley had no idea that work could be so varied and that it could call so constantly on improvisation and invention. He rose each day with zest. To the ends of their lives his children could remember him singing before his shaving mirror, "'Nita, Juanita," and "No gottee tickee, No gettee shirtee, At the Chinee laundryman's."

So it was that John Ashley ran the mine in everything but title. He learned the processes of mining coal from admirable instructors—the foremen below ground and the "Poor John" engineers *emeriti* who were as eager to share their knowledge as they were to avoid responsibility and work. This situation continued for almost seventeen years, during which the annual reports began, from the fifth year, to show small but increased profits. It continued by virtue of a conspiracy, primarily on the part of John Ashley and Miss Thoms, but involving also the men's wives. Only a John Ashley could have lent himself for so long to so difficult and even humiliating a role. Devoid of ambition or envy, indifferent to the admiration or contempt of others, completely happy in his family life at "The Elms," he "saved" Breckenridge Lansing. He not only did all he was able to conceal his superior's ineptitude from the company and the community, he played the older brother to this older man. He tried to mitigate his harshness toward his family at "St. Kitts" and to divert him from his squalid dissipations in the taverns up the River Road and on Old Quarry Pond. He involved him in his "experiments" and praised his imagined contributions to them. The beautiful mechanical drawings were signed with their combined names: The "Lansing-Ashley Spiral Shift Lock," the "Ashley-Lansing St. Kitts Primer." It was an elaborate and generous fiction; sooner or later, such fictions are exposed.

Breckenridge Lansing was murdered on the late afternoon of May 4, 1902, and John Ashley was sentenced to death for having shot him. Murders are not uncommon, but some arouse more interest than others. The escape of a convict on the way to his execution is all but unheard of. An intense search was made for the missing man. First a description, then a dim photograph, was displayed in post offices all over the country and a large sum of money was offered for information leading to his recapture and to the arrest of his six mysterious rescuers. The region's interest in these rescuers exceeded even that extended to Ashley. A man who rescues a convicted murderer brings on himself the death sentence. These six men must have been well paid. Where'd Ashley get the money? But the circumstances were otherwise amazing. One could understand six

well-paid bandits bursting into a locked railway car with blaz-
ing revolvers—but these six men, masquerading as Negro
porters, had accomplished the rescue in silence and without
weapons! This event had taken place at one in the morning at
a point a quarter of a mile south of the Fort Barry depot, where
all trains stop for ten minutes beside the water tank. Ashley's
guard consisted of five men—three sent down from the prison
at Joliet and two, including the leader Captain Mayhew, appointed by the State's Attorney's office at Springfield. After the
official inquiry all the men were removed from the police force
in disgrace. Four of them never mentioned the humiliating
occasion, but one of them could be heard telling the story far
and wide. "Blister" Hughes had come down in the world and
was selling poultry feed in the northwestern counties. He gained
a certain celebrity and increased his sales by recounting in saloons the events of that historic night.

"This porter came in the door and said the stationmaster
had a telegram for Captain Mayhew and Captain Mayhew said,
'Bring it here!' But the porter said, 'It's confidential' and 'It's
from Springfield and Captain Mayhew had to go and get it
personally himself.' Well, we thought it was a pardon from the
Governor—see what I mean? Captain Mayhew had orders not
to leave the car and he didn't know what to do. We all tried to
think what he should do and it was that moment of thinking
that made us stupid. Before we knew it the car was full of
porters. They smashed the lamps and from then on we were
crawling in broken glass. A man got hold of my feet and started
tying them together. I leaned forward to punch him, but he
was so strong that he could lift my feet up in the air and tie
them together at the same time. There were my legs pointing
to the ceiling and me lying on my shoulderblades, floundering
around like a crayfish. When he got my feet tied he flipped me
over and tied my hands behind me. We were all yelling and
Captain Mayhew was yelling the loudest: 'Shoot Ashley! Shoot
Ashley!' But how would we know which was Ashley, tell me
that? And then they gagged up our mouths and dragged us
along the aisle and laid us out like sacks of potatoes. Believe
me, they weren't from around Coaltown. They were from
Chicago or New York. They'd done it before. They'd practiced
it. You could tell that. I'll never forget it. The blinds were down,

but there was a faint light coming from somewhere and they was hopping over the backs of them seats like monkeys."

The mystery of the performance baffled the finest intelligences —from Colonel Stotz in Springfield, the newspapermen from the cities, the Sheriff playing cards with his deputies, the ladies sewing garments for the heathen in Africa, the nightly circle of great thinkers in the Illinois Tavern's saloon, down to the loungers chewing their tobacco in Mr. Kinch's livery stable and blacksmith shop. Not the least amazed by it was Beata Ashley.

There was much thereafter to stimulate the most sluggish imagination. How does an escaped convict, with four thousand dollars on his shaven head, find his way out of the country? How would such a man send messages and finally money to his penniless wife and children when every message sent to the house was intercepted by the police and every visitor closely questioned? What was he thinking? What was she thinking? What was Eustacia Lansing thinking? Questions of money played a large part in the citizens' speculations. Everyone knew how small Ashley's salary was. They had known his butcher's bills for years. The banker's wife had confided to her best friends the meager amount of his savings. The prudent and self-righteous were in ecstasy: John Ashley, for seventeen years, had been breaking one of the most implacable laws of civilization. He had saved no money. The trial had been unduly prolonged. Soon after it began Ashley courteously dismissed his lawyer and threw himself upon the defense provided by the court. The town had seen a "second-hand man" arrive from Summerville. His van had carted away furniture, crockery, window curtains and linen, the grandfather's clock from the hall, the square piano that had accompanied so many Virginia reels—even Roger's banjo. They were still eating at "The Elms"; they had their hen-house, their cow, and their garden, but there were no butcher's bills. On the last night before Ashley was put on the train for Joliet he sent his son his gold watch—the family's last convertible asset.

During the trial and the weeks following Ashley's disappearance the town watched "The Elms" with covert but breathless interest. There were few callers: Dr. Gillies; Miss Thoms, who was now temporarily carrying the whole administration on her shoulders; Miss Doubkov (Olga Sergeievna), the dressmaker;

some representatives of Colonel Stotz's office who arrived from time to time to torment Mrs. Ashley. Dr. Benson, the family's minister, did not call. He had visited the prisoner in jail, but Ashley had not shown a penitent spirit. Dr. Benson was relieved of all obligation to call again. A group of ladies from the church, after long consultation and with no encouragement from their pastor, set out to call on their friend Mrs. Ashley. They lost heart, however, twenty yards from the house. She had sewn with them in the Missionary Society; she had decorated the church with them at Easter and Christmas; she had invited their children to croquet and supper at "The Elms." But over all these years she had not addressed one of them by her Christian name. She called Miss Thoms "Wilhelmina" and Mrs. Lansing "Eustacia," but that was all. She even called her hired girl "Mrs. Swenson."

It was reported from house to house that the only son Roger, seventeen and a half, had left Coaltown. It was assumed that he had gone out in the world to make his fortune and to send money home to his mother. The daughters did not return to school in the fall. Their mother tutored them at home. Lily, almost nineteen, and Constance, nine, like their mother did not pass the front gate of "The Elms" for over a year and a half. It was Sophia, fourteen and two months, who did the shopping for the family. She was seen on the main street daily, nodding brightly to her former acquaintances, to all appearance unaware that few of her greetings were returned. Her purchases were reported from house to house—soap, flour, yeast, thread, hairpins, and "mousetrap" cheese.

The residents at "The Elms" were among the last persons in Coaltown to learn of Ashley's escape. It was Porky, twenty-one, who brought the news. Porky was Roger's best friend. Though his family name was O'Hara, he was large part Indian and belonged to the Church of the Covenant community, a religious sect that had drifted into southern Illinois from Kentucky and established itself on Herkomer's Knob, three miles from Coaltown. Porky's right foot and shin had been injured at birth, but he was a notable hunter and had taken Roger on many a hunting trip. He repaired the shoes of Coaltown, sitting all day in his little matchbox of a store on the main street. He was highly regarded by all the Ashleys, but he never entered their house by the front door and he firmly refused to sit down to a meal with them. He was taciturn and loyal; the black eyes in his square walnut-colored face were observant. On the morning of July twenty-second he appeared at the back door and uttered his signal, the hoot of an owl. Roger joined him and was told the news.

"Your mother ought to know. They'll be here soon."

"You tell her, Porky. She'll want to ask you questions."

He followed Roger into the front hall. Mrs. Ashley came down the stairs.

"Mama, Porky has something to tell you."

"Ma'am, Mr. Ashley got away. Some men piled into the car and loosed him."

Silence.

"Was anybody hurt, Porky?"

"No, ma'am, not that I heard."

Beata Ashley put her hand on the newel post to steady herself. She was accustomed to the fact that Indians waste few words. Her eyes asked him if he knew who the rescuers had been. His eyes gave no answer.

She said, "They'll be hunting for him."

"Yes, ma'am. They're saying that the men who rescued him gave him a horse. If he's smart he'll get to the river."

The Ohio is forty miles south of Coaltown, the Mississippi sixty miles west. During the long trial Beata's voice had acquired a huskiness and her breathing had become constrained.

"Thank you, Porky. If you learn anything more, will you let me know?"

"Yes, ma'am." His eyes said, "He'll get away."

There was a sound of feet mounting the front steps, accompanied by angry voices.

"They'll be asking you questions," said Porky. He went into the kitchen and left the grounds through the hedge behind the chicken run.

There was a pounding on the front door; the bell attached to it jangled furiously. It was flung open. Four men entered the hall, led by Captain Mayhew. The Ashleys' old friend Woody Leyendecker, the police chief, tried to render himself invisible.

He had been pusillanimous—and miserable—throughout the whole trial.

"Good morning, Mr. Leyendecker," said Mrs. Ashley.

"Now, Mrs. Ashley," said Captain Mayhew, "you're goin' to tell us everything you know about this." He knew that the telegram that was to dismiss him from the police force and to summon him to the capitol for trial was on its way. He knew that he was to be blamed for bringing disgrace and ridicule upon the State of Illinois. He foresaw that he and his family would retire to his wife's father's farm, where she would spend the next year weeping, and that his children would be unable to hold up their heads in whatever one-room school they would be attending. He had come to vent his rage and despair upon Mrs. Ashley. "If you hold back one thing that we ought to know, it's going to go very hard for you. Who were those men that jumped into that car and got your husband away?"

For half an hour Mrs. Ashley could do nothing but repeat quietly that she knew nothing about any plan to rescue her husband. There were few to believe her—perhaps eleven persons, including one hunted man, hiding that moment in some woods not far away. Captain Mayhew did not believe her; the police chief did not believe her; newspaper readers from New York to San Francisco did not believe her; and least of all was she believed by Colonel Stotz in Springfield. Her daughters crept down the stairs and watched their mother with awe. Roger stood beside her. Finally the investigation was interrupted. A deputy arrived from the Sheriff's office with a telegram. The men left the house. Beata Ashley went upstairs to her room. She fell on her knees beside their bed and pressed her forehead against the coverlet. No words formed themselves in her mind. She did not weep. She was the doe that hears the huntsmen's shots across the valley.

To his sisters Roger said, "Just go about doing what you were doing."

"Is Papa safe?" asked Constance.

"Well, I hope so."

"What's Papa got to eat?"

"He'll find something."

"Will he come back here when it gets dark?"

"Come on, Connie," said Sophia. "Let's look for something real interesting in the attic."

Later in the morning Dr. Gillies dropped in, as though casually. He had been a friend of the family for many years, though the Ashleys had seldom needed him professionally. On the witness stand he had testified that Ashley had been his friend and patient (he had been consulted for a brief laryngitis), that he had held many long conversations of an intimate nature with the accused (they had discussed nothing more intimate than the prevalence of silicosis, tumbles, and tuberculosis among the miners), and that he was convinced that Ashley had harbored no ill-will whatever against the late Mr. Lansing.

Mrs. Ashley received him in the dismantled living room. There were a table, a sofa, and two chairs. Looking at her, Dr. Gillies thought, as he had so often, of Milton's words: "Fairest of her daughters, Eve." He soon became aware of her hoarseness and shortness of breath. As he said to his wife later, her speech was like a "supplication between blows." He placed a pillbox on the table.

"Do what it says on the label. You must keep up your strength with all these growing girls in the house. Drop them in a little water. Just some iron."

"Thank you."

The doctor paused with his eyes on the floor. He raised them abruptly and said, "A very remarkable thing, Mrs. Ashley."

"Yes."

"Does John know horses?"

"I think he rode when he was a boy."

"Hmmmm. He'll be going south, I imagine. Does he know any Spanish?"

"No."

"He can't get into Mexico. Not this year. I expect he knows that. They're putting out a bulletin about him. They came to me about it asking what scars he had on his body. I said I didn't know any. They're putting down that he's forty. Don't look thirty-five, if he's a day. Let's hope his hair grows fast. He'll make it, Mrs. Ashley. I'm convinced he'll make it. Let me know if I can be useful in any way."

"Thank you, Doctor."

"Take the hurdles as they come. What's Roger got a mind to do?"

"I think he told Sophia that he was planning to go to Chicago."

"Yes . . . Yes . . . Tell him to come and see me tonight at six."

"I will."

"Mrs. Gillies wants to know if there's anything you need."

"No, thank you. Thank Mrs. Gillies for me."

Silence.

"Extraordinary thing, Mrs. Ashley."

"Yes," she answered faintly. An awe, as in the presence of something unearthly, hung in the air between them.

"Good morning, Mrs. Ashley."

"Good morning, Doctor."

Roger presented himself at the doctor's office as the clock in the town hall tower struck six. Doctor Gillies was taken aback at the boy's height. He was struck also by how poorly he was dressed. The Ashleys lived in all the wealth of contentment on very little money. The boy's clothes were neat and clean and homemade. He looked the country yokel. His sleeves barely reached his wrists; his pants barely reached his ankles. It was a large part of their wealth that they gave little concern to the neighbors' opinions. Roger was the first student in the high school; he was the captain of the baseball team. He was the little lord in a small town, as his father had been before him. He was solid, level-eyed, and taciturn.

"Roger, I hear you're going to Chicago. You'll find work all right. If worst comes to worst, you carry this letter to an old friend of mine. He's a doctor in a hospital there. He'll find you a job as an orderly. That work is very hard. It takes a strong stomach to do the things an orderly has to do, and to see 'em. It pays very little. Don't do it unless you have to."

Roger's only question was, "Do they give these orderlies meals?"

"This other letter is a general one. It says that you're honest and reliable. I haven't put your name in there yet. I thought maybe you'd want to change your name—not because you're ashamed of your father, but because it would save you answering a lot of foolish questions. Is there some name that's always appealed to you? . . . I must go and speak to my wife for a moment. Run your eye over the backs of these books. Pick out some names. Combine two names for yourself."

Roger weighed them. Huxley and Cook and Humboldt and Holmes . . . Robert, Louis, Charles, Frederick. He liked the color red. There was a book bound in red called *Tumors of the Brain and Spine* by Evarist Trent and another, *Law and Society*, by Goulding Frazier. Maybe he was going to be a doctor or maybe a lawyer, so he chose a name from both and Dr. Gillies added the name "Trent Frazier" to the letters.

On the morning of July twenty-sixth Roger left for Chicago. He had not thought it necessary to discuss the project with his mother. The relation between mother and daughters was an orderly landscape—clear and a little cool; the relation between mother and son was a stormy one. He loved her passionately and bore a deep resentment. She knew her fault and reproached herself. She had given all her love to her husband; there was little left over for her children. Mother and son seldom looked into each other's eyes; each could hear the other think—a relationship that does not necessarily involve tenderness. Each admired the other boundlessly and suffered. Between them had stood John Ashley, who had never been called on to suffer, who had acquired no faculty that could make him aware of suffering about him.

Sophia watched her brother pack one of two small grips left from the sale. In silence she brought the clothes his mother and Lily had washed and ironed for him and a package of sliced bread, unbuttered, but spread with homemade chestnut paste and applesauce. It was seven in the morning. They walked gravely to a portion of the croquet court hidden from the house. Roger got down on one knee, bringing his face level with hers.

"Now, Sophie, I don't want you to get downhearted one minute. I'd hate to hear that. You just stay yourself like you are. It's up to you and me."

Here he gazed at her a moment, his silence freighted with all the unspoken.

"I'm going to write Mama once a month and send her some

money. But I'm not going to give her my new name and address. Do you know why? Because the police are going to open every letter that comes to our house. I don't want the police to know where I am. That means that Mama won't be able to write me any letters; but for a whole half year and maybe more I don't want any letters from her. I've got to have my mind all fixed on just one thing, and do you know what that thing is, do you?"

Sophia murmured, "Money."

"Yes. But I'm going to write you once a month, too. I'm going to send your letter to Porky, so that nobody will know. So, listen, Sophie. The first few days after the fifteenth of the month you go down the street past where Porky's working at his window. You keep your eyes right ahead of you, but out of the corner of your eyes you look and see if he's hung up that calendar in his window—you know, the one I gave him last Christmas with the pretty girl on it. If that calendar's in the window, that means there's a letter for you. Don't go in then, but go home and get some old shoes and go into his store as if you were a customer. Nobody, *nobody*, Sophie, must know that Porky's the person we're sending letters through. We could get him into trouble, too. This is all his idea. He's our best friend. Now, every time I write you I'm going to send you an envelope all stamped and addressed to me, and I'll put a piece of paper in it for you to write me on. So you go out of the house after dark and mail it in the mailbox at Gibson's corner. That's quite a long walk, but that's the way we ought to do it. Now, Sophie, write me everything that's going on here, and I mean everything. About Mama and how you all are. And write perfectly true—that's the chief thing I ask you."

Sophie nodded quickly.

"Now, Sophie, remember this: What's happened about Papa isn't important. What's important is what starts right now. You and I. Don't you change. Don't you get silly like most girls. We'll need our wits about us." He lowered his voice. "We've got to be fighters and the fight is all about money. I wouldn't be afraid to *steal* to get Mama some money."

Sophia again nodded quickly. She understood that. It was less important than what was next on her mind. She said softly: "You've got to promise me something, Roger. You've got to promise me that you'll write me what's perfectly true. Like if you were sick or anything."

Roger stood up. "You mustn't ask me that, Sophie. It's different with a man. . . . But I promise to write pretty truthfully."

"No! No! Roger! If you got sick, very sick, or if you got terribly hungry and were alone someplace. Or if something happened to you like what happened to Papa. I won't promise to write what's true unless you promise to write what's true too. You can't ask somebody to be brave without giving them something to be brave about."

There was a struggle of wills. "All right," he said finally. "I promise. It's a bargain."

Sophia looked up at him with an expression on her face which he was to remember all his life. He was to call it her "Domrémy look." "Because, Roger I can tell you this: that if there were anything in the world you needed—like money or anything like that—I could get it. I could do anything."

"I know it. I know that." He put his hand in his pocket and brought out five dollars. "Sophie, the night Papa started off on the train he sent me his gold watch. Yesterday I sold it to Mr. Carey for forty dollars. I gave thirty dollars to Mama, and I saved five dollars for myself and five dollars for you. I don't think Mama's thinking very clear about money these days. You do the shopping, so you keep that five dollars secret until sometime you may need it."

At the same time and without an additional word he gave her his greatest treasure—three Kangaheela arrowheads of green quartz, of chrysoprase.

"Well, I better get started."

"Roger, is Papa going to write us?"

"That's what I keep thinking about. I don't see how he can without getting us into more trouble, and himself too. You know he's not a citizen any more. After a while—maybe after years—he'll find a way. I think it's best just not to think about him for a while. What we've got to do is live, that's all."

Sophia nodded, then whispered, "Roger, what are you going to do? I mean: be?" Her question meant what kind of great man was he to be and Roger knew it.

"I don't know yet, Sophie." He looked at her with a faint smile and nodded.

He did not kiss her. He took her elbows in his hands and pressed them hard. "Now you go in the house and find some way of keeping Mama out of the kitchen while I pick up my coat and go out by the chicken run."

"Roger, I'm sorry. Roger, I'm sorry, but you've got to say goodbye to Mama. You're the only man we've got in the house now."

Roger swallowed and squared his shoulders. "All right, Sophie, I will."

"She's in the sitting room sewing, like it was evening."

Roger went up the stairs the back way, pretending that he had forgotten something. He descended into the front hall and entered the sitting room.

"Well, Mama, I'd better be going."

His mother rose uncertainly. She knew how he—and all Ashleys—hated to be kissed, hated birthdays and Christmas, and all occasions that strove to bring the unspoken to the surface. Her shortness of breath returned. Her words were barely audible. Beata Kellerman of Hoboken, New Jersey, reverted to the language of her childhood.

"Gott behüte dich, mein Sohn!"

"Goodbye, Mama!"

He left the house. For the first and only time in her life, Beata Ashley fainted.

Something had hovered unspoken behind the conversation between Sophia and her brother on the croquet court.

People who couldn't pay their taxes went to the poorhouse. The poorhouse at Goshen, fourteen miles from Coaltown, hung like a great black cloud over the lives of many in Kangaheela and Grimble counties. To go to jail was far less shameful than to go to Goshen. Yet the guests at Goshen enjoyed amenities hitherto unknown to them. The meals were regular and nourishing. The sheets on the beds were changed twice a month. The view from the great verandahs was uplifting. There was no coal dust in the air. The women were set to sewing for the state's hospitals, the men worked in the dairy and vegetable gardens and in winter made furniture. It is true that there was a persistent smell of cabbage in the corridors, but the smell of cabbage is not repellent to those who have spent a lifetime in indigence. Some congenial hours might have been arrived at in Goshen, but there were no smiles and no kindness; the burden of shame was too crushing. The institution was a limbo five days a week; on visitors' days it was hell. "Are you all right, Grandma?" "Do they make you comfortable, Uncle Joe?" We are enchained and we enchain one another. To go to Goshen meant that your life, your one life, had been a failure. The Christian religion, as delivered in Coaltown, established a bracing relation between God's favor and money. Penury was not only a social misfortune; it was a visible sign of a fall from grace. God had promised that the just would never suffer want. The indigent were in an unhappy relation to both the earthly and heavenly orders.

Goshen held a peculiar fascination and horror for children. Among Roger's and Sophia's schoolmates there were a number whose relatives were in the poorhouse. They bore the brunt of the other children's cruelty. "Go to Go-shun, you!" All had heard the account of Mrs. Cavanaugh's transference. She had lived in the big house next to the Masons' Hall, mortgaged and remortgaged. No taxes had been paid for years. She had been fed by members of her Baptist church; turn and turn about, they had left packages at her back door. But the Day came. She fled upstairs and hid in the attic while a matron packed her bag. She was brought down to the street, protesting at every step, clutching at every doorpost. She was carried down the front steps, her feet not touching the ground. She was pushed into the buggy like a recalcitrant cow. It was June and the neighbors' windows were open. Many a cheek turned pale as her cries filled the street. "Help me! Isn't there anybody who'll help me?" Mrs. Cavanaugh had once been proud, happy, and well-to-do. God had turned his face away from her. Roger and Sophia knew that their mother would walk toward Goshen's buggy like a queen. They knew they were her only defense.

Sophia went to work at once. It was midsummer. She bought a dozen lemons. She pushed the little cart on which she was accustomed to tote feed for her chickens to Bixbee's ice house and bought five cents' worth of ice. She made two signs: MINT LEMONADE 3 CENTS and BOOKS 10 CENTS. She set up a counter on an orange crate at the railroad station a quarter of an hour before the arrival and departure of all five daytime trains. She set a pail of water beside her in which she washed the glasses. She placed a vase of flowers beside the pitcher of lemonade. The stationmaster himself lent her a second table on which she ranged some books she had found in the attic and in old cupboards. They were Airlee MacGregor's books and some old textbooks that her father had used at his engineering school. By the second day, she had found other objects and made signs for their sale: MUSIC BOX 20 CENTS, DOLL'S HOUSE 20 CENTS and BABY'S CRIB 40 CENTS. She waited, smiling brightly. Within hours the news of this enterprise was carried from house to house. The women were electrified. ("Did anybody buy anything?" "How much did she sell?") Men were rendered uncomfortable. It was Sophia's smile that had long offended and disconcerted. The child of shame and crime had the effrontery to smile. A spectacle of great misfortune, of happiness overthrown, of a desperate struggle for existence arouses conflicting emotions. Even those who are moved to sympathy find that their sympathy is touched with relief, even triumph; with fear or awe or repulsion. Often such reversals are called "judgments."

The crowd of loungers who made it a habit to meet the trains doubled in numbers. The little saleslady sat alone, like an actress on the stage. The first glass of lemonade was bought by Porky. He gave no sign of knowing Sophia, but stood for ten minutes beside her counter slowly enjoying his beverage. Others followed. A traveling salesman bought *A First Year Calculus* and Mr. Gregg, the stationmaster, bought Robertson's *Sermons*. The second morning a group of boys set up a game of catch the length of the station platform. Their leader was Si Leyendecker. The ball flew back and forth over Sophia's tables; it became clear that it was the boys' intention to shatter the pitcher of lemonade.

"Si," said Sophia, "you can play somewhere else."

"Go fly a kite, Sophie."

The bystanders watched in silence. Suddenly a tall man with a great curling beard strode onto the platform from the main street. He put a stop to the game with curt unanswerable authority. Sophia raised her eyes to his and said, "Thank you,

sir"—lady to gentleman. He was a stranger, but it was not new
to Sophia that it would be men and not women who would be
useful to her.

Sophia waited until the fourth day to tell her mother. She
left a note on the kitchen table: "Dear Mama, I will be a little
late. Am selling lemonade at the depot. Love, Sophia."

Her mother said, "Sophia, I don't want you to sell lemonade
at the station."

"But, Mama, I've made three dollars and ten cents."

"Yes, but I don't want you to do it any more."

"If you made some of your oatcakes, I know I could sell
them all."

"I think people will try to be kind the first days, Sophia, but
it won't last. I don't want you to do it any more."

"Yes, Mama."

Three days later her mother found another note on the
kitchen table: "Am having supper at Mrs. Tracy's."

"What were you doing at Mrs. Tracy's, Sophia?"

"She had to go to Fort Barry. She gave me fifteen cents to
cook the children's supper. Mama, she wants me to stay all night
there and she'll give me another fifteen cents. She's afraid, because Peter plays with matches."

"Is she expecting you there tonight?"

"Yes, Mama."

"You may go tonight, but when she comes back you thank
her and tell her your mother needs you at home."

"Yes, Mama."

"And do not take the money."

"But, Mama, if I do the work, can't I have the money?"

"Sophia, you're too young to understand these things. We
don't need these people's kindness. We don't want it."

"Mama, winter's coming."

"What? What do you mean?—Sophia, I want you to remember that I know best."

Three weeks after Roger's departure, on August 16, the postman delivered a letter at "The Elms." Sophia received it at the
door. She did as the Moslems do—she pressed it to her forehead and heart. She looked at it closely. It had been opened and
clumsily resealed. She carried it to her mother in the kitchen.

"Mama, I think it is a letter from Roger."

"Is it?" Her mother opened it slowly. A two-dollar bill fell to the floor. She looked at the message in a dazed way and passed it to Sophia. "Read . . . read it to me, Sophia," she said hoarsely.

"It says, 'Dear Mama, everything's fine with me. I hope things are fine with you. I'll be making more money soon. It's not hard to get work here. Chicago is very big. I can't send you an address yet because I don't know where I'll be. You'd laugh at how I'm growing. I hope I stop soon. Love to you and Lily and Sophie and Connie. Roger.'"

"He's well."

"Yes."

"Show the letter to your sisters."

"Mama, you dropped the money."

"Yes . . . well . . . put it away safe somewhere."

Sophia followed her brother's instructions precisely. She went down the main street. The calendar was in Porky's window. In the early afternoon when there are few people on the street she returned into the town carrying an old pair of Lily's shoes. A customer in stocking feet was waiting for a repair. Sophia and Porky, who had never entered a theatre, played a long scene about heels and soles and half-soles; a letter glided from his hand to hers. She continued walking south and sat down on a step of the Civil War monument. She opened the envelope. It contained a stamped envelope addressed to "Mr. Trent Frazier, General Post Office, Chicago, Illinois," a sheet of writing paper, a dollar bill, and his letter. He was well. He was growing so fast she wouldn't know him. He had begun by washing dishes in a restaurant, but he'd been promoted and now he was helping the cooks in the kitchen. Every minute they were calling, "Trent, do this," "Trent, do that." He thought maybe he'd be a clerk in a hotel next. Chicago was very big; he didn't know what all those people were doing on earth. It was a thousand times bigger than Coaltown. He kept thinking about the day when she would come and see him in Chicago. He saw a place the other day where it said "School of Nursing." "Well, that's where you're going, Sophie." Only Roger, Dr. Gillies, and her father knew that Sophia dreamed of being a trained nurse. "I guess you know I sent Mama two dollars. I can send more soon. Here's a dollar for you to put in your secret bank. Stop in at

Mr. Bostwick's and see if he won't buy some of our chestnuts. They're the only ones for miles around. Here in Chicago they're twelve cents a bushel. That's last year's. If you get short of pencils Miss Thoms will give you some. She has them to burn. Now write small, Sophie, so you can get a lot of words in. Write the very day you get this letter. I guess nobody ever was as glad to get a letter as I'm going to be when you write me. How's Mama's voice? What things have you been having to eat? When there's reading aloud, do you ever laugh any? Don't forget what I told you about being downhearted. You wouldn't be like that. We're going to win. I forgot to tell you not to let Mama know that you get letters from me, but I guess you knew that. Roger. P.S. Now I wish I hadn't changed my name. We don't care what a billion people think. Papa didn't do it. P.S. II, I think of you and Mama and the house every night at NINE O'CLOCK, so make a note of that in your think box. P.S. III, How are the oak trees Papa planted getting on? Measure them and tell me."

The days went by. The vegetable garden and the chicken-house fed them. They drank linden tea made from the petals of their own tree. Sophia bought no more coffee—a cutting deprivation for her mother, who made no comment. The money dwindled away: flour, milk, yeast, soap. . . . Long before winter Sophia began picking up coals at the edge of the railroad yards as many of the poorer sort did. Often in the early dark the women and girls of the town would stroll by "The Elms," affecting an easy nonchalance. On six evenings of the week no lights showed in the house. All Coaltown waited in suspense: how long can a widow—a virtual widow—with three growing girls exist without money?

Constance was a child. She could not understand why she was withdrawn from school or why she was forbidden to accompany Sophia on her daily trips into town. At certain hours she would steal upstairs to a window overlooking the main street. She watched her former friends go by. Lily had always been a dreamer. Even during the trial she gave little attention to what was passing before her. She was not asleep, she was absent. Three things that were essential to her were missing: music, a continuous stream of new faces, and young men whose privilege it would be to admire her. She was neither melancholy nor sullen. She did willingly and well what she was called upon to do. All the Ashley children were slow-maturing, Lily most so. Her absence was a waiting. She was like a sea anemone that lies inert and colorless until the tide returns and flows about it.

Beata Ashley held herself as straight as before. There were no idle hands at "The Elms." The house was spotlessly clean. The attic and cellar were put in order. Many discarded objects were found that could be mended and put to use. The garden, orchard, and chickenhouse were given more attention than ever before. There were lessons. Supper was early, followed by reading aloud until darkness set in. They went through their four novels by Dickens and their three by Scott, their *Jane Eyre* and their *Les Misérables*. All agreed that Miss Lily Ashley was very fine in Shakespeare. On Thursdays only French was spoken and candles burned until ten. The "Second Thursday" balls were very brilliant. There was dancing to the music that issued from the horn of the gramophone. A throng of handsome cavaliers surrounded the beautiful Miss Ashleys. On each occasion a distinguished guest of honor was present—the beautiful Mrs. Theodore Roosevelt or the French Ambassador. After dancing a delicious *souper* was served. The menu stood on a wire rack before the guests: *Consommé fin aux tomates Impératrice Eugénie*, a *Purée de navets Béchamel Lili Ashley*, and a *Coupe aux surprises Charbonville*. The exquisite viands were to be partaken with a *Vin rosé Château des Ormes 1899*. All the children had known some German since infancy. The anniversaries of German poets and composers were observed with fitting ceremony. Lectures were delivered by the eminent Frau Doktor Beata Kellerman-Ashley, who could recite Goethe, Schiller, and Heine from memory by the hour. Unfortunately the piano had been sold to the second-hand man from Summerville, but the girls had heard Beethoven sonatas and Bach preludes and fugues scores of times. A little humming brought them alive again.

The events that had befallen Beata aroused in her no sense of wonder, or even of interrogation. To her they were crushing and senseless. Yet she expressed no grief and no complaint. She showed no sign of resentment except, perhaps, in her refusal to be seen on the streets of the town. She appeared to be in full control of herself, but one faculty she had totally lost. She was incapable of planning. Her mind refused to confront the future. It slid away from any contact with the morrow, with the oncoming winter, with next year. Nor did it revert to the past. She mentioned her husband only at long intervals and with visible effort. The hoarseness that had clouded her beautiful speaking voice gradually disappeared. It returned only on the days when members of the police force called to question her—not during those brutal interviews but after them.

She bore a burden that she mentioned to no one, insomnia—the insomnia of one to whom the future seems a corridor without light and without turning, the insomnia of the unshared bed. The insomnia was woeful because she knew it would soon make her old and haggard and it was terrifying because she feared it would lead to madness. The sleepless nights were additionally hard to bear because she could not afford a light to read.

She bore another burden, a deep unease to which she could give no name. There is no precise name for it in the three languages she knew. Beata Ashley was a rigorously moral woman. She divined that she was drifting toward some peril. Listlessness? Sloth? No. Insensibility? No. One form it took was recurring irritability *at its opposite*—Sophia's will to survive, Constance's yearning to rejoin her schoolfriends, Lily's unspoken assurance that some radiant future lay ahead of her.

All mothers love their children. We know that. But maternal love is like the weather. It is always there and we are most aware of it when it is undergoing change. Meteorologists have an odd way of saying "We may expect some weather during the coming week." Maternal love at "The Elms" was little noticed. Constance was once heard to say to her best friend, Anne Lansing, "Mama loves us best when we're sick and when I broke my arm." Beata Ashley would probably have been more stricken by the loss of a child than by the disappearance of her husband, for the greatest griefs are those accompanied by self-reproach. Lily was her mother's favorite—a partiality Lily took for granted. Beata Ashley's love for her husband was of such a degree and such a nature as left little room for other affections. In addition, she brought to her relations with her daughters a vague, diffused low opinion of women—of which she was unaware. This, as so often, was inherited from her mother. Clotilde

Kellerman, *geborene* von Diehlen, held a low opinion of men, a lower opinion of women, and a large self-esteem. Beata Ashley had feared her mother, then fought and defeated her; but she had not liberated herself from her mother's attitude to women. She did not like the way women's minds worked, the things they said, the life that had been assigned to them. (The only thing that ever rendered her impatient with her husband was her knowledge that John Ashley held a directly opposite view. Conversations with men soon bored him, save when they dealt with a collaborative process. His relations with the foremen in the mine were excellent.) During the months following the dramatic reversal in her life Beata Ashley was often overcome with waves of weariness and irritation at the company she kept —at this unremitting petticoat society, at all this ignorant virginity. She reproached herself bitterly for these exasperations. She hated injustice and knew that she was unjust. This attitude did not escape the girls. They felt—even Lily—that they were in some way inadequate to her, perhaps to life itself, and it made them difficult company for one another.

Sophia had assumed that in all homes mothers and daughters were "like that"; it's fathers who love girls. It was now five months since John Ashley had crossed his doorstep. Sophia was indeed a trial to her mother. She breathed resolution. The charge laid upon her by her brother filled her with happiness. These were the months when Beata Ashley, for all her outward serenity, was turning her face to the wall. She was gliding toward some finality. Toward merciful death. She was like a woman adrift with others in an open boat at sea. Her hunger and thirst had passed into numbness and she resented the raising of a banner for rescue, the bailing out of the rising flood, and all this peering toward the horizon for the palm trees of an island.

Undiscouraged, Sophia bent all her thoughts on dollars—their beauty, their rarity, their promise. Everything her eyes rested on contributed to hope's constructive faculty. She had read in the novels of Dickens about seamstresses and milliners, but such work would find no patronage here: the stony glances of the women of Coaltown told her that. Besides, their friend Miss Doubkov was the town's dressmaker. There were two restaurants in Coaltown—the dining room at the Illinois Tavern and a bad-smelling shanty by the depot; there was no need for another. Every house in town did its own laundry; there was a Chinese laundryman for drummers and bachelors. One project presented itself to her, however, with increasing force. She viewed it from all sides. The obstacles seemed insurmountable. Nevertheless, she found one encouraging factor, then another, then another. At the southern end of the town—opposite the Lansings' "St. Kitts"—stood a vacant and dilapidated building that had once been a mansion of some pretension. High weeds filled the yard. Two soot-blackened signs hung crookedly from a pillar on the verandah: FOR SALE and ROOMS AND BOARD. It had served, long after its days as a boardinghouse, as a refuge for vagrants, for unemployed miners, for coughers and "tumblers," for the crippled and the aged. Sophia remembered reading a book called *Mrs. Whittimore's Ark*. It told of how a widow with a large family of boys and girls opened a boardinghouse by the sea. The Ashley girls had found it very funny. It contained a good deal of merriment about the threat of going to the poorhouse. The lodgers included dear old absent-minded men and fussy but kindhearted old ladies. There was a handsome young medical student who fell in love with the oldest Miss Whittimore. On one occasion this young lady went to a sinister pawnbroker's store to sell her mother's pearl locket. Sophia did not understand why this was pictured as a degrading and desperate last resource. She wished that Coaltown had a sprinkling of pawnbrokers. The book ended happily when a rich man engaged Mrs. Whittimore to be the housekeeper in his castle on the hill. Sophia found the tattered volume in the attic and read it again, this time without a smile. It contained suggestions that would be useful to her. Apparently boardinghouse keepers have difficulty with lodgers who try to steal out of the house by night without paying their bills. Mrs. Whittimore met the problem by stretching threads across the stairs and attaching cowbells to them. The absconder, terrified by the inexplicable din he had aroused, would hurl himself at the front door only to discover that the resourceful Mrs. Whittimore had covered the knob with a film of soap. If there was a lodger whom she wished out of the house (Mr. Hazeldean, who helped himself to half the meat on the platter, or Mrs. Riemer, who found nothing to her liking), the children and other allies were instructed to gaze fixedly and in alternation at their chins and shoes. The victims of this persecution—it was called "smoking them out"—soon sought less unnerving accommodations. Mrs. Whittimore spared matches in the kitchen by striking fire from flint; she offered rabbit stew as chicken; she made soap of hog fat and a distillation from wood ashes. Sophia felt that the rediscovery of this book was a happy coincidence, but the lives of the hopeful abound in happy coincidences. She resolved to open a boardinghouse at "The Elms" and she lost no time about it. She called on Miss Thoms, her father's friend at the mines' office. Miss Thoms had spent a lifetime at the margin of penury; her store of hope was barely sufficient to sustain herself. She offered little encouragement, but promised two chairs, some tableware, and a whatnot. Sophia arranged a clandestine interview with Porky. Porky thought. "Yes, Sophie," he said, "start right now having a lamp on in the front room evenings. It don't look good to have a house dark." (He left a can of kerosene at the back door the same evening.) "My mother makes rugs. I've got two to give you. I've got an extry chair.—Go right to Mr. Sorbey at the Tavern and tell him about it. You can't have him be an enemy to you. And you can't ask cheaper prices than him. Lots of times he's crowded and his guests have got to sit downstairs in the lobby all night. I think he'd send some over to you. I've got an uncle with a bed he's not using."

She called on Mr. Kenny, carpenter, housepainter, and undertaker.

"Mr. Kenny, would half a dollar and a dozen eggs be enough if I asked you to make a sign to put on a house?"

"Well, now, what kind of a sign would that be, young lady?"

Sophia drew out a piece of torn wallpaper on which she had written THE ELMS   ROOMS AND BOARD.

"I see. I see. When would you want this?"

"Could you have it by tomorrow evening, Mr. Kenny?"

"Yes, I could." (Life's funny! Spit and image of her father. So they want to take in boarders. Well, well! Not likely.) "And you can pay me around New Year's time, if you see your way to it."

"Thank you, Mr. Kenny." Lady to gentleman.

On the way down the hill she met Porky. He talked quickly. "I got a table for you. At the Tavern rooms are fifty cents and seventy cents. Breakfast is fifteen cents; with steak, twenty-five cents. Dinner is thirty-five cents. Here are some tacks. Put up a notice in the post office where those cards are about lost dogs and purses. Drummers go in and out of the post office all day. Those schoolteachers hate to eat at the Tavern. I hear them talking about it all the time. Say 'home cooking.' "

"Yes, Porky."

"Sophie, listen. You can do it, but you've got to be patient. Maybe nothing will happen for quite a while. If I have any ideas, I'll tell you. You aren't going to expect anything big right off, are you?"

"Oh, no, Porky."

Sophia saved the Ashley family through the exercise of hope. "Saved" was her brother's and sisters' word for what she accomplished.

She had had a long experience of hope. Hope (deep-grounded hope, not those sporadic cries and promptings wrung from us in extremity that more resemble despair) is a climate of the mind and an organ of apprehension. Later we shall consider its relation to faith in the life of Sophia's father, who was a man of faith, though he did not know that he was a man of faith.

Sophia, at fourteen, had lived a long and busy life, burdened with responsibilities, fraught with joy and suffering. She had administered a large hospital. She was a veterinarian. In addition to raising chickens she had made splints for the mangled paws of dogs; she had rescued cats from torture on those long summer dusks when boys don't know what to do with themselves; she had saved fledglings fallen from the nest—blue and featherless on the sidewalks; she had reared young foxes and badgers and gophers and released them to their outdoors. She knew cruelty and death and escape and new life. She knew weather. She knew patience. She knew failure.

It is doubtful whether hope—or any of the other manifestations of creativity—can sustain itself without an impulse injected by love. So absurd and indefensible is hope. Sophia's was nourished by love of her mother and sisters, but above all by love of those two distant outcasts, her father and her brother.

So defenseless is hope before the court of reason that it stands in constant need of fashioning its own confirmations. It reaches out to heroic song and story; it stoops to superstition. It shrinks from flattering consolations; it likes its battles hard won, but it surrounds itself with ceremonial and fetish. Sophia slept with the three green arrowheads beside her. There are no rainbows in the narrow gorge at Coaltown, but she had seen two in her life on picnics along the Old Quarry Road. She knew their promise. Above the secret hiding place for her money she lightly drew an arc and wrote "J.B.A." and "R.B.A." Because it is irrational, hope rejoices in evidence of the marvelous. She drew strength from the inexplicable mystery of her father's rescue. Hope—the daring—is subject to intermittent overthrow, to black hours. Sophia drew into herself, lowered her head and waited, like an animal in a snowstorm. The Ashleys attended church every Sunday, but there were no religious exercises in the home. Sophia felt that it would be a weakness to pray for any astonishing reversal. Her petitions did not extend beyond asking that she be given some "good ideas" on the morrow; she asked that her mind be "bright."

So on the night following her visit to Mr. Kenny she slipped into her sister Lily's room. In one hand she carried a lighted candle, in the other the beautiful sign reading THE ELMS   ROOMS AND BOARD. She sat down on the floor, leaning the sign against her knees.

"Lily! Lily, wake up!"

"What is it?"

"Look!"

"Sophie! What's that?" Sophia waited. "Sophie, you're crazy."

"Lily, you must help me with Mama. She listens to you. You must make her see that it's important. Lily, we've got to do it. We'll starve. And, Lily: we'd meet people. We can't go on forever without seeing anybody. There'd be old people and young people and it would be fun. You and Mama could cook and Constance and I would make the beds."

"But, Sophie, they'd be awful people!"

"Everybody isn't awful. We could have lamps all over the house. And you could sing to the people. I know where there's a piano we could get."

Lily raised herself on one elbow.

"But Mama wouldn't let strange men come into the house."

"If a man came to the door who wasn't nice, Mama could

say all the rooms were full. Will you help me with Mama, Lily?"

Lily put her head on the pillow. "Yes," she said faintly.

"I see people every day, but you and Connie don't see anybody. It's bad for you. You'll get uninteresting. Maybe you'll get ugly."

After supper the next afternoon Lily was reading aloud from *Julius Caesar*. Her mother was sewing. Her sisters were seated on the floor unraveling old baby blankets to make balls of yarn. Lily came to the end of a scene and glanced at Sophia.

"Are your eyes tired, dear?" asked her mother. "Shall I read?"

"No, Mama. Sophia has something she wants to say."

"Mama," said Sophia slowly. "This is a big house. It's too big for us. Don't you think it would be a good idea to turn it into a boardinghouse?"

"What! What, Sophia?"

Sophia brought out the sign and rested it against her knees. Her mother stared at it and rose, a distraught expression on her face.

"Sophia, I think you've lost your mind. I don't know where you get such ideas. Where did you find that dreadful thing? Put it away this minute. You're too young, Sophia, to know what you're talking about. I'm astonished at you!"

Voices were never raised at "The Elms." Constance began to cry.

Lily said, "Mama! Mama, dear, stop and think."

"Think!"

Sophia raised her eyes from the floor and looking into her mother's said with measured directness, "Papa would wish us to. Papa would want it."

Her mother stared at her as though she had been struck. "What do you mean, Sophia?"

"People who love people think about them all the time. Papa's thinking about us. He's hoping we do something just like this."

"Girls, leave me alone with Sophia."

"Mama," said Lily, "I want to stay. Constance, go into the garden a minute."

Constance flung herself at her mother's knees, "I don't want to go out of the room alone. Mama, don't send me out of the room."

The effect of Sophia's words was such that her mother, after her first outburst, was unable to control her voice. She walked to the farthest window, trembling. She felt cornered, dragged back into life.

"Mama, Papa wouldn't want us to live without lamps at night and to go around in bad clothes. He hopes we're well and happy and we hope he is. Winter's coming. You've put up all those vegetables and fruit, but we'll have to buy flour and things. Anyway, Constance ought to have some meat at her age. That's what the book upstairs says. Mama, it would be wonderful to tell Roger that he doesn't have to send us money. Maybe he needs it more than we do. It would be hard for some people, but you're such a wonderful housekeeper you'd know in a minute how to make a boardinghouse."

Lily went across the room to her mother and kissed her. "Mama, I think we ought to try," she said in a low voice.

"But, Sophia, Sophia, you don't understand: *no one would come!*"

"Mr. Sorbey at the Tavern is always very nice to me. He let me sell lemonade in the lobby one day when it rained and he said I could do it again whenever I wanted to. Sometimes the Tavern's so full that men and even ladies have to sit up downstairs all night. He used to send them to Mrs. Blake's, but Mrs. Blake broke her hip, and can't take them any more. Somebody told me that the high school teachers hate eating at the Tavern. They'd all come here to dinner. I think they'd want to live here and not at Mrs. Bowman's and Mrs. Haubenmacher's."

Her mother turned her head from side to side. "But, Sophia, we have no chairs, no bureaus, no beds, no sheets."

"Lily and I don't need our bureaus and I can sleep in Lily's bed. Miss Thoms is going to give me two chairs. Porky's going to give me a bed, a chair and a table and two rugs. He can fix that bed we found in the attic. We've got enough for two rooms. We can start."

"Let's try," said Lily.

Constance rushed to her mother and put her arms around her. "Then we can start living like other people!"

"Very well," said their mother. "Light a candle. Let's go up and look at the rooms."

"Mama," said Sophia, "I have some kerosene. Let's put a

lamp in this sitting room now. Nobody'd want to come to a house that looked like everybody was sad."

The next noon, on September 15, Lily stood on a chair and nailed the sign on an elm by the front gate. The women of Coaltown increased their evening strolls past the house to behold this evidence of a laughable delusion. "They ought to call it 'Jailbirds' Nest.'" "No, 'Convicts' Corner.'"

The next day Dr. Gillies, driving his buggy down the main street, drew up beside Sophia.

"Hey, you—Sophie!"

"Good morning, Dr. Gillies."

"Well, well! You look as happy as a butcher's cat."

"I am, a little."

"What's this about your opening a boardinghouse?"

"We are, Dr. Gillies.—Dr. Gillies, I was thinking that maybe sometime you might have a patient who was getting well and wanted to be quiet. Mama's a wonderful cook. We'd take awfully good care. . . ."

Dr. Gillies smote his forehead. "Just the thing!" he exclaimed. "Tell your mother I'm coming over to see her at seven o'clock tonight." He arranged for the convalescent Mrs. Guilfoyle to stay at "The Elms" for two weeks. "Chicken broth, some of your famous applesauce, a coddled egg every now and then."

Sophia called on Mr. Sorbey at the Tavern and told him about the project. "If the Tavern's crowded sometime, Mr. Sorbey, maybe you could send somebody to us. Mrs. Guilfoyle's at the house now and she's very contented." Three days later he sent over an itinerant preacher, Brother Jorgenson, who was making himself obnoxious by trying to save souls in the barroom.

Sophia stopped a new high school teacher on the street. "Miss Fleming, I'm Sophia Ashley. My mother's opened a boardinghouse at 'The Elms'—you can see it behind those trees there. We have dinner at twelve o'clock. It's thirty-five cents, but if you came every day of the week you'd get one dinner free. My mother's a wonderful cook." Delphine Fleming came to dinner, asked to see the rooms, and stayed two years. The news aroused displeasure in the school board, but Miss Fleming came from the east—that is, Indiana—and it was assumed that her moral discriminations were not of the finest. Some older commercial travelers discovered the place. The stewed chicken with dumplings and the *Rostbraten* began to be reported when drummers got together—as was Lily's singing. "Joe, I'm telling you the truth; I never heard anything like it. 'Mid pleasures and palaces!' A murderer's daughter, too!" A third and a fourth room were fitted out. Sophia persuaded her mother to bake tray after tray of her admired German ginger cookies. She sold them in the Tavern's lobby during holidays. She made savings, too, following Mrs. Whittimore's example. On slaughtering days she dragged her little wagon three miles down the road to the Bell Farm (Roger had hoed and hayed and milked there during his summer vacations) and returned with hog fat. She made soap from it which her mother freshened with lavender. She continued her own yeast. The stove was lit from flint and steel. Penny-pinching is anything but dull. She confronted the tradesmen without shyness. The pitying indulgence toward her began to be replaced by a surprised respect. Men greeted her cordially; a few women began to return her greetings with a curt nod. Her former schoolmates whispered and giggled when she passed. Boys jeered, "Rags, bottles, and sacks, Sophie. Y'want to buy any rags, bottles, and sacks?"

Some odd things happened.

One day, a week after "The Elms" had announced that it offered rooms and board, Eustacia Lansing, dressed in the deep mourning that so became her, called at Porky's shoe-repair store. She chose the hour of two o'clock when the streets of Coaltown are almost deserted. There was a matter of resoling one of Félicité's shoes. As she prepared to leave she said: "Porky, you see the Ashleys from time to time, don't you?"

"Once in a while I do."

"Is it true they're opening a boardinghouse?"

"People say that."

"Porky, you can keep a secret, I'm sure. I think you'll do something for me and keep it secret."

Porky's face remained impassive.

"I want you to call at my house for a large parcel and I want you to leave it at the back door of the Ashley house without anybody knowing anything about it. The parcel contains a dozen sheets and pillow cases and a dozen towels. Could you find time to do that, Porky?"

"Yes, ma'am."

"Can you pick it up just after dark? It will be behind my front gate."

"Yes, ma'am."

"Thank you, Porky. Just put this card on the parcel."

On the card was written, "From a well-wisher."

One day Miss Doubkov, the town's dressmaker, called on Porky with a troublesome shoe.

"Porky, you know the Ashleys, don't you?"

"Yes, ma'am."

"I have two chairs I don't need. Could you pick them up at my door tonight and leave them at their back door?"

"Yes, ma'am."

"And no one's to know, Porky, except you and me."

During these early weeks a rocking chair was found within the picket fence; three blankets, not new but clean and neatly mended; a large cardboard box containing all sizes of spoons, knives, and forks with cups and saucers and a soup tureen—from the women of the Methodist Church, perhaps.

Young traveling men seldom applied for admission at "The Elms." They could not afford it. They spent the night in a large drafty dormitory on the top floor at the Tavern—twenty-five cents a night. Nevertheless, Mrs. Ashley had turned a number away. There were growing daughters in the house and the town was malicious. One afternoon in January she relaxed her rule and admitted a man of about thirty carrying a grip and a suitcase of samples. At nine-thirty Beata Ashley banked the furnace, locked the front and back doors, and put out the lights. Toward two in the morning she was awakened by the smell of smoke. She roused her daughters and the mathematics teacher. They descended the stairs and traced the smoke to the kitchen. The teacher hurried on before them, crossed the room coughing, and opened the back door. Thick oddly smelling smoke was issuing from the oven, in which lay a mass of smoldering pink paper. The fire was easily extinguished. The women made themselves some hot cocoa and waited for the air to clear. When Mrs. Ashley returned to her room she found that it had been ransacked. The contents of her bureau drawers had been flung about the floor. In the cupboard the lining of her coat had been slit open. A knife had been run through her mattress;

her pillow was cut into shreds. The backs of the pictures on the walls had been torn away.

Colonel Stotz in Springfield hated the Ashleys. He was convinced that somewhere in Mrs. Ashley's room there would be information about John Ashley's rescuers. There would be letters; there might even be recent letters from the hunted man. There might be a photograph of him that could be reproduced on posters.

Throughout their married life Ashley had been only four times separated from his wife for twenty-four hours. The only letters she had from him were those which he had written her daily from the jail. These were missing. Missing, too, was her only photograph of him—a faded blue print from which he looked out laughing, holding high his two-year-old son. The following morning the daughters looked wonderingly at their mother. Her face had never shown anxiety or fear and did not show it now. The confrontation with the enemy seemed to strengthen her.

As the months went by Beata Ashley gradually emerged from her torpor. The work was unremitting. There is no day of rest for those who take lodgers. To Constance it was an exciting game. She was never tired, not even on Monday evenings after a day over the washtubs. Lily seemed to have returned from that far country where she had been moving in a dream. All day there was cooking, dusting, making beds, and dishwashing. Sophia was the only member of the family to pass the gate; Lily had no wish to; Constance longed to accompany her sister into the town, but Sophia knew that she was not yet ready to face the hostility of her school-friends. Roger's remittances to his mother rose to ten and twelve dollars a month. He reported that he was doing well, but he sent no name or address to which she might reply. Sophia did the shopping, took the lodgers' money, bought furniture, opened new rooms, and abounded in "ideas." She wrote her brother long letters. It was a proud day when she could tell him that she had paid the taxes. The town watched her activity with grudging admiration. She was said to be "sharp as a scalping knife." Auctions were rare in Coaltown, but it was often quietly circulated that a family was selling its "things"—elderly people were leaving town or a home was broken up by death. There was Sophia. When fire and the overenthusiasm of the volunteer fire department combined to make havoc of a house or the contents of an attic, there was Sophia buying bed linen, window curtains, old clothes, mattresses, and chamber pots. A Baptist church by Old Quarry Pond faltered to its end; Sophia bought the piano that had served its Sunday school—three dollars a month for five months. She bought a second cow. She began raising ducks; she suffered a defeat with turkeys. An eighth room was fitted out by the end of May, 1904. During the warm weather guests were even lodged in the Rainy Day House. Mrs. Swenson was persuaded to return as hired girl. After the occasion on which Mrs. Ashley's bedroom had been ransacked it was Lily's idea—or, to all appearances, Lily's idea—that Porky should live at "The Elms," sleeping in a small room off the kitchen. In return for his meals he did the heavy work about the house and helped the family to master those difficulties to which hostelries are particularly subject. There were heart attacks and convulsions. There was sleepwalking and drunkenness and theft. Mrs. Ashley came to know the drummer's condition: the uprootedness, the compulsion to boast, the burden of having to present all day a front of dazzling success ("Mrs. Ashley, I got so many orders today, I don't see how I'll be able to fill 'em!"), the drinking to obtain sleep, the nightmare in which existence presents a face of vacancy or derision. She came to divine the black hours when the razor blade trembles in the hand. During the early months of the venture it was the Ashleys' custom to retire upstairs after the dishes had been washed and to continue their reading aloud in Mrs. Ashley's room. But she soon learned that it was unwise to leave the lodgers to themselves at that hour; she became aware that most of the rooms contained restless, fretful, or frantic human beings. Some particular tension began to collect in them after sunset. So the evenings were spent in the large sitting room. Often Lily sang to her mother's accompaniment. One by one the roomers would creep down the stairs. Many would stay for the reading aloud. During the hot months the social hour was transferred to the summerhouse; a reader's eyes would be spared and the group would sit in silence under the spell of the moonlight or starlight on the pond and the muted complaints of Sophia's slowly gliding ducks.

Beata Ashley admirably filled the role of boardinghouse keeper. She set up a ward against disorder as many schoolmasters do—she exacted a standard of behavior of more than human height. She demanded punctuality, precedence for ladies, coats and neckties at table, decorum in speech, grace before meals, and restraint in expressing admiration for the waitresses. A number of traveling gentlemen were not accepted a second time at "The Elms." They took to boasting at the Tavern's saloon that they had been disbarred from "Rope-end Hall," but the boasts rang increasingly hollow. The legend spread—a mixture of perfect fried chicken, the best coffee in Illinois, sheets smelling of lavender, of being aroused in the morning not by kicks on the door but by angel voices repeating one's name. During the trial and the months that followed Ashley's rescue the girls were aware that their mother was giving little attention to the books read aloud in the evening, even when it fell her turn to read. A change took place in the summer of 1903, however. On Tuesday nights they read *Don Quixote* in French. Beata Ashley found not humor but truth in the adventures of the knight for whom the world was filled with evil necromancers and with those bitter injustices which a man must put right. Her needle would come to rest, suspended in meditation, at the account of his devotion to a peasant girl whom he declared to be the first of all women. They read the *Odyssey*. It told of a man undergoing many trials in far countries; to him came the wise goddess, the gray-eyed Pallas Athene, upbraiding him when he was discouraged and promising him that one day he would return to his homeland and to his dear wife. She was tired by the housework, she was consoled by the reading, and she slept.

For all their work the profits were meagre. The Ashleys held their heads just above water.

Lodgers came and went at "The Elms," but there were few callers. Dr. Gillies made professional visits and on each occasion exchanged a few words, but he did not sit down. Mrs. Gillies dropped in from time to time on a Sunday afternoon, as did Wilhelmina Thoms. There was one regular visitor, however,

Miss Olga Doubkov, the town's dressmaker. She called on alternate Wednesday evenings. She was not received with notable warmth by Mrs. Ashley, but the girls welcomed her eagerly. She brought the news of the town and of the world.

Hard circumstances had left Olga Doubkov—reportedly a Russian princess—high and dry in Coaltown. Her father, pursued by the police for revolutionary activity, had fled to Constantinople with an ailing wife and two daughters. He had joined Russian friends in a mining town in western Canada, but his wife's health was unable to sustain the climate there and he had accepted a call to Coaltown. Olga Doubkov was an orphan at twenty-one and set out to support herself by her skill as a needlewoman. Most of the women of Coaltown made and remade their own clothes and those of their younger children. Weddings had always been important affairs in Coaltown; Miss Doubkov elevated their importance. She was an authority on modes and trousseaux; her advice on every aspect of the ceremony was as much valued as her art. Few mothers had the courage to array their daughters and themselves for such occasions unaided. Weddings became Coaltown's grand opera. Her principal income, fortunately, was derived from her services at the Illinois Tavern where she was in charge of the linen room. She was a foreigner, so foreign that her idiosyncrasies were tolerated as being outside the town's ability to judge them. She smoked long yellow cigarettes. She practiced idolatry—that is, a corner of her sitting room held a number of icons with burning lamps beneath them, before which she crossed herself on entering and leaving the room. She was extremely outspoken and her "latest" was repeated from house to house in shocked undertones. She was tall and thin and carried herself straightly. Her sallow skin was drawn tightly over her high cheekbones. Her long narrow eyes intimidated children; they were thought to resemble those of a cat. Her sandy hair was piled high on her head and adorned with small black velvet bows. She dressed with elegance, tightly laced, and rustling in silk. In winter she wore a tall fur hat and a dragoon's redingote, faced with frogs and brave with epaulettes. She was poor; the whole town knew how poor she was. It was believed that she subsisted on oatmeal, cabbage, apples and tea—a chop on Sunday. Clothes and the one party she gave in the year were her only extravagances.

She invited twenty guests to a Russian Easter tea. These occasions were awesomely foreign: the great cakes, the ritual greeting, "The Lord is risen!" "The Lord is risen indeed!" the ceremonial kiss, the eggs decorated with symbolic designs, the lamps under the icons. It was known that she was saving her money to return to Russia and that she would board the train at Coaltown without one backward glance of regret. The saving of money where there was so little to be saved was a race with time. Olga Sergeievna did not intend to return to Russia a pauper. She was not a princess but a countess, nor was her name Doubkov.

Miss Doubkov had never known the Ashleys well. Her friend in town was Mrs. Lansing. Both Eustacia Lansing and her older daughter Félicité were even better needlewomen than she, but they consulted her, employed her, and enjoyed her company. Together the three of them made many elaborate and handsome garments. Miss Doubkov admired Mrs. Lansing ("Girls," she would say at a sewing session among bridesmaids, "the most important thing for a woman is charm—watch Mrs. Lansing well!"), but she detested Breckenridge Lansing and made no secret of it. She once rebuked him in his own house for a contemptuous remark he had made about his son George. She read him a lecture on the bringing-up of boys, put on her hat and tippet, bowed to Eustacia and Félicité, and left "St. Kitts," as she thought, forever. Although she did not know the Ashleys well, the whole town was aware of her admiration for them: "the children had the best manners of any in Coaltown; at 'The Elms' things were as they should be." Mrs. Ashley now distrusted these Wednesday-evening visits, coming only gradually to see that they were prompted neither by curiosity nor by compassion. The reason for the calls lay in Miss Doubkov's upbringing. She was an aristocrat. In prosperity aristocrats do not intrude upon one another; in misfortune they close their ranks. They man the walls against barbarians. During the trial, although the courtroom was full to suffocation, there were always a few vacant seats beside Mrs. Ashley and her son, perhaps out of respect, perhaps because crime and misfortune are felt to be contagious. From time to time Miss Doubkov, Miss Thoms, or Mrs. Gillies filled them—after nodding shortly toward Mrs. Ashley, as one does at funerals.

There was another reason for Miss Doubkov's fortnightly calls at "The Elms." Like Sophia, she lived suspended on hope. We have said that the hopeful find nourishment in marvels. Such, for her, was Ashley's rescue. For her it had been a repetition of the most important event in her life and it confirmed a promise of hope for her future. In Russia a sentence of death had been passed on her father. He too had slipped through the hands of the police. In Coaltown she hoped for an escape for herself that could only arrive by a miracle. She hoped to return to her native land, to present herself to her relatives, and to end her days serving her fellow countrymen. She had no desire to return in ostentatious state; she wished merely to be above condescension, commiseration, and favor. She had set aside the train fare to Chicago (three years—the first most difficult years), then the ticket to the port of Halifax in Nova Scotia (seven years), a ship's passage to St. Petersburg (twelve years). She was now saving the money, ruble by ruble, to support herself in Russia while she applied for a position as a schoolteacher or as a governess. She was fifty-two years old. This was an exercise in hope. Illness and death might intervene; fire or thieves might rob her of her savings; a nationwide devaluation of currency might wipe them out. Hope, like faith, is nothing if it is not courageous; it is nothing if it is not ridiculous. The defeat of hope leads not to despair, but to resignation. The resignation of those who have had a grasp of hope retains hope's power.

Long before that extraordinary event in the railroad yard outside Fort Barry, Olga Sergeievna had been aware of something well out of the ordinary at "The Elms." She had not been the only woman in town who had been a little in love with John Ashley, ordinary though he was to all appearances. She had been occasionally invited to supper at "The Elms"; she had exchanged greetings and general remarks with him on the street almost daily for seventeen years. The strange events that befell him in the spring and early summer of 1902 confirmed her intuition. He was chosen. He was a sign. When she called at the house now she was renewing her strength; she was warming her spirit at a flame, at a place where "real things" had been revealed. On each of these visits to "The Elms" Miss Doubkov requested that Lily sing to her. Lily was training her voice by imitating that of Madame Nellie Melba as it issued from the morning-glory horn of an almost ruined gramophone. The results were remarkable. Miss Doubkov predicted with alarming conviction that one day Lily would be a great singer with the world at her feet. She sent to Chicago—from her slowly accumulated savings—for copies of Madame Albanese's *Method of Bel Canto, Volumes I and II*. She showed her how Madame Carvalho advanced to the footlights to acknowledge applause and how La Piccolomini, in recital, stood in silence, in *recueillement*, until she had gathered all the audience's attention. The ladies at "The Elms" spoke textbook French; she introduced the more informal idioms of polite conversation. She admired Beata Ashley; she did not like her. There is nothing remarkable about that for she liked no women. She disapproved of Mrs. Ashley's refusal to appear in the streets of the town. Under similar circumstances she would have walked the length of Main Street daily, glaring crushingly at those who failed to salute her. Sophia did not interest her. She saw clearly the extent of the girl's achievement in the creation of the boardinghouse, but she offered no help or counsel. She had been through hard straits herself and assumed that persons of quality did not discuss them. Steel exists to support pressure. The truth was that she was interested only in men, despicable though most of them were. There had been no man in her life since the death of her father and the ignominious disappearance of a fiancé, but she lived only to impress men with her sharp judgments on them, her good sense, and her elegant carriage. Women were tiresome.

The linen room in the basement of the Illinois Tavern was long, low, and airless. Feeble light fell from a high grated window that was seldom washed. Several mornings a week Miss Doubkov descended to this room carrying two kerosene lanterns which she attached to hooks hanging from the ceiling. Piles of linen lay under dustcloths on shelves about the room. Under the lanterns was a long table, which she cleaned thoroughly on each of her visits. One morning in June of 1903 she was interrupted in her work by a knock on the door. She opened it a few inches; a draft would admit dust from the coalbins down the corridor.

"Wa-all?"

"Miss Doubkov?"

"Yass."

"I see that you're busy. May I come in and wait until you are free to give me a moment?"

"I'm always busy. What do you want?"

"My name is Frank Rudge. I'd like to talk to you in confidence, if you'll let me come in."

"Confidence! Confidence!—Come in. Sit down there until I finish what I am doing."

She placed him under the light and glanced at him sharply. He was a good-looking man of thirty-five and he knew it. In a moment he knew, too, that Miss Doubkov was susceptible to good-looking men and that her susceptibility would take the form of truculence and rudeness. She put him to work. There were piles of freshly laundered sheets on the floor. She directed him to heap them on the table. She busied herself at the far end of the room. Finally she lit a cigarette and addressed him.

"What do you want?"

"I want to offer you payment of thirty dollars a month for very little work."

"So!"

"And to point out to you a way of possibly earning several thousand dollars."

"Faugh!"

"I want to talk to you about John Ashley."

"I know naw-thing about John Ashley."

"You're right. For fourteen months nobody has known anything about him."

"Stop your foolishness and tell me what you want."

"The truth, ma'am. All we want is the truth."

"You are from the police! You are from Colonel Stotz's office!"

"Colonel Stotz is not in office as State's Attorney. I was in the police, but I was fired. I represent a private person."

"Colonel Stotz is an old fool."

"His office didn't handle the matter very well. We know that."

"Say what you mean! They were imbeciles!"

"Well—"

"They were idiots. You're wasting my time."

"Miss Doubkov, will you allow me to talk to you for three minutes without your interrupting me?"

"Well, first you be quiet for three minutes."

She made him wait again. She pretended to count piles of towels. Her hands were trembling slightly. She hated the police, all police everywhere. Just so the police must have closed in about her home in Russia; just so, after their departure, the police must have "smoked" about among their neighbors. But she smelt money in the air—rubles and rubles. At last she lit another cigarette and turned toward him, leaning her back against the shelves, her arms akimbo. "Say what you have to say."

"Thank you, ma'am. Ma'am, the State's Attorney's office has a section dealing with the search for missing persons—particularly for missing persons under conviction. That section has been unable to find any trace of John Ashley or of the six men who rescued him. Four thousand dollars has been offered for information leading to the arrest of either Ashley or the men."

"Three thousand."

"The price has been raised."

"Why are you telling this to me?"

"Because you are the only person who goes in and out of that house—the only observant person, Miss Doubkov! The answers to those questions are *in that house*. As soon as Mrs. Ashley gets fifty dollars together she will start making payments to those rescuers. She will soon be receiving messages and money from her husband. It is very possible she is receiving them already through some indirect means."

"Hah! So that is why the police have been opening my letters!"

"Only twice, Miss Doubkov. I didn't do it; they did it. Remember, I represent a private person. That house is being watched very closely." He rose and came around the table toward her. He stared into her eyes. "That information is going to come to light, somehow, any day now. Lots of people are going to put in a claim for the money. Why not you? Eh? If you got hold of the principal piece of information, I could arrange that your claim to the money was recognized."

"And with your low dirty minds you think I would help to send an innocent man to his death?"

"Don't be a child, Miss Doubkov. There is another governor in office. You don't suppose a new governor would put his head in that hornet's nest. Ashley would be pardoned, but he can't be pardoned until we know the truth. That's all we're after—facts."

"Why are you all so excited about a man you are ready to pardon? Just announce his pardon and he will come back."

"He might come back, ma'am, but he would never tell us who his rescuers were. I don't think you realize how many mysterious things lie back of this thing. Who organized that rescue? He didn't do it from jail, we're sure of that. Someone was ready to pay those men a lot of money to risk their lives. Who are Ashley's rich, influential friends? Try to find that out. Who's behind the boardinghouse? We know to a penny how much money Mrs. Ashley had. We know every stick of furniture that was left in the house. Even if Mrs. Ashley were a very bright woman she couldn't have got that going alone, and she's not a bright woman at all. You didn't lend her money; Dr. Gillies didn't; Miss Thoms has no money to lend her. We called on their old people: Mr. Ashley's mother's dead, but his father's still alive—runs a small bank in upstate New York. He wouldn't talk about his son; threw us out of the house. Also, Mrs. Ashley's parents. There are mysteries here, Miss Doubkov—big mysteries. When they're cleared up, Mr. Ashley can come back to his family."

Miss Doubkov walked away from him and lit another cigarette. Mr. Rudge put his business card on the table.

"You write me a letter every month on the last day of the month. Put anything into it that could have the least connection with this matter. And I shall write to you, because information is constantly turning up at our end. What is the son's address in Chicago? Through what agent is Mrs. Ashley in touch with him? Do you think Mrs. Ashley is getting messages from her husband now?"

"No!"

"You have the opportunity to find out. There is another thing you could do. You call on Mrs. Lansing, don't you? Your four thousand dollars may be there."

"What?"

"Has it never occurred to you that Mrs. Lansing may have arranged Ashley's escape?"

"What is that you say?"

"Mr. Ashley and Mrs. Lansing were—pardon my frankness—lovers."

"No, they were not."

"You cannot be sure of that. It is possible that Mrs. Lansing advanced money to start the boardinghouse. All sorts of things are possible."

Miss Doubkov gave a long low contemptuous laugh. She glanced at her visitor's card. "Mr. Rudge," she said, "you know very little about the Ashleys and the Lansings. And you don't even know what your problem is. You're barking up the wrong tree. Your business is, first, to find out who killed Breckenridge Lansing."

"There is no doubt that Ashley killed—"

"Are you a detective?"

"Yes."

"Then stop talking. Start looking and listening. Are you staying in town a day or two?"

"Well . . . I could."

"You should. Your office made a botch of the trial. Try not to make a botch of your investigation. Learn something about what took place here. Change your clothes. You look like a policeman. Go up the River Road. Pretend to get drunk at some of those places up there like Hattie's Hitching Post and The Old Brown Jug. Breckenridge Lansing spent two or three nights a week there. He certainly made some enemies. Get to know the men in the mines. Breckenridge Lansing was a pitiful administrator. He certainly made some enemies there. Get to know an old hunter around here named Jemmy. Lansing used to go off on hunting trips with him for a week at a time. Now I've earned thirty dollars of your money already. Yes, I will write the letters you want for four months. I am an honest person. If no useful information turns up in that time our agreement is over. You will pay me at the first of the month, not when you receive the letter. You will pay for my first letter now."

"I'll put a cheque in the mail this afternoon."

"No! I don't want it in writing. You'll put thirty dollars in my hand."

Rudge stayed eight days in Coaltown. He visited the linen room four times in order to discuss the Ashley Case with Miss

Doubkov. He was learning a good deal about Breckenridge Lansing, although he could not see that it threw much light on the murder. She abounded in further suggestions; she guided his investigations. As for her, she also went promptly to work, but she did not tell Rudge about whatever progress she made. An odd friendship sprang up between them. Soon they were playing cards together in the foul air and bad light of the basement. They won and lost immense fortunes in dried peas collected from the storeroom next door. They told each other the stories of their lives. Finally he confessed that he had been one of the armed guards that accompanied Ashley on the night of the rescue. Hence his dismissal from the police force. He had become a private detective and was engaged by insurance companies, banks, hotels, and jealous husbands. He had become something of an expert on arson and barn burnings. It was enjoyable work. He had been a favorite of Colonel Stotz during several of his terms of office and was now serving him in a private capacity. Colonel Stotz was a very rich man and had dug down into his own pockets to launch a manhunt: Ashley, dead or alive. Miss Doubkov drew from Rudge a detailed account of that famous rescue. Her questions drove him to search his memory for gestures and impressions that had escaped his conscious observation at the time and that he had failed to recall at the official inquiry. His account confirmed her belief in the obtuseness of the police. She did not point out to him certain deductions that seemed self-evident.

How stupid men are! Within a week she was convinced that she knew who Ashley's rescuers were. She had long been fairly certain who Lansing's murderer was.

The only person aware of these long conversations in the basement was the janitor, Solon O'Hara. Like his cousin Porky O'Hara—third or fourth cousin, cousin many times—Solon belonged to the Church of the Covenant community on Herkomer's Knob, the religious sect that had found its way from Kentucky into southern Illinois a hundred years ago. They were largely Indian stock though they bore English and Irish family names. It was thought that they engaged in strange religious rites and they were given several derisive names, but they were known to be trustworthy, irreproachable in their habits, and particularly secretive. They were employed all over

Coaltown as janitors and caretakers in the Tavern, bank, court, schools, jail, in Memorial Park, the cemetery, and the railroad yards. Except for Porky, none of them worked in stores or held sedentary jobs. Solon knocked at the door of the linen room from time to time, bringing in fresh laundry or replacing the hot irons that Miss Doubkov required when she had finished some work of mending.

Miss Doubkov set about her new task at once. She invited Mrs. Ashley and her two older daughters to "Russian Tea." Mrs. Ashley was unable to leave her boardinghouse, but the girls accepted the invitation. Lily was seen on the main street for the first time in well over a year. The appearance of a giraffe could not have caused a greater sensation. Miss Doubkov's attention to everything about her at "The Elms" was redoubled.

Lodgers came and went. Sophia's savings increased as the larger expenditures necessary to fitting out the house became fewer. Her mother did not ask to see the money or to know its amount. The second winter in the life of the boardinghouse drew near. Lily would be twenty on the New Year's Day of 1904. She had returned from her dreamy "absence," but she was not impatient for a more varied life. She seemed to be aware that she would soon have to cope with as much adulation as a young woman could sustain; she could afford to wait. Neither Mrs. Ashley nor Lily nor Sophia found anything to interest them in the procession of guests. Only Constance scanned each face and weighed each disposition. She felt curiosity about all and even affection for some. She was searching for her father. She alone of the Ashleys was demonstrative of affection. Her suffering at his disappearance from the home took the form of astonishment. She was unable to understand why her mother so seldom mentioned him. Throughout her life, even when she had forgotten him in all but the most inward sense, she retained a resentment against her mother for this silence. Mrs. Ashley sat at the head of the table in apparent serenity. She kept the conversation going, contributing the most conventional remarks, to which her beautiful speaking voice lent an air of measured reflection. Dr. Gillies's eyes often rested with concern on Sophia, his favorite, who would be sixteen next spring. She had lost weight and would be a beauty, too. At intervals they engaged in whispered conversations about her ambition to be a nurse. The thing that worried him about her was that she seemed to be developing in two different directions. There was the practical Sophia, hurrying from store to store on the main street, bargaining, selling ducks, buying her flour, sugar, and cornmeal by the barrel, or, in the house, firmly extracting the money due her from reluctant guests, behaving like a more than usually capable young woman of twenty-five; and there was another Sophia who seemed to have grown younger, who blushed and stammered in any encounter that did not involve her managerial capacity. Her air of happiness had taken on an exalted quality that disturbed him. He feared she was carrying too great a load. On the second Christmas morning of the new era he met her at the door of "The Elms" and placed a package in her hands.

"Merry Christmas, Sophia!"

"Merry Christmas, Dr. Gillies!"

"See if you like that."

She unwrapped the package, blushing, and read the title of the book, *The Life of Florence Nightingale*. As he told his wife later, "Her face went to pieces." She could not speak. She stared at him as though he were a frightening object, murmured a few words, and fled to the kitchen. "She's starved for something," he said to himself. "She misses her father and her brother." There was a lack of affection in the air at "The Elms." Each of the Ashleys lived apart from the others. "Something's going to break. Something's got to give," he thought.

Mrs. Ashley was never seen outside her house. One night two days after this Christmas of 1903 she stayed up later than usual. The boardinghouse was closed from Christmas Eve to the third of January. There was generally an old lady who was allowed to remain in the house on condition that she went to the Tavern for her dinner and suppers. Porky closed his store and went to live at his grandfather's home on Herkomer's Knob. Mrs. Ashley and her daughters took their meals in the kitchen. At this break in the routine they all became aware of an unfathomable fatigue. They slept late and went early to bed. At this break, too, Mrs. Ashley's hoarseness and insomnia returned. She was filled with longing for her husband and her son, for hope and for change. On this evening, instead of going to bed, she went into the kitchen and baked six of her famous cakes. Mr. Bostwick was always ready to give them a place of honor in his grocery store. At eleven-thirty Lily came down the stairs. She found her mother sitting on a low stool brooding before the empty oven. The cakes stood resplendent on the table.

"Mama, come to bed! Why do you have to cook now? Mama, they're beautiful, but why are you working tonight?"

"Lily, would you like to go for a walk?"

"Mama! Of course, I would!"

"Put your clothes on and call Constance. Tell her to get dressed."

"Oh, Mama, what fun!"

All was dark in the town. It was clear and cold. They went to the depot, they passed under the window of the jail, passed the courthouse. They peered through the windows of the post office, trying to see the poster with John Ashley's photograph on it. They went the length of the main street. They paused before "St. Kitts," looking long at the house where they had spent so many hours—in candy pulls, games, storytelling, and rifle practice. It would be too much to say that Beata Ashley had felt any affection for Eustacia Lansing; she had never had much to spare. The two women had had little in common—the German and the Creole—but they had got on well together. Neither was a petty woman. But now Beata Ashley was overcome with something near to love for her former friend. If they could only sit beside one another, disdaining that ugly thing that had come between them. Beata Ashley was starved for someone to talk with, to exchange silence with over a woman's life, over the passing of the years, over the fading of beauty, over the rearing of children, over the presence and absence of husbands, over the coming of old age and death.

"Come, girls."

They returned home by a side street, passing their church, passing Dr. Gillies's house. They paused for a moment on the bridge over the Kangaheela River as it flowed with a sound of suppressed laughter under its thin layer of brown ice.

"Oh, Mama," cried Constance, flinging her arms around her mother as they entered their hall, "let's do that often."

It would have been strange if they had happened to meet Eustacia and Félicité Lansing on one of those midnight walks when they, too, stood for a moment gazing at "The Elms," longing for something they had read about, for something that may not exist—friendship.

Spring is very beautiful in Coaltown. The tulips and hyacinths rise brave, though pockmarked, from the sour ground. The dandelions are briefly yellow and the lilacs promise as best they can. The Kangaheela River shakes off the last pieces of smoked glass along its shores. There is love-making in Memorial Park and, when Memorial Park is full, in the cemetery. As always in spring, there are more accidents in the mines. No satisfactory explanation has been found for this. Mr. Kenny, the carpenter-undertaker, has made those boxes throughout the winter in expectation of the spring's demands. The miners emerging from underground at six are astonished to find that there is still daylight; they take deep breaths and assemble new courage toward feeding and shoeing their families. All those men and women with tuberculosis, up Polktown way, feel better and, with Mrs. Hauserman's encouragement, pick up heart for their recovery; they resolve to cough less.

So, in its beauty, the spring of 1904 came to Coaltown and with it came Ladislas Malcolm. Few young men applied for admission at "The Elms"; those few were turned away. Neither Lily nor Constance had seen a young man save Porky for almost two years or had been seen by one. Sophia saw young men daily and was accustomed to their jeering smiles and whispered taunts; they were merely "rowdies" and "hoodlums." Yet the books the girls read were filled with heroes like Lochinvar and Henry the Fifth, or troubling apparitions—burdened with a crushing need of a thoughtful and loving woman—like Heathcliff and Mr. Rochester. The lodgers who came to "The Elms" seemed to them to be "over a hundred years old."

It happened to be Lily who answered the doorbell.

"Good afternoon, ma'am," said Mr. Malcolm, fanning himself with his straw hat. "I hope you can put me up for two nights."

Blue eyes looked into blue eyes, astonished; they hardened.

"Why, yes. Will you write your name and address in this book? Those are our terms. Your room will be Number Three—

upstairs, the second door on the left. The door is open. Supper is at six. We ask the gentlemen who wish to smoke to kindly use the plant room, there, at the end of the sitting room. If you wish for anything, you have only to call us. Our name is Ashley."

"Thank you, Miss Ashley."

Mr. Malcolm carried his grip and his samples case to Room Three; then he left the house for an hour. Soon after five o'clock unaccustomed sounds reached the ears of the women working in the kitchen. Someone was playing the piano in the living room, offering a type of music not previously heard there. It was loud; the rhythm was strongly marked and the melody was embellished by arpeggios traversing the entire length of the keyboard. Mrs. Ashley went into the front hall and appraised the newcomer. Her younger daughters followed her.

In the kitchen Constance said, "Isn't he handsome! He's like the men in books."

Later her mother said, "Sophia, I want you to wait on table tonight."

"I'll wait on table," said Lily. "It's my turn."

"But, Lily, he's not the kind of person we want in the house."

Lily looked at her mother coldly and repeated, "It's my turn."

At six o'clock Lily carried the soup tureen into the dining room. When she returned to the kitchen she said, "Mama, they're waiting for you to serve the soup."

"Dear, let Sophia finish serving at table."

"Mama, he's musical. That's my field. I'm going to wait on table and after supper I'm going to sing."

"Dear! Lily! It will only . . ."

"Mama, we never *see* anybody. You can't keep us locked up forever. They're waiting for you."

Lily had never disobeyed her mother.

It was one of the Wednesday nights when Miss Doubkov's call was expected. For the first time Mrs. Ashley had invited her to join them at supper. The girls took their meals in the kitchen; each in turn helped Mrs. Swenson in the dining room.

Mr. Malcolm was the soul of good manners. He gave his full attention to Mrs. Ashley's discussion of the weather and to Mrs. Hopkinson's account of her rheumatism. He did not raise

his eyes when Lily removed the soup plates. His glance returned often to Miss Doubkov; her eyes rested thoughtfully
on him. She had seen him surreptitiously remove a wedding
ring from his finger and place it in his vest pocket.

"You're a real musician, Mr. Malcolm," said Mrs. Hopkinson. "Oh, yes, you are! You play the piano like a professional.
But you're not the only musician in this house. Mrs. Ashley, you
must persuade Lily to sing for Mr. Malcolm after supper. She
sings like an angel, Mr. Malcolm—that's the only word for it."
In a lower voice she added, "Isn't she a lovely girl? Lovely!"

Mr. Malcolm waited until Lily had returned to the room.
He spoke modestly, "Well, I play and sing some. The fact is I
mean to go on the professional stage. I'm just traveling to earn
the money to arrange it."

After supper the company moved into the sitting room. The
two musicians performed alternately. Each commended the
other's performance. It was apparent to all that Mr. Malcolm
was swept off his feet. As we have said, Lily had neither seen
nor been seen by any young man, except Porky, for twenty
months. She had no memory of any town larger than Fort Barry.
Yet she behaved like some princess whom rude revolutionaries
had temporarily driven from her throne. She happened to be
in Coaltown, Illinois, and happened to be waiting on table in a
boardinghouse. She happened to be passing the evening with
an agreeable young man whom no princess in her senses could
take seriously—unless, perhaps, he might be useful to her. She
made light fun of the songs he sang; she made fun of the way
he kept his right foot firmly on the pedal. And yet, at the same
time, she gave the impression of quite liking him—that is to say,
he could take his place among the twenty other agreeable young
men who came in from time to time for a musical evening.

Mrs. Ashley sat tranquilly sewing until she was called upon
to accompany her daughter. Mr. Malcolm's songs were not of
the same order as Lily's, but there was nothing tentative about
them. He had a pleasant baritone voice and he sang loud. Lily
had hitherto sung with measured sweetness; on this night she
discovered that she could sing loud, too. He sang about when
the watermelon ripens on the vine and she sang about Marguerite discovering a box of jewels on her dressing table. He

sang about how stout-hearted the boys in Company B were and she sang about Dinorah dancing with her shadow in the moonlight. The shells on the whatnot trembled; the dogs in the neighborhood began barking.

Miss Delphine Fleming, the mathematics teacher at the High School, asked, "Lily, will you sing that song from the *Messiah*?"

Mrs. Hopkinson clapped. "Yes, dear. Please do!"

Lily nodded in assent. She drew herself up straight and looked gravely into the distance, quieting her listeners, as Miss Doubkov had taught her. Finally she glanced at her accompanist. She sang "I Know That My Redeemer Liveth."

A girl, a little over twenty, living in a dust-mantled town in southern Illinois, who had never heard a trained singer save through mechanical reproduction, sang Handel. Miss Doubkov's hands trembled as she listened. This was indeed a house of signs. Lily had her mother's beauty and her mother's freedom from any trace of provincialism or vulgarity; but above that she had her father's inner quiet, his at-homeness in existence. This was the voice of faith, selfless faith. John Ashley and his ancestors, Beata Kellerman and her ancestors, were contributing of their creativity, of their consciousness of freedom— hundreds of them from beyond the grave.

At nine-thirty Mrs. Ashley rose, saying it was late, very late. Miss Doubkov took her leave, kissing Lily in silence. She watched her thank Mr. Malcolm for his music and wish him good night. The Princess of Trebizond gave him her hand, a radiant smile, and tripped upstairs. He stared after her as though she had struck him.

Lily did not appear in the dining room the following evening. It was warm. Mrs. Hopkinson proposed that they adjourn to the summerhouse after supper. Lily joined the party there. The hour was not at first conducive to conversation. The group fell under a spell cast by the reflection of the starlight on the water, the lapping of the waves under the floor, the odors from the foliage, the murmurs from the circling ducks. For a moment Lily hummed a song that Mr. Malcolm had sung on the previous evening as though to offer an apology for having disparaged it. Mrs. Ashley questioned him about his childhood. His parents had arrived from Poland a year before he was born. As no one could pronounce or spell his name he had chosen that of Malcolm. He talked of his theatrical ambitions.

"How interesting! How interesting!" said Mrs. Hopkinson.

"I know you're going to be successful," said Miss Mallet.

For Mrs. Ashley his every word carried a stupefying boredom. The evening came to an end without music. He was to leave in the morning. Mrs. Ashley made it clear that his room had been promised to someone else. She would serve him at breakfast; he would not see the girls again. They went into the house. Mrs. Hopkinson, Miss Mallet, and Constance bade him an almost tearful goodbye; his eyes were on Lily. Mrs. Ashley was still shaken by her daughter's disobedience on the previous evening. Lily had gone about her duties with her accustomed efficiency, but had not once glanced in her mother's direction nor spoken an unnecessary word. She had not even wished her good night. Four times during the day her mother had sought the moment to tell Lily that she had seen a ring disappear into his pocket on the previous evening. She was now preparing to forestall a protracted leave-taking. Great was her astonishment when Lily gave Mr. Malcolm her hand, a pleasant "Good evening," and again tripped unconcernedly up the stairs.

It was a week of spring cleaning; furniture was being moved from room to room. Sophia was sleeping with Lily. After the house was dark Constance knocked at the door and entered.

"Lily? Are you awake?"

"Yes."

"Do you feel terrible? I mean, because he's going away tomorrow?"

"No."

"But you do like him a lot, don't you?"

"I'm tired, Connie."

"Well, he loves you. Anybody can see that.—Why isn't Mama nice to him?—Do you like him, Sophie?"

"Yes, but not 'Ebenezer.'"

"It's been fun. You sang wonderfully last night, Lily. As good as the gramophone. Why aren't you sorry he's going away?"

"I'm sleepy, Connie. Goodnight."

"Well . . . I think if people really like people, they come back and see them."

There was a knock at the door. Their mother entered the room.

"It's late, girls. You should get your sleep."

"Yes, Mama. I just came in to tell Lily that I was so sorry that Mr. Malcolm was going away tomorrow."

"We're used to guests coming and going, Constance. We can't look on them as friends."

"But, Mama, when can we have friends? We can't live forever and ever without friends."

"Since we're all here together, I want to tell you some things I've been thinking over. Tomorrow I'm going shopping with Sophia."

"Mama! . . . *Downtown!?*"

"Sophia and I are going to the bank. We're going to start keeping our money in the bank. We're going to think of that money as being saved up so that Lily can go to a very good teacher for her voice. I've been thinking of other things, too. Do you remember the supper parties that your father and I used to give? Well, you and I are going to give a supper like that once a month. We'll begin by asking the doctor and his wife and Mrs. Guilfoyle and the Dalziels and then on other nights Miss Thoms and Miss Doubkov. And each of you can name a friend you want."

"Mama!"

"And I think that maybe next fall Sophia and Constance can start going to school."

Constance flung herself upon her mother: "Oh, Mama! You're the best mama in the world!"

"Now, Constance, go to your room. There are some things I want to say to your sisters."

Constance left the room. Lily said, with the suggestion of a yawn, "Mama, I'm tired. I don't want to talk."

Sophia divined the extent to which the words had wounded her mother. "Mama," she said, "I think Lily's coming down with a cold. I'm going down to make her some hot milk-and-honey. I think we ought to let her try and sleep now."

All these brave projects were delayed. Three hours later Mrs. Ashley was awakened by hearing her name called in the corridor. She lit a lamp and opened her door. Mr. Malcolm, looking feverish and disheveled, asked if he could have a hot-water bottle and a mustard plaster. He refused Mrs. Ashley's offer to send for Dr. Gillies. He knew what his complaint was; he had suffered from it before. It was a "cold on the liver." He was in considerable pain, but he was manly about it.

In the morning Dr. Gillies saw the patient. Mrs. Ashley was waiting for him at the bottom of the stairs.

"What seems to be the trouble, Dr. Gillies?"

"Just a slight indigestion, I think."

"Doctor, please get him out of the house as soon as possible."

"Well—"

"I don't believe he's ill. He's not ill at all, Dr. Gillies."

"What?"

"Do help me! Send him to the hospital at Fort Barry, or get him into the infirmary at the mines or move him to the Tavern. Anyway, help me get him out of the house."

"He has a fever. It's a slight fever, but there's no doubt about it."

"He hung his head over the side of the bed. Any schoolchild can do that.—Dr. Gillies, I told him that he must give up his room, but he's fallen in love with Lily."

"I see. I see. Poor fellow!—Mrs. Ashley, we'll starve him."

"Oh, Dr. Gillies, you're a saint!"

"A cup of tea and an apple for breakfast. Chicken broth and a piece of toast for lunch and supper."

"Thank you! Thank you! Please write it down—and he's not to leave his room. Write that down, too. Quarantine the creature."

Sophia was the nurse. In the middle of the afternoon Lily called on the patient. He was sitting up in bed in a citified silk dressing gown. Lily left the door open. Her manner was as impersonal as that of royalty visiting her wounded soldiers. She read to him from the works of W. Shakespeare.

" 'There's no news at the court, sir, but the old news. That is, the old Duke is banished.' "

"Miss Ashley, I know the best teacher who could teach you dancing and everything. You could be a big star."

"You must save your voice, Mr. Malcolm. If you're not quiet I must go away. '. . . have put themselves into voluntary exile with him, whose lands and revenues enrich the new Duke. . . .' "

"Lily! Lily! Come away with me. We'll be the greatest team in the country. You're not listening to me. Within two weeks we could get engagements at club meetings and banquets."

"Do I have to leave the room, Mr. Malcolm?"

After she had left the room with a pleasant "Good afternoon," Mr. Malcolm strode to and fro in torment. Suddenly his eyes fell upon an object on his dresser. Under some tissue paper lay a large piece of marble cake. She had carried what he thought was a bag of books. She had made a few gestures of setting the room to rights.

The next afternoon more reading, more impassioned pleas, more rebukes.

"Lily, if it's serious music you want, I could get you an appointment with Maestro Lauri. He's the best teacher in Chicago. He trains singers for grand opera. I bet you he'd teach you free."

"If you get excited, Mr. Malcolm, I'll have to leave."

"Lily, you could be singing in churches and getting paid for it, right off. I've done it, but you're a hundred times better than I am."

"You must be calm!"

"I'm not calm. Lily, I love you. I love you."

"Mr. Malcolm!"

He flung himself out of bed. His fingernails dug into the carpet. "Tell me what I can do. Say something *human*! You gave me that piece of cake. You must know I'm *here*. Come to Chicago with me. In Coaltown you'll just *wither*."

She looked at him a moment in silence and wonder. She did not yet know that she was a great actress—that the knowledge of how men and women behave in extremity was at the center of her lifework. Slowly she put her hand into her bag of books and brought out a slice of the best apple pie in southern Illinois. "Get well soon, Mr. Malcolm. Good afternoon."

Ten minutes later Lily was again seen on the streets of Coaltown. She carried a pair of shoes in a paper bag. It was the busy hour. A faint smile on her face, she bowed right and left toward the gaping citizenry. She entered the post office and gazed meditatively at her father's portrait. She continued down the street and entered Porky's store. He showed no astonishment.

"Porky, I have no money, but I'll pay you back in a few

months. Will you fix these shoes so that they can stand wear? Fix them up as good as you can. Could you give them to me at the house about Friday?"

She then returned to the top of the street and climbed the stairs to Miss Doubkov's apartment. Miss Doubkov was on her knees before a dressmaker's dummy, altering the hem of a dress.

"Well, Lily!"

"Miss Doubkov, I'm running away to Chicago with that Mr. Malcolm."

Miss Doubkov rose slowly—and with no awkwardness—from the floor. "It's time for a cup of tea," she said. "Sit down."

Lily waited. Finally, when they had taken their first sips, she received the signal to speak.

"He says that he can find work for me, singing at clubs and in churches. He knows the teachers there. He says he can take me to see a very good teacher who teaches grand opera."

"Go on!"

"Nothing you can say will stop me, Miss Doubkov. I've come to you to ask you one favor. Can I tell him that he can write letters to me through you?"

"Drink your tea."

Pause.

"I can't stay in Coaltown one more month. I've got to sing and I've got to learn how to sing. Soon I'll be too old to get started right. I've got to know about life too. You can't learn much about life in Coaltown. I want to learn how to play the piano, too. Nobody could practice the piano in a boarding-house—even if I had time. I work from morning till night, Miss Doubkov."

She spread out her hands and turned them over.

"Do you love this man?"

Lily laughed, blushing slightly. "No, of course not. He's just an ignorant boy! But he can *help* me. That's all I need. He's not a bad man—you can see that for yourself. I'll go to Chicago and marry him."

"Did he ask you to marry him?"

"He . . . got down on the floor and he cried and told me he loved me."

"He didn't ask you to marry him.—Lily, he's married already."

"How do you know?"

She told her.—"Besides, I think he's a Pole and a Roman Catholic."

Lily waited a moment and said, level as her glance, "Anyway, there aren't many men who'd marry an Ashley."

"You!" said Olga Sergeievna, rising. "Drink your tea and be quiet for a moment."

She went into her bedroom and kitchen. Money was hidden about there, like a squirrel's provisions. After a few minutes she returned with a frayed silk purse.

"Here's fifty dollars. Go to Chicago. Let that man introduce you to these teachers, but don't have anything else to do with him."

"I'll borrow thirty dollars of you. I'll send it back as soon as I can."

Olga Sergeievna extracted twenty dollars and put the purse in the pocket of Lily's coat. Lily rose. "Can Mr. Malcolm send letters to you?"

"Yes.—Sit down and be quiet a moment." Deliberately, speculatively, her lower lip pressed upon her upper, she opened and examined cupboard after cupboard. "Take off your dress."

Being fitted is favorable to meditation.

"Lift up your arms. . . . Face the window!"

"Sophie should go away, too. And Connie. It's not the work that's killing us at the house. It's that Mama never goes into town and that she never mentions Papa. I'd have died long ago if it hadn't been for your visits, Miss Doubkov, and your liking my singing."

"Face the icons."

"And the reading aloud in the evening: The Shakespeare and *Jane Eyre* and *The Mill on the Floss* and *Eugénie Grandet*. . . . It's not like Mama to stay shut up in the house. At first I thought it was because she was afraid to face people; or that she just hated them. But Mama's never been afraid of anything. She doesn't care what other people think. Mama doesn't hate people; she's indifferent to everybody. To her all the boarders that come in and out of the house are just paper dolls. The first boarder she's really hated is Mr. Malcolm. She loathes him. Because he's so fiery."

"Put your elbows up, as though you were fixing the back of your hair."

"The reason she doesn't mention Papa is that she wants him all to herself. She doesn't even want us to have 'our Papa.' I think she doesn't go into the street because she doesn't want to meet Mrs. Lansing. She's afraid that Mrs. Lansing may have her own 'our Papa.' I'll tell you something I never told anybody before. Early in the trial somebody left a letter in our mailbox. There was nobody's name signed to it. On the envelope it said, 'For Mrs. Ashley.' Almost no letters came to our house; Papa and Mama never got any letters from their relations. I took the letter in to Mama, but during the trial Mama wasn't interested in anything except that. She told me to open it and tell her what it said. . . . It was all about God punishing sin and people going to hell, and it said that Papa had been meeting Mrs. Lansing for years in the Farmer's Hotel at Fort Barry. I lied to Mama. I said it was about a church bazaar. Three or four more letters came. I burned them up. . . . They were just ugly foolishness. Papa didn't go to Fort Barry more than once a year and he usually came back on the afternoon train. And Mrs. Lansing only went to Fort Barry on Sunday, with the children, so that they could go to their Catholic church. . . . But I think Mrs. Lansing did love Papa. I hope she did and I hope he knew it. You couldn't tell whether Papa loved Mrs. Lansing or not, because he had a way of liking every woman in this town. Didn't he?"

"Yes, he did. Stand up straight."

"I wouldn't be shocked if Papa and Mrs. Lansing did love each other. Mrs. Lansing's a very different kind of person. She doesn't feel indifferent to *anybody*. . . . Mama didn't see any of those letters, but maybe she knew that Mrs. Lansing felt deeply about Papa. Mama's not the kind who would be angry or jealous, but maybe she didn't go out in the street because of that. One night, late, Mama told me to get dressed and go for a walk with her, and, Miss Doubkov, we stopped for a long time in front of the Lansing house, just looking. I felt that Mama wished she could know—and yet didn't want to know— the 'Papa' that maybe Mrs. Lansing carried in her heart."

"Walk to the door and back—slowly."

"I'm to blame for a lot, Miss Doubkov. I'm the oldest. I should have changed things. I should have *made* Mama talk about Papa. I should have helped Sophie more. I should have come into town as though nothing had happened. I don't know what was the matter with me. What was the matter with me, Miss Doubkov? I was an idiot. I should have loved everybody more.—Where's Roger? What's he doing?—It's all too late now. Oh, Papa, Papa, Papa, Papa!"

"Don't spoil that silk, Lily."

"That's why I'm going to Chicago: so that I can learn to sing—so that I can do *one* thing right in this world."

"You can get dressed now."

After supper at "The Elms," Mrs. Ashley was busier than usual about the kitchen. Her daughters watched her in bewilderment. She removed all the preserves from the shelves and carried them down to the basement. Bread, cakes, and pies she carried into the dining room and locked in the sideboard.

"Why are you taking everything out of the kitchen, Mama?" asked Sophia.

"I think it's a good idea tonight."

Lily knew. She drew Sophia out of the room. "You must get some food for Mr. Malcolm, Sophie. He's *your* patient and he's starving."

When Sophie returned to the kitchen, her mother was locking the back door and the cellar door.

"I don't want you girls to come down here tonight."

After midnight Mr. Malcolm groped his way downstairs to the kitchen, where he lit his candle. The icebox was empty; the shelves were bare. The door leading to the cellar—those barrels of apples—was locked. As though in derision a small saucer of chicken feed stood on the table. It was all that Sophie had been able to find. He probed every cupboard and drawer, weeping with rage and frustration. Finally he scooped a handful of the chicken feed into his mouth. He heard a noise behind him and turned quickly. Mrs. Ashley, lamp in hand, stood watching him. She was wearing a thick bathrobe cut from some horse blanket.

"Mrs. Ashley, I'm starving."

"Oh!—Then you're better?"

"Yes, I am."

"Have you recovered from your illness?"

"Yes, I have."

"Mr. Malcolm, if you're well enough to leave the house by seven-thirty and no later, I shall give you something to eat."

She made sandwiches. She fried eggs. She placed a jug of milk beside him. She sat down, her elbows on the table, her face in her hands. She watched him eat. Her eyes kept returning to the fingers of his left hand.

"Mrs. Ashley, I love your daughter."

Mrs. Ashley made no reply.

"Ma'am, your daughter could rise right up to the top of the entertainment business. She could be what they call a star in a very short time. I know that. My idea was that we could put together an act and show it to one of these agents."

"Has my daughter told you that she's interested in these plans?"

"Ma'am, she doesn't even answer me when I talk to her. I swear to you. I don't understand her. She acts as though she didn't hear me. But, Mrs. Ashley, I love her. I love her." He beat his fists on the table. He sobbed, "I'd kill myself before I'd do anything to harm her."

"Don't raise your voice, Mr. Malcolm. Go on eating what's before you."

He looked at her, outraged, but went on eating. She loathed him.

"Has my daughter told you that she's fond of you?"

"You don't listen to me. I *told* you. I swear to you, on the soul of my dead mother, she hasn't said one word to me about anything like that. Not one word.—I've got friends who could teach her things. She'd learn fast. She's a very intelligent girl. But what's she going to learn in Coaltown? You can't keep her down in Coaltown forever. She's meant for big things."

"You're a married man, Mr. Malcolm."

His face turned scarlet. When he had recovered himself he said, "I'm sorry. I'm sorry about that. But even if I were free I couldn't marry her. She's not a Catholic." He leaned across the table. "But I'm not what you think I am, Mrs. Ashley. I'm a serious man. I'm a very serious man. I'm going to get to the top, too. I've started. I've sung at the Elks' convention! I'm going to be big. Did you ever hear of Elmore Darcy? Or Terry McCool? He's great. He was in *The Sultan of Swat*. That's where I'm going. And your daughter! Did you ever hear of Mitzi Karsch in *Bijou*? Where have you been? Well, you've heard of Bella Myerson? Who have you heard of?"

"Don't raise your voice, Mr. Malcolm."

Mr. Malcolm raised his voice and stood up. He shouted "You've heard of Madame Modjeska in *Maria Stuart*, haven't you? She's Polish, like me. These people are stars. Do you understand that—like stars in the sky? If there weren't stars in the sky we'd all be like goats with our heads down. Your daughter's a star and I think I am. There are only fifteen or twenty alive in the world at any one time. They're *chosen*. They've got a big load on their shoulders. People like that don't live like other people. Why should they? They don't care who's married and who isn't. They're only interested in one thing—doing their job better and better: *being perfect*. You're stifling your daughter down here. You ought to be glad I came."

She rose. "You've promised me that you will leave the house by seven-thirty in the morning. I will knock on your door at a quarter before seven."

She held up the lamp and indicated that he should follow her. When they parted at the door of her room, he whispered with brutal directness: "Your daughter's a big artist, Mrs. Ashley. Did you ever hear about *art*? You're a boardinghouse keeper in Coaltown, Illinois. Think it over. The sooner your daughter changes her name and gets out of here the better."

Mrs. Ashley did not flinch.

Ladislas Malcolm found a note under his door. Miss Lily Scolastica Ashley wished him a pleasant journey. She was thinking seriously of going to Chicago. He might write her, care of Miss Olga Doubkov, Coaltown, sending her any suggestions as to how she might continue her studies. She sent her regards.

During the following days Lily gave no sign of regretting his departure, but she had changed. The last vestige of that air of moving in a dream had vanished. She was more than usually considerate toward her mother, but remote. She brushed aside requests to sing in the evening. Her mother did not again mention a trip to the bank, nor did she mention that she had seen a ring on Mr. Malcolm's hand.

Three weeks later Lily left Coaltown on the midnight train—the same train that had borne her father and his guards. The handbag she carried was the same one with which Beata Kellerman had left her home, surreptitiously—also in June—twenty-one years before.

Autumn is very beautiful in Coaltown. The children return to school, exhausted by the aimless freedom of the long summer. Their mothers are rendered uneasy by the quiet; they even have some unoccupied hours and complain of headaches. The trees are clothed in heathen splendor. The days draw in. For many months the miners will live mainly by artificial light. The holidays of autumn are dreaded. George Lansing has left town, but on Halloween his troop of Mohicans will uproot the Mayor's gateposts and wrench the hands of the town clock. The stout-hearted members of the Woman's Christian Temperance Union are manfully fighting to have the saloons closed on Election Day. Philosophy quickens briefly in the mind of even the most self-sufficient householder as he stands, once again, over his pile of burning leaves. The first snowfall opens wide the eyes of the townspeople; white casts a more than usual spell in Coaltown.

Sophia and Constance did not return to school. A few adults were now nodding to Sophia on the street, but the boys and girls were still vindictive. The boys were still trying to trip her up. The younger girls had not yet tired of pretending that Sophia, like her wicked father, would shoot them dead. They crowded close about her and then, like panic-stricken doves, fled in all directions. Parents are often heard to complain that their children do not follow their example.

With Lily's departure the work became more burdensome. The weight of routine bore most heavily on Constance in the fall of 1904 and the following spring when she celebrated her twelfth birthday. February and March are the comfortless months. Constance was the only member of the family to indulge in tears and fits of temper. She longed to go to school, to church, to walk in the town. Sophia gave her charge of the ducks, her mother offered her an absorbing occupation remembered from her own girlhood in Hoboken, New Jersey: the care of the grape arbor and the making of the "spring wine"; but Constance found no interest in animals or plants. She wanted to see people—hundreds of people. It was Miss Doubkov who finally came to her rescue in July: "Beata, I think you're very wise in not exposing Constance to the rudeness of the children in town, but I feel that she needs exercise. When I was her age—in Russia—my sister and I spent whole days hunting mushrooms and picking berries. If Constance gave you her promise not to go into the center of town, why not let her go into the woods three or four times a week?"

It was wonderful. On alternate days Constance rose an hour earlier and began her scrubbing, mopping, and sweeping. At eleven she slipped out of town by the path behind the depot. She never told her mother that within three weeks she was a welcome visitor in many farmhouses. She sat in kitchens and listened, she helped her neighbors hang out the wash and listened. She sat a while with bedridden grandfathers and grandmothers. She loved to watch people's faces, particularly their eyes. She had never known shyness. She joined mowers under the trees during their lunch hour. She came upon an encampment of gypsies. At "The Elms" her tears and outbursts of anger ceased.

No Ashley had ever been seriously ill. One morning in October Sophia got out of bed, put on her hat, went downstairs, and started walking to the railway station in her nightgown. She fainted on the main street and was brought back and put to bed. Porky ran to call Dr. Gillies. Mrs. Ashley was waiting for the doctor when he came down the stairs. Her face was more stricken than on the day when her husband's conviction had been read in court. Her hoarseness had returned.

"What . . . what does it seem to be, Doctor?"

"Well, Mrs. Ashley, I don't like it. Sophie being Sophie, I don't like it. I think I've seen it coming on. She's all tuckered out, Mrs. Ashley."

"Yes."

"Now this afternoon I'm going to drive her out to the Bell Farm. Every one of the Bells loves Sophie. They've taken patients of mine before. I don't think they'll charge to board Sophie."

Mrs. Ashley put her hand on the newel post to steady herself. "This afternoon . . . ?"

"Now, Sophie don't want to go. She's angry at me. She doesn't know who'll do the shopping. She thinks the house'll fall down, if she isn't here. I've given her something so she'll rest. I'll send Mrs. Hauserman over."

"I'll do the shopping, Dr. Gillies."

"She'll be glad to hear that. I told her firmly that her father would want her to get two weeks' rest at the Bell Farm. For the first week I don't want her to have any callers—not even yourself or Connie. But I think it'd be a good idea if you wrote her once a day. Tell her that 'The Elms' is running along pretty well, but that everybody misses her.—I think we've caught it in time, Mrs. Ashley."

"Caught . . . caught what, Dr. Gillies?"

"For the first ten minutes she didn't recognize me. Old cart-horses break down, Mrs. Ashley. They can't carry loads of gravel forever. I'd like to ask Roger to come back and see us. Suggest it to him when you write.—The Bells have loved Sophie ever since she walked out and asked them for some hog fat to make soap out of. They're fond of Roger, too, him having worked there all those summers.—So I'll be back at three."

"Thank you, Doctor."

As he left the house, Dr. Gillies said to himself, "Some people go forward and some go back."

Beata Ashley went into the flower-pot room and sat down. She tried to rise several times. Waves of self-reproach swept over her. The next morning she dressed for her shopping trip into town. She descended the front steps; she reached her gate. She could go no further. She could not bring herself to face the handshakes, the greetings, the stares . . . from the citizens of Coaltown who had so often broken into gales of laughter in the courtroom . . . those jurymen, those jurymen's wives. She returned into the house. She drew up a list of things needed and Mrs. Swenson did the shopping. Nor was she able to fulfill her intention of writing every day. Her letters were lame. She could think of nothing to say.

While Sophia was at the Bell Farm she received a letter from her brother telling her that he was returning to Coaltown for Christmas. He wrote of this plan also to his mother and sent

her, for "fun," a sheaf of the articles he had published in the
Chicago papers under the name of "Trent."

One night in November of that year Beata Ashley was awakened by a noise at her window—a rattling and rustling and a
faint tapping. Her first thought was that a rain had changed to
hail, but it was a clear starlight night. She sat up in bed; she put
one foot on the floor and listened. For a moment her heart
stopped beating. Small pieces of gravel were being thrown into
her open window. She stepped into her slippers and threw her
wrapper about her. She stood against the wall looking down
through the window at the croquet ground below. As she
watched, a man's figure turned and hurried away toward the
front of the house.

She descended the stairs. Finally she opened the front door.
There was no one there. She went into the kitchen and lit a
lamp. She warmed some milk and drank it slowly.

Just so, under the cover of night, John Ashley would return.
Just so, he would announce his presence. She climbed the stairs
to her room. She removed her slippers. She walked back and
forth.

There was no gravel on the floor.

II. Illinois to Chile

1902–1905

A YOUNG man with a beard like cornsilk sat nightly from eleven to two in a café, Aux Marins, on the New Orleans waterfront. No habitual drunkards frequented Aux Marins; no altercations ever arose there. It was a place of long conversations, conducted in an undertone, about shipping and cargoes and crews. If a stranger came in the door, voices were raised slightly and the conversations turned upon politics, weather, women, and gambling. The café was watched by the police, and Jean Lamazou—Jean-le-Borgne—and his habitual customers were on the lookout for informers. They watched the young man with the silky beard. He gave little attention to what went on around him, and made no effort to enter into conversation with others. He spoke little (that little was in the French of France), but his greetings were open and friendly. He read newspapers and he studied pages torn from a *Spanish in Fifty Lessons* ("*See, sain-yore, tain-go do-see pay-sos*"). By the third week Jean-le-Borgne lost his distrust of this stranger; they were soon playing cards together for very small stakes. The young man let it be known that he was James Tolland, a Canadian. He was waiting to be joined by a friend from the north who owned a sugar plantation in Cuba.

John Ashley was a man of faith. He did not know that he was a man of faith. He would have been quick to deny that he was a man of religious faith, but religions are merely the garments of faith—and very ill cut they often are, especially in Coaltown, Illinois.

Like most men of faith John Ashley was—so to speak—invisible. You brushed shoulders with a man of faith in the crowd yesterday; a woman of faith sold you a pair of gloves. Their principal characteristics do not tend to render them conspicuous. Only from time to time one or other of them is propelled by circumstance into becoming visible—blindingly visible. They tend their flocks in Domrémy; they pursue an obscure law practice in New Salem, Illinois. They are not afraid; they are not self-regarding; they are constantly nourished by astonishment and wonder at life itself. They are not interesting. They lack those traits—our bosom companions—that so strongly engage our interest: aggression, the dominating will, envy, destructiveness and self-destructiveness. No pathos hovers about them. Try as hard as you like, you cannot see them as the subjects of tragedy. (It has often been attempted; when the emotion subsides the audience finds that its tears have been shed, unprofitably, for itself.) They have little sense of humor, which draws so heavily on a consciousness of superiority and on an aloofness from the predicaments of others. In general they are inarticulate, especially in matters of faith. The intellectual qualifications for faith—as we shall see when we consider Ashley's faith in connection with his mathematical gift and his talent as a gambler—are developed and fortified by a ranging observation and a retentive memory. Faith founded schools; it is not dependent on them. A high authority has told us that we are more likely to find faith in an old woman on her knees scrubbing the floors of a public building than in a bishop on his throne. We have described these men and women in negative terms—fearless, not self-referent, uninteresting, humorless, so often unlearned. Wherein lies their value?

We did not choose the day of our birth nor may we choose the day of our death, yet choice is the sovereign faculty of the mind. We did not choose our parents, color, sex, health, or endowments. We were shaken into existence, like dice from a box. Barriers and prison walls surround us and those about us— everywhere, inner and outer impediments. These men and women with the aid of observation and memory early encompass a large landscape. They know themselves, but their self is not the only window through which they view their existence. They are certain that one small part of what is given us is free. They explore daily the exercise of freedom. Their eyes are on the future. When the evil hour comes, they hold. They save cities—or, having failed, their example saves other cities after their death. They confront injustice. They assemble and inspirit the despairing.

But what do these men and women have faith *in*?

They are slow to give words to the object of their faith. To them it is self-evident and the self-evident is not easily described. But men and women without faith, *they* are articulate. They are constantly and loudly expatiating on it: it is "faith in life," in the "meaning of life," in God, in progress, in humanity —all those whipped words, those twisted signposts, that borrowed finery, all that traitor's eloquence.

There is no creation without faith and hope.

There is no faith and hope that does not express itself in creation. These men and women work. The spectacle that most discourages them is not error or ignorance or cruelty, but sloth. This work that they do may often seem to be all but imperceptible. That is characteristic of activity that never for a moment envisages an audience.

John Ashley was of this breed. No historic demands were laid upon him and we do not know how he would have met them. He was late-maturing and little given to reflection. He was almost invisible. For a time many tried to catch a glimpse of him through his children. He was a link in a chain, a stitch in a tapestry, a planter of trees, a breaker of stones on an old road to a not yet clearly marked destination.

Ashley had no idea who his rescuers were. Perhaps a miracle is like that—simple, natural, and unearthly. Their actions had been swift, precise, and silent. They had smashed the overhanging lamps. His guards had lunged about in the dark, shouting; they had fired a shot or two and then ceased. His handcuffs fell from his wrists. He had been led out of the car—more carried than led—into a grove. One of these friends had placed his hand upon the saddle of a horse. Another had given him a suit of worn blue overalls, a purse containing fifteen dollars, a small compass, a map, and a box of matches—all in silence and darkness. An old and shapeless hat had been placed on his head. Finally one of them lit a match and again he saw their faces. These railway porters did not look like Negroes, but like the grotesquely blackened performers in a minstrel show. The tallest of them pointed in a certain direction, then slowly his extended finger moved fifteen degrees to the right.

Ashley said, "Thank you."

They disappeared. He heard no sound of horses' hoofs.

Simple, natural, and unearthly.

Left alone, he lit a match and consulted his compass. The friend had first pointed to the southwest then to the west. Ashley knew that he was beside the railroad yard near the station at Fort Barry. Sixty miles to the west was the Mississippi River. He changed his clothes, rolling his prison garb into a bundle which he attached to the pommel. He found a bag of apples and a bag of oats hanging from the saddle.

He was filled with wonder. He laughed softly. "Gee whillikers! Gee whillikers!"

He had been prepared to die, but to John Ashley death is never now—there remains always a month, day, hour, even a minute to live. He had never known fear. Even when the sentence was read in court, even when he sat in the train on what the newspapers would certainly be calling his "last journey," he had felt no fear. To a John Ashley worst never comes to worst.

When the match was lit in the grove he had looked at the horse and the horse had looked at him. He now mounted her and waited. She moved forward slowly. Did she see a path through the thick undergrowth? Was she returning to her stall? After ten minutes he again lit a match and consulted his compass. They had been moving to the southwest. He split an apple and shared it with her. They rode on. At the end of an hour they came to a broad country road and turned right. Twice he heard riders coming from the east behind him. He had time to leave the road and conceal himself among the trees. He heard the reverberations of a wooden bridge beneath them; they went down the bank and drank from the stream. They resumed the journey at a brisker pace. Ashley felt younger hourly. He was filled with an indefensible, an impermissible, happiness. He was out of that jail where he had suffered more in body than in mind. From time to time he dismounted and walked beside the horse. He felt the need to talk. The horse seemed to like being talked to; in the diffused starlight he could see her ears rising and falling.

"Bessie? . . . Molly? . . . Belinda? . . . Someone gave you to me. It's not often one receives presents like that—a present as big as a whole life. Will I ever know why six men risked their lives to save mine? Will I die without knowing that?

"No! Your name is Evangeline, bringer of good tidings. . . . It's been strange, hasn't it? No one knew when you were foaled that you would have a part in a mysterious adventure—in an act, like this, of generosity and courage. No one knew when you were broken—it must be a black and frightening thing to be broken, Evangeline!—that one day you would carry a man on your back and give him a chance to live. . . . You are a sign. We've both been marked for something."

After these conversations he felt even more buoyant. Not forgetting to listen for oncoming riders, he even sang fragments of his favorite songs, " 'Nita, Juanita," and "No gottee tickee, No gettee shirtee, At the Chinee laundryman's," and the song of his fraternity at engineering school, "We'll be true until we die to the brothers in Kappa Psi."

The west began to brighten. Dawns are poor things in Coaltown. He was overwhelmed with the wonder of it. "Yes, that's what they mean when they say a 'new day'!" He came to a crossroad and read the signs; to the south, "Kenniston, 20 m.," to the northeast, "Fort Barry, 14 m.," to the west, "Tatum, 1 m." He passed through Tatum, blank and pallid in the early light. Two miles beyond it he turned left into a deep wood, following a brook. He found seven yards of rope attached to his saddle and tethered Evangeline. He poured some oats into the crown of his hat (blew on it, sniffed it, took some into his mouth) and set it before her. In the bag of apples he found some baked potatoes. He glanced briefly from time to time at Evangeline.

Ashley had ridden horses as a boy, spending his summer vacations on his grandmother's farm. She—the old independent eccentric gray-eyed Marie-Louise Scolastique Dubois Ashley—was the person he most loved until his twenty-first year and the person who had most rigorously loved him. She was, besides many other things, an unlicensed veterinary doctor. The farmers brought their animals to her from far and wide. She infuriated many a farmer with her denunciation of his husbandry. She moved among horses like one knowing their language. Cattle, dogs and cats, birds, deer, even skunks exchanged intelligence with her. By day and often far into the night under a kerosene lamp John helped her with injections, boluses, cataplasms; together they had delivered colts and calves; they had put many an animal to sleep. He remembered some of her injunctions: "Never look a horse or a dog or a child in the eye for longer than a few seconds; it shames them. Don't stroke a horse's neck, slap it; and after you've slapped it, slap your own thigh. Don't do anything sudden with your feet. Feet and teeth are what they use to attack their enemies and to defend themselves. Joe Dekker's always closing his stall door with a kick of his foot; his horses hate him. If you're going to have to use a whip, let the horse see you at a distance striking yourself with it. When you give him oats, sniff it first; blow it all over the place; eat some, and then give it to him as though you hated to part with it." Ashley had owned a horse and buggy in Coaltown, having paid a bottom price for Bella, an unamiable beast. He had driven Bella for ten years in a friendship to which only a ballad could do justice. He now stole some glances at Evangeline. She was no longer young, but she had been well cared for and was soundly shod.

He fell off to sleep, though he was tormented by fleas. He had written Beata daily from the jail, without mentioning the fleas. He had told her how he missed his bed and the sheets smelling of lavender. He awoke in the early afternoon. It was intensely hot, even in the deep forest. "Come on, Evangeline. Let's follow the stream and find a pool. It's time for a bath."

And there was a pool. He tethered Evangeline for the last time. He lay in the water and closed his eyes. "Beata knows now. Roger will have heard. Yes, Porky will have heard first. 'Mama, Papa got away.'" He tried to imagine his own future and to plan for it, but he was deficient in that aspect of the imagination which has to do with taking shrewd care of oneself. He had little if any faculty for making plans; he had no experience of worry. People who are habitually anxious forge plans day and night. Serener natures are incomprehensible to them; they appear to drift and procrastinate. But John Ashley was laying plans without being aware of it. He spent eight days sleeping in the woods. Each evening he awoke with a project formed in his mind. Plans were the gifts of sleep. Waking on that first evening near Tatum, it was clear to him that he was a Canadian on his way to work in the mines of Chile. He was not a mining engineer, but he was an engineer with experience in mining. He knew very little about Chile, but the little he knew suited his situation. Chile was far. It was part of the folklore in engineering schools that no bright graduate went to Chile, if he could help it. The conditions of life and work there were massively difficult. You worked the nitrate mines in intolerable heat on a desert where no rain ever fell. The best copper mines in the Andes, with one famous exception, were located above eleven thousand feet. You couldn't take a wife there. There was no entertainment. You couldn't even drink above ten thousand feet—not what a man calls drinking. His goal was Chile. Not only was Ashley going to Chile, he would become a Chilean.

The next morning he learned that he was to descend the Mississippi River on a lumber barge. Five years before he had borrowed a surrey and taken his family to see the river. The trip had been taken in the spirit of an outing, in preference to a train trip to Chicago, as being cheaper. The Ashleys had sat long on the bluffs above the stream, completely satisfied by the spectacle. They had taken a great interest in the various barges, short and squat or long and narrow, that floated down the river or laboriously chugged their way up it. A passerby informed them that the long thin ones were lumber barges from the north on their way to New Orleans. "Swedish fellas on 'em. Can't speak twenty words of American." Ashley had not been in swimming since his student days, but he thought he could swim to midstream.

On the third evening it was revealed to him that he was crossing the country too quickly. When he reached the river he must walk boldly into some rural community—as primitive a one as possible—in order to purchase some food and to sell Evangeline. He could not expose himself to that danger until his hair and beard had grown. Each morning and evening he leaned over a pool and examined his reflection. His head had been shaved in jail on the night that his sentence was pronounced, five days before his train journey. Now each morning there was greater promise of a brown plush mat. A foolish honey-colored beard was forming. He needed this to cover a scar on his left jaw; he had fallen on a hay fork thirty years ago while working on his grandmother's farm. He must remain hidden for a time in this thinly populated region. He now stayed two nights in each camping site. He massaged his scalp.

Other projects became successively clear to him—ways of reaching the southern Pacific Coast, ways of earning money. There were some problems to which the counsels of sleep offered no solution: how, in time, he would write to his wife, how he would send her money, how he would learn what was passing at "The Elms."

In the meantime the land was swarming with John Ashleys. Colonel Stotz in Springfield began receiving the first of hundreds of letters and telegrams—within the year they were to arrive from Australia and Africa—telling him where Ashley had been seen; many of them demanded their reward (it had risen to four thousand dollars) by return post. Travelers between the ages of twenty and sixty were being pulled off their horses, dragged from their buggies, pursued across fields and their hats snatched off. Sheriffs became sick and tired of all the indignant and often terrified bald men who were brought before them. Newsboys cried "Extra! Extra!" Ashley had been found living on an Indian reservation in Minnesota, his face stained with walnut juice. Ashley had been found sequestered in an expensive private institution for the insane in Kentucky. Great wealth and important connections were increasingly associated with the fugitive.

Ashley made nicks in his saddle to mark the days, but even so lost track of them. The oats and the bag of food came to an end. Berries were beginning to redden; he found watercress. A change came over horse and rider; they grew younger. When they took to the road, Evangeline picked up her heels smartly. Ashley became aware that her coat shone, even before he took to currying her with fistfuls of twigs and moss. He had the sensation that she had accompanied hunted men before, that she was no stranger to pursuit and secrecy. The traffic on the road increased. She heard the oncoming hoof beats before her master did and found hiding. When they aroused barking dogs she took to a gallop. When, for the third time, he dismounted to walk beside her she showed her displeasure and it came to him suddenly that hounds might have been put upon his scent. When his mood inclined toward dejection during the day she moved toward him and tried to distract him; she snorted into the water of the brook or she pawed the ground. When he was afflicted with diarrhea she gazed soberly into the distance; she counseled fortitude.

Riding along after midnight he would occasionally see the light of a lamp from the second story of a farmhouse. To a family man the sight suggests sitting up beside an ailing child. The thought would fill him with a tumult of emotion. He learned that he must limit the occasions when he could permit himself to think of the past. Memories pressed upon him, uncalled, all but unendurable. He held in his arms for the first time —wonder of wonders—the newborn Lily. He surprised for the first time a look of fear directed toward him on the face of his son, Roger, three years old. (He had had to be severe; he had had to spank him. The boy had twice broken away from his mother's hand and run toward the horses in Coaltown's main street.) He returned from work and was met again by Constance's clamorous welcome, and heard Lily rebuking her: "You don't have to act like a pack of dogs when Papa comes home!" From time to time it had been necessary for him to spend the night, on the mines' business, in Fort Barry—he heard Sophia saying, "When Papa's not in the house I don't sleep, really. The house is different." And Beata, the good, the patient, the silent, the beautiful. "Evangeline, I'm a family man. That's all. I have no talents. I'm not even an engineer. All I have to show, living and dying, is that I'm a family man. Girl, why did this meaningless, crazy thing happen to me?"

At Coaltown, even in his home, Ashley had not been a talkative man, yet he now talked copiously to Evangeline.

"I know why you're looking so handsome. You're thinking what I'm thinking. We can't go on this way for five hundred miles. I must sell you and you want to fetch me a good price. Goodbyes are hard. They're like death—like my grandmother's death. The only thing to do about them is to know them, to take them completely into yourself, and then put them out of your mind. They'll come back to you of their own accord when you need them. It's no good to reach out after them. . . . I told you all about my grandmother who did so much for horses. I've been thinking about her more and more on this trip we're making. She's come back to me when I need her. She taught me how not to be afraid. Have you noticed that no hunters have shown up to disturb us, no farmers have come into these woods to mark their trees, no sheriffs have been sitting up all night waiting for us to pass by? It would be a pity, wouldn't it, if this adventure of ours, that started out with such bravery and generosity—shucks, it would be a pity if it ended up with another little train ride to Joliet. But better men than you and I have been ambushed, greater hopes than ours have been brought down like a house of cards. Sure, Evangeline, if the spectacle of one defeat or of a hundred defeats discouraged a man, civilization wouldn't have gone anywhere. There'd be no justice on earth, no hospitals, no homes, no friendships like yours and mine. There'd just be moaning people, creeping about. Let's not do anything foolish."

Ashley had told her all about the trial.

"There's nothing awful about dying; the only awful thing about dying is the things you leave unfinished. Can you imagine it? I left no provision for the education of my children. How could I have been so stupid? Beata set aside a little money every week for Lily's voice training; it was eaten up by the trial, of course. I suppose I assumed that the boy could fend for himself and that I could send the younger girls to better schools when the time came. If Beata had firmly called my attention to it, I could have done something about it. I could have hunted for another job, or insisted on a raise, or have really pushed those inventions of mine. . . . Mind you, I'm not blaming Beata. The fault's mine. I was happy and stupid. Happy, asleep, and stupid."

By the end of a week he was satisfied that he had a modest stand of hair. He rubbed some dirt on his head and squeezed the juice of some purple berries on it and was astonished. He could have entered civilization two days before. His beard made him look like a wan theological student. The long thin line of his scar could be seen through it. He experimented with the saps of twigs and roots in an effort to stain it. It became manly and opaque.

They reached the river at Gilchrist's Ferry toward two in the morning of the following night. All was dark in the town. He followed a road to the south along the bluffs. After riding an hour he came upon a cluster of houses and stores, a church and a schoolhouse. He was barely able to make out a sign on the front of one of the buildings: "United States Post Office, Giles, Illinois, pop. 410." "We can't have a fine upstanding post office," he murmured and rode on. An hour later he found what he wanted. There was a general store with a long hitching rail before it, a blacksmith shop beside a dirt clearing in which stood a stake for pitching horseshoes, some shacks, some steps leading down to a landing on the river. Downstream he saw some lights on what appeared to be an island. He retraced his road to a place about a mile north of the village, sat down on the bluff, and fell asleep. He awoke at dawn. Through the mist he saw a long lumber barge descending the river. There was a light in the wheelhouse. He thought he heard voices. He imagined that he smelled coffee and bacon.

On the highest Andes a zephyr may precipitate an avalanche. It was the imagined smell of coffee and bacon that unmanned John Ashley. It brought back with it "The Elms," the job in which he delighted, the long weariness of the trial with Beata's proud drawn face ten yards from him, Lily's singing, Roger's self-reliance, Sophia's watchful gravity, Constance's boisterous love—all, all, all. He put his head between his knees. He fell over to one side, then rolled over to the other. He groaned, he lowed, he bayed. The anguish of mind in a mature man is borne in silence and immobility, but John Ashley was not a mature man.

The sun had been up several hours when he returned to the village. He tethered Evangeline to the hitching rail and stood on the bluff for a long time looking at the river, his back to the general store. He knew that an increasing number of eyes would be fixed upon him and would be appraising the horse. Finally he turned, strolled across the road, nodded to some men on the porch, and entered the store. Five men were standing or sitting about a cold stove. All but the storekeeper dropped their eyes to the floor. Ashley uttered the grunt which is the last reduction of how-do-you-do. It was returned. He purchased a box of ginger snaps, discreetly displaying some dollar bills. He ate a cookie in thoughtful silence. The curiosity about him became intense. Some more men drifted into the store.

"Where you from, son?" asked the storekeeper.

Ashley pointed north with his thumb, smiling: "Canada."

"Sight ways!" The words were repeated in a murmur around the room.

"I took it slow. Hung up in Ioway a bit. Hunting for my brother."

"Well, now!"

Ashley continued to chew meditatively. More men and boys gathered about the door. A rig drew up.

"Suppose I could buy some breakfast? Eggs, bacon? Like two bits' worth?"

"Well! . . . Emma! Emma! . . . Fix the fella some eggs and bacon and grits."

A woman appeared at the door behind the counter and stared at him. Ashley tilted his hat. "Right kind of you, ma'am," he said.

She disappeared. There was another long silence.

"Where you thinking to find your brother?"

"Got word maybe he's down to New Orleans."

"Well, now!"

Ashley looked at the storekeeper and said in scorn, "Up to Gilchrist's Ferry a man offered me twenty-four dollars for my horse!—What's this place called?"

"Just called 'Hodge's.' "

The heads of the men in the doorway had turned to gaze at Evangeline. Several sidled out through the open door to join a circle forming around her. There was talk in low tones. Ashley went out on the porch, still chewing, and looked up and down the river. Addressing no one in particular he asked, "On those lumber barges, do they ever take a man on, just for the ride?"

"Some does and some don't."

"Do they ever pull up here?"

There was a low laugh. "They keep away from the shore all right. They don't like the shore any. See that island down there? That's Brennan's Island. They stop there now and again. There's two of them there now. See them?"

A young man had pulled back Evangeline's lips and was examining her teeth. Evangeline put back her ears and snorted. Ashley did not look at her.

"I'll give you twenty dollars for the horse and saddle," said the young man in a loud voice.

Ashley gave no sign of having heard him. He re-entered the store and sat down on a nail keg, his eyes on the floor. Emma brought him his breakfast in a pewter basin. Evangeline neighed. Some women came into the store and made some purchases in a constrained manner. Evangeline neighed again. There was a stir at the door; the loungers drew back. A short solid woman of fifty marched in and placed herself before Ashley. She was wearing a jacket and skirt of the denim from which overalls are made. A man's cap, visor at the back, was pulled close over her short wiry hair. Her scuffed cheeks were red, almost as red as the turkey-red scarf tied about her throat. Her manner was brusque, but a smile seemed to come and go in her gray eyes.

"Thirty dollars," she said.

Ashley looked up at her quickly, then ate a forkful of grits. "Is that you who just come in that rig?"

"Yes."

"Let me look at your horse."

The woman gave a scornful snort. Ashley filled his mouth again slowly and went out into the road. He inspected her horse from all sides. The woman stood beside Evangeline, who bunted her sleeve and shoulder smelling oats.

"Thirty-two," said Ashley, "and you get someone to row me to Brennan's Island."

"Done!—Follow me."

Ashley paid his bill, exchanged grunts with the company, and rode after the woman's rig. At the end of ten minutes they turned in at a gate bearing the sign MRS. T. HODGE, HAY AND FEED. She called "Victor! Victor!" A boy of sixteen came running from the barn. Ashley dismounted.

"Does that horse know her name?"

"Yes—Evangeline."

"Where'd you get that saddle?"

"Friend gave it to me."

"I've only seen one like it before. It's Indian work. Victor, put Evangeline in Julia's stall and give her some oats. Then get your oars. I've got to go in the house and fetch something. Let my rig stay like it is. And bring me a jenny bag of corn."

Evangeline did not look back.

Mrs. Hodge was gone some time. She returned carrying an old carpetbag, which she handed to Ashley.

"Victor, row this gentleman over to Dinkler's. Take the corn down to the boat and wait for him."

Victor started down the steps to the dock. Mrs. Hodge took an old shapeless purse out of her pocket and put it in Ashley's hand.

"It's a fifty-dollar horse, what with that saddle. Give that corn to Win Dinkler—runs the store at Brennan's Point. Tell him it comes from Mrs. Hodge. Tell him I said to fix you up on one of those Swede barges."

She looked at him in silence for a moment. Only once before had he seen such eyes—his grandmother's. "Keep your mouth closed. Don't go shooting anybody, unless you have to. Take off your hat."

He did. She nodded, laughing in a low rumble. "Coming on. You'll not need to wash your head for a week or two."

Ashley put his hand on her wrist. He asked urgently, "After a while . . . could you think of some way to get a word to my wife?"

"Start getting down into that boat.—To torment her worse? Say to yourself: seven years. Leave impatience to boys. Goodbye. Run along."

He started down the steps. She added: "Trust women. Men won't be much help to you from now on."

She turned and went back to her house.

Ashley spent the next four days in and around Dinkler's store, which was part grocery, part chandlery, and part saloon. It sold flea and tick powder. Barges came and went. When Dinkler's was full of rivermen he stayed in his shed at the water's edge. The satchel Mrs. Hodge had given him contained socks, underwear, shirts, soap, a half-used tube of salve, a razor, a frayed copy of Robert Burns's poems, and a suit of church-going black, of old-fashioned cut and for a taller man. Thrust into the pocket was an old envelope addressed to Mrs. Tolland Hodge, Giles, Illinois. He did not finish the letter that began "Dear Bet." He decided that his new name was James Tolland, a Canadian. On the fifth day Win Dinkler put him on a Norwegian barge, forty cents a day and another twenty cents for all the akvavit you could drink. Life on a barge headed downstream is of an almost intolerable boredom. The men played cards. He won back half his passage and half his akvavit. He made friends. In their language the rivermen called him the "young one." To explain himself he told a number of lies and was allowed to resume his taciturnity. On clear nights he slept under the stars on the odorous boards. At table he repeatedly turned the conversation toward the subject of New Orleans. He learned the names of a number of *réunions* where fairly clean cards were played far into the night. He was warned to avoid a certain café, Aux Marins, which was frequented by smugglers, ammunition runners, and the like—men without "papers." He heard a great deal about the importance of "papers." Just when he was beginning to be concerned about the problem of eluding the port inspectors the solution was offered to him. Twenty miles north of the city they could expect a boat to draw up beside the barge. There would be long chaffering. They would be offered clandestine rum, mash, *sapot*, and aphrodisiac drugs. His moment came; as the boat was leaving, Ashley seized his carpetbag, jumped into the boat, shouted goodbye to his friends and was rowed ashore.

In New Orleans Ashley seldom left his room by day. He wore his overalls and went to no pains to keep them neat. He dragged his fingers through his thick hair and even rubbed grime on his face. He was a Canadian seaman looking for a job. He changed his lodgings every four days, never moving far from the neighborhood of Gallatin and Gasquet streets. There was nothing about him to arouse suspicion, but he was everywhere an object of curiosity and he knew it. But for a long time he was unaware that a preposterous thing had befallen his appearance. The curly straw-colored sidewhiskers followed the line of his jaw, descending to a short beard. Other curls played about his wide forehead. The commonplace features of John Ashley of Coaltown had taken on a strange distinction. He had come to resemble one of the Apostles—a John or a James—as they are pictured in art, particularly in bad art, on name-day cards, and votive medals, or as wax or plaster statues. People stopped to stare at him; later, in the southern hemisphere, passersby furtively crossed themselves. Ashley did not know this, or that the police—alert for the bloodthirsty assassin of Illinois who had shot his best friend in the back of the head and had fought his way, single-handed, through a posse of ten armed men—gave no second glance at this pious-looking youth.

Every night at eleven he pushed open the door of Aux Marins, murmured "*Bon soir*" cheerfully, and sat down with his newspapers. He often laid out a pack of cards and studied the card games he had been taught on the raft. Jean-le-Borgne suffered from insomnia. Night after night he postponed the hour when he must climb the circular iron staircase to wait for sleep beside his dropsical wife. He watched his Canadian customer at his games and proposed that they play together. It became custom. The stakes were small. Luck favored them in alternation. Ashley learned *la manille*, *les trois valets*, and *piquet*. There was at first little conversation, but the silences became congenial. Finally Ashley's patience was rewarded. He learned of a certain ship that would be leaving—in a week or two, or maybe a month or two—for Panama from a certain abandoned and decaying dock on an island in the Delta. Its cargo would be, ostensibly, rice.

Ashley needed money. He had the black suit altered to fit him. He put on a high stock collar. He presented himself at La Réunion du Tapis Vert and at La Dame de Pique, paid his door fee, and joined the tables. These clubs were frequented by small merchants, in slavery to cards, and by the younger sons of plantation owners who had no wish to play under their fathers' eyes at the more fashionable clubs. For the first two hours Ashley neither won nor lost; toward four in the morning he would occasionally have a sudden run of luck. When he resorted to cheating it was with limited ambition and great circumspection.

Ashley was a man of faith and did not know it; he was also a gifted mathematician—perhaps with a touch of genius—and did not know it. He was a born card player, though he had not played in twenty years. In the fraternity house at his engineering school in Hoboken, New Jersey, there had seldom been fewer than six games in progress, night and day. Ashley had no competitive sense and no need of money, but he took great interest in the play of numbers. He drew up charts analyzing the elements of probability in the various games. He had a memory for numbers and symbols. He had applied himself there to not winning overmuch and—since he was president of the fraternity—to preventing any other player from doing so. On the barge, at play with Jean-le-Borgne, and here at the clubs he learned new games; alone in his room he studied their structure.

Men of faith and men of genius have this in common: they know (observe and remember) many things they are not conscious of knowing. They are attentive to relationships, recurrences, patterns, and "laws." There is no impurity in this operation of their minds—neither self-advancement nor pride nor self-justification. The nets they fling are wider and deeper than they are fully aware of. Clarity is a noble quality of mind, but those who primarily demand clarity of themselves miss many a truth which—with patience—might become clear at some future time. Minds that are impatient for clarity—or even reasonableness—become gradually narrower and dryer. A few years after these events a relatively obscure scientist, working in a bureau of weights and measures in Switzerland, was searching—as were many others—for a formula that would express the nature of energy. He tells us that it appeared to him in a dream. He awoke and reconsidered; he laughed, for it was of a laughable self-evidence. An ancient philosopher ascribes knowledge to recollection: the delighted surprise at learning what one already knows. Ashley had no idea why he was so accomplished a gambler. He relied upon a whole series of fetishes, irrational promptings and superstitions, and was ashamed of them.

Faith is an ever-widening pool of clarity, fed from springs beyond the margin of consciousness. We all know more than we know we know.

His sailing was delayed. He waited.

Several nights a week, in grimy overalls, he explored the city. He renewed a lapsed curiosity about the lives of others. His interest was centered on the relationships in the family. With the coming on of night he set out on long walks. He became an impenitent eavesdropper. He followed married couples; he particularly lingered where he could overhear the conversation between a father and his older son or daughter. Everywhere he attempted to appraise the quality of a relationship. He turned about the homes of the prosperous as though he were planning to rob them. Most attentively he immersed himself in the lives of those in his own quarter. He came to feel like some husband, father, or uncle who returns unrecognized after years of absence—an Enoch Arden, a Ulysses beggar at his own hearth. He was driven by a need to persuade himself of the happiness of others. He shrank from the sights and sounds of brutality and disease, but, by some unhappy chance, he came upon them everywhere. In the mines at Coaltown he had learned to distinguish the cough of tuberculosis; he now heard it on all sides and saw the red spittle on the pavements. He had thrust upon him the marks of other diseases, also—the one-eyed, the ravaged noses. Everywhere prostitutes patrolled their exclusive territory, as bees are said to do. He did not venture into the half-mile square of Storeyville—famous in song, par-terre of youth and beauty, selected and fostered from among thousands. Here about him were women who could never enter Storeyville or who had outlived their service there. At dusk the world fed; there were sounds of laughter and con-tentment. This was followed by an hour of strolling, of sitting on galleries and front steps, of low-voiced courtships, of mea-sured discussions in the cafés—lofty intelligences discussing politics. By ten-thirty, however, the mood changed. An omi-nous current invaded the city. By midnight sudden cries filled the air, blows, pursuits, overturned furniture, sobbing and whimpering. In Coaltown the report that men—particularly the miners—beat their wives was matter for laughter. Here Ashley saw them. In a narrow alley he came upon a man strik-ing a woman, blow after blow; she sank gradually to her knees, taunting him as no father, as a clown of a father. Another man was beating a woman's head monotonously against the wall of a staircase. He saw children cowering under blows. A girl of six rushed from a doorway and leapt into his arms like a squirrel on a treetop. A man followed her, his head lowered, a table leg in his hand. All three fell into the gutter. Ashley hurried away. A hunted man is in no position to defend the persecuted. He longed to be at sea, to be on a mountain peak, on the Andes.

He waited.

He descended.

He ventured into other cafés. He spent an evening at Joly's, at Bresson's, and many an evening at Quédebac's. The under-world has its hierarchies. Ashley was a pariah and must accept his caste. One stratum above him was Bresson's—the resort of thieves, burglars, pickpockets, small-time confidence men, the touts at races and cockfights. These were active eager-eyed men, full of plans, heavy drinkers, loud talkers, boisterous liars. Whenever the police—in or out of uniform—strolled among the tables at Bresson's, the habitués neither lowered their voices nor glanced up. Their remarks took on a sarcastic edge; they pretended they were unaware of the intruders. These were convivial men and they admitted only convivial men to their number. Ashley was not a convivial and dared not expose himself to their sharp curiosity. Below him was the rock bottom of social life—Joly's—the pimps' café, which no other man ever knowingly enters. Pimps foregather only with one another.

In his ignorance Ashley spent an evening at Joly's. Toward the end of it Joly approached him and asked him in a low voice, "Are you from St. Louis?"

"No."

"I thought you was Herb Benson from St. Louis? You're in the *tambour*?"

Ashley didn't know why he should be in any "drum," but he compliantly said that he was.

"Where did you work?"

"Up in Illinois."

"Chicago?"

"Near it."

"Great in Chicago, eh? Great?"

"Yes."

"Well, well! Baba's Louis had to go up the river. You know Baba? She's the one just went out—the fat one. She told me to tell you it's all right, if you'd take care of her. She'd bring you thirty dollars a week—more, if you'd jump with it."

"Why would she bring me thirty dollars?"

Joly's breath stuck in his windpipe. His eyes started out of his head. "Get up and get out of here! Get out of here quick! Get! Get!"

Ashley stared at him, put down a coin, and went out the door. Joly flung the money after him down the street.

Ashley's stratum was that of those who had failed in both the orderly and disorderly life. Their café was Quédebac's—men returned from long prison sentences, unlucky housebreakers, unlucky gamblers, ex-pimps, ex-touts, spiritless men, many with tremulous hands and tremulous cheeks. They fed in the sheds at the back doors of convents. Some, intermittently, washed dishes in restaurants; some, intermittently, earned their living at the dismalest of all professions—were orderlies in hospitals. Ashley heard from them of their work and thought of applying for it. He was ready to master his repulsion; he was afraid of nothing except himself. Fastidiousness is a timidity. He did not know if hospitals demanded to see the "papers" of orderlies. In the meantime he was searching for Spanish speakers; he found one and paid for his lessons in drink. Women came and went, the last rejects of their profession.

"M'ssieu James, will you buy me a *verte*?" (Absinthe.)

"I can't afford it tonight, Toinette. You can have a beer."

"Thank you, M'ssieu James."

The word "reprobate" is used loosely; this was the world of reprobates. All speech was obscene, but not from any intention to startle or even to convey emphasis. Reprobates are incapable of anger; they have lost the right to it. They have been judged and they agree with their judges. They tell few lies. They have nothing to hide and little to gain. They are generous to one another, but not from any largeness of heart. Abjection devaluates money.

All was new to Ashley. Quédebac's made little claim on compassion, even if he had possessed a measure of it. But Quédebac's increased the turmoil of questioning within him—the constant urgent unanswerable questions. Yet he did not find the café uncongenial; he even pushed open the door with a stirring of anticipation. He was casually welcomed. The even flow of conversation was uninterrupted. The process of learning is accompanied by alternations of pain and brief quickenings of pleasure that resemble pain.

It took him a year and two weeks to reach Chile. He moved down the coast, finding passage in small ships, avoiding the larger ports when he could. There was generally work for a man who could do sums, was of open approach, and had an air of authority—provided, however, that he wore a workman's clothes. Work for a gentleman would be hard to find. He kept accounts in warehouses. He weighed produce on plantations. When questioned about his papers he told a story of losing all his belongings in a hotel fire in Panama. He was believed or indulged.

He tallied cargoes in Buenaventura.

He supervised turtle hunts on the low islands off San Barto.

Ashleys give all of themselves to whatever task lies before them. Everywhere he was asked to stay, but he moved on. He sat late in bars; he played cards. His knowledge of the seaboard dialect progressed rapidly. When there was no work to be found he even picked up a little money as a public letter writer.

He spent three months at Islaya. It is a truth well known but seldom uttered that almost any foreigner is a better foreman over a group of Ecuadorian laborers than any Ecuadorian. He slept on the stinking decks of guano boats and closely observed their management. After several trips he was put in charge of one. He was shipwrecked among silver barracudas and lost a third of his crew. It was perhaps his fault, for he pretended to a knowledge of navigation he did not possess, but bad conscience did not trouble his sleep. At the bottom of society all men are threatened with hunger, hidden reefs, and storms; all waters are shark-infested. It later became common knowledge that all the Ashleys were incorrigibly immoral.

He quickly made a place for himself in the oil fields at Salinas. He could have settled down and advanced far. Everywhere there were card games far into the night—here under the tent of netting and the hurricane lamp. Dr. Andersen, the Dane, was a pleasant fellow. There was an American, Billings, traveling in pharmaceuticals.

"Slap it down, Billings. Slap it down.—How's your rat list?"

"Slow, very slow."

"Do you know what the rat list is, Tolland?"

"No."

"It's a list of hunted men with a price on their head. Who are you looking for now, Billings?"

"Vice-president of a Kansas City bank. Run off with a hundred thousand dollars and a sixteen-year-old girl."

"Probably down here?"

"Pretty sure. Nobody's thinking of running to Mexico this year."

"What's the money?"

"Three or four thousands."

"What are his marks?"

"About forty-four. Round pink face. Two gold teeth."

"Slap it down, Billings!—Did they ever catch the judge?"

"Found him dead in Santa Marta. Took his own life, looked like. Tired of running. Seems like people got tired of feeding him, too. Two hundred pounds down to ninety.—Just got word of a new one—four thousand dollars. Man in Indiana—shot his best friend in the back of the head. Terrible type. Wouldn't want to meet him on a dark night. Shot his way free, single-handed, out of a posse of twelve men."

"Old or young?"

"Has grown children."

"Any marks?"

"I forget.—Do you know a good way to catch a rat?" Billings lowered his voice and narrowed his eyes. "All these rats have changed their names. Well, if you think you've spotted your man, you come up behind him and shout his real name 'HOPKINS' or 'ASHLEY'—like that!"

In Callao, Ashley got work in a Chinese importing firm. His employers had seldom encountered honesty outside their own race. He was advanced to a position just short of partnership. His duties, however, increasingly required his calling at important firms in Lima. He resigned.

He moved to a squalid lodging by the sea near Callao. He had journeyed thousands of miles. He had entered realms far stranger to him than those described by the geographers. He was now idle. Hitherto constant activity had concealed from him the full burden of his widening knowledge. While waiting for a coastal steamer he fell gravely ill. Despair probes the organs one by one, seeking the easiest entrance for the kill. He was saved from death by the sisters, old and young, turn and turn about by his bed. His convalescence was surrounded by gales of laughter. "Don Diego, el canadiense."

His ascent had begun, perhaps.

"That's Chile," said the Captain pointing toward the low shore.

Ashley's heart gave a leap. He had reached Chile. He was still alive. This was the land of his adoption. But he was not yet ready for Arica or Antofagasta. He asked to be rowed ashore at San Gregorio. There he learned that a Norwegian trading ship would put in at any time—in a few days or in a few months.

He was low in funds. Most of the hundred and fifty dollars he had saved in Callao had been stolen from him. A hard core of money which throughout the year he had sewn into the lining of his belt was safe; that was held intact for his final throw of the dice: his passage to Antofagasta and his presentation of himself to the mining authorities there. Once ashore in

San Gregorio he looked about for work. There was none to be found. He engaged a bed at Pablito's tavern—the cheapest to be had, a pallet under an overhang in the stables. He busied himself with removing the filth as best he could. He was the governor of his mind: He did not permit himself to be aware of hunger or to recognize the disgust he felt at the vermin he harbored. He sat in Pablito's tavern all day and far into the night.

Within a week he was playing cards with the mayor, the chief of police, and the leading merchants. He lost a little; one evening in three he gained what he had lost and more. He was blackened by the sun; his hair was long and unruly. In spite of his mastery of the dialect and abject lodging, he was "Don Diego" or "Don Jaime"—he preferred the latter. He explored the little town and its environs. He made friends. Through no efforts of his own he again became a public letter writer. His charges were moderate, a few coppers. People who had not sent a letter for years remembered their aged parents or their dispersed children. There was much correspondence about inheritances, dictated by those who had bitterly learned to avoid lawyers. Tradesmen wanted letters written in dignified *castellano*. There were love letters and threatening letters to be delivered after dark by the town's clever hunchback. He even wrote prayers that were to be hung over a child's bed as amulets. He listened to long feverish whispered stories. He advised, he consoled, he reprehended. His hands were being continually kissed. *Don Jaimito el bueno.*

From his card partners he began to pick up information about copper mining in the Andes, about the Scotchmen and Germans who worked the mines, and about the cold and heat that alternated above ten thousand feet. The city fathers returned to their homes at eleven o'clock for dinner and left Ashley to silence, warm beer, and María Icaza.

María Icaza was midwife, abortionist, *maga*, teller of fortunes, interpreter of dreams, go-between, exorcisor of devils. She was Chilean and Indian, yet there was a blue cast to her complexion; she said she was "Persian." Bluest of all were her heavy eyelids, which descended over her eyes like hoods. She said she was over eighty. The claim added to her authority; she was probably seventy. She sat against the wall and brooded about crime, disease, folly, and death. From time to time her clients consulted her or called her away. Ashley's customers likewise drew up their chairs beside him. Both held office hours in whispers. Both had dogs that would not stir a yard from their feet—María Icaza's Fidel and Ashley's Calgary—good friends for lack of better. There were fleas on the ground and gnats in the air; a slight mitigation of the heat could be felt toward two in the morning.

They exchanged salutations.

She directed one of her customers to his table; there was a letter to be written. He directed one of his customers to hers; there was a crisis to be met. Finally, they were playing cards, a pile of pebbles between them. Often no more than a few dozen words were exchanged in an hour. From time to time María Icaza would be shaken by fits of coughing. The long red scarf which she pressed to her mouth was streaked dark brown with blood. When she felt a severer fit coming on she and Fidel walked with dignity to the outhouse, whence the sounds of her agony could be heard in the long silence of the night.

"Where did you catch this cold, María Icaza?"

"High—high in the Andes."

Their friendship grew in their silences; it was cemented by their destitution; it was nourished by the prevalence of misery in San Gregorio.

The second week he was "Don Jaime," the third "Jaimito," the fourth "*mi hijo*." She frequently laid out her pack of cards in his intention or somberly studied the palms of his hands. He told her he put no faith in such things. She replied, using a vulgar idiom, that that made no difference to her.

One night, in the third week, she put her blue forefinger on a card and waited until he had looked up into her face. She made the gesture of a rope around her neck.

Looking at her interrogatively he flung the rope around his neck and pulled the end abruptly toward the ceiling.

"I don't know," she answered surlily.

One night as she laid out the cards he asked, "How many children have I?"

"Do not ask me such questions. If you doubt me, you can go and stand on your head in the excrement! You have four or five children."

"Are they well?"

"Why would they not be well?"

One night he began telling her his whole story. She interrupted him, saying, "What happens is not interesting."

"What is interesting, María Icaza?"

"God," she replied, pointing first to her forehead, then to his.

María Icaza was a singer when her health permitted. Old Pablo rarely allowed the town's prostitutes to frequent his distinguished saloon before midnight. Once in a while, when the city fathers had gone to their homes, he nodded a grave permission to one or other of the choicest—to Consuelo or Maridolores. They were required to sit sedately with a glass before them.

Occasionally it made for good business. Maridolores, the joyous one, would murmur, "María Icaza of my heart, one song! One song! Don Jaime, ask María Icaza to sing one song."

Fidel seemed to understand what was wanted. He would plant his forepaws on her lap and plead for a song. Ashley would glance at her with affectionate anticipation. Old Pablo would place a glass of rum before her with a bow.

María Icaza would begin abruptly in a voice of extraordinary volume and range. A long heart-chilling cadenza, "Aïe!" would fill the room. Then:

> "The lacemaker sits at her window
> Blind! Blind!
> Comb your hair, little one.
> There's enough sadness to come."

or:

> "Are you on your way to Bethlehem,
> My sons, my daughters?"

Fidel looked eagerly from face to face to make sure that all would rise to this privilege. At the refrain the girls beat their saucers with spoons. Maridolores leapt to the floor, her heels resounding like drumbeats. The pharmacist next door woke, dressed, and came down with his guitar. The room filled. Oh, what an hour! What passion! . . . What memories! A throng gathered in the street outside the tavern. What a clapping of hands!

"María Icaza, the beautiful—sing!"

Finally Ashley would whisper, "Don't sing any more, María Icaza! Save your breath, for the love of Christ!"

The festival would come to an end. Fidel lay down, his muzzle against his mistress's stocking, replete with pleasure. A transient happiness had descended upon San Gregorio.

María Icaza asked Ashley to tell her his dreams. He answered he could not remember them. She laughed contemptuously.

During the fourth week she said, "You look bad. You have not been sleeping. I will tell you your dreams. You are having the dream of the universal nothingness. You walk down, down, into valleys of nothing, of chalk. You stare, you stare into pits where all is cold. You wake up cold. You think you will never be warm again. And there is this nothing—*nada, nada, nada* —but this *nada* laughs, like teeth striking together. You open the door of a cupboard, of a room, and there is nothing there but this laughing. The floor is not a floor. The walls are not walls. You wake up and you cannot stop your trembling. Life has no sense. Life is an idiot laughing.—Why did you lie to me?"

He said slowly, "I could not tell anyone about them."

He went out the door and stood a long time with his hands on the parapet above the waves. When he returned she gestured to him to deal the cards.

"You have nothing to say, María Icaza?"

"Later.—Play!"

An hour later she said, "Naturally, you have these bad dreams, *mi hijo*."

"Why, naturally?"

"God in His goodness sends them to you."

He waited.

"He does not want you to be ignorant any longer. You are ignorant. You are very ignorant.—Cut the pack. I wish to read what the cards tell me."

She laid them out, yet seemed scarcely to glance at them.

"You are forty-one or forty-two years old." She drew her finger across her face. "You have no wrinkles here—from care and thought. You have no wrinkles here—from laughter. Your understanding is like a little fetus—a poor little twisting and turning fetus—trying to be born. When God loves a creature He wants the creature to know the highest happiness and the deepest misery—then he can die. He wants him to know all that being alive can bring. That is His best gift."

Ashley looked down and said in a low voice, "I have been very happy."

She swept her hands in scorn across the cards on the table, the landscape of his life. "*That? That*—happiness? No! No! There is no happiness save in understanding the whole. You are a creature whom God loves—particularly loves. You are being born."

Here she fell into a fit of coughing and drew the red scarf across her mouth. When she had recovered she put her hand into a voluminous and bulging pocket in her skirt. She drew out a small crucifix rudely carved from thornwood.

"Before you go to sleep look at it well. Think of that suffering. Not the nails. The nails are not important. There are nails everywhere. But think of the suffering—*there*!" She put her fingers on the center of her forehead. "He who held in His mind a hundred thousand San Gregorios and Antofagastas and Tiburones and—what town do you come from?"

"Coaltown."

"A hundred thousand Caltones. Look at it, then put it by your head when you sleep. You will have no more nightmares. There is no happiness for those who have not looked at the horror and the *nada*."

He took it.

He put his hand on hers and asked softly, "Have you known the highest happiness, María Icaza?"

Her spine straightened. Her chin rose. She looked out of the door, then glanced at him with a faint smile of contempt that said, "Of course, I have."

She took the crucifix out of his hand for a moment. She pointed to the red glass beads that had been affixed to it to represent the drops of blood. She looked at him. "Red. Red. Look at the red. Men, women, and children love you because of the blue of your eyes. But there is a better love than that. Blue is the color of faith. But red is love—every kind of love. Anybody can see that you have faith. So has Fidel! Faith is not enough. Maybe, if you are lucky, you will be born into love."

Ashley lowered his voice and lowered his eyes. "María Icaza, dear María Icaza! If I am born again, if I know the best and the worst, that cannot help my children. I fathered them when I was still in ignorance."

María Icaza struck his hand sharply. "Idiot! Imbecile! If God plans to give you His greatest gifts, it is because you always merited them." María Icaza had never seen an oak tree, but she quoted the Spanish proverb, "The oak tree is in the acorn." She went on, "If Simón Bolívar had fathered a child at sixteen and died next day, the child would still be the son of the Liberator."

Ashley had no more nightmares. The Norwegian trading vessel put in a few days later. Ashley had barely enough money for his passage, but he sent a flask of rum to María Icaza in the hospital. He attached to it a card all red. In his preparations for departure he lost the crucifix.

In Antofagasta Ashley found lodgings in the workers' quarter and set about planning his campaign unhurriedly. From five in the afternoon until well after midnight he sat, alternately, in the Café de la República and the Café de la Constitución, bent over one or other of the German-language newspapers published a thousand miles to the south in that province of Chile which is a new Württemberg. These cafés were in rat catchers' country; his presence was risky but necessary. All around him, hour after hour, men were talking of nitrates and copper. He soon became aware that another marginal man was frequenting the two cafés. "Old Percival" was a derelict of the fields, a former nitrate man, a former silver man, and a former copper man. He had lost an eye to love or dynamite and his wits were dim from wine and from brooding on old wrongs. He drew up to the tables of his more prosperous friends and waited to be offered a drink. It was often given him; he was often rebuffed, though never roughly. He introduced himself to Ashley: "Roderick Percival, sir, former managing director of the El Rosario Smelter. Inventor, sir, of the Percival Centrifugal Retort System —stolen from me by the Graham brothers, Ian and Robert, and I don't care who hears me say so." This was the overture to some fifty hours of soliloquy. Ashley drew his guest to less metropolitan bars. He submitted to many a repetition. He began to suspect that some of his guest's grievances were justified. Again, his patience was rewarded.

"Mr. Tolland, sir, never work at a mine that's over ten thousand feet above sea level. Why shorten your life, sir? Nobody opens their mouth to say a word; they save their breath. Up there men get melancholy. Chap blew off the top of his head at Rocas Verdes just the other day. Don't work, sir, at a mine that's far from a main line. A man can't get away for a spree. Why, there are some mines up there where the bucketline to the junction breaks down four times a summer—avalanches. Men get to hate the sight of one another. . . . Don't work at any mine that's not financed by American capital. There's the ticket. Look at El Teniente. You'd think you were at a Saratoga Springs hotel. Hot showers, if you please, day and night. Houses for married engineers! Of course, liquor's forbidden, but a smart man knows a trick or two. Why, they've got a lunchroom fifteen hundred feet down a shaft—ham sandwiches and lemonade. Look at Rocas Verdes—lot of Scotchmen and Swiss and Germans. You're lucky if you get a bowl of oatmeal. Besides a lot of the miners are Bolivian Indians—can't even talk Spanish."

Ashley saw his way. Rocas Verdes was administered by the Kinnairdie Mining Company. The representative in Antofagasta was Mr. Andrew Smith, who, at all temperatures, wore a black alpaca jacket buttoned up to his black Covenanter's beard. It required all Ashley's equanimity to stand up to Mr. Smith's piercing gaze. . . . "Mr. James Tolland, of Bemis, Alberta . . . a mechanical engineer, eager to learn copper mining . . . citizenship papers and academic certificates unfortunately lost in a hotel fire in Panama. . . . Letter of recommendation from Dr. Knut Andersen of the Salinas oil fields in Ecuador. . . ." Mr. Tolland submitted some mechanical drawings—equipment for a coal mine. Ashley might have spared his pains. Mr. Andrew Smith engaged him on the spot, delaying only to ask him about the condition of his heart and lungs. Ashley's work—to start with—was to supervise the living quarters of the engineers and the miners—heating, kitchen, sanitation—and to prepare plans for the further installation of electricity. He would receive a letter to Dr. MacKenzie recommending that he be given every opportunity to learn the processes of copper mining in all its phases. He was given instructions concerning his clothing and equipment and the money to purchase them.

"The company," said Mr. Smith, "would like ye to go to Manantiales for a week. That's just short of seven thousand feet and will prepare ye for the higher altitudes. When you coom in this afternoon to sign the contract, I'll gi' ye a letter to Mrs. Wickersham. She runs a hotel there—her Fonda, the best hotel in South America. It can be she'll take ye and it can be she'll no. She's like that. A train leaves on Friday at eight o'clock and if it doesn't leave on Friday, it leaves on Saturday. When you get to Rocas Verdes write me once a month about what you need there."

Ashley brought more questions to Roderick Percival. At first Percival was evasive about both Dr. MacKenzie and Mrs. Wickersham. Apparently he had suffered at the hands of each: he had been dropped from the Rocas Verdes mines and had been disbarred from the Fonda. MacKenzie was crazy; had lived "up there" too long; had a closed mind; thought he knew it all—conceited as an old baboon. Mrs. Wickersham was a "tartar"; ran a hotel as though it were her private home. . . . Nosey—a trouble-making gossip . . . likes to call herself the "newspaper of the Andes" . . . knows all the stories of the seventies and the eighties; awful bore, always repeating herself. Percival knew her when she was nothing but a cook for a party of emerald hunters. Anyway, she'd had one moment of good sense; set up her hotel in the only agreeable place in north Chile. She's not only got her hot springs, but the only real river within hundreds of miles. . . . "There are no streams around here, Mr. Tolland. No rain. There are children eight years old in Antofagasta that have never seen a drop of rain. Even cactus can't grow around here. . . . Surely, yes, surely, the snow and ice up there melt at the edges and big streams form, but they don't get far. Sucked up by the sun and sucked down by the soil. Why, we wouldn't have water in Antofagasta if Peter Wessel hadn't made that pipeline. A Dane—great friend of mine. He wanted to make a Tivoli Gardens here, like they have in Copenhagen. Wasn't as crazy as it sounds. With all that nitrate in the soil, your roses would grow to Heaven. All you need is water and shade. And Mrs. Wickersham's got that at Manantiales. Feeds her guests vegetables that would win first prize at any county fair in the States. Feeds her hospitals and or- phanages with them, too. . . . I'll bet she runs her institutions like she runs her hotel. 'Out you go! I don't like your face. Find some crutches; I want you out of this hospital in twenty minutes!'"

During his weeks in Antofagasta Ashley often walked about the town after sunset, as he had done in New Orleans and in port after port on his journey. Now, as though scales had fallen from his eyes, he saw only poverty, hunger, disease, and violence. Stores and houses were open to the street. Early in the evening the air was filled with laughter and terms of endearment. The bonds within the family appeared to carry a warmth unknown further north. But toward midnight the temper changed. He no longer shrank from these sights and sounds, these blows and imprecations. He even sought them out, as though there were something to be learned from them: some answer to that persistent "why?" He had never been a man of reflection. He had no vocabulary and no grammar with which to reflect on such matters, except those which he had long repudiated—the sermons delivered in Coaltown's Methodist church. He began to be afraid—an Ashley afraid!—that he would never know anything, that he would arrive at the end of his life "stump ignorant." Take this omnipresent wife beating:

Groping, he tried to recall an evening in Salinas and some remarks of Dr. Andersen. There had been a card game under the tent of mosquito netting in that house raised on piles above the shore. It was a popular saint's day and the clamor of the festivities could be heard from the distant workers' quarter. One of the players made a joke about all the wives who would be beaten that night. The doctor, speaking dryly and fastidiously, had said:

"The men can't strike us. We are foreigners, unbelievably rich, semi-divine. They can't strike their foremen—though once in a while they can ambush and shoot them. They strike one another, but they don't put their heart into it. They know they're all caught in the same desperate trap. But they can beat those who are nearest to them. The blows are aimed at circumstance, at destiny, at God. I am happy to say that even the most wretched husband and father does not strike his loved ones across the eyes or in the belly: those blows require *two* executioners; someone must unfold the cowering victim. Pedro would not permit another man to touch his treasures."

"But . . ." Ashley remembered protesting, falteringly, "the men are drunk."

"That's too easy an explanation, sir. They are devoted husbands and fathers. They get drunk in order to be brutal, to release themselves to strike at God."

"I don't understand." The game went on. Later Ashley asked, "Do they beat their wives and children in Europe?"

"In Denmark, do you mean? In my home?—Oh, Mr. Tolland! We civilized men have more refined tortures."

"What? . . . What?"

"It's your deal, Smithson.—Suffering is like money, Mr. Tolland. It circulates from hand to hand. We pass on what we take in.—It's your deal, Mr. Smithson."

Then Dr. Andersen had said something about "sometimes the chain is broken."

Now, in Antofagasta, Ashley's distress was increased by the frequent view of persons who resembled the members of his family. At first glance these short, bent, black-clothed women bore no likeness to Beata, but occasionally a gesture or a word recalled her. Like hers, their lives were centered about one man of unpredictable moods, their breadwinner, who slept beside them—a man occupied with his own interests far from their eternal kitchen; they were bringing up children; they were growing old. He saw an occasional Lily. Roger looked at him sharply and hurried by. He bought fruit syrups from Sophias. Other Sophias waited on him in restaurants. He played checkers with a Constance. More frequently he encountered a Eustacia Lansing.

The train was scheduled to arrive at Manantiales at four or five or six in the afternoon—eighty miles in eight to ten hours. For a time it careened gaily over the plain, then crept upward in zigzag. It barely moved across great spindly trestles. It made long halts in villages that came to life when it approached—parched nitrate towns clustered about a water tower whose seepage and intermittent shade had produced one pepper tree. At each stop all the passengers descended from the cars. The engineer, firemen, and conductor consented to have a glass or two with the stationmaster. Hour by hour the landscape became more awe-inspiring. The Pacific Ocean below them became a vaster platter. The peaks above them drew near and seemed to lean above the train. Ashley had seen Chimborazo from Guayaquil, rising almost twenty-one thousand feet from the sea ("Beata should see this! The children should see this!"), but these were Chile's mountains, his—henceforward his.

The wooden benches on the train were filling up long before its departure. Ashley found a place opposite and beside a large family. He exchanged no words with them after the first prim greeting. He read or pretended to sleep. Some neighbors had come to see this family off and he soon knew its names: Widow Rosa Dávilos and María del Carmen, sixteen, Pablo, Clara, Inés and Carlos. The neighbors also wore black and were accompanied by their daughters. (There is a proverb: "A daughter is a domestic calamity.") Each brought a small gift of food—accepted after such long scenes of surprise and protest that there was little breath left for thanks. When the train finally started all crossed themselves devoutly and the widow was urged for the twentieth time to submit to the will of God—an injunction that Ashley knew denoted some last numbing demand on human fortitude.

The family glanced from time to time at the gentleman. It was soon assumed that so exalted a personage would take no interest in their conversation, even if he were able to understand the dialect in which they spoke. The widow wrapped herself in desolation and leaned her cheek against the window frame. The older son, opposite Ashley, gazed somberly before him, withdrawn into contempt from the woman talk that flowed on about him. The younger children began to whimper for the food that was piled on Clara's lap. Clara, fourteen, appeared to be her mother's deputy. An hour later the children were still complaining of hunger. Finally their mother opened her eyes and said, "Eat!" Clara divided the food into five portions and gave Inés and Carlos their share. The four older members of the family denied that they were hungry. The gestures of sacrifice were transformed into a bitter quarrel. Pablo urged his mother to eat. In tones of hysterical exasperation she commanded him to eat. María del Carmen had no appetite.

"God in Heaven, why have I been given such children!"

"Mama," said Clara softly, "you've dropped your purse. Here it is."

"My purse! That's heavy, my purse! Keep it!"

"Yes, Mama."

By noon the children were again hungry. Clara told them long rambling stories about the Infant Jesus. He passes through rooms where little children are sleeping. He makes little boys manly and little girls beautiful, so beautiful. Then, still in a low voice, she told them of the wonderful life that awaited them in Manantiales.

"Do you know what Manantiales means? It means that water comes right up out of the ground. It comes hot and it comes cold. And flowers everywhere—everywhere you look. And Grandmother will say, 'Go out into the garden, Inés of my eyes, and bring me some roses to put before the Mother of God.' Do you remember what Grandmother said when she came to see Papa before he went to Heaven? She said there was an English lady in Manantiales who had a school for girls and that she would make Carmencita a laundress and, maybe, me a nursing sister and that we would bring money—money—money to Mama every Saturday of the Lord. This English lady—when a girl wants to be married, she gives her a bed and a griddle!"

"And shoes, Clara?"

"Oh, yes, shoes—and the man marries her."

"Does she do anything for boys?"

"You don't listen! When she sees Pablito, she'll say, 'I don't know what I've done that God is so good to me! I've been out of my mind looking for a strong honorable boy to take care of my mules and horses!' And when Carlos gets bigger she'll say, 'I've been watching that Carlos Dávilos for some time now. I've plans for him.'"

Here the Widow Dávilos opened her eyes, leaned forward, and gave Clara a resounding slap across the face.

"*Mamita!*"

"Hold your noise! Filling the children's ears with that nonsense! You and your English lady and your griddles and your shoes.—Tell them we have nothing to live for! Tell them that!"

"Yes, Mama."

The food was again distributed. María del Carmen accepted her share. Clara placed a portion on Pablo's knee. Barely moving, the train crossed a great trestle. María del Carmen covered her eyes with her hands and shuddered. Her mother looked at her angrily and suddenly pulled her hands from her face.

"Don't be a fool, child! Look down into that ravine! Look! It would be better for us all if we fell into that ditch."

Clara looked sternly at her mother and crossed herself. Her mother was stung. "What does that mean, little pestilence?"

"Mama, we want you to live more than anything in the world."

"For what? Tell me that—for WHAT? Your father has left us nothing. Nothing. Nothing. Your grandmother can do nothing for us. Your uncle Tomás is below worthless. She has three women in the house already. You know what became of Ana Romero's children. You know that!"

"I am ready to beg, Mama. I will take Inés and Carlito with me. They can sing." Again her mother slapped her sharply. Clara continued without flinching. "God doesn't hate beggars; He only hates the people who don't give anything to beggars. If Papa didn't leave us anything, it was the will of God."

"What's that? What's that?"

"If Papa fell and hurt his head, it was the will—"

"Your father was a saint, a perfect saint!"

Pablo threw a glance of angry scorn at his mother.

"What are you looking at me like that for? *You!* You never appreciated your father—never! Oh! If you turn out to be one-tenth the man your father was, I know someone who'll be very much surprised!"

"Mama!" whispered Clara.

"Don't you 'Mama' me!"

"Mama, you know you said to Sister Rufina how proud you were of Pablito. You said he was the manliest boy in the quarter."

"You!"

Pablo stood up and said loudly, "Papa was a stooooopid!"

"Oh, Angels in Heaven, listen to him! I was married to your father for twenty years. I bore him nine children. I was the happiest woman in Antofagasta."

"You were happy! You were happy!—Were *we* happy?"

Rosa Dávilos started to reply when Clara said to them all, authoritatively, "Papa is watching us."

Ashley wiped his forehead. He all but groaned aloud. He

seemed to himself to be dreaming—that is: present at one of those ten-act dramas of which we are simultaneously the spellbound spectator, the protagonist, and the unavowed author. A quarter of an hour later his eyes happened to meet those of Rosa Dávilos. As she looked at him expressions of astonishment and fear crossed her face. She drew herself up and assumed the air of a great lady. When the passengers descended at the next station she moved her family to another car. He walked down the village's one sunbaked street. He stood by the water tower and the pepper tree. At intervals he heard the sounds of detonation from the plain—dynamite cracking the surface to extract the nitrate that would cross the seas to furnish instruments of death and to fertilize crops. "Life affords no second chances," he thought. "Is this what growing older is—seeing always more clearly the things we failed to see?" When he returned to the train he found himself in the midst of another family—a party so large that it filled several benches. All were a little tipsy. They were celebrating the name day of a little old lady who sat opposite him, giggling sleepily. From time to time her children and grandchildren would lean down and embrace her, exclaiming noisily: "*Mamita*, you treasure!" "Abuelita, darling!" The men pressed drinks on him. He was introduced to them all and paid his compliments to the old lady. It is the diversity of life that renders thinking difficult. Many a beginning philosopher has been on the point of grasping the problem of suffering, but what sage can cope with that of happiness?

At Manantiales he rented a room in the workers' quarter. His depression lifted. He was young; he was well; he had escaped his pursuers. For the first time in a year he was in a temperate climate; the nights were cold. Best of all he was active. He repaired the flue in his landlady's kitchen; he roused her son from torpor and together they cleaned the cistern. He sang. He made himself useful in the neighborhood and was invited to dinner. Imagine a gentleman getting himself dirty at tasks like that! It was "Don Jaime" here and "Don Jaime" there.

It was said later of the Ashley children that they were all slow to mature. They were, but not as preposterously slow as their father. The principal harm in being thus fast or slow seems to be that the growing boy or girl may skip or skimp or

over-prolong one or other of the automutative phases to which
—as it were—the young are entitled. John Ashley of Pulley's
Falls, New York, had seen himself as the young Alexander
conquering one world after another, but he had not been the
boy who gives his life to working among lepers; he had been
the knight crusader of the story books, but he had not seen
himself as the statesman who would correct all the injustices in
the social order. He had been a rebel only to the extent of
erecting a wall between himself and his doting parents and of
rejecting their idols. At engineering school he had calmly declared himself to be an atheist, only to commit himself to a
more abject superstition: he had been certain that some agent
was at his beck and call; catastrophes descended upon other
people but not upon him; circumstances rushed forward to
offer him whatever he most wanted. Above all, he had barely
brushed that phase in late adolescence when every youth is an
argumentative philosopher. Ashley in Manantiales was belat-
edly suffering pains that he should have endured twenty years
before. At night he lay on the roof of his inn and gazed up at
the constellations among the peaks. Like another young man
in a story book thousands of miles away, he thought: "In infinite space, in infinite time, in infinite matter, an organism like
a bubble is formed; it lasts a short while and then bursts; and
that bubble is myself."

Another memory of his past life returned to torment him—
his relations with his parents. John Ashley had eloped with Beata
Kellerman on the day following his graduation from engineering school in Hoboken, New Jersey. His parents had journeyed
down from Pulley's Falls, New York, to be present at the exercises. They had seen him carry off the honors, prize after prize.
The next day they returned to their home; he was to follow
them within the week. At Christmas he sent them a card without return address. He never wrote them, though he considered doing so in his happiness when Lily was born. Without
resentment and with little cause for resentment both he and
Beata had cut themselves off from their families. During all the
intervening years this conduct had caused John Ashley no regret and no self-reproach. Only now, when his attention was
so urgently directed toward the family life about him, did he
begin to ask himself anxiously wherein he was to blame. Was

he an unnatural son? Had this "unnaturalness" exerted a harmful influence in the life of his own family? Would his children, in turn—self-sufficient and without affection—disappear into the throng? Had there been something amiss in the life at "The Elms"? But there had been seventeen years of loving happiness there!

Why, then, had María Icaza replied with scorn to his claim to having been happy?

His father had been an honorable man, a leader in the community, the president of the bank in Pulley's Falls. John was an only child, though he remembered that his parents had lost two children in infancy, two girls, before he was born. His father had been taciturn and undemonstrative, perhaps in reaction to his wife's effusiveness. His mother idolized her son, adored him. Even in the religious realm, these emotions often conceal an unspoken contract. Adoration of a human being, under guise of self-effacement and humility, advances large claims and is an attempt at possession. John had a good disposition; his rejection of his mother's demands on him never took the form of exasperation. He pretended to be unaware of them. He had in his life an example of the love which enlarges freedom; the summers he spent on his Grandmother Ashley's farm were the happiest days he was ever to know. It came back to him now that his father had one trait that had then seemed to him to be embarrassing but unimportant. His father had been a miser—a clandestine miser. His house was run in comfort; he made his contribution to the church; but any financial demand that exceeded his precise budget tortured him. His wife spent a great deal of time and ingenuity in attempting to conceal the extent of his idiosyncrasy from the neighbors, but stories circulated of complicated maneuvers to save a "red cent"! It now struck Ashley for the first time that his father was rich, probably very rich. In addition to his work at the bank he was constantly buying and selling farms, houses, and stores. Now, in Manantiales, Ashley realized that he had formed himself to be the opposite of his father and that his life had been as mistaken as his father's. The root of avarice is the fear of what circumstance may bring. The opposite of the miser is not the spendthrift of the parable—the prodigal son who wastes his substance in riotous living—but the grasshopper who heedlessly sings through a long summer. Ashley had lived without fear and without judgment.

He groaned aloud. "Is that what family life is? The growing children are misshapen by those parents who were in various ways warped by the blindness, ignorance, and passions of their own parents; and one's own errors impoverish and cripple one's children? Such is the endless chain of the generations?" Ashley's wonderful grandmother had been an eccentric. He knew very little about her early life. She had been born a Roman Catholic in Montreal. Marrying his grandfather, a small farmer on rocky soil, she had attended his Methodist church. She had persuaded him to move fifty miles south to better soil. But something had gone wrong between them. She had joined one of those peculiar religious sects—rigidly ascetic, yet given to emotional camp meetings and to "speaking in tongues"— that were particularly prevalent in northern New York State. Her husband had left to seek gold in Alaska. She ran her farm alone with the help of a succession of unreliable "hands" and developed her extraordinary gift for handling animals. She was strong-minded and tirelessly active; lavish in the works but not the words of love. She had sent her son to a small college from which he graduated to become the banker of Pulley's Falls— living in that world of little triumphs and vast dreads, which is a miser's life. Thereafter there had been no friendly bond between them. Had her very virtues been transmuted into her son's avarice?

Such is the endless chain of the generations?

During those summers his grandmother had taken him to the Wednesday-evening prayer meetings at her church. He was surprised to see that there was no preacher. Some sat, some stood, some knelt. There were long silences. There were short hushed hymns. There were brief requests for patience, for death, for light. All churches henceforward seemed trivial to him who had known this self-forgetting urgency. The company seemed to be waiting for his grandmother to pray. When she had spoken the meeting came to an end. She arose and addressed the Lord without closing her eyes. She spoke with a strong French accent which, when she was in deep earnest, became almost unintelligible. Many times her contribution was brief. Her thought turned always on God's plan for the universe. She asked to be shown her part in it. She complained of His slowness in its fulfillment. She asked that God be merciful to those who in wickedness or in ignorance had interfered with His great design. The air in the room became charged with electric energy. There was no doubt about it—it was *her* wickedness and ignorance that weighed her down—but all of her listeners took it on themselves. There was a murmuring and a rising and a sinking to the floor and a covering of eyes. John could not understand why his grandmother talked like that. She was the perfectest person he had ever known. Finally she consoled herself and the congregation by the conviction that God converts even our shortcomings to His own ends. She always ended by saying: "Let's sing, 'Come Holy Ghost and Make Thy Home.'"

He understood her now.

He lay on the roof of his inn and gazed up at the constellations. He was dog-tired and slept.

The moment in his growth arrived when he felt the need to admire someone. His thoughts kept returning to that Mrs. Wickersham. He visited her hospital, her orphanage, her lace-making school for the blind. These first two were municipal institutions, but the town, the sisters, and the patients had no doubt that all were hers. He had not called with Andrew Smith's letter at "the best hotel in South America"; that was rat catchers' country. He saw her riding her black horse through the streets of the town—erect, authoritative, her iron grey hair pulled back to a low bun under her wide-brimmed Spanish hat, a red rose in her lapel—doing her marketing and visiting her institutions. Storekeepers and shopgirls rushed out into the street to kiss her hand; men stood with lowered attentive heads while she harangued them. She spoke the language of the working people even better than he did. She laughed. Everyone around her laughed. Ashley seldom laughed; he did not despise laughter, but it seemed to him to be prompted by unimportant digressions that delayed the sober occupations of life. His curiosity was aroused by Mrs. Wickersham and he was ready to admire her. He came to know the hours when she was absent from her hotel. One morning he went to the door of the Fonda and asked to see her. He was told she was out. He walked by the house boy into the reception room and said that he would wait.

A number of the Conquistadores chose to end their days in the new world. It is hard to believe that they did not wish to return to that Spain of powerful compulsion—to Vizcaya, mother of seamen, even to Estremadura, whose beauties are not revealed to the hasty. They settled down in America, built themselves houses, and begot broadnosed children. But they had left a realm that was even closer to them than their birthplace and their land of adoption—the oceans which they had crossed and recrossed so many times. Their new homes were white without and within, with one exception. The walls of their reception rooms were painted blue from the floor to the level of a standing man's eyes: the lower portion of the four walls was sea-blue, the sea on a day of sun and light breeze. Mrs. Wickersham had also brought the sea and the horizon into her reception room. From the ceiling above a center table hung the model of a sixteenth-century galleon. On the wall— embattled Presbyterian though she was—she had placed an enormous time-faded crucifix. Through the open door and windows the wealth of the garden threatened to inundate the room in a many-colored tide. For Ashley the function of a room was to be serviceable; it had never occurred to him that it could be beautiful. He who lacked so many qualities—humor, ambition, vanity, reflection—had never distinguished a category of the beautiful. Some pictures on grocers' calendars had pleased him. At school he had been praised for the "beauty" of his mechanical drawings. We remember how on his flight through Illinois he had been overwhelmed by the beauty of dawn, and later of Chimborazo, and of his Chilean peaks. He sat down in a high-backed chair and looked about him. He became aware of an odd sensation in his throat: he sobbed. His eyes rested on the exhausted and submissive head on the wall before him. The world was a place of cruelty, suffering, and confusion, but men and women could surmount despair by making beautiful things, emulating the beauty of the first creation.

He rested between sleeping and waking. He was abruptly aroused by a sharp voice. Mrs. Wickersham was standing at the door looking at him. She spoke with military truculence: "Who are you?"

He rose quickly. "Is James Tolland here?" he asked.

"James Tolland? I don't know the name."

"I hoped he'd be here, Mrs. Wickersham. I'll call later. Thank you, ma'am. Good morning."

The next day he continued his journey. He had his first nosebleed at nine thousand feet. He lay down on the floor of the train. He kept laughing quietly and the laughter hurt him. At the junction for Rocas Verdes he was met by two Spanish-speaking Indians. The connecting line had been interrupted by an avalanche; they must proceed on muleback. He rode five hours, half asleep, and spent the night in a hut by the road. He arrived at the mines at noon on the following day and was put to bed for twenty-four hours by the Dutch doctor.

Several times he awoke and smelled violets or lavender. His mother's clothes had been redolent of the sachets of violet that her husband had unfailingly given her at Christmas. Beata had cultivated beds of lavender at "The Elms"; her clothes and the household linen breathed lavender. It cost nothing. At times Ashley's room was filled with people. His mother and his wife stood at either side of his bed and firmly tucked the ends of the blanket under him. They had never met, but seemed now to have entered into a close understanding. The blanket pressed upon his chest. Their faces were grave.

"You're not going to school tomorrow," his mother said in a low voice. "I shall write a note to Mr. Shattuck."

He pulled at the blanket to free himself. "Mama, I'm not a mummy."

"Sh, dear, sh!"

"I think we're going to like it here," said Beata.

"You always say that!"

"Go to sleep, dear."

"Where are the children?"

"They were here a minute ago. I don't know where they've gone."

"I want to see them."

"Sh, sh! Go to sleep now."

He awoke later at the moment when Eustacia Lansing entered the room. She was wearing one of those outrageous dresses of plum color and red, suggesting tropical flowers and fruits set in deep green foliage. There was the fascinating mole under her right eye. He verified for the thousandth time that one of her eyes was green-to-blue and the other was hazel-to-dark brown. As so often she seemed scarcely able to contain herself; some merriment, some reprehensible joke was about to convulse her.

John Ashley had made it a rule in life not to permit his thoughts to dwell on Eustacia Lansing. At most he allowed his mind in delight to glance toward her, to brush her. But altitudes play strange tricks on a man.

"Stacey!" he cried and began to laugh until his sides hurt.

"This isn't high," she said in Spanish. "The children want to go much higher."

"Stacey, you can't speak Spanish! Where'd you learn Spanish? —What children? Whose children?"

"Our children, Juanito. Ours."

"Whose?"

"Yours and mine."

He was laughing so he almost fell out of bed. His fingertips touched the floor. "We have no children, Stacey."

"Donkey! How can you say a thing like that! We have *so many* and you know it!"

Suddenly hushed, he asked hesitantly, "Have we? I only kissed you once and Breck was standing right beside you."

"Really?" she said, a strange smile on her face. "Really?" and she went out the closed door.

In this history there has been some discussion of hope and faith. It is too early to treat of love. The last appearing of the graces is still emerging from the primal ooze. Its numerous aspects are confusedly intermingled—cruelty with mercy, creativity with havoc. It may be that after many thousands of years we may see it "clarify"—as is said of turbid wine.

His colleagues were embittered men. They had left their countries and kin—they had left home life itself—and come thousands of miles to live in a barely supportable climate—all to make their fortunes. But fortunes in the field had been made in the seventies and eighties; now the fortunes from the mines were being made by men who ate steak every night beside the white shoulders of bejeweled women (these were the images that obsessed the stertorous dreamers of Rocas Verdes). The principle of the economy of energy prevailed on the mountain, including utterance. Their very card games were conducted in grunts and finger gestures. This was not entirely due to the rarity of the air; their very natures partook of ore. Sloth is like a viscous mineral. Under Dr. MacKenzie's eye they were all (except the mines' doctor) excellent workers, but sloth is not incompatible with a circumscribed diligence. Sloth breeds self-hatred and hatred; these hatreds hung in the air of the club room. Under the necessity to conserve energy they seldom reached expression. Once or twice a year a man would suddenly screech with rage at another, or would go out of his mind, biting his fists and rolling on the ground. Dr. van Domelen would administer sedatives. Dr. MacKenzie, called from his hut, would save the wretched man's face: "The fact is we've all been working too hard, especially you, Wilson. You've been doing splendid work, splendid. Why don't you go down to Manantiales for a week? Maybe Mrs. Wickersham will put you up. Even if she hasn't got a room free, she'll let you come to dinner."

Ashley, except for Dr. van Domelen, was the youngest in the club room. It gave the twenty-two engineers pleasure to look down on his youth, to raise their eyebrows knowingly at his beginner's enthusiasm and enterprise, and to sneer at the duties he performed. They regarded him as the "housekeeper." He was one degree above the Chinese cook.

Why did the men remain at Rocas Verdes? At the turn of the century mines all over the world were advertising frantically for engineers. Nineteen months later, when the great friendship had begun, Ashley put the question to Mrs. Wickersham.

"Well, mining engineers are an odd lot. They love ore and nothing else. They may think that they love the wealth that it promises to bring them, but no! they love the metal. They love the act of extracting it from the groaning, shrieking mountain. Now, Rocas Verdes is a small mine; it's at a killing altitude, *but* . . . the copper there is the best quality in all the Andes. Your friends up there are sour men, Mr. Tolland, but they're proud in their very guts to be working in a mine that produces beautiful stuff. Everyone in the world strains to be associated with what's best in its kind. It's a miners' mine. Dr. MacKenzie is known throughout the Andes as having a wonderful sense for knowing where the bloody copper is hidden and how to get it out. He could be governor of El Teniente, if he wanted to be; but he likes it at Rocas Verdes. Mining engineers are an odd lot; they like it to be difficult. Mr. Tolland, at my own table I've seen men behave in Dr. MacKenzie's presence as though they were self-conscious schoolboys in their first corduroy pants— and they were earning four and five times what he does. They work in vast millionaires' mines. They have wives and children with them, and butlers, and hot shower baths—"

"We have hot shower baths now, Mrs. Wickersham."

"And whiskey-and-sodas. But they're not really miners any more. They're merely bookkeepers. Their mines run like shoe factories. A true miner is taciturn, unsocial, single-minded. Generally, their wives have left them, as Dr. MacKenzie's did. Mind you, they don't know all these things. They think they're like other men, only better. Just as they deceive themselves about the money in it. Notice how clever your company is— automatically raising a man's salary every four years. It's like a bundle of hay in front of a donkey's nose. It gives him the illusion of getting rich. In my opinion, the real reason why the men stay there is because it's the aristocrat of mines; it's so damned unendurable, detestable, and impossible; and the copper's first class."

There was everywhere evidence of his predecessor's sloth. By the end of the second week he had cleaned the kitchen and improved the system supplying hot water. He made a friend of the cook and interested himself in the peculiarities of kitchen chemistry at high altitudes. He busied himself with doors and windows in the engineers' huts. He was again improvising as he had done in Coaltown. He turned over old lumber and broken chairs and perforated saucepans and rejected blankets. Presumably his predecessor had been shy of requesting material from the Antofagasta office. No Ashley was ever shy. John Ashley's monthly letters to Andrew Smith were filled with varied demands and the material began ascending the mountains. The men had been fed on salt pork and corned beef. He obtained permission to order meat and vegetables from Manantiales—a possibility that had not presented itself to sloth. Apples and pineapples appeared on the table. Araucanian rugs replaced Manchester drugget.

He was happiest in the miners' villages, the Chilean and the Indian. The assistants assigned to him were Bolivian Indians. He was invited to the christening of a daughter. After the banquet he asked to see the mother and child again. This was not in the customs of the tribe, but the mother and baby were brought before him. He had not held an infant in his arms for fifteen years, but his fatherhood was patent.

Dr. van Domelen was seldom called to the native villages, least of all to the Indians'. They were stoical by nature and possessed their own means of relieving extreme pain. Illness and death were less intimidating than his potions, his gleaming instruments, the brandy on his breath, and the contempt in his eyes. He had two children in the Indian village; their mother glided into his hut when he hung a lamp over his door.

Ashley saw signs of rickets. Though it was not in his province, he ordered cod liver oil from Andrew Smith by telegraph. He received permission—Indian life is surrounded with all the formality of a Spanish court—to enter their homes. He pondered ventilation, diet, and sanitation. He recommended and rebuked. In the lanes:

"Buenos, Antonio!"
"Buenos, Don Jaime!"
"Buenos, Tecla!"
"Buenos, Don Jaime!"
"Ta-hili, Xebu!"
"Ta-hili, Clez-u!"
"Ta-hili, Bexa-Mi!"
"Ta-hili, Clez-u!"

Time did what Ashley asked of it: It sped. Mrs. Hodge had said, "Seven years."

The engineers hated him. No word of appreciation was ever expressed for the improvements he had brought about in their living conditions. He was undermining the somber pleasure they derived from the rigor of their existence. They begrudged the hours when he descended into the mines in his effort to learn their profession. He seldom joined their card games after dinner, nor did Dr. MacKenzie. The managing director rose from table, bowed formally to the men, wished them good night, and went to his hut. He alone on the mountain had a hobby. He was a reader and read far into the night. He ordered the books from Princes Street, Edinburgh; they came to him around the Horn or were carried by railroad across the fens of Panama. He was interested in the religions of the ancient world. He read the Bible in Hebrew, *The Book of the Dead* in French, the *Koran* in German. He knew some Sanskrit. His days were filled with thoughts of copper, his nights with the comforting or terrifying visions of mankind. He was old and ugly, but on closer view and longer acquaintance less old and ugly than he first appeared to be. His nose had been broken, perhaps several times; he limped; his eyes and mouth were severe, but occasionally surprised the observer with some expression of deeply buried mirth or irony. He watched all the men; he watched Ashley.

One afternoon he returned to his hut to find Ashley cleaning the flue of his fireplace.

"Ah! Good afternoon, Tolland."

"Good afternoon, Dr. MacKenzie. These briquets clog up a flue in no time."

"Yes . . . yes . . . eh, Tolland, what are those tin sheets you've put up beside the latrines?"

"Well, sir, I've been thinking about solar heat. I've been trying to direct some rays on those spurs of ice—might fill a washing trough for the women in the village. The water would freeze overnight, but we could take an axe to it when the sun's up."

"Yes . . . hmm . . . I think I remember an article about collecting solar heat in some old engineering journals I have. I'll look it up. Come around after dinner tonight. Bring a cup with you and we'll make some tea."

That was the first of many cups of tea in Dr. MacKenzie's hut. These visits were an administrative error on his part and he knew it. The engineers respected their managing director as much as they hated one another. His hospitality to Ashley was without precedent. They were jealous.

One night during his sixth month on the hill, Ashley learned that a child had died in the Chilean village. On the previous evening there had been a small celebration of some miner's name day. The women and children had sat crowded together in one corner of the hut while the men drank *chicha*. The ban on alcohol brought some measure of interest into the miners' lives. During the singing and dancing and horseplay a gourd of hot *chicha* had been spilled over Martín Ramírez's week-old son. Dr. van Domelen had worked over the baby for several hours in vain. Ashley knew the parents and went to their two-family hut. He knocked at the door and entered. There were five or six women in the room, their shawls over their heads, and some children. All the men in the village were away at work, except Martín Ramírez, who sat in a corner, more angry than sorrowful. Babies die every day. Women's fuss. The baby lay on the floor wrapped in his mother's coat.

"Buenos!"

There was a murmur of greeting from the women and children. Ashley stood with his back to the door waiting for his eyes to become accustomed to the half-light. Soundlessly the visitors left the room to him, leaving the parents, and one old woman. He pressed a greeting from the father.

"*Buenos*, Martín!"

"*Buenos*, Don Jaime!"

"Come and sit here, Ana." Ana was a mere girl. She had long since lost the use of one eye. Timidly she sat down on the bed beside him. "What's the little boy's name?"

"*Señor* . . . the priest has not been here. He has no name."

The priest came once a fortnight or once a month from the larger mines to the north.

"Yes, but he has a name. You know his name."

". . . e . . . e . . ." Ana's eye moved hesitantly toward her husband. "I think . . . Martín." She began to tremble. "*Señor*, he is not a Christian."

Ashley remembered that Latin Americans barely hear what is said to them unless one touches them with one's hand. He put his fingers lightly on her wrist and spoke with surprise and reproach. "But, Ana, my daughter! You don't believe such foolish things!"

She glanced up at him quickly.

"Your Martinito has not sinned!"

"No! No, *señor*."

"You—Ana! You are not going to tell me that God-the-Eternal punishes babies who have not sinned!"

She did not answer.

"Didn't you hear that the Holy Pope in Rome went up to his golden chair and said to the whole world that that was a very wrong thought? He said that God was sorrowful that anyone would believe a thing like that." Ashley went on at some length about this. Ana's eye was fixed upon his face. Ashley was smiling. "Martinito is not here, Ana."

"Where is he, *señor*?"

"In happiness." Ashley held out his hands as though he were holding a baby. "In the greatest happiness."

Ana murmured something.

"What are you saying, *mi hija*?"

"He could not speak. His eyes were open, but he could not speak."

"Ana, I have four children. I know all about babies. You know that they can speak to us—to us fathers and mothers. You know that."

"Yes, *señor* . . . He said, 'Why?'"

Ashley put his hand firmly on her wrist. "You are right. He said, 'Why?' And he said something else, too."

"What, *señor*?"

"'Remember me!'"

Ana became very agitated. She said quickly, "Oh, *señor*, I shall never forget Martinito, never, never."

"We do not know why we suffer. We do not know why millions and millions of people suffer. But we know one thing. You have suffered. Only those who have suffered ever come to have a heart that is wise."

"What, *señor*?"

He repeated the words in a low voice. Ana looked about the room, lost. She had understood Don Jaime up to that point. But this idea was too difficult to grasp. Ashley went on. "You will have other children—boys and girls. You will become an old woman. And someday your children and your grandchildren will be all around you on your name day. They will say, '*Mamita* Ana, you treasure!' '*Mamita* Ana, *tu de oro*!' and you will remember Martinito. The only people in the world who are really loved—really loved, Ana—are those with hearts that are wise. You will not forget Martinito?"

"No, *señor*."

"You will never forget Martinito?"

"Never, never, *señor*."

He rose to go. With a glance and the slightest gesture of a hand toward the baby she asked something of him. She asked a rite. He came from the world of great people who were rich, who ate at tables, who could read and write—who had been favored by GOD and who carried magic within them. Ashley was not certain that he could make the sign of the cross correctly. He had hated everything about the Coaltown church during his seventeen years' attendance there, but above everything he had hated the prayers. Out of the children's hearing he had once muttered to Beata, "Prayers should be in Chinese." He now recited the Gettysburg Address twice, first in a low voice, then ringingly. Ana slid to the floor on her knees. He recited, "Under the spreading chestnut tree, The village smithy stands." He started off on a fragment from Shakespeare that Lily spoke so beautifully: "The quality of mercy is not strained," but he got lost. He talked to Roger and then to Sophia. "I must count on you to take care of your mother. We cannot understand now what has happened to us. Let us live as though we believed there were some meaning in it. Sophia, let us live as though we believed. Forget me. Put me out of your minds, and live. Live. Amen! Amen!"

He returned to his room. He was overcome with a great weakness. He could barely drag his feet. Closing the door behind him he fell full length upon the floor. His head struck the corner of the fireplace. When he awoke four hours later he could scarcely pass his comb through his hair. The blood had dried into a mat.

Ashley drank tea in Dr. MacKenzie's hut several evenings a month. He hoped that the managing director would discuss the problems of mining, but his host made it quite clear that he put copper out of his thoughts at sunset. By tacit consent they refrained from talking about their colleagues; neither wished to talk about himself. The walls were lined with books; there remained little to discuss except the subjects proposed by their titles—the religions of the ancient world and of the East. Ashley was ready and even eager to hear about them, but he soon learned that he was to receive neither profit nor pleasure there. Dr. MacKenzie looked upon all human activities—except mining—with irony and detachment. Ashley never employed

irony and did not understand it; nor was he prepared to view
with detachment those beliefs with which so many millions of
men had consoled or tormented themselves. It made him uncomfortable to hear accounts of human sacrifice delivered with
a remote and superior smile—maidens immolated in Carthage,
babies roasted before Baal, widows burned on pyres. Ashley
wanted to understand such practices; he did not even shrink
from trying to imagine under what circumstances he would
have participated in them. These were not smiling matters.
Another thing made Ashley uneasy during these conversations.
At each session, Dr. MacKenzie—with the regularity of one
pursuing a system—asked him a question which both men
knew to be impermissible. By time-honored convention, up-
rooted men in far places may occasionally volunteer a piece of
information about their past lives; they may not ask for any.
Dr. MacKenzie broke this law: "May I ask, Mr. Tolland—have
you ever been married?" "Were both your parents born in
Canada?" Ashley lied roundly and returned the conversation to
the ancient religions.

He heard how every Egyptian for well over ten thousand
years believed with passionate conviction that on his death,
with merit earned, he might become the god Osiris. Yes, that
his soul—"MacKenzie-Osiris" or "Tolland-Osiris"—descended
the Nile in his death boat to the hall of judgment. There, if it
had escaped the snapping crocodile and the snapping jackal, it
was weighed on a balance. Ashley listened spellbound to the
awful Negative Confession ("I have not diverted water from
where it should flow," "I have not . . ."). He heard of how
countless Indians believed, and were now believing, that they
were reborn into the world millions of times and that, with
merit earned, they would ultimately become a Bodhisattva, a
Buddha. Ashley did not find these thoughts and images very
strange. He seemed to be momentarily on the threshold of
believing them. What he found strange was Dr. MacKenzie's
way of presenting them. Question after question rose in his
mind, but he did not put them to his host. He listened. He
borrowed some books and read in them desultorily; he found
them unrewarding. But then, he had never been a reader. Beata
was the reader. One evening he ventured a question.

"Dr. MacKenzie, you say so often that the Greeks were a great people. Why did they have so many gods?"

"Well, first there's the easy answer—the one they teach us at school. Whenever a new migration poured into the country or whenever they conquered another city-state or entered into a close alliance, they made a place for the foreigners' gods among their own. Or they combined one with one of their own. Sheer hospitality. On the whole they tried to keep the principal gods down to twelve, although it wasn't always the same twelve. But I think we have to look deeper than that. Wonderful people, the Greeks."

Occasionally, as now, Dr. MacKenzie dropped his ironical tone. It was a sign of earnestness that he resorted to long pauses. Ashley waited.

"The twelve gods represent twelve different types of human beings. They looked at themselves. They looked at you and me. They looked at their wives and mothers and aunts. They made gods out of the various types of human personality. They put themselves on the altar. Look at their goddesses—mother and guardian of the hearth; lover; virgin; witch out of hell; guardian of civilization and friend of man—"

"What? What's that last, sir?"

"Athene. Pallas Athene. Minerva to the Romans. She doesn't give a damn about Hera's cooking and diapers, or about Aphrodite's perfumes and cosmetics. She gave Greece the olive; some say she gave it the horse. She wanted her city to be a lighthouse on a hill for all peoples and, by God, she did it. She's a friend to good men. Mothers are no help; wives are no help; mistresses are no help. They want to possess the man. They want him to serve their interests. Athene wants a man to surpass himself."

Ashley held his breath in amazement. "What color eyes did she have, sir?"

"Color eyes? . . . Hmm . . . Let me think: 'Then the grey-eyed Athene appeared to the far-voyaging Odysseus as an old woman, and he knew her not. "Buck up," she said. "What are you doing sniveling by the salt sea? Get some heart into you, boy, and do what I tell you. You shall yet return to your dear wife and your homeland!"' Grey eyes.—She often gets discouraged, I think."

"Why?"

"She never wins the golden apple. It's Aphrodite who wins the golden apple and starts making trouble. But Aphrodite often gets discouraged too, poor girl." Here Dr. MacKenzie was shaken by his silent laughter and had to down a whole cup of tea. Tea is inebriating at high altitude.

"Why should Aphrodite get discouraged?"

"Why, because she thinks that love is the whole of life—the beginning and the ending, and the answer to everything. She can make her gentlemen friends think so, also—for a short time. But after a while her gentlemen friends go off to build cities or fight wars or to dig for copper. She gets furious. She tears her pillow into strips. Poor Aphrodite! She can find some consolation in her mirror. Do you know why I think Venus came from the sea?"

"No."

"Because a calm sea is a mirror.—She came ashore in a shell. Do you see the connection? Pearls. Venus is obsessed with jewels. That's why she married Hephaestus. He could bring her diamonds out of the mountains."

More laughter. Ashley was beginning to have a headache. What good is conversation if it isn't serious?

"What type are *you*?" asked Dr. MacKenzie abruptly.

"What, sir?"

"Which of the gods do you take after?" Ashley had no opinion. "Oh, you're one of them, Tolland. You can't get away from that."

"Which are you, Doctor?"

"Oh, that's easy. I'm Hephaestus, the blacksmith. All we miners are diggers and blacksmiths. Always getting inside mountains, preferably volcanoes.—Now which are you? You're not one of us miners. You only play at it. Are you Apollo? Eh? Healing, poetry, prophecy?"

"No!"

"Are you Ares, the warrior? I guess not. Are you Hermes!—businessman, banker, lawyer, liar, cheat, newspaperman, god of eloquence, guide and companion to the dying? No, you're not merry enough."

Ashley was losing interest, but for politeness' sake he found a question or two.

"Dr. MacKenzie, how could a liar and a thief be of any use to people who are dying?"

"Greek, Greek. Very Greek. Each of these gods and goddesses had two sides. Even Pallas Athene can be a raging fury when she's aroused. Hermes was the god of roads and journeys and milestones. Mischievous though he was, he liked to conduct people to their destinations. Look at this picture. It's an engraved gem. See him there? He's holding his staff in the air and leading that veiled woman by the hand. Isn't that beautiful?"

Yes, it was beautiful.

"My father was a Saturn. Wise. Gave advice all day—on the street, in the home, and on Sundays from the pulpit. Bad advice, perfectly awful advice. My mother was a Hera—hearth and home, nestbuilding. But a ruler—yes, indeed. Terrible woman. I had two brothers, both Apollos. Saturns tend to beget Apollos, have you noticed that?"

"No, sir."

"Maybe I imagine it. One of them is serving a long sentence. His light—his illumination—took the form of being an anarchist. My sister was a Diana. Never grew up. Still a schoolgirl! Had three children, but marriage and motherhood couldn't touch her.—But to get back to you, Tolland. Maybe you take after a god in some other religion. The Greeks didn't know everything. There are types of personality that the Greeks hadn't observed. They were rare in Greece so they weren't elevated to gods. Take Christianity, for instance. Christianity is a Jewish religion. Most un-Greek thing in the world. Maybe that's where you come in. You Hebrews came along and tossed us off our thrones. You brought in that unhappy conscience of yours—all that damned moral anxiety. Maybe you're a Christian. Always denying yourselves any enjoyment, always punishing yourselves. Is that it?"

Ashley made no answer.

"The rest of us are fallen. We're shorn. We're decayed. It's an awful thing, Mr. Tolland, to be robbed of one's divinity—awful! There's nothing left for us to do but enjoy ourselves in our miserable way. Saturns without wisdom, like my father; Apollos without joy, like my brothers. We become tyrants and troublemakers. Or cranky and erratic, like Mrs. Wickersham."

"Dr. MacKenzie, what's the matter with those . . . those 'nestbuilders'?"

"Those Heras, those Junos? Why, they treat all their men as though they were boys—their husbands, their sons, and their fathers. Once they've produced a few babies they think they know everything. They think all the problems of the human race have been solved. Their aim is to soothe. They call it 'keeping everybody happy.' They try to rob their menfolk of sight and hearing and thought. Beware of the word 'happy' in Hera's mouth; it means 'dozing.'"

An all but insupportable pang rent Ashley's headache. He rose to say good night.

"But, Dr. MacKenzie, you don't believe . . . all this, do you?"

"No, of course not. But, Mr. Tolland, in Edinburgh we have a philosophers' club. At our dinners we talk a great deal about what others believe and have believed; but if any member uses the verb in the first or second person of the present tense, he has to pay a fine. He has to put a shilling in a skull on the mantel. We soon get out of the habit."

Time did what Ashley asked of it—it sped.

The company ruled that at the end of every eight months each engineer should descend for a month to lower altitudes to give his heart and lungs a rest. On the eve of his departure Ashley shook hands with his fellow engineers. They were unexpectedly cordial. Many persons are at their most amiable when saying goodbye. He shrank from taking formal leave of the villagers, but a deputation of men, wrapped to their noses, stood waiting for him outside the door of the club room. They gave him presents. They kissed his hands.

He called on Dr. MacKenzie.

"I hope you can stay at Mrs. Wickersham's hotel. Wait a moment! I'll write a letter to introduce you."

"Thank you, Doctor. I'm going to Santiago. I'll stop in Manantiales next time."

As Ashley was leaving the room the managing director called him back. "Tolland, don't you think it would be a good idea if you brought back a little companion?"

"What, sir?"

"A little 'hillwife.' You know what I mean. The company approves of it, makes provision for it."

Dr. MacKenzie was born to blunder. The friendship had been cooling; he killed it. In that realm no man gives advice to a man over twenty-five—asked or unasked—and Dr. MacKenzie knew it.

A dozen of the engineers, like Dr. van Domelen, had installed "native" women in the Chilean or Indian villages. The men never went into the villages; they did not take their hill wives to the lower altitudes on their vacations; they seldom saw their children. There was a general pretense that the system did not exist.

Dr. MacKenzie had blundered worse than he knew. Ashley, in his own eyes, was a family man and little else. Yet he was a family man who, for reasons beyond his control, had proved to be a total failure. Was Beata protected against insult? Did the family have enough to eat? Did the children have adequate clothing in winter? He was saving his money; he would see them again in seven years. In the meantime there was one thing he could do—one absurd impassioned thing: he could remain faithful to his wife. This was what he thought of as "holding up the walls."

Many men and women can live out their lives without any resort to superstition, magic, prayer, or fetish. They remember no anniversaries, salute no flags, and bind themselves by no oaths. They submit themselves totally to blind Circumstance, who takes away without thought what it gave without plan. Ashley's fidelity was not supported by any vow undertaken before church or state, for—as we shall see later—John and Beata Ashley were never married. The truest virtues are supererogatory: compassion not toward the good but toward the wicked, generosity to the ungrateful, fidelity without formal commitment. Continence, for Ashley, was a deprivation like blindness or immobility. He maintained it by rigorous strategy. It was to this end that he so organized his life that he went nightly to bed "dog-tired," "log-tired." He governed sharply what our ancestors called his "conversation." But any resolute person can conquer the demands of the flesh; he had a harder battle to win. He had known only one woman; he had had no experience of disassociating love from its train of attendants—companionship,

courage, consolation, unfolding knowledge, and—in parenthood
—creation. Time and time again on his trips southward these
fair promises had been extended to him. Women had seen these
expectations in his eyes. He remembered hearing in Coaltown
that Dr. Gillies was accustomed to say to patients addicted to
alcohol, "Don't deprive yourself of anything until you find
something better to put in its place." Ashley felt his deprivation
keenly; in its place he put this absurd superstition—if he failed,
the walls of "The Elms" would sway, totter, and collapse. The continent—that is, the resolute and dedicated ones, not the pining
continent—have a way of recognizing one another. Later, when
Ashley worked himself "dog-tired," repairing and reinforcing
and embellishing Mrs. Wickersham's hospital and schools, what
friendships arose with the sisters!—what laughter, what complicity—yes, what airy courtships, what coquetry!

So Dr. MacKenzie blundered. He knew he had blundered
and his contempt for Ashley turned to hate—one of those hatreds nourished by self-hatred.

"Thank you," said Ashley, "I'll think it over."

In Antofagasta he changed trains without calling on Mr.
Andrew Smith of the Kinnairdie Mining Company. His first
task in Santiago de Chile was to find work. His appearance had
altered during the eight months. He had aged—that is, he now
looked his age, which was forty-two. He was blackened by the
sun to the degree so rapidly acquired at high altitudes. His hair
had darkened and had lost its youthful curls. The pitch of his
voice was lower. He was taken for a Chilean of the Irish or
German admixture so frequent in the country. He applied
without success for work as a nursery gardener, a stable hand,
a gravedigger, a handyman at the "Eden" pleasure park. Finally
he was hired to work on the new road toward the north, toward Valparaíso and Antofagasta. When his vacation drew to
an end he left the road with regret; he had contributed to mixing and pouring the cement for twenty culverts. Again he
changed trains in Antofagasta and spent the night in the inn he
had known. The next morning he called on Mr. Andrew Smith,
who did not at first recognize him and who was displeased at
seeing a responsible engineer of his company wearing the
clothes of a laborer. He had much to talk over with Mr. Tolland, however. Whatever the company did it did cautiously

and, as far as possible, secretly. Mr. Smith and the mysterious Board of Directors would have suffered untold agonies if they had learned that loose idle talkers were spreading the rumor that Rocas Verdes was running into ever richer seams of ore, and that there were plans for large expansion. Ashley was directed to draw up designs and estimates for many more miners' huts. In fact large quantities of lime and timber were already ascending the mountains. The problems of housing were discussed at length. When Ashley prepared to take his leave, Mr. Smith's manner acquired a measure of warmth. He expressed a guarded commendation of the young man's work. He intimated that the Board of Directors might soon give concrete expression to their appreciation.

Ashley sat down again abruptly and said, "Mr. Smith, there are two things that I'd like to propose to you."

"Indeed?"

"I think that it would be a very wise measure to announce an increase in the miners' pay—even though it be a very small one." Mr. Smith stared at him angrily. "You know how many hours are lost every week because of illness."

"I do. That is malingering, Mr. Tolland. The miner is incorrigibly lazy. Dr. van Domelen has a constant struggle with them."

"No, this is different. These men are not lazy. When they are working with me on some project for their own village, it is hard to make them stop. All they need is some sign that they are respected as human beings. The Indian, sir, is subject to spells in which his mind and will 'go blank'—that's the only way I know how to put it."

"That's the way to put it—incorrigible laziness."

"His whole life stretches before him, working underground, without possibility of change. The monotony is bad enough; the loss of hope is worse. But"—and here Ashley rose—"the lack of human consideration is killing. Mining engineers, Mr. Smith, have no blood in their veins. The Indians *do* fall ill. This sense of being shut off and despised takes the form of an illness."

Mr. Smith opened and shut his lips several times; finally he said, "A man has to earn his living on this earth, Mr. Tolland, just as you and I do. A raise in their wages is none of your concern. They'd spend it in drink. They somehow manage to smuggle it in, I don't know how."

Ashley walked about the room. He approached Mr. Smith's desk and said, in a lowered voice: "*Chicha* is not the only thing that is smuggled in. Information finds its way in, too. I don't know how. Our miners have heard of the wages at La Reina and San Tomás and Dos Cumbres—especially our Bolivian Indians, who are our best workers. You are building new huts; you may have trouble filling them. The best investment in a mine is the self-respect and well-being of the miner. They have a saying, 'Ore does not come to the surface by itself.' "

Mr. Smith swallowed. He shifted the pen and inkwell on his desk. He coughed. "You said you had a second suggestion."

"There should be a priest living at Rocas Verdes. Those irregular visits aren't right."

"What do they want with their wretched priests? The priest charges them so much for a wedding and a christening that most of the miners aren't even married. They hate their priests. A visit once a month's good enough for them. Mr. Tolland, let me tell you something: Roman Catholicism is childish superstition at best; in Chile it's beneath contempt."

"I think we're all bad judges of what goes on in other people's minds about God, Mr. Smith. It's a bad thing to force a God on a man who doesn't want one. It's worse to stand in the way of a man who wants one badly. I know them! I live there!"

Suddenly Ashley was seized by a splitting headache. He closed his eyes and almost fell from his chair. Again Mr. Smith stared at him as though he had been struck. If there was to be any moralizing, Mr. Smith was accustomed to doing it. It's what he did best. Scotland is heavily populated with Saturns. No young whippersnapper from Canada could tell him anything about religious matters.

"Are you ill, Mr. Tolland?"

"Might I have a glass of water, please."

Mr. Smith watched him drink. At last he said, "How would we get a priest there? Everybody knows there aren't enough in Chile to go round. They have to ship them over from Spain."

Ashley had given no thought to this. To his own surprise he heard himself saying offhandedly—"I suppose you write to the Bishop. Maybe you give him a present. You promise to pay

the priest's salary for the first five years—something like that."
Mr. Smith stared at him somberly. Ashley went on: "Ask for a
young one. Give me permission to build him a hut; and give
me permission to enlarge the chapel. It looks like a pigsty. And
I think it'd be useful in the long run if you gave me permission
to stay one more day in Antofagasta so that I could look at
some churches and talk to some priests."

Mr. Smith struggled with himself. When he spoke, his Scots
speech, which I have omitted to reproduce, returned pro-
nouncedly: "I give you that permission. But don't be getting
too many fancies, Mr. Tolland."

At the door Ashley—totally recovered, ten years younger—
turned with a smile. "Rocas Verdes could be as beautiful inside
as it is—outside." He flung his hand into the air as though describing a coronet of peaks.

Two weeks after his return to Rocas Verdes it was announced
that the miners were to receive an increase in their monthly
pay. The news was received with doubt and distrust; the men
awaited the calamity that would surely accompany it. After the
second payment, by ones and twos, they thanked Ashley. They
connected it with his visit to the lowlands.

Ashley said to himself, "That's for Coaltown!"

He was a builder now. The villagers watched the enlarge-
ment of the chapel with awed eyes. There was a great deal of
voluntary work at night under the glare of an acetylene lamp.
Women and children couldn't be persuaded to go to bed. They
stood in the cold watching their husbands and fathers and sons
shape a dome—it was a little dome, but that's what it indubitably was. In Antofagasta Ashley had taken council with the clergy
and from his own pocket had bought a crucifix, some altar
cloths, and six hundred candles. When the itinerant priest arrived he was overwhelmed with requests for weddings and
christenings. The candlelight fell on blissful faces, and after the
services there was much parading in the lanes—spouses newly
joined in holy wedlock and persons of all ages whose right to
bear their names was now recorded in Heaven's own register.
This embracing of the sacraments was not entirely the result of
a higher wage, or the promise of a dome. A rumor had reached
the village that they were soon to have a priest of their own—
living among them, knowing them by name, remembering them

from confession to confession, being very stern with them (they hoped for that), one who also had the spirit and the authority to extend pardon—in short, a *padre*. It was for him they wished to be in fair estate, christened and married.

Four months later Don Felipe arrived.

Ashley kept out of sight. He had suggested to Dr. MacKenzie that it would be very well received if the managing director were the first to welcome the *padre* and to conduct him to his house. Dr. MacKenzie shrugged his shoulders—Christians, Mohammedans, and Buddhists were all one to him, all groveling before idols, seeking unmerited rewards. Ashley sat beside Don Felipe at dinner. He could scarcely lift his fork to his mouth. It was Roger—not a feature alike, with no resemblance in voice, but Roger—perhaps six years older, like him a little stiff, unsmiling, taciturn, intensely alive in eye and ear, concentrated; above all, independent. Like Roger he didn't want advice, he didn't want help, he didn't want friendship. (Friendship, it seems, was another of the things that can be dispensed with, when one finds something better to replace it.) Like Roger, he was of an exemplary politeness.

The priest surveyed the engineers seated at the tables around him. He became aware of their contempt. He was the youngest in the room by at least eleven years.

Dr. MacKenzie's condescension took the form of asking the "child" a great many personal questions, such as no Spanish gentleman would put to another at a first or fifth meeting. Don Felipe answered them all as Roger would, simply, and with a shade of distaste perceptible only to the well-born. He had been in South America eight months. He had served at La Paz. He had begun the study of the Indians' languages. He was born twenty-seven years ago, youngest of six children, in Seville.

"You'll find our miners a rather rough lot," said Dr. Mac-Kenzie, who was proud of his colloquial Spanish, using a word that pointed to both "disorderly" and "oafish." Ashley caught the expression that the priest turned toward the managing director; it contained a faint smile and seemed to say, "Oh, sir, not as oafish as you Protestants."

To Ashley he said, "Pedro Quiñones tells me, Don Diego, that you have done much to enlarge the church here."

Ashley choked. "The men gave their own time, Father."

Don Felipe turned his black eyes on him and made no reply.

A few minutes later he asked, "These gentlemen are from several countries?"

"Yes, Father. Our director is from Scotland. Our doctor is from the Netherlands. There are four Germans and three Swiss. The larger number are from England and the United States."

"And you, sir?"

"For reasons I cannot tell you now, I say that I am a Canadian."

Don Felipe received the statement as though he were accustomed to such peculiar locutions.

Don Felipe was young, but he suffered from no insecurity. He arranged the next day to take his meals in the kitchen, where he established the best of relations with the Chinese cook. Like Roger, he gave all of himself to the task that was set before him. That soutane whipped about the lanes as though six priests had arrived. He had a beautiful singing voice which awoke others. There were processional litanies in the bitter cold—candles under the stars. The church was too small. His sermons were like journeys into a far country, dreams from which one awoke dazed and in great need of a friendly hand. He was a remorseless enemy of sin; sin was not allowed a cranny in which to cower, and yet, it was said, when he offered absolution to the penitent, strong men fainted. His greatest innovation, and difficult for the community to grasp, was his homage to women. Within a few months its effect became evident in their carriage. It became proverbial that his parishioners walked like the women of Andalucia. A number of my readers will have recognized that we are talking of the future Archbishop Felipe Ochoa, "Pastor of the Indians," author of *Rectas Facite in Solitudine* (*Semitas Dei Nostri*).

Ashley had many brief encounters with the padre, but no conversations. Like Roger's the priest's face, in front view, was impassive; but his profile and the back of his head were vulnerable, as it is in the young. Ashley caught intimations of his homesickness for Seville (the beloved, the beautiful) and for his father and mother, of his longing for his professors and fellow students at the seminary, for the services and the music at the cathedral of his childhood, for the company of others who had also made the great decision. Ashley came to divine that he had only the vaguest notion where Scotland, Switzerland, and Canada were. His education had stored his head with far more important knowledge than that. Ashley could scarcely apprehend the extent to which he carried an irrational repulsion from Protestants. He had hitherto seen very few in his life —tourists, book in hand, impiously strolling about his cathedral as though they were in a railway station. He assumed that Protestants were a despised minority on the earth's surface, crawling about abashedly, aware of their abjection but too satanically proud to acknowledge their error.

Time sped. The next eight months drew to a close; Ashley must descend the mountains for another vacation. He received a letter from the chairman of the board informing him that he had been promoted. He was to receive the salary of a man who had worked twelve years in the mine. The Kinnairdie Company wished to retain his services. The promotion was to be guarded as an administrative secret. The projects on which he was engaged, of building and electrification, were in full swing. He dreaded the vacation. He submitted to a physical examination by Dr. van Domelen and was permitted to continue at Rocas Verdes for another two months. But May, 1905, arrived and he must leave.

He had every intention of returning to his post after this vacation . . . and yet! He longed to leave the mountains forever. He rejoiced in his work, he loved his Chileans and Indians, but he was starved for companionship—above all, for wife and child, but that did not bear thinking of. He had been tormented lately, waking and sleeping, by a recurrent dream: on a dark night, nearer to dawn than to midnight, he was standing under their elms . . . the southeast corner room . . . he was throwing some pebbles into the window. She awoke; she descended the stairs and opened the front door. But this was insane! Such rashness could only involve them all in further misery. Mrs. Hodge had said seven years—that would be July, 1909. Ashley intended to return to Rocas Verdes, yet he packed his knapsacks as though for a final departure. He sewed his paper money into his clothing; his salary checks he could cash in any large town. For the first time in his life he was gloating over money.

His leave-takings were much the same. Again he called on Dr. MacKenzie.

"This time you must stop at Manantiales—at least for a week. You must learn to know Mrs. Wickersham's hotel. I've telegraphed her that you were coming and here's a letter for her. You've heard the men talk about her?"

"A little."

"She won't have Heidrich again, or van Domelen or Platt. She says she can't stand gloomy men. There are two other passable hotels in Manantiales, but nothing on earth can compare with her Fonda. The beds, Tolland, the food, the copper-lined bathtubs, the servants! And, of course, herself. I've known her a little over thirty years. She got me my first job, in fact. In the early days she was the miners' post office and banker and even employment agency. She was more than that—she was a sort of guardian of standards. There was a German mine —it's in other hands now—called the 'Suevia Eterna.' Living conditions were bad; it was arrogant to its non-German engineers, late in its pay checks—all that; but it thought itself the best mine in the hills. She advised young men away from it. She abetted other mines in stealing its good men. Well, old 'Suevia' sent a committee to call on her. She burned the skin off their scalps; told them how to run a mine. But I'd hate to work in any mine that she ran—if she ran it as she runs her hotel. One night at the Fonda an American businessman was telling us all that the white man was the masterwork of God and that all these Indians and mixed races came into the world to be his servant help. She made him finish his dinner upstairs. He had to leave the next morning and she wouldn't let him pay his bill."

"She's English?"

"Yes, born in the late thirties, I expect. Came out here as a bride. Husband was one of these emerald hunters. She told a story once of cooking for a lot of men over in the Peruvian *oriente* where it never stops raining—in a thatched hut, holding an umbrella over her tapir stew; and of being in some diggings higher up than this, where you have to learn from scratch how to boil an egg. Husband died, leaving her with a little girl; she opened the Fonda. Three things interest her: her hospitals and orphanages; good company and good talk at her dinner table; and her reputation for knowing everything that's going on in the Andes.—By the way, have you got a cravat?"

"No, sir."

"Well, take this one. She insists on men wearing a cravat at dinner."

"Thank you.—Which of the goddesses of Greece does she resemble, Dr. MacKenzie?"

"Oh, you remember that little discussion, do you? Well, I once expounded the whole theory to her." Here Dr. MacKenzie fell into his soundless laughter. "She told me that I was an old fool. She told me each man belongs to one type: that's why we're so tiresome. But that most women were all five or six goddesses mixed up together. She said that every woman wanted to be an Aphrodite, but she had to settle for what she could get. She said that she'd been all of them—all six. She said that it's a lucky woman who graduates from Artemis to Aphrodite, to Hera and ends up as Athene. It's sad when they get stuck in one image.—Come back and tell me what you think."

On the night before he left Ashley walked through the lanes of the villages. It was intensely cold. He came to the church and pushed open the door. All was dark but for a lighted wick burning in its cup of red glass. It cast a faint reflection on the little dome above it. Don Felipe was kneeling before it, unfathomably motionless. Ashley returned to the square. He was smiling.

To himself he said, "That's for Roger."

He was filled with awe—with grateful wonder—that life permits us to pay old debts, to redeem old blindnesses, old stupidities. His grandmother had promised him that.

Ashley had no intention of going to the Fonda. He told himself he was no fool. When he arrived at Manantiales the sun was about to sink beneath the Pacific. He walked under trees and low-flying birds. The descent from the heights left him drowsy. With stealth he slowly approached the inn and entered the garden. He sank down on a bench. A fountain was rising from a pool at his feet. All was still in the house. The first lights appeared in the windows. He thought of the *sala* of white and deep-sea blue. He thought of the crucifix on the wall. Most of all he thought of Mrs. Wickersham. He was longing for someone to talk with. He was longing for friendship.

"All right," he said, rising. "I'll risk my life for it."

He straightened his shoulders and walked into the front hall. She was sitting by a lamp in her little office, bent over her account books. She looked up and saw him. Again she asked him in the tones of a drill sergeant, "Who are you?"

"James Tolland, ma'am, from Rocas Verdes. I have a letter to you from Dr. MacKenzie."

"Come in here, please." She took the green shade off the lamp so that the light would fall fully upon him. She looked him up and down. "Haven't I seen you before?"

"No, ma'am."

She looked at him hard. A slight frown crossed her face. She went into the hall, clapped her hands, and called "Tomás! Tomás!" An Indian boy came running toward her. She gave her directions in the dialect of the *sierra*. "Move Doctor Pepper-and-Salt to Number Ten damn-damn quick. Tell Teresita to make Number Four perfect like Heaven and the Angels. When Number Four is ready, carry hot water to the bath and come to me.—Mr. Tolland, your room and bath will be ready in fifteen minutes. Your room is Number Four at the top of those stairs. Here are some San Francisco papers to read while you're waiting. Dinner is at nine. You can go to sleep. Tomás will knock at your door at a quarter before nine. If you want a drink before dinner, be sure that it is half strength. The first twenty-four hours after a descent are tricky."

"Thank you, Mrs. Wickersham."

He turned and went toward the *sala*. At the door he turned his head to the right. The crucifix was no longer hanging on the wall. In his astonishment, in his consternation, Ashley let the newspapers fall from his hand. Mrs. Wickersham had been following him with her eyes. She knew very well why, three minutes earlier, she had made room for him at the Fonda. There was nothing particularly prepossessing about John Ashley; Dr. MacKenzie's telegram and letter carried little weight with her. She accepted him because he had lied to her. She remembered very well that they had seen each other before. She had forgotten whatever words they had exchanged, but she was sure of the fact. It wasn't merely the lie that arrested her now, it was the sturdiness of the lie, its "sincerity." Mrs. Wickersham was, as Dr. MacKenzie had said, "choke-full" of curiosity.

She knew that Ashley was not a liar and that he had lied to her. She wanted to know more about that.

She never joined her guests at lunch. She descended at nine o'clock wearing long trailing black dresses of silk or lace, no longer in their first youth, decked out with bugles of jet and scarlet velvet bows. The first three evenings she placed Ashley far from her at the lower end of the table. She watched him and was sorry that she had asked him into the house. He spoke very little. He listened to Swiss botanists and Swedish archae-ologists and Baptist missionaries, to businessmen and engineers (including a compatriot from Canada) and those eternal pro-fessional world travelers already composing their chapter on the "Land of the Condor." She placed him beside the Chilean doctor at her hospital and the mayor of Manantiales. He wasn't a man's man. Men merely tried to impress him with their wealth or position. Women liked him, but women like any man who will give them his whole attention. She would let him stay out the week. On the fourth night she seated him at her left and there he remained.

"Mr. Tolland, what were you doing in my kitchen today?"

"It was on fire, ma'am."

"And what did you do?"

"I put it out. I want your permission to go into the kitchen and laundry every day until they're in order. These earthquakes have shaken up your pipes and flues and boilers. I saw some places that could be dangerous."

"In Chile gentlemen don't soil their hands, Mr. Tolland. I have repairmen and plumbers of my own."

He looked her in the eye. "Yes, I've seen their work. . . . Mrs. Wickersham, I'm a tinker. And I'm miserable when I haven't anything to do. I want you to show me your orphan-ages and hospitals—all those parts that the visitors don't see. Before the boilers blow up and the drains overflow."

"Gosh!"

He changed to his workingman's clothes. He collected some assistants and tools. He was introduced to the sisters and the teachers and the cooks and the doctors. By the end of the week there was a sawing and a hammering, soldering and ditchdig-ging. By the end of the second week partitions were removed and partitions were installed. The sisters were particularly delighted when he made them shelves, dozens of shelves. He cleaned fireplaces and wells and latrines.

He sang " 'Nita, Juanita" and "No gottee tickee, No gettee shirtee, at the Chinee laundryman's."

To himself he said, "This is for Sophia."

He looked younger every day. He was greeted with blushes and laughter when he arrived in the morning, "Don Jaime, el canadiense." The wards knew him. The schoolchildren knew him. The blind girls were directed to rise and sing to him. The astonishment increased that so obviously important a personage spoke their language so well and that he deigned to labor. In the wards and on the sun terrace he would stop and talk to the amputated young and to the aged. He seemed to have a genius for remembering names. Early, before his hands and clothes were dirty, he would pick up the smallest orphans as though he had held children before. He belonged to that order of human beings from whom come hope and reassurance. What particularly struck Mother Superintendent was his deference to girls and women, an indefinable homage that was like something remembered from old legends and ballads.

Mrs. Wickersham defended her heart as best she could. The old are slow to believe that the young can repose a real friendship in them. At best the young can be polite, but are in a hurry to rejoin their coevals. Besides, they—the old—draw back from the demands that a new friendship might exact; they have seen so many fade, have begun to forget the valued ones. It may be that friendship is little more than a fatigued and fatiguing word. What then was the energy in the glance that Ashley turned toward her? Was that, really, friendship? Moreover, Ashley arrived at the Fonda at the moment when Mrs. Wickersham was losing control of her life's rudder. She had begun to weary of well doing. All those girls she had collected and trained and married—the blind whom she had taught lacemaking and weaving. Aïe, Aïe, Aïe! The times she had been awakened at four in the morning for one thing or another—to save a boy from the brutality of the police, or a member of the police force from the resentment of the workers. She was a citizen of Chile and had received ribbons of recognition from a grateful republic. She had appealed to the President himself to extend clemency to some half-mad worker who had desecrated a church or some distraught girl who had hurled her baby into a cistern. Doers of good have their seasons of weakness. They know that there is no spiritual vulgarity equal to that of expecting gratitude and admiration, but they allow themselves to be seduced by the sweet fantasies of self-pity. "No one has ever done anything for me, spontaneously." She had lost touch with the emotion which had first prompted her to these works. Sorriest of all, she had grown weary of women and woman talk, of their way of seizing on the hopeful or the alarming—exaggerating both—of their helplessness when confronting a choice between two evils. And, like all persons of resolute mind and long experience, she had become impatient at the presence of independence in others. She had become bad company to herself. She had invited cynicism into her thought; her tongue had become malicious. She had decided to devote what few years remained to her to enjoying herself—to the only enjoyments left to her: to trying to rule others' lives and to making of herself a "character." She was fashioning a mask for her face —Mrs. Wickersham, amusing, a little frightening, and always right, wise, and admirable. Some go forward and some go back. A sort of insolence in regard to the opinions of others expressed itself in her wearing, in the evening, a décolleté that had gone out of fashion for half a century and in a free application of the rabbit's foot and rouge.

And then John Ashley arrived at the Fonda and proffered his friendship.

"Mr. Tolland, do you play cards?"

"Yes, ma'am."

"Once in a while we play cards in the smoking room. We play for money. I don't want the Fonda to be known as a gambling hell, so I've made a rule: no player can win more than twenty dollars. Any profits he makes above that must go into the jar for my hospital. Do you play *dos pícaros?*"

"Yes."

"We're playing tonight at midnight."

At last Ashley could play without dissembling his skill. There were some rich men at the table—world travelers, landowners in the valley, and nitrate and copper men. He took their money. He took Mrs. Wickersham's money. A slate hung on the wall. At the end of the evening she wrote on it the sum accruing to

the hospital. Her eyes glittered. A hundred and eighty dollars!
A Roentgen-ray machine cost six hundred dollars.

A few days later:

"Mr. Tolland, do you take your breakfast on the roof?"

"Yes, ma'am."

"Come on up on the roof after dinner. I have some good
rum. We'll talk."

So began the late conversations under the stars. They sat
facing the mountains, with the jug on a low table between them.
The peaks—sightless, noble, and long enduring—seemed to
await their next event, to be leveled, or riven and folded. It was
spring. At intervals from the distance could be heard a susur-
rus, a faint thunder, and a plop—some avalanche of ten thousand tons. With the moonrise glory suffused heaven and earth.
The peaks came alive; they seemed to sway and sing, serene
fields between black pinnacles. ("Beata should see this! The
children should see this!") The conversations were about
Chile, about the early days of mining, about the hospitals and
schools, about men and women. Ashley, fatigued by the hard
day's work, rejoiced in grateful friendship, but Mrs. Wickersham was wretched and angry. Curiosity devoured all other
emotions. Who was he? What was his story? The more she
loved him the more she resented his refusal to talk about himself. She had visited his room in his absence and examined his
possessions. She had come upon some faded blue photographs
—in one a tall young woman was standing by a pond holding
a baby in her arms; three young children sat at her feet. Even
in the worn print she could read health, beauty, and harmony.
She studied it a long time with something near to bitterness.
To anyone else in the world she—the "dragon," the "tartar"—
would have put direct questions ("What are you doing down
here without your family?" "Why did you lie to me?"), but she
was a little afraid of Ashley. At moments she was so filled with
enraged frustration that she was on the point of ordering him
out of the hotel. She had had a long experience of fugitive
men; it never occurred to her that he might be of their number.
On the fifteenth night of Ashley's stay there was a long discussion at the dinner table of the "rat list"—its celebrities past and
present, the money that could be earned at rat catching, and
the unremitting attention necessary for the hunt.

Toward seven in the evening on that day an unaccustomed bustle and noise had been heard in the corridors of the Fonda, laughter from the houseboys and smothered shrieks from the girls. A favorite guest of the house had arrived, the famous Mr. Wellington Bristow, a businessman, owner of an import-export office in Santiago de Chile. He was an American citizen, he said, born in Rome of an English father and a Greek mother, but he had been heard to describe his origins differently. He carried a score of business cards in his pockets announcing that he was sole representative in Chile of certain American pharmaceuticals, of Scotch woolens, of a French perfume, a Bavarian beer, and so on. He was a general favorite and a liar, cheat, and finagler. His small head was covered with short curls and was set on the wide shoulders of an athlete. Around the card tables at midnight he looked thirty, at dinner forty, but at noon he could have passed for sixty, for his face then appeared anxious and tired, etched by innumerable small lines, not all of them the gift of laughter. He was dressed in the height of the London fashion of thirty years ago, favoring brightly colored vests and checkered trousers. He had restless jeweled hands that attracted aces. His linen was not always snowy; his cuffs were frayed. He was ceaselessly occupied in making money and often hungry. He was the best company in the world.

Wellington Bristow was every inch a businessman and a genius at it, but he loved negotiation more than money; he was of a generous nature; and he was joyous. Hence he had three strikes against him. He had to complicate a transaction, draw in third parties, bury it under provisos and "riders." He loved to accelerate a negotiation with the hint of a bribe or to threaten the recalcitrant with an intimation of blackmail. Inflating promises and concealing risks were a pleasure. He sacrificed his very commissions to render the deal more exciting. He loved business for *its own sake*. What little money he had he could not keep. He was constantly giving presents he could not afford, which is the soul of generosity. On each of his visits to the Fonda he brought Mrs. Wickersham something new and delightful from the great world—the first typewriter seen in Manantiales, the first fountain pen, the first caviar, an evening cloak by Worth. On this trip he arrived with ten bottles of champagne; there were holes in his shoes and socks. No one has ever seen a successful businessman who is joyous, for joy is praise of the whole and cannot exist where there are ulterior aims. His joy was of the purest sort; it stole its gaiety from dejection and danger. What a talker he was, what a persuader! All appearance took on whatever coloring he imposed upon it. The great persuaders are those without principles; sincerity stammers.

The first Ashley knew of Mr. Bristow's presence in the house was the sound of Mrs. Wickersham's voice, raised in indignation, from the hall below: "No, Mr. Bristow, I will not have a coffin! I don't care whether it's made of ebony or not, I will not have it in the house!"

But that was merely one of Mr. Bristow's jokes. The ten bottles of champagne had been brought into the Fonda in a long narrow box, yet . . . yet it was not entirely a joke. Mr. Bristow's thoughts ran on deathbeds, coffins, and funerals. In these matters he was not only serious, but of a high calming gravity. He haunted the dwellings of the moribund. He eased their passage and awoke a longing for the farther shore. He stepped aside for the viaticum, tapping his foot impatiently, but on many fading eyes the last image was that of a beautiful youth guiding them through flowering orchards. The people of Santiago, of all classes, would knock at his door at any hour and beg him to write words to be inserted in the newspapers with the announcement of a death. Some of them have passed into proverbial lore: "Strangers, only those who have known great joy can know our grief. Family of Casilda Romero Valdés," "Stranger, pause: death is not bitter to those who have watched the suffering of their child. Family of Mendo Cásares y Castro."

Wellington Bristow came to Manantiales three or four times a year. Manantiales was a "little Amsterdam" of the Andes, a market and outlet, mostly clandestine, for emeralds which found their way, westward bound, over the passes. An underground route to the capitals of the world passed through a number of squalid huts at the edge of the town. Mr. Bristow picked up emeralds at Manantiales, before climbing higher for chinchilla pelts. Mrs. Wickersham looked forward to his visits. He brought the gossip of the coast; he stimulated the play at the card tables; and he teased and left unsatisfied her abounding curiosity concerning himself. Who was he? Who was he, really? He published his news for her at table on the first evening. She seated him at a distance from her so that the whole company could enjoy his chronicles: trials, bankruptcies, deaths and funerals ("I don't want to hear about funerals, Mr. Bristow!"), imprisonments, hurried marriages ("Orange blossoms will burst into bloom prematurely, Mrs. Wickersham, if you light a fire under them." "I know that, Mr. Bristow"), guns fired in bedrooms, forged wills, leper wins lottery, deaths and funerals ("I don't want to hear about funerals, Mr. Bristow!"), miraculous cures before suburban altars, Inca princess unmasked as Miss Beatrice Campbell of Newark, New Jersey, the newest modes (cartwheel hats and knuckle-length sleeves), deaths and funerals ("Stop it right now!"). No wonder she charged him a mere dollar a day.

"Have you caught any rats lately, Mr. Bristow?"

"No ma'am, but a friend of mine caught a big one in Lima a few months ago."

"Mr. Tolland, do you know what the 'rat list' is?"

"Yes, ma'am."

"What's this story about Lima, Mr. Bristow?"

"Just my bad luck, Mrs. Wickersham. He'd have come south soon. I've been watching out for him for two years. He was vice president of a Kansas City bank—blue eyes, round face, pink complexion, about forty years old. He'd run off with several hundred thousand dollars and a sixteen-year-old girl."

"What's the cauliflower?"

"There'll be four or five thousand from the bank and as much from the girl's family. It was the carbuncle scars on the back of his neck that gave him away. My friend put some pills in his liquor and pulled his scarf off.—They found the Bishop."

"What Bishop was that?"

"They found him in Alaska where he was cooking in a hotel. Happy as an eel in a pie—that's what they said. He'd always wanted to cook. His wife wouldn't pay the cauliflower. She didn't want him back. She already had a cook, she said."

"How many names are on your list now?"

"Oh, hundreds, Mrs. Wickersham. Some of them go back thirty years. We're only interested in the big prizes. It keeps you on your toes. Like the man who kidnaped Mrs. Beecham in ninety-nine. He was thirty years old, then, and looked like Pete Dondrue, the jockey, they said."

"Any marks?"

"Just a little peculiarity I can't mention here, Mrs. Wickersham."

"Well, you keep your eyes open. You'll pick up some cauliflower yet."

Mr. Bristow was at his happiest at the card tables, and would have won his twenty dollars nightly but for the fact that he played neither for money nor for victory, but to circumvent the rules of the game. Ashley left it to the others to expose his cheating. Caught, Mr. Bristow would merely laugh—"I wondered if you'd see that!" All faces turned toward Mrs. Wickersham, the "dragon," who would have sent any other guest flying from the house.

"Oh, he's a rascal! I've known it for years. Play the game correctly, Mr. Bristow, or out you go!"

Mr. Bristow took a decided fancy to Ashley, who liked him in the guarded and flattered way we often do those invested with qualities opposite to our own.

Four days later Wellington Bristow left on a brief trip up in the hills. He hoped to pick up some chinchilla pelts. He looked forward to passing an evening with his old friend Dr. MacKenzie at Rocas Verdes. A departure is a pretext for a party and there was drinking and storytelling in the bar after Mrs. Wickersham had gone to bed. Ashley had never heard such storytelling. They were true stories—all of them had befallen Mr. Bristow in various parts of the world. For the first hour they had to do with narrow escapes from death. They turned on wonders and coincidences. He had escaped drowning and burning houses; he had been rescued in the nick of time from murder at the hands of brigands. Ashley was the sole listener, for the others had fallen asleep—the nitrate merchant, the botanist, and Mrs. Hobbes-Jones (author of *A Child's Asia*, *A Child's Africa*, and so on).

Finally, Mr. Bristow asked him in a low voice, "Have you ever been close to death, Mr. Tolland?"

"No," said Ashley, "I can't say I have."

Bristow then went on to stories of deaths he had witnessed that arrived opportunely, at some right moment—deaths that beautifully crowned an enterprise or averted disgrace, or that lifted an intolerable burden. His eyes glowed, he appeared younger.

"Every death is a right death. We did not choose the day of our birth; we may not choose the day of leavetaking. They are chosen."

Ashley had given little thought to death. He listened absorbedly—as his children had listened to him tell stories about Little Ib's adventures at the North Pole and Little Susanna's Trip to the Moon—and, like his children, he fell asleep.

The next morning when Bristow was leaving the Fonda, Mrs. Wickersham stopped him at the door.

"What were you doing in Mr. Tolland's room yesterday afternoon, Mr. Bristow?"

"I? I?—I don't even know where his room is!"

"I asked you what you were doing in his room."

"Oh, I remember. Was that Tolland's room? I just wanted to borrow some ink."

"What did you take from his room?"

"Nothing."

"I was told you were there twenty minutes."

"Twenty minutes! I wasn't there a second."

"I don't like my guests disturbed.—How many days will you be away?"

"Five days, six at the most."

She turned away without saying goodbye. As soon as he was gone she called Tomás. "Did Mr. Bristow leave some luggage in the storeroom?"

"Yes, Padrona."

"I want to be sure it's safe. Put it upstairs in my room."

It was not the first time Mrs. Wickersham had gone through Mr. Bristow's luggage. She found a copy of the rat list. On the last page there was an entry underscored by a red crayon.

"ASHLEY, JOHN B. Born Pulley's Falls, New York, about 1862. Five feet eight—180 lbs. Brown hair. Blue eyes. Vertical scar on right jaw. Educ. Type; Eastern accent. Mining engineer, Coaltown, Ill. Wife and 4 ch. Shot Breckenridge Lansing, his employer, in the back of the head, May, 1902. Sentenced—

Escaped from guards on way to execution at Joliet, July 22. Dangerous character, connected with criminal associates. Reward, State's Attorney's Office, Springfield, Illinois, 3000. Additional reward, 2000, J. B. Levitt, Brockhurst, Levitt, and Levitt, P.O. Box 64, Springfield, Ill."

Mrs. Wickersham leaned long over this material. She closed her eyes, as though overcome by a great weariness. It was not the first time she had asked herself the question to which she could furnish several answers—"Why are good men stupider than bad men?" During that hour she erased from her memory and her heart a speech that she had been preparing. She laid it away as some girl—hearing that her future husband had been killed—would carry a wedding dress to the attic. The speech had been shaped and embellished by many rehearsals. She had intended delivering it that night, beside the jug of rum on the roof of her hotel.

"Mr. Tolland, leave Rocas Verdes and come to Manantiales to work for me. Help me with the Fonda and with my interests in the town. You're a blessing to the schools and hospitals already. We don't know how we'll get on without you. Besides, with you I could do a great many things I haven't had the time or the wits to do by myself. The water from the Santa Catalina spring has extraordinary properties. We could bottle it and sell it by the trainload. In addition, we could build a great sanatorium. People should come and bathe here. Manantiales could be a small city of healing and happy industry."

The speech went on, even more swelling, more visionary, at each rehearsal.

"Since I've been here we've taught more than a thousand children. They marry; they have children; they open stores and inns and stables throughout the whole province. They farm. But that's not enough. What we need is a school to prepare teachers. The mixture of Spanish and Indian blood makes a very fine stock. By themselves, the Indians are crushed, resigned and suspicious, but they have a keen psychological intelligence and a readiness to help one another. The colonials are active, but they are vain and non-cooperative. Both are at their best—when they're mixed—in this climate and at this altitude. Come, Mr. Tolland, let us make a

college, a medical school, and a city of healing. Let us build for the future when Manantiales will be an example and a model for all the provinces in Chile and in the Andes."

That was the speech she never delivered.

Presently she rose, replaced the rat list in Mr. Bristow's luggage, ordered her horse to be brought to the door, put on her black Spanish hat, and pinned a red rose on her lapel. She rode into town and was closeted for an hour with Dr. Martínez of the hospital. She directed him to order a coffin generously designed for a man five feet and eight inches tall, to be placed in the farthest hut reserved for contagious patients. She had shaken off her air of weariness. Something hard and resolute had come into her voice and manner. From the doctor's office she went to that of the Mother Directress. From there she caught a glimpse of Ashley and his crew at work on the new laundry, but she stayed out of his field of vision. She had nothing, for the present, to say to him. Sister Geronima began describing to her how Don Jaime was raising the level of the troughs, "so the girls won't have back aches. And, Padrona, he lowered the desks of the lace makers. He has such a feeling for the right height!" But Mrs. Wickersham cut these praises short and talked of more important matters.

At the Fonda the guests were informed that dinner would be delayed until nine-thirty. Mrs. Wickersham dressed with more than her usual care. She wore her opal earrings and a dress which few of her guests had seen before. It was white. She had worn it on the occasion when the President of her country had conferred a decoration upon her. She wore the decoration. Her close friends (but what close friends had she? They were dead; her daughter was in India) would have known that this uncalled-for "dressing-up" was a sign of dejection—her wearing the decoration pointed to despair. She directed Ashley to sit opposite her at the foot of the table, between a Finnish botanist and his wife. Her eyes rested on him from time to time as from a great distance. At dessert the guests were served Mr. Bristow's champagne. She gave her attention intermittently to an eminent German geographer at her right. The conversation about the table became more animated. Ashley and his Finnish friends were enjoying themselves.

"What are you young people talking about down there?" she called.

"Mrs. Wickersham," said Ashley, "Dr. and Mrs. Tihonen have some splendid ideas for the trees we should plant all up and down the valley. They're going to give me a list and a map."

The table fell silent at this sound of jubilation.

"Yes, yes," cried the German geographer, clapping his hands. "There are few satisfactions greater than the planting of trees."

The Tihonens clapped their hands. Everyone clapped except Mrs. Wickersham.

Dr. von Strelow continued: "It is the planting of crops that separates man from the animal. The animal does not know there is a future; he does not know that he will die. We die, but the orchard survives. The planting of trees is the least self-centered of all that we do. It is a purer act of faith than the procreation of children. Dr. Tihonen, come with us tomorrow and show us those groves and forests we shall never see."

Again the table applauded.

"But, Mrs. Wickersham, you should do more than plant trees in this beautiful valley. You should found a city."

"What?"

"Five miles down the valley—a new town. My life study, gracious lady, is to describe the conditions favorable to man—to his body, his mind, and his industry. You have very little rain here, but you have all these hot and cold springs. There can never be a large city here; your agriculture will be limited; but you have a perfect environment for things of the mind. I can see a university here and a crown of hospitals and medical schools and hotels. I can see a concert hall and a theatre. The people from the cities on the coast will come up here to renew the spirit. There—five miles down the valley. I will show you the place tomorrow. You have done admirable things here in Manantiales, Mrs. Wickersham. Now you must do still more remarkable things *there*."

The guests raised their glasses and shouted.

"What shall we call this town of light and healing? I fear that Mrs. Wickersham is too modest to let us call it by her name. Let us call it Athens—*Atenas*. I will bequeath my library to the university."

"I will give it my collection of the plants of the Andes," Dr. Tihonen called.

"I will give five thousand dollars to it right now," said the mining engineer at Mrs. Wickersham's left.

Throughout this rhapsody Mrs. Wickersham had been clutching the edge of the table with tense fingers. She rose and said, unsmilingly, "We shall have coffee in the club room, ladies and gentlemen."

The coldness in her voice deflated the company's elation. They looked into one another's faces like children rebuked. She led the way from the room with head high and lowered eyes. When coffee was passed she said to Ashley, "I must see you on the roof at midnight. There is something I must tell you." After some struggle with herself she addressed her guests:

"I want to thank Dr. von Strelow and Dr. Tihonen for the beautiful plans they have made for the valley. And I want to thank you all for the good will you've brought to them."

She had something further to say, but could not complete her speech.

On the roof by the jug of rum, they were silent for a time. Ashley knew that there was something weighty in the air.

"Mr. Tolland, are you a man the police are hunting for?"

"Yes, I am."

"Are you on Mr. Bristow's rat list?"

"I suppose I am. I've never seen it."

"You feel fairly certain that you will not be caught?"

"No. I take the risk. I'd rather take the risk than spend my life running. I'm not running from myself. I'm innocent of the charge that was brought against me."

"Mr. Tolland, have you missed anything from your room lately?"

"Well, the fact is, I'm certain that someone stole some photographs I valued."

"Has anything else unusual happened that might be connected with that?"

"Yes, I was wondering whether I should tell you about it. A few nights ago in the club room someone put some kind of drug in my drink. I'm a very light sleeper, but that night—hours later—I was wakened by someone in my room. I could hardly drag myself awake. Someone was pulling my beard.

There was a light on—a man was moving around, maybe two men. All I knew was that I was struggling to get this man's hand off my chin. The man—or the men—were laughing. You might say, giggling. I struck back at him, but there was no strength in my arm. Then they went away. At first I thought it had been a nightmare. I could scarcely get out of bed to light the lamp. It was no nightmare. The furniture had been pushed about."

"How do you explain it?"

"Oh, I think it was some practical joke of Mr. Bristow's."

"If you're on the rat list, Mr. Tolland, there may be some scar to identify you by."

Ashley put his hand up to his right jaw. "There is." He stroked his chin, then stared at her in the darkness. "So that was it!"

"He wants to collect the money on your head, Mr. Tolland."

"How would he do it?"

"He carries some kind of document around with him. He's honorary deputy sheriff of some town in the States. It has probably no official value whatever, but it's enough to impress the police down here. It's covered with ribbons and seals and flags and eagles."

"What will he do now?"

"He's gone up to Rocas Verdes to talk you over with Dr. MacKenzie."

"Dr. MacKenzie's my friend."

"Mr. Tolland, Dr. MacKenzie would betray anyone for the sheer pleasure of it.—What time is it?"

Ashley lit a match. "A quarter past one."

"Please light the lamp. . . . I found the rat list in Mr. Bristow's luggage. I copied out the description of yourself. Read it!" He did. "Why didn't you tell me about this before? You think you are lucky. You think some special providence watches over you. There are no special providences, Mr. Tolland; there's simply our wits. Why didn't you trust me? Friendship is for those who earn it. You are in very great danger. Since you have been found out, there is only one thing to be done: James Tolland must die. John Ashley and James Tolland must die a good thoroughly certified death. The whole world must be convinced of it so that this search for you will be over. We are going to forge some documents for you. We are going to spirit you away across the desert to a little harbor called Tiburones up near the Peruvian border. Some small nitrate boats put in there. They'll take you to Central America. You'll be a Chilean who had a German mother. Have you any money?"

"I have more than I know what to do with."

"You're going to fall ill tonight. You're going to have a rare and terrible disease. I've chosen one that's not contagious; otherwise, I'd have to lock everybody up in quarantine. You've heard of poison ivy. Well, we have something ten times worse than poison ivy. You are going to die of the *tachaxa espinosa* rash, in perfect agony, Mr. Tolland. Dr. Martínez will write your death certificate. The Mayor and your friend Mother Laurencia and myself will sign it. The consul's office in the capital will register it. Newspapers all over the world will publish it. That escaped convict John Ashley—the terror of decent men and women—is dead. You will have a glorious funeral. You will be buried near me in almost consecrated ground. Then you will be born again. Drink your rum."

"I haven't finished the laundry."

Mrs. Wickersham snorted. "You haven't helped me build the new Atenas. Life is a series of disappointments, Mr. Tolland. Life is a series of promises that come to nothing.—I'm tired of talking. My voice is tired. I want you to tell me this story about your killing a man and this other story about your escaping from your guards."

He talked for half an hour. He finished the story and fell silent.

"Well!" she said. "Well!—someone else shot him."

"There was no one else around. And even if there had been, he couldn't have shot him at exactly the same second. Only one shot was heard."

"You have no idea who those rescuers were?"

"None."

"They were miners who felt indebted to you. . . ."

"Oh, Mrs. Wickersham, miners spend their lives underground. They're not quick on their feet. They're not quick in the head. They couldn't plan a thing like that and carry it out—like circus acrobats."

"Mr. Tolland, it's very strange. It makes me feel twenty years younger. I don't believe in miracles, but I couldn't exist if I didn't feel that things like miracles were happening all around me. Of course, there's an explanation for what you've told me—but explanations are for people who carry dull minds through dull lives. I feel thirty years younger. But I was very unhappy at dinner—hearing all that nonsense about building a university here and a medical school—and even a concert hall and a theatre! In all my dreaming I never got as far as that!— and of how we must found a city! And who's to do all that—a woman of seventy and you, a man who can't show his face in public? That old fool of a professor wants to locate this Atenas here in this valley where we have two hundred earthquakes a year. Earthquakes start fires. Ceilings fall in. The churches collapse so often that they don't try to build domes any more. . . . Opera! Singers can't catch their breath at this altitude. Why are idealists such ninnies?"

Mrs. Wickersham kept losing and recovering the train of her thought.

"Do you know why we have so many earthquakes? Because the Andes are rising higher. Soon they'll be higher than the Himalayas. They'll be the highest mountains ever seen. But sun and ice will reduce them again. They say the Alps are already crumbling away. It'll be as flat as your hand here before you can say 'Jack Robinson.' A few little Atenases, like the original Athens, will have had their day. Cities come and go, Mr. Tolland, like the sand castles that children build upon the shore. The human race gets no better. Mankind is vicious, slothful, quarrelsome, and self-centered. If I were younger and you were a free man, we could do something here—here and there. You and I have a certain quality that is rare as teeth in a hen. We work. And we forget ourselves in our work. Most people think they work; they can kill themselves with their diligence. They think they're building Atenas, but they're only shining their own shoes. When I was young I used to be astonished at how little progress was made in the world—all those fine words, all those noble talkative men and women, those plans, those cornerstones, those constitutions drawn up for ideal republics. They don't make a dent on the average man or woman. The wife, like Delilah, crops her husband's hair; the father stifles his children. From time to time everyone goes into an ecstasy about the glorious advance of civilization—the miracle of vaccination, the wonders of the railroad. But the excitement dies down and there we are again—wolves and hyenas, wolves and peacocks.—What time is it?"

She was ashamed of herself. She was crying. She hadn't shed a tear for thirty, maybe forty, years. Yet she was laughing, too, the long low almost soundless rumble that so often accompanied her thoughts when she was alone.

"Yes," she went on, "everything's hopeless, but we are the slaves of hope.—Well, the evening's over and I'm drunk. Mr. Tolland, you must go to bed now. You're going to wake up a very sick man. At about seven-thirty you are going to be carried through the streets on a stretcher so that the whole world can see that you're dying. Here's some red ink. Rub it on your chest and especially at the base of your throat. You will have great buboes in your armpits and in your groin. Paint them red. And here's some black ink. The inside of your mouth must turn black. When you're lying on that stretcher keep your mouth wide open. We must all see you buried before Mr. Bristow returns. I'll come and visit you tomorrow afternoon, after you're dead, to tell you what happens to you next. Good night, Mr. Ashley."

He put his glass down, still smiling. "I'll be back. We'll work on Atenas together."

"No! There'll be other fools—another Ada Wickersham, another John Ashley, and another Wellington Bristow, of course."

Soon after four in the morning Mrs. Wickersham was awakened by a loud knocking on her door. It was Tomás.

"What is it?"

"Padrona, the police are taking Don Jaime away."

"Which police?"

"Captain Rui and Ibáñez and Pancho."

"Tell Captain Rui to stay right there until I come. Who else is there?"

"Don Velantón" ("Velantón" for Wellington).

"Don Velantón went away this morning."

"He is here."

"Tell Captain Rui to wait with his prisoner in the *sala* until I come. Tell him I said to him, 'Remember Fernán.'"

Fernán was the captain's son. Mrs. Wickersham had extricated him from a grave predicament. She made them wait. She dressed slowly. Twenty minutes later she entered the *sala*. Ashley, handcuffed, was sitting between two guards. Wellington Bristow came toward her, almost sobbing.

"Mrs. Wickersham, Mr. Tolland is a famous criminal. He shot his best friend—"

"I thought you left Manantiales this morning."

"—in the back of the head. He is a very dangerous person."

"Button up your clothes!" This phrase, frequently exchanged by boys in their horseplay, is used among adults as an expression of supreme contempt.

"Mrs. Wickersham!!!"

"Captain Rui!"

"Yes, Padrona."

"How is your wife?"

"Well, Padrona."

"How are Serafina and Luz?"

"Well, Padrona."

"How is Fernán?"

The captain replied in a lower voice, "Well, Padrona."

"Good morning, Pancho. Good morning, Ibáñez."

"Good morning, Padrona."

Silence.

"I saw your mother yesterday, Pancho. I think she is recovering, I think she's doing very well."

"Yes, Padrona. Thank you, Padrona. Thank you, Padrona."

She sat down and gazed weightily before her. Her eyes avoided Ashley's and Bristow's.

"Captain Rui, I have directed a hotel in Manantiales for many years. It has not been easy. I am a woman—alone—a helpless woman. I could not have done it without the help of some strong and honorable men—like yourself, Captain Rui." ("Oh, my Padrona!") "I am a mother, with a mother's heart. Forgive my emotion!—Captain Rui, have you ever known anything scandalous or improper happening in my hotel?" ("*No*, Padrona!") "A defenseless old woman—with God's help I have run a respectable house."

Another long pause as she pressed her scarf to her eyes.

"But yesterday a shocking and a shameful thing took place.

I thought that that man—Don Velantón Bristó—was my friend. I thought he was an honorable man. He is a SERPENT!"

"Mrs. Wickersham, I can *prove* to you—"

"He entered the room of one of my guests and STOLE an object of great value! I can scarcely speak . . . for shame.— Who is *this* man, Captain Rui?"

"Padrona . . . Don Jaime Tolán."

"Yes. Who without reward—without one cent from me— has worked from sunrise to sunset for the love of the people of Manantiales. He has made the hospital fit for a king—the hospital where your dear mother is this very minute, Pancho."

"I know it, Padrona."

"Do you know what Mother Laurencia called Don Jaime Tolán? With her own sainted lips she called him an angel."

Wellington Bristow slid to his knees. "Mrs. Wickersham. That's ASHLEY—the murderer. I can prove it."

"Captain Rui, that man on the floor, that SERPENT, from his black, black heart accused that ANGEL of crimes too horrible to mention.—Remove those handcuffs and put them on the wrists of that LIAR and THIEF, and may God be merciful to him."

It was done.

"Mrs. Wickersham, have some pity on me. I'll give you half the cauliflower."

"Captain Rui, when you are taking him to jail, do not hurt him. Behave to him in a Christian way. But do not talk to him. Don't let him talk to anyone. I will call on the Mayor this morning and tell him of this treachery. Put Don Velantón in the 'coffee bin.' The first three days a little soup and bread at noon. Do not treat him unkindly, but make certain that he *talks to no one*—not even to you and your guards.—It is too late to weep, Mr. Bristow!—Don Jaime, you do not look well."

Ashley could not speak. He pointed to his throat. He unbuttoned his collar.

"Open your mouth, Don Jaime!"

Mrs. Wickersham looked into his mouth, gave a moan, and recoiled with horror. "All the saints in heaven defend us!" She whispered two words to Captain Rui, who blanched and crossed himself. She called into the hall—"Tomás! Run at once to Dr. Martínez! Tell him to come here!—Get up off the ground, Mr. Bristow. You will have time to go down on your knees in the 'coffee bin'!"

Ashley was borne through the streets and left in the shed for desperate cases. At noon all was over. The chapel bell tolled; the blind girls asked to be led in prayer; the sisters could scarcely find their way among the beds.

At noon Mrs. Wickersham visited the shed. He must have some "papers" for his new life. She brought a collection of old and new birth certificates, citizenship papers, and passports. They had been assembled from undertakers' offices, from inn-keepers, and even from pawnbrokers. They described men of all ages, and sorts—men with twelve teeth missing, with scars on their backs and moles on their chests, with hernias and hemor-rhoids and cloven palates. She brought also some penknives, bottles of ink and of acid. Ashley was in his element. They experimented with various forms of erasure, alteration, and cleri-cal penmanship. Finally, they produced a certificate—stained by weather and perspiration, barely legible—for "Carlos Cés-pedes Rojas, born in Santiago de Chile, on March 7 or 9, 1862, blue eyes, brown hair, medium height, sound teeth, bearing a scar on his right jaw, bachelor, field worker."

At midnight she returned with an old man Esteban and five mules. His journey was to Tiburones. The road was over two hundred miles—one hundred and twenty, as the bird flies, if a bird had ever flown it. Few drops of rain fell on it in a century. It crossed old nitrate beds that had been abandoned since the railroad was built. It was said to be haunted by the ghosts of the many fugitives who had died there. Water bags hung from the mules like great wasps' nests; hay was piled on their backs. There was bread, fruit, and wine for the men. Esteban held a second wide-brimmed hat like his own.

"Well, get along with you," she said.

Ashley stood looking in silence at the grey eyes in the red face, printing her features on his memory. She brought a silk scarf out of her handbag. "This is wet. Tie it about your fore-head."

He gave her an envelope. "Put that in the jar for the Roentgen-ray machine."

Silence.

"I'll let Mr. Bristow out for a few hours. He enjoys funerals so.—Mr. Tolland, did you ever hear of the English poet John Keats?"

"I've heard of him."

"He said that life is a 'vale of soul-making.' He might have added that it's a 'vale of soul-unmaking,' too. We go up or we go down—forward or back. I was slipping back. Maybe I have a few years more. A few stones for a little Atenas. Write me. I'll write you and tell you how we're getting on.—Start off, Esteban!"

Ashley took her right hand and kissed the back of it slowly. The leave-takings of the children of faith are like first recognitions. Time does not present itself to them as an infinite succession of endings.

Twelve days later Esteban returned to Manantiales by the new road. He brought Mrs. Wickersham a letter from Carlos Céspedes. The hay and water for the mules had been barely sufficient. Several weeks later she received another by slow coastal mail. He was leaving Tiburones the next day for the north. She received no more.

He was drowned at sea.

No announcement of the capture of John Ashley of Coaltown ever appeared or of his death and burial. Wellington Bristow was able to persuade the consular agent that there was something suspicious—"very fishy"—about Mrs. Wickersham's claims to have buried the notorious fugitive. Mr. Bristow continued to search for him for years.

III. Chicago

1902–1905

WHEN, TOWARD 1911, persons all over the country began asking questions about the Ashley family, it was Roger who puzzled them most. They were unable to discover any one mainspring that released and directed his energy. He exhibited no signs of ambition; he effaced himself, unsuccessfully. After the age of twenty-one he never signed an editorial in those various newspapers he was constantly buying, reshaping, and abandoning to others. He held strong views, but he was not combative. Readers recognized his voice—reasonable without being argumentative, earnest without being ponderous, and always brief. It was the voice of ethical persuasion. Finally his admirers and enemies found relief in the formula that he was "old-fashioned." He seemed to speak for the America of one's grandparents—of that age before the great city imposed itself. It was old-fashioned of him also to revive the art of platform eloquence. Up to the beginning of this century Americans had rejoiced in a passion for oratory—sitting rapt for hours in tents and halls and churches. In addition to the beautiful speaking voice they had inherited from their mother, Roger and Constance possessed that rarer form of eloquence that arises from an absence of self-consciousness. Roger consented to speak only on great occasions and on grave issues, yet never for longer than thirty minutes. The First World War was imminent. His views often ran counter to those of his readers and listeners. The façades of his newspaper offices were occasionally defaced and the windows broken; he was burned in effigy here and there; but—unlike his sister Constance—he was seldom insulted and reviled by members of his audience. He was old-fashioned, countrified, a little ridiculous, and compelling.

Roger Ashley was seventeen and a half when—on foot—he entered Chicago. He was hungry, tired, dirty, unsmiling, and resolute. He looked very much a rustic and was taken to be sixteen, but he did not know this. His blue suit, which he had outgrown, shone here and there, like a mirror. Under his arm he carried a few articles of clothing wrapped in brown paper. Like his father before him he had been the young lord of a small town. He had led all his classes and captained all his teams. He had never known fear or self-consciousness. He had leapt at runaway horses, parted fighting dogs, and rushed into burning houses as though he had been singled out to do so. He had worked all summer on Mr. Bell's farm since he was eleven and was strong. Chicago was growing fast. It was not hard to find work, poorly paid though it was. He was free to choose and he changed jobs often.

First he had to eat. Lodging was of less importance. In summer a man can sleep in parks and under bridges. Next, he had to earn money to send his mother. Above all he had to select his lifework. Sometimes he went for days with little to eat; sometimes he deliberately took less remunerative jobs, though it reduced the sums he sent to Coaltown; but he never ceased to search for his life's career—to explore, observe, weigh, and eliminate the professions. He didn't want to waste any years on a wrong choice and he wanted to start preparing himself as soon as possible.

Two other important tasks lay before him, but he was not aware of them. He must acquire an education. He must reconcile himself to the human community. He thought that education, with a little application, came of itself. He thought that the dark resentment that filled his mind and heart was the normal armor of a man who has emerged from the thoughtlessness of boyhood.

Many years later Dr. Gillies said: "Roger Ashley entered Chicago stump-ignorant. Fifteen years later, without having put foot in a classroom, he was the best-educated man in the country. Of course, he had some advantages over the rest of us. Socially, he was a pariah. Philosophically, he had just suffered the spectacle of his family being chewed up fine by a civilized Christian community. Economically, he owned nothing—he didn't even have an extra pair of shoes to pawn. Academically, he had never faced a professor."

There were a number of other advantages that Dr. Gillies failed to note.

Roger possessed little sense of humor. There was no second Roger lodged within his head. A sense of humor judges one's actions and the actions of others from a wider reference and a longer view and finds them incongruous. It dampens enthusiasm; it mocks hope; it pardons shortcomings; it consoles failure. It recommends moderation. This wider reference and longer view are not the gifts of any extraordinary wisdom; they are merely the condensed opinion of a given community at a given moment. Roger was a very serious young man. Further advantages and disadvantages will come to our attention in the course of this history.

Since he entered the city hungry he immediately sought work in restaurants. He began earning his living at the bottom of the ladder of all employment; he washed dishes. There is something comical about low tasks being performed not only adequately but to perfection. Roger knew no better, having no sense of humor. The Ashleys gave all of themselves to whatever task was set before them. He was silent without being sullen, industrious without being aggressive, and, like his father, he was inventive. He gradually instituted procedures that made for speed, efficiency, and economy. The first thing he did was to place wooden boxes in the washing troughs. All the dish-washers were getting bent backs, stiff necks, chest pains, and murderous rages from leaning over ten hours a day. He was remarked. He was called into the kitchen to supervise the mechanics of delivering and removing plates. The restaurant, like Chicago, had grown too fast. In no time he was all over the place. His name was constantly in the air, "Trent, Trent! *Wo ist der verfluchte Kerl?*" "Trent! How can I work if there's no goddamned fish here?" He was blamed for everything that went wrong, but he had a calming effect on the irritability of cooks and waiters. They cursed him during those terrible hours from noon to three and from six to nine, but when they themselves sat down to eat they heaped his plate. Emergencies arose and his work carried him into the dining rooms. He reorganized service tables and sideboards. His wages were raised once, but raises are not readily given to the silent and the undemanding. He left the restaurant at the end of three months. "Resigned" is too grand a word for those who receive seventy cents a day. Feeding the public had become distasteful to him. He felt there was something infantile about it. Besides, he was looking about for a night job that would give him an opportunity to explore Chicago by day. It would also, after a short rest, enable him to get work by day as well. "The Elms" needed money and he needed a new pair of pants. Sleep is for sloths. His fellow workers at the restaurant were aghast and even wept, but he left without regret. Everybody liked him and he liked no one.

He applied for the position of night clerk in a hotel. He was turned away from the better hotels because of his youthful appearance and his rusticity. Finally, he was given the night shift at the Carr-Bingham. He earned less money, but he was allowed to sleep in the trunk room under the eaves. He made himself tea at sunrise. He ate once a day, standing up. In any one of a dozen German saloons in the neighborhood he could help himself, for the price of a beer, to the mounds of pumpernickel, cold cuts, cheese, and pickles. The Carr-Bingham was a fourth-rate hotel. In sixth-rate hotels all is misery and vice; in a fourth-rate one there is a grain of effort and a wisp of hope. Those who are silent, self-effacing, and attentive become the recipients of confidences. He heard many life stories between ten at night and eight in the morning. From every side there was brought home to him a thing that had never come to his attention, except in the matter of Goshen: the importance of money to self-respect and, above all, to independence. It was during his first days at the Carr-Bingham that he received the letter from Sophia telling of the boardinghouse at "The Elms," about Mrs. Guilfoyle, Brother Jorgenson, and the high school teacher. He promptly went out and found a daytime job. Almost nightly one or other of the guests tried to borrow money from him. "Just fifty cents, Trent—that's a good fellow," "I'll pay you back tomorrow, honestly I will." He was no lender; he knew no greater need than his own. He appropriated a pair of shoes from the belongings of an absconding guest. He was often called upon to put drunkards to bed. On two occasions he pocketed the dollar bill or loose change that these late revelers dropped behind them on the stairs. Money, he felt, was for those who needed it. It's a spiritless son and breadwinner who does not write his own morality. He reflected further on the matter, however, when two of his three shirts, then some money, were stolen from him. Long before he left the Carr-

Bingham he decided that he would not become a hotel man. He had known a home. Night after night he was aware of the guests—the querulous breathing, the abrupt awakenings, the unrestorative sleep of the homeless.

Dr. Gillies's letter of recommendation was useful. He sold haberdashery all day, standing behind a narrow counter. He left the position after three weeks in order to catch up with sleep. When he announced his departure he was offered a promotion which he did not accept. He sorted cheques all day, seated at a table in a bank. He became a messenger in a law firm, an inter-office runner—the job was called that of "Indian." He extended and even created his own usefulness. Everywhere he observed, weighed, explored, and eliminated the professions. He watched the chiefs—their hands and eyes, their relations with their subordinates, their greetings on arrival and departure. Roger had never attended a theatre, but he had played King Herod and Ahasuerus in Sunday-school pageants, and he knew that the important thing in acting is not to be natural. Apparently the more important a businessman became the more he "acted." These men did not greet their associates in the morning; they "acted" greeting their associates in the morning. Their very smiles and frowns and clearings of the throat were calculated to convey that they were important, busy, and short of temper. It was apparent that they were somehow afraid—afraid of a non-acted word or gesture. Moreover, Roger became aware of the deformation induced by the sedentary life—the revolt of the body against the long day in the swivel chair, the sagging cheek, the paunch, the increasing fatigue in the afternoon, the strained breathing, the mounting irritation, the soda tablets, and the spittoon. Roger seldom thought of his father, but his father was serving him as the measure of a man. He had never known him to be for one moment guilty of acting. These merchants and bankers and lawyers, he asked himself, did they present a different self to their wives and children? Did they "act" being husbands and fathers? Of course, they did. He'd seen that often in Coaltown—Joel Miller's father and George Lansing's father, the great and late Breckenridge Lansing. John Ashley had begun the day singing loudly before his shaving mirror. He raised a joyful storm in the house. "Bathroom's free, little doggies! Last one to breakfast is a buffalo." His son was certain that these men did not sing in the morning. John Ashley had driven away to his office with delight and, arrived on the hill, had divided his time between office, workshop, company store, infirmary, and the shafts. Roger resolved that he would never follow a career that involved sitting down all day. In addition he gathered, in some obscure way, that a large part of all this "acting" was an attempt to make the operations of business appear more difficult than they were.

Diversity of experience does not in itself constitute an education, though the boast is often heard that it does. Contact with the suffering of others does not in itself enlarge understanding. Luck must play a part.

Roger was overwhelmed by the crowds of Chicago. He was oppressed by the multiplicity of human beings. On the way to work he would stop and gaze at the throngs on LaSalle Street. (During his first days he thought he was seeing the same persons walking back and forth.) All these men and women had souls, had "selves." All were as important to themselves as he was to himself. In seventy years everyone he was looking at— and himself—would be dead, except a few old freaks. There'd be a whole new million hurrying and worrying and laughing and talking. "Get out of my way. I don't know you. I'm busy living."

"Mr. Joch said that Peking in China was eight times as big as Chicago. Crowds make you think of death; death makes you think of crowds. . . . Nobody asked me if I wanted to be born. Trapped into life . . . Cemeteries must be awfully crowded: 'Did you enjoy your trip, son?' 'Was it a pleasant visit, ma'am?' . . . Chicago's like a big clockshop—all those little hammers going. In the street people put on a face so that strangers won't read their souls. A crowd is a sterner judge than a relative or a friend. The crowd is God. LaSalle Street is like hell—you're being judged all the time. . . . Suicide very logical.

"In Old Quarry Pond there were millions of minnows. Mr. Marden said that fish ate their own eggs when there were too many. War—not enough food to go round.

"Crowds make you think of money. Everybody has some money in his pocket. Metal and paper. Represents a certain amount of work and the quality of the work. Biggest lie under the sun. Mr. Joch telling me about the Pullman strike nine years ago. . . .

"Crowds make you think about how the sexes attract one another. On the street men's eyes never quiet, every minute looking for a pretty girl. Women put blinkers on their faces; look straight ahead. Pretend they don't see anybody. Same thing. Pull of the sexes is like a carrot hanging in front of a donkey's nose. Keeps up his interest. Like Shakespeare says, 'Lights fools the way to dusty death.' . . .

"Crowds make you think about religion. What did God mean by making so many? I'm not going to begin thinking about religion for five years. I don't know where to begin. Probably just a carrot in front of your nose. Makes people feel important. Maybe Papa's dead. But he's not dead for Sophie and me. He's alive in us even when we aren't thinking about him.

"Imagination means seeing through walls. And seeing through skulls. Eugene V. Debs in prison just a mile away. I wish I could be a fly on the wall and imagine what he thinks about people and cemeteries and lots of things."

At times he felt himself shrinking to a ghost, to a nobody— cold, meaningless, and alone. To recover himself he placed Sophia beside him. "Look, Sophie! Just look!"

He decided to appraise a life in medicine. Without presenting Dr. Gillies's letter he applied at a hospital for work as an orderly and was engaged at once. The pay was as low as the dishwasher's, but he was given his meals and a cot in a dormitory. He swabbed out operating rooms and carried out pails of flesh. He fainted once, as did the nurse beside him. He washed the moribund and held the aged and broken in his arms while the nurses changed the sheets under them. He had never been ill and prior to his arrival at the Carr-Bingham he had seen very little illness. The examples of it he had seen there were obviously the result of mistakes and general foolishness. It was some time before he was able to free himself of this assumption. Here, too, he was silent, willing, and tireless. The nurses came to take it for granted that he was always on duty. There is something comical, you remember, about performing a low job perfectly. This servant had no sense of proportion. In the wards after "lights out" he would return several times during the night to tend Mr. Kegan's fistula or the unhappy Barry Hotch-kiss's strangulated hernia. His devotion to duty was mistaken for sympathy. He neglected nothing; he forgot nothing. In previous tasks he had inspired friendship; here his comings and goings were followed with love. He loved no one. When he hastened silently between the beds at three in the morning whispers arose—as on some battlefield after a hard-fought defeat—"Trent! Trent!" He was much in demand as a letter writer. ("I have only time for about twenty words, Mr. Watson." "You already owe me for three stamps, Judge.") He was occasionally called into the women's wards. Mrs. Rosenzweig clutched his hand and said softly, "You are a good boy. God will reward you." Roger wanted none of God's recompenses. He wanted twenty dollars to send his mother.

Every month that passed saw a reduction in the number of things that could surprise him. His contacts with his fellow orderlies enlarged his experience. Dr. Gillies had refrained from telling him that they were drawn from among the all but un-employable—men fresh from prison or absent without leave from their country's armed forces, unfrocked priests, epileptics, pyromaniacs under surveillance, cryptographers working on Shakespeare's plays, collectors of dolls' clothing, weight lifters, and world reformers. The vast room was seldom quiet, for the orderlies worked in staggered shifts. Roger slept with cotton in his ears, only ostensibly because of the noise—he could have slept through battles and cyclones—but because of the conversation. The presence of woman obsessed the dormitory at all hours, resembling a cloud of gnats, invoked and repelled in cackles, guffaws, yelps, and long feverish stories.

The practice of stuffing his ears with cotton he adopted from Clem, the oldest of the orderlies. Clem spent the larger part of his free time reading; he would have spent all of it so but for his failing eyesight. For every half hour he read he sat for a half hour with his hands covering his eyes in a pose that suggested prayer or desperation. He was a philosopher. In the limited space available to him in one corner of the dormitory he had built a hermit's cell about his bed, made from packing cases marked "Jeyes' Fluid" and "Jarvis's HCHO"—walls and bookshelves. Many of the books were in Latin or in an English as impenetrable as Latin; some were in French and German:

SPINOZA . . . DESCARTES . . . PLOTINUS. Hence the cotton in his ears. Roger's eyes often rested speculatively on Clem's lowered sound-proof head.

Most of the patients left the hospital shaken, but cured. Roger received many gifts—cigars, religious medals, postcards of Chicago's waterfront, suspenders, pocket combs, grocers' calendars. ("Goodbye, Trent boy, thanks a lot," "Goodbye, Trent, you've been awful good to my husband. Now don't forget what I said: we have a room for you in our house, if ever you need it.") He was loved and he loved no one. But Roger had much to do with death. He had made a resolve not to put to himself the questions that inevitably arise from a frequent contact with death, but certain resolutions are hard to keep.

When a patient was entering on a difficult or protracted death he was lifted onto a wheeled table and rolled into a room reserved for the dying. The orderlies had an ugly name for this room that Roger never used. Priests came in and out. Relatives were permitted to stand a moment at the door. Orderlies were in the custom of dropping in and lighting a pipe. Conversation was not easy, what with all the whistling and rattling going on. Over half the patients called for their mothers—even men who appeared to be nearing a hundred. (A man's first and last words are easy to say; that *m* recurs in all languages.) A bowl of filed-down pennies stood on a shelf. Roger came to recognize fairly well the moment of death. He watched with wonder. He liked the words "gave up the ghost." (Query: where does it go?) He could look steadily into the eyes of his older patients. He averted his eyes from the young men. From time to time the weight of these experiences bore heavily on him, just eighteen. He would wait until nightfall, hoping for clear weather. In clear weather he would carry an armful of blankets to the roof of the hospital, clear away the snow, and lie down with his face to the sky. From the gorge in Coaltown one saw only a narrow portion of the heavens. It gave him a restful feeling to think that God who had made so many people had made so many stars, too. There was probably some connection. They were shining down on "The Elms" and maybe on his father, millions of them. He was becoming reconciled to the disturbing discovery of the human multitude.

Against his will his thoughts returned often to a puzzling

rigmarole told him by one of his fellow orderlies. Peter Bogardus had been a barber, but had given up the work because he was nervous; he couldn't handle knives. He was pockmarked and totally bald. He didn't drink, but he had bad habits. He was a better orderly than most—far better than Roger because he knew more. ("Quick as a fox in a crisis," said Chief Nurse Bergstrom. "He saves twenty lives a year.") He belonged to an association that made a study of the life after death and ghosts. He invited Roger to attend a meeting, but Roger refused; he was afraid he would be charged admission. Besides, he assimilated what he wanted from Peter Bogardus, free.

One late morning they were idling in the room for the dying. Roger often dropped in there to see how things were going. He'd accompanied many a patient along the road. The other orderlies noticed that he had a sort of gift for quieting the patients just before they "kicked the bucket."

("Trent, why do you always pick up the old geezers' hands?" "I don't know. Do I? I think maybe they like it.")

It was Bogardus's day on duty there. He walked back and forth smoking long brown cigarettes. At intervals he shook off the ash into the bowl of pennies.

"Trent," he said, "all men lead as many lives as there are sands in the Ganges River."

Roger waited. Finally he had to ask, "What do you mean, Pete?"

"We are born again and again. These three men here—look at them!" Roger didn't have to look at what he had seen so often—the half-open suppliant eyes, the trembling chins and cheeks. "They will be dead in a few hours. But forty-nine days from now—seven sevens!—they will be born again. And they will be born again hundreds of thousands of times."

Roger remembered hearing something about this ridiculous idea before. In Coaltown his father had put money in the collection plate at church to send missionaries across the ocean to rid ignorant people of just such notions as that. But Roger was readier than he had been to listen to old and new ideas; Coaltown had some pretty ridiculous ones of its own.

"There's a mighty ladder, boy. In each new life a man may acquire merit that will permit him to step up a rung or two, or he may fall into error and slip back. Through the merit of

Gautama Buddha himself and those who have followed him all men tend to rise. Finally, when they have lived as many lives as the sands of the Ganges, they will arrive at the threshold of supreme happiness. But—now mark my words!—arrived at that threshold, these men will not step over it. They will deny themselves supreme happiness. They will continue to be reborn. They will choose to wait until all men have reached that threshold—men as numerous as the sands of the Ganges—many of them cruel and wicked men. They move about among us now, in disguise, aiding us to ascend that mighty ladder. But even when all the men on this earth, as many as are the sands of the Ganges, have reached that threshold none of them will step over it into supreme happiness, for there are other inhabited stars, as many as the sands of the Ganges. We must wait until all the men on all the stars have purified themselves. No man can wish to be happy until everyone else in the universe is happy."

Roger stared at him, uncomprehendingly. His family had been happy at "The Elms." Peter went on:

"You can see that great staircase, Trent—that mighty staircase? Can you count all those human beings on it? Sometimes you can see a little flutter—someone has mounted four steps—Socrates or Mrs. Besant or Tom Paine or Abraham Lincoln. Sometimes there's a moment of confusion—looks like an avalanche in the Rockies—a man—a Nero or a millionaire—has tumbled and lost fifty or a thousand of his lives. None ever stands still." He continued to walk to and fro smoking his long brown cigarette. Suddenly he turned and shouted, "Free yourself of attachments! Wife and child—illusions! Your reputation among men, your honor, your dignity—vanity! Look at these men! Some men, at the moment of death, are given for half a second a memory of their former existences—a glimpse of their future existences. Boy, they lean for half a second over the vast abyss of time and see the long wretchedness of their past lives. Others look up and see the threshold in the far distance above them. They can see that someday there will be an end to living in this sorrowful world, this vale of tears."

Roger started. He had seen those lightning-quick returns to consciousness—those expressions of immeasurable horror, those visions of all consolation. Bogardus crossed and leaned toward him, lowering his voice. "Trent, know this: there is a limit even to the number of the sands of the Ganges. We shall be Buddhas when the last earthbound man and the last starbound man has sprung free."

Peter's agitation had communicated itself to two of the patients. "Judge" Bartlett's eyes were rolling imploringly from side to side. Roger could read the message of his agitated fingers on the blanket; he understood the guttural noises from his throat. He crossed the room and wiped the patient's mouth with a towel. He shouted, "I can't write a letter now, Judge. I haven't got a pencil. I'll do it tomorrow. Go to sleep. Yes, go to sleep. Get some rest." There was the suggestion of a handshake.

On another table a patient mutters. *"Hab kei Gelt. . . . Mutti. . . . Hilf'. . . . Lu . . . u . . . u . . . ft."*

"Alles gut, Herr Metzger!" cried Roger. *"Schlaf a bissl! Ja!"*

Peter Bogardus continued: "You Christians can't wait that long—no, siree. You want your supreme happiness next Tuesday. You can't wait ten billion billion years—that's Christ's fault —impatience; always announcing the end of the world, next week, next month. And Christianity inherited his impatience— kill, torture, burn, divide. Baptize 'em or burn 'em! Believe in me or go to hell. That's what hell is—impatience." He wiped the perspiration from his forehead. "Look at me—getting excited! Look at me—*attached* to trying to make you understand something. Why should I care whether a little peanut like you in Chicago, Illinois, learns anything? That's the damnable impatience I acquired when I was a Christian. Look at me— trembling!"

He sat down on the floor, cross-legged. "I must do my breathing exercises and calm myself. No! I'd better stand on my head. That's best."

Peter flung his heels to the ceiling. Roger was accustomed to this. He was still thinking about the ladder of rebirth.

"You don't really believe that, do you, Peter?"

Peter, upside down, rested his pale watery eyes on Roger and waited. "Never ask a man what he believes. Watch what he uses. 'Believe' is a dead word and brings death with it."

A new patient, purple of face, was rolled in.

"Hello, Trent. Hello, Pete," said the orderly.

"Hello, Herb."

"Y'know him?"

"Yes," said Roger. "First name's Nick. Night watchman in the Fletcher Building."

He had come to know Nick well, having served and washed him for weeks. If there was anything in the Great Ladder idea, Nick was high up, high up. Roger had never seen a patient who so made himself at home—so to speak—in the hospital and in his pain. Though dependent upon others for humiliating aid, though his bed stood among those of noisy, foul-mouthed, furious sufferers, he gazed tranquilly at the ceiling. A stag would die so. He asked for nothing. When Roger offered to write a letter for him, he dictated some words to his daughter in Boston, requesting only that the letter be mailed a week after his burial. He told her that his Mormon brothers would put his body under the ground when he was freed of it. Roger turned his chair and sat with his back to Old Nick. Nick would not wish a friend to witness his animal struggles; they were not important. And suddenly it came to Roger that his father, too, was high, high up. Throughout that long trial in Coaltown—the "Hyena trial"—his father had conducted himself just so: out of reach of curiosity and malice and to all appearances at home in the courtroom and his extremity.

Roger went out of the door and out of the building. He stood in the sunlight at the hospital's rear entrance, shivering in his white suit. He had no questions to put to his father. He had no wish to sit down at a table and talk with him; but Roger would have given much of the little he possessed to see him pass along the street. He would have followed him for blocks simply to rest his eyes on someone who was so high up.

He wanted to watch him closely too, because someday he—Roger—would have children of his own. He would leave them behind him. He would die.

He was being drawn to the human community by thoughts of the dying, the banished, and the unborn.

It was from another aspect of his family's slowness to mature that Roger suffered crushingly from homesickness. A glimpse of a woman in the distance would evoke his mother; an object, a girl's voice, a smell would recall "The Elms." Everything would go dark before his eyes. He would be obliged to put out his hand to a lamp-post or a wall and to wait until the pain subsided. From time to time, in order to suffer more intensely—that is, to embrace "The Elms" more passionately—he went to the railway station from which trains departed for Coaltown. The station was near the lake. He had never seen a body of standing water larger than a pond. The view of those innumerable waves calmed him. "When you think of all the people in the world and all the thousands of years that have gone by, I bet there must have been a lot of fellows my age who had to leave their homes for one reason or another—like going to war, for instance."

Questions, the torment of questions.

There is no true education save in answer to urgent questioning. Unease and deprivation awaken the young mind to inquiry. Roger did not realize that he and his sisters had acquired that habit of mind in their earliest years: they had struggled to survive. Like plants in a parched soil, they had sent down deep roots. From infancy they had groped hither and thither, asking "What?" and "why?" and "how?" Beata Ashley was an admirable mother; she gave her children much; she gave them everything except the essential. As we have seen (and as a result of a starvation in her own childhood) she must love only one human being. John Ashley could give his children the essential—and much besides—but he was late-maturing; the flowering of his imagination was still to come. The children did not turn in on themselves. They were saved from fruitless introspection by their father's joy in them. Lily became the princess sleeping in the cave; Sophia entered into her ministry to animals. Constance—knowing no mother—prepared herself for that extraordinary life in which she would see herself as the mother of millions, more than half of them older than herself. Roger barely escaped some obscure shipwreck. A puzzling event took place in the summer of 1891. He was six and a half. He was well known in Coaltown as a model boy—so bright, so well behaved. His parents were out of the house. Seizing his youngest sister's chair he broke five windows in the living room. He then ran away from home, weeping as from some unfathomable abandonment. He stopped only to pick up Sophia's kitten to comfort him on his long walk to China. His parents tendered scarcely one word of rebuke. Roger never gave vent to his frustration again. A change came over him. The small adventurer and babbler became taciturn. He became a listener ("what?" "why?"). The expression on his face varied little. He became the school's best student and athlete. He was liked by everyone in town and ignored their liking. He had one friend, Porky. He accepted one person's love, Sophia's. He was strengthened by confidence in his father and isolated by his passionate love for his mother.

Questions. Questions. Now—like his father, thousands of miles away—he had no vocabulary and no grammar for reflection. What unity could be found in the increasing diversity of his existence: the catastrophe in Coaltown; his mother walking beside him imperturbably to the courthouse; the mystery of his father's rescue; the noontime crowd on LaSalle Street; the deaths he was witnessing daily; God's responsibility for the suffering of children, horses, dogs, and cats; Eugene V. Debs in prison scarcely a mile away; his happiness when he looked at the waves and the stars; his fellow orderlies' views on women; his resolve to achieve a great lifework? And the working world—injustice everywhere: employers cheated the workers; workers cheated the employers and one another? He'd done some cheating himself.

One day he stopped by Old Clem's cell.

"Clem, those books you're reading—do students study them in college?"

"Yes, some of them."

"Did you go to college?"

"Yes, I did."

"What does a college education do for you?"

"It ties together the things you see."

Roger drew back as though he had been struck.

"Can a person educate himself, Clem?"

"One in a million, maybe."

"Does most of an education come out of books?"

"A man who tried to understand anything without knowing THOSE BOOKS would just be a feathered kangaroo. Like Pete Bogardus. You're wasting my time."

"Thank you, Clem."

He had no wish to go to any of those colleges, or—for a time, at least—to read any of those famous books. He had walked the streets of Chicago at all hours. He had listened to scores of life stories. Man is cruel to man and even those who are kind to those nearest them are inhuman to others. It's not kindness that's important but justice. Kindness is the stammering apology of the unjust. *The whole world's wrong*, he saw. There's something wrong at the heart of the world and he would track it down. Many of those books and colleges had been around for hundreds of years—with very little effect.

The few serious books he had looked into seemed windy, slow-moving, filled with padding—like political addresses and sermons. Like all Ashleys, he wanted no help. We shall see later how his father "invented" marriage and paternity. Roger wanted to invent the explanation for existence and the rules whereby men could live rationally side by side—to be the first philosopher, the first planner of the just community. Independence of mind (most men boast of possessing it) cannot rest. Roger had already entered on this great task. His head was full of notions and he was driven to write them down. At the Carr-Bingham Hotel he had collected wastepaper. During the long nights there, and later at the hospital, he wrote thousands and thousands of words on the backs of old account books, bills, announcements, and calendars—notions. He had never had a friend of his own age, except Porky, even more taciturn than himself. He had never, like other young men, built and unbuilt God, society, morals *in conversation*. He now drew up an explanation of the nature of things; he derived ethics from the order in the cosmos; he designed the constitution of an ideal state. One day his feverish resort to writing came to an end as abruptly as it had begun. He carried the armfuls of scrap paper to the incinerator. He had come to a dead end, not in discouragement but as the result of an insight: he discovered that he knew nothing and that he was ill equipped to learn, but that learning was possible. He was ripe for reading. We shall see how he entered reading by the back door.

After three months of hospital life Roger returned to the Carr-Bingham Hotel, promoted to day clerk. He was anxious to make more money and he had arrived at a conclusion about medicine. He had become aware of that never-ending line—from the beginning of time to the end of time—of patients waiting at the door. No bed was empty for longer than three hours. To his eyes medicine appeared to be a business of patch and shore and bolster—the temporary repair of unsalvageable vessels. He was an ignorant country boy; he had no idea that medicine could take a different view of itself.

Back at the hotel Roger came into closer contact with a group of newspaper reporters who shared a row of cubicle-like rooms on the top floor near his own. This corridor had long since lost its institutional uniformity. Most of the doors had been shattered in rage or horseplay and removed. The management had prudently replaced the chairs with benches and packing cases. For men without women a cave is sufficient.

A smell of gin, lemon peel, mash, cubebs, and medication filled the air. The men seldom ate, slept, washed, or fell silent. They were ill paid and only intermittently ambitious, but they were convinced that they belonged to the greatest profession in the world. They knew everything; all men except themselves were the dupes of appearances. They were privy to corruption in public office, the farce of philanthropy, the hypocrisy of the clergy, the wolves' raids of big business—especially of the railroads and of the stockyards. They were rich in all the knowledge they were not permitted to print. Knowledge, like courage and virtue, isolates a man; they were thrown back on one another's company. Barred from publishing what they knew, they were driven to seek out some other mode of expression: they were conversationalists. Conversation was their brightly lighted stage and their battlefield. There they knew their triumphs and their massacres. Day by day and night by night they strove for the palm of the unparalleled jest, the supreme verbal acrobacy. Under the guise of comradeship they flayed one another. They rifled the dictionaries for words and images of intoxicating precision; they demanded ever stronger accents from blasphemy and obscenity. They were untalented reporters because their ambitions lay elsewhere; they were conversationalists. Roger listened. They were quick-witted; they had a wide if heterogeneous field of information. Above all they had a point of view: the abject condition of man and the futility of his efforts to improve himself. Any confrontation with fortitude, heroism, piety, or even dignity rendered them uncomfortable. They prided themselves on being impressed by nothing. Any impulse toward admiration or compassion they promptly converted into ribaldry and persiflage. Several of these reporters had been present at the Coaltown trial and recognized the hotel clerk. They handled him roughly about it for a while, then forgot it. They could not take him seriously. He was a country yokel, a rube. He was still wet behind the ears.

Roger had two qualities, however, that recommended him to them. He was an attentive though unsmiling listener and he was reliable. Virtuosi stand in need of fresh audiences. "Old Trent listens with his eyes and ears and nose—damn it, he listens with his chin." Dissipated men need one trustworthy friend. He became their banker and their message center. "Keep this money for me until tomorrow, Trent. I don't know what will be happening to me tonight." "Tell Herb to keep out of sight. Gretchen's looking for him." "Tell Spider the caucus is at ten o'clock in St. Stephen's Hall."

If journalism was the greatest profession in the world Roger resolved to look into it. He could not understand why reporters held all action and all human beings, except themselves, in contempt. He could not understand why, seeing corruption everywhere, they were not moved to report the whole of it. One afternoon Spider, returning to the hotel, laid a large envelope before Roger. It contained scores of stories and editorials about the Ashley-Lansing case. During the trial the Ashleys read no papers. He now read these pages several times. He was astonished to see how accurately they reported the proceedings in the courthouse and yet how feeble and unfocused the editorial comment was, even when it inveighed against the verdict and the conduct of the trial. During a solemn midnight walk beside Lake Michigan Roger resolved to become a newspaperman.

Years later Roger was able to acknowledge the extent of his indebtedness to the group of reporters on the top floor of the Carr-Bingham: his introduction to journalism, to opera, to one of those devil's advocates that are so important in any education—that is, to the conversation of T. G. Speidel—and to reading.

The reporters were readers, as time permitted. There were

many books to be found on the top floor of the Carr-Bingham Hotel—under the beds, over the wardrobes, in the toilet and broom cupboard, beside the mousetrap. Most of them were pocket size—a child's pocket size. Their covers were of spongy blue paper or of imitation leather. They bore such titles as *The Wit and Wisdom of Colonel Robert G. Ingersoll*, *Great Thoughts from Plato*, *The Best Pages of Casanova*, *Nietzsche on Superstition*, *Tolstoy on Art*, *Nuggets from Goethe*, *Nuggets from Voltaire*, *Confucius on The Center*. Roger read them. He entered reading by the back door. He paid a visit to the Public Library, but was displeased with it. He began to haunt second-hand bookstores. Reading became for him a great adventure. He told no one of his rewards and of his defeats.

Even before he arrived at his decision to become a journalist Roger learned that the profession enjoys an inestimable privilege: newspapermen can occasionally obtain free admission to the theatre. One evening a reporter gave him a ticket to the opera. He attended a performance of *Fidelio*. It was an overwhelming experience.

He had endured much. He was at no time near to any breaking point, but he was starved of food for the spirit. It was time that he gazed on larger images of perseverance and constancy. A man can produce fortitude from his own vitals, but the true food of valor is example. Before the Kangaheela braves went into battle they listened—eyes fixed on the distance—to songs that recalled the exploits of their ancestors. It was perhaps not incidental that on that occasion he followed the story of a woman who descended into a dungeon to rescue a husband unjustly condemned to death. A week later another opera offered him the spectacle of a young man who endured trials of fire and water to win the hand of the girl he loved. At the end of it the young man was received into the fellowship of the wise and the just. If operas were like that—if they concerned themselves with things that really mattered (rendered all but unendurably convincing by such wonderful *noise*)—he must so arrange his life as to be constantly present at them.

He persuaded his friends on the top floor of the hotel to find work for him on a newspaper. He became a "printer's devil," or "pie monkey," as the job was called there. His hands and face and apron were covered with ink. His ears were deafened by the presses. In a maze of iron staircases he rushed copy from the reporters to the editors. He rushed copy from the editors to the typesetters. He soon learned what was needed before it was called for; he foresaw blockages; he eased the recurring crises. The halls resounded with his name. "Trent! Trent! Where's that damned Trent?" "Trent, carry this poop downstairs and be quick about it." A reporter, short of time between two stories, would thrust his notes on Roger: "Run it up! And remember WHAT, WHO, WHERE, WHEN." He was awaiting his opportunity and his opportunity came. All the reporters were out on assignment. It was learned that a man had strangled a woman behind Heffernan's Livery Stable. "Get that story and get it right! Run!" Another opportunity arose and another. In late August, 1903, he became a reporter. He had been in Chicago thirteen months. He was eighteen years and eight months old.

At last he was not only doing his duty and feeding his curiosity, he was making a *thing*. His youthful and countrified air enabled him to be present at occasions from which an older and more knowing man would have been thrown out. He stood against the wall at closed political meetings; he slipped past the guards in the training quarters of boxing champions; he re-entered his old hospital by the employees' entrance and obtained a confession from a dying man. He arrived before the police and put questions to women who did not yet know that they were widows. He was taking notes at a Greek patriotic banquet in the Olympia Restaurant while the guests, stricken with food poisoning, lay about on the floor like brightly colored clothes bags. By December, 1903, he was writing his sister, "I bet I know four hundred Chicagoans by names and faces." Soon he was submitting special articles to the editor; they were known as "pudding pieces." They were signed TRENT: "Chicagoans, Save Your Waterfront!" "Know Your Polish Neighbors," "The Swop Market on Wisconsin Avenue," "Know Your Chinese Neighbors." He sent them to Sophia. Notices would appear on the assignment board: "TF—500 words—Friday—Women's interests." The editor was bewildered by Roger's contributions and rejected half of them as unlikely to interest readers, or as capable of giving offense. When a new editor joined the paper, Roger resubmitted them. He was inventing a new kind of journalism. Readers began to keep scrapbooks of these pieces; the offices of the newspaper were plagued with requests for old issues. He received a bonus of twenty-five cents for each.

Here are some further titles. Sympathy was stirring; he was beginning to see through walls and through skulls.

"A Day at Hull House."

"A Child Goes to the Stockyards" (twice rejected).

"A Fourth-rate Hotel."

"The Statues in Our Parks."

"Thanks, Bettina!" ("Trent" interviewed the last horse to have drawn a streetcar in Chicago. The concluding sentence read: "By the time these words have been set in print Bettina's hoofs will have been bottled for glue.")

"Seagoing Adventure." (The night boat to Milwaukee.)

"Know Your Hungarian Neighbors." (The "Ungaria Eterna Association" promptly sent him an invitation to a banquet in his honor which he courteously declined.)

"Kennels for Babies." (Twice rejected. Shocked readers canceled their subscriptions.)

"Pat Quiggan and *Il Trovatore*." (A scene shifter at the auditorium gives his account of what takes place in the famous opera. Roger had little sense of humor, but an unerring ear. Truth is funnier than fiction. Like a number of the other puddings this was reprinted from coast to coast, much embellished.)

"A Pleasant Evening to You, Gentlemen." (A visit to the newly opened "St. Casimir's Home for the Aged." Roger received a letter of appreciation from the Archbishop.)

"Milly and the Treadle." (A visit to a seamstresses' sweatshop. A score of readers sent the author the text of a poem he had never read, "The Song of the Shirt.")

"Who Are Chicago's Seven Best Preachers?" (Three articles. Roger had unwittingly put his head into a hornets' nest of sectarian enthusiasm and strife. For weeks he received from fifty to a hundred letters a day.)

"A Cap for Florence Nightingale." (October, 1905. This was written in great trouble of mind to give pleasure to Sophia. Roger had just heard from Porky that she had been taken to the Bell Farm for rest. He wrote her every day, finally enclosing this "pudding" and announcing that he was returning to Coaltown for Christmas. The editor first refused this piece as too silly for print, whereupon Roger resigned, declaring that he would take his work to another paper. The editor relented. In it Trent reproduced the thoughts of a father as he watched his daughter being "capped" on graduation from a nurses' training school in Chicago. The girl was named Sophia and had lived in a house in southern Illinois called "The Elms." The father recalled his daughter's love for animals, the splints she had made for squirrels and birds, the fledglings she had fed from an eye dropper. The author seemed to know a great deal about the duties, the trials, and the rewards of nursing. The piece was widely reprinted and brought many letters. A big cake was delivered to the newspaper office; it had been baked by the sister at Misericordia Hospital who, they said, had long been praying for him.)

Roger had a rickety ink-stained table in the City Room, but was seldom there. There was a rumor in the city that he was the son of a famous criminal; it was attributed to envious gossip. Rumor also said that he was under twenty, which was preposterous. It was generally believed that he came of an old Chicago family and was well on in life. He lived in a beautiful home in Winnetka or Evanston, surrounded by a large family and many animals. Roger had a considerable acquaintance, however, among people who "worked," to whom he was known as "that boy who writes those things in the paper." He had made a number of enemies also, particularly in the sporting and political circles, and had had occasion to defend himself from violence. All this activity, to him, bore little resemblance to the lifework in journalism that was forming in his mind. He was looking forward to inventing a journalism that had never been seen before. He was not impatient. He did not take these "puddings" seriously. Besides, their spelling and grammar were deplorable. He took the precaution of submitting them to old Mr. Brant of the green eyeshade, who prepared them for print. Roger studied and digested Mr. Brant's emendations. In Chicago "Trent" was beginning to be famous, but those who have never wished for fame in early youth are slow to recognize it when it arrives and scarcely know what to do with it. As far as he was concerned he wrote solely for money.

During the spring of 1904 his face narrowed, his voice descended half an octave, his glance sharpened. His inner weather became less troubled. Perhaps he learned laughter from Demetria, Lauradel, and Izumi—of whom we shall hear more; perhaps it sprang from his pleasure in his work. His characteristic movements were swift; he crossed and recrossed the city as though he had wings on his heels. At Christmas he sent his mother a sheaf of his "puddings" and gave for the first time an address to which she could reply. He made no apology for having withheld it so long—ostensibly to escape annoyance from the police—and she made no allusion to it: at any distance this mother and son could read each other's thoughts. She expressed her pleasure in his articles. She thanked him for his remittances and assured him that they were no longer necessary. She gave him an account of the boardinghouse's success, particularly stressing Sophia's helpfulness. She told him that Lily had left Coaltown to study singing in Chicago. Lily sent her money regularly, but she did not know what name she had taken nor any address for her. (The Ashleys were odd folk.) She hoped that Roger would visit them in Coaltown before long. His room had been rented to many guests, but it would be readied for him. She made no mention of the ordeals they had undergone together two and a half years ago. She concluded her letter in German: she asked for a photograph of him.

Both had written many drafts for these Christmas letters; the emotion had been consigned to the wastepaper baskets.

The reporters spent a large part of their days and nights in Krauss's, a German saloon on Wells Street, equidistant from their several newspapers' offices. There they wrote their stories and carried on their week-long, month-long card games, and there they wrestled for the conversational crown. Roger needed their conversation, though he soon outgrew it. The rewards were intermittent as information or insight, but the vocabulary was rich. The talk turned largely on liquor (after-effects of last night's consumption), women (rapacity of, their staggering over-self-estimation, Schopenhauer's matchless essay on), politics (gorgonzola in the City Hall, populace led by the nose), their editors (exposure and downfall predicted), literature (Omar Khayyám, greatest poet that ever lived), philosophy (Colonel Robert G. Ingersoll, towering intellect of), Chicago's rich men (hands and feet in the trough), religion (farcical character of, opiate of the masses), venereal disease (wonder doctor reported in Gary, Indiana). Roger endured much browbeating. For a time they were able to ignore his rapid advancement. His youthfulness, ignorance, illiteracy, and countrified air rendered it incredible. It was assumed that some mysterious person, or persons, wrote the pieces for him. By June of 1904, however, there could no longer be any doubt. Their condescension turned to violent dislike. Twice he pushed a tormentor against the wall and demanded a retraction. He was no longer welcome at Krauss's. Before that privilege was denied him, however, he had made a friend and taken a profit. The dean and Nestor of the round tables, Thomas Garrison Speidel, "T.G.," had adopted him as audience, pupil, and doormat.

T.G. was a nihilist. For a time he had belonged to both anarchist and nihilist clubs and had addressed them—first to their admiration, then to their mounting bewilderment and fury. He was duly thrown out of both organizations. On the one hand he was eloquent on the necessity of razing all political and social institutions, but on the other he insinuated many a sneer at the enthusiasms of the revolutionary dream. His preeminence among the reporters reposed upon the purity with which he hated "everything" and upon the fact that he seldom spoke. He was a dean at forty-five and a mastiff among puppies. He had a fine head, lined and furrowed, and freckled with light blue stains like gunpowder marks. He was the son of circus performers, who had found him, at the age of five, unadapted to acrobatic training. He had been farmed out to foster homes, flogged, scalded, locked up in cupboards, and always starved. There had been a history of running away, of stealing for hoboes' dens, of reformatories, of being adopted by kindly and unkindly farmers, of more escapes. He had earned his living in many ways. He had followed county fairs and been a mesmerist in a side show. He had even dabbled in quack healing. In a camp meeting in Kentucky he had effected three cures so remarkable that a sacred rage descended on the congregations; he barely escaped their enthusiasm with his life. He never ventured into healing again. Finally he came to rest as a reporter: the occupation was not sedentary; it admitted of drinking at all hours; its demands on sustained thought were intermittent; it flattered a delusion of omniscience. He had been married four or three times. Occasionally a child or two would be waiting for him at the door of the newspaper office or at Krauss's. They were well-behaved and bright—all T.G.'s wives had been, as his daughters proved to be, exceptional women. There is a limit to the number of ten-cent pieces a drinking man can dispense on a salary of twelve dollars a week. He talked to them with gravity and great charm. (He reserved his contempt for persons whom he knew well.) The children went away pleased; they had merely wanted to look at their father.

T.G. had a tormenting secret. He was the author of some verse dramas. Throughout that stormy childhood and youth he had read books. Unfortunately, he did not so much read books as read himself into books. He was incapable of a prolonged self-forgetfulness. He had never been able to finish Rousseau's *Confessions* or even *Anna Karenina*—so great was the turbulence set up within him. Similarly, he was a victim of music. A band concert unmanned him. Even as a boy he had eavesdropped under the windows of rooms where there was singing or playing. He even slipped into churches. He made no distinction between good music and bad, but inferior music had a more rapid action. His dramas were called *Abelard* and *Lancelot* and, of course, *Lucifer*. He had never finished a play and never read a line to a human being.

The friendship between T.G. and Roger resembled an armed truce. Each needed the other. T.G. needed a fresh ear for his doctrines and a companion in total disillusion. He proselytized. Roger needed the older man's conversation: it brought to the surface, it aerated, his half-formed misanthropy. In the early days of their association, T.G.'s picture of society as a façade concealing beast, sloth, peacock, blindworm, and asp glided into Roger's mind like balm. If Roger had much to learn, he had much to unlearn. The two men were also useful to each other in a practical sense. They worked on different papers. After attending separately some trial, boxing match, or political meeting, one would pass his notes on the occasion to the other. If T.G. had been drinking, Roger wrote two accounts of the event and gave one of them to his friend. It was neither the scabrous nor iconoclastic content of T.G.'s conversation that introduced a constant strain on their relationship; it was the burden of insult and contempt that Roger was called upon to endure. "T.G." could be rendered frantic by any reply that invoked moral values or a shade of idealism. "You dreck! You donkey drool! You yellow drawers! You *have* no ideas! All you've got in your head are some clinkers from Coaltown and your grandmother's old trusses!" At this, Roger would rise, gaze at him a moment, kick over a chair, and start for the door. T.G. would call him back, tender a sour apology, and the truce would be resumed.

It was not easy to humiliate or insult the Ashleys. Their attention would be riveted, not on themselves, but on their attempt to understand the sources of malice and enmity in their persecutors. Early in her career Lily was often hissed or booed in the opera houses of Europe; she waited tranquilly through the tumult for the opinion of the majority to manifest itself and to make clear to herself, after the performance, the reasons for the antagonism. Many hotels and very many homes refused to receive Constance. She said, "After people have had the pleasure of being shocked they start to think. My best supporters began as my worst enemies. But why must that be?" One of the reasons for Roger's patience now was his search for an answer to that question: why does each of us do what we do— the petty, the favored, the aggressive, the meek? Always there lurked the fear that one's own view of truth was merely a small window in a small house. In the face of so important a concern any contempt poured on oneself was incidental.

June, 1904:

"You know why your father was such a grinning idiot, don't you? You know why the trial was a farce, don't you? Because Coaltown and everybody in it was stupefied by the fumes that came up from under the ground. You know that the miners in Coaltown are the worst paid in the country?"

"No."

"That even the miners in Kentucky and West Virginia thank their gods that they don't work in Coaltown?"

"No."

"Well, your father knew it."

"I don't think he did."

"Don't lie to me! Where was he—asleep? The facts speak for themselves. There were very few miners with less than five children. A miner with a small family could move away and find a better job. And did. Men with seven children are stuck. Especially when they're hip-deep in debt to the company stores. The Emma Goldman Mapping Battalion had posted those mines as the worst in the country. No peonage in the world could compare with the stranglehold that your father's company had on those miners."

"My father had nothing to do with the policy of the—"

"Shut your schnout! Nobody has anything to do with anything. Eighteen million dollars a year were pulled out of Coaltown and out of Dohenus and out of the Black Valley hills. Where did it go? It went to Pittsburgh and New York. It bought yachts. It hung diamonds on actresses. It bought lifetime boxes in opera houses. It bought lifetime pews in churches. And what about Coaltown? Joe started coughing. 'Sorry, Joe, we can't use you any more; you're dying.' And Dohenus: sixty-three men caught in a gas caloup. Fifty-one widows. Almost three hundred little orphans. 'Sorry! One of those accidents, boys! Sorry! Act of God! Better luck next time!'—Did you notice how few people came forward to speak a good word for your father? I went around Coaltown trying to get someone to express an opinion about the trial. 'What trial?' 'Where?' 'Who?'—Where there's injustice, there's fear. Where there's fear, there's cowardice. But the chain begins farther back: where there's money, there's injustice."

"There were no rich people in Coaltown, T.G. My father wasn't a rich man."

"Shut your damned choppers! He was on the leash from rich men. You come from the middle class, don't you? That is to say: the crawling class? You don't know how to use the words 'rich' and 'poor.' There were six in your family. You all had two pairs of shoes, didn't you?"

"Yes."

"You had meat every day of the week, didn't you? You had meat *twice a day*. Blistering cabooses! Anything you'd have to say about poverty would be like a Chinese blindman describing Niagara Falls. Remember that! There's only one qualification for talking about poverty and that's to have LIVED IT."

"My father got the company to build a clubhouse for the miners."

"Of course, he did. I could have told you that. Listen to me: philanthropy is the roadblock in the path of social justice. Philanthropy is like an infected rain from heaven; it poisoneth him who gives and him who takes."

"What do you mean, T.G.?"

"You went to the circus last week, didn't you? Well, go again. Ask the guards to let you go into the lions' cage at feeding time. Now, when the lion's got that hunk of horsemeat between his teeth, you take it away from him. You can do it. Yes, you can. You can do it, but you have to KILL him first. That's the picture of the rich man and his property. Get this straight. No rich man ever gave away a penny he could find a use for. Never has and never will. By separating themselves from a little money the rich feel justified in making a lot more. Spiders draw just enough silk out of their bowels to catch those half-dozen flies they need to feed themselves and their loved ones; but the rich make silk and silk and silk. Nothing can stop them. Their houses are stuffed with it. Their banks are stuffed with it, and it's not out of their bowels they make it, but out of the bowels and lungs and eyeballs of others. The little coins that fall from their tables make churches and libraries, don't they? Churches! That's where the soothing syrup's stored. There's no marriage tighter than that between the banker and the bishop. The poor should rest content in that situation in which God has seen fit to place them. It's God's will that they work a lifetime over a sewing machine or in a mine. Trent! Get a-holt of this: *theft is the obligation of the poor*! Over the city of Chicago hangs a poison-bloated cloud. Everybody can see it. It's fed by the unequal distribution of wealth. It poisons the child in the cradle. It befouls the home. It's so dark in the courthouse you can't see a truth two feet away. The most sacred thing in the world is property. It's more sacred than conscience. It's more untouchable than a woman's reputation. And for all its importance, no one, NO ONE, has ever attempted to put a qualifying value on it. Property can be unearned, unmerited, extorted, abused, misspent, without losing one iota of its sacred character—its religious character. They used to hang a man for stealing a loaf of bread. We don't do that now: we warp his life and maim his children. I was once given eight months for stealing a bicycle—a rich boy's toy. But I was able to escape and steal another. I NEEDED a bicycle.—Listen to me: there's going to be an earthquake. Not just one of those little tremors where Mrs. Cobblestone reports that a picture fell off the wall. Not just a little shake or two, but a real sockdologer. The earth will be shaken like a rat. Because it isn't only Coaltown that is perched above a gas leak; it's the whole world. The lie about property's gone on too long. Even the schoolchildren are beginning to see it. There's going—"

His hands were trembling. He rose and looked about him wildly. "I'm getting nervous. I've got to go to Coralie's."

July, 1904:
"Did you write this?—This is in your newspaper."

"What?"

"Says that six men were working on a cradle in Chicago harbor. 'Through an imperfection in the equipment the cradle caught fire.' Did you write that?"

"Yes."

"'Three of the men were burned to death. The other three drowned. The Magilvaney Construction Company has generously consented to pay the funeral expenses of the victims.' GENEROUSLY! What were you thinking when you wrote that? Oh, I forgot—you don't think. When you'd written that word 'generously' you ought to have gone out and hung yourself. You've joined the great Chicago Singing Society that spends its time flattering rich men. The construction company gave them a rotten piece of equipment. Six men die. 'Sorry, men. Accidents will happen. Act of God. Better luck next time!'"

July, 1904. T.G. was often able to read Roger's thoughts, to drag into the light those that Roger did not dare pursue.

"Hunkus, you've been flabbergasted by the amount of people in Chicago, haven't you? You've been thinking that there are too many people in the world. You've been thinking that most of 'em would be better off dead. Why, I'm ashamed of you—a nice American boy like you going around killing people. Don't lie to me! Well, let me tell you something. Everybody does it. Aren't you glad every time you read about a train wreck, a flood, an earthquake? Of course, you are. There'll be more room for the rest of us. There'll be more food for the rest of us. That's why people read our newspapers. 'EXTRA! EXTRA! Excursion boat sinks with all on board. EXTRA! Three cents. Read all about it!' And people read all about it. They're filled with horror. It's terrible. But, oh! a little voice inside them says, 'It was getting a little crowded at the feeding trough.' Their eyes glitter. 'I'm glad it wasn't me on that boat.' More dead! More dead! They love it. And once they get these auto-MO-biles going, what a time we'll have! It'll be great! Especially on holidays. . . . Of course, war is best of all. During the Spanish War everybody in America read his newspaper at breakfast and hoped that every goddamned Spaniard in the world had been killed the day before. Every American ate Spaniards for breakfast. The great thing about war is that it makes murder legitimate. It permits Mr. Jones and Mrs. Jones and little Junior and dear little Arabella Jones to come out of the bushes and yell 'Kill 'em!' It's called patriotism. People went to bed every night simply exhausted with the noble exertions of patriotism. In that courthouse in Coaltown, didn't you want to kill the whole caboodle?"

"Yes, I did."

"Thank you.—And they wanted to kill your father? Why—for justice? for revenge? No! They didn't care a broken horseshoe for the late Breckenridge Lansing. I found that out. They wanted, under cover of legality, to get your father out of the way. The capacity of human beings to wish their neighbors dead is unlimited. Now, mind you! I don't say that everybody wants everybody dead. We all belong to little clubs. We want the members of other clubs dead; we only want the members of our own club STUNTED. A man wants his wife stunted and vice versa; a father wants his son stunted and vice versa.

"Take fathers. You were seventeen when your father ran away. Oh, you don't know how lucky you are! Listen to me: all fathers hate their sons. They hate them—first!—because they know that their sons will be going around whistling in the sunlight when they're rotting under the ground. They know that their sons will be jangling the bedsprings with girls in their arms when the old man is wheezing in a wheelchair. That's a bitter thought. Second! They're terrified that the boys may make less of a mess of their lives than they've made. It's a terrible thought that *that* man whom you knew as a little smeller in the cradle, as an idiotic puppy, as a troublemaking pimply adolescent—him!—that he could make a better showing in life than you've done. Terrible! And as no man has EVER been successful or happy inside—inside, where his real judgment of himself sits—this becomes true of every father. No father since the beginning of time has ever given a word of advice or encouragement that would lead to his son's thinking big and planning big. No, sir-eee! Dad sweats and wrings his hands and advises caution and going slow and keeping to the middle of the road. That passes under the name of paternal affection. Everybody knows that family life is a hell, but if you want to see a family life that's really beautiful, go back to the zoo. Look at the lions and tigers and bears. They really love their young. They really do. To see the lion cubs playing under papa's chin is the most beautiful sight in the world; and mama pretending to be half asleep, keeping one eye on the cubs and one eye on the loathsome human beings on the other side of the bars. The only time when a human parent really loves its young is when the child is brought home on a shutter. Then some atavistic animal bond comes to life. Mothers are torn in two, but they're torn in two at the thought that they hadn't been able to give the little blighters any love. You see when intelligence was given to human beings it fouled up the whole picture. Intelligence brought with it the realization that there is a future and that every man's future is death. Man is the animal that plants crops, that saves money, that has old age and death.

"Yes, there are too many people in the world. Nature's only interested in one thing—to cover the earth with as thick a layer of proto-plasm as possible: plants, fishes, insects, and animals. Did you ever see a field covered with anthills? Billions of ants. Did you ever see a swarm of grasshoppers? Nature's not very bright. She doesn't care if there'll be food for all of us. She just keeps bringing us on the stage in vaster numbers. That's why we die. When we can no longer make babies we've got to go. 'Bring on another plate of murphies, Mrs. Casey.' Nature seems to be in a constant state of panic lest her big meaning-less process stop. On they come: little fishes and little trees and gophers and fleas and Ashleys. 'Bring on another plate of murphies, Mrs. Casey.'

"What's that? What's that you're saying? Listen to me: there is no sense behind the universe. There is no reason why people are born. There is no plan. Grass grows; babies are born. Those are facts. For thousands of years men have been manufacturing interpretations: life's a test of our character; rewards and penalties after death; God's plan; Al-lah's Paradise, full of beautiful girls for everybody; Buddha's *nirvana*—we get that anyway, it means 'see nothing, feel nothing'; evolution, higher forms, social betterment, Utopia, flying machines, better shoelaces—nothing but THISTLE DUST! Will you get that into your draughty head?"

Billions have believed that we are influenced variously by the sun, the moon, and the planets. Millions have scoffed at the notion. Millions have believed that the heavenly bodies have marked certain men and women as their own—often errati-cally, brokenly, even grotesquely—but indubitably. The chil-dren of the Sun reflect the characteristics of Apollo leading the muses in his train, healing, cleansing with light, dispelling mists, prophesying: Thomas Garrison Speidel.

The children of Saturn also shed their influence upon the growing man:

Roger spent the greater part of the day moving about Chicago and its environs. He returned at intervals to his table in the tumultuous City Room, where he was accustomed to receive visits from persons wanting publicity for a favorite charity, an obituary for a relative (Roger was very fine at obituaries), an ad-vertisement for a lost pet. Some came to express approval or indignation. One morning as he was leaving his desk he was approached by a grave bearded man whom he recognized as the prominent lawyer Abraham Bittner.

"Mr. Frazier?"

"Yes. Yes, Mr. Bittner. Please sit down." Mr. Bittner sat down, slowly drew off his gloves, and looked at Roger in silence. "What can I do for you, Mr. Bittner?"

Mr. Bittner's hands played with an agate fob that dangled from his watch chain. Roger's eyes kept returning to some words engraved on two sides of the stone. Seeing his curiosity, Mr. Bittner drew out the watch and fob and placed them on the table. He remained silent as Roger looked more closely at the stone.

"Are those words in Greek, Mr. Bittner?"

"They are in Hebrew."

Roger raised his eyes inquiringly.

"Those words are the motto of a society to which I belong. I am calling on you today as a representative of that society."

"What do those words say, sir?"

"Have you a Bible in this office?"

"We had one. Someone took it."

"The words, in *your* Bible, are from the Book of the Prophet Isaiah, the third verse of the fortieth chapter: 'Make straight in the desert a highway for our God.'"

"May I pick it up, Mr. Bittner?"

"You may. I represent this society and particularly its directing committee of twelve men. This committee—as a mark of esteem for what you are doing for the city of Chicago—would like to place a convenience at your disposal." He paused. "You live in Room 441 at the Thurston House. The street under your windows is noisy until late at night and is particularly so in the early morning. The view from your two windows opens on the brick wall of Cowan's warehouse. Are these things so?"

"Yes, Mr. Bittner."

"This committee wishes to rent to you for three years, at one dollar a year, an apartment on the fourth floor at 16 Bowen Street. Four of its windows look out upon the lake. There are absolutely no conditions attached to this offer. It is extended entirely in the interest of your well-being and continued productivity. The apartment is ready to receive you from this moment. Here are the keys. Here is a receipt for your signature."

Roger continued to stare at him. Finally he started to speak, but Mr. Bittner arrested him with raised hands.

"You will not know the names of these committee members. They do not wish to be thanked. All but two are men of large means—very large means. They are Chicagoans. They love this city. They are resolved to do everything in their power to make Chicago the greatest, the most civilized, the most humane, the most beautiful city in the world. They have already extended parks, built fountains, and widened avenues. They contribute largely to the universities, the hospitals, the orphanages, to the rehabilitation of prisoners. You have written of your interest in the planting of trees. The committee has planted groves of oaks in the parks and has prevented others from being cut down." He lowered his voice. A smile hovered about his lips— the smile of one sharing a secret with one who will understand its import. "They are thinking of some Jerusalem here in the future—a free Jerusalem. They are thinking of an Athens. . . . You, Mr. Frazier, are doing a work which you alone can do. You have written with sympathy of the foreign communities in the city. You have restored a measure of dignity to older men and women in the eyes of their own children. You have called the attention of your readers to deplorable things which it is in their power to alter—all this in *your* way. The committee has this fear: that you will leave Chicago, that you will carry on your valuable work in New York or in some other city."

He slowly put his watch and agate fob back into his pocket.

The door of the editor's office opened. Old Hickson appeared holding some yellow pages in his hand. He called angrily: "TRENT! TRENT! We can't print this goddamned slop. Who the hell's interested in an old tramhorse? Get on your toes! Get a bee under your tail!"

Suddenly the editor saw that Roger was entertaining a dignified visitor. He returned to his desk, slamming the door behind him.

Roger picked up the keys. "Thank you very much, Mr. Bittner, for what you've told me. Thank the members of the committee. But I . . . I . . . I'm uncomfortable when I'm given presents. I'm sorry, Mr. Bittner, but that's the way I am." He laid the keys down soundlessly on Mr. Bittner's side of the table. "Thank you, I'm sorry."

Mr. Bittner rose. He smiled and put out his hand. "I shall call on you again in November."

Two nights later Roger walked to the address on Bowen Street. The windows on the fourth floor were dark. He compared the ground plan with that of the corresponding apartment on the first floor, where the windows were lighted and open. There would be a room for Sophia; his mother could come and visit him. He looked long at the lake. But he was just nineteen. Those rooms were for a full-grown man. He didn't want to be a full-grown man yet. Mr. Bittner renewed his offer in November and was again refused. Ashleys don't take presents. But it gave him a strange feeling, a hushed feeling: he was being watched by the good and the wise. Persons who did not give their names had unlocked his father's handcuffs and given his father a horse.

He tried to recall the words engraved on the stone . . . about a road . . . about deserts.

The Archbishop of Chicago had written Mr. Frazier a letter of appreciation on "Trent's" account of the inauguration of St. Casimir's Home. He had sent a copy of "A Cap for Florence Nightingale" to his sister, who directed a hospital in Thuringia. When Roger printed a "pudding" about the midnight procession around a church on the eve of its patron's day ("A Thousand Candles, A Thousand Singers") he wrote again, inviting the author to lunch. Roger knew better than to accept invitations from the important and the well-to-do (as he put it to himself, he couldn't stand "face talk"), but the Archbishop had said there would be no other guests. Roger accepted it.

The door was opened by a young priest who stared at him in astonishment. The two had met frequently in the hospital.

"Hello!"

"Hello, Father Betz."

They shook hands.

"Euh . . . Have you come from the hospital about something?"

"No. Archbishop Krüger's asked me to lunch."

"Oh! Come in. . . . Are you sure it's today? He's expecting a man who works on a newspaper."

"That's me."

"A Mr. Frazier."

"Yes."

Roger was accustomed to this.

The Archbishop had been told that "Trent" was young. He expected to meet a man of forty. Roger expected to meet an imposing prelate. Both were astonished. The Archbishop was very old and bent; he spoke with what Roger described to himself as a "cricket's voice," for he had had an operation on his throat. Both had beautiful manners—Roger's particularly toward the old, the Archbishop's particularly toward the young. The latter was delighted, amused, and moved; Roger was delighted and moved.

"You and Father Betz have met before? Did I hear you exchange greetings at the door, Mr. Frazier?"

"Yes, Father. I met him often in the South Side Hospital. I worked as an orderly there."

"Ah, did you?" The Archbishop's conversation was interspersed—when he was pleased—with a continuous murmur of faint interjections: "Well, well," and "Truly?" and "You don't say!"

Muttering gently, his face almost below the level of his shoulders, he led his guest into the dining room. He spoke some words in Latin, crossed himself, and pointed with both hands to Roger's chair.

"It is very kind of you . . . hm, yes . . . from your busy day to give me this opportunity to express my pleasure . . . oh, a great pleasure . . . at your most sympathetic, most understanding accounts of . . . the dear sisters at St. Elizabeth's were delighted . . . were *delighted* . . . oh, yes, oh, yes . . . at your story about the *capping* exercises of young nurses. You see things . . . you *see* things in a way that others do not see them. You not only instruct us, you enlarge us. Yes, I can say that."

Roger laughed. He seldom laughed and only then where there was nothing to laugh about. He laughed now because of a certain sparkling gaiety that appeared and disappeared on his host's face. The thought occurred to him that it must be a great pleasure to have a thing he had never known: a grandfather.

It was a Friday in early Lent. They were served a little cup of soup made from greens, a trout, some potatoes, a glass of wine, and a bread pudding. Another unusual thing took place in Roger. In reply to his host's questions, he replied at length. He talked. He was asked about his early years.

"My real name is Roger Ashley. I was born in Coaltown in the southern part of the state."

He waited. The Archbishop drew in his breath. He gazed into Roger's eyes in silence.

"Did you ever hear the story of my father's trial and escape, Father?"

"I did. . . . Would you wish to refresh my memory about it?"

Roger talked for ten minutes. The Archbishop interrupted him only once. He rang a small handbell. "Mrs. Kegan, be so kind as to give Mr. Frazier that other trout. . . . You young men have a good appetite. I remember that. And do kindly finish those creamed potatoes."

"Thank you, ma'am," said Roger.

"Kindly continue, Mr. Frazier."

When Roger had finished his story, his host looked for a moment at a picture on the wall behind his guest's back. The murmured interjections had long ceased. Finally he said softly: "Those are very unusual events, Mr. Frazier.—And you do not know who your father's rescuers were?"

"No, Father."

"You have no idea who they were?"

"No, Father."

"What is your dear mother doing now?"

"She's running a boardinghouse in Coaltown."

Silence.

"You have received no news of your father . . . of any kind . . . in . . . almost two years?"

"No, Father."

Silence.

"Both your father and mother are Protestants?"

"Yes. Father took us every Sunday to the Methodist church. We went to Sunday school, too."

"Were there . . . ? Forgive me, did you have prayers in the home?"

"No, Father. My father and mother never talked about things like that."

"You plan to be a writer? You will be a writer all your life?"

"No, Father. I only write these things to make money."

"What will your life's work be, Mr. Frazier?"

"I don't see that very clearly yet." Slowly Roger raised his eyes to those of the old man. In a low voice he said, "Father, I think you have something to say about those things that happened in Coaltown."

"Do I? . . . Do I? . . . Mr. Frazier, those events are unusual. Your way of telling them is unusual. Your father's behavior was unusual. Let me say that to my eyes there are some unusual aspects that perhaps you do not see."

Roger waited.

"I think I may be able to make clear what I mean by telling you a story. A story. A number of years ago in one of the southern provinces of China there was a wave of hatred against all foreigners. A considerable number were killed. All the members of one of our missions were taken prisoner—a bishop, four priests, six sisters, and two Chinese servants. All but the servants were German. Each was placed in a small cell in a long low building made of clay and pebbles. They were allowed no communication with one another. From time to time one or another of them would be led out to be tortured. They expected that at any moment they would be beheaded. However, their execution was delayed and after a few years they were released. Can you hear me?"

"Yes, Father."

"The Bishop was placed in the central cell of thirteen. What do you think he did, Mr. Frazier?"

Roger thought a moment. "He . . . he started tapping on the walls. He counted the letters of the alphabet."

The Archbishop was delighted. He rose and went to the wall. He rapidly tapped a group of five, then another group of five, then twice.

Again Roger thought a moment. "L," he said.

"In German we think of I and J as one letter."

"M," said Roger.

The Archbishop returned to his seat.

"This could only be done very late at night and the tapping could only be heard through one wall. So, in the depth of the night messages of love and courage and faith were passed back and forth. Now the jailers had placed the two Chinese servants in the two end cells. They had been blinded by the guards so that they would not attempt to escape from those outer cells. They were Christians and they knew German, but they did not know how to read or write. The Chinese languages cannot be reduced to any pattern of tapping. How did the Bishop communicate with them?"

"I don't see how he could, Father."

"The Chinese are very musical. He directed their neighbors to tap out the rhythms of the hymns they knew and the rhythms of the spoken prayers—of what you call the 'Lord's Prayer.' They tapped back in joyous response. They had been rescued from their abandonment. Now in time several of these prisoners died. The cells were empty and the chain of communication was broken, wasn't it? But the Chinese put some other prisoners into those cells—an English silk merchant and an American businessman and his wife. They knew no German. The Bishop knew some French and some English. He sent messages from cell to cell in those languages and finally received a reply in English. He asked these prisoners kindly to transmit some messages in German to the cells beyond their own, explaining that they were words of religious comfort. Time was allotted to the newcomers. The Americans made it clear that they had no wish to partake of any religious messages, but across eight cells the husband comforted the wife and the wife the husband. How many were now transmitting patterns that were unintelligible to them?"

"All but the Bishop."

"During the early months—because of starvation, loss of consciousness, and other things—the German prisoners had lost count of the calendar. It was from the English merchant that they learned the day and the week and the month. They got back their Sundays and their Easter and their feast days—that other calendar that strengthens our steps and confirms our joy. In time another cell became vacant. It was filled by a Portuguese, a shopkeeper from Macao. He knew only Portuguese, Spanish, and Cantonese. Apparently he was an intelligent and well-disposed man. Throughout the night he tapped out messages from the right wall to the left wall and from the left wall to the right wall. Perhaps he thought his fellow prisoners were planning some escape—some attempt to murder a guard and to set the watchhouse on fire. Do you think so?"

Roger thought. "I think that, if he'd believed that, he would have got tired of it after a few weeks."

"Why did I tell you this story, Mr. Frazier?"

"You were telling me that my father and mother were like the Portuguese man."

"We all are. You are, Mr. Frazier. I hope I am. Life is surrounded by mysteries beyond the comprehension of our limited minds. Your dear parents have seen them; you and I have seen them. We transmit (we hope) fairer things than we can fully grasp."

Silence.

"Is this story true, Father?"

"Oh, yes. I have talked with one of the sisters."

"What was she like, Father?"

"What was she like? . . . Well . . . The greatest joys are those that come to us upon some confirmation of our faith—even in small fragments of faith, faith in St. Casimir's Home, in a friendship, in the survival of a family. Sister Benedikta was joyous."

To himself Roger said, "I hope Papa is joyous."

At the door, taking his leave, Roger asked and received permission to print the story for his readers. It appeared four weeks later as "A Tapping on Your Wall." At the close of it there was a pattern of vertical strokes, looking somewhat like a broken picket fence. Thousands of Chicagoans worked at it. They found: "API ESTR T E AL." The story was reprinted far and wide. It crossed the seas.

The layers of ice about Roger's heart were beginning to melt or—shall we say?—the plates of armor to fall to the ground. His freedom from isolation was accelerated by his encounters with a number of young women.

The Ashley children were widely regarded as "precocious."

Three of them had gained a certain notoriety by twenty-four. The truth is they were slow to mature in mind and body; they met the appointments of growth, however, soundly though late.

Roger's work required his crossing and recrossing Chicago daily—"like a skeeter bug on a pond," said T.G. At banquets, entertainments, athletic events he was coming to recognize and know a large number of young women. He particularly singled out those of other nations, colors, and backgrounds. These were all slightly older than himself, self-supporting, and employers of others. There were not many of this latter category at the beginning of the century. They were pioneers and were viewed askance by respectable women. Roger prolonged his conversations with them. They did most of the talking, but so intent a listener was he that they received the impression of having heard a great deal from him. They were not like other young women; he was not like other young men. It was only several years later that Roger became aware of all that he had learned from Demetria, Ruby, and the rest. Only later, too, did he realize that these associations had released him from a dangerous constraint. Mysterious are the processes of sexual selection. All the young women were vivacious, enterprising, and above all independent; only one was tall, only one was light-haired. He was expunging from his imagination—by urgent necessity—the compelling presence of the woman whom he had loved so passionately and whose failure to respond to him had come close to convincing him that he would never be loved, that he could never love. None of these women resembled his mother.

Demetria was Greek but with Turkish and Lebanese blood, twenty-six, big hipped, joyous, excitable, and ruthless in business. Like Roger, she was making her way in Chicago fast. She had begun the climb at fourteen, sewing flowers on hats for twelve hours a day in a sweatshop—foreman at sixteen, a purchaser of materials and a scout for market outlets at twenty. At twenty-one she had opened a sweatshop of her own. There was an expanding market for ugly house dresses. Every Sunday she visited her baby on a farm near Joliet. Roger first met her at the farm. (Hence Trent's article "Kennels for Babies.")

Madame Anne-Marie Blanc, from the Province of Quebec, rose and gold, short and plump, avowedly twenty-nine, was a caterer for weddings and wakes, for patriotic societies and conventions. At the conclusion of a dinner, Roger—that experienced restaurant man—would go into the kitchen and help pack up, filling the great hampers with crockery and silver. He watched Madame Blanc pay her army of cooks and waiters. He knew a genius for organization when he saw it; she knew he knew it. She asked him to stay and have a cup of coffee; she could take off her shoes and rest. She suffered from insomnia and dreaded returning to her rooms. He ventured to tell her that the food she served was less than appetizing. She burst out laughing. "Yes, yes—but *they* like it. All I want, Mr. Frazier, is money. If you will stop and think for five minutes—only five minutes, Mr. Frazier—about the life of a woman, you will understand that the first thing she wants is money. Girl, wife, or widow. Of course, I mean a sensible woman." She knew that Roger was the "writer man Trent"; she collected his pieces. She suffered from insomnia and from a despairing need to tell her story, but no one in this world listens. At first slowly, then with alarming rapidity, Roger came to learn that there were two Anne-Maries—the trenchant able businesswoman, rose and gold, given to quick short laughter; and a frightened girl barely seventeen, terrified of death and hell, haunted by memories of her childhood, athirst for a humane word, a humane ear, a humane touch. He discovered that she fortified herself in the evening with *crème de menthe* which she drank by the half pint. Before long she hurled herself at him in a storm of fear, dependence, and gratitude. Roger did not know enough to be afraid; besides, we came into this world to learn and to be useful. Lauradel, Negro, was twenty-seven, a singer and part owner of the "Old Dixie Ballroom, a Refined Dance Floor for Ladies and Gentlemen." From time to time Roger visited the establishment toward two in the morning to hear Lauradel sing "Jaybird, don't you sing that song at me" and "I walk on the water and I'm not afraid."

Ruby Morris was Japanese and Hawaiian, twenty-six. She had been adopted by some missionaries on the Islands and brought to this country, where she so profited by the public school system that she soon outgrew her foster parents, teachers, and all those tender sentimental benefactors, who—treating her always as a pretty doll—had hovered over her progress. She renounced Christianity, relearned Japanese, turned Buddhist, and struck out for herself. With help from the small Japanese community in Chicago, she opened a store for curios, kimonos, and gifts. She prospered.

He entered into each relationship with an intensity that approached violence. He pursued several simultaneously to the verge of endangering even the redoubtable store of health that had been allotted to the Ashleys. This phase of dissipation, however, came to an end almost as abruptly as it began, and without rancor. All was conducted under the sign of independence. He had made no promises and exerted no claims. Demetria and Ruby wanted to do his laundry for him; Anne-Marie and Lauradel wanted to buy him shirts and shoes; Ruby and Anne-Marie offered him a room in which to live; but he avoided any shadow of dependency.

These young women divined that something was amiss, that he was pursuing some end beyond sensuality and beyond vanity. They knew also that he was honest and that in some obscure way he was "in trouble." Without knowing it he called upon their understanding; without knowing it he afforded them an opportunity to serve. And he, in turn, brought them an exceptional gift—his ardor held a large measure of wonder and curiosity and discovery. They were accustomed to being desired; it was something new to be listened to.

Lauradel:

"I used to see you come in and sit in that dark corner. You weren't hiding from me, Junior. I knew you were listening. And you'd come up afterwards and say something gentlemanly and put twenty cents in the saucer. I don't forget anything. And then you put that piece in the paper about our 'Ballroom' and about my singing and the white people started coming to the place and we had to move in eight more tables.—Have you gone off to sleep again, big ears?"

"No, I hear everything you're saying, Lauradel."

"Go to sleep, if you want . . . Men! . . . But that thing you put in the paper about me being such a good singer that I didn't have to sing bad taste—I was mad! I wasn't sure I knew what that meant. I asked people—some said it meant vulgar and common and dirty! Oh, I was mad. You and your cat's-mess taste. The next night you came in, I wanted to go over to your table and tell you to GO HOME and take your taste with you. We didn't want you and your pweetsy-tweetsy taste here. You! . . . You! . . ."

"Stop hitting me, Lauradel!"

"Because there are only two things I like to sing about: my religion and making love. And I don't have to ask permission out of you, Mr. Tasty. I'm sorry I hit you, newspaperboy. I didn't break any of your bones. Aren't you ashamed to be lying there looking like a half-peeled radish?—Oh, you people that live in the middle of the United States and don't know anything about the ocean! Do you know where I came from?"

"Yes."

"Well, I'll tell you. I came from the islands off the State of Georgia where only the boiled shrimps are that color of you. The sun gets hot in Chicago, too, but it isn't real sun, not real. It hasn't got any *salt* in it. You're a poor little fresh-water nothing."

"I can't breathe, Lauradel. . . ."

"Taste!—Think about this for a minute. *If nobody made love for a hundred days!* Are you thinking abut that—just to please your big Lauradel? People would be creeping around the streets as though their spines had turned to jello. Even the children would stop jumping rope. You'd go in a store and ask for a pair of shoes and the man would say, 'Ma'am, shoes? Oh yes, shoes, let me see, have we any shoes?' Just imagine what people's eyes would be like—like holes you burned in wallpaper. The birds would fall out of trees; their wings wouldn't have any zupp in them. The trees would sag like old widows with female trouble. And God would get up. He'd look down. He'd say, WHAT'S GOING ON AROUND HERE? THIS HAS GOT TO STOP! I DON'T WANT ANY MORE OF MR. TRENT'S CAT'S-MESS TASTE AROUND HERE."

Roger slid out of bed and, kneeling, put his arms around her. She pushed him away, roaring with laughter, royal.

"GET LOVING, YOU SONS-OF-BITCHES, OR THE WORLD WILL TURN COLD. That's what I sing about! Now do you understand?"

"Lauradel, you're as big as a house!"

"Well, don't you start getting me mixed up in my head about what's vulgar and what's not vulgar, because *you don't know and I know.*"

Still laughing, she bent his head to the floor with her foot. "Get away from me, you little paperboy! I don't know why I go around with such a pink wart."

"You can hit me all you want to, Lauradel."

"Get back into bed and stop playing the fool on my carpet. You'll get splinters in your foot.—I told you about all the bad times I've been through, didn't I?"

"Yes, you did."

"When a person's been through ALL THAT and comes out alive—that person knows what's what."

"Tell me some more about your grandfather Demus."

"Well, first: I've got another old bone to pick with you."

"What else have I done wrong, Lauradel?"

"Mr. Trent—I mean Mr. Frazier—you hurt my feelings so bad that I don't think I'll ever get over it. And you know how you did it!" Roger was silent. "You sent back that overcoat I sent you. That wasn't honorable or decent."

"Lauradel!"

"You keep saying 'Lauradel,' but you don't love me."

"Lauradel, that's the way I am."

"When people love each other money doesn't matter. Love kills money. I love to give, Mr. Trent. I wish I had a million dollars. I'd give you a . . . shoelace. You sent back the coat I gave you. You dress bad. You don't dress any better than an old crow."

"Don't cry, Lauradel. Don't cry."

"You gave me a present: a real genuine invitation to Abraham Lincoln's funeral."

"I didn't buy that. A lady gave it to me. An old lady gave it to me because of a piece I wrote in the paper."

"But you gave it to me—in your heart you gave it to me."

"Don't cry, Lauradel. We all have to be as we're made."

"Well . . ."

"Lauradel, I have to get some sleep. I have to be at City Hall early tomorrow. Sing me to sleep, will you?"

"What'll I sing you, boy? Shall I sing you 'Sometimes I feel like a motherless child'?"

"No, not that one."

"I'll sing you one I never sang you before. It's in the language my people talked on Sea Island, Georgia. It's about why God made shells."

And Ruby:

"What are you whispering to yourself about, Ruby?"

"Go to sleep, Trent. I'm reciting the Lotus Scripture."

"I don't want to go to sleep. I want to hold your hand and hear you talk."

"Sh . . . sh . . . !"

"What is that new sign they're putting over the door downstairs, Ruby?"

"I'm changing my name and the name of the store. I've wanted to do it for two years, but I had to wait until the business was going well. Tomorrow's an important day for me, Trent. Please, will you, please, never call me Ruby again. My name is IZUMI."

He kissed the tips of her fingers and said, "Izumi, Izumi."

Weightlessly, trailing her soft robe, she left the bed and knelt on the floor. She lowered her forehead, as though acknowledging a courtesy. "You are the first person to call me by my name."

"What does the name mean, Izumi?"

"Trent, have you heard that some people believe that men and women are reborn many times?"

"As many times as there are sands in the Ganges River."

"Trent!"

"And that we either go up a great staircase to the threshold of happiness or that we sink down and drag others down with us."

"Trent!"

"We become almost-Buddhas. I forget what we are called then."

She put two fingers on his lips. "The Lady Izumi was a poet. Because her poetry was beautiful and because she loved the Lotus Scripture she became a Bodhisattva."

"Do you believe that, Izumi—that people are born again and again?"

Again she placed her finger on his mouth. "We call the world the Burning House."

"What?"

"We are born again and again in the hope that someday, someday, we shall escape from this burning house."

"You are very high up on the ladder, Izumi."

She drew herself up straight as though she were offended. Then she laid her head down upon the pillow and turned away.

"How can you tell whether a person is high up or low down? Is it when a person is good?"

"Do not use the word 'good.' Say 'free.' I am very low down on the ladder, Trent."

"*You?*"

"Yes, I have a great many weights that hold me down."

"No!—Name just one, Izumi."

She placed the knuckles of her left hand between her breasts. "*Here!* I have a great ulcer, *here*."

"Ruby! Ruby! Izumi!"

"Weights. Weights. Of anger. Of spite. I cannot forgive the people who tried to be kind to me. They hung their weights on me. Why should I be angry at them? They were ignorant. They were *Christians*! Oh, *their* burning house! To please them I was a detestable, unnatural, false little girl. They robbed me of my childhood and girlhood. See how angry I am! Go to sleep, Trent. I must say the Lotus Scripture."

"Name one more weight, Izumi."

Again she turned her head away on the pillow. She whispered, "You."

"No!" He seized her hand. "Say no."

She raised herself on her elbow and said, "You are very high on that stairway, Trent."

"I! You don't know what you're saying!"

"You are not attached to things. You do not want fame or riches. You do not want to crush people with your power. You do not envy others. You are not proud. You have no hates. You are freeing yourself from everything that is bad in your Karma. When I first knew you I thought that maybe you were a Bodhisattva. But when I knew you a little better I could see that there was a little violence in you, left over, a little violence in your Karma."

"What is Karma, Izumi?"

"It is the burden of fate that we have created for ourselves during all our thousands of past lives."

He went around to her side of the bed and knelt before her face. "I am a weight in your life. I am not helping you to climb the great ladder."

"Trent, do not be impatient. Impatience never freed a man from the burning house. I think you are helping me to forgive those people who were so kind to me. Will you go to sleep now?"

"Yes."

She returned to whispering her sacred text.

"Translate to me the words that you were saying just then, Izumi."

"I had come to the place where it tells of the plants that are reborn."

"Plants go to Heaven, too??!"

"Trent! Trent! Every living thing is a part of the nature of the One. You know that. That's why you write about animals so well. And about the planting of oak trees. We are all in the One."

The turbulence of these associations subsided. When he came to have more money in his pocket he invited one or the other out to dinner. How they talked to him and his large ears! He laughed oftener—with them and at them and at himself.

Roger's interest in the opera had abated. Reading—his new discovery—was now feeding his hunger for the noble and the heroic. He occasionally returned to the opera house, however, when his favorites were performed.

There was a late spring season in 1905. At the close of a performance Roger stood near the main entrance watching the audience disperse. His attention was attracted by a very beautiful young woman who was also lingering by a marble column. He had noticed her on a number of occasions, always seated in a box with a handsome couple of older years; he assumed she was their daughter. On this evening the mother was absent. The father had been detained in conversation by friends. The young woman had just replaced an enormous hat on her head. She was elegant, tightly laced, conspicuous, accustomed to the world's gaze and unabashed by her temporary isolation. She had acquired the art of looking through the admiring faces that turned toward her. With one gloved hand she meditatively smoothed the veil drawn over her chin, with the other she played with a feather boa thrown over her shoulders. This was not the kind of woman that Roger found attractive. What had long interested him in her, however, was her air of being upborne on some tide of supreme assurance.

Suddenly he realized that this was his sister Lily.

Her companion rejoined her and they left the theatre, Roger following. Apparently they had only a short distance to go. They talked in Italian. He heard his sister's laughter—of a kind he had not heard from her before; it ranged over an octave and a half; it echoed in the streets. They came to a grey sandstone house that bore a brass plate: "The Josepha Carrington Jones Club for Young Ladies." Lily, latch key in hand, turned and thanked her escort warmly. He continued down the street, humming. As she was unlocking the door Roger spoke her name softly.

"I beg your pardon?"

"Lily, I'm Roger."

She flew down the steps on the wings of her great cloak and threw her arms around him. "Roger, Roger! Darling Roger!— *Oh!* How tall you are! *Oh*, how you look like Papa!—I want to show you to Maestro Lauri, my singing teacher. He just left me here at the door."

How long had he been in Chicago? What did he do? Oh, how he looked like Papa—dear wonderful Papa!

"Can we go somewhere for a cup of coffee? No *man* is allowed in this building after six. Wait for me here until I change my clothes. . . . I have to kiss you again. Roger, what does it all *mean*—what happened to us?" She started up the stairs then turned back. "Roger, I have a little boy—he's *wonderful, wonderful*. Roger, how did Mama feel about my running away? I had to do it, Roger. I had to get away from Coaltown. I'm never going back—never, never. I send Mama money every month."

"I know you do."

"Soon I'll be able to send her *lots*."

Twenty minutes later they were seated in a German restaurant. Lily resembled her mother and Constance; Roger resembled his father and Sophia. For a time what they saw was more engrossing than what they said. The cascades of laughter.

"I have the most beautiful baby in the world and I'm not even married." Laughter. She raised her hand and showed him the gold band. "I bought it in a pawnshop! I'm Mrs. Helena Temple. The boy's name is John Temple. He's living with an Italian family that loves him to death. I don't know when he'll learn to speak English."

It was not new to Roger that those who ask no questions receive the fullest answers.

"I passed his father on the street yesterday. He hates me." Laughter. "He hates me because he struck me."

"What?"

"Twice, in fact. He struck me because I laughed at him. Men hate to be laughed at. He kept trying to teach me such stupid music. He wanted me to go on the vaudeville stage with him. He wanted me to practice kicking a top hat off his head. Imagine!" (Laughter.) "But—in his way—he's a perfectly nice man! I'll always be grateful to him for taking me to Maestro Lauri. I sang two of those songs I used to sing in Coaltown and the Maestro said that I was the pupil he'd spent his life hunting for. Every month I write him a receipt for the lessons I've had and when I earn enough I'll start paying him back. I sing at funerals and weddings and I sing in the Episcopal church on Sunday mornings, and in a Presbyterian church in the evenings. The funeral parlors send for me five and six times a week—Schubert's 'Ave Maria.' Fifteen dollars—take it or leave it! I won't sing 'I know a garden where roses sleep.' I'm a tartar, Roger! Weddings—Handel's 'Where'er you walk'—fifteen dollars. I won't sing *'Oh, promise me.'* Lots of people are furious at me, but I get jobs.—Roger, what do you do?"

"I'll tell you later. How did it come to an end with the father of your boy?"

"Well, he struck me a second time. There we were in that hot hotel room and he'd been trying to teach me a song and dance called 'The Way We Do the Cancan in Kentucky.' Imagine! I said I wouldn't do it *one more moment* and I laughed at him. He struck me hard. And he cried. He really loved me in a way. When he left the room I stole his amethyst ring and went to that club for working girls. For a while I washed dishes and helped cook. I showed them I knew everything about *board-inghouses*! They wanted to make me housekeeper. Then I had my wonderful baby in a Catholic hospital. I loved everything about it. I sang to the other girls. I sang even when I was having the baby. The doctor and sisters were laughing. Giovannino was born to laughter and my screeches and Mozart's 'Alleluia.' He was a seven-months baby, but he's as strong as I am. I'm going to have a hundred boys and girls—all beautiful and strong like Gianni."

Roger could not take his eyes from his sister's face. His mother, who had so beautiful a smile, seldom—never—laughed.

"But that's enough about me! Tell me, what work do you do?"

"I write for newspapers."

"Oh, do that! Do that! Someday you'll be as good as 'Trent.' Do you ever read 'Trent's' pieces?"

"Yes."

"I save them. I sent some to Mama. The Maestro thinks they're very good and Signora Lauri has collected every one of them."

"Lily, I'm Trent."

"You're 'Trent'! You're 'Trent'! *Oh, Roger, how proud Papa would be!*"

The Maestro had invited a group of friends to a musicale in his studio on the following night. He was introducing three of his pupils, including Lily. Roger had always known that the dreamy absent-spirited Lily could sing beautifully. What astonished him now was the noble utterance. The breadth. She set the windowpanes rattling with passionate declarations of joy and grief. He thought: *"How proud Mama will be!"*

Roger became a favorite in the Maestro's home. Signora Lauri enrolled him among her sons—the three living and the two dead. His chair was beside hers at the mighty nine-course Milanese dinners—the family's and the guests' anniversaries, the birthdays of Garibaldi and Verdi and Manzoni.

The Maestro was in his late sixties. Long ago he had been marooned in New York through the bankruptcy of an opera troupe which he had served as assistant conductor, chorus master, and occasional baritone. From there he was invited to Chicago to teach singing in a conservatory that had also failed.

He had stayed on and prospered. Every five years the entire family returned to Milan to visit their relatives. He was tall, thin, and as erect as a drill master. He dressed with the greatest care. He wore a *toupet*; his superb mustaches were dyed and perfumed. His expression was that of a lion tamer whose beasts were constantly in revolt; lightning flickered in his eyes. Signora Lauri's life was not an easy one. She bore the brunt of his resentment against all that went wrong in existence. She was his unsatisfactory pupils, his dyspepsia; she brought the three-day snow and drove the thermometer to one hundred and four. Yet he was boundlessly dependent on her. If she were to die, he would dwindle to a peppery, posturing old man— old and emptied. Occasionally his impotent rage against circumstance burst forth. He heaped sarcasms upon her; he denounced her for having ruined his life, she and her wagon- load of disrespectful children. She held her chin high; the glance from her eyes would wither a grapevine. The quarrels were necessary and operatic; the reconciliations were tear- drenched and very grand. Signora Lauri understood it all. That was marriage. She had the ring and a home and she had borne him ten children. Her greatest trials were his infidelities and her enormous size. She once showed her son Roger the photo- graph of a painting by a modern master. The original hung in a gallery in Rome, she said. It showed a lovely girl of sixteen, standing by a parapet over Lake Como. Roger looked up at her inquiringly; she reddened and nodded slightly. *"La vita, la vita."*

The maestro spoke a number of languages with a singing teacher's precision and with the relish of one for whom lan- guages are themselves artistic creations. It became his custom to lead Roger into his studio after dinner. He was in the mood for conversation. Lily and his daughters begged to join them, but were sternly told that the time had come for "men's talk."

Roger had found another Saturn.

What is art?

Roger had a very low opinion of art. Chicago was full of it. The homes of the rich (weddings and suicides) and the choicer brothels (mayhem) that he had penetrated as a reporter abounded in art—bronze girls holding up lamps, paintings of ladies getting ready to take a bath. There were a lot of cows in art and monks holding wine glasses up to the light. Catholic churches were full of art. *Most* art, though, was about pretty girls.

"Mr. Frazier, works of art are the only satisfactory products of civilization. History, in itself, has nothing to show. History is the record of man's repeated failures to extricate himself from his incorrigible nature. Those who see *progress* in it are as deluded as those who see a gradual degeneration. A few steps forward, a few steps back. Human nature is like the ocean, unchanging, unchangeable. Today's calm, tomorrow's tempest —but it's the same ocean. Man is as he is, as he was, as he always will be. But what are works of art?

"Let me tell you a story:

"My family has lived for centuries in Monza, a town near Milan. One day my mother decided to take us children into the city to see the paintings in the great Brera Gallery. Wherever my mother went she was accompanied by an old family servant whom we children called Aunt Nanina. Zia Nanina had never been in a picture gallery and would never have thought of entering one. Such places were for rich people, people who could read and write, who talked all the time about *l'arte*. But lo! Great heavens, suddenly, at the Brera, amid all those Madonnas and Holy Families, Zia Nanina was completely at home. She was as busy as she could be, crossing herself and bobbing up and down and saying her prayers. Did Zia Nanina think those paintings were *beautiful*? Oh, yes—but we Italians use the word *bello* four hundred times a day. For her those pictures were filled with something far more important than beauty. They were filled with *power*."

"How do you mean, Maestro?"

"There on the wall was the Virgin. One day our family—her family—was crossing Lake Como in a small boat. A terrible storm arose. We would surely drown. Who prayed like the dynamo of a great ocean liner? Zia Nanina. And the Holy Mother parted the clouds and pulled our boat safely to shore with Her own sacred hands. What power! There on the wall was a Saint Joseph. One day when I was seven a fishbone stuck in my throat. I was strangling. I turned purple. But Saint Joseph pulled that fishbone out. Zia Nanina was aware of the power of those exalted persons every day of her life—as were my mother and uncle, as are my wife and daughters to this day.

"I don't believe in God. I believe that those celebrated men and women—Mary of Nazareth and her family—are now each a pinch of dust, like all the billions of men and women who have died. But the representations of such beings are man's greatest achievement.

"You have been in this room before. Look about you. What do you see?"

"Your collection, Maestro. Statues and paintings . . ."

"I don't believe in God, but I love the gods. Each of these figures and paintings was made to represent that power, more than that: to transmit that power. Every work in this room has been at one time an object of fear or love or of urgent appeal—in most cases of all three emotions at once. Nothing here was intended for mere ornament or decoration. This is from Mexico. . . . These are the Great Twins. They have lain in the salt water about three thousand years, shipwrecked. Sailors made their last prayers to them. . . . This is an African mask worn in dances for victory or rain. . . . Here is an engraved gem. Take it over to the light. It shows Mercury—Hermes Psychopompos—leading the soul of a dead woman to the fields of the blest. Beauty?"

"Yes."

"Power?"

Roger looked at it for a time and said, "Yes."

"And this . . . a Khmer head from Angkor Wat—the half-closed eyes, the smile that never tires."

"That's Buddha," said Roger abruptly.

"Who can count the prayers that have ascended to gods who do not exist? Mankind has himself created sources of help where there is no help and sources of consolation where there is no consolation. Yet such works as these are the only satisfying products of culture.

> "Save sacred art
> And sacred song,
> Nothing endures
> For long."

There was a knock at the door. The Maestro was called to the telephone. Roger turned his back on the objects and went to the window—the lights of the city. He said to himself, "He's missed something. He's forgotten something. I'll find it. I must find it."

On Sundays Roger called for his sister at the church where she had been singing. They had dinner together at the Alt-Heidelberg restaurant and spent the rest of the afternoon in the country with little Giovannino, who, by July at nine months, was on the threshold of walking and of talking Italian. He lived in a household of adoring women and took to his uncle with clamorous delight. He seemed to have the idea that only a man could teach a man to walk. He crawled ten miles a day and was becoming thoroughly impatient with it.

Sunday dinners at the Alt-Heidelberg (June, 1905):

"My clothes? I'm a pirate. There's a girl at the club who sells them at Towne and Carruther's. I go into her department and try on a lot of dresses. She pretends she doesn't know me and says, 'Yes, madam' or 'No, madam.' And I steal the ideas and we make them at home. The materials are awfully expensive, but we know where to get mill ends. We have lots of fun. We help all the girls in the club dress and they help us. Roger, a girl alone has to be awfully bright just to live." (Roger wrote a "pudding" called "Take a Letter, Miss Spencer.")

"Roger, sometimes I think I'll go crazy because I don't know anything. I want to learn every language in the world. I want to know how women thought a thousand years ago—and what electricity is and how the telephone works—and about money and banks. I don't understand why Papa never thought about better schools for us. All sorts of people ask me to tea and dinner, but I tell them I have a sore throat. I stay home and read. Even when we're making dresses one of the girls reads aloud to us. Last night there were eight of us working until *midnight*. We were all crowded together in my tiny room and we took turns reading an English lady's *Letters from Turkey*. What do you read?"

Another Sunday (July):

"Oh, yes, I'll sing opera, but I won't really like it. Most of the heroines in opera are such geese. I'm really a concert singer and an oratorio singer. But I'll sing opera to make money."

"You could make enough money singing what you want to. Why should you make more?"

Lily looked up at him in surprise. "Why, for my children."

"Your husband would support your children, wouldn't he?"

"Roger! Roger! Don't talk to me about husbands! I'm going to have a dozen children and I'm going to love every one of their fathers, but I'm never going to be *married* to anyone. Marriage is a worn-out old custom like owning slaves or adoring royal families. I believe that there won't be any marriages in a hundred years. Besides, I pity the man who'd be married to me. I love my singing and my babies and my learning things and my plans. . . . I now have a Polish towhead. I'm going to have two Americans—twins. And a French girl. And a Spanish boy . . . and adopt so many!"

"Is that what you mean by your plans?"

She paused and looked at him gravely. She carried with her a great square velvet handbag to hold her music. She leaned over and drew from it a sheaf of what appeared to be architectural drawings. She placed several before him in silence.

"What are those?" she asked softly.

He studied them. "A hospital? Schools?"

She drew out a scrapbook. On the cover was pasted the head of the Christ child from the "Sistine Madonna." The first pages were given over to portraits of Friedrich Froebel, and Jean-Frédéric Oberlin. These were followed by cuttings from magazines and books—more ground plans and details of construction from hospitals, orphanages, hotels, villas, playgrounds. She laughed at his inquiring face. The guests in the restaurant laughed.

"That's my city of children. I'm going to go all over the world singing those silly Isoldes and Normas to make money for it." Laughter. "Isolde has a husband and a lover and all she can think about is love, but there's no word about children. Norma has some children and she prowls about with a dagger to kill them—just to spite their father. I think my city is going to be in Switzerland by a lake with mountains all around us. And I'm going to plant a grove of oak trees, like Papa's. I'm going to choose all the teachers myself.—Won't it be wonderful? Can't you hear the children from here? Now can you see why I'm happy all the time?"

"Because of your plans."

At times these conversations became strained. Lily felt driven to review their childhood, to probe into "all that" at "The Elms." Her judgments were without indulgence. Roger was not ready.

"Lily, I don't want to talk about those things."

"All right, I won't, but I've got to understand them. I don't know what you men are like, but we girls don't begin to live until we're pretty clear in our heads about our fathers and mothers."

"Please change the subject, Lily."

Her eyes rested on him thoughtfully. To herself she said, "That's Mama's fault."

Another Sunday (August):

Roger asked that they meet for dinner on the following week after her evening service instead of at midday.

"Roger, I'm not free after evening service. After it's over I go away with a friend of mine on his boat. Because of my work I can't go away on the weekend. We come back on Tuesday morning. On Monday he simply doesn't show up at his office. He's a good friend and a perfectly nice man and he teaches me things. He has a famous collection of paintings and sculpture and every Sunday night he brings some samples to the boat and lots of heavy books."

"Not the Maestro!"

"No, Roger! No! No, indeed! Someone younger. And healthier. And American. And very rich."

Other Sundays (September):

"Roger, I'm going to have to go to New York."

"To live?"

"Yes, I'll have to find another singing teacher." Laughter. "You see, I'm going to have another baby—twins, I think. I can't explain it to the club or to my congregations, so I'd better leave."

Roger waited.

"He'll be pretty glad to get rid of me, I think. Men get tired of me—not because I'm horrid, but because they can't understand me. I make them uncomfortable. I'm not impressed by the things that most men boast about. He's all confused—he's *mortified*—because I won't accept even a little pearl pin from him. For a year and a half I'll let him give me some money for the babies,—after all, the babies will be *partly* his." Laughter. "Besides, he's taught me almost everything he knows.—Roger listen: Having babies is very good for the voice. These days I'm singing better than I've ever sung in my life. I frighten myself."

"Lily, I have an idea. Papa's in Alaska or South America or Australia. He can't write to Coaltown; he can't write to us because he doesn't know where we are. You're going to get to be well-known. Maybe I will. Let's take our real names again."

"YES!"

"And to make it double sure, let's take our crazy middle names: the famous singer Scolastica Ashley, the rising newspaper man Berwyn Ashley."

"You're a genius! You're a genius!" She kissed him. She walked about the table twice. "I've always hated all that hugger-mugger about invented names. I'm Scolastica Ashley, the convict's daughter, and if they want to throw me out of their churches, let them do it. Tomorrow! Tomorrow! I'll begin tomorrow.—A letter from Papa, soon!"

"I think you should wait until after your concert. At your first concert you wouldn't want a lot of people gawking at you for *that*. Let's do it the day after your concert."

Mrs. Temple's concert was repeated ten days later by Miss Scolastica Ashley, who was also heard in Milwaukee, Madison, and Galena. Trent's readers were informed that thereafter his articles would appear over his true name. The startling announcement came too late to change the title page of Berwyn Ashley's book *Trent's Chicago*. Lily invited her mother to Chicago to attend the concert. She received an affectionate letter in return, wishing her great success. Her mother regretted that it was impossible for her to leave the boardinghouse at that time.

"Roger, can I talk about Coaltown?"
"Yes."

"Papa didn't shoot Mr. Lansing. He didn't even shoot him by accident. Someone else did. Who and how I don't know, but I'm certain of it. I went to the Public Library and read the newspapers about it—thousands and thousands of words. I was looking for an *idea*, but I couldn't find a thing. But *you* can. Someday you can clear that up. There was one thing I noticed in those papers. They were full of what a fine man Mr. Lansing was—he ran the mine, he was head of all the clubs and lodges. You know that's not true. He was a dreadful boastful creature. He was cheap, and I'll bet he was lazy. We all pretended not to see it because we liked Mrs. Lansing so much. Roger, he must have had enemies. Maybe he was hard to the miners, maybe he was cruel to them."

Roger was following her gravely. He said slowly, "Porky knew everything that went on in town. He would have told me."

"Well, now I'm going to tell you something that I've told to only one person—Miss Doubkov."

She told him about the anonymous letters. "It's all nasty nonsense. Papa didn't go to Fort Barry oftener than once a year and he came back on the afternoon train. But I now think that many people in town really believed all that. It helps explain why so few people stood by Papa and why so few people came to see Mama. I think Mrs. Lansing must have got some of those letters, too—they were so full of hatred toward her.—Who was the murderer?"

"And who were the rescuers?"

The first Sunday in November:

"Lily, you can say anything you want about the old days in Coaltown."

"I don't want to, if it makes you uncomfortable."

"I'll listen. I don't have to agree with you, but I'll listen. Shoot!—What was that you said—with a sneer—about Mama's adoring Papa? It's an idiotic expression."

"It is. I didn't say it with a sneer. It's too serious. Roger, I'm trying to get educated. I don't think a person is free to learn anything until he's begun to understand himself. And, as I said to you before, that includes understanding your father and mother. Mama worshiped Papa and as a result she was not a noticing person. Mama has many fine qualities, but Mama's a very strange woman."

"So are you!"

Lily laughed the full octave and a half. "Yes, everybody at this table is strange."

"Go on with what you were saying."

"One day, months ago, the Maestro made his youngest daughter—Adriana—leave the table. She'd merely said that she *adored* her new shoes; she thought they were *divine*. He said those were religious words and that they had nothing to do with shoes. He turned to me and said that they had nothing to do with human beings either. He warned me to beware of husbands and wives who adored one another. Such persons haven't grown up, he said. No human being is adorable. The early Hebrews were quite right to condemn idolatry. Women who adore their husbands throw a thousand little ropes around them. They rob them of their freedom. They lull them to sleep. It's wonderful to *own a god*, to put him in your pocket. That day my education took a little jump forward."

She glanced at her brother's face. It was hard and set. His eyes were angry and sullen, but he remained silent.

"Do you realize that Mama had no friends? She didn't dislike Mrs. Lansing. She didn't dislike Mrs. Gillies or Miss Doubkov. She spent hundreds—maybe thousands—of hours with them. She merely didn't care whether they existed or not. Mama cared for only one person in the world. She adored Papa.— One day I told the Maestro that I thought that most of the heroines in opera were silly geese. He said 'Yes, of course. Opera is about greedy possessive passion. The girls make one mistake after another. They're little whirlpools of destruction. First they bring death down on the baritones and basses—their fathers, guardians, or brothers; then they bring it down on the tenors. Then at half past eleven they go mad, or stab themselves, or jump into a fire, or get strangled. Or they just expire. Self-centered possessive love. The women in the audience cry a little, but on the way home they're already planning tomorrow's dinner!' Papa loved Mama, but he didn't adore her. Papa was happy, but he missed something. After you left and Mama opened the boardinghouse—"

"Sophie opened the boardinghouse!"

"Yes, Sophie did. I should have, but I was too stupid. Well, Sophie hired Mrs. Swenson to come back and help with the housework. I used to sit for hours in the kitchen, paring potatoes and stringing beans and things like that. She'd talk. I learned some things about Papa. In the early years before that *shooting*—do you remember what time we had supper at "The Elms"? We had it the latest of anybody in town—at six-thirty. We all thought that Papa had to finish up things at the mine. No, Papa got through at the mine at five and then he drove all over with that old horse. He called on the miners' families; then coming down the hill he visited homes. He'd talk. He'd repair things. He'd fix pipes and flues. He'd listen to people's troubles. He'd lend money. He'd come driving into the barn at six-thirty exactly. But this is the point: he never told Mama about all these friends. Why? There was nothing secretive about Papa. He simply didn't tell her because she wouldn't be interested. She was not a noticing woman and she was not a . . . a sympathizing woman."

Roger made no answer. He paid the bill. They got on the streetcar for the long drive south and east. The cars were crowded. Czech and Hungarian and Polish families going to visit their relatives beside the steel mills; Italian families going to visit their relatives in the marketgarden area around Codington. Families going for their last autumn Sunday at the Indiana dunes. Roger stood on the platform, a great weight about his heart. A mile of sandstone houses, homes. Miles of wooden houses, homes. Then farmhouses—apple trees in the yards, swings for the children—homes, families. They descended from the car in an Italian village. There remained half a mile to walk. They turned at the corner between a Farmacía Garibaldi and a Campo Sportivo Vittorio Emanuele. Roger's depression had lifted. He gazed about him with a faint smile on his face. Good or bad, he was on the side of homes. He was filled with the resolve to have one of his own,—damned soon, too.

On this occasion Gianni had little attention to spare for his visitors. He was engrossed. He had fairly well mastered walking and had taken up building. Being an Ashley he wanted no assistance. His mother and uncle sat in the grape arbor with glasses of wine before them, silent under the gift of the Indian summer, gazing across the long brown plain. The crops had been garnered. The soil had been turned. The day had begun with frost; now in the somnolent heat a scarcely perceptible steam arose from the earth—a promise of renewal as compelling as those in the early days of April. Presently Gianni climbed on his mother's lap and fell asleep.

Roger began slowly:

"Lily, the important thing is to be just. Even on the everyday level Mama was a remarkable mother of a family. Papa had very little money. We never knew we were poor. She worked all day, every day of her life. She was never short-tempered. She was never unfair. Even if it's true that she felt no particular friendship for those ladies, she never said a malicious thing about them. She read us the best books; she played us the best music. But that's only the smaller part of it. Not long ago the Maestro was talking to me after dinner in his studio. He said something like this: 'I'm interested in your parents—yours and Lily's—and in your ancestors. I'm interested in your childhood. I've taught more than a hundred young American men and women with fine voices. They've sung well. Some of them are now famous. But they seldom really understand what they're singing. Your sister comes to me. I teach her things about breathing and placement and so on, but in matters of style and feeling and taste I have only to say a few words to her. Somewhere else she learned how to sing nobly. She can express grief without being sentimental. She can be angry without being coarse.' He went on like that—oh, yes: he said, 'She can be coquettish without being vulgar.' He wondered where you got it. There was nothing small about Mama. Think of her walking every day to that trial. Think of her on that morning when the police came stamping into the front hall asking who rescued Papa. Mama's big. You owe her a debt as big as the Rocky Mountains. You got a lot of fine things from Papa, too, but we'll talk about them another time. . . .

"We've all got to be as we were made—as the dice fall out of the cup. We don't know what Mama's girlhood was like. I think that Papa rescued her from some difficult situation. I think what you call her 'adoration' is some kind of unending gratitude, maybe."

"*Mammi!*"

"Sì, caro. Che vuoi?"

"Mammi, cantà!"

"Sì, tesoro."

Lily sang softly the melody to which he was born. He fell asleep again.

Roger went on: "In one way, Papa was like an animal. Can you see that?"

"Oh, yes."

"Animals don't know they're going to die. You didn't see him in court every day. How many times did you call on him in the jail?"

"Three times."

"It wasn't merely being brave—for Mama and us. It was just being calm and simple about death—about life and death."

"I try to sing it."

"Look! Look at the ducks going south!"

"Hundreds of them." Pause. "Thousands!"

"A long time ago I heard Dr. Gillies make a speech, a kind of speech. It was in the Illinois Tavern on New Year's Eve of 1899. He said that evolution was going on and on. After a while— maybe millions of years—a new kind of human being will be evolved. All we see now is just a stage that humanity's going through—possession and fear and cruelty. People will outgrow it, he said."

"Do you think that's true?"

He looked out over the fields. Beautiful is the earth. He mumbled something. He put out his hand and enclosed Gianni's dusty foot.

"I didn't hear you, Roger."

"Oh, one would have to live ten thousand years to notice any change. One must feel it inside—that is, believe it."

Gianni awoke and wanted to go to his uncle. Roger hurled him up to the leafy roof of the arbor; he swung him between his legs; he hung him up by his heels. Gianni screamed between terror and ecstasy. Women don't play such games. He returned, chastened, to his mother's lap. He wasn't sure—until next time —whether he loved his Uncle Roshi or not.

Roger, still standing, continued to gaze at the fields. "I've been reading. . . . Fifty years ago in Bengal a hundred thousand peasants made a bare subsistence from weaving cotton. Soon the British government forbade them to do any weaving; Manchester was getting its cotton from America. So the Indians went down on all fours and groped for roots and bulbs to eat. Slow starvation, malformation, and death. The Civil War breaks out. No cotton for Manchester. Terrible times in Manchester—slow starvation, malformation, and death. After the war the routes are open again, but improvements in mechanical processes have eliminated twenty workers for every one that's kept on. The Negroes get down on all fours and grope for roots and bulbs. Slow starvation, malnutrition, and death. . . . The world's getting smaller. Too many people. Nobody can manage it."

"Mammi, cantà!"

Lily looked at him woefully. "What's the answer, Roger? Can't I have my ten children?"

He returned to his bench. His eyes met hers without a smile. He said sadly: "I'll let all Ashleys live."

Lily put her son on the ground. She knelt at Roger's feet and clasped her hands on his knees. "Think it through for us, Roger! Find answers to all this for us. I beg you—in Papa's name—in Gianni's name—"

A strange thing happened. Roger—Roger Ashley!—burst into tears. He arose and walked up and down the road.

"Mammi, cantà!"

Lily sang. Many times she sang the emotion that filled her on that afternoon—in Milan, in Rio, in Barcelona . . . in Manchester.

Roger returned to her, smiling. "I'm going to Coaltown for Christmas," he said.

Roger left Chicago at noon on the twenty-third of December. He felt no elation, he even fancied he was ill. He had had little rest and no vacation in two and a half years. He was encumbered with luggage, which included his and Lily's Christmas presents. He put them on the racks above him and settled down in a seat at the back of the car. He was never without a book. He opened Bagehot's *Lombard Street* and began underlining phrases, diagramming the steps of the exposition, reading each paragraph twice. He fell asleep. Many hours later he was awakened by noise and movement in the car. The train was

receiving and discharging passengers at Fort Barry. A few
minutes later it moved south for a quarter of a mile to the re-
fueling station and came to a long halt. This was where his
father had been rescued two years and five months before.
Most of the passengers descended from the cars and walked
briskly up and down the cinder path beside the water tank and
the coal sheds. There were many students on the train returning home for the holidays; they sang. The light was fading. A
few snowflakes hovered in the air. Roger's spirits revived. He
scanned the faces of those who strolled by him. His attention
was attracted by a tall thin girl of about his own age who had
separated herself from her companions and was walking rapidly
to and fro. Her eyes and complexion were dark. She wore a
sealskin cap and a collar of the same fur rose above her ears.
Her hands were clasped in a sealskin muff. An indefinable grace
and distinction invested her. He stopped and looked across the
ditch toward the clump of trees where—it was said—his father's
rescuers had given him a horse. He resumed his walk. The girl
in the sealskin hat passed him twice, then stopped before him
and said:

"Roger, I want to talk to you about something."

"I beg your pardon?"

"Not here—but when we're in Coaltown."

"I beg your pardon, but I don't know who you are."

"I'm Félicité Lansing."

"Félicité! You've grown!"

"Yes."

"I'm very glad to see you. How's your mother?"

"She's well."

"How are you all? How's George and Anne?"

"They're well. Roger, I want to talk to you about something."

Her manner was grave and urgent. Suddenly he remembered
that Sophia had written that Félicité Lansing was "studying to
be a nun." There was something nunlike in the young woman
before him: that absence of calling any attention to herself.

"What is it you want to say, Félicité?"

"It's something very important about . . . your father and
my father."

She looked over his shoulder, as at some woeful ordeal that
must be met and surmounted.

"Yes, Félicité. I think now we can find two seats side by side on the train."

"I can't tell you about it now. I'm not ready. Maybe what I have to tell you is very terrible. I didn't know that I'd be meeting you this way—on the train."

"I'll come to your house tomorrow, or you come to my house."

Félicité continued to gaze, pondering, beyond him, though not in evasion of his glance; when she looked into his face it was without reservation. Roger's heart leapt in recognition: her eyes, like her mother's, were of slightly different colors; like her mother she had a mole on her right cheekbone.

She said: "Until I'm sure of what I have to tell you—very sure—my mother mustn't know it; or your mother. George came back three nights ago. He ran away from town on the night before Father was killed. He rode on freight cars, as hoboes do. He went to California and became an actor. He's been very sick. There are many things. I have to tell you. I haven't been able to tell them to anybody."

Again she gazed over his shoulder in silence. To himself Roger said: "But I *know* her. We must have said thousands of words to one another."

"I've read some of the essays you wrote for the paper. Miss Doubkov lent them to me. I think you'll understand. I mean, I think you'll help me understand." She put out her hand. "Maybe we'll have to be very very strong and very brave."

The train gave a jerk. The whistle blew. Some girls came up to Félicité shrieking: "Filly! Filly! The train's starting. You'll be left behind."

"That's why I can't tell you with all these girls around. It's secret, very secret.—Listen! Miss Doubkov has a store on Main Street. I help her sometimes. I have the key. She said she's not going to work there on Christmas Eve. Can you come there tomorrow morning at half past ten?"

"Filly! Filly! You'll be left behind!"

"Yes, I can."

The hazel and the blue of her eyes seemed to darken. "Maybe it's not true. Maybe it's true and terrible. But if it's true we must know it. The important thing is to *prove* to everybody that your father was innocent."

She quickly put her hand in his, murmured, "Tomorrow at ten-thirty," and entered the car. Roger resumed his seat. He re-opened his book, but his eyes kept returning to the sealskin cap at the far end of the car. "What a girl!" Félicité sat motionless on the aisle; her companions babbled and fluttered about her like doves. Their voices were shrill with the excitement of the coming holiday. He heard their insistent "Filly" this and "Filly" that.

Roger said to himself: "I shall marry that girl."

IV. Hoboken, New Jersey
1883

HOBOKEN, NEW JERSEY, is a town bearing a Dutch name, once largely inhabited by people of German descent. The majority of the houses were of red brick, agreeably shaded by locust and linden trees. In good weather the citizens of Hoboken enjoyed (and still enjoy) sitting on benches along the waterfront watching the ships entering and leaving New York harbor. A great deal of beer was brewed and drunk in Hoboken, but the consumption in the various beer halls was sedate and ruminative rather than boisterous. The town contained an engineering school. Most of its students came from a distance and made fun of the town and its brewers; when they wished to enjoy themselves they took the ferry to New York, where "life" was reported to abound.

One Sunday morning in the spring of 1883 John Ashley, twenty-one years old, was sitting on a waterfront bench with Beata Kellerman, nineteen, daughter of one of the more prosperous brewers. He was wearing the new suit that he had bought for Easter. It was green—almost "bottle green." His domed hat was brown. His new shoes were yellow and shone. He wore a high stiff collar. The lapels on his light tan overcoat were of plum-colored velvet. These were the clothes of a rich man's son, but they were ill-chosen and suggested the country boy. At no time in his life was there anything remarkable to observe in John Ashley except his large nose, his attentive blue eyes, and his taciturnity. He was neither dark nor light, tall nor short, fat nor thin, handsome nor homely. His taciturnity did not proceed from shyness. He had no self-consciousness whatever. It sprang from his desire not to miss anything. He was constantly filled with wonder: mathematics and the laws of physics were wonderful; a day like this Sunday morning was wonderful; wonderful were the ships before him, the sea gulls, the clouds in the sky and the laws of vaporization that governed them; it was wonderful to be young with a long crowded life before him. Above all the girl beside him was wonderful.

She would be his wife and they would have many wonderful children. Beata's clothes also gave evidence of a rich father—from the high-buttoned shoes on her large feet to the fringed parasol in her mittened hand. Beata, however, arrested attention. She was a German version of a Greek goddess—"Junoesque," said her drawing master—with wide-set prominent blue eyes, a splendid nose, and a full cushioned chin. Beata, too, was taciturn, but for different reasons. She had recently emerged from a life in which nothing was wonderful. She had learned to know John Ashley. For her that was wonder enough.

On that morning Hoboken was very quiet. Not even church bells were heard, for an epidemic was at its height and the churches were closed. The disease had recurred for many years with varying symptoms and under different names. In 1883 it was called the "Maryland pneumonia." Door after door bore the purple notice of infection and some the crêpe of mourning. Many students had been withdrawn by their parents from the Institute. John Ashley, too, had been summoned home, but had turned a deaf ear. He was the only child of doting parents in upper New York State. Idolized sons are not noted for gratitude or obedience. He had, in addition, little acquaintance with fear. He believed that illness and accident are apportioned to those who deserve them. He was now living in an empty house. The family with whom he boarded had fled the town and were making their home with relatives on a farm in Pennsylvania. Beata's family had driven to church in New York City and would not return until evening. Beata and the servants had solemnly promised her parents that they would not leave the house during the day. She was presumably sitting in the parlor practicing a sonata by Beethoven with a brazier of smoking sulphur beside her. She was an exceptionally obedient daughter. Beata had spent her life in a prison house of many fears; from these her love for John Ashley had recently freed her. She no longer feared her mother or the mockery of her brothers and sisters or the opinion of her mother's friends. Above all she had been freed from a fear of life itself—a confused dread of "men" and "babies," and of an eternity of days spent in Hoboken. Within six weeks John Ashley had dispersed all these clouds. The crown of her love for him was gratitude.

John and Beata sat on the bench in the plague-stricken

town. They looked at the sunlight on the water. They spoke little. Any words but the most commonplace would disturb the mounting music that filled them.

"*. . . a wonderful morning!*"

"*Yes. Yes, it is.*"

We fashion our lives by the operation of our imaginations, or—as Goethe said—"Beware what you long for in your youth, for you will get it in your middle age," by which we presume he meant that we shall get it or some botched caricature of it. John Ashley's imagination was limited in some areas, but not in this: he wanted to be a husband and the father of many children; he wanted to be married by the age of twenty-two so that his older children would be passing through the teens before he was forty; he wanted to live at a distance from the Atlantic coast in a large house surrounded by verandahs—a house somewhat untidy, perhaps, because of the tumult of life within it, all those young boys and girls; he wanted a workshop near the house, filled with the proper tools and equipment, in which he could perform his experiments and make his useful and useless inventions. It never occurred to him to wish for wealth (sufficient means to maintain a family came *of themselves* to any serious-minded and diligent young man), fame (being well-known must waste a lot of a man's time), learning (he had never discovered much to interest him in books), wisdom, "philosophy," spiritual insight (things like that also came *of themselves* as one grew older, presumably). He had a fairly clear picture of his future wife: she would be beautiful and very nearly perfect—that is, without vanity, envy, malice, or deference to the opinion of others. She would be an exemplary housewife. She would be, like himself, slow to speak, but endowed with a beautiful speaking voice—that of his doting mother managed to be both nasal and flat.

There were other elements in Ashley's picture of his future that were less clear to him, but he was in no doubt about the first steps. He would lead his classes, thereby being enabled to select on graduation the job that most suited him. He would be married on the day after that graduation. As he was to reside in Hoboken for four years he resolved to search for a wife in the community. On his trips to New York he kept his eyes well open. The girls in the city seemed to him to be invested with a fatiguing vivacity; they never stopped talking; they laughed too loudly in public and they waved their hands about in the air. A small-town boy himself, he wished to marry a small-town girl.

"   . . 't's so peaceful!"

"Yes. Yes, it is."

John Ashley led all his classes and was president of his fraternity, but he took little interest in his fellow students. (He resigned from the house in his senior year and moved into private lodgings.) He was naturally endowed for sports, but did not engage in them. He lacked any competitive sense and appeared to lack ambition. But he was never idle; he explored the laws of mechanics and electricity, and he hunted women.

He intimidated his professors. Some had known gifted pupils, but none had ever seen a student who approached mechanics in the spirit of play. They gave him enlarged space in the laboratory and furnished him with expensive equipment. The energy it engendered rang bells (they played " 'Nita, Juanita") and threw numerals and letters on a grid from a clavier. He came near killing himself a number of times; he blew out windows, blackened ceilings, and almost reduced the laboratory to ashes; but grave accidents do not befall young Ashleys. His special laboratory privileges were regretfully withdrawn. As graduation approached the Dean and a number of his advisers discussed inviting the young man to join the faculty, but voices were raised against the appointment. "Inventors" were suspect and it was obvious that Ashley was of that sort. However, they hung his mechanical drawings in the school's corridors—they were of unprecedented clarity and beauty and remained there for years—and wrote handsome letters of recommendation on his behalf. Ashley also played with mechanics at his lodgings. His room resembled some eccentric scientist's cavern in a novel by Jules Verne. When, at dawn, the hands of his clock reached five-thirty a pillow fell from the ceiling on his face; in cold weather a long steel arm lowered the window, another lit a burner under a tea kettle. He played with mathematics. There were always six to ten card games in progress at his fraternity house. He drew up charts analyzing the probabilities governing whist, Jack Gallagher, and pinochle. Since he had no competitive sense, no malice, and no need of money, his interest in the card games was limited to preventing any one member of the group from winning overmuch.

If these activities reflected the spirit of play, his search for a wife was very serious indeed. He was interested only in girls of strict upbringing. An earnest hunter studies the terrain, observes the habits, runs, and feeding grounds of his quarry; he fits himself out with appropriate equipment and arms himself with patience. Soon after his arrival in Hoboken he began laying his plans. He enrolled as a student of the German language. He attended the Lutheran church. It was a general rule among the prosperous German families that their daughters would have nothing to do with the students at the Institute, and it was common knowledge at the Institute that the girls of Hoboken were heavy-footed "Dutchies," unworthy of a lively young man's attention. But John Ashley never waited to form his opinions on those of his contemporaries; his aims were above their vision and his methods beyond their patience. He followed girls on the street and learned their names and addresses. He was welcomed at the church. Introduction led to introduction. He was invited to Sunday dinners. He, in turn, invited girls (and their mothers) to lectures with lantern slides—"Our December Sky," *"Goethe und die Tiere"*—and to minstrel shows. At the close of these entertainments there was much shaking of hands in the aisles and further introductions. There were dances and balls in Hoboken long before dancing was accepted in similar communities elsewhere. He threw a wide net. Girl led to girl. He was tracking a great prize before he knew that she existed. He stalked by faith. The hunt was time consuming, but we all have time to expend on what is essential to our nature. Finally—late, when he had almost given up hope, in the second quarter of his senior year—he saw Beata Kellerman. A month later he was introduced to her. Three months later he eloped with her.

Mysterious are the laws of sexual selection. Ashley chose Beata to be his wife much as his son Roger was to choose his life's career—by elimination. He was a favorite with the mothers and younger sisters; the fathers and brothers found him uninteresting. Naturally, he kept a score card. Trude Gruber and Lisl Grau liked him very much, but they could not restrain themselves from laughing at him. Everyone could see that the other Grau twin, Heidi, was a little in love with him, but she was given to saying that she hated cooking and sewing and "all those stupid *Hausfrau* things." Gretchen Hofer (he knew four Gretchens) couldn't imagine how a girl would want to leave Hoboken to live in the West where there were nothing but Red Indians and rattlesnakes. In his third year it seemed to him that he had found what he was looking for—Marianne Schmidt. On Sunday afternoons they sat on the benches and watched the ships entering and leaving New York Harbor. Marianne was seventeen, beautiful, slow to speak, and thoughtful. She possessed the unusual ability to make Ashley talk. She wanted to know what he was learning at the Institute. Finally she confided that she wished to go to Mt. Holyoke College in Massachusetts to study chemistry. She planned to be a "lady doctor" to treat children. She had read that in Germany and France a woman could become a doctor—a real doctor, like a man. Ashley listened to her for a while, then ventured a reply. Marianne was unable at first to understand what he was saying. She couldn't believe her ears. It seemed that he thought it wasn't healthy to work among sick people all the time.

"Then who'd do it?"

"Well . . . There are enough doctors who are paid to do it. Somebody's got to do it, but not *you*, Marianne."

Marianne drew circles on the ground with the tip of her parasol. Presently she rose. "Let's go home, John. . . . John, sometimes I think that you're just plain ignorant—or rather that something was left out of you. You haven't any—*imagination*! You haven't any—!"

That eliminated Marianne Schmidt.

Lottchen Bauer had a beautiful speaking voice and was a famous cook. One day he took her skating on the *Turnverein*'s rink. They skated together with such elegance that the crowd left the ice to watch them. When at the end of the afternoon he was taking off her skates he looked up and found that she was weeping.

"Why, Lottchen! What's the matter?"

"Nothing."

"Tell me!"

"Life's awful! I had an awful quarrel with Father and Mother this morning and *I'm going to have another one tonight.*—John, you said you thought I sang beautifully."

"You do. You're the best home singer I ever heard."

"Well, I want to be an opera singer and I'm going to be an opera singer and nothing in the wide world will stop me!"

"But, Lottchen!"

"What?"

"I don't think you'd have a very good family life, if you were an opera singer. I mean: you'd have to be away evenings a lot. And I guess they must have to practice on the afternoons before the show."

Lottchen wept some more, but from prolonged laughter. That eliminated Lottchen Bauer.

He was taken to the annual concert given by the pupils of Hoboken's foremost teacher of the piano, Mrs. Kessel. Music, application, and composed nerves came naturally to these girls. Pupil followed pupil. The evening drew toward its close with exhibitions by the more advanced students, including the three Misses Kellerman. Ashley had seen these young ladies, but had never met them. Their mother Clotilde Kellerman, *geborene* von Diehlen, regarded herself as superior to the other matrons in the town and held her daughters in closer rein. Beata played last. Ashley had no way of discerning that her performance was the most brilliant but the least innately musical of the evening. It reflected not her beauty but her stony advance to the piano and her withdrawn salute to the audience. In the middle of it—*her memory failed her.* The public was electrified. This was a scandal and a disgrace and would be talked about for years. Ashley was more electrified by what followed. Beata did not recommence the work; she did not grope about among the keys for an issue. She gazed tranquilly before her, her hands raised. Then she rose and bowed to her listeners, unabashed. She left the stage with the carriage of a world-famous artist who has exceeded all expectations. The applause was generous, but did not cover the indignant comments of Ashley's friends.

"She did it on purpose!"

"Her mother will *die*!"

"She's an awful stuck-up girl and everybody knows it! She hasn't got any friends and she doesn't *want* any."

"She did it to spite her mother. She's *impossible* to her mother."

"No, she didn't do it on purpose. When she recited on Schiller's birthday she forgot the words, too."

What was it in Beata that so strongly attracted Ashley from these first moments? Was it her fortitude and imperturbability? Did he have sufficient imagination to capture in the air the cry as of one shipwrecked and drowning? Was his attention quickened toward her because of the malicious glee in the audience? (He was tending to believe that community opinion is *always* wrong.) Did he see himself as a Perseus and St. George whose mission it had been to rescue a beautiful maiden in distress? Or was it in his nature to seek a girl who—for reasons in her nature —would love him all-absorbedly, him alone?

He stalked her. The family generally attended church in New York and spent the whole Sunday there. They seldom patronized the entertainments in Hoboken. He learned that in school she had been a formidably bright student; she knew "oceans" of German poetry by heart; she and her sisters spoke impeccable French (their mother directed that only French be spoken in the home on Fridays—which left their base-born father out in the cold). She was widely disliked. She was cruelly teased by her brothers and sisters—for her aloofness, for her disdain of boys, for her large feet. The matrons lowered their voices with assumed sympathy to declare that she was "unmarriageable."

Once a year—sturdy Protestants though they were—the brewers of Hoboken gave a great pre-Lenten ball (their *Fasching*, their *Mardi Gras*) in honor of King Gambrinus, the inventor of beer. John Ashley, the hunter, attended with the Gruber family. He never failed to be attentive to the mothers and it was through Mrs. Gruber that he was introduced to Beata, who had been dancing with her brothers. She refused his invitation to dance. An hour later he sat down by the great Mrs. Kellerman. He talked of the weather and of the band. By luck he happened to mention that he had recently crossed the river to attend a performance of *Der Freischütz* at The Academy of Music. The Kellermans had held a Saturday-afternoon subscription to the opera for twenty years. Mrs. Kellerman unbent.

She invited him to dinner on the following Thursday night. She wanted him to meet her sons, one of whom was thinking of enrolling in the engineering school. Ashley again asked Beata to dance and was refused. (Later she told him that she had been aware of his following her and that she had "hated" him.) On Thursday evening, Beata was indisposed and did not join the family at dinner. Her father and brothers thought him uninteresting; her sisters thought him ridiculous. Mrs. Kellerman liked him very much. He had beautiful manners. He liked her. He listened appreciatively to her account of her childhood home in Hamburg, the great balls she had attended, the royalties to whom she had been presented. Two days later he went to New York and bought a keepsake edition of Heine's *Buch der Lieder*, bound in coral velvet, stamped with forget-me-nots. He had consulted his German professor on this important matter. He brought it to her door. Hunters leave cakes of salt in the forest. For three weeks he received no reply. Despair defends itself. Finally he was invited to coffee. That thicket of briars through which Beata groped her life away vanished into thin air.

Why? How?

He made no jokes. He didn't allude to anything in mockery. He spoke of her loss of memory at the piano. He said he understood that perfectly: that beauiful music was one thing, but that a lot of people sitting in little gold creaky chairs listening to their relatives play was *another*. He bet that she played perfectly when she was alone or with just one or two people she trusted. Ashley, who so seldom talked, talked. He told her he planned to leave the East Coast and to work in the West where he didn't know anybody. He lowered his voice to confess that he loved his father and mother, but they didn't really have the same ideas that he had.

He dropped into German: "I get along pretty well here. I get along pretty well wherever I am. But I have the feeling that I want to get away from everything that I've known. I want to start a whole new life. Do you sometimes feel like that?"

Beata was unable to speak.

"The Constitution of the United States says that we have a right to be happy. I've been happy—whenever I stayed at my grandmother's farm in upper New York State. But she died. I could be happy with you. You could make me happy. I could try to make you happy."

She gazed at him unblinkingly—blue eyes into blue. A hoarseness came into her beautiful speaking voice. She said, "I couldn't make anyone happy."

He smiled. Slowly a smile filled his face that so seldom smiled.

"Well," he said, "we could think about it."

Here begins a history of the maternal grandparents of the notorious Ashley children.

There is a theory—the folk wisdom of many countries has condensed the observation into a proverb—that gifted children inherit from their grandparents, that talents skip a generation. Some maintain that that is all nonsense: energy of mind (for good or ill) in persons and nations is primarily the result of a mixture of contrasting traits in the inheritance—a turbulent clash. The Ashley children and the Lansing children certainly had energy of mind, but the Ashley children had something more: a quality of abstraction, an impersonal passion. Where did that come from—that freedom from self-reference?

Friederich Kellerman and his bride Clotilde, *geborene* von Diehlen, arrived in America from Hamburg twenty-five years before this beautiful and soundless morning in Hoboken. Kellerman had risen from apprentice to journeyman to master in the art and science of brewing. He was stout, amiable, pusillanimous, and musical.

His wife was of another metal. She had a straight back, the carriage of a royal guardsman. Her intimidated neighbors said she looked like a weather vane, or like the figurehead on a ship —allusions to her high coloring, to her red cheeks, tufted orange eyebrows and braids, eyes of sapphire *en cabochon*. She entered public gatherings like a beadle directing a state funeral. She had been brought up in a household where parents and children (and their grandparents before them) were breathlessly absorbed in improving their social position. Her father had held a position on the administrative staff of Hamburg's Marine Institute, without being *Professor* or even *Doktor*; he was merely paymaster and superintendent of buildings and grounds. At some time in the eighteenth century—when many were doing it—his family had picked up a *von* to which they were not entitled. The von Diehlens were occasionally given cards to academic and municipal balls at which Exalted Personages were present. Young Clotilde had laid her eyes on royalties and had made her *"Knix."* She and her sisters had been taught by their mother with a sort of ferocity to imitate those Exalted Personages. They were made to ascend and descend staircases with Beethoven's *Sonatas* or atlases on their heads, to rise from a curtsy without an audible cracking of their knees, and to waltz entire evenings without reversing. Snobbery is a passion. It is a noble passion that has gone astray amid appearances. It springs from a desire to escape the trivial and to be included among those who have no petty cares, no tedious moments, among those whose very misfortunes are lofty. On starry nights the geese around the ponds below our barns hear in the upper airs the song of their migrant cousins. They imagine that all *their* diversions are magical; *they* never experience self-distaste and boredom. Clotilde's marriage to Friederich Kellerman had been a disappointment to her family and was soon to be one to her. She could not forgive herself for having married a brewer, for having followed him to a remote continent where her quality was seldom discerned, for having been betrayed by love into joining her life with that of a handsome young workman possessed of a resounding baritone voice and an easy assurance that he would be a success— one who spoke a deplorable German and one who would never, never, look well on horseback. Clotilde Kellerman, however, held her head high and looked straight ahead. She sustained the pretense of deference to the head of the house. Her children were not deceived. Perhaps the principal reason for Beata's revolt against her mother was that lady's tacit but sufficiently evident disparagement of the man she had married.

Clotilde Kellerman had other passions, too, or tended other altars. She loved her family collectively, while being in a constant state of exasperation with each individual in it. They were *hers.* She would have walked into a wall of fire for any one of them. Housekeeping, for her—like the aspiration to a higher social rank—was invested with moral values. Her aim was perfection and it took its toll of those about her. Beata was to remember all her life the occasion when her mother gazed for a moment at the roast which her maid had placed before her at the Sunday dinner table, then had seized it in both hands and hurled it to the floor. Her gesture was forceful, her voice was contained: "Tell Käthe we shall have scrambled eggs."

The von Diehlens transmitted a third passion from generation to generation, though it reached Clotilde Kellerman in an attenuated form. To them music, nightly in the home and at least twice a week at concerts, was essential to existence. Neither Clotilde nor her daughter Beata was musical, but they did not know that. They thought they were. Many color-blind persons are unaware that the world they see differs from that seen by their neighbors. They wept at slow movements; they recognized well-defined themes and rejoiced at their recurrence. Beata's father, however, had an ear. In Hoboken he was long the president of the best (of four) *Sängervereine* until he could no longer endure the banality of its programs. He grew tired of hearing forty obese men proclaim the joys of a hunter's life and bid passing birds report their breaking hearts to their beloved. He took his family to the opera in New York and wept unashamedly through the works of Wagner. His wife was very pleased to be there, though she gave little attention to the performance. She was handsome and she knew it, and very well born; it was her duty to be present and it conferred a (five-hour) privilege on those who beheld her.

Friederich Kellerman was deeply attached to his children and particularly to Beata, but his wife held strong views on parental relations. She was quick to intercept any demonstrations of tenderness. They rendered boys unmanly and girls vulgar. At mealtimes the children stood behind their chairs until their parents were seated; on going to bed they kissed their parents' hands. At heart Clotilde Kellerman had a low opinion of girls. God sent them into the world for the perpetuation of the race, but the most one could do for them was to inculcate a spine of steel, a royal carriage, a thorough knowledge of cooking, bedding, and cleaning, and to find them a husband from an estimable family. It should not be forgotten, however, that Clotilde had also acquired the merits, real or imagined, of aristocrats: never, in the presence of her children, did she say a malicious word about her neighbors. (She had other ways of conveying disapprobation.) Though she could cast a platter to the floor, she never raised her voice nor permitted her children to do so. She let it be known that she was guided by her own opinion rather than by those of her neighbors. She did not permit any discussion of the relative wealth or poverty of their friends. If her husband had entered the house one day and told her that he was bankrupt, she would have uttered no word of complaint. She would have moved to a slum and improved the tone of the neighborhood.

Beata was an exemplary student, though she was not interested in knowledge for its own sake (von Diehlen and Kellerman), an accomplished performer on the piano, a superb cook (von Diehlen). She gave all of herself to whatever task was set before her (Kellerman). She didn't give a pin for her beauty, possibly because she thought her older sisters were more beautiful. Young men left her alone. There was no one to whom she could extend affection; her dog was run over, her cat kittened. She had approached on tiptoe the possibility that she might acknowledge her love for her father and receive any, *any*, recognition in return. She tried to send some kind of message to him—the waving of a scarf from a quicksand; but Friederich Kellerman was powerless. He suggested to his wife that Beata might be sent to one of those women's colleges. "Nonsense! I don't know where you get such ideas, Fritz! Do you know what those girls wear? They wear *bloomers*!" Beata became not sullen but stony.

It would be rash to say that John Ashley came to her rescue just in time. She might have held out a year or two longer without turning to stone. Maybe he was a year or two late. We are not permitted to tease ourselves with these conditionals. The same starvation that warps one strengthens another.

Why was Beata an unhappy misfit in her own family? Because she had been formed by her parents' best principles and insights and her parents *did not recognize them when they saw them*. Parents grow old. What we have called their creativity (there is a home-building, child-rearing "creativity") loses its keenness. They are "feather-plucked" in the commerce of life. Family life is like a hall endowed with the finest acoustical properties.

Growing children hear not only their parents' words (and in most cases gradually ignore them), they hear the intentions, the attitudes behind the words. Above all they learn what their parents *really* admire, *really* despise. John Ashley was quite right in wishing to be under forty when his children were passing through their teens. His parents were both forty when he was ten—that is to say they were beginning to be resigned to the knowledge that life was disappointing and basically meaningless; they were busily clutching at its secondary compensations: the esteem and (hopefully) the envy of the community in so far as they can be purchased by money and acquired by circumspect behavior, by an unremitting air of perfect contentment, and by that tone of moral superiority that bores themselves and others but which is as important as wearing clothes.

As I shall have occasion to say when we consider the early years of Eustacia Lansing: all young people secrete idealism as continuously as the *Bombyx mori* secretes silk. It is as necessary to them as food that life be filled with wonder—that they contemplate heroes. They must admire. They must admire. The boy in the reformatory (his third conviction for burglary with assault) secretes idealism as a *Bombyx mori* secretes silk. The girl of fifteen, brutalized into prostitution, secretes idealism—for a while—as a *Bombyx mori* secretes silk. Life to newcomers presents itself as a brightly lighted stage where they will be called upon to play roles exhibiting courage, fair dealing, magnanimity, wisdom, and helpfulness. Hoping and trembling a little, they feel that they are almost ready for these great demands upon them.

In the fine acoustics of the family life Beata had imbibed from both parents a number of summonses to perfection—the responsibility and decorum of the aristocrat, and the probity and the quickness to resent oppression of the working classes. All virtues (even humility) invoke independence. Beata's mother, growing old, was relapsing into the vices of the aristocratic view of life. Beata's father, when young, had transmitted to his favorite daughter the virtues that had invested his family for generations; aging (at forty-four) he had become rudderless and obsequious. Beata's refusal to be concerned with attempts to impress the neighbors exasperated her mother; her refusal to be coerced disappointed her father. She was isolated and wretched.

John and Beata, then, were sitting on the bench watching the play of the sunlight on the waters of New York Harbor. A breeze sprang up. The ruffles on Beata's bertha fluttered in the air.

"Are you cold, Beata?"

"No. No, John."

He looked at her. Smiling, she glanced into his eyes, then lowered her own. Slowly she raised them and looked steadily into his. We remember his grandmother's warning against looking long into the eyes of a child or an animal. Hitherto these young persons had stolen quick glances at one another— blue eyes into the blue—of an almost painful sweetness and confusion. In daily life the reciprocal glance is brief; a little prolonged it is the confirmation of mature confidence or the mark of resolute antagonism. Boys play a game of outstaring one another; it soon breaks up in semihysterical laughter and a release of coltish energy. They tell us of actors experiencing a mounting panic when they are required to prolong the pose on the stage or before the camera. It is—as the photographers say—an "exposure." In love it is the dissolution of pride and separateness; it is surrender.

John and Beata gazed into one another's eyes. A force they had not foreseen took possession of them. It lifted their hands; it joined their lips; it drew them along the walk into the town.

He had not planned it. She did not distrust it. Without words they found their way to his empty house. Two months later they left Hoboken together; thereafter, for nineteen years, they were seldom separated for longer than twenty-four hours— until he was taken to jail.

On the evening following his graduation Beata left her home while her parents were entertaining friends in the front parlor. At first dark she had hidden a coat, a hat, and a small handbag under the kitchen steps.

John and Beata were never married. There was no time for it then, and a suitable occasion never presented itself. John happened to have found a bride as independent of tribal forms as himself.

Rites are instituted to aid and support the well-intentioned. Beata had long worn a thin gold band set with a garnet. John removed the stone and filed away the setting.

"Shall we go and find someone and get married, Beata?"

"I *am* married."

They arrived a few days later in Toledo, Ohio. They had stopped on the way to see the Niagara Falls. The firm that had engaged John had not been informed that he was married, but a cordial welcome was extended to the young couple and when Lily was born six months later she received many gifts in the shape of blankets, spoons, pushers, and silver mugs.

During the epidemic in Hoboken those who were shut in acquired an intensified interest in whatever could be seen from their windows. Beata's visits to the house where John lived were observed and reported. But for a long time no one dared mention them to the redoubtable Clotilde Kellerman. She was the last to learn of them. Thereafter she did not permit Beata's name to be mentioned in her presence.

It would be difficult to defend John's treatment of his parents. On the morning following his graduation he accompanied them to New York and saw them off on the train. He would write. At Christmas he sent them a card without return address. He did not tell them that he was married and a father.

John Ashley wanted all things new. He must be the first man who has earned his bread, to take a wife, to beget a child. Everything is filled with wonder—a bride, a first salary cheque, the infant in one's arms. To announce these things to persons who think they are everyday occurrences is to endanger one's own sense of their radiance.

Besides, he had had enough of advice and warning, of being commended for what a dolt could do and being ridiculed for what was hard won, for being urged to admire what he despised—his father's anxiety-ridden prudence—and being asked to deplore what he admired—his grandmother's idiosyncratic independence. He had had enough of being a son. His first year of marriage was like the discovery of a new continent. His voice descended half an octave. He walked the mile to his place of work like Adam going forth to his daily task of naming the plants and animals. On the first half mile he was filled with a storm of tenderness for what he left behind; on the second, with the gravity of one who has founded the human race and must foster and defend it. It made him uncomfortable to think that perhaps his happiness rendered him conspicuous. He had the sensation that he "shone." ("Good morning, Jack. How are you?" "Fine, Bill, how are you?") His natural taciturnity increased. That fear abated. No one noticed.

The one disappointment in his new life was the nature of his job. The machine tools he was set to design turned out to involve small changes on established patterns. He called his work "making cookie molds." There was no opportunity to fashion a new thing or to explore his own skills. By a coincidence (but the lives of such men are replete with coincidences) he heard of the position to be filled at Coaltown. The pay was poor, but the description of what would be required of him was inviting. He was replacing a "maintenance engineer" who had just died at eighty-two. The letter was signed "Breckenridge Lansing." So, after two years and two months in Ohio, the Ashleys journeyed to southern Illinois, to a life which turned out to be filled with wonder and delight and many coincidences. When they descended from the train at Coaltown's depot in September, 1885, John Ashley was twenty-three, Lily almost two, and Roger nine months old.

Each of the Ashley children was—because of the peculiar components in an Ashley—what Lily called "exhaustingly notorious"; but their separate fames were "exhaustingly" enhanced by the fact that they were brother and sisters. The admiration or antagonism they aroused was tripled; the curiosity, centupled. On one level the Sunday supplements of the newspapers published lurid stories ("Have the Ashleys a Secret?" "The Ashleys' Plans for 1911"); humorists strained themselves. On another, there were popular biographies of them. On another, amateur and professional genealogists went to extraordinary pains to trace their ancestors. Articles and brochures appeared in several languages. Presentation copies were sent to the subjects of these works, who had firmly refused to furnish any information concerning themselves. At first, Constance threw them into wastepaper baskets unread; Lily and Roger directed their secretaries to thank the authors for their interest.

John Barrington Ashley's immediate ancestors were farmers and small merchants on the western banks of the Hudson

River. As Ashley, Ashleigh, Coghill, Barrington, Barrow, and so on, they had left the Thames Valley in the 1660's, fleeing from religious persecution, and had crossed the Atlantic. For every head of a family of their persuasion and condition who steeled himself to this resolve there were ten who wavered, longed, and shrank back. ("Brother Wilkins, will ye remove with us?") Once arrived at the shores of New England they pushed westward, felling trees and building the meetinghouse and the school; then pushed further. (In the seventeenth century they were saying: "If you can see the smoke from your neighbor's chimney, you're too near." In the eighteenth they accommodated themselves, not without some stiffness, to living in a community.) They were steeled on the Lord's day by four-hour sermons that were largely occupied with sin. ("Oh my beloved brothers and sisters, consider what a terrible thing it is to fall into the hands of an angry God!") Most of the households had known a dozen children, not including the early lost. (The patriarch sleeps on the hill with his several brides beside him.) Some of the Ashley clan married into the Scots and Dutch families across the river. The Dutch families came from Amsterdam. One genealogist found an Espinosa in the line and claimed a connection with the philosopher, but there were many Espinosa-Spinozas among the Sephardim who had escaped from religious persecution in Spain. The parents of Ashley's father's mother—Marie-Scolastique Anne Dubois—had arrived in Montreal from a village near Tours on the Loire. (*"Dis, cousin Jacques! Est-ce que tu viens avec nous à Québec—oui ou non?"*) Beata's ancestors were farmers, artisans, and burghers from northern Germany. Her mother's grandmother was of a Huguenot family, weavers who had fled from religious persecution in France at the Revocation of the Edict of Nantes. They had found refuge in several of the proud and independent Hanseatic ports.

Names, hundreds of names, names from records in the town halls, church registers, from last testaments, from gravestones.

Lily sent one of these brochures to Roger: "I wish they'd hurry and find my Italian ancestors. I *know* I'm Italian. And I *know* I'm Irish.—But what's the use of all this ink?" Roger replied: "I wish I could read the annals of your descendants, and Connie's and mine." *Those* annals contain Gaels and Wops aplenty. (The word "wop" is derived from the Neapolitan-Spanish *guapo*: handsome, dashing.)

This varied documentation could be found in any large library and was at the disposal of anyone who applied for it. Soon a new kind of attention was brought to bear on the material:

There was very little intellectual heritage uncovered for the Ashleys. There were some schoolmasters and clergymen in the Coghill, McPhaill, and Van Dyke–Huysum lines. A great-great-grandmother of John Ashley was the daughter of Loris Vanderloo, the Dutch seaman whose *Voyages to China and Japan* (1770) were widely read. There was no evidence of gentle birth. Clotilde von Diehlen's presumptions were not sustained. A diligent search was made for an inheritance of musical endowment. Friederich Kellerman's presidency of the choral society in Hoboken was noted. There was a tradition in the von Diehlen family that an ancestor named Kautz had served as cellist in Frederick the Great's orchestra at Potsdam. It was confirmed. The unhappy Kautz had suffered from melancholia and had taken his own life.

It was discovered that the Ashleys drew upon a remarkable store of health in their forebears. There was a notable tendency to longevity, especially among the males. This was combined, however, with a high instance of infant mortality in the eighteenth and nineteenth centuries, but that was true in all families. Sober farmers everywhere, crossed with the superstable Hudson River Dutch—the Van Tuyls and Vanderloos (livery stables and inns)—to say nothing of the sobriety vested in the families of Hannover and Schleswig-Holstein.

Roger wrote to Constance: "They worked from before dawn to after sunset. Hardly a one of them *sat down* in daylight. No lawyers, few merchants, no bankers (*one*—your grandfather Ashley), no factory workers. They were all what you're now calling 'self-employed'." Constance wrote back: "Yes, self-employed, self-centered, and self-serving. All so proud of their independence of mind. Independent for small ends. I hate them all. It explains why darling Papa had so little imagination and Mama none."

But there was another side of the coin. There were morbid elements in both the Ashley and Kellerman lines. It was not only the strong-minded uncoercible patriarchs who were drawn to the "freedom" of the new world. The scoundrel, the fanatic, the footloose, the adventurer—fiercely independent, every one of them, and of lively imagination—that is to say: suspended on the promises of a golden future, they "skipped" to America. The genealogists found disease and insanity. That very *bourgade* outside Tours from which the Boisgelins and Dubois emigrated to the new world served as subject of a pioneering sociological study, a French counterpart of our "Jukes and Kallikaks." Moreover, it was discovered that John Ashley's own grandfather Ashley, who had run away from his Dubois wife, was hanged in the Klondike by an outraged community. Fortunately this morbid material did not reach a wide circle of readers. It was sufficiently troubling that the shadow of the Ashley case hung over John Ashley's children. Moreover it cannot be denied that many observers were of the opinion that the Ashleys were, one and all—to put it frankly—"immoral." "They haven't a glimmer of decent Christian ethical behavior." "They've made it perfectly clear that they don't give a snap of their fingers what right-minded self-respecting people think of them." There was always a certain amount of that.

But enough of these matters! Health and sanity are precarious and must be paid for. Well-being and common sense invent nothing, discover nothing; they fall back into the humus. As Dr. Gillies said during the first hour of the century (and didn't believe a word of it): "Nature never sleeps or even stands still. Her men are in constant discomfort from growing pains. What they are outgrowing causes them as much suffering as what they are acquiring."

Few of these genealogists and biographers observed—or, at least, attempted to describe—what we have called the Ashley "abstraction" or "disattachment." Perhaps it was their enemies who saw it most clearly. In particular there was a chapter on them—it was called the "Gracchi"—in a privately printed volume *America Through a Telescope* by a writer who called himself "Atticus." This "Atticus" declared himself to be happy to have left America for the shores of the Thames and the Seine. From that safe distance, having taken out British citizenship, he reviewed the horrors and absurdities of his native land. He attacked the Ashleys with surprising virulence. He appears to have known them well (especially Constance Ashley-Nishimura) and enriched his portraits with many stories not hitherto in circulation. Atticus stressed their propensity to commit social errors. It seems to have particularly annoyed him that they remained unabashed by these inelegant *faux pas*. It is true: certain discriminations were missing in the Ashleys. They were unable to distinguish shades of rank, wealth, birth, color, or servitude. In addition, Atticus felt that they were lacking in self-respect. They were slow to anger. They were serene under snub and insult. He was unable to deny their intelligence, but characterized it as lacking "suppleness" and charm. He reserved his most biting depreciation for the end of his chapter. The last paragraph developed the idea that the Ashleys were— indubitably (he hated to say it, but the truth must come out; they were indubitably) Americans.

V. "St. Kitts"

1880–1905

"WHY DID Stacey marry Breck."
Like so many others in Coaltown, Dr. Gillies often asked himself how it was possible that Eustacia Sims so far lost her senses as to marry Breckenridge Lansing. We shall hear later how Dr. Gillies explained it to himself—an explanation based on a far-fetched notion and condensed in a phrase that never failed to exasperate his wife, who said that it was in bad grammar:

"We keep saying that we 'live our lives.' Shucks! Life lives us."

Breckenridge Lansing was born in Crystal Lake, Iowa. As a boy he planned to enter the Army of the United States and to become a famous general. With his brother Fisher he did a great deal of hunting. Good Baptists cannot take life or do anything else enjoyable on Sunday, but they killed and killed on Saturdays and holidays. His marksmanship was so accurate that he aspired to enter West Point. It surprised and disgusted him to learn that future Army officers are required to have a considerable knowledge of mathematics. He repeatedly failed the entrance examinations. During his years at Brockett Baptist College he started to prepare himself for the ministry, then for medicine, then for the law. He ended up as an untrained assistant in his father's drugstore.

His father was a loud-laughing man, a leader in clubs and lodges, a good businessman, a hard contemptuous husband and father. Most of these qualifications he inherited from his father and transmitted to his sons. He held offices—from banquet manager to vice president—in the Middle States Pharmaceutical Association, and took great pleasure in attending the association's conventions. It was his habit there to sit up late, night after night, playing cards with his fellow officers. In those days every enterprising druggist tried to get into the patent medicine (or "snake oil") business. Mr. Lansing despised and feared his older son, Fisher ("Call me Fish"), who had become a lawyer; he merely despised Breckenridge, who was making a nuisance of himself in the store and in the town. Breckenridge had studied some chemistry in his premedical phase. His father set him to mixing brews in a shed behind the drugstore. He dreamed of a "Lansing Liniment" or of a "Mrs. Lansing's Wild Honey Elixir." Young Lansing got no further than establishing a strong alcohol base and writing the promises to be printed on the label. His laboratory became a social center and his experiments frequently occupied him until dawn.

One night during a card game in St. Louis a colleague offered the elder Lansing an opportunity to invest money in a new firm manufacturing some products derived from an attar of the West Indian bay tree. This essence, mixed with rum, oil of orange, and other ingredients, had a variety of medicinal and cosmetic uses. It was also reportedly consumed in large quantities by unhappy ladies who had taken the "Pledge." Lansing sold two pastures and a corner lot; he invested a considerable amount of money in the enterprise. As always, however, he had more than one end in view. He wanted to make money and he wanted to get young Breckenridge out of Crystal Lake. Taking his son with him he went to New York and called at the office of the manufacturing company. He even gave a dinner at Halloran's Steak and Lobster House. The boy made a favorable first impression. He always did. He was engaged as purchasing agent of raw materials. The oils and the rum came from the Leeward Islands. Breckenridge went to the Caribbean and it was there, on the island of St. Kitts, that he met Eustacia Sims.

This young lady came of an English family that had lived in the islands since the early eighteenth century. Generation after generation, the Simses had married into the Creole families of the Antilles. By now there was a very small measure of English blood in his veins, but Eustacia's father, Alexander Sims, was every inch an Englishman. He not only observed the royal birthdays, but on October 21 he raised the flag at dawn to commemorate the glorious victory at Trafalgar and later lowered it to half mast to mark the death of Lord Nelson. His womenfolk—there were many of them; both his grandmothers and several great-aunts lived to a hundred—had other loyalties. They were indissolubly French, British by citizenship only. They had cousins on every island from Charlotte Amalie to St. Lucia.

Guadeloupe was their ancestral Eden. Like every self-respecting Creole they claimed cousinship with Josephine, Empress of France. These ladies sat all day on the verandah of Alexander Sims's house, fanning themselves, discussing the neighbors, and waiting for the next meal. Marie-Madeleine Dutellier Sims was enormous, voluble, and unhappy. She appeared to be a self-indulgent and mindless woman. She had been reduced to this appearance by idleness, humiliation, and boredom. In large part she was responsible for her own idleness. She was so capable a manager that her family—eleven to sixteen heads, including the various dependent relatives—were admirably waited upon by five servants; four others were retained for ostentation. These servants were supposedly paid three shillings a month, but they had little need of money. Their meals, clothing, medical care, whippings, and amusement were supplied by their masters. "Madame Seems" had left herself nothing to do but to command. Her humiliations she shared with other matrons of the community. Alexander Sims had another family in Basseterre. It lived in a village of thatched roofings, barely protected from the torrential rains and often carried away by a high wind. Such a second family was required—or at least expected—of every upstanding householder. It was so numerous that one could have counted the half-clad boys and girls only if they had improbably stayed motionless for a moment. He often failed to recognize his progeny when he came upon one or other of them on the Prince Albert Wharf or on the Queen Victoria Parade. When their father—white, rich, important, quick to anger—visited their home they disappeared into the surrounding fronds. Boredom—particularly Mrs. Sims's—should not be mistaken for lethargy. Boredom is energy frustrated of outlet. She had been a woman of forceful character; little of it was left except her towering rages. Her ancestors, before they settled down to cultivate sugar, had been seamen, adventurers, and buccaneers. She believed that she came of an even more romantic ancestry.

These islands had often been landfall and first haven for the slave ships from Africa. Here they put ashore the sick and dying; here they rid themselves of their troublemakers—those whom neither blows nor starvation could subdue. These recalcitrants were generally the strongest of the young men; even emaciated they would fetch a high price on the mainland. The captains, however, were willing to sell them to the island planters at a loss. The ships had weeks ahead of them. Even in chains these men were dangerous; they disseminated unrest. One of the most famous of these was Bel-Amadé, a prince of the Ashanti, long since entered into ballad and legend. He was auctioned in Guadeloupe in about 1759. There he bided his time; he became an exemplary and almost trusted foreman. He was a mighty singer; he was mirthful. He delighted in children; children delighted in him. His master often asked him to sing for his guests —the ladies sipping *chocoli-miel* from cups of Sèvres. A ballad tells us that "His back was like the tallest cedar; his eyes were like the lightning." The ballad goes on to say that he had a hundred children—royal, all of them.

Came the Night of St. Joseph, the nineteenth of March, the night of wrath, the night of long sickles. The smoke that arose from thirteen great plantations could be seen from Martinique. So great was the force of Bel-Amadé's mind that even the faithful servants—the trusted major domo, the cook, the lady's maid, the children's *mamée*—did little to avert the massacre. The Night of St. Joseph! The night is, of course, remembered with horror. But grandeur in revolt against oppression has a way of capturing our adherence—as readers of Milton's poem know. Slavery enslaves the slaveowner and with the passage of time the proud man is revealed as a fool. Bel-Amadé was caught, castrated, and hung from a tree to die in long agony. He became a bogey with whom to threaten children, but the imagination of a people is no stickler for consistency. It was said of any tall straight young man, of any radiant bold young woman —in a whisper—"*Υ a la une goutte du sang du beau diable!*" One evening after the ladies on the verandah had been discussing the Night of St. Joseph and its instigator, Eustacia, eight years old, approached her mother.

"*Maman, est-ce que nous . . . est-ce que nous . . . ?*"

"*Quoi? Quoi, nous?*"

"*Est-ce que nous sommes descendues . . . de Lui?*"

"*Tais-toi, petite sotte. Nous sommes parentes de l'Impératrice. C'est assez, je crois.*"

"*Mais, Maman, réponds.*"

Her mother turned on her daughter a dark and heavily

powdered face. Her eyes were proud and stern. She held Eustacia's gaze a moment. Her expression said, "Of course, we are!" Aloud, she said, *"Tais-toi, petite idiote!—Et mouche-toi!"*

Eustacia Sims Lansing and her children had inherited from somewhere their violent tempers, their passion for independence, and—with the exception of Anne, who took after her father—their interesting coloring.

Alexander Sims owned and operated a general store on the waterfront in Basseterre. All his daughters were beautiful; one was intelligent. As soon as she was able, Eustacia left the society on the verandah and became her father's assistant in the store. She was seventeen. She was soon running the store and running it very well, under difficulty. Her beauty was a constant burden and trial to her. The youths of the island and the sailors of all nations laid unremitting siege; their every purchase was protracted with hesitations, whispered invitations, and declarations of love. She dressed severely; she curbed her wit. She neither expressed nor felt scorn; she merely became remote. She acquired the nickname of *"La Cangueneuse"*—a word derived from the stock collar worn by French officers in the eighteenth century, so stiff and high that the wearer was unable to lower his chin. Her capability first astonished, then delighted her father. It enabled him to fulfill an ambition; he obtained a post in the customs house where he could wear a uniform all day. He could serve his sovereign.

Twice a day Eustacia's eyes lost their unloving glaze; once—where there were few to see—at the earliest mass, and once—late at night, in treasured solitude—when she unlocked the snowy wonder of her trousseau.

She knew her vocation. She knew why she had been born into the world. It was to love; to be a wife and mother. She had seen no examples of the kind of marriage to which she aspired. She invented marriage. She raised an edifice. A bird hatched from an egg in a dark room can build a nest without having seen one. She assembled fragments from the admonitions of priests at weddings, from passages in the few *romans roses* that circulated on the island, from the very marriages she saw about her—tired, spiritless, insulted, at best resigned—from altar paintings. It is given to some to "idealize" continuously and strongly, as a *Bombyx mori* secretes silk. Eustacia Sims intended to give and receive all the plenitude of the earth by love; to grow seven feet tall by love; to have ten children—Chevalier Bayards, Joséphines—by love; to merit her beauty by love; to live to a hundred, bowed down beneath the crowns of love. She would remain simple and humble—yes, leaving her two score children and grandchildren outside the church, she would kneel in the side chapel—as she did now—only asking acceptance of a woman's life in love. She had arrived at the age of nineteen without having glimpsed a man, young or old, who could be imagined as sharing this life with her. Eustacia was as healthy in mind as in body. She did not indulge in disdain, but she knew all the marriageable young men in the region (they were all, more or less, her cousins); she knew the landscape of their minds, the good and the bad. It was certain that her husband would not come from these islands. Her interest quickened when she heard foreign languages spoken. She doubted that there were more beautiful lands in the world than her own, but she could easily believe that there were countries less steeped in vanity, malice, sloth, and contempt for women. She cast searching glances at the German, Italian, Russian, and Scandinavian officers who visited the port; but held herself aloof from their overtures. Her husband would not be a seaman absent on long voyages from the home they would build together.

She waited. Her mother, from her vast rattan chair, watched Eustacia's progress and understood her problem. She worried about her own: she had three older daughters to marry off, but the island's marriageable young men had eyes only for her youngest. She was constantly being approached by the first citizens on the island, and by the priests—"*Chère madame* . . . Jean-Baptiste's Antoine is an excellent young man . . . will inherit . . . good habits . . . very much in love with your daughter Eustacia. Could you speak to your daughter, Madame Marie-Madeleine?"

One evening she called Eustacia into her bedroom.

"Now, my daughter, for two years you've been refusing every offer that comes to us. You refuse to marry and you stand in the way of your sisters' getting married. What is it you want?"

"*Maman*, are you angry with me for working in the store?"

"No."

"Why are you angry with me? Is it my fault that Antoine and Mémé and *le petit à Beaurepaire* want to marry me? They are nice boys. I like them. I do not love them. *Maman*, they waste my time when I have work to do."

"So!—Now listen to me, Eustachie."

Apparently in France when a pretty girl must go alone on a journey, by public coach, or on one of those railway trains, she is often annoyed. She is pushed and pinched and followed by young men and old men who have no fear of God. What do those modest girls do? They brush their foreheads and their cheeks with *le vert de houx*. It does not hurt the skin. You can wash it off in a moment. It merely removes the glow of youth. It gives a gray pallor—even a faintly green tinge—to the skin. The shameless men leave the dear girls alone!

"What do you think of that, *ma fille*?"

"*Maman*, angel. *Maman*, have you some of this *vert de houx*?"

"Here on the island we have no holly, but we have something else. We have the root called *borqui*, or some call it *boraqui*. Look!"

"Quick! Quick! *Maman!* Quick, let me try it."

People began to say that Eustacia was working too hard at the store. She was beginning to look old. She would be an old maid. Her sisters were serenaded. Marjolaine was engaged to be married by Christmas.

Breckenridge Lansing had not been three days on the island of St. Kitts when suddenly Eustacia Sims regained all her lost beauty between a Tuesday and a Wednesday.

Breckenridge Lansing was good at the start of everything he started. He went from island to island organizing the delivery of bay oil and rum. Everywhere he met with success. For him barrels and carboys and kegs rolled from plantation warehouses and were stamped with the address of his company's laboratories in Jelinek, New Jersey. Entertainments were improvised for him. There were dances by candlelight in the courtyards of great estates. He was taken hunting. Mothers bedecked their daughters for him. Men soon tired of his company. He had a number of the likable traits of a boy, but these men were not accustomed to the conversation of boys. Among the women he won all hearts, including that of Eustacia Sims.

For years, thereafter, Eustacia was to ask herself, tormentedly: how? why?

One morning in early December, years before Lansing's visit, the citizens of Basseterre lifted their eyes to behold a great four-masted schooner gliding into the port. On each yard a dozen youths were standing, dressed in white, their arms outspread. This was a strange apparition, but what followed was no less spectacular. The training ship *Gdynia* of the Polish navy was making a tour of the world. It carried two hundred midshipmen between the ages of thirteen and sixteen. A people with dark hair and dark eyes, like these islanders, assume that their coloring—together with all the characteristics that accompany it—is human nature itself, is Man. It has no secrets from them. They have resigned themselves to it—perfidious, self-advertising, backsliding. But lo! the two hundred midshipmen and their officers came ashore bringing with them the wonder of another Man—the vulnerable candor of blue eyes, the promise of innocence invested in honey-colored hair. When Gregory the Great first saw British slaves in the market place of Rome, he exclaimed, "Not Angles but Angels." The fourmaster *Gdynia* continued its journey around the world, but another *Gdynia* floated, white sails furling, through the imaginations of the island women, a ship manned by incorruptible knights of rose and gold, with cerulean eyes.

Dr. Gillies, who worried ideas as a dog worries old bones, used to say: "Nature's trying to get rid of extremes. There was too much dispersion in the last million million years. I see in the paper how there aren't so many blondes left in France; they have to go to Sweden and England to fill those girly-girly shows. We'll all be brown-haired soon. The churches in Russia are hard put to it to find more basses that can make the chandeliers rock, and in Berlin there's an awful dearth of tenors. We'll all be baritones from now on. Nobody'll be tall or short or dark or light. Nature can't stand extremes. She's throwing opposites into each other's arms to hurry the business. The Bible says that ultimately—when the golden age comes—the lion will lie down with the lamb. I see it coming."

"Charles, stop it!"

"The violent man will be attracted by the gentle and prudent girl. The owl will lie down with the petrel. Ineffective somnolent wisdom will couple with stormy vitality. Eggs, eggs, interesting eggs. Look at you and me, Cora!"

"Oh, go along with you."

"Darwin's never tired of showing us how nature selected types for adaptation and survival."

"I won't have that man mentioned in my house, Charles!"

"Well, maybe NATURE after hundreds of millions of years has begun selecting for intelligence and mind and spirit. Maybe NATURE is moving into a new era. Breed out the stupid; breed in the wise. Maybe that's why Stacey married Breck. NATURE commanded it. She wanted some interesting babies for her new idea.—We keep on saying that we 'live our lives.' Shucks; Life lives us."

"That's bad grammar."

Breckenridge Lansing had the commonplace face of an Iowa druggist's assistant, but his eyes were of a light cornflower blue and hair was of a silver gold. To the business men of the Antilles he represented fair dealing; to Eustacia Sims he gave promise of children like those that hover among the clouds in altar paintings.

The office in New York was pleased with Lansing's work. He returned to the States, teeming with projects and ideas. He adroitly blocked any suggestion that he return to the Caribbean. He knew already that he was one who could not repeat a success. He was sent to the laboratories in New Jersey. He leaned over the steaming vats, half closed his eyes and murmured "hmm," judiciously. He picked up a smattering of ideas concerning the processes from the men about him. He submitted some notions for improvement, but his first reception had begun to wear thin. There are certain by-products of coal tar that are put to similar uses through similar processes. The company sent him to Pittsburgh to explore the possibilities of combined research and combined patents. The Pittsburgh company was struck with admiration for his intelligence and energy ("Best young man we've seen in a long time," . . . "bright as a penny") and offered him a position. He accepted promptly. He liked change. There were good card-playing fellows everywhere; there were animals to be shot everywhere; the kind of women he liked liked him and they could be found everywhere. Before he moved to Pittsburgh, he returned to Basseterre and married Eustacia Sims. The charming young couple spent only a year in Pittsburgh. Lansing was sent, with many a congratulatory handshake, to the "Poor John" mines in Coaltown, Illinois.

Eustacia Sims on the island spent some agonizing hours in her church. She was marrying outside her faith. But several events in the town during those last months seemed to confirm her resolve. They extended her knowledge of what could be expected by women married to a dark-haired, dark-eyed male. She sold the larger part of her trousseau; she put her hand in the store's till and withdrew what she thought was due her. Lansing never knew that she had over a thousand dollars concealed in the back of her grandmother's mirror and in the seams of her clothing. Some doubt might be entertained as to whether Eustacia Sims was ever married, truly married. She bound herself by vows in three ceremonies—one in the Queen's registry office, one in a Baptist church, and one in a church of her own faith. They were all crowded into three days, because Lansing must return to his position in Pittsburgh. The only ceremony that meant anything to her was performed in a little church on the farther side of the island. She was married by an uncle who loved her dearly. He stretched the rite as far as it could go. (Lansing had given his promise that he would receive "instruction" at the earliest possible moment.) Eustacia did not notice—or, perhaps, did not choose to notice—certain lacunae in the ceremony. She certainly heard a nuptial blessing. Lansing twice placed a wedding ring on her finger. He had bought it in New York, but unfortunately on the eve of leaving that harbor he had lost forty dollars in a card game among strangers. Eustacia—bright-eyed saleswoman that she was—knew at once that the ring was of plated brass. She dipped into her own savings and replaced it with one of purest gold.

They were very popular on the ship that carried them to New York—he for his wit, she for her beauty. (Her wit was as remarkable as her beauty, but she lost it within three days; it returned like a famished dog, eight years later.) On the seventh and last night the captain raised his glass to the most attractive couple he had ever had the privilege of conveying. The passengers rose from their chairs and shouted.

Eustacia had the sensation of climbing mountain after mountain of despair. She could perhaps become accustomed to the discovery that he was obsequious to wealth and office—a trait she had fled from in her father; that he browbeat servants—a trait that she had fled from in her mother; that he was stingy in small things and spendthrift in large. Perhaps the thing that most affronted her was the constant play in his fancy with assassination. On the deck, in the dining saloon he aimed imaginary guns at his fellow passengers: "Click! Got 'em where the camel got the needle!" "Got to raise my sights. There! Sorry, madam! Good-night!" "Wait till the old giraffe comes round again."

"But, Breckenridge, let them live."

"All right, Stacey, if you say so, honey. Just one more for the sharks."

He was silent only in sleep. It is the privilege of a bridegroom to introduce a sheltered girl to a store of witty anecdotes that has hitherto been closed to her. There is a small proportion of jokes about sexual relations that does not conceal—like a bludgeon in a bouquet—an aggressive contempt for woman. Breckenridge Lansing may have heard some of these, but his memory was not able to retain them.

The attractive young couple disembarked in New York on St. Valentine's Day, 1878. Eustacia had never seen snow; she had never felt the cold. As soon as she was able she stumbled through the snowdrifts to a church of her faith. Toward the end of the hour on her knees she assumed the yoke as punishment for her disobedience. She had made a mistake, but she trusted that the sacrament of marriage would, in some unforeseeable way, support her.

They went on to Pittsburgh and from Pittsburgh to Coaltown. Neither place could boast a salubrious climate—least of all for a daughter of sun and sea. They lost three children. We have seen how Lansing readily let the reins of administration pass first to Miss Thoms, then to Ashley. But every man must establish some area in his life where he is a success. He was a success in clubs and lodges; he was a great success in those taverns up the River Road where his laughter, stories, and horseplay reanimated a company that was not always joyous.

Several times a week he drove his team home as the sun rose. Staggering, he released his horses to the croquet lawn. It was not necessary for him to climb any stairs; he could slip into bed in an abandoned playroom on the first floor. He released his horses to the croquet lawn—an all but unimaginable example of bad husbandry—not because he was drunk, but because he was tired. He was exhausted with that multiplication of fatigue that follows exertions spent—above a ground bass of self-doubt and despair—in search of pleasure. Eustacia early learned that she had been spared one burden—her husband was not a drinking man. Alcohol disagreed with him. To Breckenridge Lansing this was a deep mortification, for heavy drinking played a large part in the image he had received in childhood of what is required of a *man*. Nevertheless, he drank and talked in large terms about his drinking. He had learned all the devices of concealment. He emptied his glass in flower pots and spittoons; he exchanged his full glasses for half-filled glasses around the table. He even carried a goose feather with which, apart, he could empty his stomach.

Lansing was proud of his wife—more than that, he had fallen obscurely in love with her; but he was afraid of her. She managed the house and his income in exemplary fashion. She dispensed with a "hired girl" and employed an occasional cleaning woman. This was much to her husband's indignation; a self-respecting householder provided his wife with "help." Eustacia's reason was that she did not wish the often stormy scenes at "St. Kitts" to be reported to Coaltown. She invested his money; she advised him in many matters; she wrote his speeches for lodge meetings and for Fourth of July celebrations. He was the foremost man in town. It was hard enough for him that Eustacia was always right; it was harder that she never alluded to her endowments; she never crowed. He loved her, but he shrank from seeing himself reflected in her eyes. On her part, she learned to endure everything in him except the failings of her father. There are few things so conducive to despair as seeing the recurrence of weaknesses in those close to you; it enables you to read the future. Her father had been indolent. She begged Breckenridge to return to the New York office; she offered him the store in Basseterre. She never descended to vituperation. The violent quarrels did not begin until she saw the way in which Breckenridge chose to bring up their son George.

The John Ashleys arrived in Coaltown in 1885. They bought the house that was thought to be haunted by the long tragedy of the Airlee MacGregors.

The Lansings lived rent free, in the house assigned to the managing director of the mines. It was of blackened red brick, without verandahs, and stood among mournful yews and cedars. Behind it a wide lawn, edged with great butternut trees, led down to the pond. Until Lansing christened it "St. Kitts," it was known in town after the name of his predecessor as the "Cayley Debevoise" house. The Debevoises, philoprogenitive and childlike themselves, lived in the happy tumult of their eleven children—six of their own and five nephews and nieces they had adopted. The rugs were in tatters, the chairs unsteady; some of the windows were sealed with brown paper for there was indoor catchball on rainy days. There was no dining room at all. Since they ate in the kitchen, the dining table was in the way of perpetual games and had been moved outdoors under the grape arbor. The clocks had broken down. The railings on the front and back porches were left unmended. Why mend them when there are always at least three children between nine and twelve? Little Nicholas and little Philippina were dressed in clothes that had been successively worn by at least three brothers or sisters or cousins. Happy Debevoises, where are you now?

From the first, Lansing admired John Ashley and imitated him, stumblingly. He went so far as to pretend that he, too, was a happily married man. Society would have got nowhere without those imitations of order and decorum that pass under the names of snobbery and hypocrisy. Ashley converted his Rainy Day House into a laboratory for experiment and invention. Lansing built a Rainy Day House behind "St. Kitts" and revived his interest in "snake oils." Perhaps it was the influence of the Debevoises, perhaps the example of the Ashleys, that enabled Eustacia to bear a child that lived, then another, then a third. The Lansings were older than the Ashleys, but their children were closely of an age: Félicité Marjolaine Dupuy Lansing (she was born on St. Felix's Day; the Iowa Lansing names had been carried to Heaven by the dead infants) and Lily Scolastica

Ashley; George Sims Lansing and Roger Berwyn Ashley; then Sophia alone; then Anne Lansing and Constance Ashley. Eustacia Lansing carried well her torch of hypocrisy or whatever it was. In public—at the Mayor's picnic, on the front bench at the Memorial Day exercises—she played the proud and devoted wife. Creole beauty is short-lived. By the time the Ashleys arrived in Coaltown Eustacia's tea-colored complexion had turned a less delicate hue; her features had lost much of their doelike softness; she was decidedly plump. Nevertheless, everyone in Coaltown, from Dr. Gillies to the boy who shined shoes at the Tavern, knew that the town could boast two handsome and unusual women. Mrs. Ashley was tall and fair; Mrs. Lansing was short and dark. Mrs. Ashley—child of the ear as a German—had no talent for dress, but a magical speaking voice, and she moved like a queen; Mrs. Lansing—child of the eye as a Latin—was mistress of color and design, though her voice cut like a parrot's and her gait lacked grace. Mrs. Ashley was serene and slow to speak; Mrs. Lansing was abrupt and voluble. Mrs. Ashley had little humor and less wit; Mrs. Lansing ransacked two languages and a dialect for brilliant and pungent *mots* and was a devastating mimic. For almost twenty years these ladies were in and out of one another's house, as were their children. They got on well together without one vibration of sympathy. Beata Ashley lacked the imagination or freedom of attention to penetrate the older woman's misery. (John Ashley was well aware of it, but did not speak.) One art they shared in common: both were incomparable cooks; one condition: both were far removed from the environment that had shaped their early lives.

For these two families the first ten years went by without remarkable event: pregnancies, diapers, and croup; measles and falling out of trees; birthday parties, dolls, stamp collections, and whooping cough. George was caught stealing Roger's three-sen stamp; Roger had his mouth washed out with soap and water for saying "hell." Félicité, who aspired to be a nun, was discovered sleeping on the floor in emulation of some saint; Constance refused to speak to her best friend Anne for a week. You know all that.

In Coaltown the principal meal, weekdays, was at noon. Supper was at six and consisted of "leftovers." No one invited friends in to a meal, with one exception: church members, in turn, invited their minister and his family to Sunday dinner. Relatives from out of town were scarcely considered to be guests; the women helped cook the dinner and wash the dishes. Beata Ashley astonished the town by inviting friends to a late meal by candlelight from which the children were absent. The Lansings were always present, occasionally Dr. Gillies and his wife, or a retired judge who had known city life, and some others. Mrs. Lansing returned the invitations. Twice a year members of the mine's Pittsburgh directorate descended on the town on a tour of inspection. They put up at the Illinois Tavern, but were invited to "St. Kitts" and "The Elms" for dinner. They received the surprise of their lives—a surprise which did not abate on repeated visits: Beata Ashley's tranquil distinction; Eustacia's wit and beauty, together with the flamboyance of her clothes and that *grain de beauté* which nature had planted with the most calculated art on her right cheekbone; the variety of subjects discussed and the quality and the originality of the food. (Their wives had to pay for it: "Isn't there anything else in the world to eat except roast beef and stewed chicken?" "Do you have to talk about the servants all the time?") At these dinners John Ashley spoke little, yet all eyes were constantly turned toward him. It was for him that the men were judicious, but easy; the women charming; and Lansing discreet. The visitors expressed to him their gratification at the improvement in the mine's returns. Casually, all but unobtrusively, he directed the commendation to Breckenridge Lansing.

One thing of remark happened during those first ten years. Eustacia Lansing fell consumedly in love with John Ashley.

As we know, John Ashley saved no money. He had married an accomplished housekeeper and had bought an orchard, kitchen garden, and henhouse. From time to time he suppressed in himself the concern as to how he would provide a better education for his children. He had a vague notion that he would be able to make some money out of the "inventions" that he was evolving in the Rainy Day House. He had become engrossed in locks. He bought up old safes collected from the ashes of buildings that had burned to the ground. He studied timepieces and firearms. Lansing, imitating him sedulously in his Rainy Day House, dropped his interests in lotions and cosmetics and tried his hand at mechanics. Ashley encouraged him warmly in these interests. The younger man followed with great concern Lansing's dissipation on the River Road, his sloth, and his neglect of Eustacia. They launched out on projects together; Ashley kept up the pretense that Lansing was an invaluable co-worker. Lansing brought to these projects his vision of their success, of the enormous amounts of money they would bring. But year after year Ashley delayed forwarding his designs to the Patent Office; to himself, he seemed always on the point of improving them. To maintain Lansing's enthusiasm he wrote their combined names, beautifully, on the various folders that contained the mechanical drawings. But tinkering with coils and springs and bits of steel was not sufficient to distract Breckenridge Lansing long from the fields where he was second to none.

Breckenridge Lansing's father treated his wife and children with contempt; his son tried to. This view was not universal in those States, but frequent. At the end of the last century the patriarchal age was drawing to a close; its majesty was cracking. We may assume that when a patriarchal order is at its height— or a matriarchal order, also—it has a certain grandeur. It contributes to the even running of society and to harmony in the home. Everyone knows his place. The head of the family is always right. Fatherhood invests him with a more than personal wisdom. His position resembles that of the king who throughout thousands of years of unquestioned and even divine sanction, receives in the cradle the capacities that make for leadership. The doctrine was so deeply instilled that the people regarded the errors, vices, and imbecilities of kings as expressions of God's will: bad kings were sent for the punishment, instruction, and edification of men. Wives and subjects perpetuated these dispensations. It is when the patriarchal order is undergoing transition—the pendulum swings in eternal oscillation between the male and female poles—that havoc descends upon the state and on the family. Fathers feel the pavement cracking beneath them. For a time they shout, argue, boast, and pour scorn upon the wife of their bosom and the pledges of their love. Abraham did not raise his voice. Women armored themselves as best they could during the transition. Guile is the shield and spear of the oppressed. Slaves cannot revolt without leaders, but slavery is a poor school for leadership. Breckenridge Lansing's mother was an example of a woman in an age of crumbling patriarchy. Her sons knew no other patterns than a bullying father and a cowed mother.

Eustacia Lansing had been brought up in a matriarchy. She was unable to comprehend the tacit assumptions that shaped family life in Coaltown. She was saved by her gift of humor. A crumbling patriarchy is tragic and very funny.

It is the growing sons who suffer most in the age of transition.

Even in the best of homes, at the best of times, a boy is always in the wrong. Boys are filled with exhausting energies; they enjoy noise; they are (or where would we be?) adventurous and inquiring. They creep out onto ledges and fall into caves and two hundred men spend nights searching for them. They must hurl objects. They particularly cherish small animals and must have them near. A respect for cleanliness is as slowly and painfully acquired as mastery of the violin. They are perpetually famished and can barely be taught to eat decorously (the fork was late appearing in society). They are unable to sit still for more than ten minutes unless they are being told a story about mayhem and sudden death (or where would we be?). They receive several hundred rebukes a day. They rage at the humiliation of being male and not men. They strain to hasten the calendar. They must smoke and swear. Dark warnings are thrown out to them about "impurity" and "filthiness"—interesting occupations which seem to be reserved to adults. They peer into mirrors for the first promise of a beard. No wonder they are happy only among their coevals; they return from their unending games (that resemble warfare) puffed up, it may be, with triumph—late, dirty, or bloody. Few records have reached us of the early years of Richard the Lion-Hearted; the story about George Washington and the cherry tree is not widely believed. Achilles and Jason were brought up by a tutor who was half-man, half-horse. Their education was all in the open air; there must have been a good deal of running involved and very little mystery surrounding the natural functions.

Breckenridge Lansing brought up his son according to a method widely advocated at the time. Its purpose was to "make a man" of him. It consisted of ridiculing the child in public and private on every occasion of his falling short in manly exercise. At five he was thrown into the water and commanded to swim. At six he was invited to play catch with his father ("the best father in the world," but all fathers are wonderful) on the lawn behind the house. Coordination of hand and eye is not fully developed at six and is further troubled by the boy's passionate and despairing attempts to be adequate. The genial games ended in tears. At seven he was given a pony; when he had fallen off it for the third time his father sold it. At nine he was introduced to the rifle. At each new trial he was overwhelmed with sneers and his failures were recounted to neighbors and postmen and delivery boys. Eustacia attempted to intervene only to be covered with similar sarcasms. Little Anne endeared herself to her father by shrieking "Sissy! Sissy!" Woeful scenes took place. Félicité paled but did not speak. When George was elected vice-captain of his school's baseball team—only vice-captain; Roger Ashley was everywhere captain—his father refused to speak to him for three days. Nature came to George's aid too late. At sixteen he was as tall as his father and far stronger. He was given to murderous rages. The day came when he advanced on his tormentor, holding a chair which he slowly broke in mid-air. From that hour his father loudly washed his hands of him. George was the product of his mother's mollycoddling. He would never be a Lansing.

His father was right. George was a Sims and a Dutellier and a Creusot. He had his mother's dark complexion. His schoolmates called him "Nig" until he thrashed it out of them. Miss Dobrey, of the high school, said that he had the "face of an angry lynx." He collected about him a gang of his friends and called them the "Mohicans." They became the terror of the town. They altered the signposts on the roads. They set the church bells jangling. They even climbed Herkomer's Knob and tried to spy on the Sunday-evening services at the Church of the Covenant. They took large allowance of the license accorded at Halloween. Chief Constable Leyendecker called several times at "St. Kitts." George never finished high school. He was sent away, briefly, to several military academies and preparatory schools.

Anne was her father's favorite and walked the earth with the assurance that such predilection confers. Life presented few obstacles which obstinacy, clamor, and rudeness could not remove. She was all Lansing—an angel of cerulean blue eye, of cornsilk hair, of inborn certitudes. She was a little lady at ten and a formidable matron at thirteen. Her best friend was Constance Ashley—Constance, who came from a home where no voices were ever raised and no claims for privileged attention ever advanced. Children arrive at amnesties that diplomats might envy. Constance made clear the limits beyond which she would not be browbeaten, but the friendship was often in jeopardy.

Félicité's mother on the island of St. Kitts had enjoyed two half-hours of happiness daily: at dawn before the altar, at midnight above her snowy trousseau. Félicité's dream was to combine them—she hoped to enter the religious life. She attended the convent school at Fort Barry until she became aware that her presence was necessary in her home. She renounced the joy she felt in the life at St. Joseph's and entered the high school in Coaltown. She resembled her mother in appearance, though taller; she had none of her mother's vivacity. She was an exemplary student and would have excelled in schoolwork many times more difficult. At the age when many girls keep diaries and guard them under lock and key, she wrote her diary in Latin. She was an accomplished needlewoman and dressed herself with a taste and distinction that astonished even her mother. It was understood in the family that no one entered Félicité's room, though the door stood open all day. She would have wished it to be white, but white rooms were labor lost in Coaltown. It was blue, with touches of deep red and purple; it was at once simple and rich. Her skill in embroidery was everywhere present, in curtains, counterpanes, table runners, and antimacassars. She had been enthralled by Miss Doubkov's icons and had imitated them in her own way. Religious pictures—set on backgrounds of velvet and surrounded with gold lace and colored beads—glowed from the walls. The silks on her prie-dieu changed with the feasts and the seasons. The room was neither a cell nor a chapel—it was a place of waiting and of preparation for great happiness. From time to time in the day's work, when Félicité was absent, her mother would lean against the door frame gazing into the room. "The children we bring into the world!"

Like her sister, Félicité had been a stormy child. She had won her contained disposition by daily struggle, year after year, winning at the same time a measure of detachment from the "world." She was moving toward abstraction. She loved her mother. She loved her brother passionately. But these loves were already imbued with the love of the *creature* which was enjoined upon her. Through these same disciplines she had found her way to a love for her father and younger sister. She had no friends. Félicité was respected, but not liked. During the stormy scenes at "St. Kitts" she never left the room—not when Anne lay rolling and screaming on the hearthrug ("I will not go to bed!" "I will not wear the blue dress!"); not when her father hurled one wounding phrase after another at his wife and son. She seldom spoke; she moved nearer to her mother and brother and listened to her father with unshaken gaze. A man's severest judges are his children and he knows it —severest of all when they are silent. She stood by her mother, but there was a barrier between them. They sewed together; they read together the classics of French literature; they partook of the sacrament side by side. They were mother and daughter in deep admiration and fellow suffering, but there was no laughter. Eustacia was born with an apprehension of the comical incongruities in life and, for all her trials, found amusement everywhere. It was an element in her nature that she could not share with her older daughter. (George caught— and could return—every inflection of his mother's wit, rare though the flashes were.) Year after year, before and after her father's death, Félicité postponed her great decision in order to be of use in the family at "St. Kitts."

Mother and daughter had more in common, however, than they were fully aware of. Both were journeying; both were waiting; both were straining to understand. They were present at a woeful drama, but they never doubted their prayers and patience and love would yield some enlightenment—for all. We came into the world to learn. They had lived among wonders all their lives. (Hadn't they, for example, mastered their ugly senseless tempers?) They never doubted that some miracle would arrive.

Fortunately, George had two friends: John Ashley and Olga Doubkov. Ashley "covered" Lansing's incompetence at the

mine by gradually assuming most of the functions of his superior and endeavored to furnish him wholesome occupation by
associating him in the experiments and inventions. (At the trial
these good offices were variously interpreted; it was charged
that he was bent on usurping Lansing's position, and that in the
experiments he made a systematic theft of Lansing's brilliant
ideas.) There was little Ashley could do, however, to correct
Lansing's method of "making a man" out of George. He did
what he could. He managed to extract from the boy a succession of plans for his lifework—at twelve he wanted to invent
flying machines; at thirteen he wanted to go to Africa to save
the lions from extermination; at fourteen he wanted to join a
circus. It was early in George's fifteenth year that an occasion
presented itself that greatly advanced the friendship.

The Lansing children were subject to illness and accident. In
the early fall of 1900 George suffered a succession of colds and
sore throats. It was decided that his tonsils should be trimmed
or removed. Lansing directed his wife to take the boy to Dr.
Hunter in Fort Barry and pass the nights before and after the
operation in the Farmer's Hotel there. Her daughters went with
her, though Félicité spent the nights at the convent school.

John Ashley seldom left Coaltown, but on that Friday—as it
happened—he had business in Fort Barry. The negotiation
dragged on and required his remaining there overnight. He
went to the railroad station and asked Jerry Bilham, the conductor, to tell Coaltown's stationmaster to inform Mrs. Ashley
that he would not be home until the morrow. The Farmer's
Hotel was full, but the great Mr. Corrigan arranged that a cot
be set up for him in the pantry. Ashley did not see Mrs. Lansing
or her son during the day, but he came upon Anne on the
hotel porch and listened to a long self-important explanation
of her presence in Fort Barry. Ashley had failed to bring sufficient pocket money to buy his dinner at the hotel; he went to
a lunchroom and ordered a bowl of soup. By ten o'clock all
were sleeping soundly except Eustacia Lansing and her son.
George was tossing and babbling in his sleep. His mother rose,
lit the gaslight, and spoke to him.

"George! George, dear! It's nothing. Hundreds of people
have their tonsils taken out every month. You'll have forgotten
all about it in a week. You won't have sore throats any more."

"Is it almost morning? What time is it, Mama?"

She told herself it was the break in routine that was unsettling. George had not slept away from his own bed more than eight times in his life—he had been Roger's guest at "The Elms"; there had been some hunting trips with his father. She had not slept ten times away from "St. Kitts" since her arrival there. She talked of the ice cream the doctor had prescribed for him, of the improvement in his condition for athletics.

They had this secret. She would tell him about the most beautiful island in the world, about the blue sky and water, about how she ran a store when she was only a few years older than he was, about her large handsome laughing mother, fanning herself on the verandah, about her father in his beautiful white uniform, about the young men on the island who were always singing and serenading. She talked of these things with no one else. It was understood that she would someday take him there; he would take *her* there, in fact. George was devout. He wanted to go to the church; he wanted to kneel at the very spot where she had knelt. From time to time she spoke of his father's visit to St. Kitts, but George made no comment. He never mentioned his father. She sang a song in her *patois* and George fell asleep. She moved over to a large wicker chair by the window and looked down at the town square. All was dark.

"Dark as my life," she thought, but caught herself short. "No! No! My life is hard but not dark. Something's coming. Something's unfolding. My mistake is going to be redeemed." How could she wish her life to have been different, if that difference would remove—would annihilate—her children? "We *are* our lives. Everything is bound together. No smallest action can be thought other than it is." She groped among the concepts of necessity and free will. Everything is mysterious, but how unendurable life would be without the mystery. She slipped to her knees and buried her face in her arms on the seat of the chair.

The moon rose.

Toward midnight George gave a loud cry and sprang up in his bed like a leaping fish. "No! No!"

"Sh, George, Mama's here."

"Where am I?"

"We're at Fort Barry. Everything's all right, dear."

George began to sob. He shook his head from side to side; he struck it against the bedstead. Anne awoke and chanted, "Crybaby! Sissy!" He refused a glass of water. He struck his mother's hand from his forehead. Half an hour later he was still weeping as from some bottomless despair. His mother paced to and fro, distraught. She thought of sending for Father Dillon. Suddenly she became aware of the sound of voices in the corridor—some guests were returning to their rooms, shepherded by the great Mr. Corrigan himself.

"Keep your voices down, gentlemen. There are a lot of people sleeping in the house . . . Joe! Joe! . . . Herb! . . . That's not your room. Come along, here . . . Lift your feet, Joe—that's right!"

Eustacia Lansing dressed and woke Anne. She told her to dress and go downstairs. "Tell Mr. Corrigan that your brother has an attack of nerves. Tell him to wake Mr. Ashley and ask Mr. Ashley to come here to talk to your brother."

Anne enjoyed her mission and performed it ably. Ashley came to their room.

"It's nightmares, John. I can't do anything with him. Dr. Hunt's taking out his tonsils tomorrow.—Anne, be quiet and get into bed."

Anne was kneeling on her mother's bed, hissing, "Sissy! Sissy!"

Ashley crossed the room and sat down beside her. He asked confidentially: "Why do you say that, Anne?"

"Boys don't cry."

"I know. That's what Coaltown thinks."

"Everybody knows that."

"Coaltown's a very small place, Anne. There are millions of people who never heard of Coaltown. There are an awful lot of things that Coaltown doesn't know. I wouldn't like to think that you and Constance are just little Coaltown girls that don't know very much—just little country girls that only think what Coaltown thinks."

"What do you mean, Mr. Ashley?"

"Didn't you ever hear that the biggest and strongest men cry sometimes?"

"No . . . Papa never cries. Papa says—"

"Abraham Lincoln cried. And King David cried. You know that. And we were just reading aloud the other night about how Achilles cried—you couldn't find a braver man than Achilles. The book said that great tears fell on his hands. Your brother's going to be a very strong man and sometimes he's going to cry."

Anne was silent. George held his breath. Ashley took the chair by George and gestured to his mother, directing her to move away as far as possible. He spoke in a low voice.

"I know about bad dreams, George. I know all about them. —You don't like having your tonsils out tomorrow?"

"No. I don't care about that. It . . . isn't that."

"Everybody laughs at dreams, but they can be very bad. And very real. I used to have them after I got this scar on my jaw. Can you see it? I got that from a pitchfork when I was haying. I was just about your age.—Can you remember your dream?"

"Not . . . all of it."

"Nobody can hear us."

"He was chasing me."

"Who?"

"It was like a giant. He had a round knife like they cut high grass with."

"A sickle or a scythe?"

"It was like a sickle."

"Do you know who it was chasing you?"

"No, it was like a giant. He was laughing like it was a game, but . . ."

"You got away all right."

"I don't want to go to sleep again. I turned around and I did something at him. And he . . . burst. It was awful, Mr. Ashley. It was all squashy under my feet, like maybe I killed him or something. I only wanted to stop him."

Here George turned his head to the wall and lay trembling.

"I see. I see. Yes, it's a bad dream you had. No wonder you're shaken up. But in a way it's a good dream, too. A man has to defend himself. It's a growing-up dream, George."

"Will he be there again, if I go to sleep?"

"Come to the window and look out. Look, the moon's just come up. See the Soldiers' Monument? See him there with his chin up? Men had to fight. They didn't want to fight and they didn't want to kill. Do you know any men who fought in the Civil War?"

"Yes, I know lots, Mr. Ashley: Mr. Killigrew at the depot and Dan May's grandfather, and, I think, Mr. Corcoran."

"Yes, he was a drummer boy. Think of what they went through, George; and yet see how quiet it is down there. Listen! . . . Take some deep breaths of that air before you get back in bed. It's better than the air in Coaltown, I can tell you that!—One of the reasons you had a bad dream is because your throat's clogged up. It's a good thing that Dr. Hunter's going to get rid of that tomorrow.—George, why don't you ever work on a farm, summers, like my boy does? You're strong already, but that kind of work makes a man really strong. You know it's hard—hoeing and haying all day and milking and carrying middlings to the pigs. Now you'd better get back into bed."

"Papa doesn't want me to. He says we're rich enough so I don't have to work."

"Your father's just joking. Money has nothing to do with it. I'm your father's best friend. I can make him see it's a good thing. Mr. Bell says that in the summer he can use every hand he can get. You're no scamooter, George. It'd be a lucky farmer that'd hire you."

"Thanks, Mr. Ashley."

"Does the sun go round the earth, George, or does the earth go round the sun?"

"The earth goes round the sun, Mr. Ashley."

"And anything else?"

"The moon, and . . . the planets, I think."

"And what's the sun doing all that time?"

"It's going very fast."

"And carrying us with it?"

"Yes."

"It's as though we were on a great ship moving through the skies." Pause. "I often have that feeling just before I fall off to sleep. We're going at that great speed and yet you saw how quiet it is down there in the square. It's a wonderful fact, isn't it?"

"Yes, sir."

"Wonderful fact!"

Ashley walked to the window and looked out; then he returned to the chair beside the bed. "What do you want to be when you grow up, George?" George was silent. "Do you still want to go to Africa and save the lions?"

"No. I . . ."

"Have you an idea?"

"I . . . If you put down your ear, Mr. Ashley. I don't want anybody to hear it.—Did you ever see a show in a theayter, Mr. Ashley?"

"Yes. Yes, I have. I've seen Edwin Booth play Hamlet."

"Did you? . . . Mama, Félicité, and I read *Hamlet* together."

"Did you?"

"Edwin Booth's brother killed President Lincoln, didn't he?"

"A high-strung family, I guess, George. Nervous."

"At one of the schools I went to they took us to see *Uncle Tom's Cabin*. . . . I want to be one of them, Mr. Ashley."

When we are talking soberly to the young we are moving in evanescent landscapes, in corridors of dreams, abysses on either side. Ashley could not know who this was he was talking to—who it was in the fullest of time.

"If you have the talent, George, and the will, you can be whatever you want to. I'll tell you about Edwin Booth someday. But if that's what you want to be, you'd better have those tonsils cleared up as soon as possible. There are no giants in the Farmer's Hotel tonight, George. Shake hands. Now tell your mother you're going to sleep so that she can get some rest, too."

Eustacia followed him to the door. She could barely find the breath to utter a word of thanks. She sat for an hour by the window, very conscious of the ship that was carrying her and her family. She rested her cheek on her hand, a faint unprompted smile upon her face. During that hour she ridded herself—she threw overboard—the last remnants of an unhappiness that had long tormented her—she ceased to envy Beata Ashley her marriage.

Almost twenty years before—on her honeymoon in New York's ice and snow—Eustacia had seen in a store window a handpainted copy of Millet's "The Angelus." It had seemed to her the most beautiful painting that a human spirit could fashion, and that to own it would introduce an unfailing benison into one's life. In an adjacent window stood an alabaster model of the Taj Mahal. She had never heard of that edifice, but a printed card told its story. It was an homage to conjugal love. Changing lights so played upon it that it seemed to be revealed now at dawn, then at noon, then in moonlight. She thought of the rich people who could afford to purchase such treasure. Slowly she had learned that beautiful things are not for our possession but for our contemplation. At "St. Kitts" she had overmastered anger. At Fort Barry she divested herself of the last pangs of envy.

George's other friend was Olga Sergeievna Doubkov. The seamstress had been a frequent visitor in the home during his early years and had remained so until that day when she had left it in indignation, denouncing Breckenridge Lansing for his treatment of his son. She had spent long hours with Eustacia and Félicité, revolving around a dressmaker's dummy, babbling happily about gores and gussets and *feuilletés* and *entrelacements*. On occasional evenings when it was certain that the master of the house would not return, she could be persuaded to stay to supper. At first the younger children resented the presence of the "sewing lady," but gradually they came to look forward to it. They found her conversation absorbing. In her home in Russia the Countesses Olga and Irena had been brought up by French, German, and English governesses. Their parents, before dressing for dinner, visited them in the nursery at the end of the day. Twice a month, however, the girls were invited, with much formality, to dine with their father and mother. The girls knew well that when their parents gave a ball, when neighbors came to dinner, when there were guests staying in the house, conversation was generally conducted in French. When they dined with their children the conversation was conducted in Russian. They never discussed the governesses, the neighbors, the daily life. Their mother talked about foreign countries and about famous painters and musicians. Their father talked about the achievements of great men— about Mr. Watt and his steam engine, Dr. Jenner and his inoculations, and about balloon ascensions. He talked about the wonders of nature—about comets and volcanoes and beehives. Above all they talked about Russia, its history, its greatness, its holiness, its future—that future that would astonish the world.

No mention was made of things that might be improved in Russia. Their father was to talk of those later, after they had crossed the border.

So it was that Miss Doubkov, seated at the supper table at "St. Kitts," talked about foreign countries and great artists, and Mr. Edison's lamp and talking machines, about what men had uncovered in the ashes at Pompeii. Moreover, Miss Doubkov found delicate ways of expressing her admiration for her hostess. It gave George great pride to hear his mother praised. His glance slid to her face to make sure that she heard these tributes. Miss Doubkov even spoke of Mr. Lansing's popularity and his importance in the town. Finally the day came when she told them about Russia, its history, its greatness, its holiness, and its future—that future that would astonish the world. She told them of the great Tsar who had built his capital on a marsh, of another who had freed the serfs, of the glories of Pushkin, of the immensity and the beauty of the country.

George asked, "Miss Doubkov, what language do they talk in Russia?"

"The Russian language."

"Will you talk some Russian to me . . . please!"

Miss Doubkov paused, looked gravely into his face and addressed him in Russian. He listened spellbound.

"What did you say, Miss Doubkov?"

"I said, 'George, son of Breckenridge'—that's the way grown-ups address one another—I said, 'You are young. You are not happy now because you have not yet discovered the work to which you will give your life. Somewhere in the world there is a work for you to do, to which you will bring courage and honor and loyalty. For every man there is one great task that God has given him to do. I think that yours will demand a brave heart and some suffering; but you will triumph.'"

There was a silence. George sat as one turned to stone. Anne looked at her brother as though she had never seen him before.

"How do you know that, Miss Doubkov?" asked Anne.

"Because George resembles my father."

Thus began the strange friendship between a boy not yet sixteen, the town's "holy terror," and a Russian spinster nearing fifty. It gathered strength quickly—at the supper table and after supper in the living room. It grew by fits and starts, for boys, like young animals, spasmodically tire even of the thing that most engages them; and because George was being sent away to one school after another. Perhaps he arranged to be expelled from them in order to return to these conversations.

"My father escaped from Russia under the very eyes of the police who were hunting for him. He shaved his beard and moustache and his eyebrows. He disguised himself as an old woman crossing the country on a religious pilgrimage. We sang hymns and begged. We were covered with religious medals. I've shown some of them to Félicité."

"Yes."

"My mother was ill. We bought a two-wheeled cart and pulled her along with us. We had money hidden on us, but to avoid suspicion we begged and slept in monasteries."

"What did your father do that was bad?" asked Anne.

"He had a secret printing press in the house. He printed pamphlets."

"What are pamphlets?"

"Keep quiet!" said George.

"He believed that the only hope for Russia was to overturn the government. He hoped to prepare the people for a revolution without violence. Already in every city and town there were men and women working with this same purpose in mind. Finally, however, my father no longer believed in his printing press and his pamphlets. People read them and did nothing. My father used to say that the Russian people talked to avoid decision. My father made other plans."

Her listeners waited. Suddenly Miss Doubkov made the gesture of hurling an object forcefully across the room.

"Why did you do that, Miss Doubkov?" asked Anne.

"Be quiet!" said George.

Eustacia said faintly, "But, surely, there are better ways of arriving at good government than that!"

"Than what, Mama?"

"Hush, dear."

"Anne, I will tell you a story. Have you ever seen a muzzle on a dog?"

"No. What's a muzzle?"

"It's a band of leather bound around a dog's nose. Sometimes it's a little straw basket strapped to his nose."

"So he won't bite anybody. But how can he eat, Miss Doub-kov?"

"The lion is the king of all beasts, Anne. He is the lord of the jungle. There is no limit to what he can do when he wishes. Once upon a time in Africa there was a great king Lion who put muzzles on all the other lions—and on the tigers and panthers, too. He put muzzles on all of them except on his family and his twenty cousins. These other animals could only open their mouths a little bit. When they were hungry they could only eat very small animals. But the great king and his family and his twenty cousins could eat all the deer they wanted—and all the antelope and gazelles. And they ate and ate. But some of those young lions found ways of loosening the muzzles on their noses, so the king thought up something else. He tied up their front paws with straps and bands so that they couldn't run fast. There was a banquet every night in the king's palace, but all those other lions went around limping, limping, with those shameful boxes on their noses. There was joy in the palace every night. Was there joy anywhere else?"

"No," cried the children.

"Was there any joy when a new lion cub was born?"

"No!—No!"

"Children! Children! You mustn't get so excited!"

"So one day the other lions met together in a remote part of the jungle to talk about their wretched life. What could they do? It seemed to them that there was only one thing to do."

"I know," said George, striking the sides of his chair. His face was white. Miss Doubkov went on as though she had not heard him.

"The worst part about the whole situation, Anne—remember!—was that the lion is the noblest of all the animals in the forest. The Russian nation is the greatest nation that has ever lived on the face of the earth. No nation loves so deeply the land in which it lives. No nation is so brave in its own defense—as Napoleon discovered and lost a mighty army. No nation is so diligent and so long-enduring. The countries of Europe are decaying daily. I have seen them. They are in a race for wealth and pleasure. They have forgotten God. But the people of Russia bear God in their hearts, like a man carrying a lantern under his coat on a stormy night." Here she paused and lowered her voice. "Russia is the Christ-bearing country. She is the Ark that will save the human race when the great floods come. Here in America you have not even a nation. Every man thinks of himself before he thinks of his country. That's why it was shameful that one lion and a few cousins— one handful of unworthy lions—could reduce all the other lions to the level of starving dogs. And my father saw that there was only one thing to be done."

"To kill him! To kill him!" cried George, rising, and going to the wall he hammered it with his fists.

"George!" called his mother.

"Kill him! Kill him!" cried George, falling to his knees and pounding the floor.

"George," said his mother. "Come finish your supper and control yourself."

George rose, hurled some bombs through the windows and dashed out of the house. Félicité slipped out after him.

"My children are so high strung, Olga. It's their Creole blood." She went to the front door, looked out, and returned with an anxious expression on her face. "My mother had a terrible temper.—And her father! Nobody could do anything with him."

"*Maman*, why did George get so excited?"

"Sh, dear. We all get a little excited when we hear about injustice."

Félicité found her brother lying face downward on the croquet court. He was panting and exhausted. They had a long whispered conversation. Finally they returned to the dining room. George stood by the door.

"Miss Doubkov, will you teach me how to talk Russian?"

Miss Doubkov looked at Eustacia, who looked at them both in turn. She could find nothing to say.

"George," said Anne, "you're crazy. You couldn't learn anything. You were the worst student in the whole school and you've been sent home from three other schools already."

"I can learn anything, if I want to learn it."

"But, George," said his mother, "you'd have no opportunity to speak it, except to Miss Doubkov."

"I'll have to speak it when I go to Russia."

"Finish your supper and we'll think about it."

"I've thought about it already."

Breckenridge Lansing was not told about these lessons. They were conducted in the linen room under the Illinois Tavern or in the Rainy Day House. Eustacia insisted on paying for them and Miss Doubkov accepted half the price offered her. Miss Doubkov had no experience of teaching languages, but she suspected that her pupil's progress was remarkable. He himself devised their form: he entered a hotel in St. Petersburg and engaged a room; he ordered a meal in a restaurant and, becoming a waiter, served it. In Moscow he bought a fur hat, a dog, a horse. He went to a theatre. He revisited the theatre by the "artists' entrance." He put questions to the leading actors. He went to church and even learned some of the liturgy in Old Slavonic. He went to taverns and fell into conversation with young men of his own age (twenty-three and twenty-four!). He discussed good and bad government with them. He reminded them that Russia was the greatest country the world had ever seen. His progress between lessons astonished his teacher. (In Russian: "*Well, Olga Sergeievna, I take walks and I talk and I pretend I'm in Russia.*") Miss Doubkov gave him the dictionary that her father had bought in Constantinople thirty-five years ago. She lent him her New Testament, which he read with his mother's French version. "Mama, it's like a different book in Russian. It's like it's more a man's book." There came the day when he asked his teacher, in a low voice, to repeat those words which she had said to him in Russian—

"Which words, George, son of Breckenridge?"

"The first words I ever heard in Russian."

She repeated them slowly, as best she could remember them. He needed no translation. To the impassioned will nothing is impossible. He was finding direction. His voice deepened. He was helpful about the house. He cleaned the eaves, hung out laundry lines, smoked out hornets' nests, dried the dishes. He was not only punctual at meals, but during his father's frequent absences he set out to replace him. He praised what was set before him. He inspirited the conversation. He had inherited his mother's gift of mimicry and told long stories about the schools from which he had been ejected. Particularly fine was his account of Dr. Kopping, a Protestant clergyman and director of the Pines Point Boys' Recreational and Educational Camp. Dr. Kopping, "just another boy himself at heart," closed each day with a short talk about the council fire, inculcating the manly virtues. Anne would run around the table and throw herself at him. "George! George! Do the housemother at St. Regis's! Do Dr. Kopping again!" The virulence of these caricatures made his mother uneasy. She had reason to be. George did not mimic his father in her presence, nor in Félicité's. When they were out of the room, however, he regaled Anne with some astonishing portraits—her father killing birds and rabbits, her father exhausted after his hard day's work at the mines, her father "washing his hands" of George, her father fulsomely endearing himself to her, to "Papa's little angel." In a very short time Anne doted on her brother; in a very short time she discovered that her father was ridiculous. Anne accepted correction from George. He seemed to know that little Russian princesses do not scream and stamp their feet, when it is time to go to bed. When they go to bed they make a curtsy to their mother and say, "Thank you, dear mother, for all that you have done for me." They curtsy also to their older sisters. And if they have been very good, one or other of the princes, their brothers, carries them upstairs to bed in his arms and says a prayer over them in Old Slavonic. If George was planning to be an actor, he did not wait for the glitter of the footlights; he played the head of a noble household at "St. Kitts."

All the Lansings were impassioned conversationalists; though Félicité's interventions were rare they were pondered. There was reading aloud; any scene from Molière or Shakespeare set in motion a long discussion. Night after night Eustacia despaired of getting them to bed at ten-thirty. It was Anne who benefited most from these hours of wide-ranging conversation. There was now a new Anne, maturing rapidly. She led her classes in school. She completed the overnight assignments in a mere quarter of an hour in order to take part in the evening's symposium. Occasionally Breckenridge Lansing returned at ten from some lodge meeting. On opening his front door he would be aware for a few seconds of the warmth and intellectual energy of this home life, and of the sudden silence introduced by his presence. One evening he admitted himself soundlessly and stood listening in the hall:

"*Maman*, Miss Doubkov says that Russian writers are the greatest writers that ever lived. And the greatest of them all

was a Negro. Papa says that Negroes aren't even people and
that it's no use teaching them to read and write." ("*Chéri*, everyone can have his opinions.") "Well, Papa's opinions are
pretty silly most of the time." ("George, I don't want you to talk
about your father like that. Your father is—") "His opinions! I
don't care what he says about *me*, but when he says about
you—" ("George! Talk about something else!") "When he says
about you that you haven't any more brains than what God
gave a gopher—" ("That's just his joke.") "It was a BAD JOKE.
And when he broke that shell on the mantel that your mother
sent you—" ("George, it was just a shell!") "He STAMPED on
it! It came from the place that you were BORN at!" ("The older
we grow, the less we're attached to things, George.") "Well,
I'm attached to my pride, *Maman*—and to YOUR pride."

Lansing did not risk eavesdropping a second time.

One of the reasons Eustacia did all she could to render these
evenings engrossing (she cut clippings from periodicals; she
sent to Chicago for books and for reproductions of paintings)
was to keep George off the streets. George inside the walls of
"St. Kitts" was a changed human being; outside them, he continued to infuriate the town. He was the "holy terror" and the
Big Chief of the Mohicans. No amount of supplication on his
mother's part could alter that. He listened to her with a stormy
face, his arms folded, his gaze on the wall over her shoulder.

"*Maman*, I've got to have some fun. I'm sorry, but I've got
to have some fun."

Eustacia knew well that the outrages were conceived and
executed with one sole purpose—to drive his father to distraction. He rejoiced in his father's contempt. He, too, seemed to
be waiting for something—for his father to strike him, or to
order him out of the house forever? Under the rain of his
father's sneers and denunciations he stood with lowered eyes,
motionless and with no shade of impertinence in his manner.

"Do you realize that you've brought disgrace on your
mother and myself?"

"Yes, sir."

"Do you realize that there's not *one* self-respecting person in
this town who has a good word to say for you?"

"Yes, sir."

"Why do you do it?"

"I don't know, sir."

"I don't know, sir! Well, in September I'm sending you to a new school I've heard about where they don't stand for any nonsense."

The Mohicans soon outgrew reversing road signs and tinkering with the town clock. They did little damage to health or property; they merely affronted decorum and right thinking. They staged complicated, well-rehearsed practical jokes that ridiculed banks, the laying of cornerstones, revivalist meetings. There was only one of the Mohicans' recreations that brought the Chief of Police to the door. It terrified Eustacia. The boys enjoyed riding "possum clancy." Hoboes, by hundreds and thousands, traveled about the country on freight trains. When a long train pulled into a railroad yard it often dropped a score of these passengers, like blackberries off a bough. When they found entrance to empty cars or lay on top of them or crouched on couplers, they were said to be riding "roost"; when they stretched out on the undersides of the cars, clutching or strapping themselves to the "riggers," they were riding "possum clancy." It was exciting and dangerous. George and his friends often traveled to Fort Barry or Summerville and back in a single night.

"George! Promise me never to ride those freight trains."

"*Maman*, you know I took a vow never to make any promises."

"For my sake! George, for *my* sake!"

"*Maman*, won't you let me give you just *one* hour of Russian lesson a week?"

"Oh, *chéri*, I couldn't learn Russian. When would I use it?"

"Well, when I'm in Russia and get settled down, you and the girls are coming over to live with me."

"George!!—Who would take care of your father?"

She begged him to stay in one of those schools—at least six months! "I want you to have an education, George."

"I'm better educated than the fellows in those schools. I know algebra and chemistry and history. I just don't like *examinations*. And I don't like sleeping in a room with three or eight or a hundred other people. They stink. And they're so babyish.— You're an education, *Maman*."

"Oh, don't say a thing like that!"

"Papa went to college and he hasn't any more education than a flea."

"Now, George! I won't have you saying such things. I won't have it."

Eustacia had a greater concern: was George subject to "fits"? Was he, perhaps, "crazy"? She had no clear idea what "fits" were, nor did she know any marks by which to distinguish insanity. At the beginning of this century such afflictions and dreads were too shameful to discuss with anyone except one's family doctor, and then in undertones. But the Lansings' family doctor was extremely hard of hearing. Even if Eustacia had respected Dr. Gridley's skill, she could not have brought herself to shout the details of George's behavior. Years ago Breckenridge Lansing had quarreled with Dr. Gillies. Dr. Gillies had contradicted him with characteristic finality on a matter of medical knowledge. Lansing did not lightly brook contradiction. He had taken a year of premedical training in his youth. His father was the best pharmacist in the state of Iowa and Breckenridge had assisted him for over two years in the family drugstore. He knew more about medicine "in his little finger" than that old horse doctor had acquired in a lifetime of practice. He refused to greet Dr. Gillies on the street. He instructed Eustacia that henceforward they would consult Dr. Jabez Gridley, the doctor serving the mine's infirmary. Dr. Gridley was a superannuated "Poor John" employee, like so many others. In addition to being "deaf as a post," his eyesight was failing. If you described your wound, burn, boil, or rash to him, he could occasionally be of service to you. Eustacia consulted her various household manuals—*A Home Book of First Aid* and *While Waiting for the Doctor*—and learned that the boy did not exhibit the classical symptoms of epilepsy. Moreover, she knew that he was so thoroughly an actor that it was difficult to distinguish between his abandoning himself to imaginative fantasies and his being out of his senses. He would beat with his fists on the floor and bay like a famished wolf; he would tear around the room in circles and dash up and down the stairs shouting "mahogany" or "begonia." In his love of danger he would balance himself on the roof and gables of "St. Kitts" under the full moon, or would climb the taller butternut trees and swing from treetop to treetop at three in the morning. He would cross Old Quarry Pond with ropes when the ice was already cracking to the accompaniment of the most musical pings. The townspeople and even his subjugated Mohicans were in no doubt that he was "crazy as a galoot." Eustacia had a high opinion of Dr. Gillies (whose wife was perfectly aware that he was "slavishly" admiring of Mrs. Lansing) and had frequently consulted him without her husband's knowledge. She paid for these visits—Félicité's anemia and Anne's ear-aches —out of her own pocket. She called on him now. Dr. Gillies consented to have a long talk with George. George gave a remarkable performance of intelligence, equilibrium, wit, and good manners. Dr. Gillies was not deceived.

"Mrs. Lansing, get that boy out of Coaltown or you'll have trouble."

"But *how*, Doctor?"

"Give him forty dollars and tell him to go to San Francisco to earn a living. He'll be able to take care of himself very well. He's not crazy, Mrs. Lansing; he's just *caged*. You run a great risk when you cage a living human being. There'll be no fee for that consultation, Mrs. Lansing. I had a very interesting talk" —whereupon Dr. Gillies gave a long low laugh.

Eustacia shrank from fulfilling the doctor's recommendation, but held ready a purse containing forty dollars.

The measure of Breckenridge Lansing's unhappiness could be gauged by the extent of his boasting. He was the happiest man in the United States. It had taken twenty years of hard work and careful management, but—by golly!—those mines were producing as they had never produced before. A well-run loving American home—that's the ticket! There's nothing like returning at the end of the day to one's own family. His listeners lowered their eyes.

He was not only unhappy but frightened. He loved his clubs and lodges, but in spite of the fact that he was the first citizen in town he was no longer elected to their prominent offices. The men in Coaltown were divided into two classes—those who wore high starched collars even in the hottest weather, and those who did not. The former group did not frequent the taverns up the River Road. They were not addressed by their first names in Hattie's Hitching Post. They did not return at dawn from Jemmy's shack where, between card games, whole nights were spent in attempts to whip up bloody fights between roosters, dogs, cats, foxes, snakes, and drunken farmhands. If a respectable family man felt the need of a little diversion and dissipation, he arranged a business trip to St. Louis or Springfield or Chicago. Lansing did not at first understand some warnings that were thrown out to him by the governors of his clubs. Within the memory of man no member had ever been ejected from those august assemblies, but a limit to their patience could be foreseen.

Lansing had set out to found that greatest of all institutions—a God-fearing American home. He held that a husband and a father should be loved, feared, honored, and obeyed. What had gone wrong? His conduct was not above reproach—he knew that; but no red-blooded man's is. His father's hadn't been. In the conduct of affairs he knew himself to be intelligent, conscientious, and diligent. He conceded that he had no talent for details. His strength lay in vision and planning; one could always leave details to spiritless drones. Lansing was wretched, frightened, and bewildered.

During the trial Breckenridge Lansing's character emerged without blemish. Humans shield humans whose frailties do not threaten their property and whose virtues do not devaluate their own. Ashley was that alien body from another climate—from the future, perhaps—who, in all times and places, has been expelled.

In the world inhabited by the Lansings of Iowa and Coaltown, it was generally understood that no man is ever sick. Sickness among males ends at fifteen and begins again, among the less hardy, at seventy. This lent a fine irony to the daily greetings— "Well, Joe, how are you?" "Just bearing up, Herb; just creeping around." When, therefore, in February, 1902, Breckenridge Lansing confessed to his wife that he wasn't feeling well, that his "food wasn't sitting good," and that there was a "sort of burning and a sort of pinching" in his stomach, Eustacia realized the extent of his suffering at once. He refused at first to see Dr. Gillies and asked for Dr. Gridley. When Eustacia pointed out that he would be obliged to shout the details of his discomfort within the hearing of half Coaltown, he consented to receive Gillies, "that old horse doctor." Eustacia was waiting on the front steps at the close of Dr. Gillies's visit.

"Mrs. Lansing, he doesn't want to tell me anything. Do you think he's feeling real pain?"

"Yes, I do."

"He wouldn't even let me palp him for more than a minute. Told me I was fooling around in the wrong area. Gave me detailed orders about just where I should palp. I told him there was a possibility that he was very ill. I advised him to see Dr. Hunter in Fort Barry, or even to go to Chicago. He said he wouldn't put foot out of this house. Where's a desk? I want to write you some instructions."

The doctor sat down and thought. Turning, he looked Eustacia in the eye. "I'm writing a list of questions about his symptoms. Send one of the children over to me every noon with a bulletin.—Mrs. Lansing, the whole town knows that your husband's refused to speak to me on the street for six years. That disqualifies me from operating on him or from being of much use. You should ask Dr. Hunter to come down and see him. The sooner the better. Does he get on well with Dr. Hunter?"

Eustacia raised her eyebrows.

"You have a hard time ahead, Mrs. Lansing. I'll do what I can."

Lansing insisted that his bed be made up on the first floor in the "conservatory" off the dining room. The word "pain" was never mentioned in the house; there was much talk about whether he was comfortable or not. He subsisted on gruel and beef tea, though occasionally he bellowed for a steak. When he was uncomfortable he was given some drops of laudanum. For days at a time he appeared to recover. At the first sign of comfort he dressed and walked the length of the main street. John Ashley called every day and brought him a large sheaf of office bulletins to sign, thus enabling him to carry on admirably his duties at the mine.

The town followed Lansing's illness with great interest. During the trial the conviction lay at the back of the judge's and jurymen's minds that Ashley and Eustacia Lansing had for months been trying to poison the murdered man.

Night after night, night after night, Eustacia sat near him or stretched herself out on a sofa. He insisted that the kerosene lamp with its wide soothing translucent green shade remain alight until sunrise. He gave up all desire to sleep; he slept in the day. He wanted to talk. Silence oppressed him. There was always hope that in talk, talk, talk he could alter the past, conjure the future, and impose an estimable image of himself upon the present. At first there were some attempts at playing checkers or parchesi or at reading aloud from *Ben-Hur*, but the patient was too occupied with his thoughts to attend those interests. Outside the glass door opening on the lawn the owls hooted, harbingers of spring; on a still night they could hear the croaking of the young frogs in the pond. Under the green lampshade Eustacia sewed or, lying on the couch, stared at the ceiling. Often her fingers turned the beads under her long shawl.

Even a healthy man, awakened by accident at three in the morning, becomes aware of his heart beating on toward its final exhaustion, of his lungs pulling his weight like a locomotive on a lonesome landscape resolutely carrying its load to the Pacific, to some ultimate discharging station. But Breckenridge Lansing, already frightened, must distract his mind in talk from those "pinchings and burnings." Finally the sky lightened. There are few human ills for which the coming of day does not seem to bring an alleviation.

Night after night they talked. At times he tended toward the maudlin, but Eustacia would have nothing of it. She could handle his self-esteem roughly. She alternated severity and balm. There is a certain comfort in being reprimanded justly— but only at intervals and within limits. He seemed eager to confess to any shortcomings that were not essential.

Three in the morning (Easter, March 30, 1902):

"Stacey!"

"What, dear?"

"Do you have to do that damned sewing all the time?"

"Oh, you know us women. Sewing doesn't take up our whole attention. We can hear and see everything that's going on around us. What did you want to say?"

Silence.

"Stacey, sometimes I've said things to you I didn't mean. I didn't mean them, really."

Silence.

"Well, say something. Don't just sit there like a dummy."

"Yes, Breckenridge, sometimes you were a very stupid man."

"What do you mean, *stupid*?"

"Well, I won't give you a big example. I'll give you a little one. Do you remember saying to me two nights ago, 'You don't know what I feel, Stacey. You've never been sick'—do you remember that?"

"Yes. It's true. What's stupid about that?"

"You forget, Breckenridge, that I lost three children. I was in what you call 'discomfort'—great 'discomfort'—for twenty and even forty hours."

Silence.

"I see what you mean. . . . I'm sorry, Stacey. Do you forgive me?"

"Yes, I forgive you."

"Don't just *say* you forgive me. *Really* forgive me."

"I do, Breckenridge. I do."

"Stacey, will you call me Breck just once?"

"You know I don't like nicknames."

"Well, I'm sick. Do me a favor. Call me Breck. When I get well you can call me anything you want."

Eustacia was playing a game for high stakes. According to her lights, within such means as were at her disposal (*faute de mieux*, as she wryly told herself), she was preparing her husband for death. She was trying to assist a soul to birth—to being born into self-knowledge, contrition, and hope. This project was conducted under peculiar difficulties. Any word faintly savoring of edification threw Lansing into a rage—a blasphemous rage. He had been for a short time a student preparing himself to be a clergyman; he was able to scent edification from afar and possessed a wide vocabulary with which to sneer at it. In addition, these conversations were often overheard by a third person. For several years George had seldom entered or left the house by any of the doors on the first floor. He came and went by his window—from the boughs of trees, by spikes driven into the wall, by climbing the back porch and swinging along the eaves. It now became his custom to prowl about the house. His mother could hear his footsteps on the soft ground of a late spring thaw. George had been described as having "the face of an angry lynx"; he had also the soft pads. Eustacia had the hearing of the felines and knew when her son's ears were glued to the half-open window. Lansing's voice was often raised in anger; he hurled objects about. George was there to protect his mother.

Eustacia's project was not only difficult, but perhaps impossible.

Three in the morning (Tuesday, April 8):

Lansing awoke abruptly from a doze. "Stacey!"

"Yes, dear?"

"What's that you're doing?"

"I'm praying for you, Breck."

Silence.

"What are you praying for—that I get better?"

"Yes. And there's a phrase in your Bible that I like: I'm praying that you be 'made whole.' "

Silence.

"I bet you think I'm going to die."

"You know very well I know nothing about such things. But, Breck, I think that you're really sick. I think you should go somewhere where you'd be better taken care of."

"I won't go, Stacey. I won't. There aren't any nurses better than you are. I'd go crazy in any other place."

"But I'd be there, too."

"They'd have some old hen in grey-and-white stripes. They wouldn't let you sit by me like this."

"I wish I were an old hen in grey-and-white stripes. I have this fear all the time that I don't *know* enough."

"Stacey, I love you. Can't you get that into your thick head: that I love you? I don't want to be off in some damned hospital where you'd only be allowed in for half an hour a day. Stacey, will you listen—just once—to what I say? I'd rather die with you near me than live forever and ever without you."

Eustacia ground her fingernails into the arms of her chair. We came into the world to learn.

Lansing forbade his children to enter the room. They were not even permitted to greet him from the door. He was temporarily indisposed; he would see them when he recovered. He forbade Eustacia to report his illness to his father, to his sister, to his brother Fisher. His mother had died. He let Ashley know that a visit every other day was sufficient. One late afternoon Eustacia was called to the front door. Beata had brought a covered dish of her famous German chicken and noodles. Lansing was furious. Gifts of food were brought only to homes that contained an invalid.

Day after day, night after night. Eustacia seldom left the room. She noticed that her patient's dreams during the day differed from those that occupied his intermittent sleep at night. By day he dreamed of hunting. He shot animals. He even imagined himself to be leading troops in the Spanish War, to great effect. He shot Spaniards. The assassination of President McKinley in the previous year preyed upon his mind—he was alternately killer and victim. At night he wandered lost, in strange places, up and down stairs, in the interminable corridors of mines. He called upon his mother.

No one at "St. Kitts" slept soundly. George prowled. Eustacia came upon her daughters sleeping in the guest room, in the sewing room, on sofas, in armchairs. There was much making of cocoa in the early hours.

Two in the morning (Wednesday, April 16):

"Girls, bring your cups into the sitting room. There's something I want to talk to you about. I've looked everywhere for George. I don't know where he can be."

Félicité and Anne sat on the floor at her feet. George suddenly made his appearance at the door and stood listening.

"*Mes très chers*, it may be some time before your father recovers his full health. We're going to do everything we can to make him comfortable, but we must think of ourselves, too. You know that vacant store on Main Street where Mr. Hicks used to sell hardware? I'm going to rent it. We're going to open a store of our own. We're going to take turns waiting on the customers."

"*Maman!*"

"The window will be arranged by Félicité, who has the best taste in the world. It will be changed often. You haven't forgotten that I ran a store all by myself when I was seventeen. Anne's inherited that. She has a very good head for management and details. She'll be our best saleslady and cash girl."

"*Maman! . . . Ange!*"

"There'll be things for George to do, too. I'll come to that in a minute.—What do young people do now after supper? They walk up and down Main Street just to pass the time. But the store windows are all dark. Besides, everybody knows what's in them. Félicité's beautiful window will be lighted until nine o'clock. One week the window will be for girls and women. I can see Félicité putting some velvet on the bottom, maybe in waves. There'll be red leather diaries with little locks on them and memory books and silks and wools. And wedding presents and birthday presents—card cases, scissors, and a thousand things. And books like those I sent to Chicago for— *Know Your Cat* and *Daisy's Trip to Paris* and *The Golden Treasury of Poetry*."

"*Maman!*"

"But when people think that our store's only for girls, they'll get the surprise of their lives. There'll be a week for boys and men. That's where George can help us. Fishing rods and flies; a geologist's hammer and the surveyor's maps of Grimble and Kangaheela counties. George will lend us his collection of minerals and Félicité will arrange them so that you can spend an hour looking at them. There'll be books—*Snakes of the Central States*, *The Indian Tribes of the Mississippi Valley*, *Mushrooms and Toadstools*, the book about how to care for your dog, and *With Clive in India* and all the Henty books. And Roger Ashley will lend us his collection of Indian arrowheads. Don't you think the young people would look in that window—and buy things?"

Anne flung her arms about her mother's knees. "Oh, *Maman*, when can we start?"

"We'd have a lending library, of course, and a lot of things that have to do with art—crayons and watercolors and books about how to draw. And when we'd made some money I think we'd open another store and—guess!—put Miss Doubkov in it! So there'd be another window lighted at night. And she could ask Lily Ashley or Sophia to help her. But that's not all—"

"Oh, *Maman*, I can't breathe!"

"Lots of people in town think that dancing's wicked. Nonsense! Coaltown's thirty years behind the times. I'd rent Odd Fellows Hall and have dancing classes twice a month."

"*Maman!* Nobody'd come!"

"Mrs. Ashley would be teacher. We'd leave the blinds up so that everybody could see. We'd have four Ashleys and three Lansings to start with. I'd ask Mrs. Bergstrom and Mrs. Coxe to be chaperones and their children could have the lessons free. Later we'd have lectures for young people. Miss Doubkov could talk about Russia and her travels. I'd talk about the six rules of French cooking. Lily Ashley would sing. Maybe we'd put on a play or a *Scenes from Shakespeare*. George could do his speeches from *Hamlet* and *The Merchant of Venice*. Lily recites beautifully, too. There's no need for Coaltown to be so narrow-minded and solemn and boring."

From across the hall and beyond the dining room came Lansing's voice: "STACEY! STACEY!"

"Yes, dear, I'm coming."

"What are you doing in there? Buzz, buzz, buzz; cackle, cackle, cackle."

"I'm coming, dear. Just a minute. Now, children, I want you to go to your beds and sleep. You can tell me tomorrow what you think about our plans."

The girls, exhausted by these visions, could scarcely reach their beds. George remained at the door, gazing at his mother with intent burning eyes.

"George, what's the matter? . . . Answer me! Why are you looking at me like that?"

"He struck you!"

"What's that you're saying? Struck me? Your father struck me? No, no, he did not."

"HE STRUCK YOU!"

"George, when do you think he struck me?"

"Last night. At this time!"

"Last night? . . . You're always imagining things. Last night your father wasn't feeling well. He was a little cross. He was waving his arms about and he knocked the water bottle off the table."

"STACEY! STACEY!"

"I'm coming, Breck.—*Mon cher petit*, you mustn't start exaggerating things, just when we need good level heads and all our patience. And, George, I want to say one other thing." She took his hand. "It's wrong to overhear the conversation of other people. It's not grown-up and it's not honorable. I don't want you to do that any more."

George pulled his hand away from hers and rushed out of the house by the kitchen door. Thereafter Eustacia was never certain whether the conversation in the sickroom was overheard or not. She knew that the Mohicans prided themselves on moving soundlessly through the darkest forests, over the dryest leaves.

"Stacey! What were you doing?"

"Just scolding the children, Breck. Nobody seems to be getting any sleep around here. It'd be a great help if you'd remember not to raise your voice. And try not to knock things over."

"I heard George's voice, too."

"Yes, I gave him a good sound lecture."

"That didn't take a whole hour. Buzz, buzz, buzz.—I guess I know what you were talking about."

Night after night, in all but the worst weather, she would draw her shawl about her, pass through the glass doors, walk along the gravel path, and stand for a moment in the main street.

His conversation was becoming more and more querulous. His need for attention took the form of trying to wound her.

"Life's just one big donkey's kick. Get that into your head, Miss Sims. And that includes a man's children. . . . You can't say I had any part in spoiling them. Filly's as stuck-up as the Queen of Sheba. George will get caught one of these days and spend the rest of his life in prison. Anne *used* to respect her father, but something's happened. . . . You and your Roman Catholic mumbo-jumbo! Just some ignorant truck you brought from those nigger islands of yours."

"Go on, Breck. I like to hear you saying things like that! You know they aren't true. You're getting rid of some old poison in you. Go on! We have a saying 'The devil spits hardest just before he has to go.' You're getting better."

"Jack Ashley! God! He's like a puppy that hasn't got his eyes open yet. He's just a milksop. And those inventions of his! He hasn't got brains enough to invent a can opener.—WHERE ARE YOU GOING?"

He dreaded being alone; he dreaded silence.

"I'm just going for a stroll outdoors."

She returned.

"What did you do?"

"Oh, nothing, Breck. Looked up at the stars. Thought."

Silence.

"You didn't have to be an hour about it."

Silence.

"What do you think about when you think?"

"All the years that I've been in this country I've missed the sea. It's like a faint toothache that never goes away. The sea is like the stars. The stars are like the sea. I don't have any original thoughts, Breck. I just have the thoughts that millions of people have when they look at the sea or the stars."

He longed to ask what those thoughts were. He shivered. He wanted to bring her thoughts back from all those stars, back to him; and, as so often, he became angry. He flung his arms about and, as so often, knocked the objects off the table beside his bed. His hand bell fell to the floor with a loud clatter. She crossed to the window and looked out.

There was a large table in the sewing room. George and Félicité would play cards, but George couldn't keep his mind on the game; he didn't care whether he won or not. He insisted on the door's remaining open. From far away they could hear the talk, talk, talk in the sickroom—the former playroom on the first floor. ("Happy Debevoises, where are you now?") When their father's voice reached them, loud in anger, or the sounds of falling objects, Félicité would put her hand on her brother's arm to restrain him. (He had "fits." Maybe he was crazy.) But he would rush from the room, descend the walls of the house, and prowl.

Often they would sit in silence for hours.

"If he strikes *Maman*, I'll kill him."

"Jordi! *Père* would never strike *Maman*. He's sick. Maybe he's in pain. He's cross. But he knows how necessary she is to him. He'd never strike her."

"You don't know."

"I do. Even if . . . if he went out of his senses, *Maman*

would understand. She'd forgive him. Jordi, you exaggerate everything so."

Half an hour of silence.

"If I thought *Maman* was safe, I'd go away for a while."

"I'd miss you, but I think it'd be good if you went away for a *short* while."

"I haven't any money."

"I've saved sixteen dollars. I'll give it to you right now."

"I wouldn't take it.—I tried to sell my gun today. Mr. Callihan would only give me twelve dollars."

"*Maman* will give you some. I'll ask her."

We have seen John Ashley's notion in the Southern Hemisphere of "holding up the walls" of his home. We have seen Sophia and Eustacia shoring up walls and roof tree. Year after year Félicité delayed her preparation to enter the life of the religious to do what she could for "St. Kitts." George, perhaps, was a little bit crazy. At all events he was in great travail of mind. Félicité knew three ways of distracting him, however briefly, from his somber thoughts. She knew that she could resort to them only infrequently; they must not be staled by repetition. She could direct the conversation to Russia; she could discuss the glorious, the dazzling life careers that lay open to both of them; she could persuade him to declaim poems and enact scenes from plays. George had told only one person of his ambition to be an actor. He had told no one of his ambition to be an actor in Russia—that ambition was too secret, too inner, too preposterous, too fraught with wonder, hope, and despair. He let his sister believe that he was still bent on saving the lions, tigers, and panthers of Africa from extermination and on living among them in a circus, exhibiting their beauty and power to audiences. Félicité had never seen a play—not even *Uncle Tom's Cabin*. But Miss Doubkov, who had instructed Lily Ashley in how to conduct herself in a concert hall, had also coached Félicité and George in the formal reading of La Fontaine's *Fables*. She had opened their eyes to how difficult it is to declaim *one verse correctly*. Passing through Paris at the time of her family's flight to the new world she had heard the greatest of all *diseuses*; she had had a glimpse of simplicity—the north star and torment of great art. Now in the sewing room, one night in four, Félicité could persuade George to work on some "pieces." They did scenes from *Athalie* and *Britannicus* (George was very fine as Nero), from *Hamlet* and *The Merchant of Venice*. George could be very funny, too, presenting Molière's miser and his casket, or Falstaff and his honor. He would forget himself and raise his voice. This would awaken Anne—a rapt and adoring audience ("Do the one in Russian, George—please!"), who could not, however, keep her eyes open long. Their mother would appear at the door and stand listening until the passage came to a close.

"Oh, my dears! Will you never get any sleep? Now, listen: each of you recite one beautiful thing for me and then promise you'll go to bed."

This was a mistake. Eustacia, who never wept under trial, became what she called "a perfect fool" in the presence of beauty.

Her son mistook the source of her tears.

Night after night:

During the last week of April there was a change in the atmosphere of the sickroom. Lansing's condition seemed to improve. There was a less frequent resort to laudanum. The patient had no wish to leave his bed, however. All-night conversation had become a habit and a cruel game. He became overbearing and, worse than overbearing, sly.

Maudlin: He loved her. Did she love him? *Really* love him? When had she loved him least? When had she loved him most? When he met that little girl on the island of St. Kitts he'd foreseen that she'd be the best little wife in the world. Oh, yes, he had. He was no fool.

Aggressive: Had she loved any other man since she left the islands? He didn't mean *misbehaved*—merely loved? Answer honestly. Would she swear to it? She didn't sound as though she meant it. He bet there was somebody. She was hiding something from him. That fellow in Pittsburgh—what was his name? Leonard something. He'd thought she was pretty neat and cute. The fellow with the big weeping-willow mustache. Was it him?

Sly (soothing digressions from which he could suddenly stage a surprise attack): The way she ran that store in Basseterre! It beat the Dutch! Smartest little head in the Caribbean. Regular little Shylock! . . . All the officers from those foreign ships. Girls go crazy for a uniform . . . He wouldn't be surprised. . . . Lot of little back rooms. . . . He'd been blind as a bat. He bet that she'd lied to him all his life. She'd gone to Fort Barry to church. Who'd she seen there?

"Now, Breckenridge, I can't stand your going on like this much longer. I'm tired. I've scarcely had what amounts to one night's rest for five weeks. I'm going to ask Dr. Gillies to send Mrs. Hauserman over to sit with you. You're simply trying to torment me. That's bad for *you*. You don't torment me, Breckenridge. You only injure yourself."

"Then give me one honest answer and we'll drop the whole subject."

"If you don't believe what I say, I'm no use to you. If you don't respect twenty-four years of married life, send me out of the room."

"WHERE ARE YOU GOING?"

"Breckenridge, I'm going to lie down in the sitting room. If you really need me, ring the bell. But don't call me in here to talk nonsense. I'll bring you your gruel at four o'clock."

But it was precisely those twenty-four years of married life that did not permit any such gesture of independence. Leaving the room was the only retaliation in her power—the only punishment; but she was not there to punish him. He rang the bell furiously. She capitulated. She resumed her chair under the green translucent lampshade. The most painful aspect of this phase was the absence of any faint intimation from the realm of the spirit; but there, too, lay its deep interest. She never doubted that the spirit was struggling behind these manifestations. Cruelty and hypocrisy are *interesting*. She felt—she *knew* —that his insistent attack was a mask behind which lay his regret for his neglect of her, for his numerous cheerless infidelities. He was trying to goad her into denouncing and reproaching him; but that was too easy. He must confront the judge within him. "The devil spits hardest just before he has to go." When self-justification is so impassioned, does contrition follow?

Dr. Hunter had directed that he should have some nourishment every four hours.

She brought him his gruel at four o'clock. Before this phase there had been moments of congeniality over the gruel. It was a game. She dusted it lightly with cinnamon or grated lemon peel. She hid two or three raisins in it. Three tears of sherry. The attentions that accompany feeding quicken both affection and repulsion. Now that game was over.

"How do I know that you went to church in Fort Barry? How do I know you aren't the talk of the county—you and Dr. Hunter?"

Her eyes kept returning to the glass doors that opened on the lawn. She arose and went quickly into the hall. Félicité was sitting on the stairs.

"Go to bed, Félicité. I don't want you *ever* to listen to what your father says when he's uncomfortable."

"I wasn't listening, *Maman*. I was sitting here so that George wouldn't listen. Sometimes he sits here for hours."

Eustacia burst out laughing. Her eyes swept the ceiling, distraught. "*Va te coucher, chérie.*"

She returned to the sickroom and stretched out on the sofa, covering her eyes with her hand. Her husband talked monotonously on. She made the slight interjections that were so necessary to him. "Well!"—"No!"—"Talk of something else!"

Yes. She had loved another man. Her conscience did not trouble her. She had surmounted the longing and the anguish. That love was a crown she wore, a medal. She could not think of it without a smile. It came to her aid often, as now. Formerly she had tormentedly asked of herself and of the night sky if she was loved in return. That no longer mattered. His glance had met hers a thousand times. Love surrounds us in many ways: he loved her.

Midnight (Saturday to Sunday, May 3 and 4):

"Here's your gruel."

"I don't want it."

"I'll warm it up for you when you're hungry."

Silence. Prolonged silence. Eustacia had learned that when he kept silent for some time it was "for effect." He was preparing a scene. There was a large element of the play actor in him. During the year in Pittsburgh Eustacia had regularly attended Wednesday matinées in the theatre. She could find a seat in the top balcony for fifteen cents and had done so for many months until her pregnancy rendered her appearance on the street "indelicate."

She loved the theatre and despised it. It calculated its effects, just as Breckenridge was doing now. This view of him as trying to outwit her, outthink her, rendered him even more pitiable.

She loved him. Yes, that's what marriage had brought her to. She loved him as a *créature*. Like most completely bilingual persons she thought in both languages. About the more superficial machinery of life she thought in English. Her inner life presented itself to her in French. In both languages the word "creature" wears two aspects; in French the two are more drastically contrasted. Her favorite French authors, Pascal and Bossuet, constantly evoked the double sense: a *créature* is an abject living thing; it is also a living thing—generally a human being—fashioned by God. Her dear uncle in marrying her had predicted that they would become one flesh; he had been right. She loved this *créature*. She could not imagine him away. Just as she shrank with horror from any desire to have wished her life to have been other. It was these children—and no other imaginable children—that constituted her boundless ineffable thanks to God. That's what destiny is. Our lives are a seamless robe. All was ordained, as the English language put it. She arrived at a position much like Dr. Gillies's. We don't live our lives. God lives us.

This very week her love for him would stab her as she looked at him—unshaven, in torment, devising ways to wound her, pitiably dependent on her, himself desperately loving her.

"Stacey!"

"Yes, Breck."

"Do you notice that I've been quiet?"

"Yes, dear. What have you been thinking about?"

"That gruel."

The air was heavy with theatre. Fifteen cents' worth.

Suddenly he leaned forward and pointed a finger at her. "I've got it!"

"What have you got?"

"The man."

"Yes, dear, what man?"

"The man you've been meeting in Fort Barry—it's Jack Ashley!"

She stared at him a moment. She burst into laughter—brief painful laughter. She was to be spared nothing.

"To think that I couldn't see it—all these years! Plain as the nose on your face. I've seen you throwing sheep's eyes at one another. And stealing off to the Farmer's Hotel in Fort Barry! Oh, Stacey! I've seen you sitting beside him at table hundreds of times, your ankles all wound up with one another.—What are you doing?"

"I'm closing the doors. Go on, Breck, go on. Go on."

"Why are you closing the doors? It's hot."

Eustacia was trembling. "I think someone may be listening. I think that some of your club members may come down and lie on the grass just to hear you talk—Mr. Bostwick of the Odd Fellows or Mr. Dobbs of the Masons. Or some of the girls from the saloons on the River Road—Hattie or Beryl. I wouldn't be surprised if that Leyendecker boy—"

"Well, they wouldn't learn anything that they didn't know already. You open those doors, Stacey!"

She closed them firmly. She then crossed the dining room and looked into the hall and sitting room. Lansing picked up one object and then another and smashed the panes in the doors. She heard the noise. It seemed as though half Coaltown must have heard it. She stood in the hall and looked up the stairs. Something like exhilaration filled her. Yes, things must come to a head. Things must get worse before they can get better. She returned to the sickroom and looked at him long and gravely.

"You and Jack have been deceiving me for years.—What are you doing now?"

"I'm going to lie down on the sofa and read. I'm putting cotton in my ears. Talk on, Breck. I hate to hear you saying nasty things."

He stared at her. Slowly she inserted the wads of cotton in her ears, lit the gaslight over the sofa, lay down, and opened a book.

Almost at once she knew that she couldn't do it. It was too cruel. You can't separate that two-in-one. Besides, it was retaliatory. She glanced at him. He was still staring at her with furious bloodshot eyes. He looked like a stricken dog. With her eyes resting on him she slowly removed the cotton from her ears.

"You and Jack have been deceiving me for years."

"Wait! Wait just one minute, Breck. A few weeks ago you said you loved me."

"I *did*! But I didn't know then what I know now. I was blind. I bet Batey knows, too. I bet she hates you."

"Oh, Breck! You said you loved me."

"*He* loves you. Comfort yourself with that: Jack loves you."

Her eyes kept returning to the doors. Again he fell silent. The play actor was preparing another fine scene.

He said quietly: "I'll kill him."

"What? What's that you're saying?"

"I'll kill Jack Ashley, if it's the last thing I do."

"Dear Breck, don't say such things!"

"Any jury in the country would acquit me. And do you know why? Do you? . . . Do you? . . . Do you? . . . Because you and he have been poisoning me. I'm not sick. I'm just poisoned!"

"Oh, Breck!"

"Cinnamon! Nutmeg and raisins!—Where are you going now?"

"I'm going to call George."

"Why call George?"

"I'm going to send him to Mrs. Hauserman's. She'll sit up with you all night after this. Tell her everything. She'll make food for you that you won't be afraid to eat. I'm no longer any use to you, Breck."

She left the room. As she mounted the stairs she heard him calling her name. She knocked at George's door. There was no answer. She opened it. The room was empty. Continuing down the hall to the bathroom she bathed her forehead and wrists in cold water, murmuring, "It's all over. I shall rest." She sank to the floor, pressing her forehead on the linoleum. "*Dieu! Dieu! Nous sommes de pauvres créatures. Aide-nous!*"

She descended the stairs. George was standing in the hall.

"George! Did you overhear what your father said?"

He made no reply. He looked over her shoulder.

"Answer me!"

"He broke the window. What did he throw at you?"

"STACEY! WHO ARE YOU TALKING TO?"

"He didn't throw anything at me. I wasn't even in the room.

He's a very sick man. Don't pay any attention to what he says."

"STACEY! ANSWER ME!"

"I'm talking to George, Breck."

"Don't you send him for Mrs. Hauserman."

She spoke softly and rapidly. "George, Félicité tells me you wish to go away for a short time. I think you should." She drew a small brocade purse from her pocket and put it in his hand. "Here are forty dollars. Go tomorrow. Write me, dear George, write me. Tell me everything that happens to you." She kissed him. "My dear treasure! My dear treasure!"

The handbell was ringing furiously. "STACEY! I'll eat this. Come back here. I'll eat this. GEORGE!" Silence. "GEORGE!"

"Yes, Papa."

"Come into the room."

George and Eustacia entered the sickroom.

"Don't you go and call Mrs. Hauserman. Do you hear me?"

"Yes, Papa."

"But I have one errand for you. Tomorrow morning early you run over to the Ashleys and ask Mr. Ashley to come here for rifle practice on Sunday afternoon—*this* afternoon. Tell him I feel better. Tell him I especially want him to come and bring the whole family."

"The children couldn't come, Papa. There's the Epworth League picnic in the park at five."

"Well, tell him to bring Mrs. Ashley."

"Yes, Papa."

"Are you and the girls going to the picnic, too?"

"Yes."

"You're Cath'lics."

"Roger's president. He and Lily invited us. Mama and Félicité have made a lot of sandwiches and cakes."

"Well, run along."

George did not move.

"What's the matter with you? I told you to go."

George had been watching his father with a closed remote expression on his face. He slowly moved to the table beside the bed, picked up the pewter bowl of gruel, and poured the contents down his throat. He left the room without raising his eyes again. Lansing stared after him in consternation. Eustacia conquered a wild impulse to laugh—to laugh for hours. Wednesday-afternoon matinée—two fifteen cents' worth.

"Why did he do that? Answer me, Stacey! What did he mean by that?"

"You've said a great many foolish and cruel things tonight, Breck. I don't want to hear any more. I want your permission to put some cotton in my ears. I'm going to sit here and read."

"But why did the boy do that?"

"When you have intelligent children, you would best behave intelligently, Breckenridge Lansing."

"What do you mean?"

She waited a moment and pointed at the broken windows.

"You mean he heard what we were saying?"

"I think he heard you accusing me of being an adulteress and a murderer. Don't you? Don't you think that's what he meant?"

He looked at her resentfully.

"He heard you threatening to kill John Ashley. John Ashley has been a very good friend to George when he needed one. Breck, why can't you be silent for even a short time? It's this talking all the time that gets you into trouble. I want your permission to put cotton in my ears for fifteen minutes. May I?"

He was grumbling: ". . . eavesdropping . . . damned impertinence . . . ought to be horse-whipped . . ."

"May I, Breck?"

He growled an exasperated "Yes . . . Yes, do what you want."

She put the cotton in her ears and lay down on the sofa with her book. Oh, blessed silence! Oh, waves lapping on the shore! Oh, sunlight on Lord Nelson's bay.

Ten minutes passed. She did not hear him repeating her name in a low voice. He got out of bed, crossed the room, and lightly touched her shoulder. She turned and looked at him. He sank to his knees and laid his forehead on her hand. She removed the cotton from her ears.

"I'm hungry!" he said.

She had forgotten his midnight gruel! She started to rise, but he restrained her. "I'll call Félicité," she said. He was weeping.

"I'm sorry, Stacey. I'm sick. Don't treat me like this, Stacey. Be kind to me. . . . I don't mean those things. You're the

best thing that ever was in my life. . . . I hate being sick and
that makes me angry at everything." Again she tried to rise,
but his forehead pinned her hand to the edge of the sofa. "I
think I was brought up wrong. Everything I do is all mixed up.
Say something kind to me, Stacey."

She looked down at that still honey-colored hair. She could
not see the eyes of cornflower blue, now bloodshot. She raised
his hand and kissed it. "Now get back into bed. You'll feel
better when you've had your gruel."

"Stay a minute. Don't go yet. Put down your ear, Stacey.
Maybe it's best that things come to an end. I wouldn't feel bad
about it. It's just like going to sleep. But I want you to pray for
me, Stacey. I'll bet most of your prayers are answered. Will you
pray that I die without an awful lot of discomfort?" ("You're
hurting my hand, Breck!") "And will you pray—Stacey, listen!
—that the things I haven't done right are gradually forgotten?
That the children remember me . . . better?" ("Breck, dear,
you're hurting my hand!") "And, Stacey, STACEY, will you
remember me . . . *in a good way*?"

He released her hand. She stroked his head. In a low voice
she said: "All this is unnecessary, Breck. Of course, I pray for
you. Of course, I always think of you with love. Now get back
into bed. The doctor said you should eat every four hours and
it's now about two o'clock. You've been better these days and
I want you to be especially well tomorrow so that the whole
family can have a pleasant time in here before the children go
off to the picnic."

Her heart was beating loudly. She drew the blanket over
him and kissed his forehead. In the kitchen she slowly stirred
the spoon in the barley. She returned to the sickroom with the
pewter bowl.

"Thank you, Stacey," he said for the first time. She had
brought a small saucer of gruel for herself.

"Are you eating this stuff, too?"

"Oh, I often steal a bit. It's good for everybody."

They ate slowly in silence.

"Are you happy sometimes, Stacey?"

"Yes, often."

"What are you happy about?"

"Just being a wife and a mother."

She caught his glance and laughed. She held his glance until he gave a low laugh in return.

"Stacey, Stacey, you're—"

She interrupted him, putting her hand on his. She said, "Oh, Breck, you have something to be so proud of and you don't know it."

"What?"

"The children!"

His face darkened. His eyes returned to his gruel.

"The children. Do you know that Anne has led all her classes for two years? And that Mother Veronica said that Félicité was the best natural student she'd ever seen? Her Latin compositions won the prize in Chicago in the whole 'Four States Contest.'"

"You're bright, Stacey. It's *you*—"

"Do you know what children are, Breck? They're the continuation of ourselves. They carry out what we wanted to be." Silence. "You're in them like the grain is in wood. They have a whole series of admirable qualities that don't come from my island people. They come from your Iowa ancestors. Sometimes I have to burst out laughing, they're so foreign to me. For instance, we island people have no perseverance. We can't concentrate on one thing for more than twenty minutes. I'm bright sometimes, but I'm only bright by fits and starts. But when Félicité sets out to accomplish something wild horses couldn't stop her. That's Iowa! That's your people! A little while ago you said that Félicité was conceited. You couldn't be more mistaken. . . . There's just one thing she lacks. She lacks one degree of self-confidence and joyousness that a father's love could give her. I'm no good for Félicité. I can't help her. She needs *you*!"

Lansing was aghast. Eustacia had drawn her handkerchief out of her sleeve. Eustacia was weeping! He put down his spoon. Almost shyly he placed his hand on hers. "Oh, you're wrong, Stacey. You're dead wrong. You're the best mother in the world. . . . I'll be better. I promise you."

Suddenly Eustacia burst out laughing. "Look at the mess I've made of my gruel. That's what they give prisoners to eat— *gruel and water*! . . . And George—you're right. He's caused us a great deal of anxiety and mortification, hasn't he? No wonder that you've been angry at him. But, Breck, I remember something you said once. You said that you Masons 'stood behind one another.' "

"We do."

"Don't you think a father should do that with his boy? When a Mason makes a mistake you let him know that it's a mistake, but you don't talk about it everywhere. You don't harp on it. You stand shoulder to shoulder letting the world see that you believe in him. . . . In seventeen years you've seldom said anything encouraging to George. George is very emotional." She leaned forward, lowered her voice, and said very distinctly: "If you started standing behind him, he would love you as *his best friend*."

Lansing was holding his breath.

"And Anne! I can understand that you don't feel her affection as you used to. Do you know why that is? It's because you continue to treat her like a little doll. You haven't seen that she's growing up very fast. She's going to be a very intelligent young woman, and she wants to be treated so, *now*. My father made the same mistake with me. I was the youngest, too. He called me his little bird and made cooing noises all the time. I was very angry and I avoided him. He changed just in time—when he saw that I was capable in the store. Now we're great friends. You've seen his letters. He misses me and I miss him."

"Stacey!"

"You asked me if I'm happy sometimes. Oh, I'm happy often, because I have a husband and these three children. And I want you to be happy in the same way."

Lansing looked about him bewilderedly. He lowered his face toward his raised knees. "Oh, Stacey, I WANT TO GET WELL! I WANT TO GET WELL!"

She rose and kissed his forehead. "You *are* better. Now let me move the lamp over to the sideboard. One sign that you're really getting better will be that you can sleep at night. See if you can catch an hour or two of sleep now. I'll be right here."

He slept until five o'clock, when he awoke and ate his four o'clock gruel, then he slept until seven-thirty. He awoke to new confidence.

"Has George been over to the Ashleys'?"

"Breck, I found a note on my dressing table this morning. George has gone off on some kind of a trip for a few days."

"There's no train until eight-fifteen."

"I'm afraid he's ridden on one of those freight trains."

"Where are the girls?"

"They're getting ready to go to Fort Barry to church on the eight-fifteen."

"Ask them to come to the door a minute before they go."

At a few minutes before eight, Félicité and Anne appeared at his door, young ladies dressed for church. He looked at them as though he had never seen them before. He could find nothing to say. They could find nothing to say. They stood, wide-eyed, waiting. They resembled the deer he had so often slain.

Finally he said, "Well, have a good time."

"Yes, Papa."

"There's a dollar bill on the dresser there. Put it on the collection plate for me."

"Yes, Papa."

"Will you have time to stop at the Ashleys' on the way to the station?" The girls nodded. "Ask Jack and Mrs. Ashley to come over about four-thirty this afternoon."

"Yes, Papa."

"You're good girls. Papa's proud of you."

The girls' testimony was heavily stressed by the prosecution. They had conveyed the invitation to John Ashley, but had not mentioned firearms. The accused calmly testified that he had assumed that he had been invited to the customary Sunday-afternoon rifle practice. Whether that had been the original intention or not, Breckenridge Lansing, seeing the gun in his guest's hand, had sent his wife into the house for his own rifle. The men tossed a coin and Ashley led off. Even in May twilight descended rapidly in Coaltown's deep gorge. Lansing had begun to tire and the light to fail when he was killed on the third round.

By the same hour the next afternoon Breckenridge's brother Fisher, the best lawyer in northern Iowa, arrived to take charge of the "arrangements," and very fine they were. The fraternal organizations marched into the Baptist Church in full regalia. The Odd Fellows' Band, standing in the street outside, played the "Dead March" from *Saul*. John Ashley could hear it from his cell. Representatives of the mines' directorate arrived from

Pittsburgh and attended the service wearing silk hats. Two pews were reserved for the foremen from the "Bluebell" and the "Henrietta B. MacGregor." The eulogies would have melted a heart of stone, but made no impression on Wilhelmina Thoms. Coaltown had never seen such a funeral.

Fisher Lansing was engaged in some important trials of his own in Iowa, but he returned to Coaltown every other week to throw his weight into the Ashley Case. During the first weeks of the trial the majority of the citizens assumed that Lansing's death would be found to have been an accident caused by a faulty mechanism in John Ashley's gun. A deep antagonism against the accused man emerged only gradually. Fisher called on the first citizens in town. He held forth nightly in the bar of the Illinois Tavern. "I'll see that that son-of-a-bitch gets *his*, if it's the last thing I do. . . . He'd been trying to rook my brother out of his job for fifteen years; finally he had to *shoot* him, the damned skunk. . . . Jess Wilbraham and what's-your-doctor's-name, keep talking about a mechanical defect—tush and nonsense! We don't talk such foolishness in Iowa. No, sir-ee, we don't. No sir."

During the selection of the jury Eustacia found on her door-step the first of a series of anonymous letters. She was grateful for them. They prepared her for her interrogation in court. She clearly but unemphatically deposed that her husband had never expressed any feeling that John Ashley bore him ill will. ("Thank you, Mrs. Lansing.") On the afternoon of the accident Mr. Ashley, seeing that her husband was recovering from an indisposition, wished to postpone the rifle practice. It was her husband who insisted that they engage in a few rounds. ("Thank you, Mrs. Lansing.")

As executor of his brother's will Fisher Lansing marched all over "St. Kitts" with an appraiser's eye. The directorate of the mines had extended Eustacia's right to live in the house rent free for five years. Much of the furniture belonged to her. In the Rainy Day House Fisher came upon some mechanical drawings: "The Ashley-Lansing Triple Drop Lock," "The Ashley-Lansing Mercury Chamber Charger," "The Ashley-Lansing Hexagon Tent."

"What are these, Stacey?"

"They worked on inventions together."

"Anything to them?"

"I don't know, Fisher. If there is, it's mostly John Ashley's work."

"They're damned good drawings. Breck couldn't do that.— Are there any patents on them?"

"No. They kept putting off sending them to the Patent Office."

"I'll take them and show them to a friend of mine."

"But, Fisher, they're John Ashley's work."

"Listen, sister, you don't have to tell me that. Breck didn't have enough brains to invent a can opener. These drawings look smart. I'll take them along. Maybe they're a property—see what I mean?"

"Fisher, they're Mr. Ashley's."

"Stacey! When we get through with John Ashley he'll be dead. Convicts aren't citizens. Alive or dead, they *have* no rights."

Fisher reverted often to Eustacia's "properties." They were considerable. Down the years she had persuaded her husband to buy here a town lot, there a meadow on the upland. It required a sharp business intelligence because Coaltown was a shrinking community and Eustacia knew it. Moreover, she had persuaded Breckenridge to open a second account in a Fort Barry bank out of the reach of the devouring curiosity of Coaltown. This procedure, together with her varied and elegant clothes, nourished the assumption that she was a very rich woman indeed. Now she had insurance and pension.

"Now, Stacey, there's enough money for you and the girls to live very well. A little bit more from these inventions wouldn't hurt. Why don't you get out of Coaltown and enjoy yourself as soon as you can?"

"I shall not leave Coaltown."

"Stay here? *Stay here?* In this God-forsaken town?"

"I shall not leave Coaltown, Fisher, and I don't want to hear another word from you about it."

"Where's George?"

"I don't know where George is. He's always had a way of disappearing for a week or two at times."

"George has always been a little bit crazy, if you ask me."

Eustacia looked at him—a long level gaze. A faint smile on her lips.

Eustacia attended the trial only on the one occasion when she was called upon to testify. Olga Sergeievna called several times a week to report its progress to her. On the afternoon when the sentence was pronounced Olga Sergeievna arrived at "St. Kitts" carrying a rose. Eustacia met her at the door. No word was spoken. Olga Sergeievna crossed herself, laid the rose on the hall table and returned to the town. On the morning of Tuesday, June the twenty-second, Eustacia and her daughters arrived at the depot to take the train to Fort Barry, to their church. Mr. Killigrew beckoned her into his telegraph office.

"Mrs. Lansing, I don't know if you've heard the news." He told her.

"Was anyone hurt, Mr. Killigrew?"

"No, ma'am. They're searching the woods. I thought you'd be interested to know."

"Thank you, Mr. Killigrew."

They continued their journey.

Eustacia also received visits from the police. She knew from the anonymous letters that she was suspected of having paid thousands of dollars to her lover's rescuers. These intruders were deferential at first, but became increasingly hard-spoken. She was a match for them. She enjoyed their visits. They afforded evidence that the great subject was still alive. There was more to come. There would be some revelation. That is what life is—an unfolding.

She continued to be seen on the streets daily, dressed in the deep mourning that so became her. She tended her husband's grave, preferring to visit it at hours when there were few to observe her. She learned from Olga Sergeievna of Sophia's selling lemonade at the depot, of the opening of the boarding-house. She sent her gifts by Porky. She expected to meet Beata momently until it dawned on her that Beata had resolved not to appear in the town. She encountered Sophia almost daily and greeted her affectionately. She invited her to supper at "St. Kitts." Sophia thanked her, saying that she had to stay at home and help her mother. Eustacia did not open the gift shop and circulating library, but she bought Mr. Hicks's abandoned hardware store and installed Miss Doubkov: "Fine Dressmaking." Miss Doubkov was instructed to engage Lily Ashley as her assistant, but Mrs. Ashley replied that Lily was needed in the boardinghouse.

Twenty months after George's disappearance—in January, 1904—Eustacia received a postal card from him. It had been mailed in San Francisco and bore a picture of the sun, in mica, setting below the Pacific Ocean. "Dear Mother, Was sick. Am all well now. Will write soon. Have a good job. Chinese food is very good and cheap. Love to you and the girls. Jordi (Leonid). P.S. All you told us about the ocean is true. It's great. *Je t'embrasse mille fois.*" That noon Miss Doubkov came hurrying to "St. Kitts." She too had received a card. It was in Russian: "Honored lady, I was sick. I am all well now. I have come to know a Russian family here and we talk the language all the time—working people's Russian. I thank you for all your great kindness. With profound respects, Leonid." There was no return address. For Easter Eustacia received a rosary carved from walrus tusks, Félicité a brightly colored poster: "The Florella Thompson–Culloden Barnes Company presents *The Girl Sheriff of Salmon Leap Falls*, with Leonid Tellier as Jack Beverly." Miss Doubkov and Anne were sent jade buttons.

Finally Eustacia received a letter. He was fine. Everything was fine. He had done his recitations in English, French, and Russian for a theatrical manager and had been engaged at once. The plays were awful. They had titles like *The King of the Opium Ring* and *Madge of the Klondike.* He was very good. He had written a play and the manager had put it on. It was called *The Boy Convict of La Guyenne.* It was an awful play, but the best scenes were stolen from *Les Misérables.* He'd send an address when he'd settled down. He directed his mother to keep the window of his bedroom open half an inch, because he might return some night and surprise them. He sent love as big as the Pacific Ocean. It was signed "Jordi (Leonid Tellier)." "P.S. Please give my regards to Mr. Ashley and all the Ashleys." Eustacia found more to disquiet than to rejoice her in this letter, but she showed no sign of it. We are as Providence made us.

Toward the end of November, 1904, Félicité was greeted on the street by Joel Miller, George's assistant sachem in the noble nation of the Mohicans. The encounter was conducted in whispers with a great air of secrecy.

"Filly, I've got a letter for you. Act as though we were talking about ordinary things."

"What kind of a letter, Joel?"

"It's from George. He says to give it to you so your mother won't know."

"Thank you, Joel. Thank you."

"Don't tell *anybody* I gave it to you."

"I won't, Joel."

She put the letter in her muff. She did not hurry her pace through the snowdrifts. She walked solemnly and with sinking heart. She foresaw that some ordeal lay before her.

GEORGE to Félicité (San Francisco, November, 1904, to February, 1905):

"*Chère* Zozo, I'm going to write you a lot of letters. I'm going to send them by Joel. I've sent him some money to rent a box in the post office. He can tell his people that it's for letters he gets about his stamp collection. Don't tell *Maman* I'm writing to you. If you tell her or Miss Doubkov or anybody else the things I'm going to tell you, I'll never write you another word. *I'll erase you from my memory.*

"I've been through some rough times, *but I'll be all right from now on*. I've got to talk to somebody and I've got to hear somebody talking to me—and that's YOU. I'm going to tell you almost everything—good, bad, and worse. *Maman*'s had enough troubles. *We know*. As soon as you get this sit down and write me EVERYTHING. How is *Maman*? What's she thinking about? Describe exactly what you do in the evenings. Do you have some good times? You don't have to tell me about *Père*'s being dead. I read that in a newspaper. *Père* was always talking about his insurance. Did they pay up quick? How's Mr. Ashley? Write me now because the company I'm acting in may be going to Sacramento or Portland, Oregon, soon. *Je t'embrasse fort.* Leonid Tellier, Gibbs Hotel, San Francisco. P.S. I tell everybody I had a Russian mother and a French father."

(Later):

"This is what happened to me. I left Coaltown riding possum clancy. In the yards outside St. Louis the train stopped with a sudden jerk. I must have been half asleep, because I fell and hurt my head. I was arrested, but I don't know any more until I woke up in an insane asylum. It wasn't bad. There were lawns and flowers. I didn't tell who I was because I didn't know who I was. One day a lady came to sing to us loonies and she sung that song that Lily used to sing about 'Home, Sweet Home.' Suddenly I remembered everything. There was a priest that used to visit us. I asked him to help me get out of there. I wanted my clothes back and the money that was in the pockets. A lot of doctors talked to me. I showed them I wasn't crazy, but just a little stupid. I told them I was a Russian orphan from Chicago. After a few weeks they let me out and gave me back my money. That was in September. In St. Louis I went to every theatre and I got to know the actors. I tried to get a job acting. They said they didn't have any parts that were my type. To save my money I got jobs working as a waiter in saloons. Three in the afternoon until three in the morning (no pay, just tips. The tips were in pennies). Like I'm going to write *Maman*, I don't drink or smoke or use bad language. You don't have to worry about me that way. I've got a worse weakness. Do you remember how *Maman* dreamed about going to San Francisco to see the ocean? All the time I had the idea that I wanted to go to San Francisco. Besides the actors said it was a fine theatre town. It is. Maybe I'll get a letter from you tomorrow. Maybe I'll never be happy one day in my life, but I don't care. Other people will be happy."

(The next weeks):

"You wrote the greatest letter a fellow ever got. . . . I was very surprised about what you told me about Mr. Ashley. I don't understand it at all. Even a baby would know that he didn't do it. Where do people think he is? Maybe he's right here in San Francisco.

". . . I'll tell you what my weakness is. I get into fights. I can't help it. It's the way I'm made. If a man says anything to me sarcastic like I was just dirt, I boil over. I insult him. I ask him, 'Did I hear you say your mother was a pig (or worse)?' and I stand on his foot. Then there's a terrible fight. I can't help it. I never win a fight because when I start fighting I get one of my dizzy spells. They beat me up and throw me in the street. I've been put in jail three times. Once I woke up in a hospital. I must have been raving in Russian, because a nurse knew some Russians and a Russian family took me into their home. Miss Doubkov is right. Russians are the greatest people in the world.

". . . The reason I write you such long letters is that I can't sleep at night until I see the sunlight coming in the window. When I sleep at night I have nightmares, almost never during the day. . . . Men in white masks come in through the keyhole. I jump out of the window and they chase me all over some mountains covered with snow. That's Siberia. I make crosses with chalk all over the walls and the door. I guess there's no hope for me. I'll have to get used to it. As long as other people are happy, *ishkabibble*.

"I know that I was born to be a very happy person, but then things happened. Sometimes, I'm so happy I could crush the whole universe in my arms for love. Doesn't last. You and *Maman* and Anne—be happy for me. Oneself doesn't count.

"I hate the manager of our company, Culloden Barnes, and he hates me. He's an old man, but until I came he played all the young heroes and he plays half of them now. He dyes his hair and wears rouge even on the street. He's an awful actor. I say all my lines real and it makes him look foolish, shouting away and waving his arms about. My young parts are all idiotic, but I study them in my hotel room until I make them sound natural. I love to work. Florella Thompson's his wife. I like her a lot. She's a bad actress, but she tries. In some of our scenes we play very well and the audience knows it. She likes to work, too. She's never too tired to come to the theatre at noon and we work. Then we have corned beef and cabbage brought in. She's always hungry. I like to see women eat, not men. She tells me a lot about her life. Now listen: some actors who live in the room next to them at the hotel say that he treats her terribly. Like I always say: *There are lots of crimes that there's no law against.* . . .

"I'm a big success now, but he doesn't pay me much because I miss performances every now and then and someone has to go on in my place. . . .

"I got fired last Saturday night. You know why. He hates me. I got a job in a saloon again. But he came and hired me back. He couldn't do without me. I'm too popular. . . .

"No, I'm not going to be an actor. I just act to make money. Acting's not serious. Maybe I'll be a detective or a wandering storyteller or a jail breaker. Can you imagine that I can cure people? When I was in that crazyhouse in St. Louis I was curing so many patients that they were glad to let me go. I even cured a girl. The men's garden or meadow or whatever you call it was separated from the women's by a high wire fence. A girl sat under a tree by the fence every morning. A lady attendant said she wouldn't talk because she thought she was a stone. I'd talk in a low voice without looking at her directly. I told her she wasn't a stone, she was a tree. Three days later she told me she was a tree and she waved her fingers in the air. I pretended not to hear her. I told her she was a beautiful animal, maybe a deer, a doe. And in a few days she told me she was a deer and she moved around all over the field. At last she became a girl. The men patients would come up to me and say 'When are we going to do "*glory, hallelujah*"?' That's the way to cure people, with dancing and singing. But I'm not going to be a healer. It gives me terrible headaches. A jail breaker is a profession I invented. It's a man who puts prisons and jails in such confusion that all the prisoners can get out. I've thought of lots of ways to do it.

"For every person who has enough to eat there are ten persons starving (maybe a hundred). For every girl and lady who goes down the street and their friends say pretty things to them, there's a dozen girls and women who've had no chance. For every good hour that a family has in a home evenings, *somebody is paying*. Somebody they don't even know. I don't mean merely that there are a lot of poor people in the world. It's deeper than that. Look at all the sick and crippled and ugly and damned. It's the way God made the world. He can't stop it now or change it. Some people are damned before they are born. You won't like that, but I know. God doesn't hate the damned. He needs them. They pay for the rest. Paryas hold up the floors of homes. Enough said."

FÉLICITÉ to George (January, 1905):

"Oh, Jordi, let me beg you once again to permit me to show your letters to *Maman*. You've forgotten what *Maman*'s like; she's strong. You say you want her to be happy. Jordi, you're stupid. Nobody wants to be happy because they're ignorant. The more *Maman* knows about anything real and serious and true, the happier she is. I beg you to give me permission. . . .

"What do you mean about being a scapegoat and a pariah? Do you go to Confession and Mass? Oh, Jordi, are you *sincere*? What do you mean that you can never be happy? How do you know? Are you trying to make a picture of yourself as an interesting tragical person!!!! It's hard to write you unless I'm certain that you're sincere. Do you remember the sermons you used to preach me about sincerity being a habit? You said that the reason why Shakespeare and Pushkin were great writers was because *from the time when they were boys they stood like policemen over their thoughts and didn't allow one small insincerity to creep in*. You used to say of a certain person that he was posing all the time. Do you remember how you hated that word. Go to church. Christians can't pose."

GEORGE to his mother (Portland, Oregon, February):

"Many thanks for your letter. I read in the paper about what happened to *Père*, but I didn't know that about Mr. Ashley. It's wonderful that somebody saved him. . . . Everything's fine with me. Yes, I eat well and sleep well. *Chère Maman*, does Mr. Wills still come to Coaltown once a month to take photographs? I'd like more than anything in the world to have a picture of you and the girls. And a big one of you alone and one of Miss Doubkov. I'm putting a five-dollar bill in this envelope. . . . I didn't write you last week because there was nothing new to say. Everything's fine. Maybe I'm going to act Shylock and Richard III. Our company's never done Shakespeare, but a Shakespeare company broke down here in Portland ten years ago. The costumes and scenery are in a warehouse and our manager can get them cheap. They're probably full of holes. I've studied the parts and I know what I'd do every minute."

EUSTACIA to George (March 4):

"Your sister and I are making costumes for your Shylock and Richard. We've studied all the illustrations we could find. Miss Doubkov is a great help, too. Give us an idea of Miss Thompson's measurements and coloring. . . . Yes, dear boy, you should hear us laugh. . . . Do assure me that you are faithful in your duties as a Christian."

FLORELLA THOMPSON to Eustacia (Seattle, Washington, May 1):

"Dear Mrs. Lansing, The dresses are the most beautiful that I've ever worn. I've grown a little stouter this spring. You very cleverly left those gussets and basted darts for alterations. They fit me perfectly now. Business has not been good in the north here and my dear husband has had to postpone the Shakespeare performances until the fall. . . . Your son Leo is a remarkable actor. You may be certain that he will go far. In addition he is such a genuine person. I can imagine what a comfort to you he must be. With many thanks from the bottom of my heart for the beautiful dresses and for having so gifted and understanding a son. Florella Thompson. P.S. I enclose a photograph of myself wearing one of the Portia dresses in *Beryl's Secret*. Do you recognize your son? That is my husband at the left."

GEORGE to Félicité (Seattle, May 4):

"Three years ago today it happened. As another actor said '*Sic semper tyrannis*.' . . . I've got a room a long way from the theatre. It's over some rocks by the ocean. When I sleep by the ocean I don't have bad dreams. I wish I could tell that to *Maman*. After the show it takes me two hours to walk to my room. I sing and shout. . . . I hate art. I hate painting and music, but I wish I could paint and write *my* art and music. Because the world is a thousand times more beautiful and *mighty* than most people can see. What they call art is not worth a bean unless it's about what I sing about when I walk to the ocean. I know that because I'm on the outside. I'm a shut-out. And Mr. Ashley knows it, too—wherever he is."

EUSTACIA to George (May 4):

"I have just returned from your father's grave. To us is given, as we grow older, the gift of understanding more fully and of loving more uncloudedly.

"My dear Jordi, I have long noticed that people who talk to those closest to them only about what they eat, what they wear, the money they make, the trip they will or will not take next week—such people are of two sorts. They either have no inner life, or their inner life is painful to them, is beset with regret or fear. Bossuet believed that there are not two such kinds of person, but just one—that people of the world occupy themselves with external things in order to escape from thoughts of death, illness, solitude, and self-reproach.

"I treasure your letters, but I miss in them any reflection of that inner life which has always been so intense and vivid and rich in you. How you used to argue—with your whole soul in your eyes and in your voice—about God and the creation and goodness and evil and justice and mercy and destiny and chance! You remember that well. At eleven o'clock I would cry out: 'Children, children, you must go to bed! We cannot settle these matters tonight.'

"Now I can only assume that you are carrying some burden that 'closes your mouth.' And I assume that that burden has to do with the events that took place here three springs ago.

"Your father was often unjust toward you. His father was unjust toward him and toward his mother. I think it very likely that his grandfather was unjust toward *his* son. And each of these sons toward his father. Oh, do not add new links to that unhappy chain. Someday you will have sons. No man can be a good father until he has understood his own.

"Try, my dear boy, to be just toward your father.

"Justice rests upon understanding *all* the facts. God, who sees all, is Justice—Justice and Love.

"When that happy day comes when I shall see you again (every night I make sure that the window in your room is raised a little) I shall tell you many things about your father. What I wish to tell you now is that during the last weeks of his life—during those nights that you so greatly misunderstood, when you thought he wished to do me harm—he saw his life with new eyes. He recognized his injustice toward you and toward all of us. In profound sincerity and deep emotion he looked forward to a new and different life.

"Then the fatal accident took place.

"Your father's last words—and above all his last *glance*—would seem unimportant to a stranger, but they showed clearly the change that was going on in him.

"You had left Coaltown the night before. On that Sunday afternoon, three years ago today, Mr. and Mrs. Ashley came over to the house as I have told you. You have probably forgotten that the Junior Epworth League of the Methodist Church was holding a picnic in Memorial Park across the hedge. The Ashley children had invited you and your sisters to be their guests. Just before the shot was fired that killed your father, the children began singing around the campfire. We all raised our heads and listened a moment.

"Your father said, 'Jack, will you thank your children for inviting ours to the picnic? You Ashleys have always been mighty good friends to us.'

"Mrs. Ashley glanced at me quickly. Mr. Ashley looked surprised. It had not been your father's habit to acknowledge kindness in anyone.

"Mr. Ashley said, 'Well, Breck, when anybody has children like your children, there's no call to thank anybody for inviting them.'

"While Mr. Ashley took his aim—you remember how serious and slow he was about it—your father looked across the lawn at me. There were tears in his eyes—tears of pride in you.

"Forgive, George. Forgive and understand.

"You will soon be playing Shylock. Think of your father when you hear Portia saying to you:

> 'We do pray for mercy,
> And that same prayer doth teach us all to render
> The deeds of mercy.'

"Your father died at the moment when his real self was beginning to find expression. But that real self is in us all from birth. It was that *real self* that I was aware of in your father throughout our long life together—which I loved and shall continue to love in eternity.

"As I do you. As I shall you."

GEORGE to Félicité (Seattle, May 10):
"Don't expect letters from me for a while. Tomorrow I'm taking a boat to Alaska, maybe. *But you write me.* I've made arrangements so that your letters will be sent on to me. Do you remember the Roman candles on Fourth of July? Well, everything here went up in a blaze of flame and sparks. I got fired. I got arrested. I got ordered to leave Seattle. The only thing I'm sorry about is Florella Thompson. She's pretty unhappy about it, I guess. I got into a fight on the stage, right in front of the audience. The fight was written in the play. Mr. Culloden Barnes is in the hospital, but he isn't hurt. I learned one thing: when I fight in a play I don't get dizzy. I win. The mayor and his wife came to see the shows often. They liked me. He's getting me

out of jail tomorrow. If I don't take the boat to Alaska tomorrow, I can take one to San Francisco two days later. It had to be. I don't regret anything except Florella's being so unhappy. Yes, I do regret it, because what I did to him didn't change anything."

FÉLICITÉ to George (May 18):

"I beg you, Jordi, by all that's precious to you, by *Maman*, by all that God has sent to St. Kitts, by Shakespeare and Puskin: write once a week without fail. Put your hands over your eyes and imagine my unhappiness if I do not hear from you regularly. Jordi, my brother, I shall ask *Maman* for a hundred dollars and I shall come out to California. I shall go to all the places where you have been. I shall hunt for you everywhere. Don't make me do that unless it is necessary. I would have to tell *Maman* that I was deeply anxious about you. She would insist on coming with me. Just one letter a week will prevent this *desperation* on our part. You and God are all we have."

GEORGE to his mother (San Francisco, June 4, 11, 18, 25, and so on into July and August):

"Everything's fine. . . . I'm working. . . . I've got a room way out by what they call the Seal Rocks. The seals bark all night. . . . I bought a new suit. . . . I've been twice to the Chinese theatre. I go with a Chinese friend and he explains it to me. I learn things. . . . I'm doing something very interesting that I'll tell you soon . . . Yes, I sleep fine. . . ."

GEORGE to Félicité (San Francisco, September 10):

"Now I'm going to tell you what I've been doing. I went back to being a waiter in a saloon again. There are about forty saloons along the waterfront where I work. Ours is a fifth-rate one. Other saloons have girly shows or singing waiters or Irish or Jewish comedians. We just have old sailors and old miners who fall asleep on the tables and don't leave any tips. Well, there's an old comic actor here named Lew. He's Greek and very good. Also, he's a kind of saint. His health is just held together with a pin. I've been paying for his drinks. Well, we started a kind of act together. In a pawnshop I found one of those tall silk hats and a ratty old overcoat with a fur collar. He comes in as a rich customer and I wait on him. We have terrible quarrels. At first the customers (and the manager!) thought it was real; then we got to be popular. He talks in Greek and I talk in Russian. Soon there were fifty people at one o'clock and two o'clock and then more and more, standing up around the walls. Sometimes I'm a sad waiter telling him my troubles, sometimes I'm a dreamy waiter or a furious waiter. We practice mornings in a warehouse. We love to practice. We're *great*. We're *wonderful*. The manager of another bigger saloon offered us ten dollars a night for four shows. The signs say LEO AND LEW, THE GREATEST CLOWNS IN TOWN. Society people come now. The reason it's funny is because we've practiced every little move and *silence*, and because people don't understand the words. Lew is great. Now I know what I want to be. I want to be a comic actor. [October 29]: Lew died. I held his hand. Everything I do falls to pieces for me, but I don't care. I don't live. I don't really live. I never will. I don't care as long as other people live. Lew told me I gave him three happy months. I heard that in India those street cleaners have to wear badges. I'm proud of mine. Don't you worry about me."

FÉLICITÉ to George (November 10):
    "Many times you have told me not to worry about you, but it has become clearer and clearer to me that you *do* want me to worry about you. That's why you write me—you want me to join you in some deep trouble. I'm not charging you with lying to me; I'm saying that you are so unhappy about *something* that you do not think clearly. Last night I sat down in my room at ten o'clock and read through all your letters slowly. It was almost three o'clock when I finished.
    "In all those letters you mention *Père* only five times (his insurance, his boasting, his killing animals—twice—and his 'bad education'). Our father was murdered. You do not mention that once. As you used to say, that is a 'very loud silence.'
    "Jordi, you have some very heavy burden on your heart. I think it is a self-reproach—a remorse of some kind. It is a secret. You want to tell it to me, but you do not. You almost tell it to me, then you run away. I know that you do not go to Confession and Mass, because you would have told me so. If I am the only person to whom you have thought of revealing this secret I am ready to hear it. Though there are many wiser than I, there is only one who loves you as much. Let me send you fifty dollars. Come! Do you remember how you used to make me read from *Macbeth*? You have not forgotten the lines:
    'Cleanse the stuffed bosom of that perilous stuff
    Which weighs upon the heart.'
Your unhappiness has somehow to do with *Père*. In some way you feel responsible for his death. That's impossible. When you suffered that concussion of your head in St. Louis some fancy became tangled and twisted in your mind. Oh, write to me! Best of all, come and tell me everything.
    "Almost six years ago you came back from the New Year's Eve

gathering in the Illinois Tavern. You waited until *Maman* had turned out her light and you woke me. You told me at that time what Dr. Gillies had said about the history of the universe. He said that a new kind of human being was going to be born, the children of the Eighth Day. You said that you were a CHILD OF THE EIGHTH DAY. I understood that. Many people in town thought you something very different, but *Maman* and Miss Doubkov and I knew. We knew what your road had been.

"What frightens me now is that you may have let some mistaken fancy ROB YOU OF FOUR YEARS OF YOUR LIFE, warp you, dwarf you. You'll slip back to the SIXTH DAY, or earlier.

"Jordi, believe what Our Lord said, 'The truth will make you free.'

"But you must tell it.

"Spring into freedom.

"I cannot imagine what crime you torment yourself with, but God forgives us all if we acknowledge our weakness. He sees billions of people. He knows everybody's road.

"You know what the deep wish of my life is. I cannot ask to take my vows until my dear brother is—as the Bible says—'made whole.' Come to Coaltown."

GEORGE to Félicité (November 11):

"You won't hear from me for a while. I think I'm going to China soon and from China to Russia. So don't be an idiot and come trying to find me in California because I won't be there."

In early November, 1905, Eustacia answered the postman's ring. It was a letter from her brother-in-law. She did not open it at once; everything about Fisher Lansing displeased her. An hour later Félicité, mopping the upper hall, heard her mother cry out in distress. She descended the stairs rapidly.

"Maman! Qu'est-ce que tu as?"

Her mother gazed at her with an imploring expression and pointed to a letter and a cheque which had fallen to the floor from her lap. Félicité took them up and read them. Fisher had submitted one of the Ashley-Lansing inventions to an expert. He had obtained a patent for it. The mechanical device had been leased to a clock-making firm. He enclosed a cheque for two thousand dollars—a first payment; royalties would follow. He was proceeding slowly in the matter of the other inventions. He was protecting her interests, she could be sure of that.

"There may be a lot in these, Stacey. Start thinking about your automobile."

They exchanged a long glance. Félicité handed the cheque to her mother, who turned her head. "Keep it. Hide it. I don't want to look at it."

After supper Anne went upstairs to do her homework for school. She would be down at eight for the evening's reading. Félicité had never seen her mother so restless—not during her father's illness nor following the receipt of a letter from George. Eustacia walked back and forth.

"*Maman!*"

"It's not mine. It's not ours."

"*Maman*, we'll think of some way to give it to them."

"Beata Ashley would never take it—never, never."

Anne appeared.

"Girls, get your hats and coats. We're going to take a walk."

The lights were going out in the homes. There was an early warning of winter in the air. From time to time Eustacia's fingers closed tightly about Félicité's wrist. For a moment she paused in deep thought before Dr. Gillies's house, then moved on slowly. They reached "The Elms." The sign gleamed faintly in the starlight. Eustacia stood a long time, her hand on the swinging gate.

Félicité whispered, "I'll go in with you."

Anne said, "*Maman*, let's!"

Their mother turned to each of them, anguished but dry-eyed. "But how—how?" she said harshly.

Eustacia opened the gate. They mounted the steps softly. They moved along the verandah and looked long into the room. Beata was reading aloud. Constance was mending some sheets. Sophia lay on the floor adding columns in her account books. An old man sat against the wall, asleep. Two others were playing checkers. An old lady was rocking a cat on her lap. Abruptly Eustacia seized her daughters' elbows and drew them into the street. They returned to "St. Kitts" in silence.

VI. Coaltown, Illinois

Christmas, 1905

THIS IS a history.

But there is only one history. It began with the creation of man and will come to an end when the last human consciousness is extinguished. All other beginnings and endings are arbitrary conventions—makeshifts parading as self-sufficient entireties, diffusing petty comfort or petty despair. The cumbrous shears of the historian cut out a few figures and a brief passage of time from that enormous tapestry. Above and below the laceration, to the right and left of it, the severed threads protest against the injustice, against the imposture.

It is only in appearance that time is a river. It is rather a vast landscape and it is the eye of the beholder that moves.

Look about you in all directions—rise higher, rise higher!— and see hills beyond hills, plains and rivers.

This history made the pretense of a beginning: *"In the early summer of 1902 John Barrington Ashley of Coaltown, a small mining center in southern Illinois, was tried for the murder of Breckenridge Lansing, also of Coaltown."* The reader has long been aware of how misleading those words are—regarded as the *beginning* of anything.

Hills beyond hills: *there* a mentally unstable family of the Loire; *there* a massacre in the West Indies; *there* a religious sect in Kentucky that moves westward. . . .

Do you see a man drowning in a wreck off Costa Rica? A great Russian actor killed in a *mêlée*, where no one gave much thought to who was slain? A funeral in Washington in 1930, with military bands and statesmen in silk hats; behind the widow and her children you can see two middle-aged women— a great opera singer and a troublemaking social reformer? (But funerals are only in appearance the end of anything.) Two old ladies sitting down to lunch in Los Angeles, enjoying the sixty-five-cent plate at The Copper Kettle ("Have the veal, Beata. You remember you liked it." "Now don't flutter at me, Eustacia!")? The children, the innumerable children . . . ?

339

History is *one* tapestry. No eye can venture to compass a hand's-breadth of it. There were once a million people in Babylon.

Then look again at a miscarriage of justice in an unimportant case in a small Middlewestern town.

December twenty-third.

The train was late. Dusk had fallen. Between the bluffs of Coaltown the snowflakes fell unhurriedly in the windless air.

A large crowd had gathered at the depot. Some came to meet relatives. Some were there because it was their custom to be there every late afternoon in the year. The larger part of the throng was present because it was rumored that Lily and Roger Ashley were returning to spend the holidays with their mother and sisters. There was a good deal of nudging and pointing. Constance and Sophia were standing at the far edge of the platform. Exciting and contradictory rumors had been circulating for many months. Some said that Lily Ashley had run away with a drummer and had been abandoned in the great city (but people will believe anything!) and that—wearing short skirts— she danced and sang in low resorts; some said that Roger frequented prize fighters and horse-racing men and Italians and Greeks and people like that; that he engaged in fisticuffs in saloons and that he wrote articles in the papers about subjects that decent people don't even think about. And yet others said that Lily—first as Mrs. Temple, and then as Miss Scolastica Ashley—sang at the weddings and funerals of Chicago's first families and that Roger had received honors and tributes from important persons and organizations. Roger was not a newspaperman for nothing; he was no stranger to the manipulation of rumor. He had forwarded clippings to Miss Doubkov and Dr. Gillies, lively advocates. They had received proof sheets of his forthcoming book. He was very conscious of being the head of the family and the defender of its damaged honor. Under such conditions one sacrifices even modesty. The most lively rumors are conflicting ones. The unhappy citizens of Coaltown did not know what to believe or whom to condemn.

Roger was dressed as a man of substance. Lily had taken him shopping. His collar scraped his chin; his coat was impressive; his handbag was new; his shoes shone. He carried a number of brightly wrapped packages. When he descended from the train his face wore a stern expression. He was endeavoring to master a constriction in his throat and an unaccustomed pounding of his heart. He was not yet ready to enter "The Elms."

Coaltown.

He looked about him in the tumultuous crowd. His sisters did not at first recognize him. He failed to see Porky, who was standing under the trees beyond the edge of the platform. He mastered his constraint and entered at once into his performance. He walked resolutely toward the stationmaster and—putting down his parcels—held out his hand.

"How are you, Mr. Killigrew? I'm glad to see you."

"Why, *Roger*! Glad to see you! Welcome home! Your sisters are here—saw them just a minute ago."

Ranges beyond ranges of hills, plains and rivers . . .

Three and a half years earlier his father—handcuffed—had obtained permission from his guards to speak to Mr. Killigrew: "Horace, will you see that my son gets this watch?" "Yes, Mr. Ashley, I'll do that." Four weeks later Sophia had set up her table and sold lemonade, three cents a glass. Here Mrs. Gillies had bowed in silence to her husband, returning with the coffin of their son, killed in a sledding accident in Massachusetts. Here the young John Ashleys had descended from the train and looked about them, all happy expectation. The platforms of railway stations! From here Olga Sergeievna will leave Coaltown forever, head high, bravely dressed for her return to her fatherland; Beata will take a train for the first time in twenty-eight years to spend a short holiday with her son and grandchildren in New York. The station platform will miss by a few hundred yards being witness to George Lansing's departure toward that astonishing career five thousand miles away (his departure was surreptitious; he leapt aboard the moving train from the heaps of coal in the station yard). Here young men departed for the First World War and returned from it. Before the second war a new highway had been built and new tracks laid eleven miles to the west of Coaltown. The station fell into disrepair. It decayed—which is a burning—and finally went up in flames one frosty November night. It burned up, like everything else in history.

Roger turned. He saw Mrs. Lansing coming toward him. "Roger! Dear Roger!" she said and kissed him as she had done several hundred times yearly during his childhood. An account of this unsuitable greeting was carried from house to house for days. He shook hands with the Lansing girls. "A merry Christmas to you all," continued Eustacia. "I hope you'll come and see us while you're here."

"I will, Mrs. Lansing. I'll come and see you tomorrow night."

Before he turned away he exchanged a glance of intelligence and connivance with Félicité. It said, "Tomorrow morning at half past ten in Miss Doubkov's store."

Shyly Sophia and Constance approached him.

Several prominent citizens came up and shook his hand. "Well, Roger! How are you? You're looking fine. Yes, sir, you're looking fine." "Why, Roger! Welcome home. How things been with you?" A number of them had behaved like skunks and weasels at the trial, but shucks! There are a lot of those in the world. Nothing to get hot about.

He shook their hands and looked into their uneasy faces. His eyes were searching for his sisters; perhaps his mother was here.

"Roger," said Sophia, softly.

How tall they were! For the first time in his life he kissed them. "Sophie! Connie! My, aren't you beautiful girls!"

"Are we?" asked Constance, eagerly. "Some of the boarders say we are."

"Is Mama here?"

"No," said Constance. "She's at home. She never comes out on the street and I almost never do." They could find nothing further to say until Constance suddenly cried, "You look just like Papa! Sophie, doesn't he look just like Papa?" She threw her arms about him in the ecstasy of embracing two.

The former mayor Mr. Wilkins (weasel and rat) came up to Roger and shook his hand. "Glad to see you, Roger. Welcome home!"

"Thank you, Mr. Wilkins."

To Sophia he whispered, "Where did you sell the lemonade and the books?"

She pointed, smiling.

"You're great, Sophie. That's all I can say about you. . . . Where's Porky?"

"Here I am."

They shook hands. "Porky, I want to have a long talk with you. After supper I'm going to have a talk with my mother and then I'm going to take a walk with Sophie. Are you going up the hill to your grandfather's house tonight?"

"No, I'll be working in my store."

Only a portion of the crowd had gone home. A number were standing about, now motionless and silent, staring at the Ashleys—"like we were two-headed chickens," thought Constance. Roger dispersed them easily: "Good evening, Mrs. Folsom. How are Bert and Della? . . . Good evening, Mrs. Stubbs. . . . Hello, Frank."

They reached the top of the main street. Roger could see a light at the corner of the house, in the dining room. He wasn't ready to enter "The Elms." "Porky, will you take these things and put them beside the front door? I'll see you at about a quarter of nine.—Girls, let's walk down the street a ways."

In front of the post office Constance said, "They took down Papa's picture off the wall."

"I've got one. A friend of mine stole it from a police station in Chicago. I cut out the picture and put it in a frame for Mama's Christmas present."

"Oh, Roger! We can have one in the house for our very own!"

It had snowed during the last weeks in Chicago; rain, sleet, and snow had been driven furiously across the city from the lake. This was the first true snowfall that he had seen this year. The snowfall of his childhood. He remembered that the Maestro's daughter Beatrice had once put to her father a question that had often occurred to himself: *"Papà Benè"* (for Benedetto), "why is the first snow in winter so beautiful . . . like music?"

"So! Well! *Bice*, listen to your father: the first months of our life we are wrapped in white, we are soothed and put to sleep in white. Later, we are told that Heaven—which is the memory of infancy—is white. We are lifted and carried about; we float. That is why we are told that angels fly. The first snow reminds us of the only times in our lives when we were without fear. A cemetery under rain is the saddest sight in the world, because the rain reminds of tears; but a cemetery under snow is inviting. We remember that world. In winter the dead are encradled."

"*Si, Papà. Grazie, Papà Benè.*"

They passed the tavern and Mr. Bostwick's grocery store. "This is Miss Doubkov's store. Mrs. Lansing owns it and Felicity works there sometimes. Here's Porky's store. Look, he's making it bigger. And this was Mrs. Cavanaugh's house—who they took away to Goshen."

Before they reached "St. Kitts" Roger turned back. "I guess Mama'll be waiting for us," he said.

Constance was now a young lady of almost thirteen and tall for her age, but under the stress of her brother's (and father's) return—on this short walk, for a few minutes—she exhibited a surprising regression. She kept tugging at Roger's sleeve, his pocket, his elbow. It became evident that she wished to be picked up and carried on his shoulder, as her father had carried her every evening when he returned from work.

Roger stopped and looked down at her with a smile: "But, Connie, you're too big to be picked up now."

A look of confusion crossed her face. "Well, let me hold your hand."

Hills beyond hills . . .

Throughout her whole life her friends and enemies used to say of her, "There's something 'little-girl' about Constance Ashley-Nishimura," or "There's a side of Constance that really never grew up; there's a silly side." In all her campaigns she relied on older men, as though they were a father or brother, and she had an unerring instinct for selecting them—two Viceroys of India, the last Khedive, Presidents, and Prime Ministers ("Codes for Landlords," "Votes for Women," "Rights of Married Women," "Supervision of Prostitution"—she advocated a sort of trade union —"Eye Clinics for Children"—she was a pioneer in preventive medicine), millionaires (all that money she collected and she was often at her wits' end to pay her hotel bill). It was the little-girl side of her that carried her through difficult times—the brutality of the police, the insults and filth thrown at her. She had the fearlessness of a little girl, not that of a mature woman. All this candor and self-

*confidence were a gift to her from her father and brother. The
fairest gifts—and the most baneful—are those of which the donor
is unconscious; they are conveyed over the years in the innumerable
occasions of the daily life—in glance, pause, jest, silence, smile,
expressions of admiration or disapproval. Constance found other
fathers and brothers. They were often exasperated, occasionally
furious; but they seldom betrayed her. . . .*

Finally, they approached the house. Roger gazed long at the
sign THE ELMS   ROOMS AND BOARD. He was remembering
Sophia's letters, his first year in Chicago, the day the taxes were
paid. He pressed Sophia's elbow against his side.

They entered the house.

"Mama! Roger's here!"

Beata came into the hall from the kitchen. She gazed at him
—a stranger! She suddenly remembered that she was wearing
an apron—which was not in the plan—and began hurriedly,
confusedly, untying it. Roger's constraint, physical discomfort,
and dread fell away from him. He grew taller. There was nothing fragile about Beata Ashley, but in his eyes she was, for the
first time, vulnerable, dependent, in need of him. During his
father's presence in Coaltown she had afforded him no opportunity to be of service to her. She wore—as always in winter
—a dark blue woolen dress of little art or grace; but there was
no doubt about it, she was the most beautiful woman in the
world. He crossed to her, took her in his arms, and kissed her
—towering over her by that half an inch which he felt to be
two feet. He was there to defend and sustain her. He had
grown up.

"Welcome home, Roger."

"You look fine, Mama."

"Mama," said Constance, "at the station Mrs. Lansing kissed
Roger. Everybody in town was there."

"Your old room's ready for you," said Beata.

"Let me look around first."

The sitting room with the pieces of furniture that Sophia
had collected one by one, all a little worn and scratched, but
gleaming; the dining room with its long table and two sideboards bristling with cruets and casters and tureens—very
"boardinghouse." They lit a lantern and visited the chicken-

house with its incubator, Violet the cow, the little shed that Porky had built for the ducks. They visited the Rainy Day House and studied the marks their father had made to record their heights annually: Lily, two years old in 1886 to her eighteenth year in 1902; Roger, one year old in 1886 to his seventeenth year in 1902; and so on. They visited the oak trees their father had planted in 1888; they gazed at them in hushed wonder. All Ashleys, save one, were interested in growth and progress and planning.

Beata, as so often, had urged Porky to join them for supper. He had never once sat down with the family in the front rooms. It was his custom to eat in the kitchen. Tonight he was absent from the house. The conversation at table avoided touching upon any serious matters. All seemed to be awaiting the inevitable discussion that Roger would have with his mother—the two alone—in the sitting room later, on that subject that was never referred to: the future. Were the girls ever to continue their education? Would their mother ever emerge from the gate of "The Elms"? Were they ever to have any friends? Roger showed some new photographs of Lily and the wonderful baby. He brought Lily's expressions of regret that she could not be with them. She was leaving for New York on the twenty-eighth, after having sung in four performances of the *Messiah*, the two in Chicago and two in Milwaukee. He talked of his work. Only Constance's questions prevented the conversation from falling into stagnant shallows. Sophia spoke not a word. When they rose from the table the girls started toward the kitchen.

Roger asked, "Mama, can the dishes wait half an hour?"

"Yes, dear. What did you want?"

"Later I'm coming into the sitting room to sit with you, but I'd like to take Sophia for a walk before it gets too late and too cold. I'll take a walk with you tomorrow night, Connie. Oldest first."

"Yes, of course, Roger. Sophia, wrap yourself up well."

They walked hand in hand, which was not an Ashley practice. Avoiding the main street, they followed the old towpath. The Kangaheela flowed by them in silence under the thickening ice.

"Sophie, I've got something to tell you. I was going to tell you on Christmas morning, but I want to tell it to you right

now. You and Porky are coming to Chicago to visit me at
Easter. I'm going to take Porky to a place where he can get a
brace fitted for his ankle, but I'm going to take you somewhere
that's more interesting still. I know a lady who's head of a
school for nurses. She liked that piece I wrote in the paper
about you. She asked me to come and see her and I told her
all about you. I showed her some parts of your letters where
you described what Mama had been teaching you and Connie
at home. She said that she'd enroll you at midterm when you're
seventeen and a half—that's a year and three weeks from today.
She's sent you some books for you to study every now and
then, to get ready."

Sophia was silent.

"Don't you like the idea?"

"Roger."

"What?"

"I couldn't go."

"Why not?"

"The . . . the boardinghouse."

"You *started* it. It's the greatest thing a girl of fourteen ever
did. But you wrote me that it's going well now. Mama and
Mrs. Swenson can run it and they can get another hired girl
when you and Connie go to school in the fall."

Sophia was silent and did not raise her eyes.

"You mean all that shopping, and sacks of flour and things?
And keeping the accounts?—Well, do you know one of the reasons why I came down to Coaltown? It was to persuade Mama
to go out into the town. You can show her how to do those
things. Mama's bright, and she's a very good housekeeper.—
Besides, I'll tell you something else. There's only going to be
one more year of the boardinghouse. Lily and I are going to
make enough money so that you and Mama won't have to work.
Now, Sophia, you listen to what I say: you're going to enter
Miss Wills's school for nurses in January, 1906, or I'm a Chinaman. And probably the boardinghouse will close its door about
six months later."

Sophia murmured, "The chickens and the ducks and the
cow."

"I'll ask Porky to give me the name of some boy you can
trust. I'll pay him to take care of the chickens and the ducks."

He talked to her about the Great Subject. After Lily, she had been the first with whom he had shared his conviction that, somewhere on the earth, their father would hear of Scolastica and Berwyn Ashley. They would receive a letter written in ambiguous terms which only they could decipher. It would say, "Please write me about my dear friend who takes care of all sick animals," or "If you know anyone who has a name that means wisdom in Greek, give that person my love." He would give an address where they could write to him. They would all go and have their photographs taken for Papa.

Roger became aware that she was scarcely listening to him. He could not know that in Sophia the faculty of hope—like a clock that had outworn its service—had broken down. She was no longer able to believe that the boardinghouse would ever come to an end, that she would ever see her father, that she would ever tend the sick, or live close—day by day—to anyone she loved.

Early in the walk Sophia had taken her hand from his. He now became aware that she was trembling.

"Roger," she said softly.

"Yes, Sophie?"

"I think . . . I ought to get back to the house."

"Are you tired?"

"Just a little."

Suddenly he remembered that she had been ill six months before—had been two weeks at the Bell Farm, where Dr. Gillies had forbidden her to receive any callers but Porky. Roger reproached himself for not having given enough attention to the report. The young tend to assume that the young are always well—a cold now and then, a twisted ankle. A vague dread awoke in him now.

"Do you eat good, Sophie?"

"Yes."

"Do you sleep good?"

"Oh, yes . . . But I'll eat better . . . and sleep better, now that you're back . . . in your room."

"We'll go in by the back door. The kitchen's warmest."

His dread was heightened by some words said to him by the Maestro a few weeks before.

Of the Maestro's six gifted children, all except his favorite daughter, Bice, were clamorous, demanding, and self-assertive. She assisted her mother in running the house; she served as her father's secretary; she asked nothing for herself. She was tireless, watchful, shielding. Family life among the Italians—as among the Irish, though with less virulence—is punctuated by grand liberating quarrels, blood-warming rhetorical baths, complete with denunciations, slamming of doors, and last words fortissimo. *These, in turn, are followed by reconciliations of an operatic beauty—tears, embraces, kneeling on the floor, protestations of penitence, humility, and undying love. These storms were greatly enjoyed by all except Bice, who, on each occasion, believed that they were real. She suffered. She alone in the family was pale and subject to migraine. During the summer of 1905 she was no longer able to conceal from her parents that she was coughing blood. Her father took her to a sanatorium in Minnesota. His character changed.*

One evening after dinner he sat alone with Roger in his studio surrounded by those works of art (that is: of power diminished to beauty) that could afford him no comfort, and said:

"Mr. Frazier, family life is like that of nations: each member battles for his measure of air and light, of nourishment and territory, and particularly for that measure of admiration and attention which is called 'glory.' It is like a forest; each tree must fight for its sunlight; under the ground the roots engage in a death struggle for moisture. We are told that some even exude an acidity that is noxious to all except themselves. Mr. Frazier, in every lively healthy family there is one who must pay."

Sophia outlived them all. When, down the years, Roger and his sisters called on her she did not recognize them. Lily would sing her favorite songs to her softly. "I had a sister who sang that song." She was under the impression that she was in Goshen. When Roger called on her she explained that many people regarded Goshen with fear and even shame, but that he could see for himself that it was delightful in every way—there were trees and lawns and birds and squirrels. She received these visitors with grave courtesy, but at the end of half an hour she informed them that she was busy, her patients required her attention. She pointed to a dozen dolls, all bedridden but convalescent. Her attendants told them that she dressed each morning with great care in expectation of

her father's visit and each night she exacted a promise that she be
awakened early the next morning for a certain reason. There was
one visitor from whom she fled and who was not encouraged to
return. Sophia detested the odor of lavender.

Roger returned Sophia to the kitchen and recommended a
glass of hot milk. He joined his mother in the sitting room.

"Mama, I'm going to stay in Chicago one more year and
then I'm going to New York. Could you run the boardinghouse
one more year—or one more year and a half—and then come
to New York?"

"Oh, Roger! I shall never leave 'The Elms.' Oh, no. Oh, no,
Roger."

"But the boardinghouse—"

"I *like* the boardinghouse."

"Next fall Sophia must go away to school."

"Oh, I shan't leave Coaltown."

"I think by that time Lily or I will have a letter from Papa."

She was silent a moment, then said in a low voice, "If that is
so, of course I shall do what your father thinks best.—I like the
boardinghouse. It brings in some money. I like to think that
that money will be useful to your father someday."

Roger leaned forward, his elbows on his knees. "Mama, will
you call with me on Mrs. Lansing on Christmas Day?"

She raised her eyes from her sewing and looked at him directly. "Roger, until your father returns I shall never leave the
grounds of 'The Elms.'"

"You hate Coaltown?"

"Oh, no."

"Why is it, then?"

"I have nothing to say to these people. They have nothing
to say to me that would interest me. All the best of my life has
been passed within these walls."

"And the worst of your life, Mama."

"I don't remember that.—A happiness such as I had lasts.
It's with me every day. I don't want things to break into it—to
trouble it."

Seven years later Mrs. Wickersham on her terrace in Manantiales
read—or rather was read to, for her eyesight was failing—that the

American diva Madame Scolastica Ashley, then singing at Covent Garden, was the daughter of the unjustly convicted John Ashley of Coaltown, Illinois. The item in the San Francisco paper reminded the readers that the real murderer had confessed his crime, but that no information had ever come to light as to the whereabouts of the fugitive. After some deliberation Mrs. Wickersham dictated a long letter—the task required the larger part of four mornings—to Madame Ashley in London. It concluded: "I am certain that if your dear father were still alive after the summer of 1905 he would have written me!" The letter was signed in a shaky hand "Ada Wickersham."

Not long after reading this letter Beata closed "The Elms" and moved to Los Angeles. She bought and repaired a dilapidated mansion on a low but steep hill near the center of the city. She put up a sign, BUENA VISTA ROOMS AND BOARD. *The very ground on which the house stood was falling away in small landslides; the neighborhood was deteriorating. Such boarders as presented themselves were an assorted lot—some office girls, rheumatic widows, asthmatic widowers, derelicts. The table she set acquired a small reputation; some business men formed a luncheon club and climbed the two long flights of uneven cement steps five times a week. Beata did not wish to run a public restaurant and only the permanent boarders sat down to dinner in the evening. Three of her children combined to offer her an income and the gift of a house in Pasadena, but Beata was resolutely independent; she accepted nothing. For half a year, in 1913, Constance and her husband—touring the hemisphere on one of their crusades—left their small half-Japanese son with her. Her happiness cannot be described. When the boy departed the separation was painful on both sides. From time to time one or other of her boarders absconded with or without some bed linen and table silver. One couple disappeared leaving a broken suitcase and a three-year-old son. Beata put the boy through deaf-and-dumb school, herself learned the manual alphabet, and adopted him. It seems that Beata came into the world to be a grandmother. Jamie helped her with the house, remained with her to her death. He and his children inherited her small savings.*

Several times a year a newspaper reporter would enter "Buena Vista" as far as the front hall. "Is it true, Mrs. Ashley, that you are the mother of Madame Scolastica Ashley, and Berwyn Ashley?"

"Thank you very much for your visit, but I'm very busy today."
"And Constance Ashley-Nishimura?" "Good morning. Thank
you for calling." "Have you had any message from your husband,
Mrs. Ashley?" "We're cleaning the downstairs rooms this morning. I'm sorry. I'll have to ask you to leave." "But, Mrs. Ashley, I
have to get a story or I'll be fired." "I'm sorry—good morning,
good morning."

Grandmotherly she was, of a German patrician rather than of
an American order. All her boarders were aware of her concern
for them. The house was spotless and she exacted a large measure
of decorum from those who lived in it. She had long talks with
addicts of tobacco and alcohol, with the despairing and the light-
minded. Behind an appearance of severity she truly "adopted"
her boarders: she lent money, she made gifts of garments and dollar watches. Her days were full. Her golden hair turned the color
of a dull straw; she long retained her erect carriage. She wore no
colors. Like many German women she came in later years to dress
with notable distinction. Passers-by on the street stopped short in
admiration at the delicate white cuffs and the snowy fichu over
the black silk or broadcloth, at the long gold chain and crystal
pendant that held a lock of a grandson's hair. When Lily arrived
in town to give a concert, or Roger and Constance to lecture, she
let it be known that she wished to sit in the back of the hall. She
refused to share a meal with them at a hotel; she invited them to
have coffee with her in the sitting room at the "Buena Vista."
These visits would have been difficult but for the fact that she had
considerable knowledge of the matters that interested them. But
there was something else:

"Mama," asked Constance one day, "you're happy, aren't you?"

"Do you remember Mrs. Wickersham's description of your father's life in Chile?"

"Yes, Mama."

"All Ashleys are happy, because we work. I'd be ashamed if we
weren't."

Late in life she had acquired a measure of humor. One day
Roger climbed the precarious steps to drink coffee with his mother.
She told him she and his father had never been married.

They both laughed.

"Mama!" he said.

"I'm proud of that."

Beata never mentioned to her children that she had joined a church—one of those independent congregations that abound in southern California, combining spiritism, Indian philosophy, and healing: it seemed to her to reflect many ideas, many affirmations, that she had acquired from her lifelong reading in Goethe.

At nine-thirty Roger gave the signal—the hoot of an owl—before Porky's store and went in. Porky resumed his work by the hot stove.

"Sophie's not well, Porky."

Porky wasted no words when a glance could better convey his sense.

"You and she are coming up to Chicago to visit me at Easter." Roger put down on the table some pamphlets illustrating braces for the feet and shins. "You stay four days; she'll stay a week. If Connie went back to school, would the children behave badly to her?"

"A few. Connie'd be all right."

"Have you got all this work to do over Christmas?"

"Most of my work I do by mail now. Drummers send me their families' shoes. Sophie ought to go to the Bell Farm again —right now—day after Christmas."

"If you say so, I'll do it. I'll take her there myself."

Bang! Bang!

"I met Felicity Lansing on the train. I think she has an idea who killed her father. Could she have?"

Bang. "Might have."

"Do you have any idea, Porky?" Porky's glance conveyed nothing. "I'd rather know who rescued my father."

It was restful to be with Porky and his hammer and his silence. "I feel I ought to be home and have a last word with Sophie. What's that drawing on the wall?"

"My cousin's building two more rooms to the store for me." *Bang. Bang.* "I'm getting married in March."

"Sure!" Roger suddenly remembered Porky's having told him in great confidence, that the young men of the Church of the Covenant on Herkomer's Knob married at the age of twenty-five. "Do I know your wife?"

"Christiana Rawley."

Roger's face lit up. He remembered Christiana at school. "Fine!" he said. They shook hands solemnly.

"I'm teaching her brother Standfast; he'll help me here. Tell your mother that when I move out of 'The Elms' he can take my room there and do the heavy work."

"I will."

They exchanged a glance. Friendship is great. It thinks of everything. Imagination.

"My grandfather wants to see you."

"Yes. Where?"

"At his house."

No one in Coaltown was ever invited to call on Herkomer's Knob.

There was something weighty in the air.

"Yes, of course, Porky. When?"

"Could you meet me here tomorrow at four? I'll have horses." Porky's lameness. An able young man could ascend the hill in forty minutes.

"I'll be here. What's your grandfather's name?"

"O'Hara. Call him 'Deacon.' And if he says anything about me, do you know my name?"

"Harry O'Hara."

"My name is Aristides."

"He's in Plutarch's *Lives*!"

"In school the teacher called me Harry. They thought the children would laugh at Aristides."

"Tomorrow at four.—I'd better get back to the house and see Sophie."

They didn't say goodnight. Just the glance, arrowlike, keener by three and a half years.

Roger entered the gate at "The Elms" and went around the house to the back. Through the window he saw his mother seated at the kitchen table, her cup of *Milchkaffee* before her, lost in thought. He returned to the front of the house and stole silently upstairs. Sophia's door was open a few inches. He stood still and listened. He whispered, "Sophie!"

"Yes! Yes, Roger?"

"Do you want to go to church with me on Christmas morning?"

"Yes."

"Like we used to do when Papa was here? You and Connie. I'll tell you a secret: Lily's sent you both some beautiful dresses to wear. Mama sent her your measurements. Then the next day we're going to the Bell Farm to see everybody there.—Now will you sleep nine hours for me tonight?"

"Yes, I will."

"I'm going to leave my door open a few inches, like Papa used to do. Remember?"

"Yes."

In the morning a copper can of hot water stood before his door. As Roger finished shaving he gazed insistently into the mirror that had so often reflected his father's face. Mirrors "hold" nothing. They don't know we're here. "T.G." used to say that the universe was like a mirror. Vacant. The smell of coffee and frying bacon filled the air. He heard his sisters stirring. He went out into the hall and shouted: "Bathroom's free! Last one down to breakfast is a buffalo!"

Constance came rushing toward him screaming: "Papa's home—I mean, Roger's home."

Sophia hid behind her door.

His mother had eaten breakfast. She brought a cup of coffee to the table and sat down beside him. She hesitated to speak. She knew that her hoarseness had returned. Besides, she could think of nothing to say. She was filled with pride in this visitor, this strange young man.

"I want to see some people today," he said. "Lily's sent down some presents for Miss Doubkov and the Gillieses."

"I've asked them to supper with us."

"That's fine. I may be a little bit late. I'm going up to Herkomer's Knob this afternoon. Porky's grandfather asked to see me.—After supper I'm going over to call on Mrs. Lansing. Have you got something to eat that I could take over for a present?"

"Yes, I have. I'll wrap up some marzipan and ginger cookies."

The girls joined them. Constance had plenty to say.

By ten-thirty Félicité had lighted the stove in Miss Doubkov's store. Roger knocked and entered. She was sitting behind the counter straight, severe, contained, like a schoolteacher—no, like a nun. She had brought Anne with her. (It was not necessary to explain that nothing escaped the eyes of Coaltown except the truth.) By previous arrangement Anne put cotton in her ears and sat down by the stove with a book.

Roger and Félicité gazed into each other's eyes a moment over something increasingly weighty; whatever it was, they were in it together. She began speaking in a low voice:

"I have two things to tell you." She told him about the money her mother had received from his father's inventions. "It's made her very unhappy. She doesn't want to keep it one day longer. She hasn't even put it in the bank. She cashed the cheque and keeps the money hidden in her room. She wanted to go to your house and give it to your mother, but she felt sure that your mother wouldn't take it. She was sure that your mother would be very angry." She paused and looked at him with a faint inquiry.

"Yes. I think she was right."

"When she heard that you were coming to Coaltown she felt a great relief. She changed in one day. She's going to put it all in your hands when you come to see her tonight. I thought I ought to tell you first so that you'd be ready. You *will* take it?"

"Surely your father did some work on the inventions?"

"Mother says she knows it wasn't very much." Félicité smiled faintly. "She says she'll ask for ten percent and give it to orphans."

Roger was unable to sit still longer. He rose and took a few steps around the room. "Papa's inventions! They've made money! . . . He always knew there was money in them, but he wouldn't do anything about it."

"Will you take it from *Maman* tonight?"

"I'll put it in the bank. You and I will be the treasurers of it. We'll use it for our sisters' education. If Papa were here, he'd want it divided equally. That's what I'll tell your mother. . . . What else did you want to talk to me about?"

Félicité's expression changed. She pressed her lips together. She looked at him imploringly. She clasped her hands tightly on the counter. "Roger, I have something terrible to tell you. I wasn't sure of it when I saw you on the train. I'm sure of it now. —Roger, what did your father do every time he fired his gun?"

"What? What do you mean, Felicity?"

"Try to remember! What did he teach you to do because he said it made you concentrate better?"

"He counted."

"And he pressed with the tip of his left shoe on the ground. Always at the same speed." Roger waited. "He said four words: 'One, two, three, *crack*!'"

"Yes?"

Félicité was silent. The blood had left her face. She looked at him with urgent appeal. "Help me," she whispered.

Suddenly he saw what she meant. "Someone else could shoot at exactly the same second!"

"From the house. From a window upstairs in the house."

"But who? Who, Felicity?"

"Someone who would know about that counting."

"*Me? You?* We were all at the picnic in Memorial Park. George had left town the night before."

She began talking very rapidly, but distinctly. "Father had been very ill for weeks and weeks. Mother sat up beside his bed every night. Sometimes he was in pain and he'd shout and throw things off his table. George thought he was striking Mother. George would wander around the house all night like an animal—like an animal going crazy. My father would never have hurt *Maman*. But he was in pain. Sometimes he called her cruel names. *Maman* understood, but George didn't. Then my father got the idea that he would shoot your father. George told me so. George said he heard him say so. My father didn't mean it. He was just suffering. Do you see? George shot my father to protect *Maman* and to save your father's life."

Roger rose slowly. He said, "That must be the way it was."

"Wait! Wait! George wouldn't have let your father go through that trial. He didn't know about the trial. He rode all night on one of those freight trains. He fell off and hurt his head. He was in an insane asylum for months. Oh, Roger, Roger! Help me!"

Roger crossed to the stove quickly and tapped Anne on the shoulder. She pulled the cotton from her ears. "Get a glass of water."

Roger and Anne stood in silence while Félicité sipped the water. Anne had never seen her sister's hands tremble. Finally Roger whispered, "Put the cotton back in your ears, Anne."

Finally he said, "Where's George now?"

"He came back four nights ago. He got into his room by the window. We didn't know he was there until the morning. Nobody's ever seen anyone so unhappy. Even my father wasn't as unhappy as that. We've always been afraid that George would become insane. And now . . . I can see now that he's trying to tell us something; but he can't tell it."

"Does your mother . . . ?"

Félicité had shed no tears. She put her hand over her mouth and a great sob broke beneath it. "Last night . . . George doesn't want to go to bed. He wants us to sit up all night with him. We read scenes from Shakespeare and French plays. And we talk. George talks. He talks strange things, a sort of nonsense. And I saw that *Maman* was trying to help him tell the thing, whatever it was. Because if he told *her* . . . do you see?"

She waited. "No, I don't, Felicity."

"He'd go to a priest. She could persuade him to go to a priest."

"Yes."

"I don't think he can *ever* tell *Maman*! He wants to tell me, but so far he arranges it that we're never alone together. Now that I've told you, Roger, I see what I can do: I can tell him that I know, that I understand. Yes. Yes." She whispered, "*Maman* knows too—I'm sure now."

"Felicity, this is what you can do. Take that money from Papa's inventions. Give it to George and tell him to go out of the country—to China, to Africa. But first have him write a full confession. When he's been gone several months we'll send the confession to the State's Attorney."

Félicité seized his hands. "Yes, Roger. YES! Then your father can come back."

Now she wept. "But I must hurry home. I'm so afraid that he'll disappear as suddenly as he came. Help me put out the fire. Anne! Anne! We're going. Thank you, Roger."

At the same time, at the same hour, George Lansing was lying full length, face down, on the floor of Miss Doubkov's sitting room, his head toward the icons. Miss Doubkov was standing beside him reading in Old Slavonic the Prayer of Contrition.

He had told his story. When his panting for breath had prevented his continuing Miss Doubkov had bound a wet towel about his forehead. Now his exhaustion was such that he could barely repeat the words after her. When she had finished she leaned down and held a crucifix before him. He kissed it.

He rose. She led him to the desk by the window and put pen, ink, and paper before him. "Write down what I dictate to you: *'I, George Sims Lansing, on the afternoon of May 4, 1902, shot and killed my father Breckenridge Lansing on the lawn behind our house. I had left town on the previous evening, but returned the next noon riding on the underside of a freight car. I hid in the woods. . . .'"*

While she was dictating she moved in and out of her four small rooms, collecting sums of money from various hiding places.

"Now address the envelope: 'The State's Attorney, The State of Illinois. . . .' Now go into the bathroom and wash your face. Sit down in my bedroom until I call you."

She wrote a letter and called him.

"You are taking the twelve-twenty train for Chicago. Go out by my back stairs. Take the path behind the courthouse. Don't get on the train at the station; jump on it when it starts to cross the bridge by the water tower. Go straight to Canada—to Halifax. Take a ship to St. Petersburg. When my father came to America from Paris we arrived in Halifax. There was a sort of Russian club there to welcome Russians and to help them make plans. Buy some workmen's clothes as soon as you can and roll in the dirt in them. You are from a small town in Alberta where my father worked for a while. Until you get to Russia you must act the part of a stupid, ignorant backwoods boy from that small Russian colony in Alberta. You know scarcely any English and your Russian's bad because you're stupid. . . . Don't get angry at anybody. Don't quarrel with anyone. Be an idiot. I have written a statement here. It says that you are an orphan . . . honest and industrious . . . a good Christian. You had a fever when you were a child that left you a little slow. The letter is written in English, but it is signed by the Pope of that small town in Alberta. When you reach Halifax look for Russians. Tell everybody you must go to Russia to find your grandmother. She is in Moscow. You do not know her address. There is her name. . . . I do not know how you will manage all this. I do not know where you will get papers, but we must leave some things to God. Here are two hundred dollars. . . . Now you have time only to write one or two sentences for your mother and sisters. I shall see your mother this afternoon. I shall tell her everything. Can I give her your promise that you will make your confession soon?"

"Yes, Olga Sergeievna."

"When you get to Russia, write me. Write in Russian. Do not write to your mother for several years." She continued in Russian: "God bless you, dear Ghyorghy. God fill your heart and soul with true repentance and free you of that great load of mortal sin. You have taken a life and you doubly owe a life to God and to His creation. The Mother of God is a source of consolation to all—particularly to us who are wanderers and exiles. May she make Herself known to you. . . . Go! Go, dear boy. . . ."

He bowed low over her hand. Without a word he left the house.

At four that afternoon Olga Sergeievna called at "St. Kitts." Eustacia knew at once from the expression on her face that grave matters were in the air. She called Félicité, who stood beside her chair throughout the half hour.

Olga Sergeievna told them everything. She laid his short note on the table. She reported his solemn promise.

"*Chère Eustachie*, when I hear from George over there I shall send his story to Springfield."

Eustacia pressed Félicité's hand. In a low voice she said, "Shouldn't you tell Beata now?"

"That's for you to decide. I should wait."

Suddenly Eustacia's sad but not stricken face lit up with joy. "I shall tell it all to Roger tonight."

Félicité said softly, "*Maman*, Roger knows almost all of it already. I had a talk with him about it this morning."

Eustacia looked at her in wonder. "Olga," she asked, "has he some money?"

"He has money. He has hope. He has courage. He has religion. He has intelligence. Go rest, Eustachie."

Eustacia kissed her, murmuring, "And pray."

Vista after vista . . . range beyond range.

The greatest Russian actor during the early years of this century first called attention to himself by behaving as a clown in the various taverns where he was engaged as waiter. He discovered an old derelict actor to work with—George speaking French; his associate, German. George played dreamy waiters, enthusiastic waiters, embittered waiters to his fastidious diner. He was particularly fine as an angry waiter, for he was said to have the face of an angry feline. George spilled soup on his guest, trod on his toes, found knives and forks in his pockets. The din was terrific; the room filled up. They were invited to cause consternation and havoc in more expensive restaurants. They were engaged as clowns in a pleasure park at the edge of the city. Posters appeared announcing "GHYORGHY." The step to the theatre followed rapidly. He was engaged as a low comedian and was particularly admired as a player of old men. Before long he arrived at a position where he was able to select his own roles. He refused all invitations to leave Russia. Visitors from abroad reported that he was—in his own translations—the finest Hamlet, Lear, Macbeth, Falstaff, Malade Imaginaire, Tartuffe they had ever seen. Olga Sergeievna, writing Eustacia from Moscow in 1911, said that she had been enjoying the company of a friend, a remarkable young "opera singer." They had talked much of their earlier lives in France—in Charbonville—remembering old days with laughter and tears and much love. Finally he wrote himself. He sent pictures of his children. The last letters from both were dated 1917. They seem to have disappeared in that turbulent time.

When Roger arrived at Porky's store at four o'clock he found Porky's cousin Stan (Standfast Rawley) in the street holding the bridles of two saddled horses. Stan was an old friend, even more taciturn than his cousin. He worked in Bilbow's livery stable. The young men shook hands. Stan disappeared. Porky and Roger mounted the horses and began the ascent.

The members of the Covenant Church in Herkomer's Knob lived in identical frame houses surrounding their tabernacle. This was one of the many communities that survived, like vestigial pockets, from the days of the Great Wilderness—moving westward from Virginia to Kentucky and Tennessee and beyond.

Their isolation was a result not only of their religious beliefs, but of the large amount of Indian blood in their veins. Since on the old frontier it was white men who married or lived with Indian women—no full-blooded Indian ever married a white girl—it was the men's names that were transmitted, spelled as they were heard. Most of the families on the Knob were named Gorum, Rawley, Cobb, O'Hara, and Ratliff. For generations they engaged in hunting and trapping, but when game became scarce their young men descended into Coaltown, first to work in the railroad yard or in the livery stables. They were sober by custom and upbringing and were known to be extremely trust-worthy and industrious. They served as janitors in the bank, the jail, the court house, and the hotel. Men of the open air and of free movement, they could not adjust themselves to working in stores, nor would they go underground as miners. In school their boys and girls—with the sole exception of Porky—made no friends outside of their own number. They were unsmiling, joyless, dogged. The older men never came to town save to pay their taxes, coins in hand. The community was known to be poor. As one of the distinguished economists in the Illinois Tavern saloon put it, they were "mouse-farm poor." The women made homespun garments and wove bed-spreads. The men made utilitarian objects from the hides of horse and deer. They did not sell these products in Coaltown (it had become apparent to some that they detested Coaltown), but carried them a considerable distance to other markets. Some of their middle-aged women came down the hill and worked as "hired girls" in homes, but always with the under-standing that they would be back on Herkomer's Knob by seven o'clock. There were many beehives on the Knob and much clover. The honey was sold elsewhere; the Ashleys and the Gillieses prized it as gifts. Their young people attended the town's schools through the eighth grade; their deportment was that of solemn little men and women. Their clothes of homespun were spotlessly clean and smelled of lye soap. Their given names were the source of much amusement. Some were taken from the Bible, but the larger number were from the two works that always accompanied the earliest adventurers from Virginia into the Wilderness: *Pilgrim's Progress* and Plutarch's

Lives. There was many a Christian and a Good Works, and many a Lycurgus, an Epaminondas, a Solon, and an Aristides. The plantation owners in the East had drawn from Plutarch the tyrannicides and warriors—Cassius, Cincinnatus, Horatius, and Brutus; the members of the Covenant Church elected the sagacious. All the boys were exceptional athletes, but were forbidden by their elders to take part in the high school's Saturday afternoon games, which were conducted under the imagery of revenge, hatred, and extermination.

Throughout the seventies and eighties the members of the community were much derided as "screechers," "jumpers," and "holy rollers," but gradually their honesty and the austerity of their lives began to command a puzzled respect. For years the young men had married girls from their own congregation and everyone on Herkomer's Knob was soon many times his own cousin. The dangers resulting from this practice were brought to their attention in the middle sixties. Dr. Gillies's predecessor—elected, as Dr. Gillies was later, to be the community's physician—explained to them the deleterious consequences of consanguineous marriage. The Elders listened to him, impassive but astonished. Fortunately, Dr. Winsted was an admirable lecturer. Thereafter it became the custom for certain elders to journey eastward visiting churches allied to their own. From these trips they brought back brides and grooms for their young people, without relinquishing any of their own. Dr. Gillies presumed, without knowing, that some money was exchanged during these negotiations.

Rumors persisted, however, that the sobriety of the congregation on Herkomer's Knob was not all that it appeared to be. It was said that their Sunday-evening services culminated in leaping and shouting and "speaking in tongues"—"downright orggies," as the eminent moral philosophers in the Illinois Tavern saloon called them. As no outsider had been within fifty yards of the tabernacle for longer than three minutes this description could not be confirmed.

Porky left Roger before his grandfather's house, leading away the horses.

The Deacon was sitting in a rocking chair on his narrow front porch. A blanket was spread across his knees. His skin was very brown, his eyes were like his grandson's of a black without luster. The faces of Indians show little change between thirty and seventy.

"Forgive me for not getting up, Mr. Ashley," he said, indicating by a gesture that Roger was to sit in the straight chair beside him.

He turned and looked long at his guest. Roger felt a prompting of awe, then of affection. He had never known a grandfather. At last the Deacon spoke:

"Did you know that your father came to the help of our Covenant Church when it needed help?"

"No, Deacon," said Roger with surprise.

There fell one of the long Indian pauses to which Roger was accustomed. They were like wholesome breathing.

"You must have been about eleven years old at the time. Our church then stood over yonder on that steep slope. Come spring there was a week of solid rain. There were mud slides all over the mountain. One night, in the middle of the night, the church rolled down into the valley. It turned over many times and broke up like kindling." Another long pause. "The next week, soon as the roads were fit to travel, your father drove up here. He gave the elders one hundred and fifty dollars." Pause. "It was a shake more than he could afford. You know that your father was not a rich man?"

"I've only come to realize that these last years, Deacon. At home Father never talked about money."

"We paid him back slowly, now a little, then a little; but every cent of the money we gave him he used in ways to help our children. Your father had eyes wide open, Mr. Ashley. Did you know it was your father who sent Aristides to Springfield to learn the shoemaking trade?"

"No, Deacon."

"Your father's mouth wasn't wide open, like his eyes were." Long pause.

"To the day he brought us that money not one of us older ones had exchanged a word with him. But he knew all our young ones. Your father had a feeling for young ones. Young ones appreciate it when it's someone not in their own family. We had been watching him and when he brought us that money we knew that he had been watching us." Pause. "Can you tell me what your father's religious views were?"

Roger hesitated. "He took us to the Methodist Church every Sunday. He didn't talk about things like that at home. He took turns reading aloud to us in the evening and there were some parts of the Bible he liked, but he didn't add any words of his own to them. I don't know how he felt inside. When he was in jail he asked Dr. Benson not to visit him again. I guess you heard that. I wish I could answer you, Deacon. I wish I knew."

The Deacon leaned forward, grasping his cane. "We felt that his wanting to give us money for our church had a special meaning. We felt that he wasn't only a kind man, but that he was meeting us as a religious man. . . . And we were right."

This was said with such solemnity that Roger asked in a low voice, "How did you know that, Deacon?"

The Deacon began, slowly and painfully, to rise from his chair. "In a few minutes I will tell you that. First, I want to show you the church your father helped us to build."

Leaning on his cane, the Deacon slowly led Roger along a level lane that followed the contour of the hilltop. It was bordered on either side by identical houses. There were no marks of wheels on the path. The stables could be seen below them. Some men, women, and children passed. They bowed their heads slightly in greeting, but no word was spoken and no one glanced at Roger. The church had once been painted brown. Over the front door was a bell tower such as is customary in country schools. It stood on level ground, but before it, beside it, and above it on the clayey slope was a field enclosed by a white picket fence. The Deacon paused with his hand on the gatepost and looked at the field.

"This is our graveyard."

There were no tombstones or markers of any kind. Roger did not voice his question.

"The dead are given new names in Heaven, Mr. Ashley. Here our names and bodies soon decay and are forgotten. My name is Samuel O'Hara; there are at least ten Samuel O'Haras in this field." His voice took on a dryness of tone. "Why should I wish an advertisement of myself here when I stand before God's face?"

Silence.

"How many billions of billions have died? No man can count them. Only one name in a vast number is remembered a hundred years. All are the humus from which the cedars of Lebanon shall lift themselves."

They went into the church. There were no Christmas decorations. There was a table and many benches. It resembled a schoolroom. The floor was streaked and scuffed as though boisterous games had been played on it. It was very cold. Roger trembled with cold and a vague apprehension. The Deacon raised one hand and pointed to a board on the wall beside the entrance. It read: "This building is the gift of John Barrington Ashley, April 12, 1896." Roger was aware of a stab of longing: to look at his father, as one would look at a stranger whom one had heard highly commended.

"Was my father ever here, Deacon?"

"No . . . You are the first person not belonging to our community who has entered this church."

A door at the end of the hall opened and three men entered carrying kerosene lamps. Seeing the Deacon, they turned and started to go out. The Deacon raised his voice and said, "You may go on with your work."

The men began attaching the lamps to hooks that hung from the ceiling. The lamps had been polished; their chimneys shone like crystal.

The Deacon and Roger returned to the house and entered the front room. A fire was burning in the small fireplace. There was a strong smell of lye soap.

"I will show you my reason for believing that your father dealt with us as a religious man." He drew a worn envelope from his pocket. "We received this letter from him four days before he started on that trip which he thought was carrying him to his death. Did your mother know anything about this?"

"I think not, Deacon. I think I can say for certain she didn't."

"You may want to read this by yourself. I think you will want to go out on the porch and read the letter. Then bring it back to me."

Roger had not felt so light-headed since the days he had made his way to Chicago, hungry. A feeling of something portentous and strange in human experience had been gathering within him. He felt as though he had walked all his life in ignorance of abysses and wonders, of ambushes, of eyes watching him, of writing on clouds. It came to him that surely life is vaster, deeper, and more perilous than we think it is. He dropped the envelope and bent over to pick it up. He was suddenly filled with fear that he would go through life ignorant —stump ignorant—of the powers of light and the powers of darkness that were engaged in some mighty conflict behind the screen of appearances—fear, fear that he would live like a slave, or like a four-footed thing with lowered head.

He went out on the porch. He put his fingers in the envelope. Stinging tears came into his eyes. He filled his lungs as though he were about to run a race and read:

"To the Elders of the Covenant Church,
    "Respected friends:
    "Apart from the members of my family you are the only persons to whom I wish to say a word at this time.
    "On the afternoon of May fourth I fired a rifle at a target. A man several yards to the left of my aim fell dead. I can find no explanation for this. I am innocent of murder in deed and intention.
    "You remember that I have felt a deep interest in the church and community on Herkomer's Knob. As a boy I attended with my grandmother a church which I believe resembled yours. Those hours of silence, self-effacement, and trust have become a part of my life. Those characteristics I have found reflected in the members of your community. Every Sunday morning in Coaltown, while attending a very different service, my thoughts have ascended the hill to Herkomer's Knob.
    "I leave a son behind me. I know no older men who could counsel, encourage, or rebuke him. At twenty-one no man wishes guidance. If prior to that age my son Roger appears to you to have fallen into discouragement, thoughtlessness, or dishonorable ways, I wish you would show him this letter.
    "I go to Joliet with my grandmother's prayer in my mind. She asked that our lives be used in the unfoldment of God's plan for the world. I must trust that I have not totally failed.
    "With deep regard,
        John Ashley."

Roger let the letter fall to his lap. He gazed at the frozen hill-side before him. The Deacon wanted him to know that it was the men from the Covenant Church who had rescued his father. They worked in the jail and on the railroad. They understood locks and handcuffs and the schedules of trains. They went unarmed; they were silent, agile, and very strong. In breaking the law they had risked their lives and—what was probably more important to them—the honor and dignity of their church. They were obedient to older laws. He had been entrusted with a grave secret. The debt was too solemn for gratitude.

He returned into the house and placed the letter on the table beside the Deacon and sat down. The Deacon was gazing intently at the home-made rug at his feet and Roger's eyes followed his. It had been woven long ago, but a complex maze-like design in brown and black could still be distinguished.

"Mr. Ashley, kindly lift the rug and turn it over."

Roger did so. No figure could be traced on the reverse. It presented a mass of knots and of frayed and dangling threads. With a gesture of the hand the Deacon directed Roger to replace it.

"You are a newspaperman in Chicago. Your sister is a singer there. Your mother conducts a boardinghouse in Coaltown. Your father is in some distant country. Those are the threads and knots of human life. You cannot see the design."

Silence.

"Have you heard of the House of Jesse, Mr. Ashley?"

"I . . . I think that Jesse was the father of King David."

The Deacon opened an enormous Bible on the table before him. The page presented a woodcut of a tall narrow tree from whose boughs, like apples, hung disks with names printed in them.

"That is the tree of the House of Jesse. There are the descendants of Jesse through David to Christ. It is good that a man think of the house to which he belongs. Did Aristides tell you that we are descended from the house to which Abraham Lincoln belonged?"

"No, Deacon."

"We are. Our forefathers came from his county in Kentucky."

Silence.

"You come from such a house. You are marked. The mark is on your forehead. There are billions of births. At *one* birth out of a vast number a Messiah is born. It has been a mistake of the Jews and Christians to believe that there is only one Messiah. Every man and woman is Messiah-bearing, but some are closer on the tree to a Messiah than others. Have you ever seen an ocean?"

"No, Deacon."

"It is said that on the ocean every ninth wave is larger than the others. I do not know if that is true. So on the sea of human lives *one* wave in many hundreds of thousands rises, gathers together the strength—the power—of many souls to bear a Messiah. At such times the earth groans; its hour approaches. For centuries a house prepares the birth. Look at this picture. Christ descended by more than thirty generations from King David. Think of them—the men and women, the grandfathers and grandmothers of Christ. I have heard a learned preacher say that it is probable that the mother of Christ could not read or write, nor her mother before her. But to them it had been said: 'Make straight in the desert a highway for our God.'"

He put his finger on the page and lowered his voice. "There are some names here of whom the Bible tells us discreditable things. Is that not strange? You and I would say in our ignorance that the men and women who were so near to bearing a Messiah would be pure and without fault, but no! God builds in His own way. He can use the stone that the builders rejected. There is an old saying, 'God moves in a mysterious way His wonders to perform.' Have you heard it?"

"Yes, Deacon."

"The sign of God's way is that it is strange. God is strange. There is nothing more childish than to think of God as a man." He waved his hand toward Coaltown—"As they do. His ways to our eyes are often cruel and laughable." He turned back a page of the Bible. "Here is the tree of Christ's descent from Adam to Jesse. When Sarah—*here!*—was told that she would bear a son she laughed. She was an old woman. She bore Isaac—which means 'Laughter.' The Bible is the story of a Messiah-bearing family, but it is only *one* Bible. There are many such families whose Bibles have not been written."

Silence. He lowered his eyes. With his cane he slowly turned up for a moment a corner of the rug at his feet—to the tangle of knots and loose threads.

"Can it be that your family has been marked? Can it be that your descendants may bring forth a Messiah, tomorrow or in a hundred years? That something is preparing? Your father fired a rifle; a man near him fell dead, but your father did not kill the man. That is strange. Your father did not lift a finger to save himself, but he was saved. That is strange. Your father had no friends, he says; but friends saved him. Your mother never left her house; she had no money; she was dazed. But a child who had never held a dollar in her hand sustained a house. Is that not strange? A great grandmother has reached out of her grave and spoken to you. Your father is right in this letter: there is no happiness equal to that of being aware that one has a part in a design." Again he pointed to Coaltown: "They walk in despair. If we were to describe what is Hell it would be the place in which there is no hope or possibility of change: birth, feeding, excreting, propagation, and death—all on some mighty wheel of repetition. There is a fly that lives and lays its eggs and dies—all in one day—and is gone forever."

He raised his eyes and gazed weightily into Roger's.

"Can it be that this country is singled out for so high a destiny—this country which so greatly wronged my ancestors? God's ways are mysterious. I cannot answer these questions."

He took back John Ashley's letter and placed it between the leaves of the Bible.

"It may be that I am deceived in these matters. It may be that I am guilty of the sin of impatience. I have read that men, dying of hunger and thirst in the desert, have visions of fountains and fruit trees. Have you read of them?"

"Yes, Deacon."

"Do you know the name of these false hopes?"

"Mirages, Deacon."

"It may be that this family and this America are mirages of my old eyes. Of my impatience. There are other lands and other 'trees' that I know nothing of. Four or five in five thousand years are sufficient to nourish hope. . . . I did not show you your father's letter, Mr. Ashley, to counsel, encourage, or rebuke you. But to share with you at this solemn season a reverent joy. I thank you for your visit."

Darkness had fallen. After Roger had passed the last house he started running down the hill. He stumbled many times; he fell; he sang. At the supper table he scanned the faces of his family and their guests. He had been reading Lucretius recently; who else here was aware of the "flaming walls of the world"? Miss Doubkov, he thought. Sophia had seen them and lost them—perhaps, Dr. Gillies, too.

Supper ended, he reminded his mother that he was to go for a walk with Constance and that he had promised to call at "St. Kitts."

"Wait," said his mother. She returned from the kitchen with a parcel of her famous ginger cookies and marzipan.

"Where do you want to walk, Connie?"

"Oh, I like Main Street best."

They walked the length of it four times. She told him that she was allowed to go berry picking, but had given her promise not to appear on the Main Street. She told him about all the people she had come to know on the farms and in the little shacks up the hill. "I don't tell Mama I know them. Lots of them are old and sick. Lots of them aren't very happy. They aren't very nice to their children."

"The Bells are happy."

"I don't go there. There are no berries there. And I guess I'm most interested in the ones that aren't so happy—and nice." Her eyes slid toward his face; there was something guilty, yet amused, in her smile.

"Are you happy, Connie?"

"I'm happy enough."

"What are the three things that you want most in the world?"

She thought. "Can I ask for four?"

"Yes."

"Papa to come back. To live near where you are. To go to school. And to know . . . to know hundreds and thousands of people everywhere."

"Well, I'll tell you a secret." Roger remembered that dolls and secrets played a large part in young girls' lives. He told her about the money from their father's inventions. That money would be used to send her and Anne Lansing to college. He would make sure that it would be a college near where he lived. He told her that those famous names Scolastica and Berwyn Ashley would surely bring word from their father. "Why do you want to know so many people?"

"I keep a list of the people I know. I know one hundred and four people. That doesn't include all the boarders. I have another list for them—the ones that I only say 'good morning' to when I'm waiting on table and cleaning their rooms. I think about people—don't you?—and the more you know the better you think. Roger, can I ask you some questions?"

"Yes, Connie. Fire ahead."

The questions! Are more people happy in a big city like Chicago than in Coaltown? Are most men happier than women? Are girls who don't get married ever happy? Does it hurt *a lot* when a person dies? Is it wrong—no, is it a bad thing to be born a girl?

"Listen, Connie. You write me every Thursday and put five questions in the letter. And I'll answer you on Sunday."

"Can I ask you one more?"

"Yes."

"Do people change any—while they're growing up?"

"Yes! I've changed—haven't I? And Lily's changed; you remember that she didn't notice anything. Today I learned that your best friend Anne Lansing has changed."

"Has she?"

"I'm going to pay a call at the Lansing house. Would you like to come with me now?"

"Oh, Roger, yes."

"Good! You go off somewhere and talk with Anne. I have to talk with her mother. And I'll tell you a secret: I think they've had some bad news today—almost as bad as we had when Papa —you know!"

They walked up to the door of "St. Kitts." Suddenly Constance threw her arms about her brother and cried, "I love you! I love you! I love you!"

Roger lifted her up, and said, "We're going to love each other a long time."

Félicité approached them from the shadows of the yew trees. She kissed Constance. To Roger she whispered: "George has gone. He told everything to Miss Doubkov. He's written out the whole story."

"And your mother?"

"Now I know she's known for a long time."

They entered the house.

"Connie," said Roger, "give Mrs. Lansing the cookies."

Eustacia came forward as though borne up on some extraordinary happiness. "Dear Roger! Dear Constance!"

Constance said, "Mama sent these and hopes that you'll have a very merry Christmas."

Soon Roger was sitting beside Eustacia. She was explaining to him about the money from his father's inventions. She was explaining to him that her son George would never have run away from his father's trial. . . .

Hills beyond hills, plains and rivers.

Eustacia went to Los Angeles. She got a job as housekeeper in a house of correction for delinquent girls. She didn't fully enjoy the work and it was not in sight of the sea. There was a privately owned Boys' Ranch at San Pedro, then a small tuna-fishing port. She became housemother.

Hills and clouds. Rise high, rise higher.

Roger and Félicité's Johnny has run away from his home in Washington for the third time. It is early 1917; a war is imminent and his father is burdened with work. Félicité has been sent to the hospital for a delivery that might prove difficult. The police of five states have been alerted to search for the child. The boy's best friend, his Grandmother Lansing, has been sent for. A week passed. Finally he was found in Baltimore asleep in a bed with two other boys of his own age. The family that harbored him read no newspapers; they assumed that he was a vagrant orphan of their own people. At one in the morning Eustacia knocked at their door and asked for a cup of tea. Johnny heard his grandmother's voice and climbed on her lap. He was now the dearest thing in the world to her. She scarcely touched him. To herself she said, "We only have what we give up." His later story was a long lamentable self-destruction.

History is *one* tapestry. No eye can venture to compass more than a hand's-breadth. . . .

Constance suffered a series of strokes in her middle forties. She sat on the terrace of her house overlooking Nagasaki Harbor. The members of her family took turns reading aloud to her. Delegations from far places called on her. Calls of adulation were limited to five minutes; she pretended she was tired. But visitors who could tell her how "the work" was going were urged to stay an hour. On her birthdays, the Emperor sent a flower and a poem.

There is much talk of a design in the arras. Some are certain they see it. Some see what they have been told to see. Some remember that they saw it once but have lost it. Some are strengthened by seeing a pattern wherein the oppressed and exploited of the earth are gradually emerging from their bondage. Some find strength in the conviction that there is nothing to see. Some

THEOPHILUS NORTH

For Robert Maynard Hutchins

Contents

I

The Nine Ambitions

I N THE spring of 1926 I resigned from my job.

The first days following such a decision are like the release from a hospital after a protracted illness. One slowly learns how to walk again; slowly and wonderingly one raises one's head.

I was in the best of health, but I was innerly exhausted. I had been teaching for four and a half years in a boys' preparatory school in New Jersey and tutoring three summers at a camp connected with the school. I was to all appearance cheerful and dutiful, but within I was cynical and almost totally bereft of sympathy for any other human being except the members of my family. I was twenty-nine years old, about to turn thirty. I had saved two thousand dollars—set aside, not to be touched—for either a return to Europe (I had spent a year in Italy and France in 1920–1921) or for my expenses as a graduate student in some university. It was not clear to me what I wanted to do in life. I did not want to teach, though I knew I had a talent for it; the teaching profession is often a safety-net for just such indeterminate natures. I did not want to be a writer in the sense of one who earns his living by his pen; I wanted to be far more immersed in life than that. If I were to do any so-called "writing," it would not be before I had reached the age of fifty. If I were destined to die before that, I wanted to be sure that I had encompassed as varied a range of experience as I could—that I had not narrowed my focus to that noble but largely sedentary pursuit that is covered by the word "art."

Professions. Life careers. It is well to be attentive to successive ambitions that flood the growing boy's and girl's imagination. They leave profound traces behind them. During those years when the first sap is rising the future tree is foreshadowing its contour. We are shaped by the promises of the imagination.

At various times I had been afire with NINE LIFE AMBITIONS —not necessarily successive, sometimes concurrent, sometimes dropped and later revived, sometimes very lively but under a different form and only recognized, with astonishment, after the events which had invoked them from the submerged depths of consciousness.

The FIRST, the earliest, made its appearance during my twelfth to my fourteenth years. I record it with shame. I resolved to become a saint. I saw myself as a missionary among primitive peoples. I had never met a saint but I had read and heard a great deal about them. I was attending a school in North China and the parents of all my fellow-students (and my teachers in their way) were missionaries. My first shock came when I became aware that (perhaps covertly) they regarded the Chinese as a primitive people. I knew better than that. But I clung to the notion that I would be a missionary to a really primitive tribe. I would lead an exemplary life and perhaps rise to the crown of martyrdom. Gradually during the next ten years I became aware of the obstacles in my path. All I knew about sainthood was that the candidate must be totally absorbed in a relationship with God, in pleasing Him, and in serving His creatures here on earth. Unfortunately I had ceased to believe in the existence of God in 1914 (my seventeenth year), my view of the intrinsic divinity in my fellow-men (and in myself) had deteriorated, and I knew that I was incapable of meeting the strictest demands of selflessness, truthfulness, and celibacy.

Perhaps as a consequence of this brief aspiration I retained through life an intermittent childishness. I had no aggression and no competitive drive. I could amuse myself with simple things, like a child playing on the seashore with shells. I often appeared to be vacant or "absent." This irritated some; even valued friends, both men and women (perhaps including my father), broke with me charging me with "not being serious" or calling me a "simpleton."

The SECOND—a secularization of the first—was to be an anthropologist among primitive peoples and all my life I have returned to that interest. The past and the future are always *present* within us. Readers may observe that the anthropologist and his off-shoot the sociologist continue to hover about this book.

The THIRD, the archaeologist.

The FOURTH, the detective. In my third year at college I planned to become an amazing detective. I read widely in the literature, not only in its fictional treatment, but in technical works dealing with its refined scientific methods. Chief Inspector North would play a leading role among those who shield our lives from the intrusions of evil and madness lurking about the orderly workshop and home.

The FIFTH, the actor, an amazing actor. This delusion could have been guessed at after a consideration of the other eight ambitions.

The SIXTH, the magician. This aim was not of my seeking and I have difficulty in giving it a name. It had nothing to do with stage-performance. I early discovered that I had a certain gift for soothing, for something approaching mesmerism—dare I say for "driving out demons"? I understood what a *shaman* or a medicine-man probably relies upon. I was not comfortable with it and resorted to it seldom, but as the reader will see it was occasionally thrust upon me. It is inseparable from a certain amount of imposture and quackery. The less said about it the better.

The SEVENTH, the lover. What kind of a lover? An omnivorous lover like Casanova? No. A lover of all that is lofty and sublime in women, like the Provençal Troubadours? No.

Years later I found in very knowledgeable company a description of the type to which I belonged. Dr. Sigmund Freud spent his summers in a suburb of Vienna called Grinzing. I was spending a summer in Grinzing and without any overtures on my part I was invited to call at his villa on Sunday afternoons for what he called *Plaudereien*—desultory conversations. At one of these delightful occasions the conversation turned upon the distinction between "loving" and "falling in love."

"*Herr Doktor*," he asked, "do you know an old English comedy—I forget its name—in which the hero suffers from a certain impediment [*Hemmung*]? In the presence of 'ladies' and of genteel well-brought-up girls he is shy and tongue-tied, he is scarcely able to raise his eyes from the ground; but in the presence of servant girls and barmaids and what they are calling 'emancipated women' he is all boldness and impudence. Do you know the name of that comedy?"

"Yes, *Herr Professor*. That is *She Stoops to Conquer*."

"And who is its author?"

"Oliver Goldsmith."

"Thank you. We doctors have found that Oliver Goldsmith has made an exemplary picture of a problem that we frequently discover among our patients. *Ach, die Dichter haben alles gekannt!*" ("The poet-natures have always known everything.")

He then went on to point out to me the relation of the problem to the Oedipus complex and to the incest-tabu under which "respectable" women are associated with a man's mother and sisters—"out of bounds."

"Do you remember the name of that young man?"

"Charles Marlow."

He repeated the name with smiling satisfaction. I leaned forward and said, "*Herr Professor*, can we call that situation the 'Charles Marlow Complex'?"

"Yes, that would do very well. I have long looked for an appropriate name for it."

Theophilus suffered, as they say (though there was no suffering about it), from that *Hemmung*. Well, let other fellows court and coax, month after month, the stately Swan and the self-engrossed Lily. Let them leave to Theophilus the pert magpie and the nodding daisy.

The EIGHTH, the rascal. Here I must resort to a foreign language, *el pícaro*. My curiosities throw a wide net. I have always been fascinated by the character who represents the opposite of my New England and Scottish inheritance—the man who lives by his wits, "one step ahead of the sheriff," without plan, without ambition, at the margin of decorous living, delighted to outwit the clods, the prudent, the money-obsessed, the censorious, the complacent. I dreamt of covering the entire world, of looking into a million faces, light of foot, light of purse and baggage, extricating myself from the predicaments of hunger, cold, and oppression by quickness of mind. These are not only the rogues, but the adventurers. I had read, enviously, the lives of many and had observed that they were often, justly or unjustly, in prison. My instinct had warned me and my occasional nightmares had warned me that the supreme suffering for me would be that of being caged and incarcerated. I have occasionally approached the verge of downright rascality, but not without carefully weighing the risk. This eighth ambition leads me into my last and overriding one:

The NINTH, to be a free man. Notice all the projects I did

not entertain: I did not want to be a banker, a merchant, a lawyer, nor to join any of those life-careers that are closely bound up with directorates and boards of governors—politicians, publishers, world reformers. I wanted no boss over me, or only the lightest of supervisions. All these aims, moreover, had to do with people—but with people as individuals.

As the reader will see, all these aspirations continued to make claims on me. As they were conflicting they got me into trouble; as they were deep-lodged their fulfillment often brought me inner satisfaction.

I was now free after four and a half years of relative confinement. Since my trip abroad, six years earlier, I had kept a voluminous Journal (from which the present book is largely an extract, covering four and a half months). Most of the entries in this Journal were characterizations of men and women I knew, together with as much of the life-story of each as I could learn. Myself was present for the most part only as witness—though occasionally an entry was devoted to an ill-digested bit of self-examination. I might almost say that for the last two years the center of my life had become that gallery of portraits. Only years later did I come to see that it was a form of introspection via extrospection. It's wonderful the way nature strives to create harmony within ourselves.

From the moment I resigned, two days before leaving the school, I discovered that several things were happening to me in my new state of freedom. I was recapturing the spirit of play —not the play of youth which is games (aggression under the restraint of rules), but the play of childhood which is all imagination, which improvises. I became light-headed. The spirit of play swept away the cynicism and indifference into which I had fallen. Moreover, a readiness for adventure reawoke in me—for risk, for intruding myself into the lives of others, for extracting fun from danger.

It happened that in 1926 it became possible for me to enter upon my new liberty earlier than I expected. Six weeks before the school's term-end an epidemic of influenza declared itself in central New Jersey. The infirmary filled up and overflowed. Beds were installed in the gymnasium which soon looked like a lazaret. Parents drove down and took their sons home. Classes came to an end and we masters were free to leave and I set out at once. I did not even return to my home in Connecticut since I had so recently enjoyed the Easter vacation there. I had bought a car from a fellow-master, Eddie Linley, on the condition that I take possession of it at his home in Providence, Rhode Island, after he'd driven it there from our school in New Jersey. I had known the car well for some time. It had belonged to the tutoring camp in New Hampshire where Eddie was also on the staff. Like all the masters we had taken turns in driving the students—usually in the larger vehicles—to church or to dances or to the motion pictures. This smaller car, known as "Hannah"—from the then popular song "Hard-hearted Hannah"—was used for short routine trips into the nearest village to the post office, to the grocery store, to the doctor, and occasionally to carry a few masters to a little apple-jack sociable. Hannah had known long service and was breaking up. Two years before, the directors of the camp had sold it to Eddie for fifty dollars. Eddie was a born mechanic. Poor Hannah asked only to lie down in a New Hampshire gully, but Eddie kept resuscitating her. He knew her "ways"; he "favored" her. She carried him to and from New Hampshire, Rhode Island, and New Jersey. I offered him twenty-five dollars for her on condition that he would give me some superficial instruction against emergencies. He agreed to this and I drove him to Trenton and back, Hannah responding admirably. He invited me to join him on his trip to Providence, but I told him that I wanted to spend a night in New York and would call at his home the next day. He consented to transport two suit-cases and some books of mine—the inconsiderable possessions I had accumulated during my years at the school. These included the last two volumes of my precious Journal. I went to New York carrying a light handbag. From that Tuesday noon I was *all* free.

I felt then that New York was the most wonderful city in the world and now, about fifty years later, I am of the same opinion. I already knew and loved many others: Rome and Paris, Hong Kong and Shanghai, where I had passed a part of my boyhood; I was later to feel no stranger in London, Berlin, Rome, and Vienna. But none have equaled New York in its diversity, its richness in surprises, and in its climate.

Its extraordinary climate contains not only those extremes of hot and cold, but those radiant days of sunlight in the intense cold and those delightful days of temperate weather with which it is blessed in July and August. Moreover I believed (and still believe) in the theory, published from time to time by so-called authorities, that there is a sort of magnetic band about a hundred miles wide and a thousand miles long extending under the soil from New York to Chicago. Persons living in that area are animated by a galvanic force; they are alert, resourceful, optimistic, and short-lived. The diseases of an overtaxed heart abound. They are offered and must accept the choice of Achilles: a brief but buoyant life as against a bland and uneventful one. Men, women, and children are aware of this force rising from the pavements of New York and Chicago—and the cities between them—particularly in spring and autumn. It has been reported by entomologists that even ants walk more quickly in this area.

I had planned to spend the night—as so often—in the national clubhouse of the fraternity to which I had belonged during my student days at Yale University and I had tried to plan an engagement for the evening. I had telephoned certain friends in New York from my school in New Jersey:

"Good morning, this is Dr. Caldwell of Montreal speaking. May I speak to Mrs. Denham?"

The butler answered. "Mrs. Denham is in North Carolina, sir."

"Oh, thank you. I shall call when I'm next in New York."

"Thank you, sir."

"Good morning, this is Dr. Caldwell of Montreal speaking. May I speak to Miss LaVigna?"

"W'ich'a Miss'a LaVigna, Anna or Grazia?"

"Miss Grazia, please."

"Grazia no live here no more. She have a job in Newark. The 'Aurora Beauty Parlor'—in the telephone book."

"Thank you, Mrs. LaVigna. I'll call her there."

These disappointments were so acute that I altered my plan. I changed trains in New York and proceeded immediately to Providence. I put up at a hotel and called for my car at Eddie Linley's house the next afternoon.

I had no very clear idea of how I would pass the summer. I

had been told that one could live inexpensively in the province of Quebec. I would stop a short time in the Boston area which I scarcely knew, look at Concord, Walden Pond, Salem; then drive north through Maine, write a postcard to my father from his birthplace . . . something like that.

It was enough that I was to be at the wheel of my own car with the roads of the northern hemisphere before me . . . and four months without a single engagement to be met.

The Nine Cities of Newport

S O IN the early afternoon I called at Eddie Linley's home to pick up Hannah and my possessions that were stored in her. I asked him to sit beside me as I drove about the city and to instruct me again in the old car's idiosyncrasies.

Suddenly I saw a sign: "NEWPORT, 30 MILES."

Newport! I would revisit Newport where seven and eight years earlier I had served—modestly enough, from private to corporal—in the Coast Artillery defending Narragansett Bay. During my free hours I had taken many long walks over the region. I had come to love the town, the bay, the sea, the weather, the night sky. I knew only one family there, hospitable friends who had heeded the injunction to "Invite a Serviceman to Sunday Dinner," and I had received a favorable impression of the townspeople. There had been little to see of the much-publicized resort of the very wealthy; their residences were boarded up and under gas-rationing few wheels were turning on Bellevue Avenue. On seeing the sign an idea occurred to me as to how I might earn my daily expenses with a part-time activity without drawing on my savings. I then returned Eddie to his door, shook hands with the members of his family, paid him the twenty-five dollars, and drove off to Newport on the island of Aquidneck.

Oh, what a day! What promises of a still-retarded spring! What intimations that I was approaching the salt sea!

Hannah behaved pretty well until we got within the city limits when she started coughing and staggering. We persevered and reached Washington Square, where I stopped to inquire the location of the Young Men's Christian Association—not the "Army and Navy Y," right before me, but the civilian "Y." I entered a store selling newspapers, postcards, etc. (The family that ran it will reappear in this history in the chapter entitled "Mino.") I telephoned the "Y" asking if there was a room available. I added buoyantly that I was under thirty, had been christened in the First Congregational Church in Madison,

Wisconsin, and that I was fairly sociable. A weary voice replied, "That's all right, buddy—calm down! Fifty cents a night." Hannah objected to going further, but was persuaded to enter Thames Street. I brought her to a stop at "Josiah Dexter's Garage. Repairs." A mechanic examined her long and thoughtfully and uttered some words that were unintelligible to me.

"How much would that cost?"

"Fifteen dollars, looks like."

"Do you buy old cars?"

"My brother does. Josiah! Josiah! Jalopy for sale!"

This was in 1926 when all mechanics, electricians, and plumbers were not only reliable but were held in high esteem as props of the self-respecting household. Josiah Dexter was much older than his brother. He had one of those faces one sees now only in daguerreotypes of judges and parsons. He too examined the car. They conferred together.

I said, "I'll sell you the car for twenty dollars, if you drive me and my luggage to the 'Y.'"

Josiah Dexter said, "Agreed."

We transferred my luggage into his car and I was about to climb in when I said, "Wait a minute!" The air made me giddy. I was about a mile from where I had spent a part of my twentieth and twenty-first years. I turned back to Hannah and stroked her hood. "Goodbye, Hannah," I said. "No hard feelings on either side—see what I mean?" Then I whispered into her nearest headlight: "Old age and death come to all. Even the weariest river winds its way to sea. As Goethe said, '*Balde ruhest du auch*.'"

Then I took my place beside Mr. Dexter. He drove a block slowly and then said, "Had that car long?"

"I have been the owner of that car for one hour and twenty minutes."

Another block. "Do you get worked up about everything you own?"

"Mr. Dexter, I was stationed at Fort Adams during the War. I'm back here. I've now been in Newport for a quarter of an hour. It's a beautiful day. It's a beautiful place. I'm a little light-headed. Sadness is just around the corner from happiness."

"May I ask what it was you said to the car?"

I repeated what I had said, translating the German ending,

" 'Soon, you too will rest.' Those are commonplace remarks, Mr. Dexter, but I have come to see lately that if we shrink from platitudes, platitudes will shrink from us. I never sneer at the poems of Henry Wadsworth Longfellow who spent so many happy weeks in and near Newport."

"I know that."

"Can you give me the address of an establishment that rents bicycles?"

"I do."

"Then I shall be at your garage in an hour to hire one. . . . Mr. Dexter, I hope that my light-headedness has not offended you?"

"We New Englanders don't go in for light-headedness much, but I've heard nothing to be offended at. . . . What were the words that German said again?"

"In a poem he was talking to himself, late at night, in a tower-room, a deep forest all around him. He wrote them with a diamond on a windowpane. They are the last words of the most famous poem in the German language. He was in his twenties. He got his rest at eighty-three."

We had reached the entrance to the "Y." He stopped the car and remained still a moment, his hands on the wheel, then said, "I lost my wife five weeks ago tomorrow. . . . She thought a lot of Longfellow's poetry."

He helped me carry my baggage into the hall. He put a twenty-dollar bill in my hand, nodded slightly, saying "Good day to you," and left the building.

Mr. Josiah Dexter was not in his garage an hour later, but his brother helped me select a "wheel," as we generally called them in those days. I continued down Thames Street and set out on the "ten-mile drive." I rode past the entrance of Fort Adams ("Corporal North, T.!" "Present, Sir!"), past the Agassiz House ("Seldom has so great a wealth of learning been so lightly borne!"), and drew up at the sea wall before the Budlong House. The wind in my face, I gazed across the glittering sea toward Portugal.

Not longer than six months before—in my exhaustion—I had been haranguing a fellow-master at the school: "Drive all those ideas out of your head! The sea is neither cruel nor kind. It is as mindless as the sky. It's merely a large accumulation of H_2O . . . and even the words 'large' and 'small,' 'beautiful' and 'hideous' are measures and valuations projected from the mind of a human being of average height, and the colors and forms which have taken on characteristics from what is agreeable or harmful, edible or inedible, sexually attractive, tactually pleasing, and so on. All the physical world is a blank page on which we write or erase our ever-shifting attempts to explain our consciousness of existing. Restrict your sense of wonder to a glass of water or a drop of dew—begin there: you'll get no further." But on this afternoon in late April all I could do was to choke on the words: "Oh, sea! . . . Oh, mighty ocean!"

I did not complete the ten miles of the famous drive, but returned to town by a short cut. I wanted to walk some of the streets I had walked so often during my first stay in the city. In particular I wanted to see again the buildings of my favorite age—the eighteenth century—church, town hall, and mansions; and to gaze again at the glorious trees of Newport—lofty, sheltering, and varied. The climate, but not the soil, of eastern Rhode Island was favorable to the growth of large and exotic trees. It was explained that a whole generation of learned scientists had derived pleasure from planting foreign trees on this Aquidneck Island and that thereafter a generation of yachtsmen had vied with one another in bringing here examples from far places. Much labor had been involved, caravans of wagons bringing soil from the interior. I was to discover later that many residents did not know the names of the trees that beautified their property: "We think that's a banyan or . . . or a betel nut tree," "I think Grandfather said that one was from Patagonia . . . Ceylon . . . Japan."

One of my discarded ambitions had been to be an archaeologist; I had even spent the large part of a year in Rome studying its methods and progress there. But long before, like many other boys, I had been enthralled by the great Schliemann's discovery of the site of ancient Troy—those nine cities one on top of the other. In the four and a half months that I am about to describe I found—or thought I found—that Newport, Rhode Island, presented nine cities, some superimposed, some having very little relation with the others—variously beautiful, impressive, absurd, commonplace, and one very nearly squalid.

The FIRST CITY exhibits the vestiges of the earliest settlers, a seventeenth-century village, containing the famous stone round-tower, the subject of Longfellow's poem "The Skeleton in Armor," long believed to have been a relic of the roving Vikings, now generally thought to have been a mill built by the father or grandfather of Benedict Arnold.

The SECOND CITY is the eighteenth-century town, containing some of the most beautiful public and private edifices in America. It was this town which played so important a part in the War of Independence, and from which the enthusiastic and generous French friends of our revolt, under Rochambeau and Washington, launched a sea-campaign that successfully turned the course of the War.

The THIRD CITY contains what remains of one of New England's most prosperous seaports, surviving into the twentieth century on the bay side of Thames Street, with its wharfs and docks and chandlers' establishments, redolent of tar and oakum, with glimpses of drying nets and sails under repair—now largely dependent on the yachts and pleasure boats moored in the harbor; recalled above all by a series of bars and taverns of a particular squalor dear to seamen, into which a landlubber seldom ventured twice.

The FOURTH CITY belongs to the Army and the Navy. There has long been a system of forts defending Narragansett Bay. The Naval Base and Training Station had grown to a great size during the War, a world apart.

The FIFTH CITY was inhabited since early in the nineteenth century by a small number of highly intellectual families from New York and Cambridge and Providence, who had discovered the beauties of Newport as a summer resort. (Few Bostonians visited it; they had their North Shore and South Shore resorts.) Henry James, the Swedenborgian philosopher, brought his family here, including the young philosopher and the young novelist. In his last, unfinished novel, Henry James, Jr., returns in memory and sets the scene of *The Ivory Tower* among the houses and lawns edged by the Cliff Walk. Here lived to a great age Julia Ward Howe, author of "The Battle Hymn of the Republic." There was a cluster of Harvard professors. The

house of John Louis Rudolph Agassiz that I had just passed
was converted into a hotel, and is still one in 1972. At a later
visit I was able to engage the pentagonal room in a turret
above the house; from that magical room I could see at night
the beacons of six lighthouses and hear the booming or chim-
ing of as many sea buoys.

Then to make the SIXTH CITY came the very rich, the empire-
builders, many of them from their castles on the Hudson and
their villas at Saratoga Springs, suddenly awakened to the realization that inland New York State is crushingly hot in summer.
With them came fashion, competitive display, and the warming
satisfaction of exclusion. This so-called "great age" was long
over, but much remained.

In a great city the vast army of servants merges into the population, but on a small island and a small part of that island, the
servants constitute a SEVENTH CITY. Those who never enter
the front door of the house in which they live except to wash it
become conscious of their indispensable role and develop a
sort of underground solidarity.

The EIGHTH CITY (dependent like the Seventh on the Sixth)
contains the population of camp-followers and parasites—
prying journalists, detectives, fortune-hunters, "crashers," half-
cracked aspirants to social prominence, seers, healers, equivocal
protégés and protégées—wonderful material for my Journal.

Finally there was, and is, and long will be the NINTH CITY,
the American middle-class town, buying and selling, raising its
children and burying its dead, with little attention to spare for
the eight cities so close to it.

I watched and recorded them: I came to think of myself as
Gulliver on the island of Aquidneck.

On the morning following my arrival I called for advice on a
person with whom I dared to presume I had a remote connection
—William Wentworth, superintendent at the Casino. Ten years
before this my brother, while still an undergraduate at Yale,
had played there in the New England Tennis Championship
Tournament and had won high place. He had told me of Mr.
Wentworth's congeniality and ever-ready helpfulness. I first
strolled through the entrance and surveyed the playing area
and the arrangements for spectators. The building was designed

—as were other edifices in Newport—by the brilliant and ill-fated Stanford White. As in every work from his hand it was marked by distinguished design and a free play of fancy. Although it was early in the spring the famous lawn courts were already a carpet of green.

I knocked on the superintendent's door and was bidden to enter by a hale man of fifty who put out his hand, saying, "Good morning, sir. Sit down. What can I do for you?"

I told him of my brother's past in the Tournament.

"Let me see, now. Nineteen-sixteen. Here's his picture. And here's his name on the annual cup. I remember him well, a fine fellow and a top-ranking player. Where's he now?"

"He's in the ministry."

"Fine!" he said.

I told him of my military service at Fort Adams. I told him of my four years of uninterrupted teaching, of my need of a change, and of a less demanding teaching schedule. I showed him the sketch for an advertisement I planned to put in the newspaper and asked him if he'd be kind enough to tack a copy on the Casino's bulletin board. He read it and nodded.

"Mr. North, it's early in the season, but we always have young people, home for one reason or another, who need tutoring. Generally, they call on the masters from the nearby schools, but those masters don't like to give the time as their term-end approaches. You'll get some of their pupils, I hope. But we have another group that might be eager for your services. Would you be ready to read aloud to older people with poor eyesight?"

"Yes, I would, Mr. Wentworth."

"Everybody calls me 'Bill.' I call every man over sixteen 'Mister.'—Do you play tennis too?"

"Not as well as my brother, of course, but I passed a lot of my boyhood in California and everybody plays it there."

"Do you think you could coach children between eight and fifteen?"

"I was coached pretty intensively myself."

"Until ten-thirty three courts are reserved for children. The professional coach won't arrive until the middle of June. I'll start collecting a class for you. One dollar an hour for each youngster. You can ask two dollars an hour for the reading aloud.—Did you bring any tennis gear with you?"

"I can get some."

"There's a room back there filled with the stuff—discarded, lost, forgotten, and so on. I even keep a pile of flannels dry-cleaned so they won't foul up. Shoes and racquets of all sizes. I'll take you back there later.—Can you typewrite?"

"Yes, Bill, I can."

"Well, you sit down at this desk here and run up your advertisement for the paper. Better rent a box at the Post Office to receive your mail. Give them the 'Y' for phone calls. I've got to go and see what my carpenters are doing."

Kindness is not uncommon, but imaginative kindness can give a man a shock. I could occasionally be altruistic myself—but as a form of play. It's easier to give than to receive. I wrote:

> T. THEOPHILUS NORTH
> Yale, 1920. Master at the Raritan School in New Jersey, 1922–1926. Tutoring for school and college examinations in English, French, German, Latin, and Algebra. Mr. North is available for reading aloud in the above languages and in Italian. Terms: two dollars an hour. Address, Newport Post Office Box No. ——. Temporary Telephone, Room 41, the Young Men's Christian Association.

I ran the advertisement in only three successive issues of the paper.

Within four days I had pupils on the tennis courts and very enjoyable work it was. (I had played the game without much interest. At the Casino I found some dog-eared manuals. "Improve Your Tennis," "Tennis for Beginners." More respected callings than was mine are supported by an element of bluff.) Within a week telephone calls and letters were arriving daily. Among the first of the letters was a summons to be interviewed at "Nine Gables," an engagement which led to complications related hereafter; another, to read aloud from the works of Edith Wharton to an old lady who had known her when Mrs. Wharton resided in Newport; and others. The responses on the telephone were more varied in character. I learned for the first time that anyone who presents himself to the general public is exposed to contacts with what is too frivolously called "the lunatic fringe." An angry voice informed me that I was a German spy and that "we have our eyes on you." A woman urged me to learn and teach Globo and so prepare the world for international and perpetual peace.

Others were more challenging.

"Mr. North? . . . This is Mrs. Denby's secretary speaking. Mrs. Denby wishes to know if you would be able to read aloud to her children between the hours of three-thirty and six-thirty on Thursday afternoons?"

I saw at once that this was the governess's "afternoon off." I was still subject to "light-headedness." For some reason I am more outspoken and even rude over the telephone than in personal confrontations. I suspect that it has something to do with being unable to look into the speaker's eyes.

"May I ask the age of Mrs. Denby's children?"

"Why . . . why, they are six, eight, and eleven."

"What book does Mrs. Denby recommend that I read to them?"

"She would leave that to you, Mr. North."

"Thank Mrs. Denby and tell her that it is impossible to hold *one* child's attention on a book for longer than forty minutes. I suggest they be encouraged to play with matches."

"Oh!"

Click.

"Mr. North? This is Mrs. Hugh Cowperthwaite speaking. I am the daughter of Mr. Eldon Craig."

She paused to let me savor the richness of my privilege. I was never able to remember the sources of my employers' wealth. I cannot now recall whether Mr. Craig was reputed to receive a half-dollar every time a refrigerator car locked its door or to receive a dime every time a butcher installed a roll of brown paper.

"Yes, ma'am."

"My father would like to discuss with you the possibility of your reading the Bible to him. . . . Yes, the entire Bible. He has read it eleven times and he wishes to know if you are able to read rapidly. . . . You see, he would like to break his record which is, I believe, eighty-four hours."

"I am thinking it over, Mrs. Cowperthwaite."

"If you are interested, he would like to know if you would be able to make special terms for . . . for such a reading."

"Special terms?"

"Well, yes—reduced terms, so to speak."

"I see. At my rate that would be over one hundred and fifty dollars. That's certainly a considerable sum of money."

"Yes. My father wondered if you could—"

"May I make a suggestion, ma'am? . . . I could read the Old Testament in Hebrew. There are no vowels in Hebrew; there are simply what they call 'breathings.' That would reduce the time by about seven hours. *Fourteen dollars less!*"

"But he wouldn't understand it, Mr. North!"

"What has understanding got to do with it, Mrs. Cowperthwaite? Mr. Craig has already heard it eleven times. Hearing it in Hebrew he would be hearing God's own words as He dictated them to Moses and the prophets. Moreover I could read the New Testament in Greek. Greek is full of silent digammas and enclitics and prolegomena. Not a word would be lost and my price would be reduced to one hundred and forty dollars."

"But my father—"

"Moreover in the New Testament I could read Our Lord's words in His own language, Aramaic! Very terse, very condensed. I've been able to read the Sermon on the Mount in four minutes, sixty-one seconds, and nothing over."

"But would it count in making a record?"

"I'm sorry you don't see it as I do, Mrs. Cowperthwaite. Your respected father's intention is to please his maker. I am offering you a budget plan: *one hundred and forty dollars*!"

"I must close this conversation, Mr. North."

"Let's say ONE HUNDRED AND THIRTY!"

Click.

So before long I was cycling up and down the Avenue like a delivery boy. Lessons. Readings. I enjoyed the work (the *Fables* of La Fontaine at "Deer Park," the works of Bishop Berkeley at "Nine Gables"), but I soon ran up against the well-known truth that the rich never pay—or only occasionally. I sent bills every two weeks, but even the friendliest employers somehow overlooked them. I drew on my capital and waited; but my dream of renting my own apartment (a dream fostering other dreams, of course) seemed indefinitely postponed. Except for a few engagements to read aloud after dark, my evenings were free and I became restless. I looked into the taverns on Thames Street and on the Long Wharf, but I had no wish to join those dim-lit and boisterous gatherings. Card-playing was permitted in the social rooms at the "Y" on condition that no money changed hands and I lose interest in card games without the incentive of gain. Finally I came upon Herman's Billiard Parlor —two long rooms containing seven tables under powerful hanging lights and a bar dispensing licit beverages, for these were "Prohibition" days. Any strong liquor you brought in your own pocket was winked at, but most of the players and myself were contented with orders of Bevo. It was a congenial place. The walls were lined with benches on two levels for on-lookers and for players awaiting their turn. The game princi-pally played at that time was pool. Pool is a concentrated rather than a convivial sport, conducted in grunts, muted oaths, and prayers, intermittently punctuated by cries of triumph or de-spair. The habitués at Herman's were handymen on the estates, chauffeurs, a few store clerks, but mostly servants of one kind or another. I was occasionally invited to take a cue. I estab-lished my identity as one who taught tennis to the beginners at the Casino. I play fairly well (long hours—in Alpha Delta Phi), but I became aware of an increasing coolness toward me. I was about to go seek another poolroom when I was rescued from ostracism by being adopted by Henry Simmons.

What a lot I came to owe to Henry: his friendship, the intro-ductions to his fiancée, to Edweena, the incomparable Ed-weena, and to Mrs. Cranston and her boardinghouse; and to all that followed from that. Henry was a lean English valet of forty. His face—long, red, and pockmarked—was brightened by dark observant eyes. His speech had been chastened by seven years in this country, but often reverted in high spirits to that of his earlier years—a speech which delighted me with its evo-cation of those characters of a similar background in the pages of Dickens and Thackeray. He served a well-known yachtsman and racing enthusiast whom he much admired and whom I shall call Timothy Forrester. Mr. Forrester, like others of his class and generation, lent his boat to scientific expeditions and explorations (and participated in them) where the presence of a "gentleman's gentleman" would have seemed frivolous. So Henry was left behind in Newport for months at a time. This arrangement agreed well with him because the woman he

planned to marry spent the greater part of the year there. Henry
was always dressed in beautifully cut black suits; only his
brightly colored vests expressed his individual taste. He was a
favorite at Herman's, to which his low-voiced banter brought
an element of extravagant and exotic fancy.

He must have been observing me for some time and connecting me with my advertisement in the newspaper, because
one evening when I had been sitting overlong on the sidelines
he suddenly approached me and said, "You there, professor!
How about three sets at two bits each, eh? . . . What's your
name, cully? . . . Ted North? Mine's Henry Simmons."

At this time of our first encounter Henry was a very unhappy
man. His master was helping a team to photograph the birds
of Tierra del Fuego and Henry hated idleness; his fiancée was
away on another voyage and he missed her painfully. We played
in relative silence. I had a run of luck or perhaps Henry disguised his greater proficiency. When the game came to an end
the rooms were emptying. He invited me to a drink. The house
reserved some cases of Bass's Ale for his use; I ordered the
usual near-beer.

"Now who are you, Ted, and are you happy and well? I'll tell
you who I am. I'm from London—I never went to school after
I was twelve. I was a bootblack and swept the barber's shop. I
raised my eyes a bit and learned the trade. Then I went into
domestic service and became a 'gentleman's gentleman.'" He
had accompanied his gentleman to this country and finally was
engaged as Mr. Forrester's valet. He told me about his Edweena,
absent as lady's maid to a group of ladies on a famous yacht. He
showed me some bright postcards he had received from Jamaica
and Trinidad and the Bahamas—meager consolations.

In turn I told him the story of my life—Wisconsin, China,
California, schools and jobs, Europe, the War, ending up with
my reasons for being in Newport. When I concluded my story
we struck our glasses together and it was understood that we
were friends. This was the first of many pool games and conversations. At the second or third of these I asked him why the
players were so slow to invite me to join the game. Was it because I was a newcomer?

"Cully, there's a lot of suspicion of newcomers in Newport.

Distrust, do you see what I mean? There are a number of types we don't want around here. Let's pretend that I didn't know that you're all right. See? I'll ask you some questions. Mr. North, were you planted in Newport?"

"How do you mean?"

"Do you belong to any organization? Were you sent here on a job?"

"I told you why I came here."

"I'm asking you these questions, like it was a game. Are you a flicker?"

"A what?"

"Are you a detective?"

I take pleasure in the modifications that words undergo as they pass from country to country and descend from century to century. "Flicker" was a bird and in 1926 it was a motion-picture. But in France a "*flic*" is a police detective; the word must have crossed the Channel, entered the slang of the English underworld, and had probably been imported to Newport by Henry himself. I raised my hand as though I were taking an oath. "I swear to God, Henry, I've never had anything to do with such things."

"When I saw in the newspaper that you were ready to teach Latin—that did it. There's no flicker ever been known that can handle Latin.—It's this way: there's nothing wrong with the job; there's lots of ways of earning a living. Once the season's begun there'll be scores of them here. Some weeks there's a big ball every night. For visiting celebrities and consumptive children, like that. Diamond necklaces. Insurance companies send up their men. Dress them up as waiters. Some hostesses even invite them as guests. Keep their eyes glued on the sparklers. Some families are so nervous, they have a flicker stay up all night sitting by the safe. Some jealous husbands have flickers watching their wives. A man like you comes to town—doesn't know anybody—no serious reason for being here. Maybe he's a flicker—or a thief. The first thing a regular flicker does is to call on the Chief of Police and get it straight with him. But many don't; they like to be very secret. You can be certain that you weren't three days in town before the Chief was fixing his eyes on you. It's a good thing you went to the Casino and found that old record about yourself—"

"It was about my brother, really."

"Probably Bill Wentworth called up the Chief and told him he had confidence in you."

"Thanks for telling me, Henry. But it's your confidence in me that's made all the difference here at Herman's."

"There are some flickers in the crowd at Herman's, but what we can't have there is a flicker who pretends he isn't. Time after time flickers have been known to steal the emeralds."

"What are some of the other types I was suspected of being?"

"I'll tell you about them, gradual. You talk for a while."

I told about what I had found out and "put together" about the glorious trees of Newport. I told him about my theory of "The Nine Cities of Newport" (and of Schliemann's Troy).

"Oh, Edweena should hear this! Edweena loves facts and pulling ideas out of facts. She's always saying that the only thing people in Newport talk about is one another. Oh, she'd love that about the trees—and about the nine cities."

"I've only made out five so far."

"Well, maybe there are fifteen. You might talk it over with a friend of mine in town named Mrs. Cranston. I've told her about you. She's said she wants to meet you. That's a very special honor, professor, because she don't make many exceptions: she only likes to see servants in the house."

"But I'm a servant, Henry!"

"Let me ask you a question: all these houses where you've got students—do you go in the front door?"

"Well, yes . . ."

"Do they ever ask you to lunch or dinner?"

"Twice, but I've never—"

"You're not a servant." I was silent. "Mrs. Cranston knows a lot about you, but she says that she would be very happy, if I brought you to call."

"Mrs. Cranston's" was a large establishment within the shadow of Trinity Church, consisting of three houses that had been so adjoined that it had required merely making openings in the walls to unite them into one. The summer colony at Newport was upborne by almost a thousand servants most of whom "lived in" at their places of employment; Mrs. Cranston's was a temporary boardinghouse for many and a permanent residence for a few. At the time of my first visit most of the great houses (always referred to as "cottages") had not yet been opened, but servants had been sent on in advance to prepare for the season. In a number of cases female domestics refused to pass the night "alone" in the remoter houses along the Ocean Drive. In addition Mrs. Cranston harbored a considerable number of "extra help," a sort of labor pool for special occasions, though she made it perfectly clear that she did not run an employment agency. The house was indeed a blessing to the Seventh City—to the superannuated, to the temporarily idle, to the suddenly dismissed—justly or more often unjustly dismissed—to the convalescent. The large parlor and adjacent sitting rooms by the entrance hall furnished a sort of meeting place and were naturally filled to overflowing on Thursday and Sunday evenings. There was a smoking room off the front parlor where legalized beer and fruit drinks were served and where trusted friends of the house—men servants, coachmen, and even chefs—gathered. The dining room was reserved for residents only; even Henry had never entered it.

Mrs. Cranston ran her establishment with great decorum; no guest ever ventured to utter an inelegant word and even gossip about one's employers was kept within bounds. I was surprised to discover that stories of the legendary Newport— the flamboyant days before the War—were not often recalled— the wars between social leaders, the rudeness of celebrated hostesses, the Babylonian extravagance of fancy-dress balls; everyone had heard them. More recent summers had not been without great occasions, eccentricity, drama and melodrama, but such events were alluded to in confidence. Mrs. Cranston conveyed that it was unprofessional to discuss the private lives of those who fed us. She herself was present every evening, but she did not choose to sit enthroned governing the conversation. She sat at one or other of the many small tables preferring that her friends join her singly or by twos or threes. She had a handsome head, nobly coiffured, an impressive figure, perfect vision, and perfect hearing. She dressed in the manner of the ladies in whose service she had passed her younger days— corseted, jet-bugled, and rustling in half a dozen petticoats. Nothing gave her greater pleasure than to be consulted on some complicated problem requiring diplomacy and thoroughly disillusioned worldly wisdom. I can well believe that she had saved many a drowning soul. She had risen through the ranks from scullery maid and slop-carrier to upstairs maid and to downstairs maid. Rumor had it—I only venture to repeat it so many decades later—that there had never been a "Mr. Cranston" (Cranston is a town a mere crow's flight from Newport) and that she had been set up in business by a very well-known investment-banker. Mrs. Cranston's best friend was the incomparable Edweena who retained in perpetuity the first-floor "garden apartment." Edweena was awaiting the long-overdue break-up and death of her alcoholic husband in distant London in order to celebrate her marriage to Henry Simmons. An advantage inherent in her possession of the "garden apartment" was apparent to a few observers; Henry could enter and depart as he chose without causing scandal.

It was a rule of the house that all the ladies—with the exception of Mrs. Cranston and Edweena—withdrew for the night at a quarter before eleven, either to their rooms upstairs or to their domiciles in the city. Gentlemen retired at midnight. Henry was a great favorite of the lady of the house to whom he paid an old-world deference. It was this last hour and a quarter that Henry (and our hostess) most enjoyed. The majority of the men remained in the bar, but occasionally, Mrs. Cranston was joined by a very old and cadaverous Mr. Danforth, also an Englishman, who had served—no doubt majestically—as butler in great houses in Baltimore and Newport. His memory was failing but he was still called in from time to time to grace a sideboard or an entrance hall.

It was during this closing hour that Henry presented me to Mrs. Cranston. "Mrs. Cranston, I should like you to make the acquaintance of my friend Teddie North. He works at the Casino and has some jobs reading aloud to some ladies and gentlemen whose eyesight is not what it used to be."

"I'm very pleased to make your acquaintance, Mr. North."

"Thank you, ma'am, I feel privileged."

"Teddie has only one fault, ma'am, as far as I know, he minds his own business."

"That recommends him to me, Mr. Simmons."

"Henry does me too much credit, Mrs. Cranston. That has been my aim, but even in the short time I've been in Newport

I've discovered how difficult it is not to get involved in situations beyond one's control."

"Like a certain elopement recently, perhaps."

I was thunderstruck. How could word of that brief adventure have leaked out? This was my first warning of how difficult it was to keep a secret in Newport, things that could easily escape notice in a big city. (After all servants are praised for "foreseeing every wish" of their employers; that requires close and constant attention. Aquidneck is not a large island, and the heart of its Sixth City is not of wide extent.)

"Ma'am, I can be forgiven for trying to be of assistance to my friend and employer at the Casino."

She lowered her head with a slight but benevolent smile. "Mr. Simmons, you'll excuse me if I ask you to go into the bar for two minutes while I tell Mr. North something he should know."

"Yes, indeed, gracious lady," said Henry, very pleased, and left the room.

"Mr. North, this town has an excellent police force and a very intelligent Chief of Police. It needs them not only to protect the valuables of some of the citizens but to protect some of the citizens from themselves; and to protect them from undesirable publicity. Whatever it was that you were called upon to do two and a half weeks ago, you did it very well. But you know yourself that it might have ended in disaster. If some such complication should present itself to you again, I hope you will get in touch with me. I have done some helpful things for the Chief of Police and he has been kind and helpful to me and to some of the guests in my house." She put her hand briefly on mine and added, "Will you remember that?"

"Yes, indeed, Mrs. Cranston. I thank you for letting me know that I can trouble you, if the occasion arises."

"Mr. Simmons! Mr. Simmons!"

"Yes, ma'am."

"Please rejoin us and let us break the law a little bit." She tapped a handbell and gave a coded order to the bar boy. As a sign of good fellowship we were served what I remember as gin-fizzes. "Mr. Simmons tells me that you have some ideas of your own about the trees of Newport and about the various parts of the town. I would like to hear them in your own words."

I did so—Schliemann and Troy and all. My partition of Newport was, of course, still incomplete.

"Well! Well! Thank you. How Edweena will enjoy hearing that. Mr. North, I spent twenty years in the Bellevue Avenue City, as most of my guests upstairs have; but now I am a boardinghouse keeper in the last of your cities and proud of it. . . . Henry Simmons tells me that the gentlemen in Herman's Billiard Parlor thought that you might be some kind of detective."

"Yes, ma'am, and some other undesirable types that he was not ready to tell me."

"Ma'am, I didn't want to put too heavy a burden on the chap in his first weeks. Do you think he's strong enough now to be told that he was suspected of being a *jiggala*, maybe, or a *smearer*?"

"Oh, Henry Simmons, you have your own language! The word is '*gigolo*.' Yes, I think he should be told everything. It may help him in the long run."

"A *smearer*, Teddie, is a newspaperman after dirt—a scandal hound. During the season they're thick as flies. They try to bribe the servants to tell what's going on. If they can't find any muck they invent some. It's the same in England—millions and millions read about the wicked rich and love it. 'Duke's daughter found in Opium Den—Read all about it!' And now it's Hollywood and the fillum stars. Most of the smearers are women, but there's plenty of men, too. We won't have anything to do with them, will we, Mrs. Cranston?"

She sighed. "They aren't entirely to blame."

"Now that Teddie's wheeling up and down the Avenue he'll begin to get feelers. Have you been approached yet, old man?"

"No," I said sincerely. A minute later, I caught my breath; I had indeed been "approached" without realizing what lay behind it. Flora Deland! I shall give an account of that later. It occurred to me that I should keep my Journal locked up—it already contained material not elsewhere obtainable.

"And the *gigolo*, Mr. Simmons?"

"Just as you wish, ma'am. I know you'll forgive me if I call our young friend by one nickname or another. It's a way I've got."

"And what are you going to call Mr. North now?"

"It's those teeth, ma'am. They blind me. Every now and then I've got to call him 'Choppers.'"

There was nothing remarkable about my teeth. I explained that I had spent my first nine years in Wisconsin, a great dairy state, and that one of its gifts to its children was excellent teeth. Henry had good reason to envy them. Children reared in the center of London often missed this advantage; his caused him constant pain.

"Choppers, old fellow, the men at Herman's thought for a while that you might be one of these—?"

"*Gigolos.*"

"Thank you, ma'am. That's French for dancing partners with ambitions. Next month they'll be here like a plague of grass-hoppers—fortune-hunters. You see, there are dozens of heir-esses here with no young men of their own class. These days the young men from the big houses go off to Labrador with Dr. Grenfell to carry condensed milk to the Eskimos; or they go off, like my master, to photograph birds at the South Pole; or they go to ranches in Wyoming to break their legs. Some go off to Long Island where they hear there's lots of fun to be had. No young man wants to enjoy himself under the eyes of his parents and his relatives. Except during Yacht Race Week and the Tennis Tournament no man under thirty would be seen here."

"No single man under forty, Henry."

"Thank you, ma'am. So when the hostesses want to give a dance for their beautiful daughters they call up their dear friend the Admiral at the Naval Station and ask him to send over forty young men that can waltz and one-step without stum-bling. They've learned from experience, the old ladies, to put a lot of pure spring water in the punch. Another thing they do is to invite house-guests for a month at a time from the embas-sies in Washington—young counts and marquesses and barons that are climbing up the first steps in the diplomatic career. That's the stuff! I came over to this country of yours, Chop-pers, as a 'gentleman' to an Honourable six removes from an earldom. He got engaged to a daughter of Dr. Bosworth at 'Nine Gables'—nicest fellow you could hope to meet but he couldn't get up before noon. Fell asleep at dinner parties; loved the meal but couldn't stand the waits between courses. Even with my tactful persuasion he was an hour late for every appointment. His wife, who was as energetic as a beehive, divorced him with a cool million—that's what they say. . . . All that an ambitious young man's got to have is a pleasant way of talking, a pair of dancing pumps, and *one* little respectable letter of introduction and all the doors are open to him, including a card to the Casino. So at first we thought you were one of them."

"Thank you, Henry."

"Nevertheless, Mrs. Cranston, we wouldn't think the worse of Mr. North here, if he found a sweet little thing in copper mines or railroads, would we?"

"I advise against it, Mr. North."

"I have no intention of doing so, Mrs. Cranston, but may I ask your reasons against it?"

"The partner who owns the money owns the whip and a girl brought up to great wealth thinks she has great brains too. I'll say no more. By the end of the summer you will have made your own observations."

I greatly enjoyed these pre-midnight conversations. If at times I thought of myself as Captain Lemuel Gulliver shipwrecked on the island of Aquidneck and preparing to study the customs and manners there I could scarcely have fallen on better luck. Telescopes are generally mounted on tripods. One leg of mine was grounded on my daily visits on the Avenue; another rested on the experience and wisdom available to me at Mrs. Cranston's; a third was still to seek.

I was not sincere in promising Mrs. Cranston to call on her aid whenever a complicated and even dangerous situation arose. By nature I like to tend to my own business, to keep my mouth shut, and to scramble out of my own mistakes. Probably Mrs. Cranston soon knew that I was engaged eight or nine hours a week at "Nine Gables"—a "cottage" where something peculiar was certainly going on; she may have suspected that I was getting involved beyond my depths at the George F. Granberrys' in a situation that might at any moment burst into a lurid conflagration of "yellow journalism."

In the matter that turned on my reading at "Wyckoff House" I did call on her for help and got it handsomely.

3

Diana Bell

S O THERE I was, bicycling my way up and down the Avenue and not only earning my living but saving money toward renting a small apartment. One morning in the middle of my third week, having come to the end of my children's class at the Casino and preparing to take a shower and change my clothes before entering on my day's academic program, I was stopped by Bill Wentworth. "Mr. North, can I see you here some time at the end of the day?"

"Yes, of course, Bill. Will six-fifteen be all right for you?"

I had come to know Bill well and with increasing admiration. He had invited me to Sunday dinner in his home with his wife and with a married daughter and her husband—sound Rhode Islanders, every one of them. I was aware that something was worrying him. He looked at me narrowly and said, "When you were at my house you told us of some adventures you'd had. Would you like to try a little expedition that's not in the regular run of things? You can turn it down flat, if you don't like the sound of it, and it won't change things between you and me. It'll call for some sharp wits, but it'll be well paid."

"Yes, I would, especially if it would be of any service to you, Bill. Send me to the North Pole."

"That might attract attention, likely. This is what they call a 'confidential mission.'"

"Just what I like."

At six-fifteen I entered his office of cups and trophies. Bill sat at his desk, passing his hand despondently over his close-cropped gray hair. He came at once to the point. "A problem has been dropped on my lap. The chairman of our Board of Governors here has been for some time a Mr. Augustus Bell. He's a New York businessman, but his wife and daughters live here a large part of the year. They go to New York for a few months in the winter. His older daughter Diana is about twenty-six; that's old for a girl in her set. They have a saying here: 'She's worn out a lot of dancing shoes.' She's high-spirited and

restless. Everybody knows that in New York she started going
around with some undesirable company. She got written up in
the papers—and you know the kind of papers I mean. Then
something worse happened. About two and a half years ago
one of those undesirable characters followed her up here. Her
family wouldn't receive him. So they eloped. She was brought
back before she got very far—police, private detectives, and all
that. The newspapers went wild. . . . The trouble is that Newport's no longer a summer resort for young men of her own
class. Newport's for the middle-aged and upward." Bill struggled with himself a moment. "Now it's happening again. Her
mother found in her room a letter from a man making arrangements to go off with her day-after-tomorrow night. Going to
Maryland to get married. Now, Mr. North, it's very difficult to
deal with the rich. Mr. Bell thinks it's my obvious duty to drop
everything and pursue two adults and somehow *block* them.
He doesn't want anything more to do with the police and with
private detectives. I will not do it and probably my job is at
stake."

"Of course, I'll do it, Bill. I'll try my best." Bill sat silent,
mastering his emotion. "Who's the man?"

"Mr. Hilary Jones, head of the athletic staffs in the school
system here. He's about thirty-two, he's been divorced and has
a daughter. He's well thought of by everybody, including his
former wife." He picked up a large envelope. "Here are some
newspaper photographs of Miss Bell and Mr. Jones and some
clippings about them. Do you drive?"

"Yes, for four summers at the camp in New Hampshire I've
driven every kind of car. Here's my driver's license; it has three
weeks to go."

"Mr. North, I took a great liberty for which I hope you will
forgive me. I told Mr. Bell I knew someone who was young,
who got on well with everybody, and who I thought was level-
headed and resourceful. I didn't tell him your name, but I said
you were a Yale man. Mr. Bell's a Yale man, too. But I don't want
you to do this for me. You're free to tell me it's a nauseating
underhand business and that you'll have nothing to do with it."

"Bill, I intend to enjoy it. I like demands on what you call
my resourcefulness. I would like to hear the whole project
from Mr. Bell's own mouth."

"He will reward you well—"

"Stop! I'll go into that with him. When can I see him?"

"Could you be in my office at six tomorrow evening? That'll leave another day for further plans."

I shall now have to repeat a good deal of the above material, but I want the reader to hear it from another angle. At six o'clock on the following evening Bill was sitting in his office. A gentleman of about fifty whom I suspected of having "touched up" his hair and mustache was striding about the room kicking chairs.

"Mr. North, this is Mr. Bell. Mr. Bell, Mr. North. Sit down, Mr. North." Mr. Bell does not shake hands with tennis coaches. "Mr. Bell, I suggest that you let me start the story. If I get anything wrong, you can correct me." Mr. Bell grunted unhappily and continued his prowling. "Mr. Bell is also a Yale man, where he had a notable athletic career. He has served at intervals on the Board of the Casino for almost twenty years which shows in what high esteem he is held. Mr. Bell has a daughter Miss Diana who's played excellent tennis on these courts since she was a child. She's a most attractive young woman with a host of friends . . . perhaps a little self-willed. Can I say that, Mr. Bell?"

Mr. Bell slashed at the window-curtains and overturned a championship cup or two.

"Mr. Bell and Mrs. Bell have discovered by chance that Miss Diana is planning to run away from home. She ran away from home once before, but she didn't get very far. The police were alerted in three or four states and she was brought home. That's quite a humiliation for a proud girl."

"Oh, God, Bill! Get on with it!"

"The Bells are, on the whole, year-round residents of Newport, but they keep an apartment in New York and spend some months there in the winter. Mr. Bell won't mind my saying that Miss Diana is a high-spirited girl, and some of those newspapermen got in the way of reporting that she was seen in public places with certain undesirable acquaintances—including the very man she was with when that pursuit was set up." I kept looking Bill in the eye. I could see that he had regained a large measure of his New England spunk and that he did not

intend to let Mr. Bell off easily. "Now Mrs. Bell happened to
come across a letter hidden in her daughter's lingeray. A man
in Newport whom I know slightly sent her the arrangements
for their meeting tomorrow night. It contained plans for a trip
to Maryland where they planned to be married as soon as
possible."

"Oh, God, Bill, I can't stand this!"

"Whose car are they driving, Bill?" I asked.

"Her car. His car is the school truck in which he carries his
teams to athletic meets. They're driving off the island on the
ten P.M. ferry to Jamestown, then the ferry to Narragansett Pier.
You can well understand that Mr. Bell doesn't wish to call in
the police a second time. Above all, the family wishes to avoid
any more of that Sunday-supplement publicity—what they call
the 'scandal sheets.'"

Mr. Bell advanced on Bill angrily: "That's enough of that,
Bill!"

"These are facts, Mr. Bell," he replied firmly. "We've got to put
the facts on the table. Mr. North must know what we're asking
him to do." Mr. Bell clenched his fists and shook them before
him. "The idea, Mr. North, is that you might intercept them
somewhere—somewhere, somehow—and bring Miss Diana
back.—You're a free man. There's no compulsion on you whatever. Miss Diana's a mature woman; she may refuse absolutely
to return to her father's home. All Mr. Bell is asking you, as a
favor—as one Yale man to another—is to try. Would you be
willing to see what you could do?"

I looked down at the floor.

I didn't believe in any sense in the universe. I thought I didn't
believe in loyalty or friendship—but there was Bill Wentworth,
maybe with his life-long job at stake. And there was that apo-
plectic bully; there was Mrs. Bell who ransacked the bureau
drawers of a twenty-six-year-old daughter for private letters—
and read them.

Of course I would do it and I would succeed. But I wasn't
going to make it easy for Mr. Bell, either.

"What's your idea that I should do, Mr. Bell?"

"Why, follow them. Better follow them beyond Narragansett
Pier so that whatever you decide to do won't happen too near
Newport. Wait to see where they stop to eat or spend the

night. Put their car out of order. Beat down their door if necessary. Point out to her what an idiot she is. The disgrace of it! She'll break her mother's heart."

"Do you know anything disreputable about this man?"

"What?"

"This Mr. Jones—do you know him?"

"God, no! He's a nobody. He's a goddam fortune hunter. He's trash."

"Have you Mr. Jones's letter on you, Mr. Bell?"

"Yes, here it is, and to hell with it!" He pulled it from his pocket and threw it on the carpet between us. Bill and I were also "nobodies" and "trash."

Bill rose and picked it up from the floor. "Mr. Bell, we are asking Mr. North to help us in a matter of strict confidence. We hope that he will be successful and that you and Mrs. Bell will wish to thank him."

Mr. Bell struggled with himself. In a choked voice he said, "I am in a very disturbed state. I apologize for throwing the letter on the floor."

I said to Bill, "We're putting this in a large envelope and sealing it with wax. Address it to Miss Bell and write: 'Received from Mr. Augustus Bell, sealed, unread, by William Wentworth and Theophilus North.'—Mr. Bell, may I ask where your daughter met Mr. Jones?"

"We live in Newport most of the year. My daughter and a number of her friends belong to a group of voluntary assistants at the hospital. Diana is crazy about children. She met this Mr. Jones when he was calling on his three-year-old daughter who was a patient there. He's a vulgar unscrupulous fortune hunter, just like the others. We've had to cope with these bastards over and over again. It's obvious."

The only thing to do with a man like that is to continue looking at him expectantly, as though he were about to say something completely convincing. Without agreement and applause such men deflate; they gasp for air.

After a pause I began again. "Mr. Bell, I must propose a few reasonable conditions. There shall be no mention of any remuneration to me whatever. I shall send a bill for the exact amount I lose for canceling my engagements here. That's compensation, not payment for a job. I want a car placed at my disposal, dark blue to black in color—one that can hold three persons in the front seat if possible. I would like a good revolver."

"Why?" asked Mr. Bell angrily.

"I won't be using conventional ammunition; I can make my own. If your daughter's car were to be found by the police at the side of a Rhode Island or Connecticut highway punctured by a bullet, it might be reported in the newspapers. I can puncture it, as you might say, naturally. I would like a sealed envelope containing ten ten-dollar bills to cover certain expenditures that might arise. I think I shall not need them; in that case I shall return the envelope unopened to Mr. Wentworth. But most important of all, if I succeed or fail, I shall say nothing about this matter to anyone outside your family. Do you agree to those conditions?"

He growled, "Yes, I do."

"I have brought a memorandum of these five conditions. Will you sign it, please."

He read the list and began signing his name. Suddenly, he looked up. "But, of course, I shall *pay* you for this. I am ready to pay you a thousand dollars."

"In that case, Mr. Bell, you must *hire* someone to kidnap Miss Bell. No amount of money could hire me to do that. I see my mission as one merely of persuasion."

He looked dazed, as though he were being led into a trap. He looked inquiringly at Bill.

"I had not heard those conditions before, Mr. Bell. I think they are reasonable."

Mr. Bell finished signing the document and laid it on the table. I shook hands with Bill, saying, "Will you keep that signed agreement, Bill? I'll be here tomorrow night at six to pick up the car." I bowed to Mr. Bell and went out.

The clerk at the reception desk of the "Y" lent me road maps of Rhode Island and Connecticut. I studied them closely at intervals during the next day. That about making my own ammunition was just bluff and swagger. In revolver practice at Fort Adams we had used cork bullets with a pin in them that penetrates the target board; I assumed that they could puncture a tire and I bought a package of them.

The car was a beauty. I crossed on an early ferry to Jamestown and waited at the dock before the second ferry until I saw Miss Bell's car enter the ferry boat. She was driving. I followed them into the vast dimly lit hull. Soon after the boat started she got out of the car and walking between the cars examined the faces of the occupants. She saw me from some distance and walked straight toward me. Mr. Jones followed her in a bewildered manner. I got out of my car and stood waiting for her, not without admiration; she was a tall handsome young woman, dark-haired and high-colored.

"I know who you are, Mr. North. You run the kindergarten at the Casino. You have been paid by my father to spy on me. You are beneath contempt. You are the lowest form of human life. I could spit on you. . . . Well, haven't you got anything to say for yourself?"

"I am here in one capacity, Miss Bell. I am here to represent common sense."

"You!"

"What you are doing now will call down a world of ridicule in the newspapers; you will ruin Mr. Jones's career as a teacher—"

"Rubbish! Nonsense!"

"I hope that you'll marry Mr. Jones—and with your family sitting in the front pew, as is fitting in a woman of your class and distinction."

"I can't stand it! I can't stand being hounded and dragged about by snooping policemen and detectives. I'm going crazy. I want to be free to do what I want."

Mr. Jones touched her elbow lightly: "Diana, let's hear what he has to say."

"Hear him? Hear him?—that yellow-bellied spy?"

"Diana! *Listen to me!*"

"How dare you give orders to me?" and she slapped his face resoundingly.

I never saw a man more astonished, then humiliated. He lowered his head. She continued shouting at me: "I won't be followed! I'll never go back to that house again. Someone stole my letter. *Why can't I live like other people?* Why can't I live my life in my own way?"

I repeated in an even voice, "Miss Bell, I am here to represent common sense. I want to spare you and Mr. Jones a great deal of mortification in the future."

Mr. Jones found his voice. "Diana, you're not the girl I met in the hospital."

She put her hand to his reddened cheek. "But, Hilary, can't you see what nonsense he talks? He's trying to cage us in; he's trying to block us."

I continued. "This crossing will take about half an hour. Will you permit Mr. Jones and myself to go to the upper deck and talk this matter over reasonably?"

He said, "Any conversation we have, I want Miss Bell to be there too. Diana, I ask you again: will you listen to what he has to say?"

"Let's go upstairs, then," she said, despairingly.

The big hall upstairs looked like a cheap dance hall, ten years abandoned. It had a sandwich and coffee counter, closed at this early season. The tables and chairs were rusty and stained. The lamps gave off a steel-blue light, such as would serve to photograph criminals. Even Diana and Hilary—fine-looking persons, both—looked hideous.

"Will you speak first, Miss Bell?"

"How could you take this nasty job, Mr. North? Some children pointed you out to me at the Casino. They *said* they like you."

"I'll tell you anything you want to know about me later. I'd like to hear you talk about yourselves first."

"I met Hilary at the hospital where I do volunteer work. He was sitting by his daughter's bed. It was wonderful the way they were talking together. I fell in love with him, just watching them. Most fathers bring a box of candy or a doll and they act as though they wished they were a thousand miles away. I love you, Hilary, and I want you to forgive me for slapping your face. I'll never *think* of doing it again." He put his hand on hers. "Mr. North, I lose control of myself every now and then. My whole life has been mixed up and full of mistakes. I was sent home from three schools. If *you*—and my father—somehow pull me back to Newport this time I'll put an end to myself—as my Aunt Jeannine did. I never want to put foot in

Newport again as long as I live. Hilary's cousin, who lives in Maryland where we're going to be married, says that there are schools and colleges all over where he can go on with his work. I have a little money of my own, left me by Aunt Jeannine in her will. It will help to pay for the operations that Hilary's daughter will need next year. Now, Mr. North, what has this common sense you keep boasting about to say about that?"

There was a silence.

"Thank you, Miss Bell. Can I ask Mr. Jones to speak now?"

"I guess that you don't know I'm a divorced man. My wife's Italian. Her lawyer told her to tell the judge that we weren't compatible, but I still think she's a very fine woman. . . . She works in a bank now and . . . she says she's happy. We both contribute from our salaries to pay Linda's hospital bills. When I met Diana she was in a sort of blue-striped uniform. When I saw her leaning over Linda's bed, I thought she was the most beautiful person I'd ever seen. I didn't know that she came from one of the big families. For lunch hours we used to meet in a corner table at the Scottish Tea Room. . . . I wanted to call on her father and mother, like most men would, but Diana thought that that wouldn't do any good . . . that the only thing to do is what we're doing tonight."

Silence. It was my turn.

"Miss Bell, I'm going to say something. I have no intention of offending you. And I'm not trying to put any obstacles in the way of your marrying Mr. Jones. I'm still talking in the name of common sense. There's no need for you to elope. You are a very conspicuous young woman. Everything you do stirs up a lot of publicity. You've run out of your allowance of elopements. I hate to say it, but do you know that you have a nickname known in millions of homes where they read those Sunday papers?"

She stared at me furiously. "What is it?"

"I'm not going to tell you. . . . It's not nasty or vulgar, but it's undignified."

"What is it?"

"I beg your pardon, but I'm not going to be part of cheap journalists' chatter."

I was lying. It was maybe half-true. Besides, I wasn't breaking any bones.

"Hilary, I didn't come here to be insulted!"

She rose from her chair. She walked about the room. She clutched her throat as though she were strangling. But she got the point. Again she cried, "Why can't I live as other people live?" Finally, she returned to the table and said scornfully, "Well, what have you got to suggest, Doctor Nosey Commonsense?"

"I suggest that when we reach Narragansett Pier we return to Newport by the same ferries. You return to your home as though you'd merely been out for an evening ride. Later, I shall have some suggestions as to how you may marry Mr. Jones in simplicity and dignity. Your father will give you away and your mother will sit duly weeping in the front pew. As many as possible of the children you have befriended will be brought to the church. Dozens of Mr. Jones's young athletic teams will also be there. The newspapers will say, 'Newport's most beloved friend of children has married Newport's most popular teacher.'"

There was no doubt that she was dazzled by this picture, but she had had a hard life. "How could that be done?"

"You fight bad publicity with good publicity. I have some newspaper friends there, and in Providence and in New Bedford. The world we live in swims in publicity. Articles will appear about the remarkable Mr. Jones. He will be proposed for 'TEACHER OF THE YEAR IN RHODE ISLAND.' The Mayor will have to take notice of it. 'WHO IS DOING MOST TO BUILD THE NEWPORT OF THE FUTURE?' There'll be a medal. Who would be most suitable to present the medal? Why, Mr. Augustus Bell, Chairman of the Board of the Newport Casino. Bellevue Avenue loves to think that it's democratic, patriotic, philanthropic, big-hearted. That'll break the ice."

I knew this was just folderol, but I had a job to do for Bill Wentworth, and I knew that a marriage between these two would be disastrous. My low strategy worked.

They looked at one another.

"I don't want my name in the papers," said Hilary Jones.

I looked Diana straight in the eye and said, "Mr. Jones doesn't want his name in the papers." She got it. She looked me straight in the eye and murmured, "You devil!"

Hilary had gained assurance. "Diana," he said, "don't you think it's best that we go back?"

"Just as you wish, Hilary," she answered and burst into tears.

Arriving at the ferry slip we learned that the boat tied up there for the night. If we wished to return to Newport, we must drive the forty miles to Providence and then the thirty miles to Newport. It was Hilary's suggestion and mine that we drive in one car and that we send for the other in the morning. Diana was still weeping profusely—she saw her life as one spiteful frustration after another—and mumbled that she couldn't drive, she didn't want to drive. So they transferred their luggage into mine. I took my place at the wheel. She pointed at me saying, "I don't want to sit by *that man*." She sat by the window and fell asleep, or seemed to.

Hilary was not only field-games director of the High School, but supervisor in all the public schools. I asked him about the prospects of the teams as we approached the crucial games of the year. He picked up animation.

"Please call me Hill."

"All right. You call me Ted."

I heard about the teams' hopes and fears—about promising pitchers who got strained tendons and great runners who got charley horses. About the possibility of winning the pennant from Fall River or the All Rhode Island School Cup. About the Rogers High School team. And the Cranston School's. And the Calvert School's. Very detailed. Very interesting. It began to rain, so it was necessary to awake Diana and to close the window. Nothing stopped Hill's flow of information. As we reached the working-class periphery of Providence it was nearly midnight. Diana opened her handbag, pulled out a package of cigarettes, and lit one. Hill turned to stone: his bride-to-be smoked!

A gas station was about to close. I drove up and filled the tank. To the attendant I said, "Joe, is there any place around here where you can get a cup of Irish tea at this hour?"

"Well, there's a club around the corner that sometimes stays open. If you see a green light over the side door, they'll let you in."

The light was on. "There's still an hour's drive," I said to my companions. "I need a little drink to keep me awake."

"Me too," said Diana.

"You don't drink, do you, Hill? Well, you can come along and be our bodyguard, if we get into any trouble."

I forget now what club it was—"The Polish-American Friendship Society" or "Les Copains Canadiens" or the "Club Sportivo Vittorio Emanuele"—dark, cordial, and well-attended. Everybody shook hands all around. We weren't even allowed to pay for our beverages.

Diana came to life. She was surrounded.

"Gee, lady, you're gorgeous."

"You're gorgeous yourself, brother."

She was invited to dance and consented. Hill and I sat at a remote table. He appeared stricken. We had to shout to be heard above the din.

"Ted?"

"Yes, Hill?"

"Is that the way she was brought up?"

"It's all perfectly innocent, Hill."

"I never knew a girl that would smoke and drink—least of all with strangers."

We looked straight before us—into the future. At the next pause in the music I said, "Hill?"

"Yes."

"You have a contract with the Board of Education or the school system, haven't you?"

"Yes."

"You're not running out on it, are you?"

Our elbows were on the table, our heads were low over our folded hands. He turned scarlet. His teeth bit into the knuckles of his right hand.

"Does Miss Bell know that?" Behind my question lay others. "Does she know that you couldn't get another job like your own in the whole country? That the only jobs you could get would be in private athletic clubs—weight-reducing institutes for middle-aged men?"

He slowly raised his eyes to mine in agony. "No."

"Have you sent in your letter of resignation yet?"

"No."

He perhaps saw clearly for the first time that his honor was at stake. "Don't you see? We loved each other so much. It all looked so easy."

The loud music began again. We averted our eyes from the sight of the young woman being snatched from one dancing partner to another. Finally he struck my elbow sharply. "Ted, I want you to help me break this up."

"You mean tonight's party?"

"No, I mean the whole thing."

"I think it's broken up already, Hill. Listen, on the way to Newport I want you to talk without stopping about your teams' football chances. Tell us what you told us before and then tell us some more. Give every fellow's weight and record. Don't let anything stop you. If you run short, give us the college teams; you'll be coaching a college team yourself one of these days."

I arose and approached Diana. "I guess we'd better get on the road, Miss Bell."

We made a big exit—renewed handshakes and thanks all round. It had stopped raining; the night air felt wonderful.

"Gentlemen, I haven't had such a good time in years. My shoes are ruined—the big brutes!"

We drove off. Hilary couldn't find his voice so I took over.

"Hill, it seems to me that you must get home pretty late every afternoon?"

"Yes."

"I'll bet your wife used to complain that she didn't see you from seven o'clock in the morning until eight o'clock at night."

"I felt terrible about that, but I couldn't help it."

"And, of course, Saturdays must have been the worst day of all. You'd come back from Woonsocket or Tiverton, dog-tired. You could go to the moving-pictures once in a while?"

"There are no moving-pictures on Sunday."

We got back to the subject of football. I nudged him and he picked up animation a little. . . . "Wendell Fusco at Washington's a real comer. You should see that boy lower his head and crash through the line. He's going to Brown University year after next. Newport will be proud of him one of these days."

"Which sport do you like coaching most, Hill?"

"Well, track, I guess. I was a track man myself."

"Which event do you like best?"

"I'll confess to you that for me the most exciting event of the year is the All-Newport relay race. You have no idea how different the men are from one another—I call them 'men'; it does something for their morale. They're all fifteen to seventeen. Each does three laps around the course, then passes on the stick to the next man. Take Bylinsky, he's captain of the blue team. He's not as fast as some of the others, but he's the thinker. He likes to run second. He knows the good and bad points of each of his men and every inch of the course. Brains, see what I mean? Then there's Bobby Neuthaler, son of a gardener up on Bellevue Avenue. Determined, dogged—kind of excitable, though. You know, he bursts into tears at the end of every race, win or lose. The other men respect it, though; they pretend they don't see it. Ciccolino—lives down at the Point, not far from where I lived when I was married—he's the clown of the red team. Very fast. Loves running, but he's always laughing. Interesting thing, Ted; his mother and older sister go to the all-night chapel at Sacred Heart at midnight before the race and pray for him until they have to go home and make breakfast. Imagine that!"

I didn't need anyone to tell me to imagine that. I felt I was listening to Homer, blind and a beggar, singing his story at a banquet: "*Then the fair-tressed Thetis raised her eyes to Zeus the thunderer and prayed for her son, even for Achilles, goodliest of men whom she bore to Peleus, King of the Myrmidons; grief filled her heart, for she knew that to him had been allotted a short life, yet she prayed that glory be his portion this day on the plains before wide-wayed Troy.*"

"Golly, I wish you could see Roger Thompson pick up that stick—just a little runt but he puts his whole soul into it. His father runs that ice-cream parlor down at the end of the public beach. Our doctor at the gym says he's not going to let him run next year; he's only just fourteen and it's not good for his heart when he's growing so fast. . . ."

On went the catalogue. I glanced at Diana, neglected, forgotten. Her eyes were open, seemingly lost in deep thought. . . . What had they talked about during those rapturous hours at the Scottish Tea Room?

Hill directed me to the door of his rooming house. While we extracted his suitcases from the back of the car Diana descended and looked about the deserted street in the Ninth City where she had so seldom put down her foot. It was well after one o'clock. Apparently Hill had not notified his landlady of his departure for he drew the front door key from his pocket.

Diana approached him. "Hilary, I slapped your face. Will you please slap mine so that we'll be quits, fair and even?"

He stepped back, shaking his head. "No, Diana. No!"

"Please."

"No . . . No, I want to thank you for the happy weeks we had. And for your kindness to Linda. Will you give me a kiss so that I can tell her you sent her a kiss?"

Diana kissed him on the cheek and—uncertain of foot and hand—she took her place in the car. Hill and I shook hands in silence and I returned to the wheel. She directed me to her home. As we drove through the great gates we saw that there was some kind of party going on. There were cars drawn up before the house with chauffeurs sleeping at the wheel. She murmured, "Everybody's mad about mahjong. It's tournament night. Please drive around to the back door. I don't want anyone to see me returning with luggage."

Even the back door had a great sandstone porte-cochère. I carried her suitcases up to the darkened entrance.

She said, "Hold me a minute."

I put my arms around her. It was not an embrace; our faces did not touch. She wanted to cling for a moment to something less frozen than the lofty structure under which we stood; she was trembling after the freezing realization of the repetitions in her life.

There were servants moving about in the kitchen. She had only to ring the bell and she rang it.

"Good night," she said.

"Good night, Miss Bell."

4

The Wyckoff Place

A MONG THE first replies to my advertisement was a note in a delicate old-world penmanship from a Miss Norine Wyckoff, such and such a number on Bellevue Avenue, asking me to call between three and four on any day at my convenience. She wished to discuss arrangements for my reading aloud to her. I might find the work tedious, and in addition she would be obliged to submit to me certain conditions which I might feel free to accept or reject.

The next evening I met Henry Simmons for a game of pool. Toward the end of the game I asked him offhandedly, "Henry, do you know anything about the Wyckoff family?" He stopped in mid-aim, stood up, and looked at me hard.

"Funny, your asking me that."

Then he bent over and completed his shot. We finished the set. At a wink from him we hung up our cues, ordered something to drink, and strolled over to the remotest table in the bar. When Tom had placed our steins before us and departed, Henry looked about him, lowered his voice, and said, "The 'ouse is 'aunted. Skeletons going up and down the chimneys like bloody butterflies."

I had learned never to hurry Henry.

"To my knowledge, cully, there have been four haunted houses among the big places in Newport. Very bad situation. Maids won't take service there; refuse to spend the night. They see things in corridors. They hear things in cupboards. There's nothing contagious like hysterics. Twelve guests to dinner. Maids drop trays. Fainting all over the place. Cook puts on her hat and coat and leaves the house. Gives the house a bad name —see what I mean? Can't even get a night watchman who'll swear to do the rounds of the *whole house* at night. . . . The Hepworth place—sold it to the Coast Guard. The Chivers cottage—it was said that the master strangled the French maid —nothing proved. They got in a procession of priests, candles and incense, the whole works . . . drove the spirits out and

422

ıld it to a convent school. The Colby cottage—deserted for years, burned down one night in December. You can go out and see the place yourself—only thistles grow there. Used to be famous for wild roses.

"Now your Wyckoff place, beautiful house—nobody knows what happened. No body, no trial, nobody disappeared, nothing, just rumors, just talk—but it got a bad name. Old family, most respected family. Rich!—Like Edweena says, could buy and sell the State of Texas without noticing it. In the old days before the War—great dinner parties, concerts, Paderewski; very musical they were—then the rumors started. Miss Wyckoff's father and mother used to charter ships and go off on scientific expeditions—collector, he was—shells and heathen idols. Be gone for half a year at a time. Then in about 1911 he came back and closed the whole place up. Went to live in their New York house. During the War both Mr. Wyckoff and his wife died decently in New York hospitals leaving Miss Norine alone—the last of the line. What can she do? She's got a lot of spirit. She comes back to Newport to open her family house— her girlhood home; but she can't get any help *after dark*. For eight years she's taken an apartment at the La Forge Cottages, but she goes every day to the Wyckoff place, gives lunches, asks people in to tea—but when the sun starts to set her maids and butler and housemen say, 'We've got to go now, Miss Wyckoff,' and they go. And she and her personal maid drive off in their carriage to the La Forge Cottages, leaving lights on all over the house."

Silence.

"Henry, you swear you don't know of anything that might have started the rumors? Mrs. Cranston knows everything. Do you suppose she has a theory?"

"Never heard her say so; and Edweena, who's the sharpest girl on Aquidneck Island—*she* don't know anything."

I arrived at the Wyckoff place the next day at three-thirty. I had long admired the house. I used to dismount from my bicycle just to rest my eyes on it, the most beautiful cottage in Newport. I had never been in or near Venice, but I recognized it as being "Palladian," as resembling those famous villas on the Brenta. Later I came to know the ground floor well. The central

hall was large without being ponderous. The ceiling wa‸
ported by columns and arches decorated in fresco. The ‸
doorways, framed in marble, opened in all directions—not‸
but airy and hospitable. An elderly maid opened the grea‸
bronze front door to me and led me to the library where Miss
Wyckoff was sitting at a tea-table before an open fire. The table
was set for a considerable company but the urn was still unlit.
Miss Wyckoff, whom I judged to be about sixty, was dressed
in black lace; it fell from a cap about her ears and continued in
flounces and panels to the floor. Her face was still that of an
unusually pretty woman and her expression was candid and
gracious and—as Henry said—"spirited."

"Thank you so much for coming to see me, Mr. North," she
said extending her hand; then turning to the maid, "Perhaps
Mr. North will have a cup of tea before he must go. If anyone
calls on the telephone, take the name and number; I shall call
them back later." When the maid had gone she whispered to
me, "May I ask you to close the door? Thank you . . . I know
you are busy so let us talk at once about my reason for asking
you to call. My old friend Dr. Bosworth has spoken to me
warmly in your favor."

A sign had been exchanged. The wealthy are like members
of the Masonic Order; they pass commendations and disap-
probations to one another by passwords and secret codes.

"Moreover, I knew that I could trust you when I read that
you were a Yale man. My dear father was a Yale man as was his
father before him. My brother, had he lived, would have been a
Yale man. I have always found that Yale men are honorable;
they are truly Christian gentlemen!" She was moved; I was
moved; Elihu Yale revolved in his grave. "Do you see those
two ugly old trunks there? I have had them brought down
from the attic. They are filled with family letters, some of them
dating back sixty and seventy years. I am the last in my line,
Mr. North. The greater number of these letters have lost their
interest by now. I have long wished to make a rapid inspection
of most of them . . . and destroy them. My eyesight is no
longer able to read handwritten material, particularly in cases
where the ink has begun to fade. Is your eyesight in good
condition, Mr. North?"

"Yes, ma'am."

"Often it will be merely necessary to glance at the beginning and the ending. My father's serious correspondence—he was an eminent scientist, a conchologist—it has gone, with his collections, to Yale University where both are safe. Would you be willing to undertake this task with me?"

"Yes, Miss Wyckoff."

"In reading old letters there is always the possibility that intimate matters might be revealed. May I ask your promise as a Yale man and a Christian that these matters will remain confidential between us?"

"Yes, Miss Wyckoff."

"There is, however, another matter about which I must ask your confidence. Mr. North, my situation in Newport is very strange. Has anyone spoken to you about it—about me?"

"No, ma'am."

"A malediction rests upon this house."

"A *malediction*?"

"Yes, this house is believed by many people to be haunted."

"I do not believe there are haunted houses, Miss Wyckoff."

"Nor do I!"

From that moment we were friends. More than that, we were conspirators and fighters. She described the difficulty of engaging domestic servants who would stay in the house after dark. "It is humiliating to be unable to ask my friends to dinner although they continue to invite me to their homes. It is humiliating to be an object of pity . . . and to feel perhaps that they hold my dear parents in some sort of suspicion. Many a woman, I think, would give up and abandon the place altogether. But it is my childhood home, Mr. North! I was happy here! Besides, many people agree with me that it's the most beautiful house in Newport. I shall never give it up. I shall fight for it as long as I live."

I was looking at her gravely. "How do you mean—fight for it?"

"Clear its name! Lift its shadow!"

"We are reading these letters, Miss Wyckoff, to find some clue to that unjust suspicion?"

"Exactly!—Do you think you could help me?"

Between one breath and another I became Chief Inspector North of Scotland Yard. "In what year did you first notice that domestic servants were refusing to work here after dark?"

"My father and mother went away on long expeditions. I couldn't go with them because the motion of the ship made me dreadfully ill. I stayed with cousins in New York and studied music. My father returned here in 1911. We meant to live here, but suddenly he changed his mind. He closed the house, dismissed the servants, and we all lived in New York. We went to Saratoga Springs for the summer. I begged him to return to Newport, but he didn't wish to. He never explained why. During the War both my parents died. In 1919 I was alone in the world. I decided to return to Newport and live in this house the whole year round. It was then that I discovered that no servants would consent to live here."

Did Miss Wyckoff have any ideas that would throw light on the matter? None. Did her father have any enemies? Oh, none at all! Did the matter come to the attention of the police? What was there to bring except the reluctance of servants and the vague rumor about a house being haunted?

"When your father was away on these expeditions who was left in charge of the house?"

"Oh, it was left fully staffed. My father liked the idea that he could return to it at a moment's notice. It was in charge of a butler or majordomo whom we'd had in the family for years."

"Miss Wyckoff, we shall begin reading the letters surrounding the years 1909 to 1912. When shall I come?"

"Oh, come every day at three. My friends don't drop in for tea before five."

"I can come alternate days at three. I shall be here tomorrow."

"Thank you, thank you. I shall sort out the letters covering those years."

The great man had the last word: "There are no haunted houses, Miss Wyckoff!—there are only excitable imaginations, perhaps malicious ones. We shall try to find out how this matter all started."

When I arrived the next afternoon the letters that might concern us were laid out in packets bound in red cord: her letters to her parents 1909 to 1912; her parents' letters to her; six letters of her father to her mother (they were seldom apart for a day); her father's letters to his brother (returned to him) and his brother's replies; letters from the majordomo at Newport (Mr. Harland) to her father; letters to and from her father's lawyers in New York and Newport; letters from friends and relatives to Mrs. Wyckoff. The reading of the domestic letters was a painful experience for Miss Wyckoff, but she stout-heartedly set many aside for destruction. Weather, storms off Borneo, blizzards in New York; health (excellent); marriages and death of Wyckoffs and relatives; plans for the following year and alterations to plans; "love and kisses to our darling girl." Miss Wyckoff and I had begun to divide the task. She found that her eyesight was able to sustain reading letters written to her by her parents and she preferred to read those to herself. So we were soon working on separate lots. I read those from Mr. Harland: leak in the roof repaired; requests from strangers to "view the house" rejected; damage to conservatory by Halloween merrymakers repaired, and so on. I began reading the letters from Mr. Wyckoff to his brother: discovery of rare shells, sent to the Smithsonian for identification, narrow escape in the Sunda Strait, financial transactions agreed upon, "delighted with news of our Norine's progress in music." . . . Finally I came upon a clue to the whole unhappy matter. The letter was written from Newport on March 11, 1911:

> I trust that you have destroyed the letter written to you yesterday. I wish the whole thing to be forgotten and never mentioned again. It was fortunate that I left Milly and Norine in New York. I wish them to retain only happy memories of this house. I have dismissed the entire staff, paid their wages and given each a generous bonus. I did not even bring the matter to the attention of Mr. Mullins [his lawyer in Newport]. I have engaged a new caretaker and some helpers who come in by the day. We shall perhaps return and reopen the house after a number of years when I shall have begun to forget the whole wretched business.

I slipped this letter into an envelope that I had prepared "For later rereading."

I had an idea of what probably took place.

While I was an undergraduate at college I had written and printed in the *Yale Literary Magazine* a callow play called *The*

Trumpet Shall Sound. It was based upon a theme borrowed from Ben Jonson's *The Alchemist*: Master departs on a journey of indefinite length, leaving his house in charge of faithful servants; servants gradually assume the mentality of masters; liberty leads to license; Master returns unannounced and puts an end to their riotous existence. Lively writer, Ben Jonson.

Mr. Wyckoff had returned to discover filth and disorder, perhaps had broken in on some kind of orgy.

But how could that have given rise to a reputation of being "haunted"—a word associated with murder? I decided that I must break my oath to Miss Wyckoff and make inquiries in another quarter. Besides, I did not want our readings to come to an end too soon; I needed the money. At the end of each week her maid, showing me out of the house, placed in my hand an envelope containing a check for twelve dollars.

I called on Mrs. Cranston soon after ten-thirty when the ladies gathered about her were beginning to withdraw for the night. I bowed to her, murmuring that there was a matter which I wished to discuss with her. Until the field was clear I sat in a corner of the bar over a glass of near-beer. In due time I received a signal to approach and I drew up a chair beside her. We temporized for a few minutes, discussing our state of health, the weather, my plan to rent a small apartment, the increasing number of my engagements, and so on. Then I said, "Mrs. Cranston, I want your advice and guidance on a very confidential matter that has come up."

I told her about the project at Wyckoff House, but made no mention of the significant letter I had discovered.

"A sad story! A sad story!" she said with ill-disguised relish, striking a handbell on the table before us. In the late evening she often partook of a tall glass of what I took to be white wine. When Jerry had served her and retired she repeated, "A sad story. One of the oldest and most respected families. Did Miss Wyckoff tell you anything?"

"Oh, not everything, Mrs. Cranston. She did not tell me what had happened to give the house a bad reputation. She assured me solemnly that she didn't know what it could be."

"She doesn't know, Mr. North. You're reading all those family letters up to the years just before the War?"

"Yes, ma'am."

"Have you come upon anything . . . sensational yet?"

"No, ma'am."

"You may."

The word "sensational" is a very sensitive word in Newport. The Sixth City lived under the white light—I should say the "yellow" light—of an immense publicity. It was bad enough to be thought frivolous, even scandalous, but it also dreaded being regarded as ridiculous.

Mrs. Cranston deliberated a moment, then picked up the telephone before her and called a number—that of the Chief of Police.

"Good evening, Mr. Diefendorf. This is Amelia Cranston . . . good evening. How's Bertha? . . . How are the children? . . . I'm very well, thank you. Thursday's my hard night, as you know. . . . Mr. Diefendorf, there is a young man here who has been engaged by a certain very respected lady in the city to make inquiries into some unhappy events in her family history. . . . No, oh, no! He has no connection with anything like that. He's merely been asked to read aloud to her from old family letters that have been stored in the attic. I think it's something that you'd like to know about. It's something that has officially never come to your attention, that needs very confidential handling. There's always the possibility that he might run across something that might get into the papers. I have full confidence in this young man, but of course he hasn't got your experience and your judgment. . . . Is there some evening when you could drop in here and see him or should I ask him to call on you in your office? . . . Oh! That would be very kind of you. Yes, he's here now. His name is North. . . . Yes, the same." (Probably the "same" who was involved in the Diana Bell elopement matter.)

It is evidence of the congeniality of our relationship that Mrs. Cranston (who seldom permitted herself to make a caustic remark about anyone) glanced at me and said dryly: "I have noticed that the Chief never refuses an excuse to leave the bosom of his family."

We did not have long to wait. I received permission to order another beer. The Chief was tall and wide. He gave the impression of being at once genial and uncomfortable. This, I was to learn, was the result of a long experience of being browbeaten by the wealthy who tend to assume that the less fortunate are unbelievably dim-witted. His defense was to assume an air of doubting the truth of any word spoken to him. He shook hands cordially with Mrs. Cranston and guardedly with me. She told him the whole story and again expressed her confidence in me.

"Mr. Diefendorf, I think that while reading those old letters the story may come to light and that maybe it *should* come to light. After all, there's nothing really damaging about it all; it doesn't reflect on the character of anybody in the family. You told me all you knew about it and I've kept my promise: I haven't breathed a word about it to a soul. If Mr. North finds something definite about it in a letter, I know he can be trusted to tell *you* about it first. Then you can decide whether Miss Wyckoff should be told."

The Chief's eyes rested on me deliberatingly: "What brought you to Newport, Mr. North?"

"Chief, I was stationed at Fort Adams during the last year of the War and I got to like it here."

"Who was the Commanding Officer then?"

"General Kalb or DeKalb."

"Did you ever go to church in town here?"

"Yes, to Emmanuel Church. Dr. Walter Lowrie was the rector."

"Did Mr. Augustus Bell pay you a large sum for handling that matter of his daughter's elopement?"

"I told him beforehand I only wanted reimbursement for the time I'd lost from my usual jobs. I've sent him a bill twice and he hasn't paid it yet."

"What were you and your bicycle doing out at Brenton's Point very early a few mornings ago?"

"Chief, I'm crazy about sunrises. I saw one of the finest I've ever seen in my life."

This caused him a little difficulty. He examined the tabletop for a few moments. He probably put my behavior down to one of the idiosyncrasies consequent on a college education.

"How much do you know about the Wyckoff House story?"

"Only that it's supposed to be haunted."

He outlined the situation as I already knew it—"Somehow the rumor had gotten round that there were ghosts in the house. . . . Now, Mr. North, just after the War our water-front life used to be much more active than it is now. Many more yachts and pleasure boats, the Fall River Line, fishing business, a certain amount of merchant shipping. Sea-going men drink. We used to collect them every night—stark, staring mad, delirium tremens. Those taverns on Thames Street used to be out-of-bounds to the men at the Naval Training Station—too many fights. One night in 1918 we had to lock up a man named Bill Owens, a merchant seaman about twenty-one years old, born and raised in Newport. He'd get very drunk, night after night, and start telling stories about the awful things he'd seen at the Wyckoff place. We couldn't have that. And we'd try to piece together what he was roaring and raving about in his cell."

Here the Chief made us wait while he lit a cigar. (There was no smoking in Mrs. Cranston's front rooms.)

"Mr. Wyckoff used to be away six and eight months at a time. He was a collector. What was it, Mrs. Cranston—sharks' teeth?"

"Shells and Chinese things, Chief. He left them to that big museum in New York." (No information was ever accurate in Newport, a matter of intellectual climate.)

"All that time he kept a kind of super-butler in charge, named Harland. Harland picked his own staff."

"Girls he found in New York, Chief. I never had anything to do with them."

"The front of the house was brightly lighted until midnight. Everything seemed to be in perfect order. Owens was a boy of about twelve, hired to empty the slops and carry the coals up to the fireplaces—odd jobs. I think Mrs. Cranston will agree with me that servants are like schoolchildren; they need a strict hand over them. When the teacher's out of the classroom they begin to raise the Old Nick."

"I'm sorry to say there's some truth in it, Chief," said Mrs. Cranston, shaking her head. "I've seen it over and over again."

"Mr. Wyckoff was a bad judge of men. His butler Harland was as crazy as they come. . . . Bill Owens said he was sent home every night at six o'clock when he'd finished his chores. But a few times he crept back to the house. The front rooms were brightly lighted, but the doors and windows of the dining room were hung with felt curtains—thick felt curtains. They

couldn't have their unholy goings-on down in the kitchen—
oh, no! They were masters and had to use the master's dining
room. Owens said he used to hide in the cupboards and peek
through the felt curtain. And he saw awful things. He'd been
telling the crowds down on Thames Street that he'd seen banquets and people taking their clothes off and what he called
'cannibals.'"

"Chief! You never used that word before!"

"Well, he said it. I'm sure he didn't see it, but he thought he
did."

"Oh, Lord in Heaven!" said Mrs. Cranston crossing herself.

"When you see half-cooked meat eaten *with their own hands*,
that's what a boy of twelve would think he saw."

"God save us all!" said Mrs. Cranston.

"I've no idea what Mr. Wyckoff saw, but he saw the felt curtains and the raw meat stains all over the floor and beastliness
in the faces of the servants, very likely. . . . Now pardon my
language, but rumor is like a stink. It took about three years
for Bill Owens's stories to pass from Thames Street to Mrs.
Turberville's Employment Agency. And rumor always gets
blacker and blacker. What do you think of it, Mr. North?"

"Well, Chief, I think that there was no murder, and not even
mayhem; there was just brutishness and somehow it got mixed
up in the popular imagination with spooks."

"And now there's nothing we can do about it. Remember, it
never reached the police desk. The ravings of a man in delirium
tremens are not a deposition. Owens shipped out of town and
has not been heard from since. I'm glad to have met you, Mr.
North."

I had got what I wanted. We parted with my usual dishonest
assurances that I would share with him any further information
that came to light. As far as I was concerned that problem was
solved, but my imagination had been occupied for some time
with a far more difficult problem: What way could be found to
dispel the "malediction" that rested on the Wyckoff House?
Explanations and appeals to reason have no power to efface
deeply ingrained and even cherished dreads.

I had glimpsed an idea.

One afternoon when I had presented myself at the door for
the accustomed reading, I found a barouche, a coachman, and

a pair of what used to be called "spanking" horses waiting in the driveway. Miss Wyckoff met me in the hall, dressed to go out. She begged my pardon, saying that she had been called to visit an invalid friend; she would be back within half an hour. Her maid was standing beside her.

"Miss Wyckoff, may I have permission to visit the rooms on the first floor? I greatly admire what I have seen of the house and would like to see some of the other rooms."

"Oh, yes, indeed, Mr. North. Make yourself completely at home. Mrs. Delafield will be glad to answer any questions, I'm sure."

It was a beautiful spring afternoon. All the doors were open. I viewed the great hall from all sides; I saw the dining room and the library for the first time. Everywhere I was arrested by some felicity of detail, but above all I was held by the harmony of the entire structure. "This is Palladio," I thought. "He himself was the heir of great masters and this is one of his descendants, just as Versailles is; but this is nearer the Italian source." When I was returning through the great hall to my work table Mrs. Delafield said, "Years ago before the master started going on expeditions, they used to give musical parties here. Have you heard of Padderooski, Mr. North? . . . He played here, and Ole Bull, the Norwegian violinist. And Madame Nellie Melba —have you heard of her? Very fine, she was. Those were lovely days. Just think of it now! It's a shame, isn't it?"

"You haven't seen or heard anything that made you uncomfortable, have you, Mrs. Delafield?"

"Oh, no, sir—not a thing!"

"Would you be willing to spend the night here?"

"Well, sir, I'd rather not. I know that maybe it's all foolishness, but we're not always in control of our feelings, if you know what I mean."

"What do people think took place here?"

"I don't like to talk about it or *think* about it, sir. Some people say one thing and some people say another. I think it's best to leave things as they are."

The readings continued. Miss Wyckoff seemed relieved that no intimation of a sinister nature came to our attention. We read on for the pleasure of reading, for the Wyckoffs were admirable letter writers. But all the time the idea of what was possible was growing in my head.

I have told of the various aspirations that had successively absorbed me when I was a very young man. A journalist's life was not among them. My father was a newspaper editor both before and after he was sent on consular missions to China. He brought a dedication to it that I was never able to share. To me it smacked too much of the manipulation of public opinion, however sincerely prompted. The idea that was developing in my head for the rehabilitation of Wyckoff House involved precisely that, but I didn't know how to go about it.

Chance opened the way to me.

The account of my relation to Wyckoff House falls into two parts. The second part led me into the Eighth City—that of camp-followers and parasites to whom I had so close an affinity. It led me to Flora Deland.

By the fifth week in Newport my schedule had begun to be exacting. The professional coach returned to the Casino and I was relieved of the second hour of instructing children, but all day I was busy with French or Latin or arithmetic in one house or another. I searched for somewhere to have lunch in as quiet a place as the town afforded. I found the Misses Laughlins' Scottish Tea Room—where Diana Bell and Hilary Jones had done their courting—in the heart of the Ninth City. It was frequented by girls from offices, some schoolteachers of both sexes, some housewives "downtown shopping"—a subdued company. The food was simple, well-cooked, and cheap. I had noticed a strange apparition there and hoped to see it again—a tall woman sitting alone, dressed in what I took to be the height of fashion. One day she reappeared. She wore a hat resembling a nest on which an exotic bird was resting, and an elaborate dress of what I think used to be called "changeable satin," blues and greens of a peacock's feathers intermingling. Before eating it was necessary that she remove her gloves and raise her veil with gestures of apparently uncalculated grace. Zounds! What was this? As before, when she entered or rose to take her departure the room was filled with the rustle of a hundred petticoats. Not only *what* was she, but *why* should she visit our humble board?

Her face was not strictly beautiful. Norms of feminine beauty change from century to century and sometimes oftener. Her face was long, thin, pale, and bony. You will later hear Henry Simmons describe it as "horsy." It can be seen in Flemish and French paintings of the fifteenth and sixteenth centuries. The kindest thing that could be said of it in 1926 was that it was "aristocratic," a designation more apologetic than kind. What was sensational about her was what we lustful soldiers at Fort Adams used to call her "build," her "altogether," her "figger."

You can imagine my surprise when on leaving she approached me with extended hand and said: "You are Mr. North, I believe. I've long wanted to introduce myself. I am Mrs. Edward Darley.—Might I sit down for a moment?"

She took her time, seating herself, her eyes resting on mine in happy recognition of something. I remembered hearing that the first thing a young actress is taught in dramatic school is to sit down without lowering her eyes.

"Perhaps you might know me better under my *nom de plume*. I am Flora Deland."

I had lived a sheltered academic life. I was one of the meager thirty million Americans who had never heard of Flora Deland. Most of the others in this thirty million had never been taught to read anything. I made appreciative noises, however.

"Are you enjoying life in Newport, Mr. North?"

"Yes—very much indeed."

"You certainly *do* get about! You are everywhere—reading aloud to Dr. Bosworth all those fascinating things about Bishop Berkeley; and reading the *Fables* of La Fontaine with the Skeel gairl. What a learned man you must be at your age! And so very clever, too—I mean resourceful. The way you managed the foolish elopement of Diana Bell—think of that! Diana is a sort of cousin of mine through the Haverlys. Such a headstrong gairl. It must have been perfectly marvelous the way you persuaded her not to make a fool of herself. Do tell me *how* you did it."

Now I have never been a handsome man. All I've got is what was bequeathed to me by my ancestors, together with that Scottish jaw and those Wisconsin teeth. Elegant women have never crossed a room to strike up an acquaintance with me. I wondered what was behind these amiabilities—then, suddenly, it struck me: Flora Deland was a smearer, a newspaper chatterbox. With her I was in the Eighth City—the parasitic camp-followers.

I said, "Mrs. Darley—how do you like to be called, ma'am?"

"Oh, call me Miss Deland," adding lightly, "You may call me Flora—I'm a working woman."

"Flora, I have not a word to say about Miss Bell. I have given my promise."

"Oh, Mr. North, I didn't mean for *publication*! I'm simply interested in cleverness and resourcefulness. I like people who use their wits. I'm a frustrated novelist, I suppose. Do let's say that we're friends. May we?" I nodded. "I lead a whole other life that has nothing to do with the newspapers. I have a cottage at Narragansett Pier where I love to entertain at the weekend. I have a guest cottage and can put you up. We all need a change from time to time, don't we?" She rose and again extended her hand. "Can I call you up at the Y.M.C.A.?"

"Yes . . . yes."

"And what may I call you—Theophilus?"

"Teddie. I prefer being called Teddie."

"You must tell me about Dr. Bosworth and Bishop Berkeley, Teddie. What a household that is at the 'Nine Gables'! Goodbye again, Teddie, and do accept an invitation to come to my dear little 'Sandpiper' for swimming and tennis and cards."

A working girl with a hundred and twenty million readers and a figure like Nita Naldi's and a speaking voice of smoked velvet like Ethel Barrymore's. . . . Oh, my Journal!

This was not a matter to submit to Mrs. Cranston. This was for a man among men. "Henry," I said, as we were chalking our cues at Herman's, "who are some of the smearers that hang around town?"

"Funny, you asked me that," he said and went on with the game. When we'd finished the set he beckoned me to the remotest table and ordered our usual.

"Funny, you asked me that. I saw Flora Deland on the street yesterday."

"Who's she?"

In all barbershops and billiard parlors there are tables and shelves bearing old and new reading matter for the customers to glance at while waiting to be called. Henry went to a pile and unerringly pulled out the Sunday supplement of a Boston paper. He opened it and spread it wide before me: "NEW YORK JUDGE BLAMES MOTHERS FOR INCREASING DIVORCE RATE AMONG THE FOUR HUNDRED, *By our special correspondent Flora Deland*."

I read it. Terrible situation. No names mentioned; certain hints that would be clearer to more experienced readers than myself.

"Cowboy," he continued (Henry presumed that Wisconsin was in the center of the Wild West), "Flora Deland comes from the oldest and most respected families of New York and Newport. None of that railroad and mining stuff—the real Old Guard. Related to everybody. Very high-spirited—'fast,' like they say. Made a few mistakes. It's all right to break up a family or two, but don't break up a family where the money's broken up, too. She ran out of her allowance of *pardonable* mistakes. Got a man disinherited. Flora's relations wouldn't see her. Are you following me, old cully? What's the poor girl to do? Can't even borrow money from Aunt Henrietta. She'd 'ad it. So she takes to pen and paper; becomes a smearer—real stuff from the inside. Like . . . like . . . many wives overspend their allowance; don't dare tell their husbands; where do you pawn your diamond tiara? In Wisconsin they eat it up. Now the stuff she writes under the name of Deland is fairly under control; but *we* know that she writes under other names too. She's got a feature called 'What Suzanne Whispered to Me,' signed 'Belinda.' Makes your eyes pop. Must make a lot of money, one way or another. Goes on lecture tours, too; 'A Newport Girlhood.' Funny stories about how we're all monkeys here."

"Does she spend the whole summer in Newport, Henry?"

"Where'd she go? The La Forge Cottages wouldn't consider it. The Muenchinger-King makes it a rule—or says it's a rule—that no guest can stay over three nights. She has a place at Narragansett Pier. The Pier is livelier than Newport—better beaches, younger set, better hideaways, clubs where you can play—all that."

"Where does she get her information from?"

"Nobody knows. Probably has plants—nurses in hospitals, for example. Patients will talk. Lots of talk goes on in beauty parlors. Servants, almost never."

"Is she beautiful, Henry?"

"Beautiful? Beautiful! She's got a face like a horse."

My invitation to visit "The Sandpiper" came through. Saturday for dinner until Monday morning: "I have plenty of swimsuits for you here. You'd only need one in the day. We often go in *au naturel* at midnight to cool off." To freeze, I suppose; the New England waters are not even tolerable until August.

I was going on the trip to enlist Flora Deland in my PLAN relative to the Wyckoff House; Flora Deland had invited me because she wished to obtain some information from me. I foresaw some form of negotiation. I had a service to ask of her. I did not take seriously the possibility that there might be a little romancing involved; I had never been in that kind of business with a woman almost fifteen years older than myself, but as the old hymn says: "Where duty calls or danger, Be never lacking there."

It was on my mind that I wished to get off the island with my bicycle without being observed by the police and others. Luck came to my aid. As I waited at the first of the two ferry slips (in those days it required two ferry rides to get to Narragansett, as the reader may recall) I heard my name called from a standing car.

"*Herr North!*"

"*Herr Baron!*"

"Can I carry you anywhere? I'm going to Narragansett Pier."

"So am I. Have you room for my bicycle, too?"

"Naturally."

This was the Baron Egon Bodo von Stams whom I had met many times at the Casino and who used to enjoy conversations in my enthusiastic hit-and-miss German. He was known as "Bodo" to everyone except Bill Wentworth and myself. He was an attaché at the Austrian Embassy in Washington on early leave for his second summer at Newport; a house-guest of the Venables at "Surf Point," even in the absence of the owners. He was the most likable fellow in the world. Two years older than I, endowed with a forthrightness and candor that approached naïveté. I climbed in and we shook hands.

He said, "I've been invited for the weekend by Miss Flora Deland—do you know her?"

"I've been invited there too."

"That's fine! I didn't know who I'd meet there."

We talked of this and that. On the second ferry boat, I asked: "Where did you meet Miss Deland, *Herr Baron*?"

He laughed. "Well, she came up to me and introduced herself at that bazaar for crippled children at the church on Spring Street."

I held my tongue for half an hour. When we approached the driveway of our hostess's cottage I said, "*Herr Baron*, stop the car a moment. I want to be sure that you understand where you're going."

He stopped the car and looked at me questioningly.

"You are a diplomat and a diplomat should always know exactly what is going on around him. What do you know about Miss Deland and what she's interested in?"

"Why, nothing much, old man" (Bodo had been to Eton), "but that she's a cousin of the Venables and she's a writer, too—novels and things like that."

I paused, then said, "The Venables haven't asked her to their house for at least fifteen years. They might be deeply offended if they knew you had visited hers. She was born into their class and circle; but she lost it. Do not ask me how; I don't know. She earns her living by writing thousands of words every week about what is called 'society.' Have you such journalists in Vienna?"

"Oh, in politics we have! They are very rude."

"Well, Miss Deland is very rude about the private lives of men and women."

"Will she write rude things about me?"

"I think not, but she will say that you were a guest in her home and that will give an air of authenticity to stories she tells about other people—the Venables, for instance."

"But that is terrible! . . . Thank you, thank you for telling me. I think I should drop you at her house and go back to Newport and telephone her that I have the influenza."

"*Herr Baron*, I think that would be wise. You represent your country."

He turned about in his seat and said to me directly: "Then why do *you* come to her house? If what she does is as bad as that, why do *you* come here?"

"Oh, *Herr Baron*—"

"Don't call me *Herr Baron*! Call me Bodo. If you are kind enough to open my eyes to this mistake, you can be kind enough to call me Bodo."

"Thank you. I shall call you Bodo *only* in this car. I am an employee at the Casino. I am a schoolmaster on a bicycle who gets paid by the hour."

"But we are in *America*, Theophilus. (What a beautiful name that is!) Here everybody calls everybody else by their given names after five minutes."

"No, we are not in America. We are in a little extraterritorial province that is more class-conscious than Versailles."

He laughed, then again solemnly asked, "Why are *you* here?"

"Well, I'll tell you another time." I pointed to the house before us. "This is a part of Newport's *demimonde*. Miss Deland is what you would call a *déclassée*. She has been ostracized, but during the summer all she thinks about is Newport—her Paradise Lost. I do not know what other guests will be at her house tonight, but the outcasts huddle together, just as you toffs do."

"I'm coming with you. I don't care what she writes about me." He started the engine, but I stopped him.

"I am interested in Flora Deland. She is a real pariah. She knows that she's engaged in a degrading business, but she has a kind of bravery about it. Do you think she's beautiful?"

"Very beautiful. She's like a Flemish ivory madonna. We own one. Theophilus, damn it, I've got to see this, too. You're quite right: I live in a little arena, like a dancing horse. I ought to know some outcasts too. If the Venables hear about it, I'll apologize to them. I'll apologize to them before they hear about it. I'll say I'm a foreigner and I didn't know any better."

"But, Bodo, your ambassador might hear about it. Tonight the guests will certainly get drunk; they'll break glass. Anything might happen. Flora intimated that we all might go swimming *mutter-nackt*. The neighbors would report it and the police would haul us off to the hoosegow. That would be a black mark for you, *Herr Baron*—Bodo, I mean."

He sat silent a minute. "But I've got to see it. Theophilus, let me come to dinner. Then I'll tell her I'm expecting a call from Washington and must return to Newport."

"All right, tell her the minute you go in the door. On Saturday night the last ferry boat leaves at twelve."

He slapped my back joyously. "*Du bist ein ganzer Kerl! Vorwärts.*"

"The Sandpiper" was a pretty little seaside cottage from one's grandmother's time—Gothic gingerbread scrollwork, pointed window frames—a jewel. A butler directed us to the guest house where a maid welcomed us and showed us to our rooms. Bodo whistled: silver-backed hairbrushes, kimonos and Japanese sandals for bathing. Toulouse-Lautrec posters on the walls, copies of the *Social Register* and *The Great Gatsby* on the bedside tables. The maid said, "Cocktails at seven, sirs."

He appeared at the door. "Theophilus—"

"*Herr Baron*, just because we are where we are I want to be called Mr. North. What is it you want to know?"

"Tell me again whom we may be meeting at dinner."

"Some Newport men install their mistresses over here for the summer—let's hope there'll be one or two of them. There'll be no jewel thieves, but there may be some detectives who've been placed here by insurance companies to catch them. There are always some young men about who are trying to get one foot in the door of 'society'—fortune hunters, in other words."

"Oh!"

"We're all adventurers, outsiders, shady, *louches.*"

He groaned. "And I have to go home at eleven!—But are you safe?"

"I'll tell you one more reason why I'm here. I'm working on a carefully thought out PLAN for which I need Flora Deland's assistance. It's one that won't do anyone any harm. If all goes well, I'll tell you the whole story at the end of the season."

"I can't wait that long."

"During dinner I'm going to grab hold of the table conversation for a short time; if you listen carefully you can get a glimpse of the first steps in my strategy."

We had been told not to dress, but Flora greeted us in a most wonderful gown—it was of yellow silk with little tabs of yellow velvet and little this-and-thats of yellow lace, each a slightly different shade of yellow. My face expressed my admiration.

"It is nice, isn't it?" she said lightly. "It's by Worth, 1910—belonged to my mother.—Baron, I'm delighted to see you. Will you have a cocktail or champagne? I drink only champagne. We must talk about Austria at dinner. My parents were presented to your Emperor when I was a gairl. I was too young, of course, but I used to see him taking his walk every day at Ischl."

Bodo made his deeply felt excuses that he must return to Newport for an important telephone call from his embassy on Sunday morning. "My Chief uses Sunday for his most important business and I have received notice that he will call me."

"What a pity, Baron! You must come some other weekend when you know you'll be free."

There were ten at the table, of whom only four were women. There was an exquisite French girl, Mlle. Desmoulins, who sat beside Bodo and who (he told me later) kept giving him little pinches to which he gallantly responded. Her chauffeur—who much resembled a bodyguard—called for her at ten-thirty and she took a tender leave of her "*bon petit Baron Miche-Miche*" (Bodo was six feet tall). There was a stout old lady—Flora whispered that she had been a famous actress in musical comedy—heavily bejeweled, who scarcely said a word, but ate and ate double portions of whatever was served. There was a young couple named Jameson from New Orleans, who had taken a cottage nearby for the summer, extremely sedate and increasingly bewildered. I sat at Flora's left and beside Mrs. Jameson. I asked Mrs. Jameson where she had met Miss Deland. "We met her by chance in the village here. She helped my husband out of some difficulty with a traffic policeman, and she invited us to dinner. Mr. North, who are these people?"

"I cannot discuss them under this roof. I leave that question to your perspicacity."

"My perspicacity is very uneasy."

"You're on the right track."

"Thank you. We shall leave as soon as it's decent. But you're all right?"

"Oh, Mrs. Jameson, I'm a salamander. I can live in air, fire, or water."

And then there were the three young men, all beautifully dressed (what to wear at an informal dinner at a famous resort), all increasingly drunk, and all very much at ease.

The conversation turned on the life at Newport during the previous season—the parties and balls to which they had or had not been invited, the famous hostesses who were too idiotic to be believed, the abysmal boredom of "all that life."

Finally the moment came when I spoke up:

"Flora, I think the wonderful thing about Newport is the trees."

"The trees?" Everyone stared at me.

I described the importations by Harvard scientists and by world travelers. I deplored the poverty of the soil and gave them a picture of long caravans of wagons bringing soil from Massachusetts (my improvisation but probable). I gave the cedars of Lebanon and the Buddha's bo tree ("If you sleep under it you'll dream of *nirvana*; I'm getting permission to do so next week"), the tara-tara tree of Chile that no bird will ever approach; the eucalyptus of Australia whose gum cures asthma; the ash tree of Yggdrasill, "the tree of life," whose berries drive away melancholy and thoughts of suicide in the young ("There's one in the garden of the Venables' house where the Baron is staying").

Bodo looked startled.

"Why, Teddie," cried Flora, "you're an angel! I could write a piece about all that!"

"Oh, there are some extraordinary subjects in Newport. There's a house that a famous Italian architect, Dr. Lorenzo Latta, has called the most beautiful house in New England—and the healthiest. Built in the nineteenth century, too. He called it 'The House that Breathes,' 'The House with Lungs.'"

"'The House with *Lungs*'! Which one is it?"

"I don't think you know it. There's a house in Newport whose great hall has such perfect acoustics that when Paderewski played in it he burst into tears; he apologized to the audience, saying that he had never played so well."

"Which house is it?"

"I'm pretty sure you don't know it. When the great Norwegian violinist Ole Bull gave a concert there he played on his Stradivarius, of course; but he said afterwards that the room itself was the best Stradivarius in the world."

"Teddie! Where do you find out these things?"

"There's a house in Newport where a simple woman lived for a while as a sort of nursing nun—Sister Colomba. She'll probably be canonized one of these days, St. Colomba of Newport. After dark, people from the working classes go and kneel before the house gates. The police don't know what to do about it. Can you arrest kneeling people for loitering?"

Flora was spellbound. The old lady stopped eating. The *jiggalas*, the crashers, and the flickers looked about wildly for strong drink.

"Flora, if you could write up these stories—"

"Why don't *you* write them?"

"Oh, I can't write, Flora. You're one of the most famous writers in the country. You've written reams and reams about Newport, but most of it has been satirical. If you began to write some pieces about the attractive things in Newport, all those cousins of yours would be very pleased—very pleased, indeed."

This sank in. She looked dazed. Then under the tablecloth she pinched me in what I suppose is called the thigh.

As we rose from table, she whispered, "You're a duck! You're a darling! *And*, I think, just a little bit, a devil!—Gentlemen, go to the smoking room. And, Baron, don't let them drink too much. We're all going in swimming later. I don't want any of you to get cramps and drown. That's happened *too* often."

Bodo and I stepped into the garden. "Teddie, give me a hint of what that was all about—I mean as a stratagem. Give me something to think about on the drive back to Newport."

"All right, I'll give you a hint. Have you a castle?"

"Yes."

"An old one?"

"Yes."

"Is it said to have ghosts?"

"Yes."

"Have you ever seen one?"

"Teddie, what do you think I am! There are no ghosts. The servants like to give themselves a thrill by talking about them."

"Do your servants stay with you?"

"Generation after generation."

"Well, I'm engaged in exorcising a supposedly haunted house where servants refuse to stay in the house after dark. All those three houses that I want Flora to write about are one house. Superstition is black magic; the only way to fight it is with white magic. Think that over."

He looked up at the stars; he looked down at the ground; he laughed. Then he put his hand on my shoulder and said, "Teddie, you're a humbug, you know."

"How do you mean?"

"You pretend that you have no aim in life."

He shook his head, smiling. Then he became very serious; I had never seen Bodo very serious: "I may have to ask you to advise me again before long. I have a real problem to face."

"In Newport?"

"Yes, in Newport."

"Can it wait?"

His gravity had become a sadness. "Yes, it can wait."

I couldn't imagine Bodo with "a real problem to face." Except for that touch of naïveté (which was really his innocence and his clear-hearted goodness) that had brought him to "The Sandpiper" he seemed to be completely endowed for the world into which he had been born. What could it be?

"I'll give you a hint. Theophilus, I'm a fortune hunter; but I'm really in love with the heiress, *really* in love—and she won't look at me."

"Do I know her?"

"Oh, yes."

"Who is it?"

"I'll tell you at the end of the season.—Now I'll say good night to Flora and catch that last boat. Remember everything to tell me later. *Gute Nacht, alter Freund.*"

"*Gute Nacht, Herr Baron.*"

I saw him off from the guest house. When I returned to "The Sandpiper," the Jamesons and Mlle. Desmoulins had left. The old lady had been helped upstairs. The three young men were singing and breaking glass.

"Is your head better?" asked Flora tenderly. I had made no mention of a headache, but I said, "I need a drink to pull me together. May I pour myself a whiskey, Flora?"

"You go and lie down in your room. I'll send you a drink. Then I'll call on you and we'll have a little talk. . . . I'll send the boys home. They're getting disorderly and it's much too cold to go in swimming. . . . No, they're staying at the Rod and Gun Club just down the road. . . . I shall change into something more comfortable. We shall talk about all those extraordinary houses—*if they do really exist, Teddie.*"

I said good night to the members of the Rod and Gun Club. Returning to my lodgings I put on the kimono and Japanese slippers and waited. I had brought with me pages and pages of notes about the three aspects of Wyckoff House. There was some truth in the first two; some outrageous invention in the second; the third was pure fantastication. They were in the form of jottings which she could consult while writing her articles. A Philippine houseboy arrived bearing a tray of bottles and ice. I poured myself a drink and went on writing. At last my hostess arrived wearing something light and comfortable under a long dark-blue cape.

"I see you have made yourself a drink. Be an angel and pour me a little champagne. The boys were beginning to be noisy and I have to be so careful of the neighbors. They make complaints when the boys fire off guns and scramble over the roof. . . . Thank you, I only drink still champagne. . . . Now tell me: who owns those houses you talked about?"

I made a long pause, then said, "They are all one house. It is the Wyckoff House."

She sat up straight. "But it is haunted. It is full of ghosts."

"I am ashamed of you, Flora. You are not an ignorant servant girl. You know that there are no such things."

"But I have so much Irish blood. I believe all ghost stories! Tell me more about it."

I brought out the sheaf of my notes. "Here's some material you might want to use in some articles sometime—articles that will *endear* you to Newport."

"Sometime! Sometime! I'll start them tomorrow morning. Show them to me."

"Flora, I'm in no mood to talk about houses now. I can only think of one thing at a time." I arose and stood above her, locking her knees between mine. "When a beautiful lady pinches a man in his thigh he is permitted to hope for other marks of her . . . good will and"—leaning over I kissed her—"her kindness."

"Oh! You men are so *exigeants*!" She pushed me away, rose, kissed me on the ear, and moved toward the bedroom.

There was no literary composition that night.

Work began the next morning at eleven.

"Read me the notes you've written," she said, laying out a pile of journalists' yellow work-paper and half a dozen pencils.

"No, I want to tell it to you first, so that I can keep looking into your beautiful eyes while I talk."

"You men!"

"First, the House with Lungs. I'm going to start a long way off the subject. Do you know New Haven, Connecticut?"

"I used to go to dances at Yale. I had glorious times."

"Where did you stay?"

"A cousin and I stayed at the Hotel Taft and another cousin came along as chaperon."

"Then you remember that corner on the New Haven Green. One day I was crossing the street with a lady under the windows of the Hotel Taft. It was cold. A wind was blowing the lady's skirts and her hat in every direction. She suddenly said something very surprising for she was a most sedate professor's wife. She said, '*Damn Vitruvius!*' All I knew about Vitruvius was that he was an ancient Roman who'd written a famous book about architecture and city planning. 'Why Vitruvius?' I asked. 'Don't you know that many New England cities were laid out according to his rules? Build your city like a great gridiron. Make a study of the prevailing winds, cross currents, and so on. Let the city breathe; give the city lungs. Paris and London awoke to his advice too late. Boston has a "green" but the streets were laid out to follow old cow-paths. Naturally Vitruvius's study reflected the Italian world which can be pretty cold, but not as cold as New Haven. Now listen to this: that corner by the Hotel Taft is the only cool refreshing spot in New Haven during the dreadful hot summer days. The very pigeons know it and gather there by the hundreds; the very bums and hoboes know it. The wisdom of Vitruvius!'"

"Really, Teddie, why are we talking about pigeons and hoboes?"

"This house was built in the style of Palladio who was a

devoted student of Vitruvius. Now I'm getting to the point. An eminent Italian architect toured New England and said this was the most beautiful and most *healthful* house he saw. New England houses were built of wood and built around a chimney in the center to heat the house in winter; but they're dreadful in summer. The corridors are in the wrong places. The first and second floors are cut up into rooms that surround it and the doors and windows are in the wrong places. The air doesn't circulate; the stale air has nowhere to go. But the builders of the Wyckoff House had the money and the good sense to build fireplaces all over the house; so the center of the house is a great high hall. It can inhale and exhale. Miss Wyckoff told me herself that she never knew anyone to have a cold there—the great American common cold! It was built in 1871 by an Italian architect who brought over a group of decorators and painters and stone-workers. Flora, it's a dream of serenity and peace—healthy lungs and a healthy heart!"

"I'll write it up! You just wait and see!"

"But that's not all. Are you fond of music, Flora?"

"I adore music—all music except those crashing bores, Bach and Beethoven. And that other fellow, Mozetti."

"What's the matter with him?"

"Mozetti? He had just *one* tune in his head and he wrote it over and over again."

I wiped my forehead.

"Well, I told you how Paderewski burst into tears at the perfection of the acoustics in the great hall. He also asked the Wyckoffs if it would disturb the family if he stayed on an hour after the guests had gone home just to play to himself. After Dame Nellie Melba sang there she persuaded Thomas Alva Edison to come up to Newport and supervise the gramophone records she made in that hall. 'The Last Rose of Summer'—it outsold all the records ever made until Caruso came along. Madame Schumann-Heink sang 'The Rosary' in that hall and had to repeat it three times. Everybody was sobbing like babies. Your first article could be called 'The House of Perfect Well-Being'; your second article you could call 'The House of Heavenly Music.' Newport will *love* you."

"Have you all those names down in these notes, Teddie?"

"But the third article is the best. Many years ago there was a

sort of saint in this town. She was never admitted into any religious order because she couldn't read or write. She was only
a lay-sister, but the working people called her 'Sister Colomba.'
All her days and nights were spent with the sick and the aged
and the dying. She calmed the feverish, she visited the sick-
rooms of those with the worst contagious diseases and never
caught a single one of them. A small boy in the Wyckoff home
had diphtheria. She nursed him daily and he recovered—
miraculously they believed. She lived in a little room across the
hall from him. When her end approached, at a very great age,
she asked that she be allowed to die in her old room. As I told
you at dinner throngs silently kneel before the gates of the
house—before Sister Colomba's room."

Deeply moved, Flora put her hand on mine. "I'll have the
sound of angel voices dimly heard by the faithful at midnight.
I'll have perfumes. . . . Bellevue Avenue . . . What was her
real name?"

"Mary Colomba O'Flaherty."

"Wait until you see what I do with that!—Great Heavens!
It's a quarter of one—my guests will be arriving for lunch. Give
me those notes. I'm going to start working on them at once."

Whatever one might think of Flora Deland, she was a diligent
hard-working woman. Bees and ants could have taken lessons
from her. My reading sessions with Miss Wyckoff were interrupted for two weeks during which she paid a visit to some old
friends at their rustic camp on Squam Lake in New Hampshire.
When she returned she invited me to tea at once. I made it a
rule to accept no social invitations, but no rule could stand in
the way of what I wished to learn about the progress of my
PLAN.

Miss Wyckoff received me in a state of considerable agitation.

"Mr. North, the most extraordinary thing has happened.
I'm at my wit's end. A newspaper woman has been publishing
a series of articles about this house! Look at the piles of letters
I've been getting! Architects want to visit the house and bring
their students. Musicians want to see the house. People from
all over the country want appointments when they may see
the house. Droves of strangers are ringing the doorbell all
day. . . ."

"What have you done about it, Miss Wyckoff?"

"I haven't answered a single letter. Mrs. Delafield had orders not to admit strangers. What do *you* think I should do?"

"Have you read that newspaper woman's articles?"

"Dozens of people have sent them to me."

"Did they make you very angry?"

"I don't know where she got all that information. There's nothing horrid in them; but there are hundreds of things about this house that I never knew before and . . . this is my home. I spent a large part of my life here. I don't know if they're true or not."

"Miss Wyckoff, I confess I read the articles and I was very surprised. But you can't deny that it's a very beautiful house. Fame is one of the consequences of excellence, Miss Wyckoff. The possession of a thing of exceptional beauty carries certain responsibilities. Have you ever visited Mount Vernon?"

"Yes. Mrs. Tucker asked us to tea."

"Did you know that certain portions of the house were open to the public on certain hours of the week? I suggest that you engage a secretary to handle this matter. Have an entrance card engraved and let the secretary send it to all those who seem to be seriously interested, stating the hours at which they may view the Wyckoff House."

"It frightens me, Mr. North. I wouldn't know how to answer the questions they might ask."

"Oh, you won't be there. Your secretary will show them about and answer their questions only in a very superficial way."

"Thank you. Thank you. I guess that's what I *must* do. But, Mr. North, there's something far more serious." She lowered her voice: "People want to bring the sick here. . . . Whole companies from religious schools want to come and pray here! I never heard of this Sister Colomba. My dear brother I told you about was a very sickly child and I think I remember that we did have some nurses from the religious orders; but I don't remember *one* of them."

"Miss Wyckoff, there's an old Greek saying, '*Reject not the gifts of the gods.*' You said that a 'malediction' hung over this house. It appears to me that that malediction is lifting. . . . I can tell you that all Newport is talking about the beauty and healthfulness of this house, and about the blessing that dwells here."

"Oh, Mr. North, I'm frightened. I've done a wicked thing. Even my old friends who've come to tea with me for years now want to see the room where Sister Colomba died. What could I do? I told a lie. I chose a room near my poor brother's where a night nurse *probably* slept."

"You foresee the next step, don't you, Miss Wyckoff?"

"Oh, dear! Oh, dear! What's the next step?"

"Servants will be clamoring to *live* in this house."

She put her hand over her mouth and stared at me. "I never thought of that!"

I leaned forward and said in a low but very distinct voice: *"Miss Wyckoff requests the pleasure of your company for dinner on such-and-such a day. At the conclusion of dinner the Kneisel Quartet with an assisting guest violist will perform the last two string quintets of Wolfgang Amadeus Mozart."*

She stared at me. She rose and clasped her hands, saying, "My childhood! My beautiful childhood!"

5

"Nine Gables"

O NE OF my first summonses to be interviewed came in the form of a note from Sarah Bosworth (Mrs. McHenry Bosworth), "Nine Gables," such and such a number, Bellevue Avenue. The writer's father, Dr. James McHenry Bosworth, it said, had employed many readers, a number of whom had proved to be unsatisfactory. Could Mr. North present himself at the above address at eleven o'clock on Friday morning to be interviewed by Mrs. Bosworth on this matter? Kindly confirm the appointment by telephone, et cetera, et cetera! I telephoned my compliance and promptly visited the "People's Library" (as it was then called) to consult various reference books about this family.

The Honorable Dr. James McHenry Bosworth was seventy-four years old, a widower, father of six and grandfather of many. He had served his country as attaché, first secretary, minister, and ambassador to several countries on three continents. In addition he had published books on early American architecture, notably Newport's. Further inquiry revealed that he lived the year round in Newport and that several of his children maintained summer homes in the vicinity—in Portsmouth and Jamestown. Mrs. McHenry Bosworth was his daughter, divorced and childless, who had resumed her maiden name under this form.

On that Friday morning in late April—the first radiantly springlike day of the year—I drove my bicycle to the door and rang the bell. The house was neither a French château nor a Greek temple nor a Norman fortress but a long rambling cottage, under weather-silvered shingles, adorned with wide verandahs, turrets, and gables. It stood in extensive grounds ennobled by mighty and far-sought trees. Within the house there was nothing rustic whatever. Through the open but latched screen door I saw a platoon of men servants in striped waistcoats and maids in uniform with flying white sashes waxing the floors and polishing the furniture. I was to learn later that the furniture well rewarded this care; here was the largest collection outside a museum of Newport's notable eighteenth-century cabinetmakers.

A formidable butler in a red striped vest and a green apron appeared at the door. I announced my business. His eyes rested with a kind of outrage on my bicycle. "Err . . . You are Mr. North?" I waited. "In general, sir, this door is not used in the morning. You will find the garden door around the corner of the house at your left."

I was willing to enter the house by the chimney or the coal cellar, but I didn't like the butler, his protruding eyes, his superfluous chins, and his tone of contempt. It was a beautiful morning. I felt fine. I didn't need the job as badly as that. I brushed my sleeve slowly and took my time. "Mrs. Bosworth asked me to call at this address at this hour."

"*This* door is not generally used . . ."

I had learned from my youth up—and in the Army—that when you are confronted with self-important authority and browbeating the procedure is as follows: smile amiably, even deferentially, lower your voice, affect a partial deafness, and talk steadily, dragging in red herrings and bushy-tailed squirrels. The result is that Sir Pompous raises his voice, becomes distraught, and (above all) attracts others to the scene.

"Thank you, Mr. Gammage . . . Mr. Kammage. I assume that you are expecting the piano-tuner, or—"

"What?"

"Or the chiropodist. What a lovely day, Mr. Gammage! Kindly tell Mrs. Bosworth that I have called as she requested."

"*My name is not* . . . Sir, take your bicycle to the door I have indicated."

"Good morning. I shall write Mrs. Bosworth that I called. *Irasci celerem tamen ut placabilis essem.*"

"Sir, are you deaf or insane?"

"Dr. Bosworth—I knew him well in Singapore—Raffles Hotel, you know. We used to play fan-tan." I lowered my voice still further—"Temple bells and all that. Punkahs swaying from the ceiling—"

"I've . . . I've . . . 'ad enough of you. *Go away!*"

It always works. Indeed, others had been drawn to the scene. The platoon of servants gazed open-mouthed. A handsome

woman of middle age appeared in the distance. A young
woman in a pale green linen dress (Persis, Persis herself!) had
descended the great staircase. I came to think of "Nine Gables"
as the house of hidden listening ears.

The lady in the distance called, "Willis, I am expecting Mr.
North. . . . Persis, this is none of your affair. . . . Mr.
North, will you follow me into my sitting room?"

The divine Persis glided between Mr. Willis and myself,
lifted the latch without glancing to right or left, and disappeared. I thanked Mr. Willis (who had lost the power of
speech) and advanced slowly down the long hall. Through an
open door I saw in one of the sitting rooms a large painting,
"The Three Bosworth Sisters," perhaps by John Singer Sargent
—three lovely girls, seated nonchalantly on a sofa, endowed
with everything, including angelic dispositions. It was painted
in 1899. Those sisters were Sarah, who had been briefly married to the Honorable Algernon De Bailly-Lewyss and was now
Mrs. McHenry Bosworth; Mary, Mrs. Cassius Marcellus Leffingwell; and Theodora, Mrs. Terence Onslowe, long resident
in Italy. Mrs. Bosworth, the eldest of the three, was in a rage
also. "I am Mrs. Bosworth. Will you sit down, please."

Gazing about I admired both the room and the lady. I noticed that a door at my left was ajar; every other door in sight
was wide open. I suspected that the eminent Dr. Bosworth was
probably overhearing this interview. Mrs. Bosworth had arranged three books beside her, each with a colorful book-
marker between the pages. I suspected that *one* marked the
page selected to eliminate the applicant.

"My father's eyes are easily tired. For one reason or another
his readers have proved unsatisfactory. I know his tastes. In
order to save your time, might I ask you to commence reading
at the top of this page?"

"Certainly, Mrs. Bosworth."

I kept her waiting. Well, well! It was the history by my old
friend Mr. Gibbon. Things were going badly in the eastern
Mediterranean, a mess of court intrigues, dozens of Byzantine
names, jaw-breakers of all kinds; but bloodwarming. I read
slowly and enjoyed myself.

"Thank you," she finally said, interrupting me in an assassination. She rose and apparently without design closed the

door beside me. "Your reading has much to recommend it. I am sorry to have to tell you that my father finds a reading with intermittent emphasis very tiring. I don't think I should waste your time any longer."

From behind the closed door an old man's voice could be heard calling, "Sarah! Sarah!" She put out her hand to me and said, "Thank you, Mr. North. Good morning!"

"Sarah! Sarah!" In the next room a handbell rang; a hurled object smote the door. It opened revealing a trained nurse. I looked about the floor as though I had lost something. Willis appeared. Persis appeared.

"Willis, go about your work. Persis, this is none of your affair!"

Whereupon the old man himself appeared. He was wearing a quilted dressing-gown; his pince-nez danced on his nose; his Vandyke beard pointed toward the horizon.

"Send that young man in to me, Sarah. Finally we have found someone who can read. The only readers you've ever found are retired librarians with mice in their throats, God help us!"

"Father, I *will* send Mr. North in to you directly. You go back to your desk at once. You're an ill man. You mustn't get excited. Nurse, take my father's arm."

For the second time I had introduced discord into "Nine Gables." I must change my ways. When the bystanders had withdrawn, Mrs. Bosworth resumed her seat and asked me to sit down. How she hated me!

"In the event that Dr. Bosworth approves of you as a reader there are some things you should know. My father is an old man; he is seventy-four. He is not a well man. His health has caused us great concern. In addition, he has a number of idiosyncrasies to which you must pay *no* attention. He tends to make large promises and to enter into extravagant projects. Any interest in them on your part could only lead you into serious difficulties."

"Sarah! Sarah!"

She rose. "I want you to remember what I have said. Have you heard me?"

I looked her in the eye and said amiably, "Thank you, Mrs. Bosworth."

That was not the answer she expected nor the tone to which

she was accustomed. She replied sharply, "Any further trouble from you and you go out of this house at once." She opened the door. "Father, this is Mr. North."

Dr. Bosworth was sitting in a heavily cushioned chair before a great table. "Please sit down, Mr. North. I am Dr. Bosworth. You may have heard my name. I have been able to be of some service to my country."

"Indeed, I know of your distinguished career, Dr. Bosworth."

"Hm . . . very good . . . May I ask where you were born?"

"In Madison, Wisconsin, sir."

"What was your father's occupation?"

"He owned and edited a newspaper."

"Indeed! Did your father also attend a university?"

"He graduated from Yale and obtained a doctorate there."

"Did he? . . . *Vous parlez français, monsieur?*"

"*J'ai passé une année en France.*"

There followed: what occupation had I been engaged in since leaving school? . . . my age? . . . my marital status? . . . what plans I entertained for later life, et cetera, et cetera.

I rose. "Dr. Bosworth, I came to this house to apply for a position as a reader. I was told that you have had many unsatisfactory readers. I foresee that I shall disappoint you also. Good morning."

"What? What?"

"Good morning, sir."

He appeared to be highly astonished. I left the room. As I progressed down the great hall, he called after me: "Mr. North! Mr. North! Kindly let me explain myself." I returned to the door of his study. "Please sit down, sir. I did not intend to be intrusive. I ask your apology. I have not left this house for seven years except to visit the hospital. We who are shut in tend to develop an excessive curiosity about those who attend us. Will you accept my apology?"

"Yes, sir. Thank you."

"Thank you . . . Are you free to read to me this morning until twelve-thirty?"

I was. He placed before me an early work of George Berkeley. When a variety of bells struck the half hour before one I finished a paragraph and rose. He said, "We have been reading from a first edition of this work. You may be interested in seeing the inscription on the title page." I reopened the book and saw that it had been inscribed by the author to his esteemed friend Dean Jonathan Swift. It took me some time to recover from my astonishment and veneration. Dr. Bosworth asked me if I had heard of Bishop Berkeley previously. I told him that at Yale University I had roomed in Berkeley Hall, that all Yale men were proud that the philosopher had left a part of his library to enrich our own—the books had been transported by bullock cart from Rhode Island to Connecticut; that moreover I had spent much of my boyhood in Berkeley, California, where we were often reminded that the town was named after the Bishop. We were pronouncing the name differently but had no doubt that it was the same man.

"God bless my soul!" exclaimed Dr. Bosworth. It is difficult for a Harvard man to believe that sober scholarly interests are pursued elsewhere.

It was arranged that I was to read for two hours on four days of the week. George Berkeley is not easy reading and neither of us had been trained in rigorous philosophical discussion, but we allowed no paragraph to be left behind without thorough digestion.

Two days later he interrupted our reading to whisper to me conspiratorially; he rose and opened the door to the great hall abruptly and peered about as though to surprise eavesdroppers; he repeated this manoeuvre at the door leading into his bedroom. Then he returned to his table and, lowering his voice, asked me, "You know that Bishop Berkeley lived three years in Newport?" I nodded. "I am planning to buy his house 'Whitehall' and fifty surrounding acres. There are many difficulties about it. It is still a *great secret*. I plan to build an Academy of Philosophers here. I was hoping that you would help me draft the invitations to the leading philosophers in the world."

"To come and lecture here, Dr. Bosworth?"

"Sh! . . . Sh! . . . No, to come and live here. Each would have his own house. Alfred North Whitehead and Bertrand Russell. Bergson. Benedetto Croce, and Gentile. Wittgenstein —do you know if he is still alive?"

"I am not sure, sir."

"Unamuno and Ortega y Gasset. You must help me draft the letters. The Masters are to have full liberty. They may teach or not teach, lecture or not lecture. They would not even be required to meet one another. Newport would become like a great lighthouse on a hill—a Pharos of Mind, of elevated thought. There is so much planning to be done! Time! Time! They tell me I am not well."

He heard—or thought he heard—a step outside the door. He put his forefinger against his mouth warningly, and we returned to our reading. The subject of the Academy did not arise again for some time. He seemed to fear that we were surrounded by too many spies.

At the end of the second week he asked if I was averse to late hours; he enjoyed a long siesta in the afternoon and felt no need to retire before midnight. This suited me very well as there were increasing requests for my time in the morning. The Bosworths gave several dinner parties a week, but it was the host's custom to rise from the table at ten-thirty—having partaken of some invalid's diet—and to join me in the library. As the season advanced these occasions became more frequent and more elaborate. It was a childish vanity on the part of the former diplomat to commemorate at these meals the national holidays of the countries where he had served; he was thus enabled to wear the decorations that had been conferred upon him. Neither our Independence Day nor the Fall of the Bastille happened to coincide with my visits to the house, but often enough he arrived resplendent in the study, murmuring modestly that "Poland had had a tragic but gallant history" or that "one could not overestimate the contributions of Garibaldi," or of Bolívar or of Gustavus Adolphus.

We continued our studies relative to *Dean* Berkeley's visit to the western hemisphere. He could see that my interest was almost equal to his own. Imagine our delight when, reading *The Analyst*, we discovered that "our boy"—now *Bishop Berkeley*—had *smashed* and *pulverized* Sir Isaac Newton and the mighty Leibnitz on the matter of infinitesimals. Both Dr. Bosworth and I were babes-in-arms in the realm of cosmological physics, but we got the point. Newton's friend Edmund Halley (of the comet) had mockingly spoken of the "inconceivability of the doctrines of Christianity" as held by Bishop Berkeley, and the Bishop replied that Newton's infinitesimal "fluxions" were as "obscure, repugnant and precarious" as any point they could

call attention to in divinity, adding, "What are these fluxions
. . . these velocities of evanescent increments? They are neither
finite quantities, nor quantities infinitely small, nor yet nothing. May we call them the ghosts of departed quantities?"
Crash! Bang! The structure of the universe, like the principles
of the Christian faith—according to the Bishop—were per-
ceived only by the intuition. It could not be said that Dr. Bosworth and I danced about his study, but the spies listening at
the doors must have reported that something strange was
going on—at midnight! These were giants indeed! Including
Swift—my patron since I had begun to think of myself as Gulliver. We were in the heart of the Second City, in the eighteenth
century.

At our first interview I had rebuked Dr. Bosworth's excessive
curiosity about myself; our intermittent conversations were
limited to historical subjects, but I was aware that he continued
to be "consumed with curiosity" about me. When the very
wealthy take a liking to any one of us belonging to the less fortunate orders they are filled with a pitying wonder as to how
we "make out" in those conditions of squalor and deprivation
to which we are condemned—to put it briefly they try to figure
out *how much money we make*. Do we get enough to eat? I was
to meet this concern over and over again during the summer.
Plates of sandwiches, bowls of fruit were constantly placed
before me. Only once (at another house) did I consent to take
as much as a cup of tea in any of my employers' homes or in
their friends' homes, though invitations to luncheons, dinners,
and parties began to arrive in considerable numbers.

I was uneasily aware that I had become an object of exag-
gerated curiosity on the Avenue by reason of the indefatigable
pen of Flora Deland. As I have related, she lost no time in endearing herself to Newport. Her nation-wide (and local) audience had been enthralled by her account of the nine cities and
the glorious trees on Aquidneck Island, and of the wonders of
the Wyckoff House. I had revisited "The Sandpiper" a number
of times, but the flower of friendship had lost its bloom; she
nagged at me and then quarreled with me. She could not understand why I did not strain every nerve to become a social success among the "cottages," presumably with herself on my
arm. I told her firmly that I had never accepted an invitation

and that I never would. But before we parted company she had published a sixth article—a glowing picture of the cultural renaissance that had taken place in this earthly paradise. This had been sent to me, but I failed to read it until long after. Without naming me she wrote of an unbelievably learned young man who had become the "rage" of the summer colony and was reading Homer, Goethe, Dante, and Shakespeare with young and old. He had revived the Browning Club and his French *matinées* were depopulating Bailey's Beach. Her article opened with a scornful repudiation of a witticism twenty years old to the effect that "the ladies of Newport had never heard the first act of an opera nor read the last half of a book." Newport was—and always has been—she affirmed, one of the most enlightened communities in the country, the foster home of George Bancroft, Longfellow, Lowell, Henry James, Edith Wharton, and of Mrs. Edward Venable, author of that moving volume of verse, *Dreams in an Aquidneck Garden.*

Nor did I know at the time that there was a less flattering reason why I had become in those circles an object of almost morbid curiosity.

It was a custom of the house that toward midnight Dr. Bosworth's guests would file into the study to take a second leave of their distinguished host. I stood against the wall in that self-effacement that became my station. Mrs. Bosworth did not accompany them, but Dr. Bosworth and Persis saw to it that I was presented to them all. Among them were some who were, or had been, my employers: I received from Miss Wyckoff a radiant smile, from Bodo (a frequent guest) a fraternal and in-elegant greeting in German. Ladies whom I had never met told me of their children's progress:

"My Michael's set his heart on becoming a tennis champion, thanks to you, Mr. North."

Mrs. Venable: "Bodo tells me that you're reading Bishop Berkeley—how fascinating!"

Another: "Mr. North, Mr. Weller and I are giving a small dance on Saturday week. To what address may I send a card?"

"That's very kind of you, Mrs. Weller, but my days are so filled that I'm unable to accept any invitations."

"No parties *at all*?"

"No—thank you very much—no parties."

Another: "Mr. North, is it too late for me to join your Robert Browning Society. I've always loved the Brownings."

"Ma'am, I don't know of any Browning Society in Newport."

"Oh? . . . Oh? . . . Perhaps I was misinformed."

The Fenwicks, whom you will meet later, were very cordial with a smile of complicity. I was presented to the parents of Diana Bell who did not acknowledge the introduction. I leaned forward to Mrs. Bell and said in a low voice but very distinctly: "I have twice sent my bill to Mr. Bell for services which he agreed upon. If he does not pay my bill, I shall tell the whole story to Miss Flora Deland and sixty million Americans will learn of that purloined letter. Good evening, Mrs. Bell."

That was low; that was unworthy of a Yale man. She stared straight ahead of her, but the bill was paid. Let him who will be a gentleman!

Among the guests I met more and more members of the family clan: Mr. and Mrs. Cassius Marcellus Leffingwell, and their older children; the Edward Bosworths and their older children; the Newton Bosworths and a child or two. All these ladies put out their hands and declared that they were delighted to meet me; these gentlemen not only refused their hands but either stared at me stonily or turned their backs. When I had been the object of hostility on repeated occasions I became aware that Gulliver was encountering some example of the *mores* on Aquidneck Island that deserved a closer study.

I was not comfortable at "Nine Gables." I had come to Newport to observe without becoming deeply involved. Among the Bosworths I felt obscurely that I was in danger of becoming extremely involved in some imbroglio out of late Elizabethan drama. I had already made two enemies in the house: Willis loathed me; when I passed Mrs. Bosworth in the hall, she lowered her head slightly but her glance said, "Beware young man, we know what your game is. . . ." Day after day I planned to throw up the job. Yet I enjoyed the readings in Bishop Berkeley; I enjoyed Dr. Bosworth's constantly recalling the Newport of the eighteenth century half a mile from where we were working. I was deeply interested in Persis, Mrs. Tennyson, though I had never been presented to her. She seemed to regard me with puzzled distrust. I wondered how was she able to live the year round in a house governed by her vindictive

"Aunt Sally." Above all I had been exalted by my employer's preposterous vision of gathering together here the greatest living thinkers—a vision he could only communicate in whispers. I had lived four and a half uneventful years in a New Jersey where there were no perils and no visions, no dragons and no madmen—and very little opportunity to exercise and explore any of those youthful ambitions that lay dormant within me. I did not resign.

It was I who unwittingly opened the next door into a deeper involvement. We had been reading aloud from Dr. Bosworth's own work *Some Eighteenth Century Houses in Rhode Island*. When we finished the chapter that contained a detailed description of Bishop Berkeley's "Whitehall" I expressed my admiration for the art with which it was written; then I added, "Dr. Bosworth, I think it would be a great privilege to visit the house in your company. Would it be possible to drive out some afternoon and see the house together?"

There was a silence. I looked up and found him gazing at me searchingly, piteously. "Indeed, I wish we could. I thought you understood . . . I have this disability. I am unable to leave this house for more than a quarter of an hour. I can walk in the garden for a short time. I shall never leave this house. I shall die here."

I returned his gaze with that impassive expression I had learned to adopt in the Army where irrationality knows no bounds and where we underlings have no choice but to make a pretense of unfathomable stupidity. To myself I thought, "He's crazy. He's around the bend." We had often sat uninterruptedly in his study for almost three hours, after which he had accompanied me unhurriedly to his front door. All I knew at that moment was that I did not want to hear one more word about it. I wanted to have nothing to do with the appealing, longing, dependent expression on his face. I was no doctor. I didn't know what I was, but Dr. Bosworth was a bad judge of men. He had assumed that I was a sympathetic listener. A miserable man cannot hold his tongue in such company and soon I was to receive the whole damnable ludicrous story.

But I must interrupt my narrative here.

I must give the reasons—which I was soon to learn—why

encounters with the guests at the close of the Bosworths' dinner parties were of so mixed a nature.

I continued to enjoy occasional late hours at Mrs. Cranston's boardinghouse now aglow with the expectation of Edweena's imminent return. Henry continued to share with us the postcards he received telling of whales, mighty storms, flying fishes, and picturing the beauties of the Leeward Islands. The conversation flowed on. For the most part I played the role of an appreciative listener. I gave them only a general idea of my activities, mentioning few names. After the retirement of the other ladies Mrs. Cranston intermittently relaxed her rule against the use of our Christian names. Generally Mr. Griffin sat with us, lost in deep thought or in vacancy, occasionally delighting us with some far-sought non-sequitur. My Journal was enriched by many of Mrs. Cranston's reflections.

"The Whitcombs!" cried Mrs. Cranston. "There's another case of the Death Watch, Henry. Oh, how I wish Edweena were here to tell Teddie about her theory of the Death Watch. You tell him, Henry. I'm tired tonight. Do now, I know it will interest him."

"Will you interrupt me, ma'am, if I get to sliding on the ice, as often happens? . . . Well, it's this way, old matey: in a dozen houses in Newport there's an aged party, male or female, sitting on a mountain of money. . . ."

"Twenty houses, Henry, at *least* twenty."

"Thank you, ma'am. Now let's call the aged party the Old Mogle—some call it Mogull, you can pronounce it either way. Newport's the only place in the country where rich old men live longer than rich old women. I've heard you make that observation, Mrs. Cranston."

"Yes, I think it's true. It's the social life that kills. The old men simply withdraw upstairs. No old woman has ever been known to withdraw from the social life of her own accord."

"And the Old Mogle has sons and daughters and grandchildren and flying nevvies and nieces, all waiting for the reading of the will. But the Old Party won't die. So what do you do? You gather around him every hour of the clock and ask him tenderly about his health—tenderly, sadly, lovingly. You call in doctors to ask him doubtfully, tenderly about his health. 'Well,

Mr. Mogle, how are we today? God bless my soul, we look ten years younger! Splendid! Let me look again at that little inflammation. We don't like that one little bit, do we? Too near the brain. Is it sensitive to the touch, Mr. Mogle?' Oh, I wish Edweena were here; she does the doctor business glorious, doesn't she, Mrs. Cranston? She says that all men over seventy can be made to be high-pepper-condriacs in zero time with a little attention from the loved ones. She says all women are, anyway."

"I'm not, Henry."

"You're nowhere near that age, Mrs. Cranston—and God gave you the constitution and the figure of the Statue of Liberty."

"I'm above compliments, Henry. Go on with your story."

"Now the Death Watch has a lot to worry about, cully—see what I mean? For instance, *favoritism*! One son over another, one daughter over another, down to the new-born grandchild. Terrible thought! Then there's always the Old Man's Folly—falls in love with his nurse or secretary. Or a beautiful divorcée arrives from Europe, pulls his beard and strokes his hands right at the dinner table. An old lady falls in love with her chauffeur; we've seen it scores of times. The Death Watch goes frantic. Frantic—and starts to act. We've seen some terrible *action* around here. Expel 'em! Crush 'em!"

"You've forgotten something else, Henry."

"Thankee, and what's that, ma'am?"

"The callers, the confidential callers, with noble causes—"

"How could I forget them! Universal peace. Colleges *named after you*! Eskimos. Fallen women—very popular. Old men are very tender about fallen women."

"Dogs' cemeteries," said Mr. Griffin.

"How bright you are tonight, Mr. Griffin!—All these things taking the food out of the mouths of his nearest and dearest."

The room seemed to have become uncomfortably warm.

"What kind of action do they take, Henry?" I asked.

"Well, they've got two lines of action, haven't they? To get rid of the favorite they've got slander—they tell stories. Even if it's their nearest kith 'n' kin. That's easy. But their 'object all sublime'—as the poet said—is to take the pen out of the great Mogle's hand—to remove his power to write checks. To drive him dotty. To get him quivering and bursting into tears. Guardianship—soften him up for guardianship."

"Terrible!" said Mrs. Cranston, shaking her head.

"They've got their doctors and lawyers all lined up. Why, we know a Mogle in this town who hasn't left his front door for ten years—"

"Eight, Henry."

"You're always right, Mrs. Cranston."

"No names, Henry."

"He's just as well as you or me. They make him think that he's got cancer of the sofa cushion. The great specialist comes up from New York—you can't do these things without specialists —specialists are the Death Watchers' best friend. Dr. Thread-and-Needle comes up from New York and tells him it's about time for another of those little operations. So the Mogle is wheeled in and they take a little piece of skin off the area. The nurses near die of laughing. 'Ten thousand dollars, please.' "

"Henry, I'd say you were sliding on the ice a bit."

"I'll be forgiven if I exaggerate. Teddie's new to the town. You never can tell when he might come up against an example of things like this."

"Let's talk about something more cheerful, Henry. Teddie, who have you been reading aloud to lately?"

"Mostly I've been getting children ready to return to school, Mrs. Cranston. I've had to turn down a number of jobs. I think there's a craze on to trace a family's genealogy to William the Conqueror."

"That's always been true."

The conversation flowed on.

I returned to my room thoughtfully.

My next engagement at "Nine Gables" was on the following Sunday morning. Dr. McPherson had suddenly decided that the late-hour sessions were inadvisable. I was surprised to see Dr. Bosworth fully dressed to go out. He was arguing with his nurse. "We shall not need your company, Mrs. Turner."

"But, Dr. Bosworth, I must obey Dr. McPherson's orders. I must be near you at all times."

"Will you leave the room and close the door, Mrs. Turner?"

"Oh, dear! I don't know what to do!" she answered and left.

To me he whispered, "Listening! Always listening!" His eyes searched the ceiling. "Mr. North, will you climb up on that chair and see if there's some kind of gramophone up there listening to what's said here?"

"No, Dr. Bosworth," I said, raising my voice, "I was engaged to read aloud here. I am not an electrical engineer."

He put his ear to his bedroom door. "She's telephoning all over the house. . . . Come, follow me."

We started down the great hall to the front door. As we approached it Mrs. Leffingwell came floating down the staircase.

"Good morning, Papa dear. Good morning, Mr. North. We're all coming over to lunch. I came early to see if Sally wanted to go to church. She can't make up her mind. But I'd much rather listen to the reading. Mr. North, do persuade my father to let me join you. I'll be as quiet as a mouse."

Something in her voice astonished and pained him. He stared at her for a moment and said, "You too, Mary?" then added harshly, "Our discussion would not interest you. Run off to church and enjoy yourselves. . . . We are going to the beech grove, Mr. North."

It was a most beautiful morning. He had brought no book with him. We sat for some time in silence on a bench under the great trees. Suddenly I became aware that Dr. Bosworth's eyes were fixed on me with an expression of suffering—of despair.

"Mr. North, I think I should explain my disability to you. I suffer from a disorder of the kidneys which the doctors tell me may be related to a far more serious illness—to a fatal disease. I find this very strange because—apart from certain local irritations—I have experienced no pain. But I am not a medical man; I must rely on the word of certain specialists." His eyes now bored into mine. "As a side aspect of this wretched business, I suffer from a compulsion to urinate—or try to urinate—every ten to fifteen minutes."

I returned his gaze as solemnly as he could wish.

"Why, Dr. Bosworth, you and I have sat in your study for hours at a time without your leaving the room once."

"That's the ridiculous part about it. Perhaps it's all in the mind—as Bishop Berkeley is constantly insisting! As long as I'm in my own house—keeping quiet, so to speak—I am not inconvenienced. I am assured that it is not the usual old man's affliction; it is not prostate trouble. It's something far graver."

(Oh, hell! Oh, crimson tarnation! Resign right now!—

Besides, every two weeks I'd sent my bill to Mrs. Bosworth, my ostensible employer, and she'd made no reply. This was my fifth week. She owed me over sixty dollars!)

The old man went on: "For many years I served my country in the diplomatic life. Public functions tend to be long drawn out. State funerals, weddings, christenings, openings of parliament, national holidays. Unforeseen delays! Snowstorms in Finland, hurricanes in Burma! . . . Waits at railway stations, waits on grandstands. I was the head of my delegation. . . . I have always been a healthy man, Mr. North, but I began to get a dread of that—that little necessity. Now I know that it's all in the mind. Bishop Berkeley! Doctors laugh at me, I know, behind my back. One doctor fitted me out with a sort of goat's udder." Here he covered his face with his hands, murmuring, "I shall die in this house or in their wretched hospital."

There was a silence. He lowered his hands and whispered, "The worst of it is that the idea is getting around that I'm crazy. Do *you* think I'm crazy?"

I raised my hand for silence and got it. I was as authoritative as a judge and solemn as an owl. "Dr. Bosworth, none of this is new to me—this kidney trouble. I know all about it."

"What's that you say?" He clutched my sleeve. "What's that you say, boy?"

"One summer I left Yale and went to Florida and got work as a swimming and sports director at a resort. One of the hurricanes came along. The tourists canceled their bookings. I was out of a job. So I became a truck driver. Long drives—Miami to Winston-Salem, Saint Petersburg to Dallas, Texas. Now the three things that truck drivers think about are: the bonus for speed of delivery, falling asleep at the wheel, and kidney trouble. There's something about sitting all day in that shaking truck that upsets a man's waterworks—irritates it. Driving is hell on the kidneys. Some men get the fear of retention—afraid that they'll never piss again. Others have what you have—the constant itch. Of course, they can get down when they want to, but nothing comes. Now I have an idea."

"An *idea*? What . . . what idea?"

"I have very few pupils tomorrow. I'll cancel them. I'll go to Providence to the truck drivers' stop. They sell stay-awake pills and a *certain gadget*. It's got a very vulgar name that I won't repeat to you. I'll bring it back to you and one of these days we'll drive to 'Whitehall' and try it out."

Tears were rolling down the old man's face. "If you do that, Mr. North, if you do that, I'll believe there's a God. I will. I will."

I had never been to Florida since the age of eight. I had never driven a truck farther than twenty miles—it was the summer school's carry-all. But in the Army barracks a man picks up a lot of desultory information, a great deal of it scatological.

"I have three pupils in the morning. I shall have to charge you for the canceled lessons, as well as for the cost of the trip to Providence and for the gadget I hope to find. I live on a strict budget, Dr. Bosworth. I think I can do the whole thing for twenty dollars. Maybe the gadget costs more. I shall submit an itemized account. Shall I send it to you or to Mrs. Bosworth?"

"What?"

I continued firmly. "I have sent Mrs. Bosworth a bill for our readings every two weeks, but so far I have received no payment whatever. She has the bills."

"What? I don't understand it!"

"I shall need some money to go to Providence."

"Come in the house. Come in the house at once. I am shocked. I am grieved, Mr. North."

He started for the house like a runaway horse. He met Willis at the door. "Willis, tell Mrs. Bosworth to bring my checkbook to my study and Mr. North's bills also!"

Long wait. He smote his handbell. Enter Persis.

"What is it, Grandfather?"

"I wish to speak to your Aunt Sarah."

"I think she may be at church."

"Hunt for her. If she's out of the house, go to her desk and bring me my checkbook or her checkbook. She has failed to pay Mr. North's bills."

"Grandfather, she has given strict orders that no one may open her desk. May I write a check for you?"

"It's *my* checkbook. *I* shall open her desk."

"I'll see if I can find her, Grandfather."

While we waited I filled in the time with further graphic

accounts of the discomfitures of truck drivers. Presently there was a knock at the door and Willis entered, nobly bearing a bronze tray on which lay a checkbook and my two envelopes, opened. Dr. Bosworth asked me to state the total sum for my past and future services. He recalled my full name and wrote the check. I receipted the bills.

Mrs. Bosworth entered the room. "Father, you directed me to keep the accounts of this house."

"Then keep them! Pay them!"

"I assumed that a monthly payment for Mr. North would be sufficient."

"Here is your checkbook for the household accounts. I have paid Mr. North for our readings and for some errands he is doing for me. Kindly return to me my own checkbook for my own private use.—Mr. North, is it agreeable to you, if we return to our former evening schedule?"

"Yes, Dr. Bosworth."

"Father, Dr. McPherson is convinced that the late hours are harmful to you."

"My compliments to Dr. McPherson . . . Let me see you to the door, Mr. North. I am too agitated to continue our work this morning. May I expect you Tuesday evening?"

In the hall we passed Mrs. Bosworth. She said nothing, but our eyes met. I bowed slightly. In the Orient, they believe that hatred, in itself, kills; and I was brought up in China.

At the door her father whispered feverishly: "Perhaps I shall live again."

The next morning at the "Y" I fitted myself out, with the help of some acquaintances in the corridor, with a dirty sweater, some dirty pants, and a battered hat. I was a truck driver. At the truck drivers' stop in Providence I bought—as a pretext— some stay-awake pills and asked where was the nearest drugstore frequented by us road men. It was across the street, "O'Halloran's." I bought some more stay-awake pills and had an intimate conversation with Joe O'Halloran about some inconveniences I suffered on the road.

"Let me show you something, Jack. First they invented this for babies. Then they made 'm bigger for hospitals and insane asylums, see what I mean? Lots of incontinence in insane asylums."

I bought the medium size. "Mr. O'Halloran, I get a kind of ache in my wrists and forearms. Have you some mild—real mild—painkiller? Nothing potent, you know. I've gotta drive over four hundred miles a day."

He put a bottle of scarlet pills on the counter. "How many should I take?"

"Driving like you do, not more than one an hour."

Was I taking a great risk? I weighed the matter thoroughly. Medicine had never been among my youthful ambitions, but it had always been high among my curiosities. I had no doubt that Dr. Bosworth had been for years the victim of a carefully staged conspiracy that had taken advantage of an insecurity frequently found among diplomats, policemen on all-night guard duty, performing artists. Among my fellow-soldiers in the barracks I had heard ex-chauffeurs telling hilarious stories of the "perfect hell" of driving ladies out shopping in midtown where there was no place to park. When Dr. Bosworth and I were immersed in the eighteenth century it was apparent that he was as filled with well-being as with intellectual delight and as with self-esteem. It was only when the obsession descended upon him that he became a pitiable man. The risk I was taking was a risk for me, not for him. I was in a condition to assume a risk and to relish it.

I was back in Newport at four in the afternoon. I'd swallowed two of the red pills, very bitter with little effect—perhaps a slight numbness in the neck. I telephoned my employer.

"Yes, Mr. North? Yes, Mr. North?"

"I have a message for you. Can I give it to you on this line?"

"Wait a minute. I must think. . . . Tell me your number. I will call you back from the gardener's house."

He did. "Yes, Mr. North?"

"Dr. Bosworth, in a quarter of an hour a telegraph boy is going to call at your house with a parcel for your hands only and for your signature. Don't let anyone intercept it. I think you'll want to use what's inside. You take a walk around the garden at five, you told me. When you start out take one of those red pills. Thousands of men take them on the road every day. After about ten minutes you may feel a little itching, but it'll go away. Ignore it. The other thing is just a safeguard. You'll be able to throw it away after a week or two."

His voice was trembling. "I don't know what to say. . . . I'll be at the front door. . . . I'll report to you Tuesday night."

When I entered his study Tuesday night, he clutched at me excitedly, then closed both the doors. "First afternoon, half an hour! This morning, half an hour! This afternoon, forty-five minutes!"

"That's fine," I said calmly.

"*Fine?* FINE?" He wiped his eyes. "Mr. North, can you drive with me to 'Whitehall' next Sunday morning or afternoon?"

"I am sorry I am engaged with Colonel Vanwinkle on Sunday mornings. I would feel it to be a great privilege to go with you on Sunday afternoon."

"Yes, I shall take my granddaughter with me this Sunday."

There was a knock at the door. "Come in!"

Mrs. Bosworth entered. "Forgive me interrupting you, Father. I must discuss our dinner Tuesday week. The Thayers have been called to New York. Whom would you like in their place?" Her father muttered something agitatedly. "I'm sorry, Father, but I *must* know whether you prefer the Ewings or the Thorpes."

"Sarah, how many times must I tell you *not* to disturb me when I am at work?"

She stared at him. "Father, you have been behaving very strangely lately. I think these readings and those *walks* have overexcited you. Shouldn't you say good night to Mr. North and—?"

"Sarah, you have your car and driver. I do not wish to interfere with your life. Tomorrow I want you to arrange for the rental of a car and a driver for my use. I wish to go for a drive tomorrow after my nap—at four-thirty."

"You are not going to—?!"

"What you take for my *strange behavior* is an improvement in my health."

"A drive! Without Dr. McPherson's permission! Your doctor for thirty years!"

"Dr. McPherson is *your* doctor. I do not now feel the need of one. If I do, I shall call in that young Dr. What's-his-name that Forebaugh was telling me about. . . . I wish now to return to my studies."

"But the children . . . !"

"Edward? Mary? What have they to do with it?"

"We are all deeply concerned. We love you!"

"Then you'll be glad to hear that I feel much better. I would like to speak to Persis."

Persis appeared almost at once. This was "the house of listening ears."

"Persis, can you arrange to take a short drive with me in my car every afternoon after my nap?"

"I'd love to, Grandfather."

"The Sunday after next we will take Mr. North with us and show him 'Whitehall.' "

The roof had fallen down about Mrs. Bosworth's ears. She did not even glance at me. Her manner suggested that the time had come for stronger measures.

Our readings in the works of Bishop Berkeley continued, though with a relaxed concentration. Dr. Bosworth was filled with an irrepressible elation. They now were enjoying the famous "ten-mile drive" daily. He hoped soon to revisit Providence; they would put up for the night at the hotel "without Mrs. Turner." He was dreaming of going to New York in the fall—plans for the Academy . . .

A storm was gathering about my head.

I enjoyed the flashes of lightning.

Increasingly the Leffingwells were present at every dinner party at "Nine Gables" and on each occasion joined the late parade into Dr. Bosworth's study. Mrs. Leffingwell extended her hand to me in greeting; her husband stared into my face and seemed about to address me, but the war within him between rage and decorum silenced him. (I always thought of Cassius Marcellus as "Vercingetorix or The Dying Gaul"—the only mustached head known to me in ancient sculpture— probably straw-blond.) One evening there was—as in all parades —a halt in the line. The Leffingwells were marking time directly in front of me. Mrs. Leffingwell and I discussed the weather, the beauty of Newport, and her father's improved health until even her conversational resources were exhausted. She fanned herself with her handkerchief, smiling sweetly. Her husband growled, "Get on with it, Mary. Get on with it!"

"I can't, Cassius. Mrs. Venable is holding up the line."

At last Cassius found his tongue. He stretched his head toward me and said between his teeth (right out of *The Curfew Shall Not Ring Tonight*): "One of these days, North, I shall horsewhip you."

His wife overheard him. "Cassius! Cassius, we shall not wait to see my father any longer. We shall go upstairs."

But he balked; he wanted to drive his point home more forcefully. "Remember my words: horsewhip!"

I looked at him gravely. "Are they still horsewhipping in the South, Mr. Leffingwell? I thought that went out fifty years ago."

"Cassius, follow me!"

It was an order and he obeyed. The trouble with him was that he hadn't had enough to drink.

A few nights later I found a note waiting for me at the Y.M.C.A. *"Dear Mr. North, I have heard that a member of a family— where you read—has been talking wildly all over town—about doing you harm. A freind of mine—you met him—has arranged to have a car call for you at midnight Friday. Do not leave the house until you are told that a car and driver are waiting for you at the door."* It was signed *"A Freind on Spring Street."* Freinds indeed: Amelia Cranston—more for Newport's sake than for mine—had arranged with the Chief of Police to prevent the summer residents from getting into trouble.

There was no dinner party on Friday. Dr. Bosworth and I read Benedetto Croce on the subject of Giambattista Vico. My employer's knowledge of Italian was superior to mine and it gave him pleasure to help me over the difficult passages. It gave him pleasure, too, to believe that the author would soon be his guest and neighbor in the Academy of Philosophers. It gave me pleasure because author and subject were new, astonishing, and big. I forgot that I was to be called for.

At a quarter before twelve Persis Tennyson knocked at the door and was asked to enter. "Grandfather, I wish to drive Mr. North home in my car tonight. Please let him leave a little early because it's late."

"Yes, my dear. Do you mean *now*?"

"Yes, Grandfather, please."

As I was preparing to take my departure Mrs. Bosworth appeared at the door. She had overheard her niece's proposal. (At

"Nine Gables" no one went to bed until that abominable Mr. North was out of the house.) "That will not be necessary, Persis. It is unsuitable that you drive about town at this hour. I've arranged for Dorsey to drive Mr. North home in my car."

"Well, my friend," said Dr. Bosworth in Italian, "everybody wants to see that you get home safely tonight."

Willis appeared at the door and announced that Mr. North's car was waiting. . . .

"What car is that, Willis—mine?"

"No, madam, a car called for by Mr. North."

"Well," said Persis, "let's all go and see Mr. North to the door . . . !"

We made quite a procession advancing down the hall. From the foot of the staircase Mrs. Leffingwell approached us agitatedly. "Sally, I can't find Cassius anywhere. I think he's out of the house. Please help me find him. If we can't find him I shall drive Mr. North home in my own car.—Willis, have you seen Mr. Leffingwell anywhere?"

"Yes, madam."

"*Where* is he?"

"Madam, he is in the bushes."

"Yes, Aunt Mary," said Persis. "I saw him lying in the bushes. That's why I asked to drive Mr. North home. He had something in his hand."

"Persis, that will do," said Mrs. Bosworth. "Hold your tongue. Go to your room."

Willis said to Mrs. Bosworth, "Madam, may I speak to you at one side for a moment?"

"Talk up, Willis," said Dr. Bosworth. "What are you trying to say? What is it that Mr. Leffingwell has in his hand?"

"A gun, sir."

Mrs. Leffingwell was too well brought up to shriek. She squeaked. "Cassius is playing with guns again. He will kill himself!"

The driver who had called for me stepped forward. "Not at present, madam. We have taken the gun from him." And he held it under our noses.

"And who are you?" asked Mrs. Bosworth grandly. The driver flipped his lapel and showed his badge.

"God bless my soul!" exclaimed Dr. Bosworth.

"*And*," asked Mrs. Bosworth, who enjoyed beginning a question with "and," "what authority have you for trespassing on this property?"

"Mr. Loft . . . Mr. Left . . . the gentleman in the bushes . . . has been overheard in three places threatening to kill Mr. North. We can't have that, madam. Is Mr. Leveringwall a resident of Newport?"

"Mr. Leffingwell lives in Jamestown."

"The Chief told us not to press charges, if the gentleman lives outside Aquidneck County. But he must agree not to appear in this township for six months. Felix, call him in."

Mrs. Leffingwell said, "Officer, please do not call him in now. I am his wife and I will stand guarantee that he will not return here. We have a farm in Virginia, also, *where a man may carry a gun in self-defense wherever he goes*."

That's what's called the last word. She delivered the line grandly and couldn't have looked handsomer.

My rescuer ("Joe") had had free ingress to all motion-pictures and knew how to behave in great houses. "If Mr. North is ready to go, the car is waiting for him. We have a call to the Daubigny cottage. Good night, ladies and gentlemen, we are sorry to have been an inconvenience to you."

I bowed in silence to the company and left.

Outside Joe said to his companion, "Let's see where the gook's gone."

"He's knocking at the side door, Joe. Do you think he needs any help, Joe?"

"They'll find him. . . . The Chief says to have as little to do with these people as possible. They're crazy as coots, he says. Let them wash their own sheets, he says."

If I'd had a grain of decent feeling in me, I'd have resigned the next morning; but what's a little family unpleasantness compared to discovering Bishop Berkeley, Croce, Vico, and letting one's eyes rest on Persis Tennyson?

When the hour arrived for the Sunday drive to "Whitehall" Dr. Bosworth and his granddaughter were waiting at the door. It was a beautiful afternoon in August (but I remember no others; on Aquidneck Island rain fell—considerately—only when the inhabitants were sleeping).

Persis said, "I shall sit in front with Jeffries. Mr. North, will you sit with Grandfather. He likes to drive slowly and I know he wants to talk to you."

"Mrs. Tennyson, I have never had the pleasure of being introduced to you?"

"What!" said Dr. Bosworth.

"We have exchanged greetings," I said.

Persis laughed. "Let us shake hands, Mr. North."

Dr. Bosworth was bewildered. "Never met! Never introduced! What a house I live in! Cassius lying in the bushes—policemen passing around guns—Sarah and Mary behaving like . . ." He began laughing. "Makes an old man feel like King Lear."

"Let's forget all about it, Grandfather."

"Yes." He began pointing out to me some eighteenth-century doors and fanlights. "There are some beautiful houses all over town—going to rack and ruin. Nobody appreciates them."

"Dr. Bosworth, I've discovered a resident in Newport who could have helped us with those metaphysical passages in Bishop Berkeley."

"Who's that?"

"Someone you know well—Baron Stams. He has a doctorate from Heidelberg in philosophy."

"Bodo? God bless my soul! Does Bodo know anything?"

"He also has a doctorate from Vienna in political history."

"Do you hear that, Persis? He's a pleasant fellow, but I thought he was just one of these dancing-partners that Mrs. Venable collects for her parties. You always found him rather empty-headed, didn't you, Persis?"

"Not empty-headed, Grandfather. Just difficult to talk to."

"Yes, I remember your saying that. Surprised me. He seems to be able to talk easily to everybody he sits by except you. A regular *gigolo*. Your Aunt Sally always seats him by you and Mrs. Venable always seats him by you, I hear."

Persis remained silent.

Dr. Bosworth again addressed me confidentially. "I always thought he was one of these fortune hunters, if you know what I mean—title, good looks, and nothing else."

I began laughing.

"Why are you laughing, Mr. North?"

I made him wait for it and laughed some more.

"You find something droll about it, Mr. North?"

"Well, Dr. Bosworth, it's Baron Stams who has the fortune."

"Oh? He has money, has he?"

I looked Dr. Bosworth in the eye and I didn't lower my voice. "A fortune: excellent brains, excellent character, a distinguished family, an assured career. He has been decorated by his country for bravery in battle and he almost died of his wounds. His castle at Stams is almost as beautiful as the famous monastery at Stams—which you must know. In addition, he's lots of fun." Again I laughed. "That's what I call a fortune."

Persis had turned her profile toward us. She appeared to be annoyed and bewildered.

We arrived at "Whitehall." I had to hold my breath from awe.

Bishop Berkeley was the author of the line "Westward the course of empire takes its way." There we were, pilgrims from the East.

In spite of kind invitations I never drove out in Dr. Bosworth's car again; though I was taken for a drive in Persis Tennyson's—an account of that starlit encounter I must defer. It will be found in a later chapter entitled "Bodo and Persis" whom it more closely concerns. Persis became her grandfather's constant companion—running head on into the danger from which I was escaping, "favoritism." Mrs. Bosworth's tone became increasingly sharp to her, but Persis held firm. One afternoon I called on Dr. Bosworth at his request for a short talk following his daily drive. While waiting in his study for him to change his clothes I overheard the following conversation in the hall.

"You must be able to see, Aunt Sally, that these drives agree with Grandfather."

"You are an ignorant girl, Persis. This activity will *kill* him."

"I asked Grandfather as a favor to me to submit to an examination by Dr. Tedeschi. Dr. Tedeschi recommended the drives."

"How could *you* take such a responsibility? Dr. Tedeschi is a puppy, and an Italian puppy at that."

Dr. Bosworth reentered his study. He was overflowing with ideas that had occurred to him. He was preparing to present the great project to a still unselected board of directors. There was to be an administration building with two lecture halls, a large and a small; a well-stocked library; at least nine separate residences; large annual grants to the Masters; a dormitory and dining hall for whatever students the Masters consented to accept. Further expenditures were added in pencil along the margins. . . . The project called for millions and millions. Very exhilarating.

Two evenings later I arrived at the usual hour. Persis was waiting outside the house. She put her fingers on her lips, raised her eyebrows, and pointed toward the hall. There was trepidation and a shade of amusement on her face. She spoke no word. I rang the bell and was admitted by Willis. Mrs. Bosworth met me in the hall at some distance from her father's study. She addressed me in a low voice but very distinctly. "Mr. North, since you entered this house you have been a constant source of confusion. I regard you as a foolish and dangerous man. Will you explain to me what you are trying to do to my father?"

I replied even more quietly. "I don't understand what you mean, Mrs. Bosworth."

It worked. Her voice rose. "Dr. Bosworth is a very sick man. These exertions may kill him."

"Your father invited me to accompany him to 'Whitehall.' I assumed that he had his doctor's permission."

"*Assumed!* It is not your business to assume anything."

I was now almost inaudible. "Dr. Bosworth spoke of his doctor's approval."

"*He refuses to see his doctor—the man who has been his physician for thirty years.* You are a trouble-maker. You are a vulgar intruder. Mr. North, it was I who engaged you to come to this house. Your engagement is terminated. Now! *Now!* Will you tell me what I owe you?"

"Thank you . . . Dr. Bosworth is expecting me. I shall go to his study to say goodbye to him."

"I forbid you to take one step further."

I had one more trick up my sleeve. Now I raised my voice. "Mrs. Bosworth, you are very pale. Are you unwell? Can I get you a glass of water?"

"I am perfectly well. Will you lower your voice, please?"

I started dashing about, shouting, "Mr. Willis! Mr. Willis! Is anybody there? Mrs. Turner! Nurse!"

"Stop this nonsense. I am perfectly well."

I ran the length of the hall, calling, "Smelling salts! Help! Asafoetida!"

I overturned a table. Persis appeared. Mrs. Turner appeared. Willis appeared. Maids emerged from the kitchen.

"Do be quiet! I am perfectly well!"

"Call a doctor. Mrs. Bosworth has fainted." I recalled a smashing phrase from eighteenth-century novels, "Unlace her!"

Willis pulled up a chair behind Mrs. Bosworth so abruptly that she sank into it, outraged. Persis knelt and patted her hands. Dr. Bosworth appeared at the door of his study and the room fell silent. "What's the matter, Sarah?"

"Nothing! This *oaf* has raised a great noise about nothing."

"Persis?"

"Grandfather, Aunt Sally suddenly felt unwell. Fortunately Mr. North was here and called for help."

Now it was like grand opera—that relief in the air *when things crack open*. Mrs. Bosworth rose and advanced toward her father —"Father, either that monster leaves this house or I do!"

"Willis, call Dr. McPherson. Sarah, you're tired. You're overworked. Mrs. Turner, will you kindly take Mrs. Bosworth up to her room. Go to bed, Sarah; go to bed! Persis, I want you to stay here. Willis!"

"Yes, sir."

"I will have a whiskey and soda. Bring one for Mr. North, too."

Whiskey! It was that request that made it clear to Mrs. Bosworth that her authority was at an end. After years of gruel, *whiskey.* She started for the stairs, brushing Mrs. Turner aside. "Don't touch me! I can walk perfectly well by myself."

"Dr. Bosworth," I said, "I have great respect for Mrs. Bosworth. I shall certainly discontinue my visits here since they are so unwelcome to her. May I remain a few minutes to thank you for the privilege it has been to meet with you here?"

"What? What? We must talk this over. Persis, will you please join us?"

"Yes, Grandfather."

"Mr. North feels that he must leave us. I hope he will be able to meet me from time to time at the 'Reading Rooms.'"

Willis entered with our drinks. Dr. Bosworth raised his glass, saying, "Dr. Tedeschi recommended today that I have a little whiskey in the evening."

Persis and I exchanged no glances, but I felt that we shared a sense of something accomplished.

That was my last engagement at "Nine Gables."

Both Mrs. Bosworth and I left the house—she to visit a dear friend in England, I to offer my services elsewhere. But, as I have already told the reader, I had not yet entirely terminated my relations with all the residents at "Nine Gables."

Toward the end of the summer I met Dr. Bosworth by chance. He was as cordial as ever. He confided to me that he was too old to cope with the numerous details involved in setting up an Academy of Philosophers; he had another project in mind—still a secret; he was planning to build and endow a clinic for that "excellent young physician Dr. Tedeschi."

6

Rip

LATE IN June I was surprised to discover that someone I had known fairly well at college was living in Newport's Sixth City. One late afternoon I was wheeling homewards along the Avenue when I was startled to hear a voice from a passing car calling "Theophilus! Theophilus! What the hell are you doing here?" I drew up beside the curb. The car which had passed me did so also. A man alighted and walked toward me laughing. Still laughing he slapped me on the back, punched me in the thorax, seized my shoulder, and shook me like a rat. It took me some minutes to recognize Nicholas Vanwinkle. All his life—through school, college, and military service—he had naturally been called "Rip." There was a legend in his family that Washington Irving had known his grandfather well and had written him one day asking permission to use the name Vanwinkle, applying it to a likeable old character in a story he was writing about the Dutchmen living in the Catskills. He was given cordial permission and the result became known around the world.

And once again the name "Rip Van Winkle" attained a wide celebrity, for the man who was handling me roughly on Bellevue Avenue was the great ace in the War, one of the four most decorated veterans on "our side" and The Terror (and tacitly acknowledged admiration) of the Germans. He had been a member of the class of 1916, but the men who received their degrees in 1920 included many who had left school long before to take part in the War—some enlisting in Canada before our country was involved; some like my brother and Bob Hutchins joining ambulance units in France and the Balkans, then later transferring to our services. Many among the survivors of these dispersed students returned to Yale to complete their undergraduate education in 1919 and 1920. I had not known Rip well; he had moved in far more brilliant circles; he was the very flower of the *jeunesse dorée* and an international celebrity in addition; but I had conversed with him many times in the

Elizabethan Club, where he could very well represent for us the figure of Sir Philip Sidney, the perfection of knighthood. Tall, handsome, wealthy, preeminent in all the sports he engaged in (though he did not play football or baseball), and endowed with a simplicity of manner far removed from the stiffness and condescension prevalent in his own *coterie*, sons of the great steel and investment banking houses.

By chance I ran into him in Paris one noon on the Avenue de l'Opéra in the late spring of 1921, soon after I had finished my year's study in Rome. We crossed near the entrance to the Café de Paris and he promptly asked me to lunch there. His simple spontaneity was unaltered. He was returning to America the next day, he said, to marry "the finest girl in the world." It was a delightful hour. Little could I perceive that the price of our meal was from the bottom of his pocket. I had not seen him nor heard anything about his private life in the intervening five years. Five years is a long time in one's late youth. He was now thirty-five, but looked well over forty. The buoyancy of his greeting soon gave way to an ill-concealed dejection or fatigue.

"What are you doing, Theo? Tell me about yourself. I've got to go out to dinner, but I have a whole hour before I have to dress. Can we sit down and have a drink somewhere?"

"I'm free, Rip."

"Come on—the Muenchinger-King! Put your bike in the back seat. Gee, I'm glad to see you. You've been teaching somewhere —is that right?"

I told him what I had been doing and what I was doing. I pulled out of my purse a clipping of the advertisement I had placed in the Newport paper. There was something refreshing and moving about the selflessness of his attention, but I was soon aware that it was precisely the relief of not talking or thinking about himself that he was enjoying. Finally I fell silent. His eyes kept returning to the clipping.

"You know all these languages?"

"Hit or miss and a bit of bluff, Rip."

"Have you a good number of students or listeners, or whatever you call them?"

"Just about as many as I can handle."

"You know German, too?"

"I went to German schools in China when I was a boy and have kept up my interest in it ever since."

"Theo?—"

"Call me Ted, will you, Rip? 'Theophilus' is unmanageable and 'Theo' is awkward. Everybody calls me Ted or Teddie, now."

"All right . . . listen, I have an idea. Next spring, in Berlin, there's going to be a banquet and two-day reunion for the men on both sides who fought in the air. Bury the hatchet, see what I mean? Hands across the sea. Gallant enemies. Toasts to the dead and all that. I want to go. I've got to go. And I want to get a little practice in the German language first. I had two years of German in prep school and I had a German grandmother. Now at that meeting I'd like to be able to show that I can at least stumble around in German. . . . Ted, could you find two two-hour lessons a week for me?"

"Yes. Early morning all right for you? Eight o'clock? I'm giving up some of those tennis coaching hours now that the pro's come back."

"Fine."

He looked down at the table a moment. "It won't go down well with my wife; but this is a thing I *want* to do, and, by Jesus, *I'll do it.*"

"Your wife doesn't like anything that has to do with Germany?"

"Oh, it isn't that! She has a hundred reasons against my going. Leaving her alone with the children in New York. She thinks that any recall of the War makes me nervous and high-strung. God damn it, this trip would make all that easier for me. And there's the *expense*, Ted—the useless *expense*! Mind you, I love my wife; she's a wonderful woman, but she hates useless expense. We have the New York house and we have this cottage. She thinks that's all she can manage. But, Ted, I've got to go. I've got to shake their hands. Bury the hatchet, see what I mean? They tell me I'm as well known over there as Richthofen is over here. Can you understand how I feel about it?"

"Yes, I do."

"Gee, it's great seeing you again. It gives me the strength I need to put this thing through. Don't you think I owe them the courtesy of making an attempt to speak German? You can start me picking it up again this summer; and I'll work like a fool on it for the rest of the year. God knows, I have nothing else to do."

"What do you mean by that, Rip?"

"I have an office. . . . The idea was that I was to manage my wife's property. But the money kept getting bigger and the advisers at the bank kept getting more and more important— so that there was less and less for me to do."

I got the idea and answered quickly, "What would you like to do?"

He rose and said, "Do? Do? Suggest something. I'd like to be a streetcar conductor. I'd like to be a telephone repairman!" He brushed his hand across his forehead and looked about him almost feverishly; then concluded with forced joviality, "I'd like to break my engagement tonight and go out to dinner with you, *but I can't*," and he sat down again.

"Well," I said in German, "I'm not leaving town. We can have dinner some other night."

He pushed his glass backward and forward broodingly, as though that possibility was doubtful. "Ted, do you remember how Gulliver in the land of the little people—"

"In Lilliput—"

"In Lilliput was tied to the ground by thousands of small silk threads? That's me."

I rose and looked him straight in the eye: "You're going to that banquet in Germany."

He returned my seriousness, lowering his voice. "I don't see how. I don't see where I'll get the money."

"I always thought you came of a very well-to-do family."

"Didn't you know?" He named his birthplace. "In 1921, in my city three large companies and five prominent families went bankrupt."

"Did you have any inkling of that when I saw you in Paris?"

He pointed to his head. "Oh, more than an inkling. But fortunately I was engaged to a girl with considerable means. I told her that I had nothing but my severance pay. She laughed and said, 'Darling, of course, you have money. You're engaged to look after my property and you'll be very well paid for that.' . . . I spent my last hundred dollars getting to the church."

In 1919 and 1920 and in the years immediately following I came to know a large number of combat veterans—to say nothing, for the present, of those whom it was my duty to interrogate in a later war. (My part in "Rip's war," as has been said, had been safely passed among the defenders of Narragansett Bay.) As could be expected the marks left by that experience on the veteran varied from man to man; but in one group the aftereffects were particularly striking—the airmen. The fighting men on land and sea in early youth experienced what journalists called their "glorious hour"—the sense of weighty responsibility bound up with belonging to a "unit," exposure to extreme fatigue, to danger, and to death; many carried the inner burden of having killed human beings. But the "hour" of the first generation of combat aviators comprised all this and something in addition. Air combat was new; its rules and practice were improvised daily. The acquisition of technical accomplishment *above the earth* filled them with a particular kind of pride and elation. There were no gray-haired officers above them. They were pioneers and frontiersmen. Their relations with their fellow-fliers and even with their enemies partook of a high camaraderie. Unrebuked, they invented a code of chivalry with the German airmen. None would have stooped to attack a disabled enemy plane trying to return to its home base. Both sides recognized enemies with whom they had had encounters earlier, signaled to them in laughing challenge.

They lived "Homerically"; that was what the *Iliad* was largely about—young, brilliant, threatened lives. (Goethe said, "The *Iliad* teaches us that it is our task here on earth to enact hell daily.") Many survivors were broken by it and their later lives were a misery to themselves and to others. ("We didn't have the good fortune to die," as one of them said to me.) Others continued to live long and stoic lives. In some cases, if one looked closely, it was evident that a "spring had broken down" in them, a source of courage and gaiety had been depleted, had been spent. Such was Rip.

There was some discussion as to where Rip and I could meet for an eight o'clock class. "I'd like you to come over to my place, but the children would be having their breakfast and my wife would be running in and out to remind me of things I should do."

"I think Bill Wentworth would let us use one of those social rooms behind the gallery at the Casino. We might have to move from room to room while they're cleaning up. I've never seen you in the Casino, but I assume Your Honor is a member there."

He grinned and held his hand beside his mouth as though it were an unholy secret. "I'm a life-member. They don't let me pay any dues," and he poked me as though he'd stolen the cookie jar.

So the lessons began: an hour of vocabulary and grammar followed by an hour of conversation, in which I played the role of a German officer. Rip owned a collection of books in both languages describing those great days. No session passed without his being called to the telephone from which he returned with an enlarged list of the day's agenda, but he had a notable gift for immediately resuming his concentration. There was no doubt that he derived great enjoyment from the work; it touched some deep layer of self-recovery within him. He studied intensively between sessions; and so did I. ("Did his homework," as he called it.) My daily program permitted little time for desultory conversation at the close of the lesson, nor did his. When he rose he consulted the list of errands he must do: register certain letters at the Post Office; take the dog to the vet's; call for Miss So-and-so, his wife's part-time secretary; take Eileen to Mrs. Brandon's dancing class at eleven and call for her at twelve. . . . Apparently Mrs. Vanwinkle needed her car and chauffeur the greater part of the day. His appearance began to improve; he laughed more frequently, with some of the buoyancy of our first meeting on Bellevue Avenue. But there was no word that he had received permission to go to Germany.

One evening I paid my respects at Mrs. Cranston's.

"Good evening, Mr. North," Mrs. Cranston said graciously, eyeing a straw box I was carrying. It was lined with moss and contained some jack-in-the-pulpits, trilliums, and other flowers whose names I did not know. "Wild flowers! Oh, Mr. North, how could you know that I value wild flowers above all others!"

"I believe, ma'am, that it's against the law to dig some of these up, but at least I rode outside the city limits to gather them. I've also borrowed a trowel and a flashlight and am ready to replant them around your house at any point you indicate to me."

Henry Simmons happened at that moment to enter from the street.

"Henry, look at what Mr. North has brought me. Henry, help him replant them under Edweena's window where she will find them when she returns. A gift like that is a gift to us all and I thank you heartily for my share in it." She tapped her table bell. "Jerry will bring you a pitcher of water. That will make the flowers feel at home at once."

Neither Henry nor I was an experienced horticulturist, but we did our best. Then we washed our hands and returned to the parlor where some illicit refreshment was waiting for us.

"We have missed you lately," said Mrs. Cranston.

"We thought you had shifted your affections to Narragansett Pier, Teddie, I swear we did."

"And I missed you, ma'am, and you, Henry. I have some late-evening students now; and on some days my schedule is so crowded that I fall into bed at ten o'clock."

"Now you're not going to overwork and make a dull dog of yourself, are you, cully?"

"Money! Money!" I sighed. "I'm still hunting for that little apartment. I've looked at a dozen, but the rent is more than I'm ready to pay. A number of my older students have offered to make me a present of a very acceptable apartment in their former stable or an empty gardener's house, but I have learned the rule that the relations between landlord and tenant should be as impersonal as possible."

"It's a very good rule, but admits of an occasional exception," replied Mrs. Cranston, tacitly alluding to Edweena's possession of the "garden apartment" and probably to a number of her other lodgers.

"I think I've found the real right thing. It's not in an elegant neighborhood. The furnishings are modest but neat and clean; and it's within my means, after I've done a bit more haggling. I am not of a spendthrift nature, Mrs. Cranston, being wholly New England on my father's side and almost wholly Scottish on my mother's. In fact, I am what New Englanders call 'near.' Schoolboys say 'chinchy.'"

Mrs. Cranston laughed. "In Rhode Island we often say 'close.' I am not ashamed to say that I am fairly 'close' in my dealings."

Henry was indignant. "Why, Mrs. Cranston, you are the most generous person I've ever known. You have a heart of gold!"

"I never liked that expression, Henry. I would not have been able to run this house and keep my head above water, if I had not been 'careful.' There's another word for you, Mr. North. I hate close-fisted stinginess, of course; but I certainly recommend a firm grasp on what money should and should not do." She sat back in her chair, warming up to the subject. "Now twenty and thirty years ago Newport was famous for reckless spending. You wouldn't believe the amount of money that could be thrown away in a single night—to say nothing of a single season. But also you wouldn't believe the stories of miserliness, penny-pinching, meannesses—what's the word that's the opposite of extravagance, Mr. North?"

"Parsimony?"

"That's it!"

"Avarice?"

"Listen to that, Henry: That's what comes of a college education; hitting the nail on the head. Edweena's fond of saying that extravagance—give me another word, Mr. North."

"Conspicuous waste."

"Oh, what a beauty!—that conspicuous waste and avarice are related; they're two sides of the same desperateness. 'Newport avarice,' she used to say, 'was of a special kind. They all had millions, but their behavior was like a fever-chart: it would go up and down.' There was one hostess who would send out invitations for a big party—two hundred on gold plate; catering and additional staff from Delmonico's or Sherry's. But four days before the party she'd come down with an attack of some kind and cancel the whole thing. When this had happened a number of times her dearest friends made plans for an 'emergency dinner' in case of another cancellation. She was the same lady who went through two seasons in two evening gowns; she appeared in the black or the purple one. She'd write orders for dresses to be sent up from New York, but she'd forget to mail the letter. These people think that no one notices! There's some demon inside them that robs them of the ability to look an expenditure in the face. It's a sickness, really."

Here followed some staggering examples of penuriousness and "trimming."

"Why," said Henry, "there's a woman in town now—a very young woman, too. She's married to a man as famous as General Pershing—"

"Almost, Henry."

"Thank you, ma'am. 'Almost as famous' as General Pershing."

"No names, remember! A rule of the house."

"She has one all-absorbing interest: cruelty to animals. She's given half a dozen shelters to communities around here and pays their upkeep. She's on the National Anti-carve-'em-up Society. She gets hysterical about feathers on hats. But the stories—"

Mrs. Cranston broke in: "Mr. North, she does much of her own shopping. She puts on a thick brown veil, gets in her car, and goes down to those shipping supply shops; sends her chauffeur inside to tell the butcher that 'Mrs. Edom' would like to speak to him outside. Mrs. Edom was the woman who *used* to be her housekeeper. She buys a whole side of beef from the salt-barrel. Takes two weeks to soak the salt out of it—*half*-soak the salt out. That's what the national hero and his children eat. She drives out to the Portuguese market and buys great milk cans of their kale soup with their *linguiça* sausages in it. When her servants protest and resign she scarcely gives them a civil letter of recommendation. She replaces them from those immigrant employment agencies in Boston and Providence. But she comes of an old Bellevue Avenue family and she must keep up her social position. About every ten days she gives a dinner party—catering from Providence; spends all the money she skimped for. Oh, it makes me boil—to think of that wonderful husband of hers and her children living on corned beef and kale soup while she spends thousands on dogs and cats!"

"Well, Mrs. Cranston, we have a saying in the Old Country: kind to animals, cruel to humans."

"It's a kind of sickness. Mr. North, let's talk about something pleasant."

I came to know the limits to which Mrs. Cranston could go in discussing any unfavorable aspect of the Newport she loved.

The lessons went on in fine shape, but the sweeping and dusting and the telephone calls from Rip's home were no small inconvenience. One day Rip asked me: "Do you ever take pupils on Sunday morning?"

"Yes, I have."

"Could you manage one of my sessions every Sunday morning about eleven? My wife goes to church then; I don't. . . . Would that be all right? . . . So I'll pick you up at the 'Y' next Sunday at a quarter before eleven. I'll take you to a classroom where we won't be disturbed. I belong to a club called the 'Monks' Club'; it's a sort of shooting, fishing, drinking, and dining club, with a little dice-rattling on the side now and then. It's just over the line in Massachusetts, beyond Tiverton. It belongs to a little group of the lively set. No ladies allowed, but every now and then you see some girls there— from New Bedford or Fall River. No one ever shows up before sunset, especially not on Sunday. The Monks have pretty much given up hunting." He added with his confidential grin, "Very expensive membership, but they made me an honorary member —*no dues*! . . . A great place for our work."

The thought of a quarter of an hour's drive disturbed me a little. I'd come to like and admire Rip more and more, but I didn't want to hear his "story"—how Gulliver came to be bound supine by a thousand small silk threads. It was a woeful situation, but there was nothing I could do about it. I felt in my bones that he was burning to tell me the story—the whole sorry business. So far I had never met Mrs. Vanwinkle and had no wish to. I have a ready interest in eccentrics and my Journal was filled with their "portraits," but I shrank from those borderline cases that approach madness—raging jealousy, despotic possessiveness, neurotic avarice. Rip's wife appeared to me to be stark staring mad. This view had been confirmed by a strange event that happened to intrude itself into my daily routine.

I had a pupil whom I was preparing for the college entrance examination in French, a girl of seventeen. Penelope Temple and I were working in the library when Mrs. Temple entered hurriedly:

"Mr. North, please forgive me, but the upstairs telephone is in use and I want to answer a call here. I think it will be very brief."

I rose. "Shall we go into another room, Mrs. Temple?"

"It's not necessary. . . . It's a woman I never met. . . . Yes, Mrs. Vanwinkle? This is Mrs. Temple speaking. I'm sorry to have made you wait, but Mr. Temple is expecting an urgent call on the other telephone. . . . Yes . . . Yes . . . It is true, those were egret feathers I was wearing at the ball when that photograph was taken. . . . Excuse me, let me interrupt. . . . Those feathers belonged to my mother. They are at least thirty years old. We have preserved them with great care. . . . Excuse me interrupting you: the feathers are now falling to pieces and I shall destroy them, as you request. . . . No, kindly do *not* send Mr. Vanwinkle to this house. Any home in America would be proud to receive Mr. Vanwinkle, but he is too distinguished a man to go about town picking up dilapidated feathers. . . . *No*, Mrs. Vanwinkle, I wish you to do me the credit of *believing* me when I tell you that I will destroy the wretched feathers *at once*. Good morning, Mrs. Vanwinkle, thank you for your call. . . . Excuse me again, Mr. North. Penelope, I think the woman's insane."

Twenty minutes later the front door bell rang and down the hall I heard Rip's voice in conversation with Mrs. Temple.

Naturally, I did not mention this episode to Rip.

Our first Sunday morning drive into Massachusetts was on a beautiful day in early July. Rip drove like Jehu, as all *retired* aviators do. Even in that aging car he exceeded the speed limits in city and country. The police never interfered; they were proud to receive a wave of his hand. In order to forefend any confidential communications about the enslaved Gulliver, I plunged into my overworked theory about the nine cities of Troy and of Newport. I made a considerable digression about the great Bishop Berkeley as we passed near his house ("I lived in Berkeley Oval in my freshman year at college," he said). I had just about come to the end of my exposition when we drove up to the door of the Monks' Club. He brought the car to a standstill but remained at the wheel gazing before him.

"Ted?"

"Yes, Rip?"

"You remember that you asked me what I'd like to *do*?"

"Yes."

"I'd like to be a historian. . . . Is it too late?"

"Why, Rip, you've got your niche in history. It isn't too late to pour out all you know about that—begin there and then broaden out."

His face clouded over. "Oh, I wouldn't want to write anything about that. It's what you were saying about the eighteenth century in Newport—Rochambeau and Washington and Berkeley—that reminded me that I'd always wanted to be a historian. . . . Besides, a historian works in a study where he can close the door, doesn't he? Or he can go to some library where there's a SILENCE sign on every table."

"Rip," I ventured, "in New York is your life much like this—a lot of errands during the day and dinners out every night?"

He lowered his voice. "Worse, worse. In New York I do most of the shopping."

"But you have a housekeeper!"

"We *had* a housekeeper—Mrs. Edom. Oh, I wish she were back. Capable, you know—quiet and capable. No arguments."

The Monks' Club had been an important roadside tavern before the Revolution. Many alterations had been made since. It had served as a storehouse, as a home, and as a school, but much of the original structure remained, built of hewn stone with high chimneys and a vast kitchen. The front room must have been originally designed for dancing; there was a fiddlers' gallery opposite the great fireplace. The "Monks" had furnished and adorned it as a luxurious hunting lodge, complete with some masterpieces of taxidermy. We worked upstairs in the library surrounded by maps, files of sporting magazines, law manuals of the Commonwealth of Massachusetts relative to shipping and game-hunting. The room overlooked the front entrance and was large enough for us to stride up and down in during our mock international dialogues. It was ideal for us. At one o'clock we used to collect our textbooks and reluctantly return to Rhode Island.

During our second Sunday morning session the telephone rang at the bottom of the stairs.

"I know who that is! Come along, Ted, I want you to hear this."

"I don't want to hear your private conversations, Rip."

"I *want* you to. You're a part of this—you're a part of my campaign.—Anyway, leave the door open. I swear to you, I *need* you to back me up! . . . Hello? Yes, this is the Monks' Club. . . . Oh, is that you, Pam? I thought you were at church. . . . I told you: I'm having a German lesson. . . . I know it's a sunny day. . . . We went over that before. The children are perfectly safe at Bailey's Beach. There are three lifeguards there—one on a scaffold and two in rowboats; and on the beach there are at least thirty nurses, nannies, governesses, *Fräulein, mademoiselles*, and *gouvernantes*. I cannot and will not sit there for three hours amid a hundred women. . . . Rogers can bring them back, can't he? . . . Then arrange with Cynthia or Helen or the Winstons' chauffeur to bring them. Pamela, I have something to say to you: I shall never go to Bailey's Beach again. . . . No, the children will not drown. Both of them hate to go in the water. They say it 'thtinkth.' . . . No, I don't know where they picked up that word. They say that all the children say so. They want to go to the Public Beach where there's real surf. . . . I will not be disturbed in my lesson. . . . No, there's no one else in the building as far as I know; the staff have gone to church. . . . Pam, be yourself; talk like yourself; don't talk like your mother! . . . I don't want to discuss that over the telephone. . . . Pamela, be your sweet, reasonable self. . . . I have never said anything more disrespectful about your mother than you have said many times. . . . I will be back well before one-thirty. This long-distance call is costing a good deal of money. . . . Yes, I'll pick up some ice cream at the dairy. No, it's got to be at the dairy where I can charge it, because I haven't a penny in my pocket. . . . I have to go back to my lesson now, but I don't wish to hang up on my dear wife, so will you please hang up first? . . . Yes . . . Yes . . . No . . . Goodbye, see you soon."

He rejoined me with raised eyebrows, saying: "Gulliver and the hundreds of silk threads. Every day I cut a few of them."

I made no comment and we went on with our work. He seemed to be reinvigorated, or should I say, proud of himself.

I was getting caught up in a situation that was more than I could handle. What I needed was not advice—which I have seldom found profitable—but more facts; not gossip but facts. I thought I knew the reason why Rip was a diminished man. I wanted to know more about his wife. I wanted to be sure that I was being just to her; to be just you must seek out all the facts you can get. I felt that I had reached the end of what Mrs. Cranston and Henry Simmons could tell me.

Where could I go for solid facts about Pamela Vanwinkle?

Suddenly I thought of Bill Wentworth. I asked him for a half hour of his time. Again at the end of the day I found myself in his office among the shining trophies. I told him about the German lessons, the constant interruptions, and the sheer servitude to which my friend had been reduced. "Bill, how long have you known Colonel Vanwinkle?"

"Let me see. Pamela Newsome—as I knew her—brought him here in the summer of 1921 soon after they were married."

"Had you known her long?"

"Since she was a child. During the summer she was in here every day; since her marriage she scarcely appears here at all. Her parents are old Newporters."

"Are many Newporters aware of the tight reins she holds over him?"

"Mr. North, they're the laughing-stock of the town."

"How is it that she has so much money in her own name?"

"The Newsomes are not so much a family as a corporation. Every child on reaching twenty-one gets a large bundle of stock —well over a million, they say—and continues to get more annually. . . . She was a very difficult girl. She never got on with her parents. Perhaps that's the reason why—when she became engaged in the fall of 1920—they gave her their Newport cottage and themselves started going to Bar Harbor for the summer."

"Excuse my frankness, Bill, but is she as miserly and hard-driving as they say?"

"My wife was a long-time friend of their housekeeper, Mrs. Edom, a fine woman, a strong character. Mrs. Edom used to call on Mrs. Wentworth on an occasional Sunday morning. It broke her heart to see what Pamela was doing to the Colonel. You wouldn't believe what went on in that house. Mrs. Edom used to come to my wife for comfort."

"Bill, why has the Colonel so few friends?"

"Everybody likes him—not only admires him, but likes him. But both men and women are made uncomfortable by the picture they see. Mr. North, before the war there were many young men around here who did nothing—simply enjoyed themselves and nobody thought the worse of them. But times have changed. They have jobs, even if they don't need the money. Idleness is out of fashion; it's made fun of. And everybody can see the bad effects of it. We've seen it before—a poor man married to a very rich girl; she cracks the whip and he jumps through the hoop like a monkey."

I gave him my picture of the young man who had had his "glorious hour" too early in life and whose vitality or willpower had been broken by it. I went on to tell him how Rip was beginning to lean on me to help him get some freedom.

"Well, if you have any influence on him urge him to get a job. If what I've heard is right, he hasn't a penny. He has to crawl to her for an allowance which she can give or she can withhold. Now I'm going to tell you a story that I've never told to a soul, and I'm trusting you. The second summer he was here the Board of Governors made him an honorary member of the Casino. I asked him to call on me the day before so that I could explain to him how we were setting up the ceremony. I told him that perhaps his wife might want to come, but he telephoned me later that she would be present at the ceremony, but that on that rehearsal morning she was busy with one of her 'cruelty to animals' committees. Well, he arrived; it's always a pleasure to meet him—a fine fellow, and all that. I told him a photographer would be present; we wanted the picture to hang on our walls. There it is! We never give out publicity photos for the newspapers, except during the Tennis Championship Week. I told him the Governors would be pleased if he wore his uniform and his medals. He said he had his uniform and a few medals. He'd sat beside the Mayor on the grandstand at the Fourth of July parade. Which medals did they want? I told him they hoped he'd wear the American 'big three' and the French and English ones. 'I haven't got them, Bill.' Then he grinned. Do you know his grin?"

"Oh, yes, whenever he talks about his war record or his celebrity he grins."

"He said that he'd wanted to buy a birthday present for his wife on her first birthday since their marriage, and that he'd borrowed money on them as security from those medal and trophy dealers in New York. Now, I'll tell you one thing more: *she didn't come to the ceremony.* She hates his fame; she's afraid it may 'go to his head' and spoil him. Mr. North, urge him to get a job. He'll be a different man."

"Thanks, Bill. Has he been offered any?"

"Of course he has—with that famous name of his. Corporation directorships, things like that. She won't let him consider them. You know he comes from western New York State. The Governor wanted to create one for him, provided that he'd move to Albany. I heard it was about twenty thousand a year, State Marshal. His wife laughed at it. To her that's peanuts. She said it was degrading."

"Is it true that she feeds the family mostly salt beef and kale soup?"

"Oh. The town makes up stories about her. But she does buy canned goods by the gross."

So it is profitable to go to the right person for advice, after all.

The next Sunday morning we were up in the library at the Monks' Club having a breezy time, breaking irregular verbs. Rip had arrived at that borderline in learning a new language when words hitherto only recognized in print become vocables—an exhilarating feeling.

"Na ja, Herr Major, ich kenne Sie."

"Und ich kenne Sie, verehrter Herr Oberst. Sie sind der Herr Oberst Vanderwinkle, nicht wahr?"

"Jawohl. War das nicht ein Katzenjammer über dem Hügel Saint-Charles-les-Moulins? Dort haben Sie meinen linken Flügel kaputt gemacht. Sie waren ein Teufel, das kann man sagen."

Rip glanced out of the window. "Jesus! There's my wife." Sure enough, there was the car and the chauffeur was coming up the walk. The doorbell rang. "Go downstairs. Pretend you're the club steward or something. Say that I gave orders not to be disturbed until one o'clock."

I put on my blazer ("YALE 1920"). "I can't be a steward in this. I'll pretend I'm a member. I'll work something out." I descended the stairs slowly and opened the door.

"Sir, Mrs. Edom is calling and wishes to speak to Colonel Vanwinkle."

I caught a glimpse of "Mrs. Edom" in a deep brown veil sitting in the car. I said loudly, "I think he gave orders that he was not to be disturbed on any account. Has something serious happened in his home? Fire? Appendicitis? Mad dog bite?"

"I don't . . . think so."

"Wait. I'll see if he can be seen. Tell Mrs. Edom that his German professor is very strict about interruptions. He's a holy terror."

Rip was waiting for me on the stairs. "She says she's Mrs. Edom and she wishes to speak to you."

"She'll come in. Nothing can stop her."

"I'm going to lock the door leading upstairs. It's half-past twelve already. I'll stay down and keep her company."

"Damn it, I want to hear what you say. I'm going to stretch out on the floor of the fiddlers' gallery. She can't see me from there." I went down to the front room, locked the inner staircase door, put the key in my pocket, picked up a copy of *Yachting*, and sat down to read it. There was a noise up in the gallery. Rip had pulled a coverlet about himself and was lying down. The doorbell rang again. I opened the door and faced a determined woman. She had thrown the veil up about her hat—a very good-looking young woman, furious. She pushed the door open and passed me into the front room.

"Good morning."

"Good morning, madam. Forgive me if I say that it is a rule of the club that ladies are not admitted here. There is no reception room for women."

"Kindly tell Colonel Vanwinkle that Mrs. Edom wishes to speak to him."

"Madam, as the chauffeur told you . . ."

She sat down. "Excuse me, are you the steward of the club?"

"No," I said, deeply offended.

"Who is in authority here? . . . Are there no servants here?"

"The caretaker and his wife seem to have gone to church."

"Sir, will you kindly tell me whom I am addressing?"

I was amiability—dare I say: charm?—itself. "Mrs. Edom, surely you know something about men's clubs. It's a rule of the club that *no* member may be addressed by the name he bears in private life. We are addressed by the name given us by the Abbot. I am Brother Asmodius. The member to whom you have been referring is Brother Bellerophon."

"Childish nonsense!"

"Since the Middle Ages and the Crusaders' Orders. I happen to be a Mason and the member of a fraternity. In each club

I have been assigned a name to be used in that club. You surely know that monks in a religious order do the same. My wife finds it hard to forgive me that I do not tell her every detail of our ceremonies. . . . I think I remember hearing that you are the housekeeper in Brother Bellerophon's home."

She glared at me in silence. Then she rose, saying, "I *will* speak to the Colonel." She went to the door leading upstairs and shook the knob.

I was cleaning my fingernails. "That German professor locked it, I expect. I wouldn't put anything beyond him."

"I shall sit here until the Colonel comes down."

"Would you like something to read, Mrs. Edom?"

"No, thank you."

I resumed my reading in silence. She looked about her. "I see that you monks—as you call yourselves—shoot deer, foxes, and birds. Contemptible sports!"

"There's less and less of that now. You can understand why." She stared at me in silence. "Out of respect for Brother Bellerophon's wife." Silence. "Surely, you know of her crusade for the prevention of cruelty to animals. . . . What a fine woman she must be! Saves the lives of dogs and cats and wild animals every year! A great heart! A big heart!"

I strolled across the room to straighten a picture. Nonchalantly I added, "Having heard what an intelligent woman she is—and what an excellent wife and mother—I have always been surprised that she permits her children to go to Bailey's Beach. My wife wouldn't let our children be seen dead there."

"What is unwise about that?"

"I am surprised you ask, Mrs. Edom. The transatlantic sea lane and the Gulf Channel both pass a few miles from that point. Hundreds of ships in each direction go by all day and night. And by some unfortunate combination of land, tides, and currents the rubbish thrown overboard finds its way to Bailey's Beach as to a magnet. Each morning the employees rake up baskets of trash: seamen's boots, decaying fruit, dead parrots, picture postcards unsuitable for children, and other things too distasteful to mention."

She stared at me appalled. "I do not believe that to be true."

"It is very discourteous of you to say that, Mrs. Edom. In this club gentlemen do not call one another liars."

"I beg your pardon. I meant to say that I find that difficult to believe."

"Thank you . . . I have also heard that the lady about whom we are talking is careful about the diet furnished to her family and staff. Do you know my wife and I think that kale soup is one of the most nutritious—and delicious—dishes that exist." (Pause.) "But a very experienced doctor advised us not to let children under twelve eat that highly spiced *linguiça* sausage that is cooked in it at the Portuguese market. . . . And beef and pork soaked in brine—excellent! The British Navy served it to their seamen for centuries and ruled the sea. The Battle of Trafalgar was said to have been won on corned beef. That same doctor advised my wife, however, that too much of that salted meat is not to be recommended for young children, even after weeks of soaking in clear water."

"Does Brother Bellerophon—as you call him—come often to this club?"

"Not as often as we'd like. I think I can say that he is the most beloved and admired member here. The club members, who are all very wealthy men, became aware that his family is less fortunately *provided* than themselves. They made him honorary member which requires no dues. Four of them, including myself, offered him high positions in their companies and enterprises. Brother Prudentius has offered him a vice-presidency in an insurance company in Hartford. Brother Candidus is developing resident areas in Florida. Brother Bellerophon's name on the letterhead, his presence, his famous probity, would bring the firm millions of dollars which they would be glad to share with him. And so the rest of us. Brother Bellerophon is too deeply attached to his family; his wife does not wish to move to Connecticut or to Miami. I am hoping that he will change his mind and join my company from sheer necessity."

"What business are you engaged in, sir?"

"I'd rather not say, Mrs. Edom. But considering his distinguished service to our country, the Federal Government would not be inclined to examine our operations too closely." I lowered my voice. "Do you think I can hope that he will?"

"Brother Asmodius, I have no desire to continue this conversation."

"A man must work. A man must stand up on his own feet, ma'am."

"I will pound on that door!"

"Oh, Mrs. Edom, don't do that! You would wake up the girls!"

"*Girls!* What girls?"

"Naturally on the weekends there are some convivial times here. A little drinking. And some pleasant company from New Bedford and Fall River. The members return to their homes at a very late hour. But we allow their charming friends to sleep later. They will be picked up in a limousine at two."

"*Girls!* Do you mean to tell me that the Colonel is upstairs now among a lot of Jezebels?"

I looked thoughtful. "I don't recognize the name. . . . I met an Anita, a Ruth, a Lilian, an Irene. And a Betty."

"I am leaving this minute.—No! I *will* pound on that door."

"Madam, as a member of this club I must restrain you from creating an unseemly disorder." I added bitingly, "I had always heard that Mrs. Edom conducted herself as a woman of distinction, which has not always been said of her mistress."

"What do you mean by *that*?"

I pointed to the clock. "You have only a quarter of an hour to wait."

"What did you mean by that unpleasant remark?"

"It was not an unpleasant remark. It was a tribute to yourself, Mrs. Edom."

"I am waiting—"

"If you sit down and stop abusing this club, I shall . . . give you a short explanation."

She sat down and glared at me, expectantly. I returned to polishing my nails, but I began to speak offhandedly: "My dear wife does not engage in gossip. I have never heard her repeat a malicious remark—but once. By the way, we took the doctor's advice. We no longer serve the children kale soup and beef in brine."

"You were about to tell me some remark about Mrs. Vanwinkle."

"Oh, yes." I lowered my voice and moved my chair toward hers. "There is a nickname that is going around about that otherwise *wonderful* woman."

"A nickname!"

"My wife heard it from Mrs. Delgarde who heard it from Lady Bracknell who heard it from Mrs. Venable herself."

"Mrs. Venable!"

I rose. "No! I don't circulate things like that. I've changed my mind."

"You're a very exasperating man, Brother Asmodius. You'd better finish what you began."

"All right," I sighed, "but promise not to repeat it—least of all to Mrs. Vanwinkle."

"I will *not* repeat it."

"Well, Mrs. Venable heard that Mrs. Vanwinkle sent her husband—that great man—to Mrs. Temple's house to pick up a thirty-year-old egret feather, because she refused to believe Mrs. Temple's promised word that she would destroy it herself. Mrs. Venable said, 'I shall not give another penny to those animal shelters until Mrs. Vanwinkle is locked up. She's a Delilah!'"

"Delilah!"

"You remember that Delilah cut short the mighty Samson's hair whereby he lost his strength—so that his enemies could rush into his tent and blind him. She beat on cymbals and tambourines and danced on his prostrate body. Scholars of the Old Testament know very well that the story means that she performed a far more serious operation on him."

Mrs. Vanwinkle had turned as white as a sheet. She was speechless.

"Shall I get you a drink of water?"

"Yes, please do."

When I returned from the kitchen, Rip had climbed out of the fiddlers' gallery, descended the stairs, and was pounding on the locked door. I opened it.

Husband and wife stared at one another in silence. She accepted the glass from my hand without taking her eyes off Rip. Finally she said, "Nicholas, will you ask this dreadful man to leave the room?"

"This is my German professor, Pam. I'm driving him back to Newport in a few minutes. Ted, will you go upstairs and wait until I call you?"

"I'll start walking into town, Rip. You can pick me up on the road. Good morning, ma'am."

And I went out the front door. As I passed the threshold I heard Mrs. Vanwinkle break into a convulsion of weeping.

It was a beautiful day. I walked for a quarter of an hour. Soon after I passed Tiverton I saw Mrs. Vanwinkle's car go by. She had lowered her veil but her head was held high. Not long after Rip stopped for me. I climbed into the car.

"You were very tough, Ted. . . . You were very tough." He started the car. After a few minutes he said, "You were very tough."

"I know I went too far, Rip, and I apologize."

We drove in silence for a while.

Ten miles in silence. Then he said, "I told her you were an old joker way back in college days and that all that about Mrs. Venable was just horse-feathers. . . . But how the hell did you know about Mrs. Temple's goddamned feather?"

"I won't tell."

He stopped the car and cracked my skull against his.

"Oh, you're an old son-of-a-bitch, Ted—*but I got a thousand dollars to go to Berlin!*"

"Well, you gave me a wonderful lunch at the Café de Paris—when you were low in funds, remember?"

7

At Mrs. Keefe's

THE EVENTS that led to my obtaining an apartment occurred during my sixth week in Newport, perhaps later. I was living at the "Y," contentedly enough; my relations there were impersonal and left me time to prepare for my classes. I was on good terms with the superintendent—unjustly called "Holy Joe," for he was not at all sanctimonious. From time to time, for a change, I would descend to the "library" where card games of the family type, like hearts and three jacks, were permitted and desultory conversation tolerated.

It was in this library that I met a remarkable young man whose portrait and unhappy predicaments I find recorded in my Journal. Elbert Hughes was a reedy youth, barely twenty-five, belonging to that often wearisome category of human beings known as "sensitive." This adjective once meant intensely aware of aesthetic and spiritual values; then it took on a sense of someone quick to resent slights; recently it has become a euphemism for someone incapable of coping with even the smaller demands of our daily practical life. Elbert chiefly fulfilled the third description. He was short but delicately proportioned. His eyes were deeply set under a protruding forehead, lending an intensity to his gaze. His fingers were much occupied with a tentative mustache. He was something of a dandy and on cool evenings wore a black velveteen jacket and a flowing black tie, recalling the students I had seen near the Beaux-Arts Academy when I lived in Paris. Elbert gave me a partial account of his life and I presently discovered that he was a sort of genius—subdivision, calligraphic mimicry. He was a Bostonian and had followed courses in a technical high school there, devoting himself passionately to copperplate writing and to lettering, with a particular interest in tombstone inscriptions.

By the age of twenty he had secured a profitable job at a leading jeweler's establishment where he furnished the models for engraved inscriptions on presentation silver, for formal invitations and calling cards. For another firm he wrote diplomas

on parchment and honorary tributes to retiring bank presidents. He made no claims to originality; he imitated scripts
from standard "style books" or from admired early English
and American "plate" in museums and private collections. But
that was not all. He could copy any signature or individual
penmanship after a moment's profound "absorption" in a
model before him. He could furnish a receipt in the hand of
almost any signer of the Declaration of Independence at a moment's notice. He was a wonder.

It was not new to me that these "sensitives" are an unhappy
mixture of humility and boldness. One evening he asked me to
write a sentiment and to sign it. I wrote (in French, of which
he did not know a word) a *maxime* of the Duc de la Rochefou-
cauld and signed it with my own name. He studied it gravely
for a few minutes and then wrote: "*Mr. Theodore Theophilus
North regrets that he will be unable to accept the kind invitation
of the Governor of the Commonwealth of Massachusetts and of
Mrs. So-and-so for such-and-such an evening.*" It was in my own
hand, staggeringly in my own hand. Then he wrote it again
and passed it over to me, saying lightly, "That is how Edgar
Allan Poe would have written it. I like to do his handwriting
best. When I do his handwriting I feel him moving my hand.
People say I look like him. Can you see that I look like him?"

"Yes. But I never heard that he was much of a draughtsman."

"We're a lot alike though. We were both born in Boston.
. . . The thing I like to draw best is the lettering on tomb-
stones. There's a lot about graves and tombs in Poe's writings.
He's my favorite writer that ever lived."

"What are you doing in Newport?" I asked.

"Much the same kind of work I did in Boston. A man named
Forsythe saw some presentation copies I had made on vellum
of a poem by Edgar A. Poe in Poe's handwriting, and some
alphabets I had drawn up in several styles. He said he was an
architect and building contractor with an office in Newport.
He offered me a pretty good salary to come down here and
work for him. I do lettering for the fronts of buildings—post
offices, town halls, things like that. I do gravestones for masons
too. I like that best."

I had been staring at our (mine and Poe's) replies to the
Governor.

"I'll show you something else," he said. He extracted from a portfolio beside him a leaf of the Governor's personal stationery —seal embossed—and wrote the invitation for which he had twice written the reply.

"Is that the Governor's own handwriting?"

"I've done lots of work for both his office and his mansion. I've worked for all the best stationers and I collect samples. I've got a trunk full of the best stuff. There are collectors all over the world, you know—they keep it secret. I trade duplicates." He laid before me: "The White House," "L'Ambassade de France," "John Pierpont Morgan," "The Foreign Office," Enrico Caruso's cartoon of himself as a letterhead, a bookplate by Stanford White. . . .

"Are you doing that kind of work for Forsythe here in Newport?"

"Not very much," he answered, evasively, returning the "samples" to their portfolio. "We do something like it."

He changed the subject.

Elbert Hughes might have been, *should* have been, good company, but he wasn't. He suffered like many of his kind from alternations of vitality and depletion. He would launch forth on a subject with enthusiasm only to fall silent in a short time like a deflated bellows. He was engaged to be married. Abigail was a wonderful woman; she was (he whispered) divorced; she was six years older than he was and had two children. He added, with abated enthusiasm, that he had saved up three thousand dollars to buy a house (where they would presumably live gloomily ever after). One couldn't help admiring and even liking Elbert, but I began losing interest in him; I tend to avoid the disconsolate. I am indebted to him, however, for awakening my interest in an aspect of Newport that I had neglected. Elbert took to bringing down to our little library the work he was doing; he said that the light was better than that provided in our rooms upstairs, as indeed it was. I would occasionally use the library for my own "homework," when it was not also occupied by a conversational gathering. One evening I asked permission to see what he was engaged upon. He answered confusedly that it was just "some nonsense he was doing for fun." It was a letter from the eminent historian George Bancroft inviting the equally eminent Louis Agassiz to an evening

of "punch and good talk." Elbert seemed to have given himself
the enjoyment of writing Agassiz's reply to this attractive invitation.

"Where are the originals of these letters?" I asked.

"Mr. Forsythe has a big collection. He says he advertises for
them and buys them from the owners."

Entirely apart from Elbert's "fun" with such documents, I
was delighted with them. That was Newport's Fifth City—the
city that had disappeared leaving little trace behind it—the
Newport of the mid-nineteenth-century intellectuals. My various jobs were nourishing my interest in the Second City, the
Sixth City, and the Seventh City; I was living in the Ninth City.
In my early twenties I had fancied myself as an archaeologist.
Here was a field for excavation. Dr. Schliemann had possessed
a large private fortune; I had not a dollar to spare. I reminded
myself of an old saying I had read somewhere: "To the impassioned will nothing is impossible."

There were still a few half-mornings and half-afternoons free
in my schedule. I prepared myself by visiting the "People's Library," and "reading up" on the period. Then I visited the an-
tiquaries and second-hand stores. I nursed the hope that I might
come upon things that no one else had spotted. I concentrated
on letters and manuscripts—diaries, correspondences, job-lots
of books and papers from old houses, family photograph al-
bums, the emptyings of attics. . . . The James family, the
Agassiz families (the great father and the great son), the Ban-
crofts, Longfellow. Longfellow spent his summers at Nahant,
but he often visited his friend George Washington Greene at
West Greenwich near Narragansett Bay and Greene's parents
who lived in Newport. Two of his best-known poems show his
interest in our First City, "The Skeleton in Armor" and "The
Jewish Cemetery at Newport."

The "antique shops" were still selling objects from the First
and Second Cities. The vogue for taking a half-condescending
pleasure in the furniture and decoration of the Victorian age
was still twenty years in the future. Here and there I found
collections of daguerreotypes, framed letters or poems signed
by the notable men of the time; but these had already been
discovered and were beyond my means. I descended to the
second-hand stores and received permission to climb ladders

with a flashlight, to poke in old barrels and open old dressers, the flotsam and jetsam of the years: here a clergyman's wife had sold a lifetime of her husband's sermons for rag paper, a thrifty merchant's family their father's account books, and so on.

Almost at once I made a small discovery. It was a schoolgirl's "memory book," bound in coral velvet, moth-eaten, mouldy. There were faded blue photographs of picnics and birthday parties, dance cards and autographs. On one page H. W. Longfellow had copied out "The Children's Hour," "for my dear young friend Faith Somerville." With a show of casual interest I bought the book for two dollars; the following autumn I sold it in New York for thirty. I found bundles of Somerville papers and bought them for forty cents a pound. My idea was that somehow I might penetrate that magic world (my father used to call it "plain living and high thinking") and glimpse those enchanted late afternoons in Newport when professors played croquet with their children until fireflies hovered over the wickets and a voice called, "Come in, children, and wash your hands before supper."

I knew that any first edition of a work by Edgar Allan Poe was among the greatest prizes in all American book-collecting and that any letter from his pen was eagerly sought. Poe had paid an extensive visit to Providence, only thirty miles away; but there was no record of his having visited Newport. If I could discover a bundle of Poe's letters—what a lively interest for me and, later, what an addition to my capital savings! (No biographer had yet drawn up the wide spectrum of *that* boyhood's ambitions: poet, detective, gentleman, actor perhaps [like his mother], metaphysician ["Eureka!"], cryptographer, landscape gardener, interior decorator, tormented lover—too great and diverse a load for any American to carry.)

I found no Poe letters, but his name was brought to my attention repeatedly. One evening I found under my door a copy of his poem "Ulalume," signed by the poet and a triumph of Elbert Hughes's art. Meeting Hughes by chance in the hall I thanked him; but I tore the counterfeit up.

There was no night watchman prowling the corridors of the "Y," but a night clerk, Maury Flynn, tended the front desk. Maury was a cheerless old man in poor health. Like many night attendants in hotels and clubs he was a retired policeman. One night toward three in the morning I was awakened by a knock at my door. It was Maury.

"Ted, are you a partickler friend of Hughes in 32?"

"I know him, Maury. What's the matter?"

"Fellow in the next room says he's been having nightmares. Groaning like. Falling out of bed. This fellow telephoned me. Would you go in and see if you could calm him down, sort of?"

I threw on a bathrobe and got into some slippers and went down to Room 32. Maury had left the door ajar and the light on. Elbert was sitting on the edge of his bed, his head bent over his knees.

"Elbert! Elbert! What's the matter?"

He raised his head, gazed at me vacantly, and resumed his former position. I shook him brusquely but he made no response. I looked about the room. On the center table lay an unfinished example of his accomplished art. It was the opening of "The Fall of the House of Usher." On the bedside table stood a half-empty bottle of "Dr. Quimby's Sleeping Syrup." I sat down and watched him for a while, repeating his name in a low insistent voice. Then I went to the washstand, dipped a washrag in cold water, and applied it to his face, the nape of his neck, and to his wrists—as I used to do to drunken companions in Paris in 1921. I now did this several times.

At last he raised his head again and mumbled, "Hello, Ted. Nothing . . . Bad dreams."

"Get up, Elbert. I'm going to walk you up and down the corridor a few times. Breathe, breathe deep."

He fell back on the bed and shut his eyes. More cold water. I slapped his face and struck his shoulder sharply. At last we were walking the corridor. We must have done a quarter of a mile. We returned to the room. "No! You remain standing. Take some more deep breaths. . . . Tell me about your dreams. . . . Yes, you can hold on to the wall."

"Buried alive. Can't get out. Nobody can hear me."

"Do you take this syrup all the time?"

"Don't sleep very good. Don't want to sleep because . . . *they* come. But I've got to sleep, because when I don't, I make mistakes in my work. They take it off my pay."

"Do you know Dr. Addison?"

"No."

"Why don't you? He's the 'Y's doctor. He's in and out of the building all the time. I'm going to send him to see you tomorrow night. Talk to him; tell him everything. And don't drink any more of this stuff. Will you give me permission to take this bottle away? . . . And, Elbert, don't read any more Edgar Allan Poe. He's not right for you—all those crypts and vaults. Do you think you'll be able to sleep calmly now? . . . Do you want me to read aloud to you for ten minutes?"

"Yes, will you, Ted?"

"I'm going to read to you in a language you don't understand. All you have to know is that it's serene and beautiful like the printing of the Elzevirs."

So I read him from Ariosto and he went off like a baby.

I lost touch with Elbert for about ten days. Dr. Addison gave him some sleeping pills and some stern advice about his diet; he had been scarcely eating at all. I continued my search for the Fifth City. In another store—now down almost at the rags-bottles-and-sacks level—I had another stroke of luck: the rejected sketches of the elder Henry James's commentary on a work of Swedenborg. They were resting in a barrel together with bundles of old letters to the family. I separated the letters from the theology and bought them for very little. I had first become interested in the writing Jameses while reading (in my earliest phase), with mounting dissatisfaction, William James's *Varieties of Religious Experience*; more recently I had read a number of his brother's novels. The James family lived in Newport throughout the Civil War. The two eldest sons had left to join the Army. William, Henry, and their sister Alice all had had nervous breakdowns in 1860 and enlistment of those brothers was out of the question. The letters had little to tell me, but I felt I was on the trail.

Within two weeks my teaching schedule became so heavy that I had to give up those researches entirely. What little free time I had was devoted to hunting for an apartment. This was limited to opportunities within my means—among the jerry-built workmen's homes on the streets leading up the slope from the further reach of Thames Street. I rang every doorbell whether there was an advertisement of lodging or not. I had a clear idea of what I wanted: two rooms or one large room, a bath, a cooking facility however simple. I wanted the rooms to be on the second story, entered by an outside stairway so that (yet not the only reason) I would not be required to come and go through the landlord's residence and family. I did not object to crying babies, boisterous children, a location above a kitchen, a sloping roof, proximity to a firehouse or to a convivial fraternal organization or to church bells. This requirement of a separate entrance was not as uncommon as might appear. These old houses were beginning to be subdivided into family apartments; elderly lodgers were increasingly afraid of fires, frequent enough in this run-down area. I was shown many apartments and derived considerable enjoyment from the encounters this search involved.

One morning I found my apartment. I had surveyed the premises and seen the exterior stairway. The mailbox said "Keefe." The door was opened by a thin distrustful woman in her middle fifties. Her face was lined but retained the high coloring characteristic of those living by a northern sea. I learned later that on the death of her husband over twenty years ago she had opened a rooming house and raised two sturdy sons to become merchant seamen. In spite of many disappointments she had never been able to free herself of the idea that a rooming house should have the character of a home. She was distrustful but eager to trust.

"Good morning, Mrs. Keefe. Have you an apartment to let?"

She paused a moment. "I have and I haven't. How long would you want it?"

"All summer, ma'am, if it suited me."

"Are you alone? . . . What is your work?"

"I'm a tennis instructor at the Casino. My name is Theodore North."

"Do you attend any church regularly?"

"I've only been a short time in Newport. During the War I was stationed at Fort Adams. I used to walk into town to attend the evening service at Emmanuel Church."

"Come in and sit down. Excuse my dress; it's early and I'm housecleaning."

She led me into a sitting room that should have been preserved in a museum for generations yet unborn.

"What exactly were you looking for, Mr. North?"

"One large room or two small ones; a bath and some simple kitchen facility; some housecleaning and a change of linen once a week. And I'd like it to be on the second floor with an exterior stairway."

She had been looking me up and down. "How much would you be willing to pay, Mr. North?"

"I was thinking of twenty-five dollars a month, ma'am."

She sighed and examined the floor in silence. I remained silent too. With each of us every penny counted; but she had a weightier anxiety on her mind. "It is occupied at present, but I have told the men there that they must be prepared to give it up on two weeks' notice. They agreed to that."

"You don't find them satisfactory, Mrs. Keefe?"

"I don't know what to think. They don't sleep there. They had me take the beds away. They used it like it was a business office. They brought in a big table to work on. They say they're architects, working on some problem, some prize-contest they want to win. Like a plan for a perfect town, something like that."

"Do they give you any trouble?"

"I don't see them or hear them for a week at a time, except sometimes when they come and go up their back stairs. I never see any of them face to face except when he pays the rent. They keep the doors locked all day and night. They do their own cleaning up. Never any letters; never any telephone calls. Mr. North, they're like ghosts in the house. Never say good morning; never exchange the time of day. I don't call that *roomers*."

She was looking at me with a first sign of confidence, even of appeal.

"Did they give any kind of reference in town when they came? Any other address?"

"The oldest one, I guess he's the head of 'em, gave me the number of his postbox at the Post Office—Number 308. One Sunday noon I saw them all eating at the Thames Street Blue Star Restaurant."

"Have you taken other people up to inspect the apartment?"

"Yes, two married couples. They didn't like it—no beds, hardly any chairs. I guess it didn't look like an apartment to them. Besides, there's the smell."

"Smell!"

"Yes, it's getting all through the house. Some chemical they use."

"Mrs. Keefe, I think you have reason to be worried."

"How do you mean?"

"I don't know yet. Can you take me up there now?"

"Yes . . . Yes, I'd *like* to."

That amazing detective Chief Inspector Theophilus North had sprung to life again. I followed her up the stairs and when she had knocked loudly at the door I gestured to her, smiling, to stand at one side. I put my ear to the crack in the door. I heard a muffled oath, whispered commands, rapid motions, a falling object. Finally the door was unlocked and a tall man with a southern colonel's mustache and goatee, very angry, faced us. He was wearing a white linen coat that I associate with surgeons.

"I'm sorry to disturb you, Mr. Forsythe, but there's a gentleman here who'd like to look at the apartment."

"I asked you to arrange these interruptions at the noon hour, Mrs. Keefe."

"My visitors have to make these calls at their own time. They visit five and six apartments every morning. I'm sorry; that's the way it is."

It was a large room filled with the sunlight that I would seldom be able to enjoy—seeming all the larger because of the sparseness of the furniture. A long trestle-like table ran the length of the room. On one end of it rested what I think would be called a "mock-up" of an ideal village in miniature, a delightful piece of work. The four men stood against the wall as though they were undergoing a military inspection.

To my great surprise the youngest of the men was Elbert Hughes. He was as astonished as I was, and extremely frightened. In my role as detective I knew that it was my task to appear as unsuspicious as possible. I strolled over to Elbert and shook his hand. "Good morning, Hughes. Too bad to be indoors on a fine morning like this. We'll get you out on the tennis courts yet." I gave him a blow on the shoulder. "You look kind of thin and peaked to me, Hughes. *Tennis*, man, that's what you need!—What! Making children's toys? Awfully pretty village that. Excuse me, gentlemen, while I see if there'd be room in these cupboards for my collection of tennis cups."

There was a row of china cupboards, faced with glass and lined with silk. I grasped at their handles, but they were locked. "Locked?—Well, don't take the trouble to unlock them now." I strolled into the bathroom and kitchen. "Just right for me," I said to Mrs. Keefe. "Funny smell, though. I also have a collection of rocks—an old hobby of mine, semiprecious stones. I'd like a good deal of cupboard space for them, too." Returning into the main room I looked about me genially. It appeared as unlike an architect's *atelier* as possible. *There were no wastepaper baskets!* It was as neat and uncluttered as a business office in a department store window—except for one thing: across the open windows were strung sheets of paper, delicately fastened together; they were damp and had been hung out to dry. They had been dyed the color of blond tobacco.

I smiled to Mr. Forsythe and said, "Laundry day, eh?"

"Mrs. Keefe," he said, "I think the gentleman has had time enough to inspect the apartment. We must get back to our work."

I assumed that the making of counterfeit money and the engravers' and etchers' art would require a bulky press and pots of blue and green ink, but nothing of the kind was to be seen. The sheets of paper in the window were certainly being "aged." But I was getting "hot."

"There are some more cupboards for my collections up in that corner," I cried eagerly. They were not furnished with locks. I could hardly reach their handles, but I made two jumps for them. They swung open. To break my fall I clutched at the stacks of paper they contained, bringing down cascades of leaves that covered the floor—yes, "Thick as autumnal leaves that strew the brooks in Vallombrosa." All four men rushed forward to pick them up, but not before I saw that they were copies in a delicate old-fashioned calligraphy of "The Battle Hymn of the Republic," signed by Julia Ward Howe, once resident in Newport. As I lay flat on the floor over them I could see that each was inscribed to a different recipient—"For my dear friend . . . ," "For the Honorable Judge So-and-so . . ." I showed no sign of finding anything remarkable. "Gee, gentlemen, I'm sorry about this," I said, picking myself up. "I hope I haven't sprained my ankle!—I'm ready to go now, Mrs. Keefe. Thank you very much for your patience, gentlemen."

As I started limping out of the door, Mr. Forsythe said, "Mrs. Keefe, I hope you'll allow us to retain the rooms until the end of August—without interruptions. I was about to propose an arrangement of this matter."

"We'll talk that over at another time, Mr. Forsythe. Now I'll leave you to your work."

At the bottom of the stairs I asked, "Can we talk somewhere else—in the kitchen, maybe?"

She nodded and started down the corridor. I turned back and opened the front door, saying loudly: "I'm sorry, Mrs. Keefe, I can't consider it. It would take weeks to get rid of that unpleasant odor. Thank you for your trouble. Good morning, Mrs. Keefe!" I then slammed the front door loudly and followed her on tiptoe to the kitchen.

She watched me open-eyed. "You think they're undesirable roomers, Mr. North?"

"They're forgers."

"*Forgers*, God bless my soul! *Forgers!*"

"They don't make counterfeit money. They make antiques."

"Forgers! I've never had them before. Oh, Mr. North, the father of the Chief of Police was a good friend of my husband's. Shouldn't I go to him?"

"I wouldn't make a big thing of it. They're not harming anybody. Even if they sold a hundred fake letters of George Washington only fools would buy them."

"I don't want them in the house. *Forgers!* What should I do, Mr. North?"

"When is their month up?"

"Like I said, they've agreed to go any time on two weeks' notice."

"You shouldn't let them suspect that you know what they're doing. They're ugly customers. Let everything go on for a few days just as usual. I'll think of something."

"Oh, Mr. North, help me get them out. They pay thirty dollars a month. I'll give it to you for twenty-five. I'll put the beds back and some nice furniture." Suddenly she burst out, "My sister said I should have gone back to Providence when my husband died. She said I wouldn't be happy here. There's an element in this town, she said, that's riff-raff and that attracts riff-raff, and I've seen it over and over again."

I knew her answer, but I asked, "You mean the other side of Thames Street?"

"No! No!" She tossed her head toward the north. "I mean up there: Bellevue Avenue. No fear of God. *Filthy money, that's what I mean!*"

I comforted her as best I could and drove off on my bicycle to a hard day's schedule, whistling. I'd found my apartment and I'd heard the voice of the Ninth City.

At about nine that evening as I sat brushing up my New Testament Greek for one of my students there was a knock at my door. I opened it to Elbert Hughes. He wore the look of the unhappiest man in the world.

"What can I do for you, Elbert? Nightmares again? . . . Well, what is it? Sit down."

He sat down and burst into tears. I waited.

"For God's sake, stop crying and tell me what's the matter."

Sobbing he said, "You know. You saw it all."

"What do I know?"

"They said if I told anyone, they'd crush my hand." He extended his right hand.

"Elbert! Elbert! How did a decent American boy like you get mixed up with a gang like that? . . . What would your mother think, if she knew what you were doing?"

It was a shot in the dark, but it went home. Heavy precipitation. I got up and opened the door: "Stop crying or leave this room!"

"I'll . . . I'll tell you."

"Take this towel and clean up. Drink a glass of water at the washstand and begin at the beginning."

When he'd pulled himself together, he began, "I told you how Mr. Forsythe offered me the job to work for him. Then I found out it wasn't lettering they wanted, but . . . that other thing. They'd bought a lot of first and second editions of *Hiawatha* and *Evangeline* and made me inscribe them to the writer's friends. At first I thought it was a kind of stunt. Then I copied the poems and did the same thing. And short letters by a lot of people. He keeps thinking up new things, like Edgar Allan Poe. Lots of people collect the signatures of the Presidents of the United States."

"Where do they sell these?"

"They don't talk much about it in front of me. By mail, mostly. They have a stamp that says 'John Forsythe, Dealer in Historical Documents and Autographs.' They get a lot of letters every day from Texas and places like that."

For two months he had been working at this, eight hours a day, five and a half days a week. The men wanted him under their eyes every day and night. They lived in a commercial hotel on Washington Square. He was not a man of strong will, but Elbert had won a small battle; he had insisted on living at the Y.M.C.A. They surrounded him as in a cocoon. He couldn't go out for a meal or to a lecture without one or other of them in amiable attendance. When he announced that he was going to Boston for a weekend to see his mother and his fiancée, Mr. Forsythe said, "We're all taking a vacation in September." He pulled from his pocket the lengthy contract that Elbert had signed in which he agreed to a "*continuous residence in Newport, Rhode Island.*" Mr. Forsythe added, kindly, that if Elbert broke that contract he could be sued in court for all the salary that had been paid him. "A team is a team, Elbert; a job is a job." I had long noticed that one or other of the team spent a large part of the evening in the lobby of the "Y" reading or playing checkers *and watching the stairs.*

No wonder that he dreamed of being buried alive, of walls closing in.

"What does the curly-haired one do?"

"He makes the watermarks, and ages the paper. He makes stains on the paper and sometimes he makes burns on it."

"And the other one?"

"He frames the writing and puts glass over them. Then he takes the boxes to the Post Office."

"I see. . . . What's this about smashing your hand?"

"Well, he said it just as a joke, of course. One day I said that I was really interested in lettering—and that's what they hired me for—and that I wanted to go down to Washington, D.C., for two weeks to study the lettering on the public buildings there, like the Supreme Court and the Lincoln Memorial. He said he wanted me right here. He said, 'You wouldn't want anything to happen to your right hand, would you?' and he pushed my fingers way back, like this. . . . He said it with a smile, but I didn't like it."

"I see. . . . Do you want to break away from them, Elbert?"

"Oh, Ted, I wish I'd never seen them. Help me! Help me!"

I looked at him for a few minutes. Damn it, I was caught. I was caught in a trap. It looked as though I were the sole person responsible for the welfare of this helpless incapable half-genius. If we called in the police, these men, sooner or later, would retaliate on Elbert or on me, or on Mrs. Keefe, or on all three of us. I had a busy schedule; I could not drop what I was doing to extricate this unhappy maladept from his predicament. I must throw the baby on someone else's lap—and I had an idea.

"Now, Elbert, things are going to change for you. You go back to work just as usual—and continue working so for a few days. Don't you give any sign that there's going to be a change or you'll ruin the whole plan."

"I won't. I won't."

"Now you go back to your room and go to sleep. Did Dr. Addison give you something to help you about that? Are you getting some sound sleep?"

"Yes," he said, unconvincingly. "He gave me some pills."

"Now you've got all wrought up. I can't read to you tonight. Take one of Dr. Addison's pills, and what have you got to think about to calm you down?"

He looked up at me with a confidential smile. "I think about designing a good gravestone for Edgar Allan Poe."

"No! No!—Forget Poe! Think about what's ahead for you —freedom, your marriage, Abigail. Get a good rest now. Good night."

"Good night, Ted."

There was a telephone at the end of the corridor. I called up Dr. Addison. "Doc, this is Ted North. Can I drop in and see you in about ten minutes?"

"Sure! Sure! Always ready for a little prayer-meeting."

As I have said the "Y" had its own doctor, Winthrop Addison, M.D., a tall trunk of walnut, over seventy. His professional notice was still attached to the post of his verandah, but he told all strangers that he had retired; no patient he had ever served, however, was turned away. He cut his own hair, cooked his own meals, tended his own garden, and, as the ranks of his former patients were thinning, he had plenty of free time. He liked to linger in the front room of our building and talk with any resident who chose to approach him. I greatly enjoyed his company and was assembling a portrait of him for my Journal. He had a fund of stories not always suitable for his younger listeners.

I ran down to Thames Street and bought a flask of the best, then came back up our street and rang his doorbell.

"Come in, professor. What is it now?"

I offered my present to him. As he knew I didn't drink hard liquor, he put the bottle to his lips murmuring, "Heaven, sheer Heaven!"

"Now, Doc, I've got a problem. You're under the oath of Hippocrates not to say a word about it for six months."

"Agreed, lad. Agreed! I can clean you up in two months. I should have warned you about going to 'Hattie's Hammock.'"

"I don't need a doctor. Listen: I need smart, experienced grade-A advice."

"I'm listening."

"What did you think of Elbert Hughes?"

"He needs rest; he needs food; he needs backbone. Maybe he needs a mother. He's got some load of misery. He won't talk."

I told him about the forgery ring, about Elbert's extraordinary gift; about his condition of slavery. Doc loved it and took a deep swig. "Elbert wants to get away from them without their suspecting that he'll talk to the police or to anyone. They're very ugly types, Doc. They've already threatened to maim him, to *smash his right hand*. Could you give him some disease that would put him to bed for six weeks? That would put them out of business and they'd leave town. He's all they've got. He's their pot of gold."

Doc laughed long and loud. "That reminds me of a case that I had twenty-five years ago—"

"Save it! Save it!"

"This man's wife had hives—cruel! What I call 'thistle-patch hives.' He told me he wanted an excuse not to sleep in the same bed with her. She said she couldn't sleep a wink without his being by her side."

"Doc, save it. Please save it. I want the *whole* story another time. Remember we're writing a book together." (It was to be called *Coughing Up the Diamonds: The Memoirs of a Newport Doctor*; the best of it is in my Journal.) "Get your mind back to Elbert Hughes. What's that disease that makes your hand tremble? Or could you sort of make out that he's blind for a while?"

Dr. Addison held up his hand to stop me. He was deep in thought.

"I've got it!" he cried.

"I knew you'd think of something, Doc."

"Last month Bill Hinkle was doing his laundry down in the basement. He got his hand caught in the mangle—get the picture? His hand came out as flat as a playing card. Well, I pushed the knuckles back in place and separated the fingers. He'll be playing poker by Christmas. I'll give Elbert a plaster cast as big as a wasps' nest."

"You're a wonder, Doc. Now you've got to say 'No Visitors Admitted' because those gangsters will want to call on him. They're so furious they'll tear off the plaster cast and wreck his hand. He's fouled up their game. They'd follow him to China. Doc, could you write a letter to 'Holy Joe' to make sure that no visitors could be admitted to his room?"

"When do you want me to put the cast on?"

"Today's Tuesday. I want him to go to work a few days as usual. Say Saturday morning.—Doc, does your daughter like poetry?"

"She writes it—hymns mostly."

"I'll see she gets a copy of 'A Psalm of Life,' framed in glass, practically signed by the author."

"She'd appreciate that. 'Life is real! Life is earnest! And the grave is not its goal.' Eyewash, but talented." Here he fell into deep thought again. "Wait a minute! 'Holy Joe's' not got spunk enough to prevent gangsters moving about his house. Elbert's not safe there."

"Oh, Doc, if you could hide him in your house. Elbert's saved up a lot of money. He could pay for a husky male nurse to watch him when you were out."

"Out or in, I'm too old to rassle with thugs. I might kill one of them, unintentional. Hide him in New Hampshire or Vermont."

"You don't know Elbert yet. He can't cope with anything except the alphabet. He'd get in touch with his mother and his fiancée and these fellows know their addresses. Somebody's got to do his thinking for him. He's not all there. He's a genius; he's a little bit crazy. He thinks he's Edgar Allan Poe."

"Great Jehoshaphat! I've got it. We'll give out that he's crazy. A friend of mine has a mental hospital twenty miles away that's as hard to get into as a Turkish harem."

"Wouldn't that be complicated? Couldn't you think of a simpler idea?"

"Hell! You're only young once. Let's make it as complicated as possible. Saturday morning we kidnap him. We'll call it brain fever."

"That's great, Doc. I knew I'd come to the right place. Now we've got Elbert out of the way of mayhem. But we have another problem and I want your ideas. Take a swig; you'll need inspiration—real inspiration. We want *them* out of town quick. We don't want to call in the police. We want to scare them out."

"I've got it," said Doc. "The only way these men can be charged and indicted is by the Post Office Department. They're shipping fraudulent goods through the mail. No wonder they don't get letters or telephone calls at Mrs. Keefe's. They had to give a local address to rent that post office box. So they probably gave the Union Hotel on Washington Square, where they're staying. This Forsythe isn't there at any time during the working day, is he? Well, tomorrow morning I'm going to drop in there and ask in a heavy manner for Mr. Forsythe. 'Not in.' 'Tell him a representative of the United States Post Office Department called on him and will call again.'"

"Wouldn't the hotel know you, Doc?"

"I haven't answered a call from that hotel for twenty years. Then *you* find time in the afternoon before five to do the same thing. Then I'll ask a patient of mine to do the same thing—a retired gardener, solemn as a judge. That'll get them rattled. I'll tell Mrs. Keefe to tell him that a representative of the P.O. Department called on him in the evening. That'll put a bur under his tail."

"Good!—Now I've been cooking up another idea to add to yours. Let me read you a letter from the Governor of Massa-chusetts that I've got ready for Elbert to forge on the Governor's own stationery. Take a swig. *'Mr. John Forsythe, Dealer in Historical Documents and Autographs, Newport, Rhode Island. Dear Mr. Forsythe, As you may know, my office in The State House is hung with portraits of worthies in our history. Those belong to the Commonwealth. I have a smaller reception room, however, on whose walls I have hung autographed letters from my own collection. A mimeographed sheet of your very interesting offers for the autumn of 1926 has just been brought to my attention by a friend who found it in a hotel room in Tulsa, Oklahoma. There are some lacunae in my collection that I would like to fill, particularly letters from Thoreau, Margaret Fuller, and Louisa May Alcott. In addition I would like to replace a number that I own—those of Emerson, Lowell, and Bowditch—with letters of more significant content. Would you kindly send me the address of your office or showroom in Newport, so that I may send an expert to report to me about the properties you have in stock. This is an unofficial letter and I request that you regard it as confidential. Faithfully yours,'* et cetera, et cetera."

"That'll smoke 'em out."

"I'll wake Elbert at six o'clock tomorrow morning so that he can copy it out before he goes to work. How'll I get it mailed in Boston?"

"My daughter'll mail it. Leave it at my door as soon as it's finished. Tomorrow's Wednesday; they'll get it Friday morning. Elbert must be out of the way before they read it."

"Anything else occur to you, Doc?"

"Yes. Do you think Elbert can afford to pay about thirty dollars for his rescue?"

"Sure of it."

"I'll have a friend of mine walk up and down in front of Mrs. Keefe's house. He needs the money and he'll love the work. He's a former actor. When that messenger of theirs goes to the P.O. carrying all those boxes Nick will follow him and stick his nose into everything this fella does. Then he goes back to Mrs. Keefe's house and when the forgers quit work, he'll give them the Hawkshaw eye and they'll see him writing all their comings and goings in a notebook—see what I mean?"

"Beautiful!"

"You telephone Mrs. Keefe that he's out there protecting her. They'll order a van and get out of there Saturday morning

or I'm a Chinaman. Tell Mrs. Keefe to telephone me the minute they announce they're leaving and I'll go down and sit in
the hall to see that they don't do any damage. Nick and I could
take turns sitting up all night, if need be."

And that's the way it happened. I moved in the next week.
The stink didn't last long.

8

The Fenwicks

MY FAVORITE among the pupils in the early morning tennis classes at the Casino was Eloise Fenwick. She was fourteen —that is, as the spirit moved her—of any age between ten and sixteen. Some days when I approached the courts she seized my left elbow with both hands and required me to drag her to the back line; some days she preceded me, the only female world's champion who was also a lady, Countess of Aquidneck and the Adjacent Isles. In addition, she was intelligent with breathtaking surprises; she was deep and kept her counsel; she was as beautiful as the morning and showed no sign that she was aware of it. At first we had few opportunities for desultory conversation, but we were acknowledged friends without that. Friendship between one of Shakespeare's heroines at the age of fourteen and a man of thirty is one of life's fairest gifts, only occasionally available to parents.

Eloise bore a burden on her shoulders.

One day she said, "I wish my brother Charles would take lessons with you, Mr. North." She surreptitiously indicated a young man who was practicing his tennis shots against a wall reserved for such exercise at the farthest end of the courts. I had observed him for some time. He was, I assumed, about sixteen; he was always alone. There was something defensively arrogant about him. His face was covered with the pimples and discolorations usually associated with late puberty.

"Tennis lessons, Eloise? Mr. Dobbs teaches students of that age."

"He doesn't like Mr. Dobbs. And he wouldn't take lessons from you because you teach children. He doesn't like anybody. No—I just wish you would teach him something."

"Well, I can't until I'm asked, can I?"

"Mama's going to ask you."

I glanced down at her. The tone of her voice and the carriage of her head said as plain as words that she, Eloise, had arranged it as she probably arranged many things that came to her notice.

At the conclusion of the next lesson two days later, Eloise said, "Mama wants to talk to you about Charles." Her eyes indicated a lady sitting in the spectators' gallery. I had already remarked Charles back at the practice board. I followed Eloise who introduced me to her mother and withdrew.

She was indeed Eloise's mother. She had come to take her children home after their strenuous exercise and was heavily veiled for motoring. She put out her hand.

"Mr. North, may I speak with you for a few moments? Please sit down. Your name is well known in our house and in the houses of a number of my friends with whom you read. Eloise admires you very much."

I smiled and said, "I had not dared to hope so."

She laughed softly and our reciprocal confidence was sealed.

"I wanted to talk to you about my son Charles. Eloise tells me that you know him by sight. I was hoping that you could find time to coach him in French. He has been accepted for school in the fall." She mentioned a highly esteemed school for Roman Catholic students in the vicinity of Newport. "He has lived in France and speaks the language, after a fashion, but he needs to apply himself to the grammatical constructions. He has a *bloc* against learning the genders of nouns and the tenses of verbs. He admires everything that is French and I have the impression that he really wishes to bring it up to a higher standard." She lowered her voice slightly. "It embarrasses him that Eloise speaks much more correctly than he does."

I paused a moment. "Mrs. Fenwick, for four years and three summers I have taught French to students most of whom would prefer to do anything else. It is like dragging loads of stones uphill. During this summer I resolved not to work so hard. I have already rejected a number of students who are required to improve their French, German, and Latin. I must have the student's own expression of readiness to study French and to work on it with me. I would like to have a short talk with your son and hear him make such a commitment."

She lowered her eyes a moment, then rested them on her son in the distance. She finally said, sadly but directly: "That is a good deal to ask of Charles Fenwick. . . . I find it difficult to say what I must. I'm not a bashful woman, I'm not a bashful-minded woman at all, but I find it very hard to describe certain tendencies—or traits—in Charles."

"Perhaps I can help you, Mrs. Fenwick. In the school where I've been teaching the Headmaster has got into the way of calling my attention to any boys who don't fit into the pattern of the 'All-American Boy' he wants in the school—boys who seem to have what he calls 'problems.' My telephone will ring: 'North, I want you to have some talk with Frederick Powell; his housemaster says that he's been walking and groaning in his sleep. He's in *your* parish.' My parish comprises sleepwalkers, bed-wetters, boys who are so homesick that they cry all night and can't hold down their food; a boy who seemed to be pre-paring to hang himself because he failed in two subjects and foresaw that his father would not address a word to him throughout the whole Easter vacation—and so on."

"Thank you, Mr. North . . . I wish you had room in your parish for Charles. He has none of those problems. Perhaps he has a worse one: he has a disdain, almost a contempt, for ev-eryone he has come into contact with, except perhaps Eloise, and several priests whom he has come to know in his religious duties. . . . He is far closer to Eloise than to his parents."

"What are the grounds for Charles's low opinion of the rest of us?"

"Some posture of superiority . . . I have found the cour-age to give it a name: he is a snob, an unbounded snob. He has never said 'Thank you' to a servant, or even raised his eyes to one. If he has thanked his father or myself when we have taken some pains to please him, the thanks are barely audible. At mealtimes when the family is alone (for he refuses to come downstairs when there are guests) he sits in silence. He takes no interest in any subject but one: our social standing. Neither his father nor I care one iota about that. We have our friends and enjoy them—here and in Baltimore. Charles is intensely anxious as to whether we are invited to what he regards as im-portant occasions; whether the clubs his father belongs to are the best clubs; whether I am what the papers call a 'social leader.' He is driving his father mad with questions about whether we

have more means than the So-and-sos. Charles has a low opinion of us because we don't stretch every nerve to—oh, I can't
go on with this—"

She was blushing intensely under her veils. She put her hands
to her cheeks.

I said quickly, "Please go on a moment more about this,
Mrs. Fenwick."

"As I said we are Roman Catholics. Charles is serious about
his religious life. Father Walsh, who is in our home quite often,
is fond of Charles and pleased with him. I have talked over
with him this . . . this preposterous worldliness. He does not
see it as of much importance; he thinks Charles will outgrow it
soon."

"Will you tell me something of Charles's education?"

"Oh!—At the age of nine Charles developed a form of heart
trouble. Baltimore and Johns Hopkins Medical School is a
center for many distinguished doctors. They treated him and
cured him; they tell me he is completely well. But at that time
we took him out of school and ever since his education has
been entirely in the hands of private tutors."

"Does that explain why he has so few friends, why he seems
to be always alone?"

"Somewhat—but there is always his disdainful manner too.
The boys don't like him and he thinks the boys are coarse and
vulgar."

"Do the blemishes in his complexion have a part in this self-
isolation?"

"That condition has only developed in the last ten months.
He has been under treatment by the best dermatologists. His
attitude to us is of long standing."

I smiled at her. "Do you think he can be persuaded to come
over here and talk to me?"

"Eloise can persuade him to do anything. You can imagine
our gratitude to God that that little girl of fourteen is so helpful and so wise."

"Then I will go inside and cancel my next appointment.
Please ask Eloise to persuade him to come to this table and talk
with me. Could you and Eloise leave us alone together for half
an hour on some pretext?"

"Yes, we have shopping to do." She beckoned to Eloise and

told her of this plan. Eloise and I exchanged a glance fraught with meaning and I went off to telephone. When I returned Charles was seated in the chair his mother had left; he had turned it about so that only his profile was presented to me. In the school I had attended and the school where I had taught students rose when a master entered the room. Charles, without a glance at me, merely lowered his head in acknowledgment of my presence. He had good features, but the cheek he presented to me was marred by a number of cones and craters.

I sat down. There was no possibility of his shaking hands with the lowest menial at the Newport Casino.

"Mr. Fenwick—I shall call you that at the beginning of our conversation, then I shall call you Charles—Eloise tells me that you have spent much time in France and have had several years of tutoring. Probably all you need is a few weeks putting some polish on the irregular verbs. Eloise certainly surprised me. She could get an invitation tomorrow to one of those châteaux for a weekend and pass the test with flying colors. As you probably know, French people of real distinction refuse to have anything to do with Americans who speak their language incorrectly. They think we're savages. In a few moments I am going to ask you if you would like to work with me on this matter, but first I think we should know each other a little better. Eloise and your mother have told me a number of things about you: aren't there some questions you'd like to put to me about myself?"

Silence. I held the silence so long that presently he spoke. His manner was offhand and freighted with condescension. "Did you go to Yale . . . is it true that you went to Yale?"

"Yes."

Same prolonged pause.

"If you went to Yale, why are you working at the Casino?"

"To make some money."

"You don't look . . . *poor.*"

I laughed. "Oh, yes, I'm very poor, Charles—but cheerful."

"Did you belong to any of those fraternities . . . and clubs they have there?"

"I was a member of the Alpha Delta Phi fraternity and of the Elizabethan Club. I was not a member of any one of the Senior Societies."

For the first time he glanced at me. "Did you try to get into one?"

"Trying has nothing to do with it. They did not invite me."

Another glance. "Did you feel very badly about it?"

"Maybe they were wise not to take me in. Maybe I wouldn't have suited them at all. Clubs are meant for men who have a lot in common. What kind of clubs would you like to be a member of, Charles?" Silence. "The best clubs are built around hobbies. For instance there's a club in your own town Baltimore—a hundred years old—that I think must be the most delightful in the world and the hardest to get into."

"What club is that?"

"It's called the 'Catgut Club.'" He couldn't believe his ears. "It's always been known that there's a close affinity between medicine and music. In Berlin there's a symphony orchestra made up of physicians alone. Around your Johns Hopkins Medical School there are more great doctors than in any place of its size in the world. Only the most eminent professors belong to the 'Catgut,' but they're also pianists, violinists, violists, cellists, and possibly a clarinetist. Every Tuesday night they sit down and play chamber music."

"What?"

"Chamber music. Do you know what that is?"

A strange thing was happening. Charles's face already a mottled red and white had turned scarlet. He was blushing furiously.

Suddenly I remembered—with a bang—that to very young Americans the word "chamber," through association with chamber pots, was invested with the horror and excitement and ecstasy of the "forbidden"—of things not said openly; and every "forbidden" word belongs to a network of words far more devastating than "chamber." Charles Fenwick at sixteen was going through a phase that he should have outgrown by the age of twelve. Of course! He had had tutors all his life; he had little association with boys of his own age who "aerate" that suppressed matter in giggles and whispers and horseplay and shouting. In one area of his development he was "arrested."

I explained what chamber music was and then I laid another trap for him to see if my conjecture was right.

"There's another club, also very select, at Saratoga Springs, whose members own racehorses and bet on races, but seldom ride them. There's an old joke about them; some people call it the 'Horses and Asses Club'—the members don't sit on their horses, they sit on their asses."

It worked. The crimson flag went up. At chapel services in the school where I had taught, the Bible readings occasionally reminded us that Abraham or Saul or Job had lost a large number of asses. The air in the auditorium would become tense; in the seats reserved for the smaller boys there would be agonies of suppressed laughter, convulsion, and desperate coughing. I went on serenely. "Which club would you rather belong to?"

"What?"

"The Baltimore doctors wouldn't give a pin to get into the millionaires' club at Saratoga Springs and the horse-owners wouldn't be caught dead listening to a lot of chamber music. . . . But I'm wasting your time. Are you ready to say that you'd be willing to work with me on the finer points of the French language? Be perfectly frank, Charles."

He swallowed and said, "Yes, sir."

"Fine! When next you're in France you and Eloise may be asked to some noble's country house for a pleasant weekend and you'll want to feel secure about the conversation and all that. . . . I'll sit here and wait until your mother returns. I don't want to interrupt your practice any longer." I put out my hand; he shook it and rose. I grinned. "Don't tell that little story about Saratoga Springs where it might cause any embarrassment; it's all right just among men." And I nodded in dismissal.

Mrs. Fenwick returned followed by Eloise.

"Charles feels that he'd like to try a little coaching, Mrs. Fenwick."

"Oh, I'm so relieved!"

"I think Eloise had a large part in it."

"Can I come to the classes, too?"

"Eloise, your French is quite good enough. Charles wouldn't open his mouth if you were there. But you can be sure that *I'll* miss you. Now I want to discuss some details with your mother." Eloise sighed and drifted off.

"Mrs. Fenwick, have you ten minutes? I want to lay a plan before you."

"Oh, yes, Mr. North."

"Ma'am, are you fond of music?"

"As a girl I seriously hoped to become a concert pianist."

"Who are your favorite composers?"

"It used to be Bach, then it was Beethoven, but for some time I have become fonder and fonder of Mozart. Why do you ask?"

"Because a little-known aspect of Mozart's life may help you to understand what is making life difficult for Charles."

"Charles and Mozart!"

"Both suffered from an unfortunate deprivation in their adolescence."

"Mr. North, are you in your senses?"

(I must now interrupt this account for a brief declaration. The reader has not failed to notice that I, Theophilus, did not hesitate to invent fabulous information for my own amusement or for the convenience of others. I am not given to telling either lies or the truth to another's disadvantage. The passage that follows concerning Mozart's letters is the easily verifiable truth.)

"Ma'am, half an hour ago you assured me that you were not a bashful-minded woman. What I am about to say requires my discussing what many people would regard as vulgar and even distasteful matters. Of course, you may draw this conversation to a close at any moment you wish, but I think it will throw some light on why Charles is a closed-in and unhappy young man."

She stared at me in silence for a moment, then clutched the arms of her chair and said, "Go on."

"Readers of Mozart's letters have long known of a few that he addressed to a cousin living in Augsburg. Those that have been published contain many asterisks indicating that deletions have been made. No editor or biographer would print the whole, feeling that they would distress the reader and leave a stain on the image of the composer. These letters to his *Bäsle*— a German and Austrian diminutive for a female cousin—are one long chain of childish indecencies. Not long ago the famous author Stefan Zweig bought them and printed them, with a preface, for private distribution among his friends. I have not seen the brochure, but a musicologist I know, living in Princeton, gave me a detailed account of them and of Stefan Zweig's introduction. They are what is called scatological—having to do with the bodily functions. As I was told, there is little or no allusion to sexual matters; it is all 'bathroom humor.' They were written in the composer's middle and late teens. How can one explain that Mozart who matured so early could descend to such infantile jokes? The beautiful letters to his father, preparing him for the news of his mother's death in Paris, were written not long after. Herr Zweig points out that Mozart never had a normal boyhood. Before he was ten he was composing and performing music all day and far into the night. His father was exhibiting him about Europe as a wonderchild. You remember that he climbed on Queen Marie Antoinette's lap. I have not only been a teacher at a boys' school, I have earned my living during the summers as counselor at camps and have had to sleep in the same tent with seven to ten urchins. Boys pass through a phase when all these 'forbidden' matters obsess them—are excruciatingly funny and exciting and, of course, alarming. Girls are supposed to be given to giggling, but I assure you boys between nine and twelve will giggle for an entire half hour if some little physiological accident takes place. They give vent to the anxiety surrounding the tabu by sharing it in the herd. But Mozart—if I may put it figuratively—never played baseball in a corner lot, never went swimming on a boy scout picnic." I paused. "Your son Charles was cut off from his contemporaries and all this perfectly natural childish adjustment to our bodily nature was driven underground; and has festered."

She addressed me coldly, "My son Charles has never uttered a vulgar word."

"Mrs. Fenwick, that's the point!"

"How do you know that something is *festering*?" There was a sneer in her voice. She was a very nice woman, but she was being hard pushed.

"By sheer accident. In our conversation he gave me pretty hard treatment. He asked me if I had belonged to certain extremely exclusive clubs at Yale, and when I told him I had not, he tried to humiliate me. But I have had a lot of experience. I was beginning to think very well of him; but I could see that he was living in a capsule of anxiety."

She put her hands over her face. After a moment she regained possession of herself and said in a low voice, "Go on, please!" I told her about the musical club in Baltimore and about Charles's crimson reaction. I told her that I had made an experiment and invented a club for card-players which offered rewards for the best and the worst players called the "Tops and Bottoms Club" and aroused the same response. I explained that for boys—and probably girls—during certain years the English language was a mine-field sown with explosives—words, dynamite; I said that I had remembered Mozart's letters and that Charles had been brought up by tutors, cut off from the life usually led by boys. I said that he was entrapped in a stage of development which he should have outgrown years before and that the trap was *fear* and that what she had called his snobbery was his escape into a world where no shattering word was ever spoken. I had asked him if he would like to work with me in the hope of bringing his French up to Eloise's standard—and that he had agreed to it and that before he left he had shaken my hand and had looked me in the eye.

"Mrs. Fenwick, you may remember Macbeth's question to the doctor concerning Lady Macbeth's sleepwalking: 'Canst thou not . . . Cleanse the stuffed bosom of that perilous stuff Which weighs upon the heart?'"

With no tone of reproach she said, "But you are not a doctor, Mr. North."

"No. What Charles needs is a friend with a certain experience in these matters. You cannot be sure that doctors are also potential friends."

"You believe that Mozart outgrew his 'childishness'?"

"No. No man does. He outgrows most of his anxiety; the rest he turns into laughter. I doubt that Charles even knows what it is to smile."

"Oh, Mr. North, I've hated every word you've said. But I think I can see that you are probably right. Will you accept Charles as a pupil?"

"I must make a proviso. You must discuss it with Mr. Fenwick and Father Walsh. I could teach French syntax to Tom, Dick, and Harry, but now that I have glimpsed Charles's predicament, I cannot spend all those hours without trying to help. I couldn't teach algebra—as a friend of mine was paid to do—to a girl who was suffering from religious mania; she was secretly wearing hair shirts and sticking nails into her body. I want your permission to do a thing that I would not dream of doing without your permission. I want to introduce into each lesson a 'dynamite word' or two. If I had a student whose mind and heart was absorbed by birds, I would build French lessons about ostriches and starlings. Learning takes wings when it's related to what's passing in the student's inner life. Charles's inner life is related to a despairing effort to grow up into a man's world. His snobbery is related to this knot inside him. He won't realize it, but my lessons would be based on these fantasies of his—of social grandeur and of the frightening world of the tabu."

She had shut her eyes, but opened them again—"Excuse me; what is it you want?"

"A message from you that I may occasionally use low earthy images in the lessons. I want you to trust me not to resort to the prurient and the salacious. I don't know Charles. He may develop an antagonism against me and report to you and to Father Walsh that I have a vulgar mind. You probably know that ailing patients *also* cling to their illnesses."

She rose. "Mr. North, this has been a painful conversation for me. I must think it all over. You will hear from me. . . . Good morning."

She extended her hand tentatively. I bowed saying, "If you agree to my proviso, I can meet Charles in the blue tea room behind us for an hour every Monday, Wednesday, and Friday at eight-thirty."

She looked about confusedly for her children, but Eloise and Charles had been watching us and hurried forward. Eloise said, "Mr. North won't let me come to the classes, too; but I forgive him." Then she turned and threw her arms about her brother's stomach and said, "I'm so glad Charles is going to have them."

Charles, standing very straight above his sister's shining head, said, "*Au revoir, monsieur le professeur!*"

Mrs. Fenwick stared at her children with a distraught air and said, "Are you ready to go to the car, dears?" and led them off.

Two days later Eloise approached me at the close of the last of my tennis classes and gave me a note from her mother. I put it in my pocket.

"Aren't you going to read it?"

"I'll wait. Just now I'd rather take you to the La Forge Tea Rooms for a hot fudge sundae. . . . Do you think this note engages me or dismisses me?"

Eloise possessed three forms of laughter. I now heard the long low dove's ripple. "I shan't tell you," she said, having told me. This morning she had chosen to be all of twenty years old but she slipped her hand into mine—in full view of Bellevue Avenue, astonishing the horses, shocking the old ladies in their electric phaetons, and very definitely opening the summer season.

"Oh, Mr. North, is this really our last class? Shall I never see you again?"

We didn't sit on high stools before the soda fountain, as once before, but at a table in the furthest corner. "I was hoping that you'd have a hot fudge sundae with me every Friday morning at exactly this time—just when I finish my lesson with Charles." We were hungry after all that exercise and addressed ourselves to our sundaes with a will.

"You really do know a lot about what's been going on, don't you, Eloise?"

"Well, no one ever tells a young girl anything so she has to be a sort of witch. She has to learn to read people's thoughts, doesn't she? When I was a little girl I used to listen at doors, but I don't do that any more. . . . You grown-ups suddenly woke up about Charles. You saw that he was all caught in . . . a sort of spider's web; he was afraid of everything. You must have told Mother something that made her frightened, too. Did you tell her to ask Father Walsh to dinner?" I remained silent. "He came to dinner last night and after dinner Charles and I were sent upstairs, and they went into the library and had a council of war. And way upstairs, miles away, we could hear Father Walsh laughing. Mother's voice sounded as though she had been crying, but Father Walsh kept shouting with laughter.—Please read the letter, Mr. North—not to *me*, of course, but to yourself."

I read: *"Dear Mr. North, Reverend Father says to tell you that when he was young he had worked as a counselor at a boys' camp, too. He told me to tell you to go ahead—that he'll do the praying and you do the work. It comforts me to think of the lady in Salz-*

burg for whom things worked out so well. Sincerely, Millicent Fenwick."

I don't believe in unnecessarily hiding things from young people. "Eloise, read the letter, but don't ask me to explain it to you yet."

She read it. "Thank you," she said and thought a moment. "Wasn't Beethoven born in Salzburg? We went there when I was about ten and visited his house."

"Is it hard to be a witch, Eloise? I mean: does it make living harder?"

"No! It keeps you so busy. You have to be on your toes. . . . It keeps you from growing stale."

"Oh, is that one of your worries?"

"Well, isn't it everybody's?"

"Not when you're around.—Eloise, I always like to ask my young friends what they've been reading lately. And you?"

"Well, I've been reading the *Encyclopaedia Britannica*—I discovered it when I wanted to read about Héloïse and Abelard. Then I read about George Eliot and Jane Austen and Florence Nightingale."

"Some day turn to *B* and read about Bishop Berkeley, who lived in Newport, and go and visit his house. Turn to *M* and read about Mozart, who was born in Salzburg."

She slapped her hand to her mouth. "Oh, how boring it must be for you to talk to young girls who are so ignorant!"

I burst out laughing. "Let me be the judge of that, Eloise. Please go on about the *Encyclopaedia*."

"For another reason I read about Buddhism and glaciers and lots of other things."

"Forgive me asking so many questions, but why do you read about Buddhism and glaciers?"

She blushed a little, glancing at me shyly. "So that I'll have something to talk about at table. When Papa and Mama give luncheons or dinner parties Charles and I eat upstairs. When relatives or old friends are invited we are invited, too; but Charles *never* comes to table if anyone else is there—except Father Walsh, of course. When just the four of us are there he comes to table but he scarcely says a word. . . . Mr. North, I'm going to tell you a secret: Charles thinks he's an orphan; he thinks Papa and Mama adopted him. I don't think he really believes that, but that's what he says." She lowered her voice. "He thinks he is a prince from another country—like Poland or Hungary or even France."

"And you're the only one who knows that?"

She nodded. "So you see how hard it is for Papa and Mama to make conversation—and in front of the servants!—with a person who acts as though he were so far away from them."

"Does he think that you are of royal birth also?"

She answered sharply. "I don't let him."

"So at mealtimes you fill in about Buddhism and glaciers and Florence Nightingale?"

"Yes . . . and I tell them the things you've told me. About the school you went to in China. That filled a whole lunchtime —I embroidered it a little. Do you always tell the truth, Mr. North?"

"I do to you. It's so boring to tell the truth to people who'd rather hear the other thing."

"I told how in Naples the girls thought you had the Evil Eye. I made it funny and Mario had to leave the room he was laughing so."

"Now I'm going to tell you something. Dear Eloise, if you see that Charles is cutting his way out of that spider's web a little, you can tell yourself that it's all due to you." She looked at me in wonder. "Because when you love someone you communicate your love of life; you keep the faith; you scare away dragons."

"Why, Mr. North—there are tears in your eyes!"

"Happy tears."

So I met Charles at eight-thirty on the following Monday. In the intervening time he had relapsed somewhat into his haughty distrust; but he deigned to sit in his chair facing me. He was like a fox watching a hunter from behind a screen of foliage.

My Journal does not contain an account of our successive lessons, but I find, pinned into it, an almost illegible schema of our progress—the day's syntactical problem and the "dynamite words" at my disposal: auxiliary verbs, the subjunctive, the four past tenses, and so on; *derrière, coucher, cabinet,* and so on. I find no notations for my campaign against snobbery, but it was never long absent from my mind. The day usually began with a little shocker, then went on to forty minutes of pure grammatical grind, concluding with free practice in conversational French. The entire lesson was conducted in French which—for the most part—I shall translate here. (Every now and then I'll give the reader a little run for his money.)

In the earlier lessons, I used restraint in upsetting his modesty during those conversational twenty minutes—though I became increasingly exacting during the grammatical grind—to which he responded admirably.

"Charles, what are these odd-looking kiosks in the streets called—these constructions for the convenience of men only?"

He had some difficulty in recalling the word "*pissoirs*."

"Yes, they also go by a more elegant and more interesting name *vespasiennes*, after the Roman emperor to whom we are indebted for the happy idea. Now that you're older and will be circulating more with maturer persons over there you will be astonished at the lack of embarrassment with which ladies and gentlemen of even the most refined sort refer to such matters. So be prepared for that, will you?"

"Yes, sir." . . .

"Charles, I hope that you will be a student in Paris in your twenties, as I was. We were all poor, but we had a lot of fun. Be sure that you live on the Left Bank, and *pretend* that you're poor. Don't drink too much Pernod; the only time that I was ever beastly drunk was on Pernod—watch that, will you? What times we had! I'll tell you a story—it's a little risqué, but you don't mind a bit of that when it's not disgusting, do you? . . . To save money we used to press our pants by putting them under our mattresses; that gave them a razor-edge crease, see? Well, my roommate was a music student and one afternoon his professor invited us both to his home for tea with his wife and daughter—delightful people. And Madame Bergeron commented on the elegance of his clothing and especially that brilliant crease. 'Thank you, madame,' he said, 'Monsieur North and I have a secret about that. Every night we put our trousers under our *maîtresses*.' Madame Bergeron, laughing heartily, waved her hands in the air, and then politely and smilingly corrected him."

That was a dynamite word. Charles was so stunned that it took him ten minutes to think it over. Maybe it was on that

occasion that for the first time I saw the ghost of a smile on his
face.

One morning Charles brought me a message from his
mother. She invited me to an informal Sunday supper with the
family at the end of the week.

"Charles, that is very kind of your mother and of you all. I
shall write her a note. I shall have to explain that I'd made a
rule to accept no invitation whatever. I want you to read the
note I shall write to her and I know you both will understand.
But it's very hard to refuse this kindness from your mother. May
I tell you in confidence, Charles, that my work carries me into
many cottages in Newport and I've met a number of the admired hostesses in this town. *In confidence*, not *one* can hold a
candle to your mother for distinction and charm and what the
French call *race*. I'd always heard that the ladies of Baltimore
belonged to a class apart and now I know it to be true." I
struck his elbow. "You're a lucky man, Charles. I hope you live
up to that privilege. I like to think of you finding a hundred
delicate ways of expressing not only your affection, but your
admiration and gratitude to so remarkable a mother—as all
French sons do, and—I'm sorry to say—all American sons
don't. You do, don't you, Charles?"

"*Oui . . . oui, monsieur le professeur.*"

"I must say I'm glad that this kind invitation wasn't brought
to me—face to face—by Eloise. The man hasn't been born
who could refuse a request from Eloise." I added in English,
"Do you understand what I mean?"

He returned my deep glance into his eyes—"Yes," he said,
and for the first time he laughed deeply. He understood.

But there was still much work to be done.

"*Bonjour, Charles.*"

"*Bonjour, monsieur le professeur.*"

"Today we're going to work with the conditional mood,
with verbs ending in *ir*, and with the second person singular
tu. You use *tu* to children, to your very old friends, and to
members of your family, though I've been told that until about
1914 even husbands and wives addressed one another as *vous*.
You notice that I always address you as *vous*; if we haven't
quarreled in the meantime, I might address you as *tu* five years

from now. Often in French, and always in Spanish, God is addressed as *Tu*, capital *T*. Of course, lovers call each other *tu*; all such conversations in bed are in this second person singular."

Up ran the scarlet flag.

Forty minutes of grammar drill.

Then at ten minutes past nine: "Now for some practice in conversation. Today we're going to have some man-to-man conversation. We'd better move to that table in the corner where we won't be overheard."

He looked at me in alarm and we moved to the corner. "Charles, you've been in Paris. After dark you must have often seen certain women of the street strolling singly or in couples. Or you've heard them addressing passing gentlemen in a low voice from doorways and alleys—what do they usually say?"

The scarlet flag was high on the mast. I waited. At last he murmured, strangulatedly, "*Voulez-vous coucher avec moi?*"

"Good! Since you're very young, they may say, '*Tu es seul, mon petit? Veux-tu que je t'accompagne?*' Or you're sitting alone at a bar and one of these *petites dames* slides up beside you and puts her arm through yours: '*Tu veux m'offrir un verre?*' How do you answer these questions, Charles? You're an American and a gentleman and you've had some experience with these encounters."

Charles was in a crimson agony. I waited. Finally he ventured, "*Non, mademoiselle . . . merci.*" Then added generously, "*Pas ce soir.*"

"*Très bien*, Charles! Could you make it a little more easy and charming? These poor souls are earning their living. They're not exactly beggars, are they? They have something to sell. They're not contemptible—not in France, they aren't. Can you try again?"

"I . . . I don't know."

"At the school where I've been teaching there's a master who teaches French. He loves France and goes to France every summer. He hates women and is afraid of them. He prides himself on his virtue and righteousness and he's a really dreadful man. In Paris he goes for strolls in the evening just so that he can humiliate these women. He told the story to us fellow-masters to illustrate what a tower of Christian morality he was. When he's spoken to by one of these women he turns on her and says, *'Vous me faites ch————!'* That's a very vulgar expression; it's far worse than saying 'You make me vomit.' He told us that the girl or girls sprang back from him aghast crying, *'Pourquoi? Pourquoi?'* He'd had his little triumph. What do you think of that?"

"It's . . . awful."

"One of the most attractive aspects of France is the universal respect for women at every level of society. At home and in public restaurants a Frenchman smiles at the waitress who's serving him, looks her right in the eye when he thanks her. There's an undertone of respectful flirtation between every man and woman in France—even when she's a woman of ninety, even when she's a prostitute.—Now let's act a little one-act play. You go out of the room and come in the door as though you were strolling in one of those streets behind the Opéra. I'm going to pretend I'm one of those girls."

He did as he was told. He approached me as though he were entering a cage of tigers.

"*Bonsoir, mon chou.*"

"*Bonsoir, mademoiselle.*"

"*Tu es seul? Veux-tu t'amuser un peu?*"

"*Je suis occupé ce soir. . . . Merci!*"

He threw a wild glance in my direction and added, "*Peut-être une autre fois. Tu es charmante.*"

"*A-o-o! A-o-o! . . . Dis donc: une demi-heure, chéri. J'ai une jolie chambre avec tout confort américain. On s'amusera à la folie!*"

He turned to me and asked in English, "How do I get out of this?"

"I suggest you make your departure quick, short, but cordial: '*Mademoiselle, je suis en retard. Il faut que je file. Mais au revoir.*' And here you pat her elbow or shoulder, smile, and say, '*Bonne chance, chère amie!*' "

He repeated this several times, elaborating on it. Presently he was laughing.

Make-believe is like dreams—escape, release.

I came to notice that on the days when the lessons began with heavy skirmishing in the "mine-field" area my pupil's memory and resource were quicker. He could laugh; he could skate over depth-bombs, and he could make conversation from recollections of his own past. Besides, he was working hard on his grammar exercises between classes—and his complexion was clearing up.

Another session from the following week, after we'd had a smart run-through of the gender and plural of three hundred nouns in frequent use:

"Now we're going to have another one-act play. The scene is laid in one of the great restaurants of Paris, *Le Grand-Véfour*. Charles, France is a republic. What became of the royal and imperial families—the Bourbons and the Bonapartes? . . . Oh, yes, they're around still. . . . What name do they give to the real King of France who is not permitted to use that title and to wear his crown?—He is called the Pretender, the *Prétendant*. In English that means an impostor; not in France, where it means merely claimant. He calls himself the *Comte de Paris*. In this play you are he. You are addressed as *Monseigneur* or as *Votre Altesse*. In your veins flows the blood of Saint Louis, king and saint, and of Charlemagne—your own name Carolus Magnus—and of all those Louises and those Henris."

His face was getting very red.

"Your secretary has made a reservation for dinner. You arrive exactly on time—punctuality is called 'the courtesy of kings.' Your three guests have arrived before you—that is etiquette and woe to the guest who's late. You're very handsome and you carry yourself with extraordinary ease. Naturally the staff of the restaurant is at the highest pitch of excitement. I shall play the proprietor—let's call him Monsieur Véfour. I am waiting at the door. The porter is standing in the street and gives a secret signal when your car is seen approaching at exactly eight o'clock. Now you go out the door and come in."

He did. He was like a person dazed.

I bowed and murmured, "*Bonsoir, Monseigneur. Vous nous faites un très grand honneur.*"

Charles, alarmed, was at his loftiest. He responded with a slight nod. "*Bonsoir, monsieur . . . merci.*"

"One moment, Charles. The greatest noblemen and many of the kings have long established a tone of easy familiarity that would surprise even the President of the United States. Over there the greater the social status, the greater the democratic manner. The French have a word for cold, condescending self-importance: *morgue*. You would be horrified if you thought your subjects, the great French people, attributed that quality to you. Now let's do it again." Like a stage director I whispered some suggestions to him—some business, some lines. Then we did it again. He began to add some ideas of his own.

"Do you want to try it again? Let's go! Do anything that occurs to you, as long as you remember that you're the King of France. By the way when you meet me, you don't shake hands, you pat me on the shoulder; but when you meet my son you shake his hand. *Allons!*"

He entered the restaurant, wreathed in smiles; he handed his imaginary cape and top hat to an imaginary attendant, saying, "*Bonsoir, mademoiselle. Tout va bien?*"

I bowed and said, "*Bonsoir, Monseigneur. Votre Altesse nous fait un très grand bonneur.*"

"*Ah, Henri-Paul, comment allez-vous?*"

"*Très bien, Monseigneur, merci.*"

"*Et madame votre femme, comment va-t-elle?*"

"*Très bien, Monseigneur, elle vous remercie.*"

"*Et les chers enfants?*"

"*Très bien, Monseigneur, merci.*"

"*Tiens! C'est votre fils? . . . Comment vous appelez-vous, monsieur? Frédéric? Comme votre grand-père! Mon grand-père aimait bien votre grand-père.—Dites, Henri-Paul, j'ai démandé des couverts pour trois personnes. Serait-ce encore possible d'ajouter un quatrième? J'ai invité Monsieur de Montmorency. Ça vous gênerait beaucoup?*"

"*Pas du tout, Monseigneur. Monsieur le Duc est arrivé et Vous attend. Si Votre Altesse aura la bonté de me suivre.*"

Charles was agitated; he was blushing but with a different kind of blush. "*Monsieur le professeur* . . . can we ask Eloise over to see it? She's sitting there, waiting to go home."

"Yes, indeed! Let me invite her.—Give it the works, Charles! Hoke it up! . . . Eloise, we're doing a little one-act play. Would you like to be our audience?"

I explained the scene, the plot, and the characters.

Charles surpassed himself. With his hand on my shoulder he told me how his mother had first brought him to this restaurant at the age of twelve. Was it true that I served a dish named after his mother? On his way to the table he recognized a friend (Eloise) among the guests. "*Ah, Madame la Marquise . . . chère cousine!*"

Eloise made a deep curtsy, murmuring, "*Mon Prince!*" He raised her up and kissed her hand.

At his table he apologized to his guests for being late. "*Mes amis, les rues sont si bondées; c'est la fin du monde.*"

The Duc de Montmorency (myself) assured him that he had arrived exactly on time. And so our entertainment came to an end. Eloise had watched it in open-eyed wonder. To her there was nothing funny about it. She rose slowly, the tears pouring down her face. She threw her arms around her brother and kissed him with poignant intensity. All I got was a look from her, over his shoulder, but what a look! She couldn't see me, but I could see her.

"Charles," I said, "at our next class I'm going to give you the examination for those who have completed three years of French. I'm sure you'll pass it splendidly and our lessons will be over."

"Over!"

"Yes. Teachers are like birds. The moment comes when they must push the young out of the nest. Now you must give your time to American history and physics which I can't teach you."

On the following Friday I met Eloise for our visit to the tea room. On this morning she was neither the ten-year-old nor the Countess of Aquidneck and the Adjacent Isles. She was dressed all in white, not the white of the tennis courts but the white of snow. She was someone else—not Juliet, not Viola, not Beatrice—perhaps Imogen, perhaps Isabella. She did not put her hand in mine but she left no doubt that we were true friends. She walked with lowered eyes. We sat down at our removed table.

She murmured, "I'll have tea this morning."

I ordered tea for her and coffee for myself. Silence with Eloise was as rewarding as conversation. I left it to her.

"Last night there were no guests. At table Charles brushed away Mario and held the chair for Mother. He kissed her on the forehead." She looked at me with a deep smile. "When he sat down he said, 'Papa, tell me about your father and mother and about when you were a boy.'"

"Eloise! And you were all ready to tell them about the Eskimos."

"No, I was all ready to ask them about the Fenwicks and the Conovers."

We both burst out laughing.

"Oh, Eloise, you are a child of Heaven!"

She looked at me wide-eyed. "Why did you say that?"

"It just sprang to my lips."

We drank our tea and coffee in silence for a few minutes and then I asked, "Eloise, how do you see your life as it lies before you?"

Again she looked at me wonderingly. "You're very strange this morning, Mr. North."

"Oh no, I'm not. I'm the same old friend."

She reflected a moment and then said, "I'm going to answer your question. But you must promise not to say one word about it to anyone."

"I promise, Eloise Fenwick."

She put her arms on the table and, looking straight into my eyes, said: "I want to be a religious, a nun."

I held my breath.

She answered my unspoken question. "I'm so grateful to God for my father and mother . . . and brother, for the sun and the sea, and for Newport, that I want to give my life to Him. He will show me what I must do."

I returned her solemn gaze.

"Eloise, I'm just an old Protestant on both sides of my family. Forgive me if I ask you this: couldn't you express your gratitude to God while living a life outside the religious orders?"

"I love my parents so much . . . and I love Charles so much, that I feel that those loves would come between me and God. I want to love Him above all and I want to love everybody on earth as much as I love my family. I love them *too much*."

And the tears rolled down her cheeks.

I did not stir.

"Father Walsh knows. He tells me to wait; in fact I must wait for three years. Mr. North, this is the last time we'll meet here. I am learning how to pray and wherever I am in the world I shall be praying for Papa and Mama and Charles and for you and"—she pointed to the guests in the tea room—"for as many of the children of Heaven as I can hold in my mind and heart."

During the rest of the summer our paths crossed frequently. She was disattaching herself from love of her family—and naturally from friendship—in order to encompass us all in a great offering that I could not understand.

9

Myra

ONE DAY toward the middle of July—shortly before I was able to take possession of my apartment—I was called to the telephone at the "Y."

"Mr. North?"

"This is Mr. North speaking."

"My name is George Granberry. I should say George Francis Granberry because I have a cousin in town named George Herbert Granberry."

"Yes, Mr. Granberry."

"I'm told that you read aloud in English—English literature and all that."

"Yes, I do."

"I'd like to make an appointment with you to discuss reading aloud some books to my wife. My wife's a sort of invalid this summer, and it would . . . sort of . . . help her pass the time. Where could we meet and talk about it?"

"I suggest tonight or tomorrow night at the bar of the Muenchinger-King at six-fifteen."

"Good!—Tonight at the 'M-K' at six-fifteen."

Mr. Granberry was about thirty-five, young for Newport. He belonged to the category that journalists like Flora Deland call "sportsmen and men-about-town." Like many others of his kind he had a face that was handsome but wrinkled, even strangely ridged. I first thought this condition was the result of exposure to wind and wave in early youth—yacht races, Bermuda Cup trials, and so on; but later decided it was acquired on dry land and indoors. He had been designed to be a likable fellow, but idleness and aimlessness are erosive too. I received the impression that this interview with a "professor" was discomfiting, perhaps intimidating, and that he had been drinking. He offered me a drink. I accepted Bevo and we withdrew to the window-seat overlooking Bellevue Avenue and the Reading Rooms.

"Mr. North, my wife Myra is the brightest girl in the world. Quick as a whip. She can talk rings about anybody, see what I mean? But when she was a young girl she had an accident. Fell off a horse. She missed some years of schooling. Schoolteachers came to the house and taught her—terrible bores; you know what schoolteachers are like.—Where was I? Oh, yes: as a result of all this she hates reading a book. The way she puts it, she can't stand nonsense—*The Three Musketeers* and Shakespeare and all that. She's a very realistic girl. But she likes being read to, for a while. I've tried to read aloud to her, and her nurse, Mrs. Cummings, reads aloud to her, but after ten minutes she says she'd rather talk instead. Well—where was I? One of the results of this interruption in her education is that sometimes in general conversation she doesn't do credit to herself. You know that 'I-hate-Shakespeare' stuff and 'Poetry is for sheep.' . . . Newport's full of us Granberrys who think all that's just bad education and middle-western yap. It's a little embarrassing for me and my mother and all those cousins I have around. . . . As I told you, just now she's something of an invalid. She's pretty well got over that fall from the horse, but she's had two miscarriages. We're expecting a child again in about six months. The doctors have ordered her to get a little exercise in the morning and she's allowed to go out to dinner several evenings in the week, but all the afternoon she's got to spend resting on a sofa. Naturally she gets pretty bored. She has a bridge teacher twice a week, but she doesn't enjoy that . . . and a French teacher."

There was a pause. I asked, "Friends come to call?"

"In New York they do; not here. She's a great talker, but she says that in Newport people just talk *at* her. She told the doctor to give orders that she's not to receive callers—except me. I love Myra, but I can't spend all my afternoons just listening to her. It's those afternoons she finds hard. . . . Besides, I'm a sort of inventor. I have a laboratory in Portsmouth. That takes up a good deal of my time."

"An inventor, Mr. Granberry!"

"Oh, I tinker at some ideas I have. I hope to come on something important some day. . . . Until then I keep it pretty secret. So . . . uh . . . would you be willing to read aloud to her, say three afternoons a week from four to six?"

I took my time. "Mr. Granberry, may I ask you a question?"

"Oh, sure. Go ahead."

"I never take a student unless there is some assurance that the student wants to work with me. I can't get anywhere with an indifferent or an antagonistic student. Do you think she'll resent me as she does the bridge teacher?"

"I tell you frankly, it's a risk. But my wife's older now. She's twenty-seven. She knows that she's missed something . . . and that some of those ladies think she's a little . . . unfinished. Myra's not stupid—oh, no!—but she's strong-minded and very sincere. If you put her before a firing-squad and asked her to name five plays by Shakespeare, she'd say, 'Go ahead and shoot!' She's got a skunner against Shakespeare. She thinks he's piffle. So do I, rather, but I know enough to keep my mouth shut about it. She was born in Wisconsin and up there they don't allow anybody to tell them anything."

"I was born in Wisconsin."

"*You were born in Wisconsin?*"

"Yes."

"You're a Badger!"

"Yes."

All the states have their totems, but the middle-western states are particularly conscious of the animals with which they identify themselves.

"Oh, that'll be a big recommendation. Myra's very proud of being a Badger. . . . Oh, that's fine! Well, do you think you could try it, Mr. North?"

"Yes, but under one condition: the minute that Mrs. Granberry loses interest or becomes impatient, I must resign."

"I'd be awfully grateful if you'd give it a try. You may have to be a little patient with her at the beginning."

"I will."

We arranged a schedule. I thought the interview was over, but he had something further on his mind.

"Have another Bevo, Mr. North. Have something stronger. Have anything you want. I'm part owner of this hotel."

"Thank you, I'll have another Bevo."

We were served.

"I think I ought to tell you that one reason I've asked you to help me about Myra's reading is the way you behaved in that Diana Bell matter." I showed no sign of having heard him. "I mean that you made an agreement to say nothing about it and wild horses haven't been able to drag a word out of you about it. In Newport all they do is talk and talk—gossip, damned gossip. Can I make the same agreement with you?"

"Certainly. I never talk about my employers."

"I mean: you may be meeting me here and at the house. You met a friend of mine out at dinner, a very charming girl. She enjoyed talking French with you."

"Sir, I haven't been out to dinner *once* in Newport—except at Bill Wentworth's home."

"It wasn't here. It was at Narragansett Pier, at Flora Deland's."

"Oh, yes. Miss Desmoulins, a very charming young lady."

"You may be meeting her again over there. I just happen to have missed you twice at Flora Deland's. I'd appreciate it if you didn't mention it . . . in certain quarters—you see what I mean?"

"I'd like to return to the subject of Wisconsin again. Did you meet Mrs. Granberry there?"

"Lord, no! She lived way up in the north near Wausau. Only been there once in my life, the days before the wedding. Met her at parties in Chicago—she has cousins there and so have I."

The conversation floundered about like a rudderless ship. As I rose to go, he took one more look out of the window and said, "Ah! There she is!" A car had drawn up to the curb; the chauffeur had alighted and opened the door to a lady. Except for her white straw hat she was all in rose from the veils that covered her head to the tips of her shoes.

He muttered to me, "You go first!" and I opened the front door. French women are taught from the cradle to express delighted surprise at meeting any man—from twelve to ninety—whom they have met before.

"*Ah, Monsieur Nort, quel plaisir de vous revoir! Je suis Denise Desmoulins . . .*" et cetera. I expressed my moved admiration of what I saw before me, et cetera, and we parted with expansive hopes of meeting again soon at Narragansett Pier.

At the appointed afternoon I wheeled up to the door of "Sea Ledges," was received and led into Mrs. Granberry's "afternoon room." That lady, as beautiful as the morning but not as shy as the dawn, was lying on a chaise-longue. A stout pleasant-looking nurse sat near her knitting.

"Good afternoon, Mrs. Granberry. I am Mr. North. Mr. Granberry has engaged me to read aloud to you."

The lady glared at me in astonishment and silence, probably rage. I was carrying two volumes which I put down on the table beside me. "Will you kindly introduce me to your companion?"

This was another surprise. She murmured, "Mrs. Cummings, Mr. North."

I crossed and shook hands with Mrs. Cummings. "Are you from Wisconsin too, ma'am?" I asked.

"Oh, no, sir. I'm from Boston."

"Are you also fond of reading?"

"Oh, I love reading, but I don't get much time for it, you know."

"Surely some of your patients—as soon as they begin to feel better—like a bit of reading? Something light and amusing?"

"We have to be careful, sir. When I was in training the Mother Directress told us about a Sister who had read aloud *Mrs. Wiggs of the Cabbage Patch* to a surgical case. Had to re-stitch him, they did. She tells that story to every graduating class."

"It's a lovely book. I know it well."

Perhaps it was time that I gave my attention to the lady of the house. "Mrs. Granberry, I don't want to read anything that's boring and certainly you don't want to hear anything that's boring, so I suggest that we draw up some rules—"

She interrupted me curtly. "What exactly did Mr. Granberry say when he asked you to come and read to me?"

"He said that you were a very intelligent young woman who had lost a year or two of education because of an accident in your childhood; that you had routine teachers during your convalescence who had given you a prejudice against poetry and some of the standard classics."

"What else did he say?"

"I don't remember anything else, except his distress that you had to pass these afternoon hours without any interest or occupation."

The expression on her face was strong. "What are these rules that you propose?"

"I suggest that I start reading a book and that you let me read it for a quarter of an hour without interruption. Then I look at you and you give me a sign that I may go on for another quarter of an hour, or a sign that I start some other book. Does that rule seem unreasonable to you, ma'am?"

"Don't call me 'ma'am.' Let me make it clear to you, Mr. West, that there's something behind all this that I don't like. I don't like being treated as an idiot child."

"Oh, then," I said, rising quickly, "there's been some misunderstanding. I'll say good afternoon. Mr. Granberry gave me the impression that you might take some pleasure in being read aloud to." I went over to Mrs. Cummings and shook her hand. "Good afternoon, Mrs. Cummings. I hope I may meet you at another time. Please recall me as Mr. North, not Mr. West."

The lady of the house said sharply, "Mr. North, it's not your fault that I don't like the whole idea. Mr. Granberry asked you to come here and read to me, so please sit down and begin. I agree to your rules."

"Thank you, Mrs. Granberry."

I sat down and began reading: "*Emma Woodhouse, handsome, clever, and rich, with a comfortable home and happy disposition, seemed to unite some of the best blessings of existence; and had lived nearly twenty-one years in the world with very little to distress or vex her.*"

"Excuse me, Mr. North. Will you read that again, please."

I did.

"Who wrote that?"

"Jane Austen."

"Jane Austen. She doesn't know anything about life."

"You find it hard to believe, Mrs. Granberry?"

"Twenty-one!—I wasn't ugly; I wasn't stupid; my father was the richest man in Wisconsin. I had a comfortable home and the disposition of an angel. I lived to the age of twenty-three and *most* of the time was sheer hell. Excuse my language, Mrs. Cummings. The only time when I felt happy was when I was out riding my horse and the four days when I ran away to join the circus. Ask any woman who's honest and she'll tell you the same thing. . . . But I agreed to let you read for a quarter of an hour. I keep my bargains. What comes next?"

I was a little uncomfortable. I remembered that Jane Austen lets us know that any girl with a grain of sense has a rough time in life. I read on. My listener was certainly attentive. When we made the acquaintance of Miss Bates and her mother, she murmured, "Why do people write about old fools? It's a waste of time!" At four thirty-five I looked up and received permission to continue. At six I closed the book and rose.

"Thank you," she said. "Next time start some other book. It's *starting* a book that kills me. Once it's started I can go on by myself. Is it a long book?"

"In this edition, it's in two volumes."

"Leave them here and bring another book next time."

"I'll say good evening, Mrs. Granberry."

I took leave of Mrs. Cummings also, who said in a low voice, "You read lovely. I had to laugh. Was that wrong?"

At the next session Mrs. Granberry was more amiable. For the first time she gave me her hand. "Are all those Austen books about the feeble-minded?"

"It has often been said that she had a fairly low opinion of men and women."

"She should know some people I know.—What's this new one called?"

"*Daisy Miller*. It was written by a man who lived in Newport when he was young."

"In Newport? In *Newport*?"

"Not far from this very house."

"Then why did he write books?"

"I beg your pardon?"

"If he was so rich why did he take the trouble to write books?"

I didn't answer at once. I looked her straight in the eye. She blushed slightly. "Well," I said slowly, "I think he got tired of buying and selling railroads, and building hotels and naming them after his family, and gambling at Saratoga Springs and betting on horses, and sailing his yacht into the same old ports, and going out to dinner and balls, meeting the same people every night. So he said to himself 'Before I die I want some real enjoyment. . . . Damn it!' He said—excuse my language, Mrs. Cummings—'I'm going to write it all down—how people behave in the world. The fat and the thin, the happy and the unhappy.' He wrote and wrote—over forty solid volumes about men, women, and children. When he died the last book—still unfinished on his desk—was a novel laid in Newport, called

The Ivory Tower, about the emptiness and waste of the life here."

She looked at me, caught between anger and puzzlement. "Mr. North, are you trying to make me look ridiculous?"

"No, ma'am. Mr. Granberry told me that you don't always do justice to yourself—that sometimes out of sheer boredom you say the first thing that comes into your head. As we used to say in Wisconsin, I was just waving a feather under your nose."

She struggled with herself a moment, then directed me to begin. After listening for an hour she said, "Excuse me, but I'm tired today. I'll finish that by myself. I've finished *Emma* so you can take that back. Does it cost much when you take a book from the library?"

"No. They're free."

"*Anybody* can go in and take books home? Don't people steal a lot of them?"

"In winter almost three thousand books go in and out every week. Maybe they miss a few from time to time."

"In *winter*! But there's nobody here in winter."

"Mrs. Granberry, you do not always do yourself justice."

By the end of the second week we had read the openings of *Ethan Frome* (written by a lady who had lived three summers in a cottage nearby), *Jane Eyre*, *The House of the Seven Gables*, and *David Copperfield*. She made few comments, but the sufferings of young David dismayed her. She was thinking of the son she was expecting. "Of course, they were very poor," she added, as though dismissing the matter. I looked at her fixedly a moment. Again she blushed, recalling that the early years of the daughter of the richest man in Wisconsin had been described as "sheer hell." She stared me down, refusing to concede a fractured logic. I was somewhat in doubt as to whether she had read all those books to the end. I found a moment alone to ask Mrs. Cummings.

"Oh, Mr. North, she reads all the time. She'll ruin her eyes."

"But *you* never learn how the stories turn out."

"She tells me, sir; it's as good as a moving-picture! Jane Eyre! What happened to her! Tell me, sir, was that a true story?"

"You know more about life than I do, Mrs. Cummings. *Could* it be a true story?"

She shook her head sadly. "Oh, Mr. North, I've known worse things."

One day as we were entering upon the long reaches of *Tom Jones*, there was a knock at the door. For the first time we received a call from Mr. Granberry.

"Can I come in?" He kissed his wife, shook hands with me, and greeted Mrs. Cummings. "Well, Myra, how are things going?"

"Very well, darling."

"What are you reading, dear?"

"It's called *Tom Jones*."

Vague memories of his college education returned to him. He turned to Mrs. Cummings. "Er . . . er . . . is that always suitable for—I mean—a lady's reading?"

"Oh, sir," said Mrs. Cummings from an unshakable professional authority, "if anything unsuitable happened in a book, I'd ask Mr. North to return it to the library at once. The important thing is that Mrs. Granberry is really interested, isn't it? When she's read aloud to she never gets fretful. I don't like it when she gets fretful."

"Well, I'll just sit here for ten minutes. Don't pay any attention to me. Forgive my interrupting you, Mr. North." So Mr. Granberry took a chair in a corner of the room, crossed his long legs, and laid his cheek on his hand, as though he were listening to a burdensome lecture on philosophy back at Dartmouth College. He stayed for a quarter of an hour. Finally he rose with his fingers on his lips and took his leave. Thereafter he returned about once a week, not always able to keep his eyes open. Myra read the whole of *Tom Jones* over a long weekend, but could not be drawn into any comment on it.

On another day, I arrived with *Walden* under my arm.

"Good afternoon, Mr. North. . . . Thank you, I'm very well. . . . Mr. North, you made a rule—the fifteen-minute rule. I want to make a rule too. My rule is that after the first forty-five minutes we take half an hour off for talk."

"As you wish, Mrs. Granberry."

There was an ormolu clock on the table beside her. At a quarter of five she interrupted me. "It is now talking time. What did you mean two weeks ago when you said something about 'the emptiness and waste' of life at Newport?"

"Those were not my words. I was reporting to you what Henry James said."

"In Wisconsin we don't quibble. You said it and you meant it."

"I don't know Newport life well enough to make any judgment about it. I have been here only a few weeks. I have no part in Newport life. I come and go on a bicycle. Most of my students are children."

"Don't quibble with me. You must be twenty-eight years old. You've been to college. You've been in dozens of Newport cottages. You sit up half the night at 'Nine Gables.' You get drunk at the Muenchinger-King bar. Stop running away from my questions."

"Mrs. Granberry—!"

"Don't call me 'ma'am' again and don't call me 'Mrs. Granberry.' Call me 'Myra.'"

I raised my voice. "Mrs. Granberry, I make it a rule that in all the houses where I *work* I use only family names and I wish to be called by my own."

"You and your rules! *We're from Wisconsin.* Don't be an Easterner. Don't be a stuffed owl."

We glared at each other.

Mrs. Cummings said, "Oh, Mr. North, I wish you would make an exception in this case—seeing"—and she gave me a significant glance—"that you are both Badgerers."

"Of course, I shall obey any request from Mrs. Cummings—but in this room only and in her presence only. I have a great admiration for Mrs. Cummings. She is an Easterner and I wish you would apologize to her for having called her a stuffed owl."

"Oh, Mr. North, Mrs. Granberry was just joking. I don't mind at all."

I looked sternly at Myra and waited.

"Cora, I admire you and am deeply indebted to you and I apologize if I have hurt your feelings in any way."

Mrs. Cummings covered her face with her knitting.

"Theophilus, I promise not to interrupt you if you tell us

about your life in Newport—your friends, your good times, your enemies, and if you're making any money."

"This is not in my contract and I don't like it, but I shall obey. If I mention any names they will be 'made up' names. I live at the Young Men's Christian Association and am saving up money to rent a small apartment. I do not make friends easily, but to my surprise I have already made several in Newport whom I highly value." I told them about the superintendent at the Casino, about an unoccupied valet named "Eddie" ("who talks just like some of the characters in *David Copperfield*"), about some of my tennis pupils—including a girl named "Anemone" who was just like some of the girls in Shakespeare's plays—and about "Mrs. Willoughby's" boardinghouse for domestic servants. I did full justice to "Mrs. Willoughby's" decorum and generosity. When I came to a close there were tears in Myra's eyes. There was a pause.

"Oh, Cora, I wish I were a maid. I wish I lived at Mrs. Willoughby's. I'd be happy. My baby would be born as simply and sweetly as a . . . as a lamb. Theophilus, couldn't you take Cora and me to Mrs. Willoughby's some night?"

"Oh, Mrs. Granberry," said Cora righteously, "I'm a registered nurse. I'm not allowed to do anything like that."

"You go out to dinner parties with me."

"Yes, I sit upstairs until you are ready to go home."

"Myra," I said quietly, "it wouldn't be possible. Everybody likes to be with his or her own kind."

"I wouldn't talk. I know that just to look at it would be good for my baby."

I nodded and smiled and said, "Conversation time is up."

At the following session's conversation break I asked Myra to give me an account of her friends, her good times, and her enemies. She thought a moment. Her face took on a somber cast.

"Well, I grow older. I wait for my baby. I eat breakfast. Then the doctor calls and asks if I've been good. He gets ten dollars for that. Then if it's a sunny day Cora and I go to Bailey's Beach. We sit well wrapped up in a sheltered corner so as not to have to talk to people. We sit and watch the old boots and orange crates drift by."

"I beg your pardon?"

"My father owns hundreds of lakes. If any one were as dirty as Bailey's Beach he'd drain it and plant it with trees. What do we do then, Cora?"

"You go to luncheon parties, Mrs. Granberry."

"Yes, I go to luncheon parties. Ladies. There are men there only on Sundays, all named Granberry. During the week the ladies stay on and play cards. I'm allowed to go home early for my nap because I'm in an 'interesting condition,' as the lady in *Jane Eyre* was. Then my tutors arrive. Several evenings a week I go out to dinner and see the same people—as your Henry James said. Again I come home early and I read as long as Cora lets me. And I can't think of anything else to tell you."

I turned to Mrs. Cummings. "May we ask what you do in your free time?"

She glanced at me for reassurance. I nodded and maybe I winked at her.

"Well, I have an old friend in Newport. She went through training with me—Miss O'Shaughnessy. She's assistant director of nursing at the hospital. At six o'clock on Thursdays Mrs. Granberry kindly has me driven to the hospital in her car. And Miss O'Shaughnessy and I—and sometimes some friends of hers—go to dinner at a restaurant near the beginning of the Cliff Walk. We tell stories of our training days and, Mr. North —being off duty—we have a little bit of the Old Irish and we laugh. I don't know why it is but mostly nurses laugh when they're off duty. And Sunday mornings four of us go to Mass together. Rain or shine—we like the walk too. But I'm always glad to get back to this house, Mrs. Granberry."

Myra was staring at her. "I know Miss O'Shaughnessy. During my second summer here George let me join the Ladies Volunteer Workers at the hospital. I loved it. I couldn't do it the other summers because the doctor wouldn't let me. I hope Miss O'Shaughnessy remembers me; I hope she liked me. Couldn't I come with you some Thursday night?" There was a silence. "I never see anybody that's fun. I never see anybody I like. I never laugh, do I, Cora?"

"Oh, Mrs. Granberry, you forget! You laugh and you make me laugh. When I go to the kitchen they sometimes ask me, 'What do Mrs. Granberry and you laugh about all the time?'"

"Myra," I said, with a shade of severity, "it wouldn't be any holiday for Mrs. Cummings to have dinner with you on Thursday nights. You have dinner together on many evenings."

"It doesn't have to be Thursday nights. I still have my Volunteer's uniform. Mr. North, will you be so kind as to ring that bell?" A servant appeared. "Please ask Madeleine to bring down my Hospital Volunteer's uniform—and to lay it out in the dressing room down here. I won't want the shoes and stockings, but tell her not to forget the cap. Thank you. You've never seen me in my uniform, Cora.—It wouldn't have to be on a Thursday night. We could go on some other night and have a bit of the Old Irish and laugh. The doctor says that a little whiskey wouldn't be bad for me at all.—Besides, I love being in disguise. Cora, you could call me 'Mrs. Nielson.' Can't we go? Maybe Miss O'Shaughnessy could get an extra leave on another night. My husband's on the Hospital Board; he can do *anything*."

We talked reassuringly about the project. Myra murmured meditatively, "When you're in disguise you feel more free."

There was a knock at the inner door and a voice said, "The uniform is ready, Mrs. Granberry."

Myra rose saying "I'll only be a minute," and left the room.

Mrs. Cummings confided to me. "The doctor says we're to let her do anything she wants within reason. Poor child! Poor child!"

We waited. Presently she returned smiling, downright radiant, *free*, in that uniform, in that cap. We clapped our hands.

"I am *Miss* Nielson," she said. She leaned over Mrs. Cummings and asked soothingly, "Where does it hurt, dear? . . . Oh, that's just wind. You must expect that after an operation. It's a sign that all's going well. Your appendix will never trouble you again." She resumed her place on the chaise-longue. "I'd have been happy as a nurse, I know I would.—Mr. North, let's not read any more today. Let's just talk."

"Very well. What shall we talk about?"

"Anything."

"Myra, why do you never make any comment on these novels we've been reading?"

She blushed slightly. "Because . . . you'd make fun of me. You wouldn't understand. They're all so new to me—*those lives, those people*. Sometimes they're more real than life. I don't want to talk about them. Please talk about something else."

"Very well. Are you fond of music, Myra?"

"Concerts? Heaven help us! In New York we go Thursday nights to the opera. The German ones are the longest."

"The theater?"

"No. I went a few times. It's all 'made up.' It's not at all like the novels; *they're* real. Why are you asking me these questions?"

I paused a moment. What was I doing in that house? I told myself that I was earning twelve dollars a week (though my fortnightly bills had not yet been paid); that I derived some satisfaction from introducing a bright but inadequately educated young woman to good reading—a pastime to render less painful her husband's neglect. But I was discouraged—as I was with others I worked with on the Avenue—by association with those who had more than their share of the disadvantages of their advantages.

She had asked me why I asked her those questions.

"Because, Myra, there is a theory that expectant mothers can prepare themselves to bear beautiful well-conditioned children by listening to beautiful music and gazing at beautiful objects."

"Who says that?"

"It's widely held. Italian mothers believe it especially, and everyone can see that their boys and girls look as though they had stepped out of those famous Italian paintings."

"Are there any in Newport—those paintings?"

"Not that I know of—except in books."

She was sitting up straight and looking at me fixedly. "Cora, have you ever heard of such an idea?"

"Oh, Mrs. Granberry! Doctors are always urging ladies in this condition to have lovely thoughts—oh, yes."

Myra continued to stare at me almost angrily. "Well, don't just sit there like a stick. Tell me what I can do."

"Please lie down and shut your eyes and let me talk to you." She looked about her as though annoyed and then did as I requested. "Myra, Newport is often said to be one of the most beautiful towns in this country. You drive up and down Bellevue Avenue and pay visits in the cottages of your friends. You go to Bailey's Beach and you have told me what you think of it. Do you often take the ten-mile drive?"

"It's too long. If you've seen one mile you've seen them all."

"The architecture of the so-called cottages is the laughing-stock of the nation. They are preposterous. There are only three that can be said to be truly beautiful. . . . Now let me tell you my idea of Newport." So I told her about the trees and —at considerable length—about the Nine Cities of Troy and the Nine Cities of Newport. Mrs. Cummings let her knitting fall to her lap, motionless. "Moreover, the view of the sea and the bay from the Budlong place, five miles from here, is one of which you could never grow tired—at dawn, at noon, at dusk, under the stars, and not least, in wind and rain. There you can see the circling beams of six lighthouses that give security to sailors and hear the voice of many buoys saying, 'Steer clear of these rocks and you will have a safe journey.' All of Newport is interesting in one way or another; the least so is the Sixth City."

"You mean *here*?"

"And the most interesting and beautiful is the Second."

"I forget which that is."

"That of the eighteenth century. I'll leave a marked map for your driver. Now can we go back to *Walden*?"

She put her hand to her forehead. "I'm tired today. Will you excuse me, if I ask you to leave now? I want to think. We'll pay you just the same. . . . But stop! Before you go write down the names of those painters in Italy that help make beautiful children, and some pieces of music that are good for that too."

I wrote down: "Raphael. Da Vinci. Fra Angelico," and added an address in New York where the best prints could be obtained. Then: "Gramophone records by Mozart: *Eine Kleine Nachtmusik. Ave, verum corpus.*"

There was a knock at the door. Mr. Granberry entered. Greetings.

"How's my dear little squirrel today?"

"Very well, thank you."

"What are you reading now?"

"*Walden.*"

"*Walden*, oh, yes—*Walden*. Well, that wouldn't interest us much, I think."

"Why not, George?"

He pinched her cheek. "We wouldn't be happy on thirty cents a day."

"I like it. It's the first book I want to read all through in class. George, this is a list of all the books I've read. I want you to buy every one of them for me. Mr. North has to go and get them at the People's Library. They're not very clean and people have written silly things in the margins. I want my own books so that I can write my own silly things in the margins."

"I'll see to that, Myra. My secretary will send for them tomorrow morning. Is there anything else I can do for you?"

"Here are the names of some painters who lived in Italy. If you want to be an angel, you can buy me some pictures by them."

He gasped. "Why, Myra, any pictures by one of these men would cost a hundred thousand dollars."

"Well, you pay more than that for those boats you never use, don't you? You can buy me one and Papa will buy me another. Here's the name of a man who wrote some good music. Please buy me the best gramophone that you can find and those records. . . . I'm a little tired today and I've just asked Mr. North to cut short the reading. I told him we'd pay him just the same . . . but don't *you* go."

Then something very painful happened.

Two days later I was met at the door, as usual, by the butler, Carel, a Czech—as distinguished in appearance as an ambassador but as self-effacing as an ambassador's personal secretary. He bent his head and whispered, "Mrs. Cummings wishes to speak to you here, sir, before you enter the morning room."

"I'll wait here, Carel."

Carel and Mrs. Cummings must have arranged some system of coded signals, for she appeared in the hall. She spoke hurriedly. "Mrs. Granberry received two letters this morning which have upset her *badly*. I think she wants to tell you about them. She wouldn't go for a drive. She has scarcely said a dozen words to me. When you leave, please tell Carel anything I should know. Wait three minutes before you knock on the door." She pressed my hand and returned to the morning room.

I waited three minutes and knocked on the door. It was opened by Mrs. Cummings.

"Good afternoon, ladies," I said buoyantly.

Myra's face was very stern. "Cora, I have something that I must discuss with Mr. North and I must ask you to leave the room for five minutes."

"Oh, Mrs. Granberry, you mustn't ask me to do that. I'm an R.N. and I must obey every word of the doctor's orders."

"All I ask is that you go out on the verandah. You can leave the door ajar, but you must not try to hear a single word."

"I don't like it at all; oh, I don't like it at all."

"Mrs. Cummings," I said, "since this seems to be an important matter to Mrs. Granberry I shall stand by the verandah door where you can see me every minute. If any subject arises that has to do with medical matters I shall *insist* on repeating it to you."

When Mrs. Cummings had withdrawn to a distance I stood waiting like a sentry.

"Theophilus, Badgers always tell the truth to Badgers."

"Myra, I am my own judge of what truths I shall tell. The truth can do just as much harm as a lie."

"I need help."

"Ask me some questions and I shall try to help you so far as I am able."

"Do you know a woman named Flora Deland?"

"I have dined at her house at Narragansett Pier three times."

"Do you know a woman named Desmoulins?"

"I have met her at dinner there once and I have met her by chance on the street in Newport once."

"Is she a harlot and a strumpet and that other thing in *Tom Jones*—a doxy?"

"No, indeed. She is a woman of some refinement. She is what some people would call an 'emancipated' woman. I would never think of applying those ugly words to her."

"'Emancipate' means to free the slaves. Was she a slave?"

I laughed as cheerily as I could. "Oh, no.—Now stop this nonsense and tell me what you are trying to get at."

"Is she better-looking than I am?"

"No."

"Badger?"

"Badger!"

"BADGER?"

"BADGER!—She is a very pretty woman. You are a very beautiful woman. I'll go and call Mrs. Cummings."

"Stop!—Have you had dinner almost every Thursday night with my husband and Miss Desmoulins at the Muenchinger-King?"

"No. *Never*. Please get to the point."

"I have received two an-anonny-mous letters."

"Myra! You tore them up at once."

"No." She lifted a book on the table and revealed two envelopes.

"I'm ashamed of you. . . . In the world—and especially in a place like Newport—we are surrounded by people whose heads are filled with hate and envy and nastiness. Once in a while one of them takes to writing anonymous letters. They say it comes and goes in epidemics, like influenza. You should have torn them into small pieces—unread—and put them out of your mind. Do they say that I had dinner with those two persons at the M-K?"

"Yes."

"Well, that's a sample of the lies that fill anonymous letters."

"Read them. Please read them."

I debated with myself: "Hell, I'm resigning from this job tonight anyway."

I studied the envelopes carefully. Then I glanced through the contents; I can read fast. When I came to the end of the second I burst out laughing. "Myra, all anonymous letters are signed either by 'A Friend' or 'Your Well-Wisher.'" She burst into tears. "Myra, no Badger cries after the age of eleven."

"I'm sorry."

"Years ago, Badger, I planned to make my life-career that of being a detective. When boys are ambitious they really are ambitious. I read all the professional handbooks about it—hard, tough books of instruction. And I remember that the tracing down of anonymous letter writers was an important section. We were taught that there are twenty-one 'give-away' clues to every anonymous letter. Give me these letters and in two weeks I'll find the writer and drive him—or her—out of town."

"But, Theophilus, maybe *him* or *her* is right. Maybe my husband loves Miss Desmoulins. Maybe my baby has no father any more. Then I might as well die. Because I love my husband more than anything else in the world."

"Badgers don't cry, Myra—they fight. They're smart, they're brave, and they defend what they've got. They also have something that I find missing in you."

She looked at me, appalled. "What?"

"They're like otters. They have a sense of fun and laughter and *wicked tricks*."

"But, Theophilus, I've always had them too. But lately I've had so much illness and lonesomeness and boredom. Believe me, my father used to call me his 'little devil.' Oh, Theophilus, put your arm around me one minute."

Laughingly I squeezed her hand hard and said, "Not one second!—Now promise me that you'll put this whole wretched business out of your head for a week. . . . Badgers always catch the snake. Can I call Mrs. Cummings now? . . . Mrs. Cummings, it's school time. Mrs. Cummings, you're a wonderful friend and you should know what we talked about. Mrs. Granberry heard an ugly bit of gossip. I told her that no one who's intelligent and beautiful and rich has ever escaped gossip. Aren't I right?"

"Oh, Mr. North, you're very right."

Naturally that about the twenty-one clues was sheer kite-flying. In my hasty glance at the letter I read that Mr. Granberry entertained Mlle. Desmoulins at dinner in one of the small dining rooms at the Muenchinger-King every Thursday night. It went on to tell of Flora Deland's dinners, mentioned myself, bloodwarmingly, as an "odious person," then rambled on in a grieved self-righteous way. I judged that they had been written by a woman, some former friend of George Granberry, that unoccupied planless inventor—perhaps by a Granberry. I returned to our classroom work as though nothing had intervened to upset it. We read *Walden*.

I needed help—that is to say, I needed to know more.

I arranged to meet Henry for a pool game at Herman's. During an interval I asked him if he knew George F. Granberry. He was chalking his cue thoughtfully and said, "Funny, your asking me that," and went on with the game. When the set was over we paid up and withdrew to a corner and ordered our usual.

"I don't like to mention names. We'll call the party Longears. Choppers, under idleness all men and women become children again. Women cope with it better than men, but all men become babies. Look at me: when my Chief's away I have to fight it every minute. Fortunately, just now I'm busy. Edweena and I are exchanging letters and making plans. We're the Governors of the Servants' Ball at the end of the season and that takes a lot of hard work. . . . Longears belongs to a very large family. He could get a job any minute in the family's firm, but it's stuffed already with a dozen members of the same name, all of them brighter than he is. They don't want him. He doesn't need the money. Before the War there were scores of young and middle-aged men like him in New York and Newport, rich, and idle as tailors' dummies. In 1926 you can count 'em on one hand. When I arrived here he was already a divorced man—so maybe the blight had set in early. Everybody said he used to be intelligent and popular. For some reason he couldn't get into the War. He married again—a girl from the Wild West, like Tennessee or Buffalo. She has poor health. Nobody sees her much. Men like that take to drink or women or gambling. A few take to boasting, to setting themselves up as some kind of superior person—something special. Longears pretends that he's an inventor. He has a workshop out in Portsmouth—very secret, very important. Rumors—some say he's making bread out of seaweed or making gasoline out of manure. Anyway, he *hides* there. Some people say that he doesn't do anything more than play with electric trains or stick postage stamps into his collection. . . . Used to be a fine fellow. He was my Chief's best friend, but now my Chief just wags his head when he's mentioned."

"Was it the divorce that broke him up?"

"I wouldn't know. I think it's merely nothing-to-do. Idleness is dry rot. . . . He has a girl hidden in the bushes here somewhere—he's not the only one who does that, of course. . . . That's all I know."

At the next session I appeared with a satchel under my arm. Among the books it contained were three school editions of *Twelfth Night* and three of *As You Like It*. I had worked for hours on them, selecting scenes for group reading. "Good

afternoon, ladies. Today we are going to try something new."
I drew out the copies of *Twelfth Night*.

"Oh, Theophilus—not Shakespeare! *Please!*"

"You dislike his work?" I asked in hypocritical wonder. I
began cramming the copies back into the satchel. "That surprises me, but you remember we agreed at our first meeting
that we'd not read anything that bored you. Excuse me! My
mistake is due to my inexperience. Hitherto I've tutored only
boys and young men. After a short resistance I'd found that
they take to Shakespeare enthusiastically. I've had them striding up and down my classroom pretending to be Romeo and
Juliet and Shylock and Portia—eating it up! . . . I remember
now how surprised I was when Mr. Granberry also said that he
had always thought Shakespeare to be 'piffle.' Well, I have another novel here to try."

Myra was staring at me. "Wait a minute! . . . But his plays
are so childish. All those girls dressing up in men's clothes. It's
idiotic!"

"Yes, a few of them. But notice how Shakespeare has arranged
it. The girls have to do so because they're destitute; their backs
are against the wall. Viola is shipwrecked in a foreign country;
Rosalind is exiled—thrown out into the wilderness; Imogen
has been slandered in her husband's absence. Portia dresses
like a lawyer to save the life of her husband's best friend. In
those days a self-respecting girl couldn't go from door to door
asking for a job. . . . Let's forget it! . . . But what girls they
are: beautiful, brave, intelligent, resourceful! In addition, I've
always felt they have a quality that I've found . . . a little
. . . missing in you, Myra."

"What's that?"

"A humorous mind."

"A *what?*"

"I don't know exactly what I mean, but I get the impression
that they've observed life so attentively—young though they
are—that they don't shrink from the real; they're never crushed
or shocked or at their wit's end. Even when the big catastrophe
comes their minds are so deeply grounded that they can face it
with humor and gaiety. When Rosalind is driven out into that
dangerous wilderness she says to her cousin Celia:

Now go we in content
To liberty, and not to banishment.

I wish I'd heard Ellen Terry say that; and soon after Viola had lost her brother in that shipwreck someone asks her about her family and she—dressed as a boy and now called Cesario—says:

I am all the daughters of my father's house,
And all the brothers too.

I wish I'd heard Julia Marlowe say that."

Myra asked me harshly, "What good does it do you—this famous 'humorous mind'?"

"Shakespeare places these clear-eyed girls among a lot of people who are in an incorrect relation to the real. As a later author said, 'Most of the people in the world are fools and the rest of us are in great danger of contagion.' A humorous mind enables us to accommodate ourselves to their folly—and to our own.—Do you think there's something in that, Mrs. Cummings?"

"Oh, Mr. North, I think that's why nurses laugh when they're off duty. It helps us—like you might say—to survive."

Myra was staring at me without seeing me.

Mrs. Cummings asked, "Mrs. Granberry, can't we ask Mr. North to read to us a little out of Shakespeare?"

"Well . . . if it's not too long."

I put my hand tentatively into the satchel. "My idea was that we all take parts. I've underlined Myra's part in red, and Mrs. Cummings's in blue, and I'll read the rest."

"Oh," cried Mrs. Cummings, "I can't read poetry-English. I couldn't do that. You've got to excuse me."

"Cora, if that's the way Mr. North wants it, I suppose we must let him have his way."

"God bless my soul!"

"Now slowly, everybody—*slowly*!"

Within the week we had done scenes from those plays—and repeated them, switching roles—and the balcony scene from *Romeo and Juliet* and the trial scene from *The Merchant of Venice*. Mrs. Cummings astonished herself as Shylock. It was Myra who, at the end of each scene, said, "Now let's do it again!"

One afternoon Myra greeted me at the door with an air of suppressed excitement. "Theophilus, I asked my husband to come here at four-thirty. We're going to do the trial scene from *The Merchant of Venice* and I'm going to make him play Shylock. You be Antonio, I'll be Portia, and Cora will be everybody else. Let's rehearse it once before he comes. Cora, I want you to be splendid as the Duke."

"Oh, Mrs. Granberry!"

We put our hearts into it. *Myra had memorized her lines.*

A knock on the door: enter George F. Granberry II. Myra was silken. "George darling, we want you to help us. Please don't say no because it would make me very unhappy."

"What can I do?"

She put the open book in his hands. "George, you must read Shylock. Go very slowly and be very bloodthirsty. Sharpen the knife on your shoe. Mr. North is going to lean backward over that desk with his chest exposed and his hands tied behind him."

"Now, Myra, that's enough! I'm no actor."

"Oh, George! It's just a game. We'll do it twice so you'll get the hang of it, and *go slowly.*"

We started off haltingly, groping for our words on the page. As Shylock leaned over me, an ivory paper-cutter in his hand, he said under his voice, "North, I'd like to cut out your gizzard. Something's going on here that I don't like. You've fouled up the whole air around here."

"You engaged me to interest your wife in reading and especially in Shakespeare. I've done that and I'm ready to resign when you pay the three two-week bills I've sent you."

That took his breath away.

During the first rehearsal Myra had made a show of reading indifferently and stumbling over her words. On the second time around we played for all we were worth. Myra laid aside her book; at first she represented the young lawyer Balthasar with a slight playful swagger, but she grew in authority speech after speech.

George was caught up into the spirit of the thing. He roared for his "bond" and his pound of flesh. Again he leaned over me, savagely, knife in hand. Then something extraordinary took place.

PORTIA: *Do you confess the bond?*
ANTONIO: *I do.*
PORTIA: *Then must the Jew be merciful.*
SHYLOCK: *On what compulsion must I? Tell me that!*

Here George felt a hand rest on his shoulder and heard behind him a voice saying—gravely, earnestly, from some realm of maturity that had been long absent from his life:

PORTIA: *The quality of mercy is not strained,*
             It droppeth like the gentle rain . . .
             . . . We do pray for mercy;
             And that same prayer doth teach us all to render
             The deeds of mercy. . . .

George straightened up and threw down the ivory knife. He said confusedly, "Go on with your reading. I'll see you . . . another time," and he left the room.

We looked at one another surprised and a little guilty. Mrs. Cummings took up her sewing. "Mr. North, play-acting is a little too exciting for us all. I haven't said much about it, but Mrs. Granberry always stands up and moves about the room. I don't think the doctor would like that. We haven't had a talk-time lately. You told Mrs. Granberry you'd tell her sometime what it was like when you went to school in China."

I vowed that I'd send in my resignation that night—before I was fired—but I didn't and I wasn't. I was more than half in love with Myra. I was proud of her and proud of my work. A check arrived for me in Monday morning's mail. We began *Huckleberry Finn*. On Friday another surprising thing happened. I bicycled up to the portal of the house. I saw a young man of about twenty-four strolling on the lawn, smelling a long-stemmed rose. He was dressed in the height of fashion—straw hat, blazer of the Newport Yacht Club, flannels, and white shoes. He approached me and put out his hand.

"Mr. North, I believe. I am Caesar Nielson, the twin brother of Myra Granberry. *How* d'you do?"

Zounds! Holy cabooses! It was Myra.

God, how I hate transvestism! I shuddered; but never contradict a pregnant woman.

"Is your sister at home, Mr. Nielson?"

"We've ordered the car. We thought it would be nice to drive to Narragansett Pier and ask your friend Mademoiselle Desmoulins for a cup of tea."

"Sir, you forget that I am employed here to read English literature with Mrs. Granberry. I am only here under the conditions of my contract. Will you excuse me? I don't wish to be late for my appointment.—Would you like to join us?"

I looked up at the house and saw Mrs. Cummings and Carel, stricken, watching us from the drawing-room windows. Faces were similarly framed in many windows of the upper floors.

Myra came nearer to me and murmured, "Badgers fight to defend what they've got."

"Yes, but since nature made them small she made them clever. No well-conditioned badger or woman destroys her home to preserve it. Please precede me, Mr. Nielson."

She entered the house disturbed, but chin up. As I followed her through the hall Carel said to me in a low voice, "Mr. Granberry has been in the house for half an hour, sir. He returned by the coachhouse drive."

"Do you think he saw the show?"

"I'm sure he did, sir."

"Thank you, Carel."

"Thank you, sir."

I followed Myra and Mrs. Cummings into the morning room. "Myra, please change your clothes quickly. Mr. Granberry is in the house and will probably be here in a few minutes. He will probably dismiss Mrs. Cummings and me, and your next few months will be very dreary indeed."

"Shakespeare's girls did it."

"Please leave the door of your dressing room open two inches so that I can talk to you while you are changing your clothes.— Can you hear me?"

But we were too late. Mr. Granberry entered the room without knocking. "Myra!" he called. She appeared at the door, still Caesar Nielson. She returned his angry gaze unabashed.

"Pants!" he said, "PANTS!"

"I'm an emancipated woman like Miss Desmoulins."

"Mrs. Cummings, you are leaving the house as soon as you can pack. Mr. North, will you follow me into the library?"

I bowed low to the ladies, opening my eyes wide in smiling admiration.

In the library Mr. Granberry was seated behind the desk like a judge. I sat down and crossed my legs composedly.

"You broke your promise to me. You told my wife about Narragansett Pier."

"Your wife told me about Narragansett Pier. She had received two anonymous letters."

He blanched. "You should have told me that."

"I was engaged by you to be a reader of English literature, not a confidential friend of the family."

Silence.

"You're the biggest nuisance in town. Everybody's talking about the hell you kicked up among the Bosworths at 'Nine Gables.' And Heaven knows what's going on at the Wyckoff place. I'm sorry I called you in.—God, I hate Yale men!"

Silence.

"Mr. Granberry, I hate injustice and I think you do too."

"What's that got to do with it?"

"If you dismiss Mrs. Cummings as incompetent in her profession, by God, I shall write a letter to the doctor or to whatever agency sent her telling them what I found here."

"That's blackmail."

"No, that is a deposition in a suit for slander. Mrs. Cummings is obviously a superior trained nurse. In addition—as far as I can see—she has been your wife's only friend and support in a difficult time." I put a slight emphasis on the word "only."

Another silence.

He looked at me somberly. "What do you suggest I do?"

"I seldom offer advice, Mr. Granberry. I don't know enough."

"Stop hammering that 'Mr. Granberry.' Since we hate each other I suggest we use first names. I'm told that you are called Teddie."

"Thank you. I don't give advice, George, but I think it would help you if you just talked to me at random about the whole situation."

"God damn it, I can't live like a monk half a year *again*, just because my wife's under doctor's care. I know a pack of men who have someone like Denise in the woods. What did I do wrong? Denise was a friend of a friend of mine; he passed her over to me. Denise is a nice girl. The only trouble with her is that she cries half the time. French people have to go back to France every two years or they expire like fish on ice. She misses her mother, she says. She misses the smell of the Paris streets— imagine that! . . . All right, I know what you're thinking. I'll give her a pack of Granberry stock and send her back to Paris. But what the hell will I do here? *Play Shakespeare all day?* . . . Well, say something. Don't just sit there like an ox. Jesus!"

"I'm trying to get some ideas. Please go on talking a little longer, George."

Silence.

"You think I neglect Myra. I do and I know I do. Do you know why? I . . . I . . . How old are you?"

"Thirty."

"Married? Ever been married?"

"No."

"I can't stand being loved—loved?—worshiped! Overestimation freezes me. My mother overestimated me and I haven't said a sincere word to her since I was fifteen years old. And now Myra! She suffers and I know she suffers. I wasn't lying to you when I told you I loved her. Wasn't I right when I told you she was intelligent and all that?"

"Yes."

"And suffers all the time . . . four years of suffering and I'm the only person she gives a damn about. I can't stand it. I can't stand the responsibility. When I come into her presence I freeze. Teddie, can you understand that?"

"Can I ask you a question?"

"Go ahead. I'm numb anyway."

"George, what do you do in the laboratory all day?"

He rose, threw me an angry glance, sauntered about the room, then placed his hands on the lintel above the door into the hall and hung there—as boys with their excess energy do (and to hide their faces).

"Well," he said, "I'll tell you. The principal reason is to hide myself. To wait for something, to wait for things to get worse or to get better. 'What I do' is to play war-games. Since I was a boy I've played with tin soldiers. I wasn't able to get into war service because of some malfunction of the heart. . . . I have dozens of books; I do the Battle of the Marne, and the whole lot. . . . I do Napoleon's and Caesar's battles. . . . You're famous around here for keeping secrets, so please keep that secret."

Tears filled my eyes and I smiled. "And soon you'll have to face another ordeal. In about three years a little girl or a little boy is going to come into the room and say, 'Papa, I fell down and hurt myself. Look't, Papa, look't!' and someone else will love you. All love is overestimation."

"Make it a girl, professor; I couldn't stand a boy."

"I see your next step, George. Learn to accept love—with a smile, with a grin."

"Oh, God!"

"Can I be a fool and give a piece of advice?"

"Keep it short."

"Go down the hall into the morning room. Stand up straight in the door and say, 'I'm sending Mademoiselle Desmoulins back to France with a nice goodbye present.' Then go and get down on one knee by the chaise-longue and say, 'Forgive me, Myra.' Then look Mrs. Cummings in the eye and say, 'Forgive me, Mrs. Cummings.' Women won't forgive us for ever and ever, but they love to forgive us when we ask them to."

"You mean that I should do that now?"

"Oh, yes—now.—And, by the way, ask her to dinner Thursday night at the Muenchinger-King."

He left the room.

As I went out the front door I shook hands with Carel. "This is the last time I shall be in this house. If you have an opportunity, could you express to Mrs. Granberry and Mrs. Cummings my admiration . . . and affection? Thank you, Carel."

"Thank you, sir."

10

Mino

AT THE bottom of Broadway, at a corner of Washington Square and across the street from Old Colony House, there stood a store that I visited daily. It sold newspapers, magazines, picture postcards, maps for tourists, toys for children, and even Butterick patterns. It was very Ninth City. It was run by one family, the Materas—father, mother, son, and daughter took turns serving the public. I was to learn that their name was far more complicated; when the parents emigrated to America they adopted the name of their birthplace to simplify the formalities at Ellis Island. They came from the desolate impoverished part of the instep of Italy's boot that the government of Rome and—as we are told in Carlo Levi's fine book *Cristo si è fermato a Eboli*—God forgot. The title does not mean that Christ stopped at Eboli to enjoy the environs, but that in despair He went no further.

I love Italians. My friendship with the Materas began with my attempts to ingratiate myself by speaking their language, however haltingly. I barely made myself understood. I then tried the Neapolitan dialect even more haltingly (yet how I relished it!), but the the dialects of Lucania are impenetrable to the outsider. We conversed in English.

High among the glories of Italy are the mothers of Italy. Their whole self is delivered over to husband and children. Through sheer selflessness they become wonderful selves. Maternal love there has no element of possessiveness; it is a hearth-fire of astonished wonder, ever renewed, that those lives are bound up with their own. It can be just as dangerous for the growing girl and especially the growing boy as devouring maternal love—so often prevalent in other parts of the world—can be; for what young person can wish to break away from the warmth and support of all that devotion, laughter, and cooking?

Mamma had love and laughter to spare. I stopped in at the store daily to buy my New York paper, and pencils, ink, or other incidentals. I bowed to the parents with due deference and to the children with comradely liveliness and before long came within the orbit of Signora Carla's generous heart. The Materas were of a dark complexion (the Saracen invaders of Calabria). Rosa, twenty-four, seemed to be unaware that some might regard her as plain; helping her parents and brother was quite sufficient to fill her life with buoyancy. Benjy, twenty-two —when it was his turn to mind the store—sat cross-legged on a shelf beside the cash register. All spoke English, but all non-Italian names seemed equally unpronounceable to Signora Matera; the only ones she knew well (and revered) were "Presidente Vilson" and "Generale Perchin." Except very occasionally I am not going to attempt to reproduce the *signora*'s pronunciation. After a certain time we cease to notice a valued foreigner's "accent"; the communications of friendship transcend the accidents of language.

One late afternoon I returned to the "Y" and was informed by the desk clerk that a lady was waiting for me in the little reception room off the lobby. What was my surprise to discover Signora Matera sitting majestically at ease, with a six-weeks-old clipping of my newspaper advertisement in her hand. I greeted her delightedly.

She was amazed. She waved the clipping. "*You . . . you* are Mr. Nort'?"

"Yes, *signora*. I thought you knew my name."

She repeated with heart-felt relief: "*You* are Mr. Nort'!"

"Yes, *cara signora*. What can I do for you?"

"I come for Benjamino and myself. Benjamino wants to take lessons with you. He wants to study Dante with you. He makes money; he can pay you very well. He wants to read Dante with you for eight hours—that is sixteen dollars. You *know* Benjamino?"

"Yes, indeed, I know Benjamino. I see him almost every day in your store and I often see him at the People's Library where he is surrounded by dozens of books. But, of course, we are not allowed to talk in the library. Tell me about him. Why is he always up in one place by the cash register?"

"You did not know he is a cripple? He has no feet."

"No, *signora*, I did not know that."

"When he was five he ran into a train and lost his feet."

Her memory of that terrible occasion was all in her eyes and

I met it; but she had lived so many days since in wondering astonishment and love of her son that the grief had been transmuted into what she was about to tell me. "Benjy is a very bright boy. He wins prizes every week. He does all the puzzles in the papers. You know how many papers and magazines we have. He wins all the contests in the advertisements. Checks come in the mail every week, five dollars, ten dollars, once twenty dollars. He wins clocks, bicycles, big cases of dog food. He won a trip to Washington, D.C.; when he told them he was a cripple they sent him the money. But that is not all." She pointed to her forehead. "He is very smart. He makes up puzzles for the papers. Papers in Boston and New York pay him to send them puzzles—arithmetic puzzles, joke puzzles, chess puzzles. And now something new has happened. He has invented a new kind of puzzle. I do not understand it. He makes patterns of words that go up and down. *Sindacatos* want to buy them for the Sunday papers.—Why do they call them *sindacatos*, Mr. Nort'?"

"I don't know." (To her, *sindaco* meant a mayor or town magistrate.)

"How much schooling has he had, *signora*?"

"He went through grammar school—always top of his class. But the High School has stone steps. He goes to school in his little wagon, but he did not want the boys to carry him up and down those big steps twenty times a day. The boys like him very much; *everybody* loves Benjy. But he is very independent. Do you know what he did? He wrote to the Department of Education at Providence to send him the lessons and examinations that they have for students in hospitals—for TB students and paralyzed students. And he passed High School, top of his class. They send him a diploma with a note from the Governor!"

"Wonderful!"

"Yes, God is good to us!" she said and burst out laughing. She had long steeled herself not to weep, but one has to do something.

"Does Benjamino want to go to college?"

"No. He says he can do studies by himself now."

"Why does he want to read Dante?"

"Mr. Nort', I think he has played a trick on me. I think he knew all the time that you were the Mr. Nort' in this advertisement. I think he liked the way you talked to him. He has many friends—school friends, teachers, his priest; but he says they all talk to him as if he were a cripple. I think he thought you knew he had no feet, but you did not talk to him as if he were a cripple. The others pat him on the back and make loud jokes. He says they don't talk to him *natural*. Maybe you talked to him natural." She lowered her voice. "Please do not tell him that you did *not* know he had this trouble."

"I won't."

"Maybe he wants to learn what Dante says about people who've had accidents—about why God sends accidents to some people and not to other people."

"*Signora*, tell Benjamino that I am not a Dante scholar. The study of Dante is a vast subject to which hundreds of men have devoted a whole lifetime. Dante is full of theology—*full* of it. I know very little theology. I'd be ashamed. A brilliant boy like your son would ask me questions every minute that I couldn't answer."

Signora Matera looked stricken. I can't endure calling forth a stricken look on an Italian mother's face.

"*Signora*, what time do you all go to church on Sunday?"

"The seven o'clock Mass. We have to sell the Sunday papers at eight-thirty."

"I have a Sunday morning appointment at a quarter before eleven. Would it be inconvenient if I came and sat with Benjamino at nine o'clock?"

"*Grazie! Grazie!*"

"No lesson. No money. Just talk."

I was punctual. The store was filled with customers buying their Boston or Providence Sunday papers. Rosa slipped out of line and led me through the door connecting the store with the house. Finger on her lip, she pointed to the door of her brother's room. I knocked.

"Come in, please."

His room was as small and neat as a ship's cabin. He was sitting cross-legged on some pillows at the head of his bed. He was wearing a trim sea-captain's coat with silver buttons. Across his knees was a drawing-board; this was also his workroom. A carpenter had built shelves on three sides of the room, including those at his right and left within reach of his long arms. I saw dictionaries and other works of reference and piles of paper ruled with grid lines for the making of puzzles. Benjy was a very handsome fellow, his large head covered with curly brown hair and his face lit up by his Saracen-Italian eyes and the Matera smile. But for his accident he would have been an unusually tall man. His level gaze and deep bass voice gave the impression of his being older than he was. For me there was an armchair at the foot of the bed.

"*Buon giorno, Benjamino!*"

"*Buon giorno, professore!*"

"Are you disappointed that we aren't going to read Dante?" He made no answer, but continued smiling. "I thought of Dante yesterday morning. I drove out to Brenton's Point on my bicycle to see the sunrise. And

> *L'alba vinceva l'ora mattutina,*
> *che fuggía innanzi, sì che di lontano*
> *conobbi il tremolar della marina.*

Do you know where Dante says that?"

"At the beginning of the *Purgatorio*."

I was taken aback. "Benjamino, everybody around here calls you Benjy. That sounds a little too street-corner and ordinary for you. May I have your permission to call you Mino?" He nodded. "Do you know of anyone else who was called Mino?"

"Mino da Fiesole."

"What was 'Mino' probably short for in that case?"

"Maybe Giacomino—or Benjamino."

"Do you know what Benjamin means in Hebrew?"

" 'Son of the right hand.' "

"Mino, this is beginning to sound like a classroom examination. We must stop that. But I do want to go back to Dante for a moment. Did you ever take the trouble to learn any passages in Dante by heart?"

The reader may think this was reprehensible on my part, but one of the rewards of being a teacher is watching a brilliant student display his knowledge. It is like putting a promising young racehorse through his paces. A good student enjoys it.

Mino said, "Not very much—just the famous passages, like Paolo and Francesca or La Pia and some others."

"When Count Ugolino was locked up in the Tower of Famine with his sons and grandsons, without food, and days and days went by—what do you think that much-disputed verse means: '*Poscia, più che 'l dolor, potè il digiuno*'?'" Mino gazed at me in silence. "How would you translate it?"

"'Then . . . hunger . . . had more power than . . . grief.'"

"What do you think we are to understand?"

"He . . . ate them."

"Many distinguished scholars, especially in the last century, think it means 'I died of hunger which was even stronger than my grief.' What makes you think as you do?"

Suddenly his expression became one of passionate intensity. "Because the whole passage is full of *that*. The son says to his father, 'You gave us this flesh; now take it back!' And all the time he is talking—in all that ice at the bottom of Hell—he is gnawing the back of his enemy's neck."

"I think you're right, Mino. The nineteenth-century scholars refused to face the cruel truth. The *Divine Comedy* was translated in Cambridge, Massachusetts, by Charles Eliot Norton and again by Henry Wadsworth Longfellow—with notes—and by Thomas Carlyle's brother in London; they refused to see it as you do. It should teach us that Anglo-Saxons and Protestants have always misunderstood your country. They've wanted the sweetness without the iron—without the famous Italian *terribilità*. Evasion, shrinking from the whole of life. Haven't you found people pretending that you never had an accident?"

He gazed at me earnestly, but made no answer. I smiled. He smiled. I laughed. He laughed.

"Mino, what do you miss most because of the accident to your feet?"

"That I can't go to dances." He blushed. We both burst out laughing.

"If you'd lost your eyesight, what would you have missed most?"

He thought a minute and replied, "Seeing faces."

"Not reading?"

"There are substitutes for reading; there are no substitutes for not seeing faces."

"Damn it, Mino! Your mother was right. It's too bad about your feet, but you're certainly all right in the upper story."

Now, reader, I know what he wanted to talk about, you know

what he most wanted to talk about (at two dollars an hour), and I suspect that his mother knew what he most wanted to talk about—there had been a certain emphasis in her report of his complaint that the boys and men he knew did not talk to him "natural." By what appears to be a coincidence (but the older I grow, the less surprised I am by what are called coincidences) I came to this interview with Mino prepared—armed—with a certain amount of experience acquired five years previously.

The following recall of this experience in 1921 is no idle digression:

When I was discharged from the Army (having defended, unopposed, this very same Narragansett Bay) I returned to continue my education; then I got a job teaching at the Raritan School in New Jersey. In those days at no great distance from the school there was a veterans' hospital for amputees and paraplegics. The hospital had a hard-worked staff of nurses and recreation directors. Ladies in the neighboring towns volunteered their services in the latter department—and stout-hearted ladies they were, for it is no easy thing to enter suddenly into a world of four hundred men, most of whom have lost one or more limbs. They played checkers and chess with the men; they gave lessons in the mandolin and guitar; they organized classes in watercolor painting, public speaking, amateur theatricals, and glee club singing. But the volunteer workers fell all too short. Those four hundred men had nothing to do for fifteen hours a day but to play cards, torment the nurses, and to conceal from one another their dread of the future that lay before them. Moreover there were few male volunteers; American men were back at home from war, hard at work, picking up their interrupted lives. And naturally no man would willingly enter that jungle of frantic wounded men unless he had himself been a soldier. So the superintendent of the hospital sent out word to the headmasters of the private schools in the nearby counties asking for ex-military volunteers to assist the recreation director. Transportation would be provided. A number of us from the Raritan School (including T. T. North, corporal, Coast Artillery, retired) piled into a weapons-carrier and rattled off thirty miles to the hospital on Monday mornings and Friday afternoons.

"Gentlemen," said the recreation director, "a lot of these fellows think they want to learn journalism. They think they can earn a million dollars by selling their war experiences to the *Saturday Evening Post*. Some don't want to think about the War; they want to write and sell Wild West stories or cops-and-robbers stories. Most of them never got out of high school. They can't write a laundry list. . . . I'm dividing you volunteers into sections. Each of you has twelve men. They've signed up eagerly; you don't have to worry about that. Your classes are called Journalism and Writing for Money! They're eager enough, but let me prepare you for one thing: their attention gets tired easily. Arrange so that every fifteen minutes *they* have a chance to talk. Most of them are real nice fellows: you won't have any trouble with discipline. But they're haunted by fear of the future. If you finally get their confidence you'll get an earful. Now I'm going to talk frankly to you men: they think they can never get a girl to marry them; they're afraid they can't even get a whore to sleep with them. They think most of the outside world looks on them as sort of eunuchs. Most of them aren't, of course, but one of the effects of amputation is the fancy that they've been castrated. In one ward or another every night someone wakes up screaming in a nightmare *about that*. All they think about, really, is sex, sex, sex—and just as desperately: the prospect of being dependent all their lives on others. So every fifteen minutes take a conversation-break. Your real contribution here is to let them blow off steam. One more word: all day and most of the night they use foul language to one another—New York smut, Kentucky smut, Oklahoma smut, California smut. That's understandable, isn't it? We have a rule here; if they talk like that within the hearing of the nurses or the padres or you volunteers, they're penalized. They get their cigarette allowance cut or they can't get their daily swim in the pool or they can't go to the movie show. I wish you'd cooperate with us in this matter. You'll get their respect by being severe with them, not easy. Give them an assignment. Tell them you want an article or a story or a poem from each one of them when you return a week from today. Miss Warriner will now lead you to your tables in the gym. Thank you, gentlemen, for coming."

"Mino, I think it's great the way you struck out for yourself and are on the way to making yourself self-supporting—first solving the puzzles and then inventing new ones. Tell me how that happened?"

"I began doing them when I was about twelve. Schoolwork wasn't very hard so I used to read a lot. Rosa would bring me books from the library."

"What kind of books then?"

"I thought then that I'd be an astronomer, but I began that too early. I wasn't ready for the mathematics. I am now. Later I wanted to be a priest. Of course I couldn't, but I read a lot of theology and philosophy. I didn't understand all of it, but . . . that's when I learned a lot of Latin."

"Couldn't you find anyone to talk those things over with?"

"I like to figure things out by myself."

"Hell, you wanted to read Dante with me."

He blushed and murmured, "That's different . . . then I began doing puzzles to make money to buy books."

"Show me some puzzles that you've been making."

Most of the shelves within reach of his hand were like those in a linen closet. He drew out a sheaf of leaves; the puzzles were written with India ink on art paper. "*Opus elegantissimum, juvenis!*" I said. "Do you get a lot of pleasure out of this?"

"No. I get pleasure out of the money."

I lowered my voice. "I remember my first paycheck. It was like a kick in the pants. It's the beginning of manhood. Your mother told me you were inventing some new things."

"I have designs for three new games for adults. Do you know Mr. Aldeburg?"

"No."

"He's a lawyer in town. He's helping me take out patents for them. The whole field of puzzles and games is full of crooks. They're crazy for new ideas and they'd steal anything."

I leaned back. "Mino, what are the three most important things you want to do when the real money starts coming in?"

He reached toward another shelf and brought out a manufacturer's catalogue—hospital equipment, wheelchairs for invalids. He opened it and held a page toward me: a rolling chair, propelled by a motor, nickel-plated, with a detachable awning for protection against rain, snow, or sun—a beauty. Two hundred and seventy-five dollars.

I whistled. "And after that?"

Another catalogue. "I get fitted for some boots. They're attached to my legs above and below the knee by a lot of straps. I'd still have to use crutches, but my feet wouldn't swing. Through my legs I could put some of my weight on the ground. But I'd have to use some kind of cane to prevent my falling on my face. I think I could invent something after I'd got used to the boots."

Such was his mature control that he might have been talking about buying a car. But there was one element of confidence still lacking. I went right to the point. "And after that you want to rent your own apartment?"

"Yes," he said surprised.

"Where you can entertain your friends?"

"Yes," he said and looked at me sharply to see if I had guessed what was in his mind. I smiled and repeated my question, holding his glance. The courage ebbed out of him and his eyes fell away.

"Can I look over your books, Mino?"

"Sure."

I rose and turned to the shelves behind me. The books were all second-hand and appeared to have suffered long use—longer than his life. If he had bought them in Newport he must have ransacked the same second-hand stores that I had come to know when I was "excavating" the Fifth City. Maybe he had ordered them from the catalogues of such dealers in the larger cities. On the bottom shelf were the *Britannica* (eleventh), some atlases, star charts, and other large works of reference. The majority of the shelves were filled with works on astronomy and mathematics. I took down Newton's *Principia*. The margins were covered with notes in fine handwriting and in faded ink.

"Are these notes yours?"

"No, but they're very sharp."

"Where's your *Divina Commedia*?"

He pointed to two shelves within his reach: the *Summa*, Spinoza, the *Aeneid*, the *Pensées* of Pascal, Descartes . . .

"You read French?"

"Rosa's crazy about French. We play chess and go and parcheesi in French."

I had been thinking of Elbert Hughes. So there was another half-genius in Newport; maybe a genius. Maybe a late blooming of the Fifth City. I remembered having heard that in Concord, Massachusetts, almost a century before, groups used to devote an evening to reading aloud in Italian or Greek or German, or even in Sanskrit. In Berkeley, California, my mother used to read Italian aloud with Mrs. Day on one evening in the week and French with Mrs. Vincent on another. She attended German classes at the University (Professor Pinger), because we, her children, had learned some German in two successive German schools in China.

It was on the tip of my tongue to ask Mino if he had any wish to go to either of the two universities nearby. I saw that his rigorous independence not only forbade his relying on others to help him move about from place to place, but that his deprivation had shaped his mind toward becoming an autodidact. ("I like to figure things out by myself.") I remembered how the father of Pascal had come upon the young boy reading with delight the First Book of Euclid. The father had other plans for his son's education. He took away the volume, scarcely begun, and shut the boy in his room; but Pascal wrote the rest of the book himself, deducing the properties of the rectangle and the triangle, as a silkworm produces silk from his own entrails. But in the case of Mino I was saddened. In the twentieth century it is not possible to advance far as an autodidact in the vast fields of his interests. I had already known such solitary men—and in later years discovered others—who, having early repudiated formal education, were writing a *History of the Human Intelligence* or *The Sources of Moral Values*.

I sat down again. "Mino, have you seen any girls you like lately?"

He looked at me as though I'd struck him or ridiculed him. I continued looking at him and waited.

"No . . . I don't know any girls."

"Oh, yes you do! Your sister brings some of her friends here to see you." He couldn't or didn't deny it. "Didn't I see you talking to one of those assistant librarians in the magazine room at the People's Library?" He couldn't or didn't deny it.

At last he said, "They don't take me seriously."

"What do you mean, they don't take you seriously?"

"They talk for a minute, but they're in a hurry to get away."

"God damn it, what do you want them to do: start taking their clothes off?"

His hands were trembling. He put them under his buttocks and continued to stare at me. "No."

"You think they don't talk naturally to you. I'll bet you don't talk naturally to them. A fine-looking young man like you, with top-quality first-rate brains. I'll bet you play your cards wrong." There was a breathless silence. His panic was contagious, but I plunged on. "Sure, you have a handicap, but the handicap isn't as bad as you think it is. You build it up in your imagination. Be yourself, Mino! Lots of men with a handicap as bad as yours have settled down and got married and had kids. Do you want to know how I know this *personally*?"

"Yes."

I told him about the veterans' hospital. I ended up almost shouting, "Four hundred men in wheelchairs and wagons. And some of them still send me letters and cards. With photographs of their family—their own *new* family around them. Especially on Christmas cards. I haven't got any of them in Newport, but I'll send home for some to show you. But, Mino, understand this: they're older than you. Most of them were older than you when they were wounded. What the hell are you so impatient about? The trouble with you is that you're building up an anxiety about the years ahead; you've got 1936 and 1946 planted in your head as though they were tomorrow. And the other trouble with you is that you want the Big Passionate Bonfire right now. A man can't live without female companionship, you're damn right about that. But don't spoil it, don't ruin it by building up a lot of steam too early. Begin with friendship. Now listen: the Misses Laughlins' Scottish Tea Room is just eight doors from your father's door. Have you ever eaten there?" He shook his head. "Well, you're going to, you and Rosa. I'm inviting you and *some girl you know* to lunch with me next Saturday noon."

"I don't know any girl *well enough* to ask."

"Well, if you don't bring a girl to lunch on Saturday, I'll clam up on the whole matter. It'll always be a pleasure to me to come and call on you and talk about Sir Isaac Newton and Bishop Berkeley—I'm very sorry to see that you haven't got any of his works on your shelves—but I'll never open my damn mouth on the subject of girls again. We'll just pretend we're eunuchs. My idea was that you ask one girl this Saturday with the three of us—just to break the ice—and that the following Saturday you ask *another* girl, all by yourself. I guess you can afford it, can't you? They serve a very good seventy-five-cent blue-plate lunch. You were ready to throw away sixteen dollars on some lousy Dante lessons with me.—Then the following Saturday I'll give another party and you bring still a different girl."

A terrible struggle was going on within him. "The only girls I know . . . I know a little . . . are twin sisters."

"Great! Are they lively?"

"Yes."

"What's their name?"

"Avonzino—Filumena and Agnese."

"Which do you like better?"

"They're just the same."

"Well, Saturday you sit by Agnese and I'll bring a friend of mine to sit by Filumena. You know what Agnese means in Greek, don't you?" He made no sign. "It comes from *hagne*—'pure, chaste.' So put the damper on those lascivious ideas of yours. Keep calm. Just a pleasant get-together. Just talking about the weather and about those puzzles of yours. We'll give the girls a big thrill talking about your new inventions and patents. Is it a deal?" He nodded. "You aren't going to backslide, are you?" He shook his head. "Remember this: Lord Byron had to strap up his misshapen foot in complicated boots and half the girls in Europe were crying their eyes out for him. Put that in your pipe and smoke it. What does King Oedipus's name mean?"

"Swell-foot."

"And who did he marry?"

"His mother."

"And what was the name of that splendid daughter of his?"

"Antigone."

I burst out laughing. Mino managed a hesitant laugh. I continued, "I've got to go now. Shake hands, Mino. I'll see you next Sunday at this time; but *first* I'll see you next Saturday at twelve-thirty at the Scottish Tea Room. Wear just what you're wearing now and be ready to have a good time. Remember, you don't win the right kind of girls by dancing with them and playing tennis; you win them by being a fine honorable fellow with a lot of zzipp in your eyes, and enough money in the bank to feed the little Antigones and Ismenes and Polyneiceses and Eteocleses. 'Nuff said."

Passing through the store I told Rosa about the Saturday engagement. "Will you come?"

"Oh, yes! Thank you."

"See that Mino gives the invitation to the Avonzino girls. He may need a little help from you, but leave as much of it to him as you can.—Signora Matera, you have the brightest boy on Aquidneck Island."

"Datt'a wot I tole you!" And she kissed me in the crowded store.

I shook hands with her husband. "Goodbye, Don Matteo!" (In southern Italy respected heads of families even in the working classes are addressed as "Don"—vestige of centuries of Spanish occupation.)

I reached a telephone and having called the Venable house asked to speak to the Baron.

"*Grüss Gott, Herr Baron!*"

"*Ach, der Herr Professor! Lobet den Herrn!*"

"Bodo, we had dinner in the Eighth City—remember?"

"I'll never forget it."

"How'd you like to have lunch in the Ninth City?"

"*Schön!* When?"

"Are you free next Saturday at twelve-thirty?"

"I can get free."

"You'll be my guest. You'll be enjoying the seventy-five-cent blue-plate lunch at the Scottish Tea Room on Lower Broadway at twelve-thirty *punkt*. Do you know where that is?"

"I've seen it. Will there be any police interference?"

"Bodo! The Ninth City is the most respectable of all the nine cities of Newport."

"Have you got another of your plans on your mind?"

"Yes. I'll give you a hint. You won't be the guest of honor. You won't even be a baron. The guest of honor is a twenty-two-year-old genius. He has no feet."

"What did you say?"

"A train ran over him when he was a baby. No feet. Like you, he reads the *Summa* and Spinoza and Descartes before breakfast —in the original. Bodo, if you had no feet, would it make you a little shy about meeting girls?"

"Ye-e-es. Maybe it would, a little."

"Well, there are going to be three charming Ninth City girls there. Don't dress too elegant, Mr. Stams. And no pinching, Mr. Stams."

"*Gott hilf uns. Du bist ein verfluchter Kerl.*"

"*Wiederschaun.*"

On Saturday morning I dropped in at the Tea Room and had a word or two with my esteemed and straight-backed friend Miss Ailsa Laughlin.

"There'll be six of us, Miss Ailsa. Can we have the round table in the corner?"

"We never hold reservations, Mr. North. You know that. Five minutes late and you must take your chances with the other guests."

"When I listen to you, Miss Ailsa, I have to close my eyes— just to listen to that Highland music."

"It's Lowland, Mr. North. It's Ayrshire. The Laughlins were neighbors of Robbie Burns."

"Music, perfect music. We'll be here exactly at twelve-thirty. What is being offered?"

"You know perfectly well that on Saturday noons in summer we have shepherd's pie."

"Ah, yes, *agneau en croûte*. Kindly convey my shy admiration to Miss Jeannie."

"She won't believe it, Mr. North. She thinks you're a fickle deceiver. You and Miss Flora Deland behaving scandalously in our house!"

We are all prompt, but the Materas were promptest. They arrived five minutes early so that we did not see Mino rise from his rolling chair, adjust his crutches, and swing himself into the

Tea Room—Rosa's hand in the small of his back as leverage. I arrived just in time to seat them. Rosa was the kind of girl who appears more attractive at each successive meeting; happiness casts a spell. Mr. Stams and the Avonzino girls followed immediately. Filumena and Agnese were bafflingly identical and so beautiful that the world was enhanced by the duplication. They were enchantingly and even alarmingly dressed. Rosa, who sat at my right, informed me that they were wearing the dresses and hats which they had made themselves from a Butterick pattern, five years before, to serve as bridesmaids at an older sister's wedding. These were of tangerine organdy and they had "built" wide-brimmed hats of the same material, stretched on fine wire. When they went down a crowded street passers-by formed two hedge-rows to watch them. Each had embroidered the initial of her first name over her heart to help us to identify her. Agnese wore a wedding ring. Her name was Mrs. Robert O'Brien; her husband, a naval warrant officer, had been drowned at sea three years before.

I made the introductions. "We're all going to call one another by our Christian names. Beside me is Rosa; next is Bodo —he is from Austria; next is Agnese; next is Mino, who is Rosa's brother; next is Filumena. Bodo, will you repeat these names, please."

"They're all such beautiful names, except mine, that I'm ashamed. But we are Theophilus, Rosa, poor old Bodo, Agnese, Mino, Filumena."

He was applauded.

It was a warm day. We began the meal with a glass of Welch's grape juice with a "scoop" of lemon sherbet in it (ten cents extra). Two of my guests—Mino and Bodo—were intimidated, but the twins were raving beauties and knew that everything would be permitted them.

"Bodo," said Filumena, "I like your name. It sounds like the name of a very nice dog. And you look like a very nice dog."

"Oh, thank you!"

"Agnese, wouldn't it be nice if we could build a big kennel in our back yard and Bodo could live with us and keep naughty men away. Mamma would love you, Bodo, and feed you very well."

"And," said Agnese, "Filumena and I would make flower-chains to put around your neck and we'd go for walks on the Parade."

Bodo barked happily, nodding his head up and down.

Agnese continued, "But Mamma loves Mino best, so you mustn't be jealous, Bodo. Mamma loves Mino because he knows everything. She told him the date of her birth and he looked up at the ceiling a moment and said 'That was a Monday.' Papa asked him why a leap-year comes every four years and Mino made it as clear to him as two-times-two-makes-four."

I said, "Mino has given me permission to tell you a secret about him."

"Mino's going to get married!" cried Filumena.

"Of course, Mino's going to get married. So are we all, but Mino's too young yet. No, the secret is that he's getting out patents for some games he's invented and they're going to sweep the country like mahjong. They're going to be in every home like parcheesi and jackstraws and he's going to be very rich."

"Oh!" cried the girls.

"But you aren't going to forget us, are you, Mino?"

"No," said Mino, dazed.

"You aren't going to forget that we loved you before you were rich?"

"Another secret," I announced. "He's started inventing a practical boot so that he can climb mountains and go skating—and *dance*!"

Applause and cheers.

The shepherd's pie was delicious.

Agnese said to Mino, "And you're going to give Bodo some beautiful dog biscuits, and you're going to give Filumena a sewing machine that doesn't break down all the time?"

"And," continued Filumena, "you're going to give Agnese some singing lessons with Maestro del Valle, and you're going to give your sister a turquoise pin because she was born in July. What are you going to give Theophilus?"

"I know what I want," I said. "I want Mino to invite us all to lunch the first Saturday in August, 1927—the same place, the same people, the same things to eat, the same friendships."

Bodo said "Amen"; everybody said "Amen" and Mino added "I will."

Now we were eating prune whip. The conversation became less general. While I was talking to Rosa Bodo was asking Agnese about her interest in singing. All I was able to overhear was the name of Mozart. Bodo was suggesting to her a riddle that she was to put to Mino. He did not tell her the answer.

"Mino," she said, "you must answer this riddle: what connection is there between the names of our host today and the composer I love best, Mozart?"

Mino looked up at the ceiling a moment and then smiled. "*Theophilus* is one who loves God in Greek and *Amadeus* is one who loves God in Latin."

Applause and delighted wonder, especially mine.

"Bodo told me to ask you," she added modestly.

"And Mozart knew it well," added Bodo. "Sometimes he would sign his middle name in Greek or in Latin or in German. What would the German be, Mino?"

"I don't know much German, but . . . *liebe* . . . and *Gott* —oh, I have it: *Gottlieb.*"

More applause. Miss Ailsa had been standing behind me. The Scots love learning.

Agnese addressed Mino again. "And does my name mean 'lamb'?"

Mino shot a glance at me, but turned back to her. "It could come from that, but many people think it comes from an earlier word, from the Greek *hagne* that means 'pure.' "

Tears started to her eyes. "Filumena, please kiss Mino on the forehead for me."

"Indeed, I will," said Filumena and did so.

We were all a little exhausted by these surprises and wonders and fell silent while the coffee was placed before us. (Five cents extra.)

Rosa whispered to me. "I think you know someone who's sitting over there in that corner."

"Hilary Jones!—Who's he with?"

"That's his wife. They've come together again. She's Italian, but she's not Roman Catholic. She's Italian and Jewish. She's Agnese's best friend too. We're all best friends. Her name's Rachele."

"How's Linda?"

"She's home with them. She's out of the hospital."

When my guests took their leave (Bodo whispering, "You should hear the conversation I'm accustomed to at luncheon!") I crossed and shook hands with Hill.

"Teddie, I'd like you to meet my wife, Rachele."

"Very happy to meet you, Mrs. Jones. How's Linda?"

"She's much better, much better. She's at home with us now."

We talked about Linda and Hill's summer job in the public playgrounds and about the Materas and the Avonzino sisters.

Finally, "I want to ask you a question, Hill—and you, Mrs. Jones. I trust you not to think it's just vulgar curiosity. I know that Agnese's husband was drowned at sea. There must be many such widows in Newport, as there are all up and down the coast of New England. But I feel that she carries some particular burden—some additional burden. Am I right?"

They looked at one another in a kind of dismay.

Hill said, "It was terrible. . . . Nobody talks about it."

"Forgive me. I'm sorry I asked."

"There's no reason you shouldn't know," said Rachele. "We all love her. Everybody loves her. You *do* see why everybody loves her, don't you?"

"Oh, yes."

"We all hope that *that* and her wonderful little boy and her singing—she sings beautifully, you know—will help her forget what happened. You tell Mr. North, Hilary."

"Please . . . you tell him, Rachele."

"He was on the crew of a submarine. It was way up in the north, like near Labrador. And the submarine struck a reef or something under the water and the machinery broke down. And the ice began to crush it. And the compartments got closed. They had air for a while, but they couldn't get into the galley. . . . They had nothing to eat."

We all looked at one another in silence.

"Airplanes were looking for them, of course. Then the ice moved away and they were found. Their bodies were brought back. Bobby's buried in the Naval Cemetery on the Base."

"Thank you.—I'm only free on Sunday afternoons. Can I call on you a week from tomorrow and see Linda?"

"Oh, yes. Please come to supper."

"Thank you, I can't stay to supper. Please write down your address, Hill. I'll look forward to seeing you all at four-thirty."

Throughout the following week I met one or other of the Materas every noon when I picked up my New York paper. Italians, all of us. On Sunday morning I called on Mino at nine.

"*Buon giorno, Mino.*"

"*Buon giorno, professore.*"

"Mino, I'm not going to ask you if you kept your promise to invite a girl to lunch yesterday. I don't want to hear a word about it. From now on that's your business. What shall we talk about today?"

He was smiling with a more than usual air of "a man who knows where he's going" and I was answered. Young people are eager to be made to talk about themselves and to hear themselves discussed, but there is a limit—as they approach twenty—beyond which they shrink from such talk. Their interest in themselves becomes all inward. So I asked, "What shall we talk about today?"

"*Professore*, will you tell me what a college education gives a man?"

I spoke of the value of being required to devote yourself to subjects that at first seem foreign to your interests; of the value of being thrown among young men and young women of your own age, many of whom are as eager as you are to get the best of it; of the possibility—it's only luck—of being brought into contact with born teachers, even with great teachers. I reminded him of Dante's request to his guide Virgil. "Give me the food for which you have already given me the appetite."

He was looking at me with urgent intensity. "Do you think I should go to college?"

"I'm not ready to answer that question. You are a very remarkable young man, Mino. It is very possible that you have outgrown what an American university could give you. You have the appetite and you know where to find the food. You have triumphed over one handicap and the handicap was spur to the triumph. It may well be that you will triumph over this other handicap—the lack of a formal higher education."

He lowered his voice and asked, "What do you think I lack most?"

I laughed and rose to go. "Mino, centuries ago a king in one of the countries near Greece had a daughter he loved very much. She seemed to be wasting away with some mysterious illness. So the old man journeyed to the great oracle at Delphi, bringing rich gifts, and asked the sibyl, 'What can I do to make my daughter well?' And the sibyl chewed the bay leaves and went into a trance and replied in verse, 'Teach her mathematics and music.' Well, you have the mathematics all right, but I miss in you that music."

"Music?"

"Oh, I don't mean what we call music. I mean the whole vast realm that's represented by the Muses. You have your Dante— but the *Divina Commedia* and the *Aeneid* are the only works that I've seen here that are inspired by the Muses."

He smiled at me, almost mischievously. "Wasn't Urania the Muse of astronomy?"

"Oh, yes. I forgot her; but I stick to my point."

He was silent a moment. "What do they do for us?"

I said briskly, "A school of the sympathies, of the emotions and passions, and of self-knowledge. Think it over. Mino, I can't come next Sunday morning, but I'd like to be here the Sunday after that. *Ave atque vale!*" At the door I turned and asked, "By the way, do Agnese's son and Rachele's Linda come to call on you here?"

"They come and see Rosa and my mother, but they don't come to see me."

"Do you know much about the death of Agnese's husband?"

"He was drowned at sea. That's all I know."

He was blushing. I guessed that he had invited Agnese to lunch on the day before. I waved my hand airily and said, "Cultivate the Muses! You are an Italian from Magna Graecia— you have probably lots of Greek blood in you also. Cultivate the Muses!"

In my Journal, from which I am refreshing my memory of these encounters, I find that I was assembling a "portrait" of Mino, as of so many others in these pages. I come upon a hastily written notation: "Mino's handicap involves restrictions I had not foreseen. Not only is he aware that people do not talk to him 'naturally,' he has never received visits from the young children of his sister's two best friends, and has probably not even seen them. The implication is that the children would be affected 'morbidly' by his accident. That consideration would not have arisen in Italy where the disfigured, the scrofulous, and the maimed are visible daily in the market-place—generally as beggars. Moreover, Mino seems not to have been told those details of Warrant Officer O'Brien's death that had so distressed the Hilary Joneses and that were rendering life all but unendurable to his widow. In America the tragic background of life is hidden in cupboards, even from those who have come most starkly face to face with it. Should I some day point this out to Mino?"

On the following Sunday afternoon I called on Linda and her parents, carrying a small old-fashioned bouquet nestling in a lace-paper frill. Hilary, reunited with his wife, had become family-proud, which is always an engaging thing to see. Rachele's family had come from the north of Italy, from the industrial region near Turin where girls of the working classes are brought up to enter the widening field of office workers and, when possible, to become schoolteachers. The little apartment was spotless and serious. Linda was still convalescent and a little wan, but delighted to receive company at tea. I was surprised to see what used to be called a "cottage piano" or a "yacht piano," lacking an octave at the upper range and an octave in the bass.

"Do you play, Rachele?"

She let her husband answer. "She plays very well. She's very popular at the boys' clubs' rallies. She sings too."

"Usually on Sunday afternoon Agnese drops in with her Johnny. You don't mind, do you?" asked Rachele.

"Oh, no," I said. "I liked the Avonzino twins at once. Will you and Agnese sing for me?"

"We do sing duets. We each take two lessons a month from Maestro del Valle and he made us promise to sing every time anyone seriously asks us to. Are you serious, Theophilus?"

"Am I!"

"Then you'll hear four of us. Our children have heard us practice so often at home that they know the music and sing with us. First we'll sing alone, then we'll sing again and they'll join in. Please act as though it were a perfectly natural thing. We don't want them to become self-conscious about it."

Presently Agnese arrived with Johnny O'Brien, also almost four. I'm sure Johnny was a firehouse of energy at home, but like most fatherless small boys he was intimidated by two full-grown men. He sat wide-eyed by his mother. Agnese, apart from her vivacious sister, was subdued also. We talked about the lunch at the Scottish Tea Room and the glowing picture I had painted of Mino's future. I assured them it was true. Agnese asked who Bodo was and what he "did." I told them. All girls like one surprise a day.

"Then it was shocking our talking about him as a dog."

"Oh, Agnese! You could see how pleased he was."

When we'd finished tea I asked the girls to sing to us. They exchanged a glance and Rachele went to the piano. Each mother turned to her child, put her finger to her lip and whispered, "Later." They sang Mendelssohn's "Oh, That We Two Were Maying." Mino should have heard that.

"Now we'll do it again."

The mothers sang softly; the children sang unabashed. I glanced at Hilary. So this was what he almost lost for Diana Bell!

Agnese said, "For a bazaar at my church we learned some parts of Pergolesi's *Stabat Mater*."

They sang two terzets of that; first alone, then with the children. Pergolesi should have heard that.

Newport is full of surprises. I was learning that perhaps the Ninth City is nearer to the Fifth—perhaps to the Second—than any of the others.

When we had taken our leave I walked to her house door with Agnese, hand in hand with Johnny.

"You have a beautiful voice, Agnese."

"Thank you."

"I think that Maestro del Valle must have ambitious plans for you."

"He does. He has offered to give me regular lessons without fees. With my pension and my daily job I could pay for them, but I have no ambition."

"No ambition," I repeated, meditatively.

"Have you ever suffered terribly, Theophilus?"

"No."

She murmured, "Johnny, music, and submission to the will of God . . . they . . . they hold me."

I ventured a very rash remark, still meditatively. "The War left behind many hundreds of thousands of young widows."

She answered quickly, "There are some aspects of my husband's death that I cannot talk about with anybody—not with Rosa or Rachele, not even with my mother or Filumena. Please, don't . . . say . . ."

"Look, Johnny, do you see what I see?"

"What?"

I pointed.

"A candy store?"

"Open on Sunday too! When I went to call on Linda I took her a present. I didn't know that you were going to be there. Come up to the window and see what you'd like."

It was what used to be called a "notions" store. In one corner of the window were toys—model planes, boats, and automobiles.

Johnny began pointing, jumping up and down. "Look! Look, Mr. North! There's a submarine, my daddy's submarine. Can I have that?"

I turned to Agnese. She gave me a harrowed glance of appeal and shook her head. "Johnny," I said, "today's Sunday. When I was a boy my father *never* let us buy toys on Sunday. Sunday we went to church, but no games and no toys." So I marched in and bought some chocolates. When we reached the Avonzino home, he said goodbye nicely and went into the house.

Agnese stood with one hand on the swinging gate. She said, "I think you have urged Benjy—I mean, Mino—to ask me to lunch?"

"Before I ever knew that the Avonzino sisters existed, I urged him to bring any girl or girls he knew to the Scottish Tea Room. I then urged him to bring any girl, preferably a different girl in order to widen his acquaintance, on the following Saturday. He said no word to me about inviting you."

"I have had to tell him that I cannot accept such invitations again. I admire Mino, as we all do; but weekly meetings in a public place like that are not suitable. . . . Theophilus, do not tell anyone what I am about to say: I am a very unhappy woman. I am not capable even of friendship. Everything is just play-acting. I shall be helped, I know"—and she pointed with forefinger from an otherwise motionless hand to the zenith—"but I must wait patiently for that."

"Please go on play-acting for Johnny's sake. I don't mean by going to lunches with Mino, but by seeing some of us in groups from time to time. I think Bodo is planning a kind of picnic, but his car can hold only four and I know he wants to see Mino and yourself again. . . ." She did not raise her eyes from the ground. I waited; finally I added, "I do not know your intolerable burden, Agnese; but I do know that you do not wish it to be a shadow on Johnny's life forever."

She looked at me, frightened; then said abruptly, "Thank you for walking home with us. Oh, yes, I am happy to meet Mino anywhere when there are others in the company." She put out her hand. "Goodbye."

"Goodbye, Agnese."

At seven o'clock I telephoned Bodo. You could always catch him dressing for some dinner party.

"*Grüss Gott, Herr Baron.*"

"*Grüss Gott in Ewigkeit.*"

"What time is your dinner engagement tonight?"

"Eight-fifteen. Why?"

"When could I meet you in the Muenchinger-King bar to lay a plan before you?"

"Is seven-thirty too soon?"

"See you then."

Diplomats are punctual. Bodo was wearing what we used to call in college his "glad rags." He was dining at the Naval War College with some visiting "brass," admirals of all nations—decorations (known to the lower ranks as "fruit salad") and everything. Quite a sight!

"What's your plan, old man?" he asked with happy expectation.

"Bodo, something very serious this time. I must talk fast. Do you know the Ugolino passage in Dante?"

"Naturally!"

"You remember Agnese? Her husband was lost in a submarine at sea." I told him the little I knew. "Maybe the men died of suffocation within a few days; maybe they lived on for a week without food. The boat was finally liberated from the ice. Do you suppose the Navy Department informed the widows and parents of the men of what they may have found?"

He thought a minute. "If it was appalling, I don't think they did."

"The possibilities haunt Agnese. They are robbing her of the will to live. She does not suspect that I know what is haunting her."

"*Gott hilf uns!*"

"She tells me that she is filled with thoughts that she cannot tell her sister, her best friends, or even her mother. When people say a thing like that it means that they are longing to tell them to someone. Mino has asked her to lunch several times since our party at the Scottish Tea Room. She tells me she cannot accept any more invitations from him *alone*. Don't you think Mino a fine fellow?"

"I certainly do."

"I want to give a sunset picnic at Brenton's Point next Sunday. Are you free to come between five and eight?"

"I am. It is one of my last days in Newport. They're giving a reception for me at nine-thirty. I can make it."

"I shall provide the champagne, the sandwiches, and the dessert. Will you, as a Knight of the Two-Headed Eagle, come with us and lend us your car? You and Agnese and Mino will sit in the front seat and I will sit in the rumble seat with the ice-bucket and the provisions. I don't want to appear to be host. Will you be the ostensible host?"

"No! For shame! I shall *be* the host. Now I too must talk fast. In my guest house there are always bottles of champagne in the ice-box. I shall bring along a little portable kitchen with a hot dish. Any Swiss can open a hotel with one day's notice; we Austrians can do it in a week. If it's raining or cold we can go to my guest house. You have supplied the idea—that's quite enough from you.—Now tell me your plan. What is the idea?"

"Oh, Bodo, don't ask me. It's only a hope."

"Oh! Oh!—Give me a hint."

"Do you know *Macbeth*?"

"I played in it at Eton. I was Macduff."

"Do you remember Macbeth's question to the doctor about Lady Macbeth's sleepwalking?"

"Wait!—'*Canst thou not . . . Pluck from the memory a rooted sorrow. . . ?,*' and something about '*Cleanse the stuffed bosom of that perilous stuff Which weighs upon the heart?*'"

"Oh, Bodo!—That's what will win you Persis; that's what we must do for Agnese."

He stared at me. He whispered, "Persis too? Did her husband die in a submarine?"

"Only the happiness that is snatched from suffering is real; all the rest is merely what they call 'creature comforts.'"

"Who said *that?*"

"One of your Austrian poets—Grillparzer, I think."

"*Schön!*—I must run. Send me a note about where to pick up my guests and all that. *Ave atque vale.*"

The invitations were sent through Rosa and accepted. "Rosa, we would love to invite you and Filumena, too, but you know the size of his car." Rosa's eyes showed she understood—perhaps understood the whole stratagem. "Will you show me, Rosa, where you put your hand on Mino's back to help him in and out of doorways and cars?"

Her mother watched us laughing. "I do'no w'at you are tinking now Signor Teofilo, but I no afraid."

The great day arrived. The weather was perfect. Mino was seated in the car by skilled hands. Agnese preferred to be picked up at the Materas' store, in order—I assumed—that her son's disappointment would not be enhanced by his longing to accompany her on an automobile ride. When we arrived at Brenton's Point that great hotel-man Baron Stams whisked out two portable service tables, spread them (with a flourish) with linen, and proceeded to uncork a bottle. Mino and Agnese remained in the car with trays on their laps while the other two cavaliers drew up beside them on folding chairs.

Mino said, "Now I can say that I've tasted champagne twice. I've tasted Asti Spumante at my brothers' weddings. The only time I had champagne before was at your wedding, Agnese."

"You were only fifteen then, Mino. I'm glad you did." She

spoke like someone treading on ice. "My husband's family live in Albany, New York. They came and stayed at our house. They brought three bottles of champagne. . . . Do you remember Robert well, Mino?"

"I certainly do. His boat didn't come in to the Bay often, but he once asked me if I wanted to go on board and, of course, I was crazy to. But on that day there was a big storm blowing up and I couldn't have managed the ladders and the gangway. He told me he'd take me another time. He was my idol. My mother thought he was the handsomest man she'd ever seen—and the nicest."

Agnese looked about her distraught.

Bodo asked, "Did the Navy give him special leave for the wedding?"

"Oh, he'd saved up his shore leave. We went to New York. We saw everything. We took a different El and a different subway to the end of the line every day. Robert knew that I loved music, so we went to the opera three times." She turned to Mino and looked up into his face. "Of course, we had to sit way up high, but we could see and hear everything perfectly. And we went to the zoo and to Mass at St. Patrick's." There were tears in her eyes, but she added with a little laugh, "We went to Coney Island too. That was fun, Mino."

"Yes, Agnese."

"Yes . . . Theophilus, what is Bodo doing?"

Bodo was busy over a chafing-dish. "I'm cooking supper, Agnese. It won't be ready for a while so have another glass of champagne."

"I'm afraid that it'll make me tipsy."

"It's not very strong."

"Agnese," I asked, "has Maestro del Valle given you any songs that you can sing without piano accompaniment? You know he wants you to sing if anyone asks you seriously. I can promise you we're all serious."

"Well, there's an old Italian song. . . . Let me recall it a minute."

She put her hand over her eyes and then sang "*Caro mio Ben, Caro mio Ben*," as purely as a swan gliding over the water. In the second verse she broke down. "I'm sorry I can't go on. That was one of the three songs he loved best. . . . Oh,

Theophilus, oh, Bodo . . . he was such a good man! He was just a boy really and he loved life so much. Then that dreadful thing happened to him—under the ice, without food. I suppose they had water, didn't they? . . . but nothing to eat . . ."

Bodo started speaking, distinctly but without emphasis, his eyes on the work before him. "Agnese, during the War I lay in a ditch for four days without food. I was so wounded that I could not get up to look for water. I kept losing consciousness. When the doctors found me they said that I had died several times, but that I was smiling. You can be sure that the men in the boat—*with so little air*—lost consciousness. Air is more important than even food and water."

She stared at him startled, a gleam of hope. She put her hand to her throat and murmured, "No air. No air." Then she threw her arms about Mino; she laid her cheek on the lapel of his coat and sobbed, "Mino, comfort me! Comfort me!"

He put his arm around her and repeated, "Dear Agnese, beautiful Agnese . . . dear Agnese, brave Agnese . . ."

"Comfort me!"

Bodo and I stared at one another.

Suddenly Agnese collected herself, saying, "Forgive me, forgive me, everybody," and drew a handkerchief from her handbag.

Bodo said loudly, "Supper's ready."

II

Alice

DURING MY earlier stay in Newport—at Fort Adams in 1918 and 1919—I had belonged to the Fourth City, that of the military and naval establishments. In this summer of 1926 there was little likelihood—nor did I seek any—that I would have any contact with those self-sufficient enclosures.

Yet I did come to know and delight in one very humble member-by-alliance of the United States Navy—Alice.

From time to time I am overcome by a longing for an Italian meal. I had received invitations to dinner at the homes of the Materas, the Avonzinos, and the Hilary Joneses, where I was promised an Italian meal; but the reader knows of my resolve to accept no invitations whatever. My life was so gregarious and fragmented that only a strict adherence to that rule could save me from something approaching breakdown. I ate alone. There were three restaurants in Newport purporting to be Italian, but like so many thousands in our country they offered sorry imitations of true Italian cooking. My favorite was "Mama Carlotta's" at One Mile Corner. There one was able to obtain, in a teacup, a home-grown wine popularly called "dago red." About once in two weeks I wheeled the mile to "Mama Carlotta's" and ordered the *minestrone*, the *fettuccine con salsa*, and the bread; the bread was excellent.

This restaurant was across the road from one of the half-dozen entrances to the vast high-fenced Naval Base. It adjoined the many acres of barracks—six apartments to a house—in which lived the families of sailors many of whom worked at the Base, the majority of whom were often absent for many months at a time. Ulysses, King of Ithaca, was separated from his wife Penelope for twenty years—ten of them fighting on the plains before Troy, ten of them on the long voyage home. These men in Newport, their wives and children, lived in a densely crowded area of identical dwellings, identical streets, identical schools and playgrounds, and identical *conventions*. Since 1926 the area has grown many times in size, but with the increase of air travel home leave is granted more frequently and even the families are transported for a time to similar "compounds" in Hawaii, the Philippines, and elsewhere. In 1926 there were hundreds of "shore widows." Density of population increases irritability, lonesomeness, and a censorious view of the behavior of others, all exacerbated at that time by walled enclosure. Penelope's was a hard lot and she must have been surrounded by the wives of absent seamen, but at least, being a queen, not *every* moment of her daily life was exposed to the eyes of women as unhappy as herself.

Residents on the Naval Base were permitted to leave the enclosure at will, but they seldom ventured into the town of Newport—they had their own provision stores, their own theaters, clubhouses, hospitals, doctors, and dentists. Civilian life did not interest and perhaps intimidated them. But they enjoyed escaping briefly from what they themselves called the "rabbit warren" and the "ghetto" to certain locations outside the walls. "Mama Carlotta's" was one of a group of restaurants and licit bars at One Mile Corner that they felt to be theirs. It consisted of two large parallel rooms, the bar and the restaurant. The bar was always crowded with men, though there were tables for ladies (who never came singly); the restaurant at noon and evening was generally well filled. The naval families seldom spent money for meals away from home, but occasionally when parents and relatives arrived for a visit they were offered the treat of a meal off the Base. A warrant officer or a chief petty officer came here, out into the world, to celebrate an anniversary. It is proverbial among the other services that professional seamen, from admirals down, marry goodlooking women, not conspicuously intelligent, and that they find them in our southern states. I was able to confirm this rash generalization over and over again, notably at "Mama Carlotta's."

Early one evening, soon after I had entered into possession of my apartment, I was enjoying a meal at "Mama Carlotta's." It was my custom to read a paper or even a book at table. The fact that I was alone and reading was sufficient to mark me a landlubber. On this evening for reasons unknown I could not be served with wine and was drinking Bevo. I sat alone and exposed at a table for four, though the crowd was so great that the feminine portion of it had overflowed from the bar into the restaurant where it stood, two by two, glass in hand, engaged in animated conversation.

This chapter is about Alice. I never knew her married name. During the few hours I saw her I learned that she came from a large, often starving, family in the coal-mining region of West Virginia and that she had run away from home at the age of fifteen with a gentleman-friend. I shall not attempt to reproduce her accent nor to indicate fully the limitations of her education.

Alice and her friend Delia (from central Georgia) were standing, touching two of the empty chairs at my table. They were talking to be seen talking—not for my benefit only, but for the benefit of the public. Almost everyone in the room knew everyone else in the room and was keeping watch on everyone else in the room. As an author of a later day has said, "Hell is *they.*" I have unusually sharp hearing and became aware of an alteration in their tone. They had lowered their voices and were debating whether it would be "out of place" to ask me if they could sit in the empty chairs at my table. Presently the elder, Delia, turned to me and asked with chilly impersonality if the seats were taken.

I half-rose and said, "No, indeed, ladies. Please sit down."
"Thank you."

I was to learn later that even my partially rising from my chair was positively exciting. In the circles where they moved men did not under any occasion rise to acknowledge the presence of a woman; that was what gentlemen did in the movies, hence the excitement. I resumed my reading and lit a pipe. They turned their chairs face to face and continued their conversation in their earlier manner. They were discussing the election of a friend to the chairmanship of a committee responsible for supervising a charity bingo tournament. I had the sensation of listening to a scene from one of those old-fashioned plays wherein—for the audience's benefit—two characters inform one another of events long known to each of them.

It went on for some time. Delia was pointing out that it was ridiculous that a certain Dora had been elected. Dora, in a former high office, had made a perfect mess of organizing a farewell tea-party for a couple transferred to Panama; and so on.

"She tries to make herself popular by telling fortunes from palm-reading. Do you know what she told Julia Hackman?"

"No." Some whispering. "Alice! You made that up!"

"Cross my heart to die."

"Why, that's *terrible*!" (Stage laughter.)

"She'll do anything to get talked about. She said there was a Peeping Tom outside her bathroom; she opened the window suddenly and threw a soapy wet sponge in his face—in his *eyes*."

"Alice! That's not true."

"Delia, that's what she says. She'll say anything to get famous. That's the way she gets votes. Everybody knows her name."

I had now the opportunity to observe them surreptitiously. Delia was the taller, dark and handsome, but discontented and even embittered; I took her to be about thirty. Alice was scarcely over five feet, about twenty-eight years old. She had a pretty, birdlike, pointed face, of a pallor that suggested ill-health. Under her hat some wisps of lusterless straw-colored hair could be seen. But all was rendered vivid by dark intelligent eyes and an almost breathless eagerness to extract enjoyment from life. Her drawbacks were two: her native intelligence led her into a constant irritation with those less quick of mind than herself; the other was an unprepossessing figure which, like her pallor, was probably the result of malnutrition in childhood. In spite of the difference in their ages Alice exerted an ascendancy over her friend.

They emptied their glasses. Almost without raising my eyes I spoke to them in a low voice: "May I offer the ladies a glass of beer?"

Each stared into the other's face, frozen—as though they had heard something that *cannot be repeated*. Neither looked at me. Having established the audacity of my overture, Delia assumed the responsibility of answering me. Without smiling, she lowered her head and murmured, "That's very kind of you."

I arose and gave a barely audible order to the waiter and returned to my book.

Convention! Convention! That rigorous governor of every human assembly, from the Vatican to the orphanage sandpile, is particularly severe on "shore widows," for a sailor's advancement is also conditioned by his wife's behavior. We were being observed. We were under fire. Convention demanded that no smiles be exchanged. The important thing was to give no impression that we were enjoying ourselves—for envy plays a large part in censorious morality. When the glasses were placed before them the girls nodded slightly and resumed their conversation. But before I returned to my reading Alice's eyes met mine—those superb dark eyes in the body of that early-aging hedge-sparrow. Quicksilver began coursing through my veins.

After a few minutes I ostentatiously spilled some of my beer on the table—"I *beg* your pardon, ladies," I said, mopping up the beer with my handkerchief. "Excuse me. I'd better have my eyes examined. Have I spilled any on you?"

"No. No."

"I'd never forgive myself, if I'd spilled anything on your dresses." I pretended to dry the hem of my jacket.

"I have a scarf here," said Delia. "It's an old thing. Use it. It'll wash out easily."

"Thank you, thank you, ma'am," I said earnestly. "I shouldn't read in a place like this. It's bad for the eyes."

"Oh, yes," said Alice. "My father used to read all the time—at night, too. It was terrible."

"I'd better put my book away. I sure need my eyes every minute of the day."

We were solemn enough to satisfy the severest critics.

Alice asked, "Do you live in Newport?"

"Yes, ma'am. Seven years ago in the War I was stationed at Fort Adams. I liked the place and I came back here to find work. I work on the grounds of one of the places."

"*On the grounds?*"

"I'm a kind of handyman—furnaces, leaves, cleaning up the place—like that."

In the services "cleaning up the place" denotes a form of punishment that resembles chain-gang labor; but they had decided that I was a civilian and were merely confused. Delia asked, "Do you live at the place you work at?"

"No, I live alone in a little apartment just off Thames Street—not really alone because I have a big dog. My name is Teddie."

"A dog? Oh, I love dogs."

"We're not allowed to keep dogs on the Base."

I invented the dog. There's an American myth, diffused by the movies, that a man who keeps a *big* dog and smokes a pipe is all right. Things were going very fast. What had not yet been conveyed was which girl I liked best. Alice and I knew, but Delia was not markedly bright.

"Would you ladies like to be my guests at the nine o'clock show at the Opera House? After the show I could bring you back here in a taxi."

"Oh, no . . . Thank you."

"It's far too late."

"Oh, no!"

I could swear on a pile of Bibles that Delia pushed her shoe against Alice's and Alice pushed Delia's shoe according to some prearranged code. Delia said, "You go, Alice. We could leave here together and the gentleman could meet you later up the street a ways."

Alice was horrified. "How could you think of such a thing, Delia!"

"Well," said Delia, rather grandly, rising. "Thoughts are free. I'm going to the little girls' room. Excuse me. I'll be back in a minute."

Alice and I were left alone.

"I think you're from the South," I said with the first smile of the evening. She did not smile; in fact, she glared at me. She put her head forward and began speaking in a low voice, but very distinctly. "Don't smile! In a few minutes I have to introduce you to some of the girls. I'm going to pretend that you're a doctor, *so be ready*—I'd better say that you're an old friend of my husband's. Were you ever in Panama?"

"No."

"In Norfolk, Virginia?"

"No."

"Well, where have you been all your life? I'll say Norfolk. . . . Delia can't go downtown because her husband's coming back next week and she don't dare go anywhere. *Stop smiling!* This is a serious conversation. *When Delia and I leave here you say goodbye to us. Then five minutes later you go out through the kitchen and then out the back door. Then go up the road—not down toward Newport—and I'll meet you where the streetcar stops opposite Ollie's Bakery."*

These instructions were given me in a manner of being very angry at me. I began to get the idea. Whatever followed would be dangerous.

"When I say goodbye to you what do I call you?"

"Alice."

"What's your husband's first name?"

"George, of course."

"I see. My name's Dr. Cole."

Alice's face had become flushed through the exertion of her generalship and through exasperation at my stupidity.

Delia rejoined us. From time to time the girls had exchanged greetings with members of the audience. Alice now raised her voice. "Hello, Barbara, hello, Phoebe. I want you to meet Dr. Cole, an old friend of George's."

"Pleased to meet you."

"Pleased to meet you, Barbara—and you, Phoebe."

"Imagine, George told him, if he was in Newport to call me up. He did and Dr. Cole said he'd meet me here. Hello, Marion, I want you to meet Dr. Cole, an old friend of George's. So Delia and I sat here trying to decide who looked like a doctor. Isn't that a sit-you-ation! Hello, Annabel, I want you to know Dr. Cole, an old friend of George's, just passing through town. He asked Delia and I to go to the movies with him, but of course we can't, it being so late and everything. He knew George at Norfolk before I did. George told me about this doctor he knew. Were you a doctor then, Teddie?"

"I was in my last year at Baltimore. I have cousins in Norfolk."

"Imagine that!" said Barbara and Marion.

"What a coincident!" said Phoebe.

"The world's a very small place," said Delia.

"Well, you'll want to talk over old times," said Barbara. "Happy to have know'd you, Doctor."

I had risen. The girls withdrew to talk it over.

"That'll go like a grass-fire," said Delia.

Alice rose. "Finish your beer, Delia. I'm going to put my hat straight."

Now Delia and I were alone.

"Alice tells me your husband will be in next week, Delia. Congratulations." Delia looked at me hard and waggled her hands. "How long has he been gone?"

"Seven months."

"Gee, it must be very exciting."

"You said it!"

"What ship is it?"

"Four destroyers . . . More'n two hundred men on 'em have homes right in this town."

"Have you children, Delia?"

"Three."

"Wonderful for them too."

"They've faced it before. I'm taking them to my mother's. She lives in Fall River. I'm lucky."

"I don't understand."

"Doctor, when the men get off the ship, we're down there waving. See? They kiss us and all that. And then we go home to wait for them. They go straight off to the Long Wharf."

"Oh."

"You can say that again."

I was learning things. Ulysses returned to his home in disguise. None of those tear-stained embraces. They get rip-roaring drunk on the Long Wharf. No sight for children. Reunions require more courage than partings. The institution of marriage was not designed by Heaven to accommodate long separations.

"Has Alice some children?"

"Alice—Alice and George?"

"Yes?"

(It is characteristic of communities like a naval base that their residents believe their customs and affairs are what the earth revolves about; anyone who does not know them is stupid.)

"Married for five years and no children. It's driving Alice wild."

"And George?"

"Says he thanks God it's that way and gets drunk."

"When does she expect George's return?"

"He's here now." I stared. "He got here a week ago. Stayed here three days. Then went up to Maine to help his father on the farm. He has three weeks' shore leave coming to him. He'll be back soon."

"Does everybody like George?"

Everything I said exasperated her. In certain walks of life the question of liking or not liking—short of downright villainy—does not arise. One's neighbors, including one's husband, are simply there—like the weather. They're what mathematicians call "given."

"George is all right. He drinks, but who doesn't?" She meant males. Men are expected to drink; it's manly. "If Alice goes to the movies with you, see that she gets back to the gate by one."

"What'd happen if she got back after one?" She gave me a look of exhausted patience. "Wives must often get back later when they've been visiting their parents—trains late and all that?"

"They don't kill you, if that's what you mean. But they remember it." That mighty word "they." "I don't think Alice has ever been out after eleven so they might overlook it. You ask a lot of questions."

"All I know about is the Coast Artillery. I don't know anything about the Navy."

"Well, the Navy's the best and don't you forget it."

"I'm sorry I've made you angry, Delia. I didn't mean to."

"I'm not angry," she said shortly. Then she looked me in the eyes and said something between her lips that I couldn't understand.

"I didn't hear what you said."

"There's something that Alice wants more than anything in the world. Give it to her."

"What? . . . What?"

"A baby, of course."

I was thunderstruck. Then I was very agitated. "Did she tell you to say that to me?"

"Of course not. You don't know Alice."

"Has Alice led other men downtown for this?" I was so urgent that I struck her knee with my knee under the table.—I had pictures of troops and parades.

"Take your knee away!—She only made up her mind that she had to last week. The evening after George went to Maine

Alice and I went to the Opera House to see a movie. She got talking to a man that sat next to her. They didn't like the movie and went out to get something to eat. She whispered to me not to wait for her. She told me later that the man had a boat tied up by the Yacht Club. She went along, but she wouldn't go aboard. She said that while she was walking Jesus told her the man was a bootlegger, a rum-runner, and that he'd tie her up and start the boat and she'd be in Cuba for weeks. She wouldn't walk up the gangway and when he began pulling her she screamed for the Shore Patrol. He let hold of her and she ran most of the way home."

"You swear you're telling the truth?"

"You're hurting my knee! Everybody's looking at us!"

"Swear!"

"Swear what?"

"That you're telling the truth."

"As God is my judge!"

"And Alice would have no idea that I knew any of this?"

"As God is my judge!"

I leaned back exhausted, then I leaned forward again. "Would George think it was his baby?"

"He'd be the proudest man on the Base."

Alice rejoined us. She had touched up her appearance considerably; there were sparks in the air.

"Well, Delia, it's *late*. We'd better be going. It's very nice to have met you, Dr. Cole. I'll tell George."

"Goodbye, girls. I'll write him."

"He'll be sorry to have missed you."

Each of these remarks was repeated several times. I gathered that shaking hands would have been excessive. Left alone, I ordered another beer, relit my pipe, and resumed reading. Others sat down at my table. When the moment came I obeyed Alice's instructions, though I had to steal around to the side of the restaurant to pick up my bicycle. Alice was waiting at the streetcar stop. She said, moving away from me and scarcely turning her head, "I'll sit in the front of the car. Don't you want to bicycle down to Washington Square?"

"No. At night they let you put the bike on the back platform."

"I don't want to go to the movies. I know a kind of quiet

bar where we can talk. It's by the telegraph office. If I see anybody I know on the car, I'll tell them I'm going to the telegraph office to get a money order from my mother. You follow me down Thames Street about a block behind me."

"My apartment's not many blocks beyond the telegraph office. Couldn't we go there?"

"I didn't say we were going to your apartment! Where did you get that idea?"

"You said you liked dogs."

"The name of the bar is 'The Anchor.' While I'm in talking to the telegraph man you stand just inside the door of 'The Anchor.' Ladies can't go in there unless they're with a gentleman-friend." She looked at me fiercely. "This is all very dangerous, but I don't care."

"Aw, Alice, can't we go straight to my apartment? I have a little rye there."

"*I told you!* I haven't made up my mind yet."

The streetcar came rattling and squealing down the road. A very dignified Alice boarded it and advanced to the front seat. At the One Mile Corner stop she was joined by some friends, a chief petty officer and his wife.

"*Alice darling, what are you doing?*"

Alice launched into a long narrative filled with disasters and miracles. She held them spellbound. All passengers descended at Washington Square. She was overwhelmed with good fellowship. "I hope everything comes out all right. Good night, dear. Tell us all about it next time we see you."

Again I followed her instructions. Through the great window of the telegraph office I could see her telling another thrilling story to the night clerk. Finally she started toward me with determination, her heels clicking on the brick paving. Suddenly halfway across the street she was accosted by two reeling sailors. Alice managed to do three things at once: she signaled to me to go back into "The Anchor," she reversed her direction as though she had forgotten something in the telegraph office, and she had dropped her handbag.

"Alice, you cutey! Wha' you doin' in the beeg city?"

"Alice, where's George? Where's old Georgie, the old skunk?"

"Oh my, I've lost my purse. Mr. Wilson, help me find my purse. I left it in the telegraph office, I know. Oh, isn't that terrible! I'll *die*! Mr. Westerveldt, help me find my purse."

"Here it *is*. Lookit! Now do I get a lil kiss—just a lil lil kiss?"

"Mr. Wilson! You never said a thing like that before. I won't tell George this time, but don't you ever say such a thing again. I had to hurry and send a postal money order off before *closing time*. Mr. Westerveldt, please . . . take . . . your . . . hand . . . away. I just saw the Shore Patrol following me down Thames Street. I think you'd better go up to Spring Street. It's after nine."

Thames Street was out of bounds to Navy seamen after nine. They took her advice and tumbled up the hill.

With set face she marched resolutely into "The Anchor," put her arm through mine—single women are not allowed in the taverns on the *north* side of Thames Street—and propelled me to the last booth at the back of the room. She sat against the wall and shrank to the size of a child. Between her teeth she muttered, "That was a close call. If they'd seen me with you, I don't know what would have happened."

I whispered, "What shall I order for you?"

Again I was to be regarded as an idiot child. She lowered her head and said, "A Rum Floater, of course."

"Alice, please understand I'm not a Navy man. I don't speak Navy language. Please don't be like Delia. I'm not stupid; I'm only ignorant. I haven't been to Norfolk or to Panama. I've been to lots more interesting places than those."

She looked surprised, but remained silent. Alice's silences were weighty; to borrow a schoolboy's expression, "You could hear the wheels go round." The Rum Floaters turned out to be rum in ginger ale, a combination I couldn't abide. She fell on hers like one famished.

"What was Panama like?"

"Hot . . . different."

"What were you doing in Norfolk?"

"I was a waitress in restaurants." She had turned morose. I waited for the rum to take effect. Looking straight before her she said, "I shouldn't have come. . . . You've been telling lies to me all night. You don't 'clean up places'; you live in them.

You're one of those rich people. I know what you think of me, *Dr. Cole.*"

"*You* made me say I was a doctor. *You* made me say I was an old friend of your husband's. I'm not rich. I coach children to play tennis. You don't get much for that, I can tell you. Don't let's quarrel, Alice. I think you're a very bright girl and very attractive too. I think you've got knock-out eyes, for instance. You have a personality that sends out electric shocks all the time, like doorknobs when a storm's coming on. Alice, don't let's quarrel. Let's have another Rum Floater and then I'll take you back to the gate in a taxi. There are some taxis standing in the Square every hour of the day and night. Forget all that I said about going to my apartment. Damn it, I hope you and I are grown up enough just to be friends. I can see that you've got some trouble on your mind. Well, leave that trouble behind at the Base."

She had been looking at me fixedly.

"What are you looking at?"

"When I look at a man I try to figure out what movie star he looks like. I can almost always find it. You don't look like any I've seen. You're not very good-looking, you know. I don't say that to hurt your feelings; I just say it because it's true."

"I know I'm not good-looking, but you can't say I have a lowdown mean face."

"No."

I got the barman's attention and put up two fingers.

I asked, "What movie star does your husband look like?"

She turned to me sharply. "I won't tell. He's a very good-looking man and a very good man."

"I didn't say he wasn't."

"He saved my life and I love him. I'm a very lucky girl.—Oh, it would have been awful if those men had seen me with you. I'd never have forgiven myself. I'd have just died, that's all."

"How do you mean—George saved your life?"

She gazed before her broodingly. "Norfolk is an awful town. It's worse than Newport. I got fired out of five restaurants. It was awful hard to keep a job. There were a million girls for every job. George was beginning to kind of court me. He'd come back to eat at the same table where I was serving. He'd

leave twenty-five cents every time! . . . The men who ran the
restaurants were always trying to take advantage of the girls;
they'd act fresh in front of the customers. I didn't want George
to see anything like that . . . and just when I'd given up *hope*
he asked me to marry him. And he gave me twenty-five dollars
to buy some nice things, because he had a brother there in the
Service too. George knew that he'd write home about me. I
owe everything to George." Suddenly she brushed my hand
with hers. "I didn't mean to hurt your feelings with what I said
a while ago. You haven't got a lowdown mean face at all. Every
now and then I *say* things—"

Suddenly Alice disappeared. She slid from our bench and
crouched under the table. I looked about and saw that two
sailors wearing the armband of the Shore Patrol had entered.
They greeted a number of the guests affably and, leaning
against the bar, discussed at length a certain fracas that had
taken place the night before. The public joined in. The conversation threatened to be interminable. Soon I became aware
that some little fingernails were scratching my ankles. I leaned
over and brushed them away angrily. There are certain tor-
ments a man cannot put up with. I heard a giggle. Finally the
Shore Patrol left "The Anchor." I whispered, "They're gone,"
and Alice hoisted herself onto the bench.

"Did you know them?"

"*Know them!*"

"Alice, you know everybody. You'd better make up your
mind whether you'll let me take you back to the Base, or
whether you'll come and see my apartment."

She looked at me without expression. "I don't like big dogs."

"I was lying to you. I haven't any dog at all. But I have a
pretty nice little present for you." I had three younger sisters.
Girls love presents, especially surprise presents.

"What is it?"

"I won't tell."

"Where did you get it?"

"At Atlantic City."

"Will you give me a hint?"

"It glows at night like a big glowworm. So when you're
lonesome at night it'll be a comfort to you."

"Is it a Baby Jesus picture?"

"No."

"Oh!—It's one of those wrist-watches."

"I couldn't afford to give anyone a radium wrist-watch. . . . It's about the size of a pin-cushion. It's friendly."

"It's one of those things that keep papers from blowing away."

"Yes."

"You don't wear a wedding ring."

"In the part of the country I come from men don't wear them—only Catholic men wear them. I've never been married anyway."

"If I go to your apartment you won't act fresh or anything?"

It was my turn to look hard and blank. "Not unless someone scratches my ankles."

"I was just *tired* of sitting on the floor."

"Well, you could have said your prayers."

She was staring before her in deep thought. You could "hear the wheels go round." She leaned up against my shoulder and asked, "Is there a roundabout way to your house?"

"Yes. First, I'll pay the bill. Then you follow me."

We got there and crept up the outside staircase. I opened the door and turned on the light, saying, "Come in, Alice."

"Oh, it's big!"

I put the paperweight on the center table and sat down. Like a cat she circled the room inspecting everything within reach. Talking to herself in short admiring phrases. Finally she took up the paperweight—a view of the Atlantic City boardwalk, picked out with bits of mica, under an isinglass dome.

"Is this what you said I could have?" I nodded. "It doesn't . . . glow."

"It can't glow as long as there is one bit of sunlight or electric light around. Go into the bathroom, shut the door, turn out the light, keep your eyes closed for two minutes and then open them."

I waited. She came out, threw herself on my lap, and put her arms around my neck. "I'll never be lonesome any more." She put her lips against my ear and said something. I thought I heard what she said but I couldn't be certain. Her lips were too close; perhaps shyness muffled her speech. I thought I heard her say, "I want a baby." But I had to be sure. Holding her chin with one hand I moved my ears two inches from her lips and asked "What did you say?"

At that moment she heard something. Just as dogs hear sounds that we cannot hear, just as chickens (I had worked on farms as a boy) could see hawks approaching from a great distance, just so Alice heard something. She slid off my lap and pretended to be busy straightening her hair; she picked up her hat and—resourceful actress that she was—said sweetly, "Well, I'd better be going. It's getting late. . . . Did you really mean that I could keep this picture for my own?"

I sat motionless watching her play the scene.

Had I said anything to offend her? No.

Made a gesture? No.

A harbor sound? A street quarrel? My neighbors at Mrs. Keefe's?

In 1926 the invention known in my part of town as the "raddy-o" was present in an increasing number of homes. On a warm evening through open windows it diffused a web of music, oratory, and dramatic and comic dialogue. I had become habituated and deaf to this, and certainly Alice on the Base had become so also.

"You've been very sweet. I love your apartment. I love your kitchen."

I rose. "Well, if you must go, Alice, I'll follow you as far as the Square and pay your taxi-man to drop you at the gate. You don't want to meet any more of the thousand people you know."

"Don't you move *one inch*. The streetcars are still running. If I meet anybody I'll tell them I've been to the telegraph office."

"I could walk with you perfectly safely along Spring Street. It's darker and the Shore Patrol will have swept it up pretty well by now. Here, I'll wrap up the paperweight."

Mrs. Keefe had furnished my room according to her own taste which called for a wide selection of table runners, lace doilies, and silk table covers to support vases and so on. I picked up one of the latter and wrapped it around the gift. I opened the door. Alice was now very subdued and preceded me down the stairs.

Then I heard it—another music that had escaped my ears,

but not hers. During the summer a small frame house near Mrs. Keefe's had been turned into "The Mission of the Holy Spirit," a fervent revivalist sect. A meeting was in progress. While working on farms in Kentucky and Southern California I had attended many camp-meetings of a similar kind and knew well some of their hymns, seldom heard in urban churches. Surely these hymns had been built into the lives of boys and girls growing up in rural West Virginia where the camp-meeting was the powerful center of the religious, social, and even "entertainment" life of the community. What Alice had heard was the hymn that precedes the "offering of one's life to Jesus": "*Yield not to temptation; Jesus is near.*"

We turned up the hill to Spring Street. It was deserted and I stepped forward and walked beside her. She was weeping. I enclosed her tiny hand in mine.

"Life is hard, dear Alice."

"Teddie?"

"Yes."

"Do you believe in hell?"

"What do you mean by hell, Alice?"

"That we go to hell when we do bad things? When I was a girl I did a lot of bad things. When I was in Norfolk I had to do a lot of bad things. I had a baby but I haven't got it any more. It was before I knew George but I told him about it. Since I married George I haven't done a bad thing at all. Really, I haven't, Teddie. Like I told you, George saved my life."

"Has George ever struck you, Alice?"

She looked up at me quickly. "Do I have to tell the truth? Well, I will. He gets very drunk after he comes back from a long tour of duty and he does strike me. But I don't hate him for it. He has a reason. He knows that he . . . he can't make babies. He makes love, but no babies get to be born. Wouldn't that make you kind of upset?"

"Go on."

"Every now and then I thought I'd get a baby with another man without George's knowing about it. I don't think going to bed with another man once in a while is very important. . . . Even though it was a lie, it would make George very happy. He's a good man. If it made him feel good to be a father, that wouldn't be a very bad sin, would it? Like what they call in the

Bible adult'ary. Sometimes, I think I'd go to hell for a long time if it would make George happy."

I turned her hand over and over in mine. We reached Washington Square. We crossed the street and sat down on a bench farthest from the street lights.

I said, "Alice, I'm ashamed of you."

She said quickly, "Why are you ashamed of me?"

"That *you*—who know that the heart of Jesus is as big as the whole world—you think that Jesus would send you to hell for a little sin that would make George happy or a little sin that you had to do to keep alive in a cruel city like Norfolk."

She put her head against my shoulder. "Don't be ashamed of me, Teddie. . . . Talk to me. . . . When I ran away from home my father wrote me that he never wanted to see me until I had a wedding ring on my finger. When I wrote him that I was married he changed his mind. He said he never wanted to see a hoor in his house."

I'm not going to put down here what I said to Alice almost fifty years ago. I reminded her of some words that Jesus said and maybe I invented some. And then I said, "I'm not going to say any more." Her hand in mine had become calmer. I could hear "the wheels going round."

She said, "Let's go over nearer to the street lights. I want to show you something."

We moved to another bench. She had taken something out of her handbag, but kept it hidden from me.

"Teddie, I always wear a chain and locket around my neck, but when I came out tonight with Delia I took it off. You can guess who gave it to me."

I looked at the picture in the locket. It had been taken several years before. A sailor about eighteen years old—the sailor who could have sat for any recruiting poster—was laughing into the camera; his arm was about Alice. I could imagine the occasion:

"Step up, ladies and gentlemen! Just twenty cents for the picture and a dollar for the locket and chain. You two there—you're only young once. Don't miss this opportunity."

I looked at it.

She looked at it.

Again she whispered in my ear. "I want a baby—for George."

We rose and walked back to my apartment. As we got near the stairs I said, "It's very important that George doesn't know. That's the whole point. Will Delia talk?"

"No."

"Can you be sure?"

"Yes. Delia knows how important that is. She's said so over and over again."

"Alice, I don't know your last name and you don't know mine. We must never meet again." She nodded. "Twice tonight you've had narrow escapes. You can go to 'Mama Carlotta's'; I'll never be there again."

Two hours later we returned to the Square. She peered around the corner as though we'd robbed a bank. She whispered, "The movie's over." She giggled.

I left her in a doorway and went up to a taxi. I asked the driver how much it cost to go to One Mile Corner.

"Fifty cents," he said.

I went back and put half a dollar and two dimes in her hand. "Where will you say you've been?"

"What do they call that place where they were singing hymns?"

I told her. "I'll stay here at this corner and see you off."

She kissed her finger tips and put them on my cheek. "I'd better not keep that picture of Atlantic City."

She gave it back to me. She took some steps toward the taxi, then returned to me and said, "I won't be lonesome at night any more, will I?"

Off she drove.

I thought suddenly, "Of course, all those twenty years Penelope had Telemachus growing up beside her."

12

"The Deer Park"

THIS CHAPTER might also be called "The Shaman or *Le Médecin malgré lui*."

One day I found a note in my mailbox at the Post Office
asking me to telephone a Mrs. Jens Skeel, such and such a
number, on any day between three and four.

"Mrs. Skeel, this is Mr. North speaking."

"Good afternoon, Mr. North. Thank you for calling. Friends
have spoken to me with much appreciation of your reading
with students and adults. I was hoping that you could find
time to read French with my daughter Elspeth and my son Arthur. Elspeth is a dear sweet intelligent girl of seventeen. We
have had to take her out of school because she suffers from
migraine. She misses school and particularly misses her courses
in French literature. Both my children have been to school in
Normandy and in Geneva. They speak and read French well.
Both of them adore the *Fables* of La Fontaine and wish to read
all of them with you. . . . Yes, we have several copies of them
here. . . . The late morning would suit us very well. . . .
Eleven to twelve-thirty, Mondays, Wednesdays, and Fridays—
yes. May I send a car for you? . . . Oh, you prefer to come by
bicycle. . . . We live at 'The Deer Park'—do you know it?
. . . Good! May I tell the children that you will be here tomorrow? . . . Thank you so much."

Everyone knew "The Deer Park." The father of the present
Mr. Skeel had been a Dane engaged in international shipping.
He had built this "Deer Park" not in imitation of the famous
park in Copenhagen, but in affectionate allusion to it. I had
often dismounted before the high iron grille enclosing a vast
lawn that ended in a low cliff above the sea. Under the glorious
trees of Newport I could catch glimpses of deer, rabbits, peacocks—alas, for La Fontaine, no foxes, no wolves, not even a
donkey.

I was met in the front hall by Mrs. Skeel. "Elegance" is too
brilliant a word for such perfection of presence. She was dressed

in gray silk; there were gray pearls about her neck and in her ears. All was distinction and charm and something else—anguish under high stoic control.

"You will find my daughter on the verandah. I think that she would prefer that you introduce yourself.—Mr. North, if at any time you see that she is suffering from fatigue, will you find an excuse to draw the lesson to a close? Arthur will help you."

Like mother, like daughter—though the anguish was partially replaced by an extreme pallor. I addressed her in French.

"Mr. North, may I ask that we read in French? But it tires me to speak in it." Her hand lightly indicated the left side of her forehead. "Look! Here comes my brother."

I turned to see a boy of eleven scrambling up the cliff in the distance. I had seen him often on the tennis courts, though he had not been among my pupils. He was the lively freckled American boy so often pictured on grocers' calendars to illustrate Whittier's poem. He was called "Galloper," because his middle name was Gallup and because he talked so rapidly and never walked when he might run. He sped toward us and came to an abrupt halt. We were introduced and shook hands gravely.

"Why, Galloper," I said, "we've met before."

"Yes, sir."

"Are you called by that name here too?"

"Yes, sir. Elspeth calls me that."

"I like it. May I call you so?"

"Yes, sir."

"Are you fond of the *Fables* also?"

"We're both very interested in animals. Galloper spends many hours watching a tidal pool. He's come to know some of the fish and shellfish and he's given them names. We talk over everything together."

"I'm very happy, Miss Skeel, that you wish to read the *Fables*. I haven't read them for some time, but I remember my admiration for them. They are small but somehow great, modest but perfect. We shall try and find out how La Fontaine manages that. But before we begin, kindly let me have a moment to become accustomed to this beautiful place—and to those friends I see there. Would it tire you if we took a short walk?"

She turned to the nurse who came toward her. "Miss Chalmers, may I take my morning walk now?"

"Yes, Miss Elspeth."

The deer enjoyed a pavilion at our right within a grove of trees; the rabbits resided in a village of hutches; the peacocks reigned in an aviary, a portion of which could protect them throughout the winter.

"Should we have some biscuits in our hands?"

"The caretaker feeds them several times a day. They don't expect anything from us. It's best that way."

The deer watched us approach, then slowly drew nearer. "It's best not to put out your hand until they've touched us first." Presently the deer were beside us and between us and before us and behind us. We were taking a walk together. Even the fawns who had been lying in the shade of a tree struggled to their feet and joined the procession. The older deer began brushing us—bumping us, ever so slightly. "What they like most is to be talked to. I think they live most in their eyes and ears and muzzles. *That's the most beautiful baby, Jacqueline. I remember when you looked just like her. You must be careful that she doesn't fall over the cliff, as you did. You remember the splints you had to wear and how you hated them. . . . Oh, Monsieur Bayard, your antlers are growing fast.* They like it when you stroke their horns. I think their horns itch when the velvet is growing on them. The rabbits hope that we'll come over and visit them too. They stay away from the deer. They don't like hoofs. *Oh, Figaro, how handsome you are!* The deer will leave us soon; they find the company of humans exhausting. . . . See, they are drifting away already. . . . It's terrible to see them on the Fourth of July. Of course, no one has ever shot at them, but they carry some memory of hunters in their blood—do you think that's possible? . . . It's too early to see the rabbits play. When the moon's come up they tear around as though they'd gone out of their mind."

"Mademoiselle, why do the deer push against us that way?"

"I think, maybe . . . Will you excuse me if I sit down for a minute? Please sit down too. Galloper will tell you what we think about that."

I had noticed that bamboo chairs with wide armrests, such as I had known in China as a boy, were placed, two by two, at intervals on the lawn. We sat down. Galloper answered for his sister. "We think that we must imagine their enemies. We have a picture in the hall—"

"I think it's by Landseer."

"—of stags and does huddled together in a mass surrounded by wolves. Before there were any men with guns on the earth, the deers' enemies were wolves or maybe men with spears or bludgeons. The deers must have lost some, but they defended themselves that way—with a sort of wall of antlers. They don't like to be patted or stroked; it's nearness they like to feel. That's different from the rabbits. The hare has been thumping the ground to warn the others that we are coming. But if there is no shelter near, they 'freeze' wherever they are; they 'play dead.' They have enemies on the ground too, but they mostly fear hawks. But hawks hunt singly. Either way, the deer and the rabbits lose a few of their kind—"

"What I call 'hostages to fortune.'"

"But they do what they can for their kind."

Elspeth looked at me. "Do you think that there is something in that idea?"

I looked at her with a smile. "I'm your pupil. I want to hear what you say."

"Oh, I'm just beginning to try to think. I'm trying to understand why nature is so cruel and yet so wonderful. Galloper, tell Mr. North what you see in the tidal pool."

Galloper answered reluctantly. "It's a battle every day. It's . . . it's terrible."

"Mr. North," said Elspeth, "why must that be? Doesn't God love the world?"

"Yes, He surely does. But we must talk that over later."

"You won't forget?"

"No.—Mademoiselle, have you ever seen deer in their wild—I mean, their natural—state?"

"Oh, yes. My Aunt Benedikta has a camp in the Adirondacks. She's always asking us to visit her in the summer. There you can see deer and foxes and even bears. And there are no fences or cages at all. They're *free*! And so beautiful!"

"Are you going there this summer?"

"No . . . Father doesn't like us to go there. And besides, I'm not . . . I'm not very well."

"What are some of the other things about animals that you talk about together?"

"Yesterday we had a long talk about why nature placed the eyes of birds on the sides of their heads."

"And why," added Galloper, "so many animals' heads are bent to the ground."

"We love WHYS," said his sister.

"And what did you decide?"

Galloper, after a glance at his sister, released her from the effort of answering. "We knew that herbivorous animals had to keep their eyes on the plants beneath them and that the birds had to be alert for enemies on all sides of them; but we wondered why nature couldn't have worked out a better way—like the eyes of the Crustacea in my tidal pool."

"The difficulty of thinking," murmured his sister, "is that you have to think of so many things at once."

She had been carrying a copy of the *Fables*. It fell from the wide armrest of the chair. (Had she pushed it?) We both leaned over to pick it up from the ground. Our hands met and struggled for it a moment. She drew in her breath hastily and shut her eyes. When she opened them she looked into mine and said with unusual directness: "Galloper says that your pupils at the Casino say that you have electric hands."

I think I blushed furiously and was furious at myself for blushing. "That's absurd, of course. That doesn't mean anything."

Hell! Damnation!

Every once in a while it rains in Newport. Sometimes a shower would fall during those two early hours when I was coaching tennis at the Casino. I never had more than four pupils at a time; my other pupils would be playing against one another on courts nearby. And we would all run for shelter to one of the social rooms behind the spectators' gallery. My pupils, all between eight and fourteen, made a very pretty sight, dressed in spotless white, radiant with youth, delicately fostered, and expending their energy. They would gather about me, crying, "Mr. North, tell us some more about China!" or "Tell us some more stories like 'The Necklace'"—I had once held them hushed and dismayed by de Maupassant's story. The ever-watchful Bill Wentworth—himself a father and grand-father—knew well that children of that age love to sit on the floor. He would spread out some sail cloth about the "teacher's chair." Galloper had not been among my pupils; but he joined the circle and even some older players hesitantly drew up their chairs. It was there that I had first beheld Eloise Fenwick and it was for her dear eyes and ears that I had first retold Chaucer's story of "The Falcon." It was for Galloper that I told of Fabre's discovery of how a wasp paralyzes a grub or a caterpillar and then lays its egg upon it to nourish the future insect. Was it Rousseau who said the primary function of early education was to expand in children the faculty of wonder?

I felt no prompting to caress the children about me. I do not like to be touched myself, but children must pet and stroke and tease and even buffet any older person who has gained their confidence. When the shower was over there was a great dragging of me to return to the courts and a great dragging of me to stay and tell one more story because "the grass is still wet." And one child after another claimed to discover that I had "'lectric" hands, that my hands gave off sparks. I took a severe attitude toward this. I forbade such remarks. "That's silly! I don't want to hear any more about that." Then one day things got out of bounds. In the tumultuous rush to the courts, Ada Nicols, aged nine, was flung to one side; striking her head against a post she lost consciousness. I leaned over her, parting her hair where the bruise seemed to be and repeating her name. She opened her eyes, then closed them again. The whole group was staring down at her anxiously. She pulled my hands to her forehead murmuring, "More! More!" She was smiling vacantly. Finally she said happily, "I'm hypmertized," and then, "I'm a angel." I picked her up and carried her to Bill Wentworth's office which was frequently called upon to serve as a first-aid station. From that hour I became a far sterner and more matter-of-fact coach. No more Uncle Theophilus's stories. No more mesmerism.

But Ada's story spread.

I have already told the reader in the first chapter of this book that I knew I possessed a certain faculty and that I wished to ignore it. I had often parted furious dogs; I could calm frantic horses. During the War and elsewhere, in bars and taverns, I had only to lay my hands on the shoulders of quarrelsome men and to murmur a few words in order to establish peace. I take no interest in the irrational, in the inexplicable. I am no mystic. Besides, I had already learned that—whether it was a "real" thing or not—it inevitably led me to a certain amount of imposture and quackery. The reader knows that I'm no stranger to imposture, but I want to practice deceptions when I please to, not when they're forced upon me. I want to engage in life in the spirit of play, not in leading others by the nose, not in rendering others ridiculous in my own eyes.

And here this wretched business of my "electric hands" had raised its head at "The Deer Park" in the presence of that rare and suffering girl and that keenly intelligent boy.

HELL! DAMNATION!

For two afternoons we read the *Fables* and analyzed them by the French method called "*l'explication de texte*." I stayed up half the night doing my "homework" preparation for the sessions. I brought forward all the professional commonplaces: the art with which homely speech is elevated to poetry; the energy imparted by the insertion of short verses among the long (condemned by a number of La Fontaine's most distinguished contemporaries); the irony conveyed by the heroic alexandrines; the redoubled simplicity when the poet closes the fable with its edifying or instructive moral.

At my arrival for the third session I was met by Galloper who told me that his sister was suffering from a migraine that day and could not come downstairs.

"Well, Galloper, shall we have our class just the same?"

"Sir, when Elspeth isn't well . . . I can't keep my mind on books and things. My mother told me to tell you that we'll pay you as usual."

I looked at him hard. He was indeed in great distress.

"Galloper, would it be any relief to you if you gave me a half hour of your time now to show me your tidal pool?"

"Oh, yes, sir. Elspeth would like me to do that—sir." He looked back at the house calculatingly. "We have to go down the cliff behind the caretaker's house. Father's at home and he doesn't like me to be interested in the tidal pool. He . . . he wants me to go into the business, I mean his shipping business."

We took the roundabout way almost stealthily. On the descent I asked him, "Galloper, do you go to a military school?"

"No, sir."

"Then why do you feel that you must address me as 'sir' *every* time you speak to me?"

"Father likes me to do it to him. His father was a count in Denmark. He's not a count because he's an American; but he likes it when important people call him 'Count.' He wants Elspath and me to be like his father and mother."

"Oh, so you must be very much a lady and a gentleman?"

"Oh, *yes*, s- s-"

"Do you ever have headaches? . . . No? . . . Forgive me asking so many questions. In a minute you're going to tell me all about this pool. Is your Aunt Benedikta very much a countess too?"

"Oh, no. She lets us do anything we want to do."

We knelt over the pool. We saw the anemones opening to welcome the incoming tide; we saw the crayfish lurking ominously in their caves. He showed me the marvels of protective coloration—the waterlogged sticks that were not sticks, the pebbles that were not pebbles. He showed me the fury with which tiny fish, when near their eggs, can fight off predators many times larger than themselves. I, too, was revived by the inflowing tide of wonders. My wonder included the small professor. At the half hour's close I asked him to accompany me to the front door. As we rose I said, "Thank you, sir. I haven't been so filled with the excitement of science since I read *The Voyage of the Beagle*."

"We think that's the best book in the world."

As we crossed the lawn the deer gathered about us as though they had been waiting. They bumped me and even pushed me from side to side. I stopped and talked to them in French. Galloper stood apart and watched this. When we moved on he said, "They don't do that to me or even to their keeper—not so much. They only do it to you and to Elspeth. . . . They know you have galvanic hands."

"Galloper! Galloper! You're a scientist. You know there are no such things."

"Sir, there are a lot of mysteries in nature, aren't there?"

I made no reply. At the door I asked if he felt that his sister was improving. He looked up at me. He was fighting back tears. "They say she has to go to Boston for an operation soon."

I shook his hand in goodbye, then put my hand on his shoulder. "Yes . . . Yes . . . There are a lot of mysteries in nature. Thank you for reminding me of that." I leaned down and said, "You're going to see one. Your sister is going to get better.—Put this in your pipe and smoke it, Dr. Skeel: your sister has no trouble with her eyesight; and she can go down those verandah steps without losing her balance."

At the next session Elspeth seemed much improved. She volunteered to recite a *Fable* she had newly committed to memory. I cast a glance toward her brother to see if he had caught the significance of this achievement. He had.

She said, "Galloper, will you tell Mr. North what we decided yesterday to ask him?"

"My sister and I decided that we don't want to read any more of the *Fables*. . . . Oh, we like them very much; but we don't want them now. . . . We feel that they're not really about animals; they're about human beings and my sister has always had a strong feeling that animals should not be . . . ?"

He looked at her. She said, "—regarded as persons. We went through ten of the most famous *Fables* and underlined the places where La Fontaine seemed to have his eye really on the fox and the pigeon and the crow . . . and we didn't find very many. Oh, we admire him, but you told Galloper to read Fabre. And Mother ordered the books from New York and we think they're almost the best books we ever read."

There was a silence.

I said, with a gesture faintly implying withdrawal, "Well, you don't need me to read Fabre with you."

"Mr. North, we haven't been quite honest with you. Galloper persuaded Mother to invite you to read with us. Galloper wanted me to meet you. We wanted you just to come and talk with us. Won't you do that? We can pretend that we're reading La Fontaine."

I looked at them gravely, still with the attitude of one about to rise from his chair.

She added, bravely, "And he wanted you to put your hands on

my head. He told me about Ada Nicols.—Almost all the time I have such pain. Will you put your hands on my forehead?"

Galloper was staring up at me with an even more intense urgency.

"Miss Elspeth, it is unsuitable that I put my hands on your head without permission from your nurse."

As before she beckoned to Miss Chalmers who came toward her. I arose and descended some steps of the verandah. I heard Miss Chalmers say something about . . . "most unladylike . . . cannot take the responsibility for such unsuitable behavior. . . . You are my patient and I do not wish you to be agitated. . . . Well, if you insist, you must ask your mother. If she asks me I must tell her that I emphatically disapprove. . . . I think these readings have been most harmful to you, Miss Elspeth."

Miss Chalmers withdrew, bristling with indignation. Galloper arose and entered the house. His absence was prolonged. I assumed that Mrs. Skeel was being told for the first time of the Ada Nicols incident. While we waited I asked Elspeth where she had attended school and if she had enjoyed it. She named one of the best-known girls' finishing schools.

"Every moment you had to remember what you were supposed to do. It was like being in a cage; you were being trained to be a lady. . . . It was like those horses that they teach to waltz. . . . When I'm at Aunt Benedikta's camp in the Adirondacks, I can see real deer in the wild. A deer jumping is one of the most beautiful sights in the world—these deer have never really leaped over anything. There's no room and no reason for their jumping, is there? . . . Mr. North, do you ever have a nightmare about being in prison?"

"Yes, I have. It's the worst dream a man can have."

"Next year my father wants me to do what they call 'come out in society.' I think it's not a coming out but a going in. The girls at school talked about the Christmas and Easter vacations—three dances a night and tea-dances . . . and being stared at by a *wall* of young men all the time. Don't you think that's like animals in the zoo? Whenever I think about it my head begins to ache.—And Father wants me to take the name 'Countess Skeel.'"

"Haven't you things to think about to drive away those nightmares?"

"I used to have music . . . and the books Galloper and I read together, but . . ." She put her hand to her forehead.

"Miss Elspeth, I'm not going to wait for your mother's permission. Miss Chalmers lives in a very small cage. I'm going to put my hand on your forehead," and I rose.

At that moment Galloper returned. He went directly to Miss Chalmers with his message; then came to our table.

"Mother says you may place your hands on Elspeth's forehead for a few minutes."

What to do?

Play the charlatan.

Elspeth shut her eyes and lowered her head.

I arose and said in a matter-of-fact tone, "Please, look toward the sky, Miss Elspeth, and keep your eyes open. Galloper, will you please place your hands on your sister's right forehead." I placed my hands lightly on her left forehead. I looked down into her open eyes and smiled. I did two things at once: I concentrated on forcing "some kind of energy" into my finger tips and I spoke to her as unemphatically as I could. "Look up at the cloud. . . . Try to feel the earth slowly turning under us. . . ." Her hands rose to my wrists. She could not keep her eyes open. She was smiling. She murmured, "Is this dying? Am I dying?"

"No. You are feeling the earth turning.—Now say anything that comes into your head. . . . Give me your right hand." I enclosed it between mine. "Say anything that comes into your head."

"Oh, *mon professeur*. Let us go away, the three of us. I have some money and some jewels that were given to me. Aunt Benedikta has a camp in the Adirondacks. She has asked me to come at any time. We would have to escape without anyone knowing. Galloper says he does not know how to arrange it, but you and he could together. If I am taken to Boston, they will kill me. I am not afraid to die, but I don't want to die in their way. Mr. North, I want to die in your way. Hasn't everyone a right to die in the way they choose?"

I stopped her by increasing the pressure above and below her hand. "You are going to Boston, but the operation is going to be postponed. Gradually your headaches are going to go away.

You are going to spend the rest of the summer at your Aunt Benedikta's camp." Then I spoke in French, "Please say 'Yes, professor' very slowly. Remember—the clouds and the ocean and the trees are listening."

Slowly, "*Oui, monsieur le professeur!*" Then more loudly, "*Oui, monsieur le professeur!*"

We remained motionless for a full minute. An overpowering weakness invaded me. I doubted that my legs could carry me to the front door and to my bicycle. I withdrew my hands. I made a gesture to Galloper to stay where he was and I stumbled and swayed through the house. I caught a glimpse of Miss Chalmers on her feet staring at her patient. The butler and some servants were peering through the drawing-room window. Their heads turned toward me as I hurried by. I fell off my bicycle twice. I had difficulty keeping to the right side of the road.

A weekend elapsed. I rang the bell at "The Deer Park" on the following Monday morning at eleven. I was ready to resign, but I wanted to be dismissed. At the door the butler informed me that Mrs. Skeel wished to see me on the verandah. I bowed to her. She put out her hand, saying, "Will you please sit down, Mr. North?" I sat down and kept my eyes on her face.

"Mr. North, when I first telephoned you I was not quite honest with you. I did not tell you the whole truth. My daughter Elspeth is very ill. For several months we have driven her to Boston twice a month for consultations with Dr. Bosco—examinations and X-rays. The doctor fears that she has a tumor of the brain, but there are many aspects of the case that puzzle him. As you will have noticed she has no difficulty in speaking, though it pains her to raise her voice. She has no impairment in her vision or in her sense of balance. She suffers from lapses of memory but they can be attributed to her difficulty in sleeping and to the medication that she is given." Her hands were grasping the arms of her chair as though she were clinging to a raft. "Dr. Bosco has decided that he must perform a major operation on her brain next week. He wishes that she enter the hospital on Thursday. . . . My daughter feels that this is all unnecessary. She is convinced that you have the power to heal her. . . . Of course, the doctor's assistant could give her an

injection and she could be transported to Boston . . . as
. . . as she says, 'like a mummy.' She says that she would fight
him 'like a dragon.' You can imagine how distressing that
would be for the whole household."

I continued to listen gravely.

"Mr. North, I would like to make a request of you. I ask this
not as an employer, but as the suffering mother of a suffering
child. Elspeth says she will consent to go to Boston 'quietly,' if
the operation is postponed for two weeks and if I can obtain
your promise to visit her there twice."

"Certainly, ma'am, if the doctor permits it."

"Oh, thank you. I'm sure I can arrange it; I *must* arrange it.
A car and chauffeur will be placed at your disposal on both
days for your trip and return."

"That will not be necessary. I can find my way to Boston
and to the door of the hospital. Please write down the hours
when I am to call, the length of the visit, and enclose a letter
which I am to present to the office of admission at the hospital.
I shall send you a bill for whatever expenses I may incur, including the cost of the engagements I must cancel here. I do
not wish any remuneration except those basic expenses. I think
such an interview would be easiest for us if your son Arthur
were present at the same time."

"Yes, you can be sure of that."

"Mrs. Skeel, since my visit last Friday has Miss Elspeth had a
return of the migraine?"

"She was greatly improved. She said she slept 'like an angel'
all night. Her appetite improved. But last night—Sunday night
—the pain returned. It was terrible to see. I longed to telephone to you. But Miss Chalmers and our Newport doctor were
here. They believe you to be the cause of the whole trouble.
They forget that this happened over and over again before you
ever came here. And her father was here. The Skeels, for generations, have known very little illness. I believe his suffering to
be worse than mine, for I have grown up among many . . .
such illnesses."

"Are we to have a class today?"

"She is sleeping. She is blessedly sleeping."

"When does she go to Boston?"

"Even if the operation is postponed—as I shall insist—she will leave here Thursday."

"Please tell Miss Elspeth, I shall be here Wednesday and that I shall visit her in Boston at whatever hour you name. . . . Mrs. Skeel, do not hesitate to call on me any hour of the day or night. It is often hard to reach me by day, but I shall leave you here a schedule of telephone numbers where I can be reached. You and Miss Elspeth must have the courage to face those who resist my visits."

"Thank you."

"I wish to say one more word, ma'am. Arthur is a very remarkable young man."

"Isn't he! Isn't he!"

And for a moment we laughed, astonishing ourselves. At that moment a gentleman appeared at the door. There was no mistaking the former Count Jens Skeel of Skeel.

He said, "Mary, kindly go into the library. This foolishness has gone on long enough. This is the French tutor's last visit to this house. Will the French tutor kindly send me his bill as promptly as possible. Good morning, sir."

I smiled sunnily into his outraged face. "Thank you," I said nodding in the manner of a clerk who has been accorded a long-wished-for vacation. "Good afternoon, Mrs. Skeel. Kindly convey my deep regard to your children." Again I smiled at the master of the house, raising my hand in a manner of saying "Don't trouble to see me to the door. I know the way." Only an accomplished actor can be thrown out of a house and leave a room as though a favor had been conferred upon him—John Drew, say; Cyril Maude, William Gillette.

I was expecting a late telephone call that night, so I sat up reading. The call came at about one-thirty.

"Mr. North, you told me I might call you at any hour."

"Yes, indeed, Mrs. Skeel."

"Elspeth has been in great distress. She wishes to see you. Her father has given his permission."

I wheeled to the house. There seemed to be lights in every window. I was led to the sickroom. Servants in breathless dismay, but dressed as though it were high noon, could be seen lurking in shadows and behind half-open doors. Mrs. Skeel and a doctor were standing in the upper hall. I was introduced to him. He was very angry and shook my hand coldly.

"Dr. Egleston has given me permission to call you."

At a distance I saw Mr. Skeel, very handsome and furious. Mrs. Skeel opened a door a few inches and said, "Elspeth dear, Mr. North has called to ask how you are."

Elspeth was sitting up in bed. Her eyes were bright and fierce after what I presumed to be a prolonged battle with her father and the doctor. My smile included all the bystanders. There was no sign of Miss Chalmers.

"*Bonsoir, chère mademoiselle.*"

"*Bonsoir, monsieur le professeur.*"

I turned back and said in a matter-of-fact tone, "I would like Galloper to join us."

I knew that wherever he was he would hear me. He came forward quickly. Over his pajamas he was wearing a thick dressing-gown bearing the insignia of the school he attended. I let the onlookers see me take out my Ingersoll watch and place it on the bedside table. At a gesture from me Galloper opened wide the door into the hall and another into an inner room where Miss Chalmers was probably boiling.

"You have been in pain, Miss Elspeth?"

"Yes, a little. I don't let them give me those *things.*"

I turned back to the door and said calmly, "Anyone may come in who wishes to. I shall be here five minutes. I only ask that no one come in bringing anger or fear."

Mrs. Skeel entered and took a chair at the foot of her daughter's bed. An elderly woman who had been turning the beads of a rosary in her hand—probably Elspeth's nurse since childhood—came in with an air of defying some order. She knelt in a corner of the room, still fingering her beads. I continued to smile about me as though this were a very usual call and as though I were an old friend of the family. Indeed, it was so unusual an occasion that the household servants gathered about the door, unrebuked. Several even entered the room and remained standing.

"Miss Elspeth, as I came up the Avenue on my bicycle, not a person could be seen. It was like a landscape on the moon. It was very beautiful. I was looking forward to seeing you. I was a little *exalté* and I heard myself singing an old song that you must surely know: '*Stone walls do not a prison make, Nor iron bars a cage.*' Those lines, written almost three hundred years ago, must have brought comfort to thousands of men and women—as they have done to me. Now I am going to talk to you in Chinese for a moment. You remember that I was brought up in China. I shall give you the translation too. '*Ee er san*'—with a downward, then upward glide—'*see. Gee—den—gaw*'—with a rising inflection. '*Hu*' (a descending note) '*li too bay. Nu chi fo n' yu*' and so on. The first seven words are all the Chinese I know. They mean: 'one, two, three, four, chicken—egg—cake.' Mademoiselle, this means: 'All nature is one. Every living thing is closely related to every other living thing.' Nature wishes every living thing to be a perfect example of its kind and to rejoice in the gift of life. That includes Galloper's fish and Jacqueline and Bayard and everybody here, including you and Galloper and me." Those were not the words of Confucius or Mencius, but a paraphrase of something remembered from Goethe.

I leaned forward and spoke to her in a low voice. "Let them drive you to Boston. The operation is going to be postponed and postponed. I am not only going to Boston to see you; I am going to see Dr. Bosco. Has he ever been here to see 'The Deer Park'?"

"Yes. Yes, he has."

"I shall tell him that you have been like a beautiful deer in the deer park, but that you want to be outside that iron fence. Your headaches are your protest against those bars. I shall tell Dr. Bosco to send you to your Aunt Benedikta's camp among those deer who have never known a cage."

"*Can* you do that?"

"Oh, yes."

"I know you can!—Will you come to see me there too?"

"I will try. But a man of thirty has cages and cages. Don't forget I shall see you more than once in Boston and for the rest of the summer I shall write you often. Now I have one minute left. I am going to put my hand on your forehead . . . and all the way home my thoughts will be on you, like a hand, and you will fall asleep."

There was a hush. . . . Sixty seconds of silence on the stage is a long time.

"*Dormez bien, mademoiselle.*"

"*Dormez bien, monsieur le professeur.*"

I may not have galvanic hands but I can put on a galvanic performance. This time I chose as my model that of Otis Skinner in *The Honor of the Family*, after Balzac's story. Moving toward the door I smiled commandingly on those within the room and outside it, on the tear-stained face of Mrs. Skeel, on the Greek chorus of awestricken servants, and on the angry and frustrated faces of Mr. Skeel, Dr. Egleston, and Miss Chalmers who had joined them. I gained two inches in height, a cylinder hat rose from my head at a jaunty angle. I carried a short riding-crop with which I thrashed the jamb of the door. I was all assurance to the degree of effrontery—Colonel Philippe Bridau.

"Good morning, ladies and gentlemen. Good morning, Galloper—Charles Darwin expects every man to do his duty."

"Yes, sir."

"Good morning, all." I called back into the sickroom, "Good morning, Miss Elspeth. '*Stone walls do not a prison make, nor iron bars a cage.*' Please say 'No, they don't!'"

Her voice rang out, "*Non, monsieur le professeur!*"

I advanced bowing to right and left and descended the staircase two steps at a time, singing the Soldiers' Chorus from *Faust*.

Hope is a projection of the imagination; so is despair. Despair all too readily embraces the ills it foresees; hope is an energy and arouses the mind to explore every possibility to combat them. On the bicycle ride to "The Deer Park"—through that mysterious landscape on the moon—*I had had an idea.*

It was arranged that I call at the hospital on the following Friday afternoon at four o'clock. I wrote Dr. Bosco, asking for a five-minute appointment to see him at that time to talk to him about his patient Miss Elspeth Skeel. I wrote that I had enjoyed many congenial talks with his great friend and colleague Dr. de Martel at the American Hospital at Neuilly near Paris. Dr. de Martel was another of the three greatest surgeons in the world. I had never met that eminent man, but hope leaps over obstacles. He had, however, performed an operation on a friend of mine, six days old. Besides, he was the son of the novelist "Gyp" (the Comtesse de Martel), a zestful writer with eyes wide open.

Dr. Bosco received me with a cordiality that immediately turned to professional impersonality. During the entire interview his secretary stood behind him, notebook in hand, open.

"What is your work, Mr. North?"

"I am tutor in English, French, German, and Latin; and children's tennis coach at the Newport Casino. I do not wish to waste your time, Doctor. Miss Skeel has confided to me that she dreads going to sleep because she is afflicted by nightmares of being caged. She is dying of cultural claustration."

"I beg your pardon?"

"She is an exceptional human being with a quick adventuring mind. But at every turn she is met by the tabus and vetoes of genteel society. Her father is her jailor. If I were talking again to your friend Dr. de Martel, I would say, 'Dr. de Martel, your brilliant mother wrote that story over and over again. She believed in the emancipation of young women.' "

"And so?"

"Dr. Bosco, may I make a request of you?"

"Be quick about it."

"Elspeth Skeel's Aunt Benedikta—the former Countess Skeel of Denmark—has a camp in the Adirondacks where the deer roam freely and even the foxes and bears come and go as they wish—and where even a girl of seventeen will never hear a brutal and a life-denying word." I bowed and smiled. "Good afternoon, Dr. Bosco. Good afternoon, ma'am."

I turned and left the room. Before the door closed I heard him say, "I'll be damned!"

A few minutes later I was led to Elspeth's room. She was sitting in a chair by the window overlooking the Charles River. Her mother was sitting beside her; her brother was standing by the bed. After the greetings Elspeth said, "Mother, tell Mr. North the good news."

"Mr. North, there is to be no operation after all. Dr. Bosco made the examination yesterday. He thinks the condition that alarmed us is clearing up of itself."

"Isn't that splendid! When are you returning to Newport?"

"We're not returning to Newport at all. I told Dr. Bosco

about my sister-in-law's camp in the Adirondacks and he said, 'Just the place for her!' "

So all my play-acting and heroics and prevarication had not been necessary. But I had enjoyed them. Elspeth's smile as her eyes rested on mine was reward enough. It implied that we shared a secret.

There was nothing left to do but to talk small-talk: the Harvard students sculling on the river; the departure for the Adirondacks at the end of the week; the wonderful nurses (from Nova Scotia)—small-talk. My mind began to wander. For me small-talk is a wearisome cage.

A nurse appeared at the door. She asked, "Is a Mr. North here?"

I made myself known.

"Dr. Bosco's secretary has called. He will be here in a few minutes. He wishes you to remain here until he comes."

"I shall be here, ma'am."

Zounds! What now?

Presently the doctor appeared. He gave no sign of having recognized me. He spoke to Mrs. Skeel. "Mrs. Skeel, I have been thinking over your daughter's case."

"Yes, Dr. Bosco?"

"I think it advisable that she be given a longer rest and change than this summer in the Adirondacks. I recommend that she spend eight to ten months abroad—in the mountains, if possible. Have you friends or relatives in the Swiss Alps or in the Tirol?"

"Why, Doctor, I could take her to an excellent school we know in Arosa. Would you like that, Elspeth?"

"Oh, yes, Mother." Her glance included me. "If you write letters to me there."

"Indeed, we shall, dear. And I shall send Arthur over to you for the Christmas holidays.—Dr. Bosco, could I ask you to write Mr. Skeel telling him that you strongly advise this plan?"

"I'll do that.—Good afternoon again, Mr. North."

"Good afternoon, Dr. Bosco."

"Mrs. Skeel, Mr. North deserves some kind of medal. He asked me for five minutes of my time. He called on me and finished his business in three minutes. That has never happened to me in my long experience. Mr. North, I telephoned my wife

that you were a good friend of our friend Dr. de Martel. She is
fonder of Thierry de Martel than she is of me. She asked me to
bring you home to dinner tonight."

"Dr. Bosco, I told a lie. I have never met Dr. de Martel."

He looked around the room and shook his head in amazement.

"Well, come just the same. It won't be the first time we've
had liars to dinner."

"But, Dr. Bosco, I'm afraid that I'd have nothing to say that
could interest you."

"I'm accustomed to that. Kindly be waiting at the entrance
to this building at six-thirty."

That stopped me. I had heard many stories of Dr. Bosco and I
knew that I had received more than an invitation—a command.

When he had left the room, Mrs. Skeel said, "That's a great
privilege, Mr. North."

Elspeth said, "He's very interested in you, *monsieur le professeur*. I told him about your hands and how you had driven my
headaches away and how wonderful you had been about Ada
Nicols, and how people said that you cured Dr. Bosworth of
cancer. I think he wants to know what you *do*."

My eyes popped out of my head with horror, with shame.
HELL AND DAMNATION! . . . I had to get out of the building.
I had to get by myself and think. I toyed with the idea of throwing myself into the Charles River. (It's too shallow; besides I'm
an expert swimmer.) I hastily shook hands with the Skeels, thank-
ing them, et cetera, and wishing them many happy days in the
Adirondacks. To Galloper I whispered, "Someday you'll be a
great doctor; start learning now how to give orders like that."

"Yes, sir."

I walked the streets of Boston for two and a half hours. At
six-thirty I was waiting as directed. An unpretentious car drove
up to the curb. A man of fifty, more resembling a janitor than
a chauffeur, alighted and crossing the pavement asked me if I
was Mr. North.

"Yes. I'd like to sit up in front with you, if you don't mind.
My name's Ted North."

"Glad to know you. I'm Fred Spence."

"Where are we going, Mr. Spence?"

"To Dr. Bosco's house in Brookline."

"Dr. Bosco's gone home already?"

"On Friday afternoons he don't operate. He takes his students around the building and shows them his patients. Then I call for him at five and take him home. On Friday nights he likes a guest or two for dinner. Mrs. Bosco says she never knows what he'll bring home." That "what" implied stray dogs or alley cats.

"Mr. Spence, I wasn't invited to dinner. I was ordered. Dr. Bosco likes to give orders, doesn't he?"

"Yes. You get used to it. The doctor's a very moody man. I take him to the hospital at eight-thirty and I take him home at six-thirty. Some days he don't say a word the whole time. Other days he don't stop talking about how everything's in bad shape and everybody's stupid. Been like that since he came home from the War. He likes his guests to go home at ten, because he has to write everything down in his diary."

"Mr. Spence, I've got to take a train from South Station at ten-thirty. How'd I get there?"

"Dr. Bosco's arranged for me to drive you to Newport or to anywhere you want to go."

"To Newport!—I'll be very obliged to you, if you'll drive me to South Station after dinner."

Entering the house I was met by Mrs. Bosco—of generous proportions, gracious, but somehow impassive.

"Dr. Bosco would like you to join him in his study. He is making you one of his famous Old-Fashioned cocktails. He doesn't drink them himself, but he likes to make them for others. I hope you aren't hungry, because the doctor doesn't like to sit down to dinner until a quarter before eight."

In the afternoon, in his white coat, he had the head of a lean Roman senator; in a dark suit his features were more delicate and ascetic—the vicar-general of a religious order, perhaps. He shook hands in silence and returned to the matter that was occupying him. He was making me an Old-Fashioned. I got an impression of a crucible, a mortar and pestle, some vials— Paracelsus making an alchemical brew. He was totally absorbed. I was not asked if I wished an Old-Fashioned nor was I asked to sit down.

"Try that," he said finally. It was indeed rich and strange. He turned and sat down—with a plan in his head, as though con-versation were also a totally occupying discipline.

"Mr. North, why did you represent yourself as a friend of Dr. de Martel?"

"I felt that it was urgent that I have a few minutes of your time. I felt that you should know *one* of the reasons for Miss Skeel's migraines—a reason that no one in the family was in a position to tell you. I felt that a great doctor would want to know every aspect of the case. I have since learned that you had already recommended her removal from her home and that my call on you was unnecessary."

"No. It opened my eyes to the part that her father was play-ing in her depressed condition." He passed his hand wearily over his eyes. "In my field of work we often tend to overlook the emotional elements that enter into a problem that faces us. We pride ourselves on being scientists and we do not see how science can come to grips with such things as emotions. . . . Apparently *that* is an aspect of these problems that you have interested yourself in." I pretended not to have heard him, but there was no evading any step in the conversation that Dr. Bosco had planned to pursue. "You *do* engage in healing?"

"No. No, Dr. Bosco. I have never made claim to any capac-ity for healing. Some *children* have talked some nonsense about my having 'electric hands.' I hate it. I don't want to have any-thing to do with it."

He gazed at me fixedly for a moment. "I am told that you enabled Dr. Bosworth to leave his house for the first time in ten years."

"Please change the subject, Doctor. I just talked common sense to him."

He repeated thoughtfully, "Common sense, common sense. —And this story about a girl Ada—Ada somebody—who struck her head against a post?"

"Doctor, I'm a fraud. I'm a quack. But when a person is suffering right under your eyes what do you do? You do what you can."

"*And what is it that you do?* You hypnotized her?"

"I never saw a person hypnotized. I don't know what it is. I merely talked soothingly to her and stroked the bruise. Then I

carried her to the superintendent of the Casino who has a lot
of experience in first-aid. There was no real concussion. She
came back to class two days later."

"If I ask Mrs. Bosco to join us, will you tell us the full story
of Dr. Bosworth's recovery? There's still half an hour before
dinner."

"There are some homely vulgar details connected with it."

"Mrs. Bosco is used to such details from me."

"I am a guest in your house," I said discouragedly. "I shall
try to do what you wish me to do."

He refreshed my glass and left the room. I heard him calling,
"Lucinda! Lucinda!" (It was not an invitation but an order.)
Mrs. Bosco slipped into the room and sat by the door. The
doctor sat at his desk.

"All right," I said to myself, "I'll give him the works." I gave
him the background of the Death Watch, my first interview
with Mrs. Bosworth, our readings in Bishop Berkeley, my increasing awareness of a "house of listening ears," the family's
efforts to persuade him that he was condemned and going
crazy, my trip to Providence disguised as a truck driver, the
attempt on my life.

Toward the end of the story Dr. Bosco had covered his face
with his hands, but not in boredom. When I had finished, he
said, "No one tells me anything. . . . I am the specialist who
is called in at the end of the game."

A servant appeared at the door. Mrs. Bosco said, "Dinner is
ready."

Dinner was delicious. The doctor was silent. Mrs. Bosco
asked me, "Mr. North, would it bore you to tell us the story of
your life and interests?"

I spared them nothing—Wisconsin, China, California, Oberlin College, Yale, the American Academy in Rome, the school
in New Jersey, then Newport. I mentioned some of my interests and ambitions (omitting the *shaman*).

"Lucinda, I shall ask Mr. North to join me in my study for
coffee."

It was a quarter before ten.

"Mr. North, at the close of the summer I wish you to come
to Boston. I am appointing you to be one of my secretaries.
You will accompany me on my rounds. I shall tell each patient

that I have full confidence in you. You will visit them regularly. You will report to me on each patient's intimate life-story, and on any strains he or she may be living under. Get to know them by their first names. I have seldom known a patient by his or her Christian name. What is yours?"

"Theophilus."

"Ah, yes, I remember. That is a beautiful name. It carries connotations that were once real to me; I wish they were today. Are you returning to Newport tonight?"

"Yes, Doctor."

"I have arranged that Fred Spence will drive you there." (It was an order.) "Here is a five-dollar bill you will give him at the end of the journey. It will make you feel more comfortable about the trip. Do not answer now about the proposal I have laid before you. Think it over. Let me hear from you by a week from today. Thank you for coming to dinner."

I said good night to Mrs. Bosco in the hall. "Thank you for coming and for bringing those soothing hands with you. The doctor's not often as patient as he's been tonight."

I slept all the way home. At Mrs. Keefe's door I gave Fred Spence the honorarium and climbed up my stairs. Three days later I wrote Dr. Bosco—with many expressions of regard—that my return to Europe in the autumn would prevent my accepting the position that he had offered me. I thought the whole damnable *shaman* business was at an end, but ten days later I found myself in a mess of trouble.

I rejoiced in my apartment, but I was seldom there. My daily work became more and more difficult and I spent many evenings at the People's Library preparing for my classes. At midnight I found notes under my door from my good landlady: "*Three ladies and a gentleman called for you. I let them wait for you until ten in my sitting-room, but I had to ask them to go home at ten. They did not wish to leave their names and addresses. Mrs. Doris Keefe.*" On another night, the same message speaking of eight people. "*I cannot have more than five strangers waiting in my sitting-room. I told them they must go away. Mrs. Doris Keefe.*"

Finally on a Thursday evening I was at home and received a telephone call from Joe ("Holy Joe"), the supervisor at the Y.M.C.A. "Ted, what's going on? There are twelve people

—mostly old women—waiting for you in the visitors' room. I told them you didn't live here any more. I couldn't tell them your new address because you never gave it to me. . . . There are some more coming in the door now. What are you doing—running an employment agency? Please come over and send them away and tell them not to come back again. There've been a few every night, but tonight beats everything. This is a young men's Christian association, not an old ladies' home. Come on over and drive the cattle out."

I hurried over. The crowd now overflowed the visitors' room. I recognized some of the faces—servants from "Nine Gables" and from "The Deer Park" and even from "Mrs. Cranston's." I started shaking hands.

"Oh, Mr. North, I suffer from rheumatism something terrible."

"Oh, Mr. North, my back hurts so I can't sleep nights, not what you'd call sleep."

"Mr. North, look at my hand! It takes me an hour to open it in the morning."

"Ladies and gentlemen, I am not a doctor. I don't know the first thing about medicine. I must ask you to consult a regular practicing physician."

The wails mounted:

"Oh, sir, they take your money and do nothing for you."

"Mr. North, put your hand on my knee. God will reward you."

"Sir, my feet. It's agony to go a step."

I had spent a part of my childhood in China and was no stranger to the unfathomable misery in the world. What could I do? First, I must clear the lobby. I rested my hand here and there; I grasped an ankle or two; I drew my hand firmly down some spines. I gave particular attention to the napes of necks. I made a point of *hurting* my patients (they yelped, but were instantly convinced that that was the "real thing"). Gently propelling them to the front door, I planted the heels of my hands on some foreheads, murmuring the opening lines of the *Aeneid*. Then I said, "This is the last time I can see you. Do not come back again. You *must* see your own doctors. Good night, and God bless you all."

I returned to my own address and dispersed a group that had gathered there.

I dreaded the following Sunday night and had reason to. I made my way to the "Y" and from afar I could see that they had all come back and brought others; a line extended from lobby to sidewalk. I called them all together and held a meeting in the middle of the street. "Ladies and gentlemen, there's nothing I can do for you. I'm as ill as you are. Every bone in my body aches. Let us shake hands and say good night." I hurried back to Mrs. Keefe's house where another crowd had gathered. I dismissed them with the same words. Mrs. Keefe was watching us from a window. When the strangers had gone she unlocked the front door to me.

"Oh, Mr. North, I can't stand this much longer. When I lock the door they wander around the house knocking on the windowpanes like beggars I've shut out in a snow storm. Here is a letter for you that was brought by hand."

"*Dear Mr. North, it would give me much pleasure to see you this evening at ten-thirty, your sincere friend, Amelia Cranston.*"

At ten-thirty I hurried to Spring Street. The rooms were emptying quickly. Finally no one was there but Mrs. Cranston, Mr. Griffin, and Mrs. Grant, her principal assistant in running the house. I sat down by Mrs. Cranston who appeared to be unusually large, genial, and happily disposed.

"Thank you for coming, Mr. North."

"Forgive me for being absent so long. My schedule gets heavier every week."

"So I have been informed . . . bicycling up and down the Avenue at two in the morning and feeding the wild animals, I presume." Mrs. Cranston enjoyed giving evidence that she knew everything. "Mrs. Grant, will you kindly tell Jimmy to bring the refreshments I set aside in the icebox." We were served the gin-fizzes I had come to recognize as a mark of some special occasion. She lowered her voice. "You are in trouble, Mr. North?"

"Yes, I am, ma'am. Thank you for your letter."

"Well, you have become a very famous man *in certain quarters*. My visitors Thursday night and tonight talked of little else. Somehow or other you put new life in Dr. Bosworth and now he's bounding about the country like a lad of fifty. Somehow or other you brought relief to Miss Skeel's headaches. Servants watch their employers very closely, Mr. North. How many patients were waiting for you tonight?"

"Over twenty-five in one place and a dozen in the other."

"Next week the waiting line will stretch around the block."

"Help me, Mrs. Cranston. I love Newport. I want to stay until the end of the summer. I haven't got 'electric hands.' I'm a fake and a fraud. That first night I couldn't *drive* them out of the building. You should have seen their eyes: It's better to be a fake and a fraud than to be . . . brutal. I didn't do them any harm, did I?"

"Put your hands down on the table, palms upward."

She passed five finger tips over them lightly, took a sip from her glass, and said, "I always knew you had something."

I hastily hid my hands under the table. She went on speaking evenly with her calm smile: "Mr. North, even the happiest and healthiest of women—and there are very few of us—have one corner of their mind that is filled with a constant dread of illness. Dread. Even when they're not thinking about it, they're thinking about it. This is not true of most men—you think you'll live forever. Do you think you'll live forever, Mr. North?"

"No, ma'am," I said, smiling. "I'll say, 'I've warmed both hands before the fire of life; It sinks and I am ready to depart.' But I'd like to have seen Edweena before I departed."

She looked at me in surprise. "It's funny your saying that. Edweena's back from her cruise. She's been in New York a week, making arrangements for her fall season there. Henry Simmons has been to New York to bring her back here. I'm expecting them tonight. Edweena knows all about you."

"About *me*?!"

"Oh, yes. I wrote her all about your problem a week ago. She answered at once. It's Edweena who's had the idea about how you can get free of this mess you're in. It's Henry Simmons and I who have arranged it at this end." She took up an envelope from the table before her and waved it before my nose as you'd wave a bone before a dog.

"Oh, Mrs. Cranston!"

"But let's say one more word about your new situation in Newport. Women never put their full confidence in doctors.

Women are both religious and superstitious. They want nothing less than a miracle. You are the latest miracle man. There are many *masseurs* and manipulators and faith-healers in this town. They have licenses and they take money for their services. Your fame rests on the fact that you take no fees. That inspires a confidence that no doctor can inspire. If you pay a doctor you buy the right to criticize him as though he were any other huckster. But everybody knows that you can't buy miracles and that's why you are a miracle man. There is no sign that Dr. Bosworth or the Skeels gave you an automobile or even a gold watch—and yet look what you did for them! *You still go about on a bicycle!*"

I didn't like this talk. My eyes were fixed on the envelope. My tongue was hanging out of my mouth for that bone. I knew that Mrs. Cranston was teasing me, perhaps punishing me—for not having called on her for help earlier, for having been absent from "Mrs. Cranston's" so long.

I got down on one knee. "Please forgive me, Mrs. Cranston, for having been away so long. I'm indebted to you for so much."

She laughed and put her hand on mine for a moment. Well-conditioned women love to pardon when they're asked. "In this envelope is a document. It's not official, but it *looks* official. It has a ribbon and some sealing-wax and is on the stationery of a health organization that has long since been absorbed by others." She took it out and laid it before me:

> To whom it may concern: Mr. T. Theophilus North, resident in Newport, Rhode Island, has no license to provide medical service of any kind or manner unless the patient appears before him with the written permission of a physician duly registered in this city. Office of the Superintendent of Health, this day the ——— of August, 1926.

"Oh, Mrs. Cranston!"
"Wait, there is another document in this envelope."

> Mr. T. Theophilus North, resident in Newport, Rhode Island, is hereby given permission to make one visit, not lasting longer than thirty minutes, to Miss Liselotte Müller, resident at ——— Spring Street, and to furnish her such aid and comfort as seems fitting to him.

This was signed by an esteemed physician in the city and bore the date of the previous day.

I stared at her.

"Miss Müller lives here now?"

"Could you see her now? This building is really three buildings. The third and fourth floors of the building on this side have been fitted out to be an infirmary for very old women. They have spent their lifetimes in domestic service and many of them have been well provided for by their former employers. Most of them cannot negotiate even one flight of stairs, but they have a terrace where they can sun themselves in good weather and social rooms for all weather. You will see sights and smell smells that will distress you, but you have told us of your experiences in China and you are prepared for such things." Here I heard her short snort-like laugh. "You have accepted the truth that much of life is difficult and that the last years are particularly so. You are not a green boy, Mr. North. Few men pay calls in that infirmary—occasionally a doctor, a priest, a pastor, or a relative. It is a rule of the house that during such calls the door into the sickroom is left ajar. I am sending you upstairs with my assistant and friend, Mrs. Grant."

I asked in a low voice, "Will you tell me something about Miss Müller?"

"Tante Liselotte was born in Germany. She was the eleventh child of a pastor and was brought to this country at the age of seventeen by an employment agency. She has been the nanny in one of the most respected houses here and in New York for three generations. She has bathed and dressed all those children, spent the entire day with them, paddled and powdered and wiped their little bottoms. I have selected her for your visit because she was kind and helpful to me when I was young, lonesome, and frightened. She has outlived all the members of her family abroad who would take any interest in her. She has been much loved in her station, but she is a strict rigid woman and has made few friends except myself. She is sound of mind; she can see and hear; but she is racked by rheumatic pains. I believe them to be excruciating because she is not a complaining woman."

"And if I fail, Mrs. Cranston?"

She ignored the question. She went on: "I suspect that your

fame has preceded you upstairs. The guests in this house have many friends in the infirmary. News of miracles travels fast. . . . Mrs. Grant, I should like you to meet Mr. North."

"How do you do, Mr. North?"

"I think we shall be speaking German tonight, Mrs. Grant. Do you understand German?"

"Oh, no. Not a word."

"Mrs. Cranston, after these meetings I am sometimes very weak. If Henry Simmons returns before I come down, will you ask him to wait for me and walk home with me?"

"Oh, yes—I think both Edweena and Henry Simmons will be here. Your visit to Tante Liselotte is also Edweena's wish."

I was staggered.

Again I was to learn: happy is the man who is aided by what folklore calls "the wise women." That is a lesson of the *Odyssey*. "Then the gray-eyed Athene appeared to Odysseus in the guise of a servant and he knew her not, and she spoke unto him. . . ."

I followed Mrs. Grant upstairs. The women I passed on the landings and in the corridors lowered their eyes and shrank against the walls. On the third and fourth floors all wore identical "wrappers" in gray and white stripes. Mrs. Grant knocked at a half-open door and said, "Tante Liselotte, Mr. North has come to call on you," then she sat down in a corner, folded her hands, and lowered her eyes.

"*Guten Abend, Fräulein Müller.*"

"*Guten Abend, Herr Doktor.*"

Tante Liselotte appeared to be a skeleton, but her large brown eyes were bright. She seemed barely able to turn her head. She wore a knitted cap and a comforter over her shoulders. The linen and the entire room were spotless. I continued in German. "I am neither a doctor nor a pastor—merely a friend of Mrs. Cranston and of Edweena." I had no idea what I was going to say. I made my mind go blank. "May I ask where you were born, Tante Liselotte?"

"Near Stuttgart, sir."

"Ah!" I said with delighted surprise. "A Swabian!" I knew nothing about the region except that Schiller was born there. "In a moment I want to look at all these photographs on the

walls. Forgive me if I put my hands on yours." I took her infinitely delicate right hand between mine and rested all three on
the counterpane. I began to concentrate all the energy I could
assemble.

"I speak German so badly, but what a wonderful language it
is! Aren't *Leiden* and *Liebe* and *Sehnsucht* more beautiful words
than 'sufferings' and 'love' and 'longing'?" I repeated the German words slowly. Tremors were passing through her hand.
"And your name *Liselotte* for Elizabeth-Charlotte! And the diminutives: *Mütterchen, Kindlein, Engelein*." I felt prompted
to push our three hands all but imperceptibly toward her
knee. Her eyes were wide, staring at the wall opposite her.
She was breathing deeply. Her chin was twitching. "I think of
the German hymns I know through Bach's music: '*Ach, Gott,
wie manches Herzeleid*' and '*Halt' im Gedächtnis Jesum Christ*.'
'*Gleich wie der Regen und Schnee vom Himmel fällt . . .*' They
can translate the words, they cannot translate what we hear
who love the language." I remembered and recited others. I
was trembling because I was recalling Bach's music which so
often has something multitudinous about it—like waves and
generations.

I was aware of much tiptoeing in the corridor but at first no
whispering. A large group was gathering outside the door. I
suspect that the custom of lowering lights at such a late hour
had been set aside because of my visit. I gently withdrew my
hands, rose, and started on a tour of the room; pausing before
the pictures. I stood before two silhouettes—probably a hundred years old—her parents. I glanced at her and nodded. Her
eyes were following me. A faded blue snapshot of Tante
Liselotte seated between two perambulators in Central Park.
In every photograph—first as a happy young woman with a
square plain face, then as a woman in middle age, inclining to
stoutness—she was dressed in a uniform that resembles what
we in this country know as the garb of a deaconess, surmounted
by a bonnet tied under her chin with a wide muslin band. On
her feet she wore stout "hygienic" shoes that had undoubtedly
aroused discreet laughter throughout her long life:

Tante Liselotte in an old-world "bath chair" with children at
her feet—in faded ink "Ostende, 1880";

A large party on the deck of a yacht gathered about the

German Kaiser and the Kaiserin; at the edge of the picture stood Tante Liselotte with a baby in her arms and her young charges beside her. As though talking to myself I said, "Their Imperial Majesties have graciously requested that I present to them Miss Liselotte Müller, a much valued member of our household"—"Kiel, 1890";

Tante Liselotte on the Cliff Walk in Newport, always with children;

A wedding picture, bride and groom and Liselotte, "Love to Nana, from Bertie and Marianne—June, 1909." I said aloud to myself in English, "You were present at my father's wedding too, weren't you, Tante Liselotte?"

Photographs in the nursery. "Nana, can we go hunting for shells today?" "Nana, I'm sorry I was naughty about the over-shoes this morning. . . ." "Nana, when we go to bed will you tell us the story about the carpet that flies in the air?"

All my movements were slow. My eyes returned to hers at each improvisation. I went back to my chair and placed our three hands against her knee. She shut her eyes but suddenly opened them wide in great alarm or wonder.

The throng that had gathered in the corridor was filling the doorway. There was a sound now of sighing and groans and the chittering of bats. An old woman on crutches lost her balance and fell face downward on the floor. I paid no attention. Mrs. Grant came forward and lifted the woman from the floor and with the help of others led her from the room. During the disturbance another woman, not a patient, had entered the room and had sat down in Mrs. Grant's chair. Tante Liselotte drew her hand from between mine and beckoned me to lean nearer to her. In German she said, "I want to die. . . . Why does God not let me die?"

"Oh, Tante Liselotte, you know the old hymn and Bach's music for it, '*Gottes Zeit ist die allerbeste Zeit.*'"

She repeated the words. "*Ja . . . Ja . . . Ich bin müde. Danke, junger Mann.*"

I rose with effort. I looked about, drowsy with fatigue, for Mrs. Grant. My eyes fell on the woman who had taken her place—on one of the nine faces dearest to me that I have known in my life, though I was to know her such a short time. She rose smiling.

I said, "Edweena," and the tears rolled down my face.

"Theophilus," she said, "you go downstairs. I will stay here a little longer. Henry is waiting for you. Can you find the way?"

As I leaned against the door I heard Edweena ask, "Where is the pain, dear Tante?"

"There is none . . . none."

I wanted to reach the staircase, but my way was barred. I could scarcely keep my eyes open; I longed to lie down on the floor. I slowly walked as through a field of wheat. I had to unfasten hands from my sleeves, from the hem of my coat, even from my ankles. On the flight of stairs between the second and third floors I sat down on a step, leaned my head against the wall, and fell asleep. I don't know how long I slept, but I woke much refreshed and found Edweena sitting beside me. She had taken hold of my hand.

"Do you feel better?"

"Oh, yes."

"It's nearly midnight. They'll be hunting for us. We'd better go downstairs. Can you walk all right? Are you yourself?"

"Yes. I think I had a long nap. I'm all rested."

On the second-floor landing, under a light on the ceiling where we could see each other's face, she said, "Can you bear a bit of good news?"

"Yes, Edweena."

"About five minutes after you left, Tante Liselotte died."

I smiled, I started to say, "I killed her," but Edweena put her hand on my mouth. "I understand a little German," she said. " 'Ich bin müde. Danke, junger Mann.' "

Together we entered the front rooms on the ground floor.

"Well, you've been quite a while," said Mrs. Cranston. "Mrs. Grant has told me about the ending. You've performed your last miracle, Dr. North."

"I'll walk you home, cully," said Henry.

I said good night to the ladies. As I was going out the door, Mrs. Cranston called, "Mr. North, you've forgotten your envelope."

I returned and took it. I bowed and said, "And thank you, ladies."

On the way home, buoyed up by good old Henry and by the consciousness of having made a new friend in Edweena, I recalled a theory that I had long held and tested and played with—the theory of the Constellations: a man should have three masculine friends older than himself, three of about his own age, and three younger. And he should have three older women friends, three of his own age, and three younger. These twice-nine friends I call his Constellation.

Similarly, a woman should have her Constellation.

These friendships have nothing to do with passionate love. Love as a passion is a wonderful thing but it has its own laws and its own histories. Nor do they have anything to do with the relationships within the family which have their own laws and their own histories.

Seldom—perhaps never—are all eighteen roles filled at the same time. Vacancies occur; some live for years—or for a life-time—with only one older or younger friend, or with none.

What a deep satisfaction we feel when a vacant place is filled, as it was by Edweena that night. ("Then felt I like some watcher of the skies when a new planet swims into his ken.")

During those months in Newport I found one sound older friend, Bill Wentworth; two friends of my own age, Henry and Bodo; two younger friends, Mino and Galloper; two older women, Mrs. Cranston and (though meeting seldom) Signora Matera; two women of about my own age, Edweena and Persis; two younger women, Eloise and Elspeth.

But we must remember that we also play a part in the Constellations of others—which is a partial replacement in our own. I was certainly a younger friend necessary to Dr. Bosworth, though so self-centered a man could never meet the need of an older friend for me. "Rip" Vanwinkle and even George Granberry were ghosts of their former selves (the test is laughter; their resources for laughter were spent or quenched). I hope I was an older friend in Charles Fenwick's Constellation, but he was struggling to arrive at his rightful age and the struggle left him with little to give in the free exchanges of friendship.

Of course, this is only a fanciful theory of mine—not to be taken too literally, nor to be dismissed hastily. . . .

At the end of the summer I met Galloper at the Casino. We shook hands solemnly as usual.

"Have you got a minute to sit down over here in the spectators' gallery, Galloper?"

"Yes, Mr. North."

"How's the family?"

"They're all very well."

"When do your mother and sister leave for Europe?"

"Day after tomorrow."

"Please tell them I wish them a happy voyage."

"I will."

Comfortable pauses.

"You don't end every sentence with 'sir' any more, do you?"

He looked at me with what I had come to know as his "interior smile." "I told my father that American boys call their father 'Dad' or 'Papa.'"

"*Did* you? Was he very angry?"

"He threw his hands up in the air and said that the world was going to pieces. . . . I call him 'sir' the first thing in the morning, but most of the time I call him 'Dad.'"

"He'll come to like it."

Comfortable silences.

"Have you decided what you're going to be in life?"

"I'm going to be a doctor. . . . Mr. North, do you think Dr. Bosco will still be teaching when I get to medical school?"

"Why not? He's not an old man at all. And you're a sharp student. You'll skip a class or two. I see where a fellow graduated from Harvard the other day at the age of nineteen. . . . So you're going to be a brain surgeon, eh? . . .

"Well, that's one of the most difficult professions in the world—hard on the body, on the mind, and on the spirit. . . . You come home tired at night after a couple of four- or five-hour operations hanging between life and death. . . .

"Marry a calm girl. See that she doesn't laugh outside, but inside, as you do. . . . Many great brain surgeons have a hobby to escape into when the burden gets too great—like music or collecting books about the early history of medicine. . . .

"Many great surgeons have to set up a kind of wall between themselves and the patients. To shield their hearts. See if you can change that. Put your face near to the patients when you talk to them. Pat them lightly on the elbow or the shoulder and smile. You're going down into the valley of death together, see what I mean? . . .

"Many a great Dr. Sawbones—do you mind the word?"

"No."

"Many a Dr. Sawbones tends to withdraw into himself. To save his energy. They become domineering or eccentric—always a sign of an inner loneliness. Pick out a few friends—men and women, of all ages. You won't have much time to give them, but that doesn't matter. Dr. Bosco's best friend lives in France. He only sees him once in every three or four years, at congresses. They steal away and have a choice and expensive dinner together. Great surgeons tend to be great gourmets. After half an hour they discover that they're laughing together.—Well, I have to go now."

We shook hands solemnly.

"Keep well, Galloper."

"You, too, Mr. North."

13

Bodo and Persis

T HIS CHAPTER might also be called "Nine Gables—Part Two," but it has seemed advisable to place it here among these later chapters. It is therefore out of its chronological order. The events recounted here took place after the drive with Dr. Bosworth and Persis to Bishop Berkeley's "Whitehall" (when I explained that Bodo was not a fortune hunter but was himself a fortune) and before my last visit to "Nine Gables" (and that smashing ultimatum from Mrs. Bosworth: "Father, either that monster leaves this house or I do!").

I have not yet entered into possession of my apartment. I am still at the Y.M.C.A.

I had no classes on Monday nights. After supper in town on a certain Monday evening I returned to the "Y" at about eight. The desk clerk gave me a letter which I saw resting in my pigeon-hole. Standing at the desk I opened and read it. "*Dear Mr. North, I often take a late drive. I hope you will not be too tired to join me tomorrow night when you've finished reading with my grandfather. You can place your bicycle in the back seat of my car and I can return you later to your door. There is something urgent I should tell you. This needs no answer. I shall be at the door of 'Nine Gables' when you leave. Sincerely yours, Persis Tennyson.*" I put the letter in my pocket and was starting upstairs when the desk clerk said, "Mr. North, there's a gentleman over there who's been waiting to see you."

I turned and saw Bodo coming toward me. I had never seen his face stern and taut before. We shook hands.

"*Grüss Gott, Herr Baron.*"

"*Lobet den Herrn in der Ewigkeit,*" he replied unsmilingly. "Theophilus, I've come to say goodbye. Have you time to talk for an hour? I want to get a little bit drunk."

"I'm ready."

"I left my car up at the corner. I have two flasks of *Schnapps.*"

I followed him. "Where are we going?"

"To Doheney's, down at the Public Beach. We need ice. *Schnapps* is best when it's very cold."

We started off. He said, "I shall never come to Newport again, if I can help it."

"When do you go?"

"The Venables are giving a small dinner for me tomorrow night. When the guests are gone, I'll start driving to Washington and shall drive all night."

His unhappiness was like a weight and a presence in the car. I remained silent. Doheney's was a "straight" bar, that is to say no illegal liquor was sold there. The curtains at the windows were not drawn. Guests could bring their own. It was as friendly as Mr. Doheney himself and it was almost empty. We sat at a table by an open window and ordered two teacups and a small pail of ice. We embedded the flasks and the teacups in the ice.

Bodo said, "Danny, we're going for a walk on the beach while the stuff gets cold."

"Yes, Mr. Stams."

We went out, crossed the road, and started walking toward the bathing pavilion—shut up for the night—our feet sinking in the sand. I followed like a familiar dog. Bodo ascended the steps and stood with his back against one of the pillars on the verandah. "Sit down, Theophilus; I want to think aloud for a few minutes."

I obeyed and waited. Something awesome was going on in Bodo.

It is a universally held opinion of our day that full-grown men do not shed tears. I'm quite a weeper myself, but I'm not a sobber. I weep at music and at books and I weep at the movies. I never sob. I have told in Chapter 7 how Elbert Hughes—who was not a full-grown man—cried like a baby and how exasperating it was. At college I had a friend who was about to be dismissed from the university for having published a plagiarized story in the undergraduate magazine of which I was an editor. His father was a clergyman. The scandal and disgrace would be overwhelming and would shatter his life. Perhaps I shall tell that story some day. The spectacle of his abasement was all the more devastating because he had been innocent of any intention to deceive. When I was at Fort Adams I knew a soldier, drafted from his farm in Kentucky. He had never been farther from his dirt-floor cabin, from his parents and his eight brothers and sisters than a visit to the nearest county seat. ("Till I was drafted I'd never wore a pair of shoes except on Sunday; my brother and I took turns wearing the shoes to church.") Sobbing of homesickness. At the American Academy in Rome I cut down a friend who had been trying to hang himself in the shower because he had contracted a venereal disease—sobbing rage.

There's a vast amount of suffering in the world—a small, but important, part of it, unnecessary.

Bodo's condition was something else. It was soundless, motionless, and tearless. Even in that diffused starlight I could see that his jaws were clenched and white; his gaze was not fixed on me nor on the wall behind me. It was turned inward. Here was my best friend—well, with Henry Simmons my best friend—in extremity. That starts a fellow thinking.

At last he spoke. "I called at 'Nine Gables' this afternoon to say goodbye. I had the foolish notion that I might—just possibly might—ask Persis to be my wife. She showed a little more animation than usual, but we're all relieved when someone who bores us to death comes to say goodbye. Her grandfather, however, showed a real interest in me for the first time; wanted to talk about philosophy and philosophers; wouldn't let me go. . . . I don't understand her. . . . I can understand a woman not liking me, but I can't understand a total absence of any reaction whatever—just politeness, just evasive good manners. . . . We've spent so many hours together. We've been thrown at one another—by Mrs. Venable and Mrs. Bosworth and half a dozen others. We have *had* to make talk. Of course, I've asked her out to dinner, but there's no place on this island to go to dinner except the damned Muenchinger-King and she says that she doesn't like dining in public places. So we make talk at formal dinners. Each time, I'm knocked over by the fact that she's not only a very beautiful woman, but a superior one. She knows all about music and art and even *Austria*. She speaks three languages. She's reading all the time. She dances like Adeline Genée—I'm told that she sings beautifully. What's more, my instinct tells me that she has great capacity for life and love . . . and life. I love her. I love her. But she gives me no sign of recognizing that I am a living, breathing, possibly loving, human being. All that talk and nothing catches fire. You know how I like children and *children like me*. I turn the conversation to her three-year-old son, but even then nothing catches fire. . . . Sometimes I wish she showed annoyance, or downright dislike; I wish she'd snub me. I look around the dinner tables; she's the same with every man. . . . Perhaps she's grieving for her husband—but she's out of mourning; perhaps she's in love with someone else; perhaps she's in love with you. Don't interrupt yet! So I'm leaving Newport forever. I'm erasing Persis from my mind and heart. I'm renouncing something that I was never offered. Let's go see if the *Schnapps* is cold."

We returned to our table. He lifted a flask and the cups out of the pail and poured. We exchanged a hearty "*Zum Wohl!*" and drank.

"Old man, I've wanted for a long while to clear up something between us. When I told you at Flora Deland's that I was a fortune hunter you must have thought that I was a contemptible skunk, as they say over here. Now don't answer me until you hear my story. In fact, before we part you're going to talk to me tough and straight. This is the situation: I am the head of my family. My father was aged and broken by the War. My older brother went off to Argentina and is selling automobiles. He has renounced his title and taken Argentine citizenship to help him in his business. He has a family of his own and cannot send back much money to the *Schloss* and my parents don't want him to. My mother's a wonderful manager. During the summer and especially during the winter she takes in paying guests. More and more people are interested in the winter sports resorts nearby. But it's hard work and the profits are small. The castle needs repairs all the time—roof, drainage, heating. Try and imagine all that. I have three sisters—angels every one of them. They have no *dots* and I must and will see them married comfortably and happily in their own class. Legally, the castle is mine; morally, the family is mine.—*Zum Wohl, Bruder!*"

"*Zum Wohl, Bodo!*"

"I shall marry within a year. In Washington young women are pushed at me all the time—attractive, charming girls, with visible *pecunia*. I've selected two, either one of whom I could come to love and whom I could make happy. I'm old for marriage. I want to have children who will know my parents; I want my parents to know my children. I want a *home*. . . . For two years I've been having a love-affair with a married woman who wants to divorce her husband and marry me; but I can't take her to my parents—she's had two husbands already. She's very accomplished and for the first year she was delightful, but now she cries most of the time. Besides I'm tired of little hotels in the country and signing idiotic names. And something more—I'm a Catholic; I'd . . . I'd like to try harder . . . to be a good Catholic."

Here for the first time tears appeared in my friend's eyes.

"*Zum Wohl, Alter.*"

"*Zum Wohl, Bursche.*"

"So within a year I shall be married to a girl with a fortune. Can I call that an act of filial duty or am I still a skunk?"

"I am a Protestant, Bodo. My father and my ancestors went about grandly telling others where their duty lay. I hope that will never be said of me."

He threw back his head, laughing. "God in Heaven, what fun talking is—maybe I mean unloading."

"Are you drunk or can we get back to the subject of Persis? I have no right to call her that, but I shall while talking to you."

"Yes, oh yes! But what is there left to say about her?"

I put my elbows on the table, clasped my hands, and looked him in the eye gravely.

"Bodo, don't laugh at what I'm about to say. It's a hypothetical case, but I'm trying to make a point of urgent importance."

He sat up straight and returned my gaze, somewhat disturbed. "Go on! What's on your mind?"

"Suppose—just *suppose*—that two and a half years ago there had been a hushed-up scandal in your Foreign Affairs Office. Some secret documents had disappeared and it was thought that someone in the Foreign Office had sold them to the enemy. And suppose that a shadow of suspicion rested on you, just a shadow. There was of course a very thorough inquiry and you were completely cleared. The heads of the government departments went out of their way to invite you to the most important functions. The Foreign Secretary seated you beside him at a very high council or two. You were ostentatiously declared innocent. There was no trial, because there were no charges—but there was *talk*. A retired diplomat once told me that the two worst cities that he'd served in, for gossip and malicious tongues, were Dublin and Vienna. Everything damaging about you—real or imagined—was kept alive decade after decade. You'd be a 'man under a cloud,' wouldn't you?"

"Why are you asking me these questions?"

"What would you do about it?"

"Ignore it."

"Are you sure? You have a very delicate sense of honor. Your wife and children would also learn that there was a faint bad odor connected with the family. You know how people talk. 'There was more to that matter than met the eye.' 'The Stams are so well connected that they could hush anything up!'"

"Theophilus, what are you driving at?"

"Maybe Persis Tennyson is a 'woman under a cloud.' You know and I know and God knows that she could not have been capable of anything dishonorable. But as Shakespeare says somewhere, 'Be thou as . . . pure as snow, thou shalt not escape calumny.'"

Bodo arose, glared at me with something between fury and despair. He strode about the room; he opened the door onto the road as though to fill his lungs with fresh air. Then he returned and flung himself into his chair. His eyes resting on me had now taken on the air of a trapped animal.

"I'm not trying to torment you, Bodo. I'm trying to think of some way that you and I can help that splendid unhappy young woman locked up in that 'Nine Gables,' that spiteful, loveless house. . . . Isn't that just the way a woman of impeccable feeling would behave toward any man she respected— maybe loved—who approached her as a suitor; she wouldn't want to bring a suspicion of malodor into his family. Think of your mother!"

He was now looking at me with a terrible intensity.

I went on brutally: "You know that her husband killed himself?"

"All I know is that he was a crazy gambler. He shot himself over some debts."

"That's all I know. We must know more. But we do know

that the town is busy with hateful gossip. 'There's more in that case than meets the eye.' 'The Bosworths have enough money to hush anything up.'"

"Oh, Theophilus! What can we do?"

I pulled the letter out of my pocket and laid it before him.

"I know the urgent thing she wants to talk to me about. She wants to warn me that there are Bosworths who are planning to do me harm. I know that already. But maybe what she wants to do is to tell me the story of her husband's death—the true full story—so that I'll put it in circulation. Take heart and hope, old Bodo. We know that Mrs. Venable admires and loves her. Mrs. Venable looks upon herself as the guardian of correct behavior on Aquidneck Island. Mrs. Venable must know all the facts. She does everything she can to shield and protect Persis. But it's possible that Mrs. Venable hasn't enough imagination to see that it's not enough to take Persis under her wing. There may be some details relative to Archer Tennyson. She thinks that silence is the best defense; *but it isn't.* . . . Bodo, I have a hard day tomorrow. I must ask you to drive me home. Can I propose something?"

"Yes, of course."

"What time is your dinner over tomorrow night when you start driving for Washington?"

"Oh—about eleven-thirty, I should think."

"Could you postpone your departure for two hours? Persis will drop me at my door at about one-thirty. Could you be waiting in your car up around the corner? I may have the *facts* to tell you. We'll have something to go on. Don't you think that to rescue a damsel from injustice is one of the noblest jobs a young man can have?"

"Yes! Yes!"

"Well, you fall asleep in the car. I hope to have something for you to think about as you drive through the night."

At my door I said, "We're sure that Archer Tennyson didn't kill himself because of any imperfection in his wife's behavior, aren't we?"

"Yes! Yes, we are!"

"Well, take heart! Take hope!—What were Goethe's dying words?"

"Mehr Licht! Mehr Licht!"

"What we're looking for is more light. Thanks for the *Schnapps*. See you tomorrow night."

The next day held a crowded schedule. I hadn't come to Newport to work so hard, but I checked up fourteen dollars before supper. Then I took a short nap and wheeled out to "Nine Gables" for my ten-thirty appointment.

Since the alarming improvement in his health Dr. Bosworth had felt the need of some refreshment during the evening. This took the form of a French *tisane* and biscuits (I declined with thanks) that Mrs. Turner brought to him at about eleven-thirty. It did not escape me that these interruptions in our work were designed to afford an occasion for desultory conversation. My employer was longing to talk. We were now reading (for reasons best known to ourselves alone) Henri Bergson's *Deux sources de la morale et de la religion* when Mrs. Turner arrived with her tray.

What followed was something more than a conversation: it was a military foray, a diplomatic maneuver, with some of the character of a chess game. I had noticed earlier that he had tardily concealed an *aide-mémoire*, an "agenda," such as he had drawn up so often in his career. I put myself on the alert.

"Mr. North, September is the most beautiful month in the year in Newport. I hope you are not planning to leave the island then, as so many do." Silence. "I would be very sorry to hear it. I would miss you very much."

"Thank you, Dr. Bosworth," et cetera, et cetera.

"Moreover, I have some projects involving yourself that could most profitably occupy you here. I wish to employ you on the planning staff of our Academy. You have a quick apprehension and grasp that would be invaluable to me." I bowed my head slightly and remained silent. "During the winter months my circle of friends narrows. Now that I am able to drive about there is much that I can explore—*we* could explore—in this part of New England. It is a great joy to me that my granddaughter takes pleasure in these drives also. I have begun to share with her some aspects of what I call my 'Athens-in-Newport.'" (Silence.) "Mrs. Tennyson strikes some people as a 'reserved' person. She is, but I assure you that she is a woman of marked intelligence and wide culture. She is also an accomplished musician—did you know that?"

"No, Dr. Bosworth."

"On winter nights, I shall hear much fine music. Does music appeal to you, Mr. North?"

"Yes, sir."

"Oh, yes. Up to the time of her husband's tragic death she continued to take lessons of the best teachers in New York and abroad. Since that unhappy occasion she refuses to sing for my guests or for Mrs. Venable's. Had you heard of the unfortunate circumstances of Mr. Tennyson's death?"

"I know only that he took his own life, Mr. Bosworth."

"Archer Tennyson was a very popular man. He derived great enjoyment from living. But there was also in him, perhaps, an element of eccentricity. The whole unhappy business is best forgotten." He lowered his voice and added significantly, "On winter evenings the three of us could make rapid progress on the design for our Academy."

The game of chess was being played very rapidly and recklessly. There was no need of any subtlety on my part. I advanced my black knight boldly.

"Sir, do you think that Mrs. Tennyson has put out of her mind any intention of marrying again?"

"Oh, Mr. North, she is a superior woman. What younger men are there around here—or even in New York!—who could interest her? We have a few yachtsmen; we have a few of that type that is called 'the life of the party'—tiresome quips and gossip. She now refuses her Aunt Helen's invitation to join her for a few weeks in the winter season. She refuses all those opportunities to attend concerts and the theater. She has turned in upon herself. She lives only for her small son, for her reading and her music—and, I am happy to say, for her devoted kindness to me." Again he lowered his voice. "She is all I have— Persis and the Academy. Her Aunt Sarah has lost all patience with her and I am at my wit's end. I would be happy if she married anyone, *wherever* he came from."

"She must have many admirers, Dr. Bosworth. She's an exceptionally beautiful and charming woman."

"Isn't she?" He advanced his white queen the length of the

board, again lowering his voice. "And, of course, very well off."

"*Is she?*" I asked with surprise.

"Her father left her a large fortune and her husband another."

I sighed. "But if the lady gives no sign of encouragement, there's not anything a gentleman can do. I have the impression that Baron Stams is most deeply and sincerely interested in Mrs. Tennyson."

"Oh, I've thought of that. Especially since you opened my eyes to his excellent qualities. He called on us here to say good-bye yesterday. I've never been so mistaken in a man in my life . . . and such interesting connections! Did you know that his mother's sister is a marchioness in England?" I did not know this and shook my head. "It was she who put him through Eton College, as they say. To think that he knows so much about philosophy and philosophers. If he were a little older I could consider appointing him Director of our Academy. But I must tell you something: Persis became quite cross with me—quite firm—when I spoke of him, last night, with high commendation. I couldn't understand it. Then I remembered that there have been a number of disappointments among our friends in the matter of international marriages—especially with European aristocrats. My daughter Sarah had a most unhappy time—perfectly nice fellow, but couldn't keep his eyes open. I don't think a foreigner would be very welcome, Mr. North."

This foolishness had gone on long enough. I brought my rooks and bishops forward. I spoke lightly, "I wouldn't know anything about such obstacles, Dr. Bosworth. I'm just a Wisconsin peasant." It was my turn to lower my voice. "I have been engaged to be married for some time, but I must tell you in confidence that I am slowly and painfully dissolving that engagement. A young man cannot be too careful. Even in my walk of life a man would hesitate to marry a woman whose former husband took his life in her presence."

Dr. Bosworth gasped like a harpooned whale. "It wasn't in Persis's presence! It was on a ship. He shot himself in the head on the top deck of a ship. I told you he was *eccentric*. He was eccentric. He enjoyed playing with firearms. No reproach was brought up against dear Persis." The tears were pouring down his face. "Ask anyone, Mr. North. Ask Mrs. Venable—ask anyone . . . some insane person sent around those anonymous letters—wicked letters. I think they broke my dear child's heart."

"A very tragic situation, sir."

"Oh, Mr. North, that's what life is—tragic. I am almost eighty years old. I look about me. For thirty years I served my country, not without recognition. My domestic life was all that a man would wish for. And then one misfortune followed upon another. I won't go into details. What is life?" He grasped the lapel of my jacket. "What is life? Can you see why I wish to found an Academy of Philosophers? Why are we placed on this earth?" He began drying his eyes and cheeks with an enormous handkerchief. "How rich this book of Bergson's is! . . . Alas, time is passing and there is so much to read!"

There was a knock at the door.

Persis entered, gloved and veiled for motoring. "Grandfather, it is a quarter past midnight. You should be in bed."

"We've been having a very good talk, dear Persis. I shall not go to sleep easily."

"Mr. North, I was wondering if you were in the mood for a short drive before retiring. I can deliver you at your door. The night air has a wonderful way of clearing the head after a difficult day."

"That's very kind of you, Mrs. Tennyson. I would enjoy it very much."

I said good night to Dr. Bosworth, and Persis and I started down the long hall. I have described "Nine Gables" as "the house of listening ears." Mrs. Bosworth emerged from one of the sitting rooms. "Persis, it is most unsuitable for you to drive at this hour. Say good night to Mr. North. He must be tired. Good night, Mr. North."

Persis said, "Get a good rest, Aunt Sally. Climb in, Mr. North."

"Persis! Did you hear what I said?"

"I am twenty-eight years old, Aunt Sally. Mr. North has spent forty hours in learned talk with Grandfather and can be regarded as an established friend of the family. Get a good rest, Aunt Sally."

"Twenty-eight years old! And so little sense of what is fitting!"

Persis started the motor and waved her hand. We were off.

The reader may remember from the opening chapter of this book that I was somewhat afflicted by the "Charles Marlow complex"—not, fortunately, to the extent of Oliver Goldsmith's hero. I did not stammer and blush and keep my eyes lowered in the presence of nice well-brought-up young women, but Persis Tennyson certainly presented the image (the lily, the swan) of what most intimidated me. I suffered that ambivalence which I had read was at the heart of every complex; I admired her enormously and wished I were many miles away. I was rattled; I floundered; I talked too much and too little.

She drove slowly. "I thought we'd go and sit on the sea wall by the Budlong place," she said.

"At the end of the day I'm usually too tired to drive anywhere. But I don't need much sleep. I get up early and ride out there to see the sun rise. It's still quite dark, of course. At first the police used to think I was on some nefarious business and would follow me. Gradually they came to see that I was merely eccentric and now we wave our hands at one another."

"I often take a late drive at this hour and the same thing happens to me. The police still feel they must keep an eye on me. But I've never been out at dawn. What's it like?"

"It's overwhelming."

She repeated the word softly and reflectively.

"Mr. North, what magic did you use to bring about such a change in my grandfather's health?"

"No magic at all, ma'am. I saw that Dr. Bosworth was under some kind of pressure. I've been under pressure too. Gradually we discovered that we shared a number of enthusiasms. Enthusiasms lift a man out of himself. We both grew younger. That's all."

She murmured, "I think there must have been more to it than that. . . . We feel deeply indebted to you. My grandfather and I would like to give you a present. We have been wondering what you would like. We wondered if you would like a car?" I did not answer. "Or the copy of *Alciphron* that Bishop Berkeley presented to Jonathan Swift? It was written at 'Whitehall.'"

I was disappointed. I concealed my bitter disappointment under a show of effusive thanks and some friendly laughter. "Many thanks to you both for your kind intention," et cetera, et cetera. "I try to live with as few possessions as possible. Like the Chinese a bowl of rice . . . like the ancient Greeks a few figs and olives." I laughed at the absurdity of it, but I had also indicated a firmness in my refusal.

"But, surely, some token of our gratitude?"

The privileged of this world are not accustomed to take no for an answer.

"Mrs. Tennyson, you did not invite me to join you on this ride to talk about presents but to give me an urgent message. I think I know what that is: There are some persons in and near 'Nine Gables' who wish me *out*."

"Yes. Yes. And I am sorry to say that there is something more than that. They are working on a plan to do you harm. There are some very rare first editions on the shelves behind my grandfather's chair. I overheard a plan to remove them gradually and replace them with later editions of the same works. These last years you are the only person who has come into the house who would realize their value. Their idea is that the suspicion will fall on you."

I laughed. "Thrilling!" I said.

"I anticipated their project and substituted the volumes. The originals are in my jewel safe. If some unpleasant talk starts up about you I shall produce them.—Why did you say 'thrilling'?"

"Because *they* are coming into the open. *They* are beginning to make mistakes. I thank you for removing those volumes, but even if you hadn't, I'd have enjoyed the showdown. I'm not a fighting man, Mrs. Tennyson, but I hate slander and malicious gossip—don't you?"

"Oh, I do. *How* I do! People talk—people talk hatefully. Oh, dear Mr. North, tell me how a person can defend himself."

"Here we are at the Budlong place.—Let's get out and sit on the sea wall."

"Don't forget what you were about to tell me."

"No."

"You will find a lap robe in the back seat to throw over the stone parapet."

An untended field of wild roses was at our back. The flowers were entering their decline and the perfume was heavy. Our faces were swept by the beams of the lighthouses; our ears were lulled by the dull booming and wailing and tinkling of the buoys. Above us the sky was like a jeweled navigators' chart. It was here that a few afternoons before Bodo had brought Agnese and Mino and me to his picnic.

As usual there were a number of cars in which were couples younger than ourselves.

"You advise me to resign from the work at 'Nine Gables'?"

"You have brought us that great benefit. All that is left for you is the danger of certain persons' ill will."

"You inherit it—conspicuously."

"Oh, it doesn't matter about me. I can bear it."

"With that spitefulness? You have your small boy to think of. Excuse my question, but why have you continued to live in that house?"

How calm she was! "Two reasons: I love my grandfather and he loves me—insofar as he can love anyone. And—where would I go? I hate New York. Europe? I have no wish to go to Europe for a while. My mother left my father long ago—before his death—and has been living in Paris and at Capri with a man to whom she is not married. She seldom writes letters to any of us. Mr. North, I often think that a large part of my life is over. I am an old widow-lady living only for my son and grandfather. The humiliations I am sometimes subjected to and the boredom of the social life do not touch me. They merely age me. . . . You were going to tell me how to get the better of malicious tongues. Did you mean it?"

"Yes . . . Since we are talking about matters that concern you closely, may I—just for this hour—call you Persis?"

"Oh, yes."

I took a deep breath. "Have you reason to believe that in some quarters you have been the object of slander?"

She lowered her head then abruptly raised it. "Yes, I know I am."

"I have no idea what these people are saying. I have never heard any reference to you that was not in terms of admiration and respect. I was told that your husband took his own life, alone, on the top deck of a ship at sea. I assume that malicious interpretations were circulated about that tragic event. I am convinced that nothing discreditable could ever be attributed to you. You asked me how one would go about defending oneself against slander. My first principle would be to state all the facts—the truth. If there is someone involved whom you feel you must shield, then one must resort to other measures. Is there such a person involved in this case?"

"No. No."

"Persis, do you wish to drop the whole subject and talk of other things?"

"No, Theophilus. I have no one to talk to. Please let me tell you the story."

I looked up at the stars for a moment. "I don't like secrets—unhappy family secrets. If you place me under an oath not to repeat a word of this, I must ask you *not* to tell it to me."

She lowered her voice. "But, Theophilus, I want all those talkers and letter-writers and . . . to know the simple truth. I loved my husband, but in a moment of utter thoughtlessness—of madness really—he left me under a cloud of suspicion. You can tell the story to anyone, if you thought it would do any good."

I folded my hands on my lap. In the diffused starlight she could see the welcoming smile on my face. "Begin," I said.

"When I left school I was, as they say, 'presented to society.' Dances, balls, tea-dances, debutante parties. I fell deeply and truly in love with a young man, Archer Tennyson. He had not been in the War because he had had tuberculosis as a boy and the doctors wouldn't pass him. I think that was at the bottom of it all. We were married. We were happy. Only one thing disturbed me; he was reckless and at first I admired him for it. He drove his car at great speeds. On shipboard once he waited until after midnight to climb the masts. The captain rebuked him for it in the ship's bulletin. I gradually came to see that he was a compulsive gambler—not only for money; that, too, but that did not matter—for life itself. He gambled with his life—skiing, motor-boat racing, mountain-climbing. When we were in the Swiss Alps he would descend only the most dangerous *pistes*. He took up lugeing which was fairly new then: tobog-gan descents between walls of packed ice. One day when my attention was distracted he picked up our one-year-old baby, placed him between his knees, and started off. I saw then for the first time what was in his mind: he wanted to raise the stake in his duel with death; he wanted to place what was nearest and dearest to him in the balance. First he had always wanted me beside him in the car or in the boat; now he wanted the baby too. I used to dread the approach of summer because each year he tried to break his record driving from New York to Newport. He broke everyone's record driving to Palm Beach, but I wouldn't go in the car with him. And all the time he betted on everything—horses, football games, Presidential elections. He'd sit in his club window on Fifth Avenue and bet on the types of automobiles that happened to pass. All his friends begged him to take a position in his father's brokerage office, but he couldn't sit still that long. Finally he began taking flying lessons. I don't know if wives go down on their knees to their husbands any more, but I did. I did more than that—I told him that if he went up in the air alone, I would never give him another child. He was so astonished that he *did* give up flying."

She paused and showed uncertainty. I said, "Continue, please."

"He was not seriously a drinking man, but he spent a great deal of time in bars where he could play the role of daredevil and—I'm sorry to say—could swagger. The story is almost over."

"May I interrupt a moment? I don't want the story hurried. I want to know what was going on in your mind during those years."

"In me? I knew that in a way he was a sick man. I loved him still, but I pitied him. But I was afraid. Do you see that he needed an audience for all this show of daring and risk? I had the front seat at the show; a large part of it—but not all of it—was to impress me. A wife can't scold all the time. I did not want to put a gulf between us. . . . He thought of it as courage; I thought of it as foolishness and . . . cruelty to me. One night we were standing on the deck of a ship going to Europe and we saw another ship approaching us in the opposite direction. We had been told that we would pass close to our sister-ship. He said, 'Wouldn't it be glorious if I dived in and swam over to her?' He kicked off his dancing pumps and started to undress. I slapped him hard—very hard—on one cheek and then on the other. He was so shocked that he froze. I said, 'Archer, I did not slap you. Your son did. Learn to be a father.' He

slowly pulled up his trousers. He picked up his jacket from the
deck. Those were not words that came to me at that moment.
They were words I had said over and over to myself on sleepless nights. There were more: 'I have loved you more than you
love me. You love defying death more than you love me. You
are killing my love for you.' I shouldn't have been weeping but
I was, terribly. He put his arms around me and said, 'It's just
games, Persis. It's fun. I'll stop whatever I'm doing any time
you say.' . . . Now I'll finish my story. It was bound to happen that he'd meet someone with the same madness, someone
even madder. It was two days later. Of course, he met him in
the bar. It was a War veteran with a wild look in his eye. I sat
with them for an hour or two while that man crushed my
husband with the narrow escapes he'd been through in combat. What fun it had been, and all that! A storm was rising. The
barman announced that the bar was closing, but they gave him
money to keep it open. I kept trying to persuade Archer to
come to bed, but he had to keep up with this man, drink for
drink. This other man's wife had gone to bed and finally, in
despair, I went to bed, too. Archer was found on the top deck
with a revolver in his hand and a bullet through his head. . . .
There was an inquiry and an inquest. . . . I testified that on
several evenings my husband and this Major Michaelis had
talked about Russian roulette, as though it were a joke. But
nothing of that came out in the serious newspapers and very
little, as far as I know, even in 'sensational' papers. My grandfather was greatly respected. He knew personally the publishers
of the better papers. The incident was briefly reported in the
inside pages. Even then I begged my grandfather to see that
my testimony was published; but the Michaelises also belong
to those old families that move heaven and earth to keep their
names out of the papers. And it was that silence that's done me
so much harm. It was closed with the verdict that my husband
had committed suicide in a state of depression. I had no one to
advise me or help me—least of all the Bosworth family. Mrs.
Venable has been a dear and close friend to me since I was a
child. She joined the family in soothing me: 'If we don't say
anything it will soon be forgotten.' She knows the Michaelises.
She stays with cousins near them in Maryland. She knows the
stories about him down there—that the neighborhood com-

plains of his carrying on revolver practice at three in the morning and bullying the men at his country club about Russian roulette. . . ."

"Mrs. Venable *knows* this? Really knows it?"

"She confided it to my grandfather and to my Aunt Sally—to comfort them, I suppose."

I strode up and down before her. "Why didn't she *confide* it to everybody—to her famous Tuesday 'at homes'? . . . Oh, I hate the cliquishness and the timidity of your so-called privileged class. She hates unpleasantness. She hates to be associated with anything unpleasant, is that it?"

"Theophilus, I'm sorry I told you the whole story. Let's forget it. I'm under a cloud. There's nothing that can be done about it now. It's too late."

"Oh, no, it's not. Where are the Michaelises now?"

"The Major's in a sanatorium in Chevy Chase. I suppose Mrs. Michaelis is in their home nearby in Maryland."

"Persis, Mrs. Venable is a kind woman at heart, isn't she?"

"Oh, very."

"Heaven knows she's influential and likes being influential. Can you explain to me why she hasn't used her kindness and her knowledge and her sense of justice to clear up this fog about you long ago?"

Persis did not answer at once. "You don't know Newport, Theophilus. You don't know what they call the 'Old Guard' here. In those houses nothing disturbing, nothing unpleasant, may ever be mentioned. Even the grave illness or death of old friends can be alluded to only in a whisper and a pressure of the hand when saying goodbye."

"Cotton wool. Cotton wool.—Someone told me that she invites the heart of the 'Old Guard' to luncheon every Thursday. Some people call it 'The Sanhedrin' or 'The Druids' Circle' —is that so?—Are you in it?"

"Oh, I'm not old enough."

I hurled an empty beer bottle into the sea. "Persis!"

"Yes?"

"We need an ambassador to persuade Mrs. Venable and 'The Sanhedrin' that it's their responsibility and their Christian duty to tell *everybody* what undoubtedly happened on that ship. . . . They should do it for your *son's* sake." She must often have thought of that for she clasped her hands tightly to conceal their trembling. "I think our ambassador should be a man— one for whom Mrs. Venable has a particular regard and who has the authority of an acknowledged social position. I have come to know the Baron Stams much better. He is a man of far solider character than you and your grandfather first believed, and let me assure you he hates injustice like the devil. For parts of two summers he has been Mrs. Venable's house guest. Have you observed that she has a real esteem and affection for him?"

She murmured, "Yes."

"Moreover, he has a very real and deep admiration for you. Do you give me permission to tell him the whole story and to urge him to be this ambassador?—But you don't like him."

"*Don't . . . don't* say that! Now you understand why I had to be so cold and impersonal. I was under a cloud. Don't talk about it. . . . Do—do what you think best."

"He was leaving Newport today. He is staying over. He will have half an hour talk with Mrs. Venable tomorrow morning. You should hear him talk when he's on fire with a subject. It's late. I must ask you to drive me home. I'll drive as far as my door."

I picked up the lap robe and held open the right front door of the car for her. The starlight fell on the face she turned toward me. She was smiling. She murmured, "I am not accustomed to the agitations of hope." I drove slowly, taking neither the longest nor the shortest way home. A police car discreetly followed the great heiress into the town, then turned off.

Her shoulder rested against mine. She said, "Theophilus, I made you cross earlier this evening when I suggested a choice of presents from Grandfather and from myself as an expression of our appreciation. Will you explain that to me?"

"You mean it?"

"Yes."

"Well, as this is to be a soothing little lecture I shall address you as Mrs. Tennyson. Let me explain, Mrs. Tennyson, that each of us is conditioned by our upbringing. I am a member of the middle class—in fact, of the middle of the middle classes— from the middle of the country. We are doctors, parsons, teachers, small-town newspaper editors, two-room lawyers. When I was a boy each house had a horse and buggy and our mothers were assisted in running the house by a 'hired girl.' All the sons and many of the daughters went to college. In that world no one ever received—and, of course, never gave—elaborate presents. Such presents were obscurely felt to be humiliating— perhaps I should say, ridiculous. If a boy wanted a bicycle or a typewriter he earned the money for it by delivering the *Saturday Evening Post* from door to door or by cutting his neighbors' lawns. Our fathers paid for our education, but for those incidentals so necessary at college—such as a 'tuxedo' or trips to dances at the girls' colleges—we worked during the summer on farms or waited on table at summer hotels."

"Did nothing unpleasant ever happen in the middle classes?"

"Oh, yes. People are the same everywhere. But some environments are more stabilizing than others."

"Are you telling me all this to explain to me why you were displeased about the present we wished to make you?"

"No." I turned to her with a smile. "No. I'm thinking about your son Frederick."

"Frederick?"

"In 1918 a woman who worked on Bellevue Avenue—and whom I think you know well—said to me, 'Rich boys never really grow up—or seldom.' "

"Oh, that's . . . superficial. That's not true."

"Have you heard Bodo describe his home—his father and mother and sisters? Provincial nobility. Where the castle is part farmhouse—where the servants have stayed with them generation after generation. Now they take in paying guests. Everybody is busy all day. Austrian music and laughter in the evening. Mrs. Tennyson, what an environment for a fatherless boy!"

"Did he send you to tell me these things?"

"No—on the contrary. He told me he was leaving Newport in despair and that he would never again put foot on this island if he could help it."

We had arrived at my door. I lifted my bicycle from the back seat. She walked around the car to take her place in the driver's seat. She put out her hand to me, saying, "Until that cloud of suspicion is lifted I have no word to say. Thank you for coming with me on this drive. Thank you for listening to my story. Is one permitted to exchange a friendly kiss in the middle class?"

"If no one is looking," I said and kissed her slowly on the cheek. She returned it, as to Ohio born.

Presently I joined Bodo. He had not fallen asleep, but leaped from his car.

"Bodo, could you possibly stay in Newport until tomorrow noon?"

"I have already received permission."

"Could you possibly have a private conversation with Mrs. Venable tomorrow morning?"

"We always have Viennese chocolate together at ten-thirty."

I told him the whole story, and ended up with the job which was now on his shoulders. "Can you do that?"

"I've got to and, by God, I'll succeed—but, Theophilus, you idiot, we still don't know if Persis can love me."

"I can vouch for it."

"How? . . . How? . . . How?"

"Don't ask me! I *know*. And one thing more: You will be back in Newport on August twenty-ninth."

"I can't.—Why? . . . What for? How do you know?"

"Your Chief will send you. And bring an engagement ring with you. You've found your Frau Baronin."

"You're driving me crazy."

"I'll write you. Get a good rest. Don't forget to say your prayers. I'm dog-tired. Good night."

I walked back to my door. I had had an inspiration. Edweena would help me find the way.

14

Edweena

WHEN IN Tante Liselotte's room my eyes fell on Edweena and the tears rolled down my cheeks, my relief sprang not only from seeing a replacement; I was also seeing an old and loved friend. I *knew* Edweena—I had known her in 1918 as Toinette and as Mrs. Wills. During all the weeks at Mrs. Cranston's when she had been referred to so often—Henry's fiancée and Mrs. Cranston's "star boarder" in the garden apartment —she had never gone under any other name than Edweena. Yet I knew at once that my old friend must be the long-expected Edweena.

This is how I had come to know her:

In the fall of 1918 I was twenty-one years old, a soldier stationed at Fort Adams in Newport. On my advancement to the grade of corporal I was given a seven-day leave to return to my home to show my new-won stripe to my parents, to my sisters, and to the public. (My brother was overseas.) I returned to my station via New York and embarked on a boat of the Fall River Line for Newport. Old-timers still remember those boats with sighs of deep feeling. They offered all that one could imagine of luxury and romance. Most of the cabins opened on the deck by a door faced with wooden slats that could be shifted to temper the air. We had seen such accommodations in the motion-pictures. We could imagine that at any moment there would be a tap at the door, we would open it to confront a beautiful heavily veiled woman whispering imploringly, "Please let me in and hide me. I am being pursued." Ah! We were traveling under blackout. Dim blue lights indicated the entrances to the interior of the vessel. I stayed up on deck for an hour, barely distinguishing the Statue of Liberty, the outlines of Long Island's coast, and perhaps the lofty joy-rides of Coney Island. All the while I was aware by a prickling down my spine that our progress was being observed through the periscopes of enemy submarines—baleful crocodiles below the surface of

the water—yet knowing that we were not sufficiently important game to induce them to reveal their presence. Finally I
entered the hull of the boat, which consisted of a vast brightly
lit dining saloon, a bar, and a series of social rooms where all
was carved wood, polished brass, and velvet drapery—the Arabian Nights. I went to the bar and ordered a Bevo. I noticed
that other passengers were refreshing themselves from flasks
carried in their hip pockets. (I was not then a drinking man
unless opportunity arose, having solemnly taken the Pledge of
life-long abstinence at the age of eight under the deeply moved
eyes of my father and an official of the Temperance League in
Madison, Wisconsin.) I sat down to dinner, hovered over by
stately waiters in white coats and gloves. I denied myself the
"Terrapin Baltimore" and ordered dishes from the less expensive items on the menu. The dinner cost me half a week's pay,
but it was worth it. A soldier's pay was weightless. The government provided all his necessities; a portion was automatically
deducted and sent to his loved ones; he was under the impression that the end of the War was, like his middle age, unimag-
inably remote. I had been told that the boat was completely
filled. It would reach Fall River at about nine when passengers
for Boston and the north would disembark. Those with tickets
for Newport had to go ashore at six in the morning. I was in
no hurry to go to bed and having finished my blueberry pie *à
la mode* I returned to one of the many tables near the bar and
ordered another near-beer.

At the table next to mine was an elegantly dressed couple
quarreling. The chair of the woman was back to back with mine.
At that time—to counteract the routine of my work at the
Fort—I was assiduously keeping my Journal and was already
composing an account of this trip in my mind. I have no com-
punction about overhearing conversations in public places and
this one I could not fail to overhear without moving to another
table.

The man may have been drinking, but his articulation was
precise. I had the impression that he was "beside himself," he
was crazy. His wife, sitting very straight, was attempting to
make her remarks both soothing and admonitory. She was at
the end of her tether.

"You've been at the back of it all for years. You've been try-ing to put them against me the whole time."

"Edgar!"

"All this talk about my having ulcers. I haven't got ulcers. You've been trying to poison me. You're in cahoots with the whole family."

"Edgar! The few times I've seen your mother and brothers during the last three years have always been in your presence."

"You *telephone* them. When I leave the house you telephone them by the hour." Et cetera. "*You* got me blackballed at that damned club."

"I don't know how a woman could do that."

"You're sly. You could do anything."

"You lost your temper at Mr. Cleveland himself. The vice-president of the club—in front of everybody.—Please go to bed and get some rest. We have to get off this boat in seven hours. I'll sit here quietly for a while and slip into the cabin when you're asleep." A woman had approached them. "You can go to bed, Toinette. I shan't need you until the ship whistles for landing."

Apparently Toinette lingered. There was a shade of insis-tence in her voice. "I have some sewing to do, madam. The light is better here. I shall be sitting by the bandstand for an hour. I heard them say there might be some bad weather to-night. I shall be in Cabin 77, if you should need me."

The man said, "That's right, Toinette. Tell the whole boat your cabin number."

"Tomorrow, Edgar, I shall ask you to apologize to Toinette. You forget that you were brought up to be a gentleman—and the son of Senator Montgomery!"

"Women's voices! Women's voices! Insinuations, innuen-does! Nagging! I can't stand any more. You can sit here quietly until the boat sinks. I'm going to bed and I'm going to lock the door. I'll put your dressing-case in the corridor. You can bunk with Toinette."

"Toinette, here's my key to the cabin. Will you kindly pack my necessaries in my dressing-case.—Edgar, please remain at this table until Toinette has collected my things. I shall not say a word."

"Where's that waiter? I want to pay the bill. Waiter! Waiter! —What are you doing with my purse?"

"If I'm to arrange for another cabin I shall need some money. I'm your wife. I shall pay your bill here too."

"Stop! How much are you taking?"

"I may have to bribe the purser for a cabin."

Edgar Montgomery rose and strolled moodily the length of the saloon. I caught a glimpse of his dark tormented face. He had what we used to call a "weeping willow" mustache. He peered into the card room and the coffee rooms (scarlet damask and gilt mirrors).

Toinette returned with the dressing-case. I turned and saw her descending the great staircase. She was dressed in what I assumed to be a French maid's uniform for street-wear in winter. It was a jacket and skirt in the severest dark-blue wool, probably to be worn under a long swinging cape. It was close-fitting and the edges were "piped" (is that right?) in black braid. If you have an eye for simplicity, it was exceedingly elegant. But what smote me was her carriage. At the age of twenty-one I had no wide experience in such matters, but I had seen "La Argentina" and her company dance in San Francisco when I was sixteen and had saved up my money in the New Haven years to see Spanish dancing—what I called to myself the "spine of steel" of Spanish women, the "walk of the tigress," the "touch-me-not" arrogance of the dancer relative to her partner. Toinette came down those stairs not only without lowering her eyes to her feet, without lowering her eyes below the level of the horizontal regard. Zowie! Olé!! What deportment! She soon passed out of my line of vision.

"Madam," she said in a low voice, "I'd be very happy if you used my cabin. It's not for long and I've often sat up the night."

"I wouldn't think of it, Toinette. Will you sit here by the dressing-case while I go down to the purser's office? The trip was a mistake. Both the doctor and I thought he was so much better. Toinette, don't give a thought to me. You go to bed when you're ready."

Mr. Montgomery made as though to approach them, then changed his mind and ascended the great staircase. Apparently a number of the cabins had doors that opened on the gallery as well as on the deck. He entered his and shut the door resolutely.

Toinette whispered something into his wife's ear.

"That's all right, Toinette. I did as the doctor told me. I emptied the *things* and put some blank cartridges in the chambers."

Mrs. Montgomery sat in silence for a moment. She then turned and looked briefly at me as I did at her. A very handsome woman. After a pause she turned again and said, "Sergeant, have you a cabin to yourself?"

"Yes, madam," I said, rising to military attention.

"I'll give you thirty dollars for it."

"Madam, I'll clear out at once and give you the key, but I'll take no money for it. I'll get my gear and be back in a moment."

"Stop! I won't accept it."

She left the hall, descending the steps to the purser's office. I turned and saw Toinette's full face for the first time—a fascinating triangular face of what I took to be some Mediterranean origin, dark eyes, dark lashes, and an air of mock gravity over the distressing situation that had brought us together.

"Madam," I said. "If I give you the key to my cabin, I think she'd accept yours. I have some friends on the boat. They're sitting up all night and have asked me to play cards with them. I've often sat up all night playing cards."

"Corporal, we must let these people work things out in their own way."

"It's hard to believe that Mr. Montgomery is a grown-up man."

"Rich boys never really grow up—or seldom."

I started. I'd been warned strongly for years against making generalizations. I was ready to weigh Toinette's.

"Madam, what was that I heard about guns?"

"May I ask your name, sir?"

"North, Theodore North."

"My name is Mrs. Wills. May I take you into my confidence, Mr. North?"

"Yes, madam."

"Mr. Montgomery has always played with guns. Though I have never heard of his firing one except at cardboard targets. He thinks he has enemies. He keeps a revolver always in the drawer by his bedside table. All rich boys do. Mr. Montgomery has little nervous breakdowns from time to time. Mrs. Montgomery was advised by his doctor last week to substitute blank cartridges for real bullets. They're almost noiseless—just cork and feathers, I think. He's a little disturbed tonight—that's the way we put it. If Mrs. Montgomery insists on sitting up all night, I shall sit up too."

I said firmly, "I'll sit up too. Excuse me, Mrs. Wills—what do you think will happen?"

"Well, I know he's not going to sleep. Maybe in half an hour he's going to come to his senses and be ashamed of himself for throwing his wife out of his cabin. Anyway, he'll come out to see the effect of his big noise. Sooner or later he'll break down —tears, apologies.—They're dependent, men like that. He'll consent to take a *piqûre*. Do you know what a *piqûre* is?"

"A puncture—I mean, an injection."

"All those words have soothing names around here. We call it a little sleeping-aid."

"Who gives it to him?"

"Mrs. Montgomery, mostly."

"It must be an exciting life for you, madam."

"Not any more. I've given Mr. Montgomery notice that I'm leaving in two weeks. While we were in New York I arranged for some new work."

"I'm going to sit here where I can see him come out of that door on the balcony. If he's as what you call disturbed as that, we may see some action. I wish you'd sit where you could see it too and where I could catch your eye."

"I will. You're a planner, aren't you, Corporal?"

"I never thought of it that way, ma'am. Perhaps I am. *Now* I am when I see you mixed up in a thing like this. Even dummy bullets can cause a bit of trouble."

I couldn't take my eyes off her and our eyes were constantly meeting with little sparks of recognition. I sent up a trial kite. "Mr. Wills must be glad that you're resigning from an unpleasant situation like this."

"Mr. Wills? That's another piece of business I did in New York this last week. I put my husband on a ship for England. He was homesick for London. He didn't like America and took to drinking. The mistakes we make don't really hurt us, Corporal, when we understand every inch of the ground."

I was losing my distrust of generalizations.

Mrs. Montgomery reappeared. It was apparent that her inquiries had been fruitless. I again offered her my key. "There are all-night card games at Fort Adams every Saturday night. I've often joined them."

She looked at me directly. "Would you like to play cards?"

"Very much. There are some friends of mine in the next room. If Mrs. Wills would play with us we'd only need one of them."

"I don't play cards, Corporal North," said Toinette.

"There are two soldiers there that play well and would appreciate playing with a lady."

"Corporal, my name is Mrs. Montgomery. My husband has had many things to worry him lately. When I find that he's moody I often leave him alone to rest."

"I'll get the cards and the men, Mrs. Montgomery. We'd better play bridge for low stakes. When men return from leave they generally have very little money in their pockets."

What was in my mind was that they might take her over the barrel.

"You're very kind, Corporal."

The men I selected were eager to play with a lady. I dug into my uniform and pulled out two ten-dollar bills. "Low stakes, fellas—just to pass the time. Lady's husband's a little off his head but not dangerous.—Mrs. Montgomery, this is Sergeant Major Norman Sykes. He was wounded overseas and has been sent back to build up cadres over here. This is Corporal Wilkins. He's a librarian in Terre Haute, Indiana."

With no apparent effort on my part I seated myself in direct view of the Montgomery cabin. I placed Mrs. Montgomery at my left. By turning her head Mrs. Montgomery could see her cabin door; as far as I was aware she did not glance at it once. She was charming; so was the sergeant. Wilkins ran off to find a cleaner pack of cards.

"From what state do you come, Sergeant Major Sykes?"

"I'm a Tennessee wildcat, ma'am. I had only a short lick of schooling, but I was reading the Bible at six. I'm in the Army for life. I got a bit of steel in my shoulder, but the Army's found work for me to do. I've got three little wildcats of my own. Young children take a lot of feeding, as you may know, ma'am. . . . I had the good fortune to marry the brightest, prettiest schoolteacher in Tennessee."

"I think the good fortune was equally divided, Sergeant."

"That was very pleasant-spoken, ma'am. We have a good number of Montgomerys in Tennessee and I've noticed they're all pleasant-spoken."

"That is not always true of the Montgomerys of Newport, I'm sorry to say."

"Well," said the sergeant soothingly, "civil manners come hard to some folks."

"How true!"

Wilkins returned with fresh cards and we were soon engrossed in tense play. From time to time I exchanged glances with Toinette. She was engaged—or perhaps pretended to be—in mending or altering a skirt.

Neither of us missed the moment at which Mr. Montgomery stepped out of his cabin onto the gallery. He had changed into a burgundy-colored velveteen smoking jacket. He gazed down for a few moments on the congenial foursome. Nothing irritates a bully like seeing others having a good time without him. There's a generalization for you. I could swear that Mrs. Montgomery was aware of his presence also. She raised her voice and said, "Three no trumps! Sergeant, we must pull ourselves together."

"Ma'am," he said, "I'm a slow warmer-upper. We'll take their shirts yet. Pardon the expression."

Mr. Montgomery slowly passed along the balcony and as slowly descended the great staircase. He crossed to the bar and ordered a set-up, reached into one pocket, then the other, and brought out a flask. He poured from its contents into his glass which he carried to a table. He sat down, facing us directly, and gazed at us somberly.

To myself I said, "He's going to goof."

The majority of the passengers had dispersed to their cabins, but there was a large group of intermittently noisy drinkers at the bar. Eight strokes of the ship's bell were clearly audible.

"Midnight," said the sergeant.

"Midnight," said I.

I glanced at Toinette. Still smiling she performed an odd bit of pantomime. She leaned toward the right as though she were about to fall out of her chair and then dropped her piece of sewing from her right hand to the floor. I got the idea at once.

"It's your play, Corporal North," said Mrs. Montgomery.

The game continued for a few moments. Then slowly Mr. Montgomery's hand went to his right pocket. His wife rose. "Excuse me, gentlemen, I must speak to my husband."

At that moment he fired. A wad of cork struck my right shoulder and fell on the table before me.

I fell off my chair and lay dead on the floor.

"Edgar!" cried Mrs. Montgomery.

"Corporal!" cried Toinette and rushed to my side. "He's wounded! Corporal! Corporal! Can you hear me?"

Mr. Montgomery was panting. He doubled up, retching. The sergeant strode over to him and tore the gun out of his hand; he cocked it and dropped the cartridges on the table.

"Duds!" he said, "goddamned DUDS!"

Toinette was slapping my cheeks. "Corporal, can you hear me?"

I sat up. "I guess it was just the shock, ma'am," I said, blissfully.

The barman's chin hung like a swinging satchel. The noisy revelers had observed nothing.

Mrs. Montgomery leaned over her husband. "Edgar, you're tired. We're both tired. It's been a very pleasant trip, hasn't it? —but *wearing*. You've been simply splendid. Now I think you might have a very small sleeping-aid. We'll have forgotten all about it by tomorrow. Say good night to all these friends. Barman, will five dollars cover my husband's bill? Here, Sergeant, take this for my share in our losses; if it's too big, give the rest to your church."

Mr. Montgomery had raised his head and was peering about him. "What happened, Martha? Was anybody hurt?"

"Corporal North, will you take Mr. Montgomery's other arm? I can carry the dressing-case, Toinette. I won't need you. Edgar, don't stop for the flask now. Let's leave it for these gentlemen who kindly asked me to join their game."

Mr. Montgomery didn't want the help of my arm. "Please go away from me, sir. . . . Martha, *what happened*?"

"You and your schoolboy jokes! You made us laugh. . . . Turn right, Edgar. . . . No, the next door. Good night, gentlemen. Thank you all."

"I don't want his gun," said the sergeant, "or his liquor neither. I took the Pledge."

"So did I," said the corporal.

"I'll give them to him in the morning," said Toinette, dropping them into her sewing bag.

The corporal swept up the dummies and said to the sergeant, "Let's get out of here before they start asking questions."

The barman must have pressed a button summoning the night watchman. The two approached the table where Toinette and I were sitting.

"What was that fracas that was goin' on over here?"

"Oh, you mean *that*!" I said laughing. "One of the passengers played a schoolboy's joke. Had a black bat made of rubber. Tried to scare the ladies.—Barman, can I have two soda-water set-ups?"

"Every night something crazy," said the watchman and left.

So there we sat, face to face, over that table, looking into each other's eyes. I can go out of my mind about a pair of fine eyes. Mrs. Wills's were unusual in several ways. Firstly there was a slight "cast"—so mistakenly called a "flaw"—in her right eye; in the second place you couldn't tell what color they were; thirdly, they were deep and calm and amused. When I go swimming in a pair of eyes I am not fully master of what I may say.

"Please, what color are your eyes?"

"Some people say they're blue in the morning and hazel at night."

My attention is almost as consumedly drawn to hands. I was to learn later that Toinette was five years older than I. I now saw that her hands gave evidence that in earlier life they had been engaged in hard manual labor—scullery work, maybe— probably accompanied by malnutrition and harsh treatment. She had suffered and in all other aspects of her mind (and body) she had surmounted those trials; she had come through.

To the eyes of friendship and love the coarseness of her hands had become spiritualized. She did not attempt to hide them.

"Excuse me asking questions.—Are you English?"

"I think so. I was found."

"Found?"

"Yes, found in a basket."

I was so filled up with delight that I laughed at the good fortune. "Do you have any idea—?"

"Theodore, do come to your senses. I was less than a week old. Do you know Soho?"

"It's a part of London where there are foreign restaurants and where artists live. I've never been there." I was bewildered. I could see the orphanage; I could see the scullery. Like Henry Simmons she had risen from the hardest stratum of London life, but—unlike Henry—her accent had been consciously schooled. She spoke the English of a "lady" with the faint suggestion of speaking a foreign language. (My conjecture was an apprenticeship in a hairdresser's establishment, perhaps in the theater . . . she had known what it was to be a protégée here and there—just long enough to confirm her outstanding trait of independence; a quick learner.)

A fine gold wire was strung between our eyes and some kind of energy was passing back and forth. Our hands were clasped before us on the table as though we were good children at school. But my hands were moving toward hers—without pushing, as on a Ouija board.

"I think I'm part Jewish and part Irish."

Again I overflowed with laughter. "That's a great situation for an orphan; you get all the good of it without having to listen to the advice." The golden wire went zingazingaling. "The blight of family life is advice." Who was making generalizations now? "Can I ask what new work you're going into?"

"I'm going to open a shop in New York—and maybe in Newport later. Things for ladies to wear, not dresses, not hats, but just pretty things. It will be a great success." She did not stress the word "great"; it would be a great success and that was that. I learned that mark of maturity from her, then and there.

"What are you going to call it?"

My finger tips had reached one of her knuckles.

"I don't know. I'm going to change my name. Maybe I'll choose a simple name like Jenny. Everything in the shop is going to be simple but perfect. Maybe for the first weeks nobody will buy anything, but they'll come back and look again."

She lifted her glass to her lips. Then put her hand back on the table where it had been touching mine.

"What do you do, Mr. North?"

"I'm a college student. When the War's over I'm going back to college."

"What do you study most?"

"Languages."

"You have nice friends. Are many of the men at Fort Adams like that?"

"Yes. For one reason or another the Army hasn't given us orders to go overseas. My eyes are all right, but they're just below the grade for overseas duty."

By now the fingers of my right hand were intertwined with those of her left. What with eyes and hands, I was finding myself again.

She asked, "After you've learned those languages what are you going to do?"

She seized my restless hand firmly, flattened it on the table, and laid her hand over it to keep it still.

"In New York day before yesterday I had a narrow escape. A cousin of my mother's is in the business of importing silk from China. Big office. Typist girls tiptoeing around like whipped mice. He offered me a job when I graduate. He says the War is going to end in a month, so I'd graduate in 1920. He's a Scotchman and doesn't say a word he doesn't mean. He promised me that I'd be making five thousand dollars a year in five years. I wrestled with temptation for three minutes flat. Then I thanked him properly and got out. On the street I frightened the New Yorkers by shouting, 'AN OFFICE! AN OFFICE!!' *No*, I can make money without sitting in a chair for forty years."

"Theodore, not so loud!"

"I'm going to be an actor or a detective or an explorer or a wild animal tamer. I can always make money. What I want to see is a million faces. I want to *read* a million faces."

"Sh—sh!"

I lowered my voice. "I guess I've read a million and so have you."

She was laughing interiorly.

"But you're a new face, Miss Jenny. If a man travels enough he'll run into the Bay of Naples or Mount Chimborazo or something. He'll run into a surprise like Mr. Edgar Montgomery . . . or a great surprise like Miss Jenny," and I leaned down and kissed her hand. I kissed it again and again.

The barman called out, "The bar's closing in about five minutes, ladies and gentlemen. We don't want that kind of business in here, soldier. You heard me say 'ladies and gentlemen' and I meant it."

I rose grandly and said, "Barman, I don't like your tone of voice. This lady and I have been married for three years. I wish you to apologize to my wife at once or I shall report you to Mr. Pendleton, passenger agent of this line and my own cousin."

Even the revelers heard this.

The barman said, "I didn't mean no offense, ma'am, but I'm ready to tell Mr. Pendleton or anybody else that wherever your husband is, some peculiar things start to happen. He laid out dead here just twenty minutes ago."

Mrs. Wills said, "Thank you, barman. Surely, you know that soldiers must be given consideration on the short leave that's given them before they cross the sea to offer their lives for us."

The revelers applauded.

She rose, glass in hand, and said splendidly, "My husband is a very distinguished man. He speaks twelve languages better than he speaks English."

More applause. I put my arm around my dear wife and shouted, "Iroquois! Choctaw!"

"Eskimo!" she cried.

"Jabberwocky!"

"Mulligatawny!"

There were cries of "Give 'em a drink!" . . . "Sprekkenzy Doysh?" . . . "Me likee Chinee girl, she likee me!"

Flushed with success, we sat down—the picture of conjugal love and pride.

Suddenly, however, world events took the matter out of our hands. The night watchman appeared at the head of the staircase, wearing a sou'wester and swinging a hurricane lantern. He had heard town-criers as a boy and put his whole soul into it. "Ladies and gentlemen, quiet please! Word has just come over the wireless that the War has come to an end. The Arnstiss— the Armystiss—what they call it!—has been signed. The skipper has tole me to tell you in the saloon, but not to wake anybody up that's gone to bed. There's high seas runnin' and the boat will be delayed, maybe, dockin' at Newport and Fall River.—Tommy, the skipper says the Line offers a free drink to anybody that's sittin' up. I gotta go down to the engine room."

All hell broke loose. The revelers began hurling crockery about the hall. Cuspidors are too heavy to hurl, but they can be rolled on their rims for quite a distance. The card-players poured into the saloon.

"Jenny," I said.

"What?"

"Jenny, let's not separate."

"I didn't hear what you said."

"Yes, you did! Yes, you did!"

"Why, where did you ever get such an idea!"

"Jenny!"

"Well, we don't see a war come to an end every day. In about ten minutes come down to Cabin 77. I have an alarm clock set for five-thirty."

I whirled her about. When I restored her to the floor, she went downstairs to the cabins reserved for servants; I went upstairs and packed my gear.

"*Charmes d'amour, qui saurait vous peindre?*" as Benjamin Constant wrote on setting out to describe a similar encounter. "Enchantments of love, what artist can picture you?" The generosity of the woman, the bold tenderness of the grown man—the fathomless gratitude to nature for its revelation of itself, yet with some reminder that death is the end of all, death accepted, death united with life in the chain of being from the primal sea to the ultimate cold. "*Charmes d'amour, qui saurait vous peindre?*"

She must have turned off the alarm clock instantaneously for it did not wake me. When I woke at the ship's whistle she had taken all her possessions and was gone. On the mirror was written with soap, "Don't change." I dressed and was about to leave the cabin when I turned back and flung myself on the bed again and buried my head in the pillow, alone and not alone.

I was among the last to disembark. From the gangplank a strange sight met my eyes. There was a great bonfire in Washington Square. Hundreds of men and women and children, hastily dressed, in a tumult of distraught dogs, were dancing about it. "The War's over! The War's over!" Everyone in the Ninth City was hugging and kissing everyone else, particularly the few service men who were disembarking or who had come to the center of the town. Maybe I was hugged and kissed by the Materas and the Avonzinos and by Mrs. Keefe, and the Wentworths and Dr. Addison, but this was November, 1918, and I knew only seven civilians in all the Nine Cities. The apparatus of the Newport Fire Department was dashing up and down in the streets in an ecstasy of uselessness. In the little park where Alice and I were to see each other for the last time, sporadic religious revivals and scandalous orgies were contaminating each other. Nicolaidis's All Night Café, having run out of coffee and frankfurter buns, was jammed and was being looted by enraged customers. Reader, it was gorgeous!

No, I was not the last to leave the boat. I saw Mr. Montgomery, having aged thirty years in a few hours, unsteady on his legs, being met by his doctor, his valet, and two chauffeurs. His wife took her place beside him looking very fine indeed in sables. The second car was so filled with luggage that Toinette had to sit on the valet's knees.

I disentangled myself from the embraces of a grateful populace and started my walk to Fort Adams under the dawn's early light, only two miles, but the longest trek I remember ever having taken. At reveille about ninety percent of the soldiers were absent without leave.

That was the famous "False Armistice."

All discipline broke down. During the intervening days before the end of the War was officially declared, the Headquarters Company had time to run up *pro forma* papers for the soldiers' separation from the service and I had time to obtain my travel orders and to brace myself for endless peace and the serious business of living. I made no attempt to get in touch with the Montgomery household which I assumed to be in as chaotic a condition as that about me.

So it was that—almost eight years later—it was not Toinette, not Jenny, but Mrs. Edweena Wills who followed me downstairs from Tante Liselotte's room and found me asleep against the wall between the second and third floors.

The summer was drawing to a close. Many of my "pupils" were occupied with plans for the fall and our lessons drew to a close. I welcomed the increase in my free time. I spent long contented hours in my apartment bringing my Journal up to date, filling in "portraits" of the persons I had known—pages which refreshed my memory and on which I am now drawing so many years later in the composition of this book. I had worked very hard and the "professor" experienced little difficulty in refusing invitations from his former "pupils," however kindly intended.

I saw Edweena and Henry almost every day. They were engaged to be married as soon as Mr. Wills in far-off London had drunk himself to death on the allowance his wife continued to send him. I loved Edweena and I loved Henry and I'm proud to say they loved me. Never for a moment, in company or alone, did Edweena and I make any reference to having met previously. Even Mrs. Cranston, whom little escaped, had no inkling of it. Edweena had prospered. Her shops, first in New York, then in Newport, were a great success. She had selected and trained assistants and presently handed the management over to them, because a more satisfying and even more remunerative career opened up for her. No name could be found for it, but she was delighted when (from my fund of "twelve languages") I offered and explained to her the words *arbitrix elegantiarum*, "The woman who dispenses the laws of good taste," as Petronius Arbiter did at the Emperor Nero's court. She continued to insist that she was a lady's maid, but she turned down all invitations to serve as maid to any one lady; how far that designation falls short of the role she played in New York and Newport. No ball, no dinner of great occasion was imaginable without Edweena's presence in the *boudoir* reserved for the ladies. Many guests brought their own maid with them, but no guest was completely sure of her presented self until Edweena had approved of it. It was her sternly upheld doctrine of *nothing too much* that had changed the modes of dress. She proffered counsel only when she was asked for it; many a dame, supremely sure of herself in Chicago or Cleveland or even in New York, would start down the great staircase like a galleon in full sail, only to discover that confidence was ebbing step by step, and would remount the stairs. Insecurity as to how one looks can be a torment, particularly in a time of transition; the baroque was passing into the classic. Edweena had not created the new; she had felt the shifting tide "in her bones" and rode the wave.

Edweena was more than a judge of what was fitting, however. She was a refuge and a comforter and a source of encouragement to old and young; she knew or divined everything: incipient hysterics, rages, domestic jars, feuds, confrontations of a man's wife and his mistress, the terror of brides introduced into this scene for the first time. ("If you feel tired at any time, Mrs. Duryea, come up and sit by me for a while.") Before long her career extended itself. She was invited into homes to plan trousseaus for marriage or mourning. She was engaged by women to advise them on their entire wardrobe. She enjoyed the work; the remuneration was considerable, but the basis of her contentment was her love for Henry and her friendship with Amelia Cranston.

This is the Edweena I encountered in the middle of August. I was now able to be a more frequent guest at Mrs. Cranston's in the late evening. Edweena served tea every afternoon at four-thirty in the "garden apartment" and I was duly reproached when I failed to appear. Edweena loved conversation. Often we were joined by Mrs. Cranston when her duties permitted. After dispensing tea Edweena would stretch out on the long sofa, her shoulder resting against Henry's—Henry sitting straight and proud.

I remained reticent about my encounters on the Avenue. I had little doubt that Mrs. Cranston had received partial accounts of my involvements with the Bosworths, the Granberrys, the Vanwinkles, perhaps—as she had had of my involvement with the Skeels. But she respected my silence. Then when I was beginning to feel that my summer tasks were coming to an end I was confronted with the nearest and weightiest of them all: the matter of Persis and Bodo.

What had I meant when I said to Bodo, "You will be back in Newport on August twenty-ninth"? I don't know. That's the kind of irrational impulse to which I am prone. I knew that something had to be done quickly and if it had to be done, it could be done.

From the moment Bodo left Newport my imagination began groping for a solution; it continued to grope even while I slept. I have said before that both despair and hope invoke the imagination. In response to hope the imagination is aroused to picture every possible issue, to try every door, to fit together even the most heterogeneous pieces in the puzzle. After the solution has been found it is difficult to recall the steps taken— so many of them are just below the level of consciousness. I began to feel that somewhere there must be public confirmation of Major Michaelis's obsession with Russian roulette. I began to be visited with images of Bodo's return to Newport to create a *divertissement* at the Servants' Ball in Mrs. Venable's own cottage. I began to see that in some way, somehow, Edweena could help me.

The very day after Bodo left I appeared punctually at the "garden apartment" for tea.

"We're going to have a visitor today, Teddie. . . . Yes, a most respected one—Chief of Police Diefendorf. Mrs. Cranston and I have a little matter to discuss with him. Poor helpless women though we are, we have been able to be of real service to the Chief on a number of occasions and, of course, he's been many times of service to us."

"Edweena, my love, before you returned from shipwrecks and sharks I took the liberty of telling my old pal of what a wonderful detective you were."

Indeed, he had. It was a blood-warming story.

Servants live in terror of being unjustly dismissed from a situation without a letter of recommendation. This usually takes the form of being charged with having stolen objects of value. As the reader knows I shrink from making a generalization, but when I do it's a bold one: persons endowed with enormous inherited wealth tend to be more than a little unbalanced. So would you or I. They know they are marginal citizens—a very small portion of the inhabitants of this industrious or idle, mostly starving, often much-enduring, often rebellious world. They are haunted by the dread that what destiny, chance, or God has given them, destiny, chance, or God may as mysteriously withdraw. They are burdened by the problem of their merits. They assume (often with reason, often with none) that they are the object of envy (one of the uglier sins), of hatred, or of ridicule. They herd together for company. They know that something is wrong, but who began it? Where will it end? Hysteria lurks under the surface.

Masters and servants live under one roof in a close symbiosis, a forced intimacy. A woman's jewels (*precious* stones) are the outward and visible symbol that someone loves her, even if it's only God. A number of the ladies on Bellevue Avenue no longer trusted the safes in their own bedrooms. They had what Edweena called "the squirrel complex." When they returned from a ball they hid their emeralds and their diamonds in old stockings or behind picture frames or in electric light sconces and *then forgot where they'd hidden them.* (There's something in one of Professor Freud's books about that.) The next morning they'd be frantic. They'd give orders that every servant in the house be present in the dining room at ten o'clock. "A thing I value very much for association's sake has disappeared. You are to remain in this room while the housekeeper and I search through your rooms. If it is not found by us or restored by one of you—by noon today—every one of you except Watson, Wilson, Bates, Miles, and the kitchen staff will be dismissed without a letter of recommendation. While I am gone now you may sit down." In some cases the lady called up the police, but most of the ladies regarded the police as bumbling yokels. One of the suspected criminals would creep out of the dining room and call up the police. But the police could do no more than ring the doorbell and ask permission to enter. Chief Diefendorf then telephoned "Miss Edweena" who was permitted to enter and who, with transcendental tact, was permitted to join the searching party. Four times out of five she found the missing object very soon, but pretended for a whole half hour —to save the poor woman's face—that the case was hopeless.

In many ways the Chief was deeply indebted to Edweena and
treated her with an old-world admiring deference, as he did
Mrs. Cranston.

Edweena lowered her voice to tell me that this expected visit
of the Chief did not have to do with a supposed theft but with
another problem that appears from time to time in this Seventh
City. "It concerns a housemaid Bridget Trehan who is being
persecuted by the master of the house where she is employed.
She has resigned from her position, but the Chief and I have
ways of extorting from her former mistress—who is furious—
an excellent letter of recommendation!"

"Golly," I said in awe. We both nodded. "Edweena, can I
ask you what your plans are for the Servants' Ball this year?"

"You know in general what it's like, don't you?"

"I only know that Mrs. Venable lends her ballroom for
the occasion and that you and Henry are chairwoman and
chairman of the committee. And I know that you and Henry
made the rule two years ago that no one of the summer colony
can come and look down on you from the balcony as they
used to."

"Teddie, I have no plans. I have no ideas. We're all tired of
fancy-dress balls. We've had enough pirates and gypsy flower
girls. We've had enough of the 'Gay Nineties' and the gas-lit
era. There are fewer and fewer young people among the domestic servants. We all have a good time, but we need a fresh
idea. Couldn't you think up some idea, Teddie?"

Heaven sent me an idea. I pretended to be reluctant. "Well,
I haven't an idea . . . but I have a dream. The trouble with
your ball and many of the balls I hear about is that the same
people step out on the same floor with the same people they
stepped out with the last time. In Vienna the most enjoyable
ball is called the 'Fiaker Ball'—the ball for the cabmen of the
city. And the people from the highest society enjoy going to it
and they all mingle together. . . . My dream is this: that you
begin gradually and invite two guests of honor from Bellevue
Avenue—a young man and a young woman—good-looking
and charming and particularly admired for their friendly appreciation of servants. Honor them and they will feel honored.
Tactfully make it clear to them that you would be much pleased
if they wore their most elegant ballroom dress."

"Teddie, you're crazy. Would they want to come? Why?"

"Because that's the kind of persons they are. They've long wanted to know the servants better. I know just such a gentleman who often comes to dinner at a house where I have a pupil. My pupil and I aren't in the dining room, but I can hear him when he arrives at the front door chat with the man who takes his coat. I can hear him exchanging comradely greetings with all the staff. He's never accepted a barrier between employer and employee."

"Who is it, Teddie?"

"I know a young lady who dines twice a week at the very house where you're holding your ball. The household staff has known her since she was a child. She calls them all by name and asks after their relatives. Edweena, she knows you well and loves you. She doesn't call you 'Miss Edweena'—at least not to me; she calls you affectionately 'Edweena.' Who—together with you—is the most attractive woman on Aquidneck Island?"

"Who is it, Teddie? Teddie, you're like a child blowing soap-bubbles. Whoever they are, they wouldn't think of accepting the invitation. Henry, ask Teddie who he has in mind."

"Teddie, speak up. Who do you have in mind?"

"Baron Stams and Persis Tennyson."

Henry stared at me for a moment, then he struck the table. "God help me, he's right! I thought he meant Colonel Vanwinkle, but his wife wouldn't let him come, and I thought he meant young Mrs. Granberry, but she's expecting a baby. I don't think the Baron and Mrs. Tennyson would come, but that's the most happy-barmy dream I ever heard."

"Do you give me permission to sound them out or must you consult your committee?"

"Oh, we're the committee," said Edweena. "You should remember that servants—as individuals or as a class—have very little experience in taking the initiative. They're glad to leave all of that to us. But, Teddie, isn't Persis—whom I love dearly and whom I practically introduced into society—isn't dear Persis a ghost of herself since that tragic death of her husband?"

Mrs. Cranston had slipped into the room some time before, refusing tea, and had been listening to us.

"Mrs. Cranston, have I your permission to break a rule of the house and to name names while telling a story? The lady in question expressly asked me to tell the truth about something that had been unwisely hushed up."

"Mr. North, I trust you."

I told them of Archer Tennyson's desperate compulsions and of their unhappy consequence. When I had finished they were silent a moment.

"So that's what happened!" said Mrs. Cranston.

"Oh, the unhappy child!" said Edweena rising. "She'll receive no proposals of marriage except from the wrong kind of man. Mrs. Cranston, I want to see Chief Diefendorf. I think there's something that can be done about this."

"Edweena, you forget. He'll be here in a minute when he can get away from his office."

And he knocked on the door. There were sedate greetings on all sides. He refused tea, but was given permission to smoke. He conferred with the two ladies about the Bridget Trehan matter and arrived at a satisfactory procedure.

"Chief, are you in a hurry or might we consult you on a matter we think you should know?"

"I'm completely at your disposal."

"Chief, Mr. North has come across some very interesting light on the tragic death of Mr. Archer Tennyson. He wants you to know about it because you're so resourceful and because you helped him so splendidly once before. Mr. North, will *you* tell the Chief what you learned?"

I told him the whole story. I made a point of talking quickly but very distinctly. At the end I said, "I wish Miss Edweena would now point out to you the consequences of that game of Russian roulette as they affect the life of Mr. Tennyson's widow."

She did so. He thought a moment and then said, "May I do what I would do if the whole thing had happened to my own daughter?"

"We hope you will, Chief."

"May I use your telephone? . . . I shall make a long-distance telephone call using the code number reserved for the police. The rest of you can go on talking or remain silent, as you wish."

First he called his own office. "Lieutenant, Chevy Chase, Maryland, is on the border of the District of Columbia. Will you find for me the nearest station-house to Chevy Chase, its telephone number, and the name of the Chief of Police?" He took out his notebook and jotted down the information given him. He then called the distant number. He gave his own name, office, and code number. "Chief, I'm sorry to call you so late in the afternoon. I hope I have not caused you inconvenience. . . . A problem that has arisen in Newport requires my asking you what you can tell me of Major James Michaelis." The conversation continued for almost ten minutes. Chief Diefendorf continued writing in his notebook. "Thank you again, Chief Ericson, and forgive me for intruding on you at this hour. If you will send me as much of that material as was rendered available for the public record, I shall be very indebted to you. Good evening, sir."

Chief Diefendorf was very pleased with himself—and with reason.

"Ladies and gentlemen, two years ago Major Michaelis was asked to resign from the Chevy Chase Country Club, popularly known as the 'golf club of Presidents.' He had brandished a revolver in the billiard room and attempted to induce a number of the club members to engage in a game of Russian roulette with him. His resignation was also required of him by the Army and Navy Club in Washington. He was obviously becoming more and more unbalanced. He comes of an influential family and no reference to this appeared in the Washington papers. Last year his wife instituted a suit for divorce. She was interviewed by the reporter of a Takoma Park paper published near her home. Among the grounds for her suit she specifically mentioned her husband's obsession with that desperate game. Official and unofficial copies of that material will be in my hands in a few days. I hope that will take a load off Mrs. Tennyson's mind."

"Yes, and take her out of Coventry, Chief," said Edweena.

Three mornings later I telephoned "Nine Gables" and asked Willis, who answered, if I might speak to Mrs. Tennyson.

"Mrs. Tennyson is seldom here in the morning, sir. She is in her own cottage beyond the greenhouses." He gave me the telephone number.

"Thank you, Willis."

I had frequented "Nine Gables" all those weeks without

learning that Persis had a residence of her own. She retained an apartment at her grandfather's and spent much time there but even more with her son and his nurse and her books and her piano in her own cottage, "The Larches." This was merely another example of the stifling reticence that Mrs. Bosworth had introduced into her father's home. No words were wasted that could convey any intimation of a family existence. Coventry, indeed.

"Good morning, Mrs. Tennyson."

"Good morning, Theophilus."

"This morning I am leaving some documents at your door. Might I call on you this afternoon about five to discuss them?"

"Yes, indeed. Will you give me a hint as to what I may find in them?"

"Is Frederick well?"

"Oh, yes—very well."

"Some day he will be glad to know that there is official evidence that his father did not take his own life in a fit of depression but in one of foolish but hopeful high spirits."

"Ah! . . ."

At five o'clock I drove my bicycle to her door. "The Larches" was built in the style of "Nine Gables" and was often referred to as the "little cottage." Diminutives were constantly misapplied in Newport. The door was open and Persis came forward to greet me. Again she was wearing a linen dress, this time in crocus yellow. There was a string of pale amber beads around her neck. My expression involuntarily expressed my admiration. She was accustomed to such expressions of admiration and met them with a light disculpatory smile—as much as to say "I can't help it." Her small son peered at me from behind her and fled—a sturdy young citizen with enormous eyes.

"Frederick's shy. He'll lurk about and gradually try to make friends with you later. . . . Let us have a cup of tea first and then discuss the surprising material you left at my door."

I was led into a large sitting room with tall windows open to the sea air. I had often seen them when passing on the Cliff Walk. Two elderly maids were busying themselves with the tea urn, the sandwiches, and the cake.

"Mr. North, this is Miss Karen Jensen and Miss Zabett Jensen."

I bowed. "Good afternoon, good afternoon."

"Good afternoon, sir."

"Your name is very well known in this house, Mr. North."

"I think I have had the pleasure of meeting the Miss Jensens at Mrs. Cranston's."

"Yes, sir. We have had that pleasure."

As Mrs. Cranston had said, I was a very famous person "in certain circles."

When the tea things had been cleared away Persis asked, "Please tell me what I am to think about these clippings and documents."

"Mrs. Tennyson, you will soon become aware that the climate that surrounds you is undergoing a change. Those who enjoyed—*enjoyed*—putting a malicious interpretation on your situation at the time of your husband's death must find some other victim for their spite. You are no longer a woman who drove her husband to desperation; you are a woman whose husband was imprudent in the choice of his friends. Mrs. Venable has received a copy of these papers; Miss Edweena, who is in and out of many cottages these days and who has always been your devoted champion, is *hard at work clearing the air*. You are in the situation of many women a century and a half ago whose husbands were killed in duels over foolish quarrels about racehorses or card games. Do you feel that the climate is changing within yourself?"

"Oh, yes, Theophilus, but I can scarcely believe it. I must have time."

"Let us not talk about it any more," I laughed. "We can be certain that a considerable number of people are talking about it at this very moment. There is something else I want to talk to you about. But first!" I rose. "I am incapable of seeing music on a music rack without wanting to know what has been studied or played."

I walked over to the piano and saw Busoni's transcriptions of six Bach organ chorale preludes. I glanced at her. With her same "disculpatory" smile she said, "My grandfather's very fond of Bach. For the coming winter evenings I've been preparing these for him."

"There is very little good music on the island of Aquidneck. I'm starved for it. Could you *try* these on me?"

"Oh, yes, if you wish it."

She was indeed accomplished. She was ready for Schloss Stams. The music blew away spite and condescending self-righteousness and the presumed shelter of worldly gratifications. . . . She set ringing the carillon of "*In Dir ist Freude*"; she found voice for the humility of "*Wenn wir in höchsten Nöten sein*." Frederick crept back into the room and sat down under the piano.

When she ceased playing she rose and said, "Frederick, I'm going into the garden to pick some flowers for Granddaddy. Don't let Mr. North go away while I'm gone," and she left the room.

I rose hesitantly from my chair. "Did your mother say she wanted me to go away, Frederick?"

"No!" he said loudly, coming out from under the piano. "No . . . you *stay!*"

"Then we must play the piano," I answered in a conspiratorial manner. "You sit here on the bench and we'll play church bells. You play this note softly, like this." I put his finger on the C below middle C and showed him how to repeat it slowly, softly, and on count. I put my foot on the damper pedal and I released the overtones of the note, including the dissonances in the higher registers. Then I reached over and played the C in the bass. This is an old musical parlor-trick. The novice has the sensation of playing many notes and of filling the air with Sunday morning chimes. "Now a little louder, Frederick." He looked up at me with awe and wonder. What did that Frenchman say? "The basis of the education of the very young is the expansion of the sense of wonder." There is also an element of fright in awe. His eyes fell on his mother standing motionless at the door. He ran to her, crying, "Mama, I'm making piano!" He'd had enough of that disturbing Mr. North and fled upstairs to his nurse.

Persis advanced smiling. "The Pied Piper of Hamelin!" she said. "I just invented that visit to the garden. Frederick doesn't have an opportunity to see many gentleman callers in this house.—What else did you want to discuss with me?"

"A notion.—I have become a close friend of Edweena Wills and Henry Simmons. Just now because of Edweena's delayed return from that almost disastrous cruise in the Caribbean they are very busy with their plans for the Servants' Ball. They've engaged the Cranston High School Band again. They've sold many cards already, but they're searching for a novel idea that will make the thing take on new life. I suggested they invite some guests of honor, beginning with the Chief of Police and six gallant young members of his force and Chief Dallas and six gallant young firefighters. They certainly are public servants."

"What a good idea!"

"Then I told them about Vienna's famous 'Fiaker Ball' where all levels of society mingle happily together. Then it occurred to us to begin gradually with an idea like this: to invite a young gentleman and a young lady of the summer colony— the best-looking, the most charming, and particularly those who had shown themselves most appreciative of the servant community. They didn't have much confidence about this, but they took a straw vote in their committee for such a gentleman and the votes were unanimous: Baron Stams. Have you noticed how his beautiful manners include *everyone*?"

"Indeed, I have."

"Well, I sounded him out. Did he feel it was beneath his dignity to be such a guest, or did he think it would bore him? On the contrary! He said he'd long wanted to meet the staff at Mrs. Venable's, *socially*, and the staff at 'Nine Gables' and at Mrs. Amis-Jones's and those other houses where he's dined so often. But he didn't see how he could get away. His Chief couldn't spare him from the embassy. Edweena laughed at that. Edweena and Mrs. Venable are not only valued friends but are often fellow-workers on projects that make Newport a congenial place for those who both work and play here. She is sure that she has only to suggest that she call the Ambassador. 'Dear Ambassador, could I ask a small favor of Your Excellency? We wish to institute a sort of Fiaker Ball here. Could you lend us Baron Stams who has been chosen as the most popular guest of the summer season? Vienna-in-Newport, that kind of thing?' Don't you think that could be done?"

"It's a charming idea."

"Then the committee cast votes for the young lady guest of honor. They chose you."

"Me? . . . *Me*? But that's impossible. I hardly go out to dinner at all! They don't know I exist."

"Persis, you know better than I do that the domestic servants in Newport seldom change from year to year. They are like a silent spellbound audience watching the brilliant world they serve. How often you 'great folk' are astonished at all they know. They have long memories and deep sympathies, as well as deep resentments. The misfortune that happened to you happened to them also. They remember you in your happiest years—so few years ago. They remember that you and Mr. Tennyson won the cup for the best dancers at the benefit ball for the Newport Hospital. But most of all they remember your graciousness—you may have seemed removed and impersonal to your fellow-guests, but you were never impersonal to *them*."

She put her hands to her cheeks. "But I'd disappoint them so. I can understand their admiring Bodo, but as I told you, I'm just a dreary old widow-lady 'under a shadow.' "

"Well," I said sadly, "I told them it was doubtful that you would wish to accept their invitation; that your Aunt Sarah would feel that you were *degrading* yourself, and all—"

"No! No! Never!"

"May I present their ideas a little further? The grand march is set for midnight. Henry and Edweena would advance down the center of the hall to a march by John Philip Sousa, followed by the members of the committee, two by two. Then Chief Diefendorf and his six gallant men and Chief Dallas and his six gallant men in their dashing uniforms. Then you and Bodo in your finest clothes, smiling to right and left. When you reached the head of the line Henry would raise his staff (with all those ribbons) as a signal to the band which would start playing softly the 'Blue Danube Waltz.' You two would make a tour of the room dancing. Then the band would fall silent; Miss Watrous would take her place at the piano and you two would encircle the room first with the polonaise, then the polka, then the varsovienne, dancing like angels. Then the band would come in again with the 'Blue Danube Waltz' and you two would pick a succession of partners from right and left. Finally you would bow to the assembly, shake hands with Henry and Edweena—and then you could go home. . . . No one would ever forget it."

There were tears in my eyes. I am never so happy as when

I'm inventing. Bodo had not yet heard a word of this. The Ambassador had not yet received the request.

Just sheer soap-bubbles.

Just sheer kite-flying.

But that's what finally happened.

Edweena and Henry and Frederick and I were invited to attend one morning a dress rehearsal of those dances at "The Larches." Persis wore a many-layered dress of pale green tulle that billowed about her in the waltz ("as danced in Vienna"), although dresses of that sort were not in fashion in 1926. After the close of the rehearsal and after the Master and Mistress of Ceremonies had praised the dancers, Edweena and Henry sat on in silence for a moment.

Henry said, "Edweena, my love, that show could have gone on at the Queen's Jubilee in the Crystal Palace, I swear it could."

Frederick was practicing the polka all around the room. He fell down and hurt himself. Bodo returned, picked him up in his arms, and carried him upstairs to his nurse—as one accustomed.

As we rose to go, Henry said, "Now, Teddie, old Choppers, couldn't you tell a little lie just once and say that you were a servant? We'll give you a card and let you into the show tomorrow night."

"Oh, no, Henry. You made the rule: There are those who go in the front door of the house and those who don't. I can picture you all in my mind's eye and shall do so many times."

We were standing on the gravel path before the cottage.

Edweena said, "I think you're trying to say something, Teddie."

I raised my eyes to Edweena's. (It was true; they were more blue than hazel in the morning.)

I said hesitantly, "I always find it hard to say goodbye."

"So do I," said Edweena and kissed me.

Henry and I shook hands in silence.

15

The Servants' Ball

FOR SOME weeks I had felt intimations of autumn in the air. Some of the leaves of Newport's glorious trees were changing color and falling. I found myself murmuring the words of Glaukos in the *Iliad*: "*Even as are the generations of leaves so are those of men; the wind scatters the leaves on the earth and the forest buds put forth more when spring comes around; so of the generations of men one puts forth and another ceases.*" The summer of 1926 was coming to an end. I had called at Mr. Dexter's garage and had paid the two final installments on my bicycle, up to and including the last day of my stay. In addition I had bought from him a jalopy at a price somewhat higher than I had paid for "Hard-hearted Hannah"—who in the meantime had been restored to further usefulness and was watching this transaction.

"I only use her myself," said Mr. Dexter. "I know what to do. Did you want to say a few words to her?"

"No, Mr. Dexter. I'm not so light-headed as I was."

"I heard you had some troubles. Everything gets around in Newport."

"Yes. True or false, it gets around."

"I heard you had a theory that Newport was like Troy—nine cities. When I was a boy our baseball team was called the Trojans."

"Did you mostly win or lose, Mr. Dexter?"

"We won mostly. In boys' schools Trojans were always the favorite team because in the story they didn't win. Boys are like that."

"What years were those?"

"Ninety-six, ninety-seven. All of us took Latin and some of us took Greek. . . . When would you like to pick up your car?"

"After supper next Thursday night. If you could give me the key now I could drive off without disturbing you."

"Now, professor, this isn't a new car and it isn't an expensive car; but it'll give you a lot of miles if you handle it right. I'd like to go on a short drive with you and give you some pointers."

"That's very good of you. I'll be here at eight and turn in my bicycle. Then we can drive to Mrs. Keefe's and pick up my baggage and go for that ride. Will you put in a big can of gasoline, because I'll be driving to Connecticut all night."

So on the night of the Servants' Ball I took Mrs. Keefe and her daughter-in-law to the "Chicken Dinner Church Sociable" at the Unitarian Church. I saw many new faces and was introduced to their owners. Unitarian faces are pleasant reading. Mrs. Keefe and I had become good friends, New England–fashion, and no moving words were necessary at our leave-taking. I finished my packing, stowed my baggage by the front gate, and bicycled down to Mr. Dexter's garage.

Lessons began at once. He showed me how to start and how to stop; how to back as smoothly as nodding to a neighbor; how to save gas, how to spare the brakes and the batteries. As in violin-playing there are secrets you can learn only from a master. When we had returned to his garage, I paid for the additional gasoline and put it in the car.

"You must be in a hurry to be off, professor."

"No. I have nothing to do until a few minutes before midnight when I want to pass under the windows of Mrs. Venable's house to hear the grand march at the Servants' Ball."

"Since my wife's death I have a second home down here up in the loft. Could we sit there and have a little old Jamaica rum while you're waiting?"

I'm not a drinking man but I can take it or leave it. So we climbed the stairs to the attic. It was filled with portions of dismantled automobiles, but he had partitioned off a neat clean little three-room apartment with a big desk, a stove, some comfortable chairs, and some well-filled bookshelves. My host brought some water to the boil, added the rum, some cinnamon sticks, and half an orange. He filled our mugs and I settled down for an hour of New England taciturnity. I resolved to hold my tongue. I wanted to hear more from him. I had to wait for it.

"Have there been any more cities at Troy since the nine that Schliemann found?"

"Seems not. He found a scrubby village called Hissarlik and that's all there is still. You'd think it might have prospered being only four miles from the mouth of the Dardanelles, but it didn't. Probably no underground water left."

Silence. Wonderful rum.

"Started me thinking about what changes might take place here—give a hundred or a thousand years. . . . Likely the English language would be almost unrecognizable. . . . The horse is almost extinct already; they're thinking about pulling up the train tracks to Providence. . . ." He flapped his arms. "People will come and go on wings like umbrellas." He passed his hand over his brow. "A thousand years is a long time. Likely we'll be a different color. . . . We can expect earthquakes, cold, wars, invasions . . . pestilences. . . . Do ideas like that trouble you?"

"Mr. Dexter, after I graduated from college I went to Rome for a year to study archaeology. Our professor took us out into the country for a few days to teach us how to dig. We dug and dug. After a while we struck what was once a much traveled road over two thousand years ago—ruts, milestones, shrines. A million people must have passed that way . . . laughing . . . worrying . . . planning . . . grieving. I've never been the same since. It freed me from the oppression of vast numbers and vast distances and big philosophical questions beyond my grasp. I'm content to cultivate half an acre at a time."

He got up and walked the length of the room and back. Then he picked up the jug from the stove and refilled our mugs. He said, "I went to Brown University for two years before I came back here and got in the livery stable business." He pointed to his bookshelves. "I've read Homer and Herodotus and Suetonius—and still do. Written between twenty-eight hundred and eighteen hundred years ago. Mr. North, *one* thing hasn't changed much—*people!*" He picked up a book on his desk and put it down again. "Cervantes, 1605. They're walking up and down Thames Street—as you say—'laughing and worrying.' There'll be some more Newports before we slump into a Hissarlik.—Could we change the subject, Mr. North? I'm not yet freed from the oppression of time. After forty we get kind of time-ridden around here."

"Sir, I came to this island a little over four months ago. You were the first person I met. You may remember how light-headed I was, but underneath I was exhausted, cynical, and aimless. The summer of 1926 has done a lot for me. I'm going on to some other place that may be unrecognizable three hundred years from now. There'll be people in it, though at this moment I don't know a soul there. Thank you for reminding me that in all times and places we find much the same sort of people. Mr. Dexter, will you do a favor for me? Do you know the Materas? . . . and the Wentworths? Well, I'm a coward about saying goodbye. When you meet them will you tell them that among my last thoughts on leaving Newport was to send them my grateful affection?"

"I'll do that."

"Five persons that I love will be at the Servants' Ball tonight. They got the message already. Tonight, sir, will be among my happy memories." I rose and held out my hand.

"Mr. North, before I shake your hand I have a confession to make. I buy old cars, as you know. My young brother cleans them up. Some weeks we get four or five. He's a careless soul; he dumps old things he finds under the seats, in the linings, under the rug—all kinds of things—in a barrel for me to sift out later. Sometimes I don't get to look at it for weeks. About six weeks ago I found a sort of story. No name on it; no place mentioned except Trenton, New Jersey. The license on your car was New Hampshire. After talking to you tonight I think that story was by you."

I had turned scarlet. He reached down to a lower drawer in his desk and pulled out a long entry from my Journal—the account of an adventure I'd had with a shoemaker's daughter in Trenton. I nodded and he handed it over to me.

"Will you accept my apology, Mr. North?"

"Oh, it's of no importance. Just some scribbling to pass the time."

We looked at one another in silence.

"You made what happened pretty vivid, Mr. North. I'd say you had a knack for that kind of thing. Have you ever thought of trying to be a writer?" I shook my head. "I'll see you down to your car."

"Good night, Josiah, and thank you."

"Drive carefully, Theophilus."

I didn't wait under the trees outside Mrs. Venable's cottage to hear the Sousa march and the "Blue Danube Waltz."

Imagination draws on memory. Memory and imagination combined can stage a Servants' Ball or even write a book, if that's what they want to do.

AUTOBIOGRAPHICAL
WRITINGS

Chefoo, China

IT USED to be said that to have lived in China during those years between the Boxer Rebellion and the 1911 Revolution was to have enjoyed a foretaste of Heaven. Skilled and tireless servants could be engaged for six to ten dollars a month. There were superb cooks and inspired gardeners; there were tailors able to copy faithfully the fashion plates from Paris and London. International trade and diplomatic relations were expanded. Chinese officials had been rendered tractable by the "foreign devils." In fact the Empress Dowager had finally deigned to accord ambassadorial rank to representatives from those late-appearing, those barely civilized powers of Europe and America. Vast new markets had been opened; money could be made easily. Clerks and accountants could be taught the methods of the western world, though the beads of the abacus continued to be heard clicking in the back rooms of offices. In the Imperial City and in the treaty ports the privileged were borne from place to place in the two most soothing conveyances obtainable since the womb: first, the sedan chair suspended from men's shoulders; then—after the introduction of rubber tires—the jinrickisha. There was leisure for talk at the clubs on the Bunds, at the eternal tiffins, and teas, and dinners. There were numerous celebrations in the international compounds: Independence Day, Bastille Day, royal birthdays. There were boating parties, polo matches, and picnics "in the hills." Even in the missionary compounds there were cricket games on St. George's Day among the Anglicans and *Kaffeeklatsches* with the Lutherans and open-house concerts at the orphanages and institutions for the blind. "Old China hands" still refer to those days as sheer Heaven. "You didn't have to raise a hand." My own father—a rugged individualist from the state of Maine—returning to America after fifteen years was unable to tie his own shoes without a spasm of annoyance.

And yet:

There was another saying often heard up and down the China Coast: "Living ten years in China either makes or breaks a man."

My father as Consul-General had to ship home scores of "broken men," alive or dead, or to bury them in some potter's field. Any head-shaking tongue-clicking moralist (that is to say, any American) can see why living in this earthly paradise might lead a man to lose a grip on himself. But there were other elements in the China scene that contributed to breaking a man. There was the spectacle of omnipresent misery,—untended, ignored, and uncomplainingly endured.

To consider the second of these first:

A Scandinavian diplomat's wife wrote her sister: "We live a charmed life in the international city. There is no need for us to leave its enclosure. The tailors, the jewelers, the dealers in works of art bring their wares to our homes. Even when we drive out into the country we pass along a wide avenue shaded by great trees. Many of us have been here for years without advancing more than a few yards into the native city. Our husbands forbid us to enter it . . . Finally Lady B. and I rebelled. We made expeditions every Thursday morning. We selected certain trusted houseboys as guides and unnecessary guards . . . Oh, Marie! What shall I say? On one day we seemed to see mostly goitres and tumors; on another only leprosy and scrofula; and on another the *children*; and always emaciation, skeletal arms and legs, blindness—flies swarming upon the poor sufferers' eyes." Another testimony: a missionary's wife told my mother that when she arrived many years before in one of the treaty ports her life was made miserable by the sight of a group of old people and young women with babies who camped, night and day, before the barred gate of the compound where she lived. One evening, during her husband's absence and to the loud consternation of her servants, she directed that a dozen cups of condensed milk and a large platter of rice and dried fish be carried out to them. Within an hour a howling mob of hundreds had gathered before the gate. In the end the treaty port's police had to drive them away *with bamboo poles*. In the larger missionary compounds there were rice-kitchens, but doles were arranged under complicated systems. "Some of us have been destined to starve, some to eat." Even the bright young men sent out from Europe and America to work in the banks, import-export offices, and law firms— even the attractive young brides who came out in due time to join them—could not long remain entirely unaware of the ocean of suffering around them. A slow creeping apprehension is more disintegrating than a brutal confrontation.

Consider then the human multitude in China.

Years later, in Algiers, during the Second World War, we found ourselves in a plague of locusts. We were cloaked and bonneted and shod in locusts; our jeeps careened from side to side in haystacks and puddings of locusts. We were filled with wonder at nature's fecundity. Yet what is many, what is few? What is large, what is small? We have been told that there are more stars in the firmament than all the men and women born into the world since its creation; more than all the locusts. Heraclitus said, "Man is the measure of all things." It is frightening to contemplate another measure; perhaps a star or an atom can be better said to be the measure of all things: it obscurely undermines a man's self-esteem. This multitude was another confrontation that tended to make or break men in China. New York or London was a larger city than Nanking or Foochow (not to consider Peking, where no reliable census has ever been or could ever be taken) but the Chinese population lives in the street, spills into the street. Even in the coldest weather it surges about you, it encumbers you, it is underfoot . . .

But that's not all. All those hundreds of thousands of eyes rest on you for a moment, really see you (you are the "foreign devil") and in those two glances is neither antagonism nor admiration nor even indifference,—there is a touch of curiosity and some amusement. There is something that is more chilling for an occidental. The Chinese have lived in this density of population for tens of centuries (even the villages convey a shoulder-to-shoulder density); their customs are fashioned by it; their religion has been moulded by it. Those glances reflect also the reason for the omnipresent untended misery: they devaluate the importance of *any one individual life*.

Associated with my father's work in Shanghai was a delightful and thoughtful American, Judge Thayer of the International Court. Someone once asked him his opinion of that often quoted phrase about life in China either making or breaking a man.

"Well," said the Judge, turning his level quizzical gaze on the questioner, "living thirty-three years anywhere on the earth either makes or breaks a man, doesn't it? Maybe China merely accelerates it."

Even small boys are affected by these confrontations.

In 1906 my father—through connections he had made at Yale College—was appointed American Consul-General in Hongkong, China. At the time of this appointment he was editor and owner of a newspaper in Madison, Wisconsin, which he had bought with borrowed money, a loan which he was still struggling to repay many years later. He took his wife and four children—another child was to be born four years later—across the Pacific Ocean on what was then a month's journey. Mrs. Wilder and the children were to enjoy the "sheer heaven" I have described for only six months. The educational opportunities in Hongkong appeared to my father to be unsatisfactory and he sent his family back to Berkeley, California. When he was transferred to Shanghai three years later some of us rejoined him. Thereafter like a chess-player he moved his wife and five children about the world, sending some to Europe, some to America, and some to north China—always in the interest of the young people's education.

My sister Charlotte and I were sent to the China Inland Mission Boys' and Girls' Schools at Chefoo in Shantung Province, on the coast some 450 miles north of Shanghai. All our fellow students were missionaries' children. Missionaries hated the consuls; consuls hated the missionaries. My father was the only American (or even European) consul within memory who admired, who venerated missionaries. The duties of a consul (apart from salvaging or burying human derelicts) were largely given over to ratifying contracts and facilitating international commerce. Consuls were selected "at home" for astute business sense, for an unsentimental attitude toward drifters and wastrels, and for representing their native lands' character as congenial and even convivial good fellows. Consuls hated the missionaries for their clamorous demands (missionaries could not see why the consuls should not personally relieve all China's sufferers from drought, flood, and famine), for their pride in their calling (it appeared to be arrogance), for their stern disapproval of consular ways (that is, smoking, drinking, cardplaying, absenting themselves from church attendance, and otherwise misrepresenting before the Chinese people the great countries from which they came), and for their passion for martyrdom,—in troubled times they had to be rescued by river gunboats, literally dragged from their besieged churches and compounds. The missionaries hated the consuls. When it became known up and down the Yangtse Kiang River that Dr. Wilder at Shanghai fell over himself in order to be serviceable in any possible way to those "noble Christian men and women," there was great rejoicing. It was assuredly this reputation for serviceability that enabled him to have us enrolled in those schools. I suspect my father selected Charlotte and myself as the two of his children most in need of the edifying influences we would find there. Besides, the board and tuition was very cheap.

It was a good school. All the teachers and administrators were English or Scottish. Of the one hundred and twenty students in the Boys' School one hundred were English, about a dozen were American; there were a few Scandinavians. Much attention was given to religion, but there was none of the "hell-fire" evangelism that I was later to encounter occasionally at Oberlin College and even at Yale. The background was not primarily of the Anglican Church but of those denominations they called "chapel,"—Methodist, Congregational, Presbyterian, and so on; hence there was little class-consciousness. In a history recently published dealing with Henry Luce and his publications the writer quotes from Luce's letters telling of floggings and of that tyrannizing of older over younger boys that was called "fagging." Harry was at the school longer than I was. I heard of only one flogging, before my time; a boy had stolen a watch. In the classes we were often given short written tests; the three students who received the lowest grades were thwacked smartly over the palm of the hand with a ruler. I had many occasions to compare my rising welts with those of my fellow-students.

It was a very English school, modeled on those "at home." Games—cricket and soccer—were compulsory. Latin phrases abounded: permissions to leave the grounds were accorded us on *exeat* days. We were addressed by our last names; if a number of students bore the same family name they were known as Smith Major, Smith Minor, Smith Tertius . . . Quartus . . . Quintus . . . and so on, to Smith Minimus. The sons of an eminent medical missionary in Peking, Dr. George Wilder, arrived at the school before and after me. I was Wilder Minor. Wilder Major and Wilder Tertius were to be my best friends among my fellow students, as well as five years later at Oberlin College.

All the students (and teachers) had nicknames. I was called "Towser," though the nickname at home had been Todger.

Every Sunday the students of both schools marched into the great city of Chefoo,—two by two, in long "crocodiles," as the English say—to attend the Church of England services there. Sunday is not a day of rest for the Chinese. The long procession was often held up in the narrow streets by a blockage of one kind or another. There we saw on either side: the goitres, the tumors, the abscesses, the flaking white stumps of a leper's arms and legs, the blind, the skeletal children . . .

The life of a missionary in China is a difficult one. The missionary must be an exemplary Christian, an exemplary representative of the nation from which he came, an exemplary representative of that triumph of human development WESTERN CIVILIZATION. In addition—following the steps of St. Paul— he should be an inspired orator in an appallingly difficult language, and a profound student of the Chinese thought-world, the Chinese *ethos*. Many missionaries labored for years without making a single convert other than those unhappy adherents they had rescued from destitution and who were universally called "bowl-of-rice converts." The missionary was fortified throughout these disappointments by his sense of his mission. He had received a "call" to preach to those who walk in darkness. Now there is no doubt that there is much that the great Chinese people can learn from the Christian dispensation,— but how? Occasionally there appeared a missionary, a joyous man, who learned and reveled in the language, who had slowly and wonderingly entered into that subtle, disciplined, tradition-buttressed world: the Chinese mind. I have known some of these men and their families; I have attended their churches.

The majority of the American missionaries came from small colleges and seminaries in our middle southern states. Their religion turned largely upon SIN. The early translators of the Bible into Chinese found difficulty in translating that word. The Chinese knew all about wickedness and injustice, but when these "foreign devils" harangued them from street corners, beseeching them to confess their sins to God and be saved, they could only listen with blank wonder. The Chinese are not introspective. They had not diverted irrigation canals; they had not "stripped" copper coins; they had not stolen their neighbor's piglets. My father was once rendered very angry by a chance remark of a fellow-consul who held that "the missionaries had introduced sin into China." Only an occasional missionary was able to render Christianity *attractive* to his native listeners, to himself, or to his family.

I was assigned to Room 7, North Corridor. The room was on the second floor; its large window looked on the school's paved quadrangle; it contained four beds,—all for Americans. I settled in easily, for novelty quickens rather than intimidates me. In class work Americans were at a disadvantage. English students begin the study of Greek, Latin, algebra and geometry several years before Americans do; moreover they were well advanced in those basic studies, the history and geography of Great Britain and its empire. We were frequently rebuked and derided for speaking the English language incorrectly. We gave the impression of being stupid, ill-educated, and uncouth. There was little possibility of our ever, ever growing up to be gentlemen.

I was introduced to two of my roommates, a third arrived a week later. Wilkins was a fat boy, easily excited by anything unusual, given alternately to giggling and bursting into tears. Like many of the smaller boys he was often poignantly homesick. They missed those compounds in remote stations, those parents who had received so awe-inspiriting a Call, those amahs of boundless understanding, devotion, and noble firmness. Smith Sextus was gloomy, bilious, and very religious. Fortunately for me, they were loquacious; they introduced me to all the customs, taboos, written and unwritten laws of the community. They put me in possession of the idiosyncrasies of our overseers,—the masters, the prefects. Two weeks later, delayed by the mumps, our fourth member arrived,—Dawson Minor, like myself a "new boy." His older brother was seventeen and had been in the school for five years. He was in the sixth form, a prefect and a pillar of the school, a captain in soccer and even in cricket. He took his turn in conducting prayer meetings, impressively. He would have been Head Boy, if he had been a little better in his studies and if he had spoken the English language more intelligibly, for the Dawson brothers were of Tennessee stock and their speech was difficult for any of us. They were tall and knotty. Dawson Major was a model boy; Dawson Minor, fifteen, was of a very different sort. He had a square, uncheering face. His eyes weighed appraisingly, even distrustfully, everything that was said to him. There was an insolence and a suggestion of violence under his control.

After lunch the students were granted a twenty-five minute break in the day's routine during which we were permitted to return to our rooms. We entered Room 7 to discover Dawson Minor standing in tense fury before our house mother, Miss Cunningham, who was unpacking his suitcase. He had not fore-seen this procedure. Most boys have secrets—secret treasures —that are not to be revealed to the prying adult: fossil shells, a faded admission card to the St. Louis World's Fair, pages torn from the Sears-Roebuck catalogue displaying unobtainable delights in shotguns or Brownie cameras, a dog-eared copy of *My Forty Years as a Wild Animal Trainer*—fetishes for comfort in a dark hour.

"Dawson Minor, these are your roommates. This is Smith Sextus and this is Wilkins. We all wish they were better stu-dents, don't we? But they seem to teach things differently in America. I suppose that's because it's a *new* country. And this is Wilder Minor. He's only been here a fortnight and we hope he'll learn our ways.—You may sit down, you other boys. —Now let's see what your dear mother has sent. I hope she read care-fully the list of recommendations . . . American mothers seem to have their own ideas. I don't know why that is. Oh, dear me, I find only five undergarments; and I see only *five* pairs of stockings . . . There's been a good deal of mending here, hasn't there? . . . I hope they hold together in the laundry. . . . Collars, yes. Shorts for games. Singlets.—Bless my soul, what are these? Look, boys,—*beads*! Really, Dawson Minor, at the *Boys'* School we don't play with beads. Beads! I think you'll outgrow them soon. Ha-ha-ha-ha!"

Miss Cunningham had managed in a very short time to dis-parage his mother and his native land, to expose his poverty, to cast doubt on his manliness and to violate a sanctuary in his heart. The prayer beads were a gift from his amah at a leave-taking of all but unbearable pain.

"Why, they're *Chinese*! Are you sure they're clean? One can never be too careful. You must know that we have very little to do with the Chinese at this school, Dawson Minor. All of us—and all of your parents, except Wilder Minor's—are here to *help* the Chinese, to show them the Truth and the Way, but . . ."

And so on.

Many boys and girls of that age, all over the world, go through hell a part of the time in their relations with adults, another part of the time in their relation with their coevals. Hell.

The moment after Miss Cunningham left the room Dawson Minor went to the window, overlooking the large square that served for recreation between classes. It was enclosed on three sides by the main building of the school,—classrooms, assembly hall, dining room and kitchen on the first floor; dormitories, linen rooms, and so on, on the second. Opposite our window the square was bounded by a high white-washed stone-and-rubble wall; beyond the wall the ground rose toward the Girls' School and the mountains. Standing at the window Dawson Minor could see at his right the great entrance gate. Without turning his head he asked, "Is that big door locked at night?"

"Yes."

"Did any of you ever get over the wall?" None of us answered. "Is there some other door you can get out of at night?"

Wilkins asked, "Where would you go?"

"To town."

"Even in the day you're not allowed to go to town. Even on *exeat* days you're not allowed to go farther than the playing fields."

"You don't know anybody that ever went to town at night?" The idea was so preposterous that we didn't even shake our heads. He continued addressing Wilkins. "How long have you been at this school?"

"Three years."

"You don't know *anybody* who got out at night?"

Wilkins was so intimidated that his voice cracked. "My first year a boy was caned for even going downstairs at night. In front of the whole school."

"How caned?" Wilkins leaned over and made a gesture of lowering his trousers.

"What was he doing downstairs?"

"He tried to get in the kitchen."

"Don't you get enough to eat here?"

We all nodded slowly and gravely. Again Wilkins piped up. "He said he had to have a lot of treacle and sulphur. He had worms."

Dawson Minor's eyes kept examining the room. "What time do they turn the lights out?"

"Nine-thirty."

"Do the masters walk up and down at night and look in the rooms?"

"There's a master on duty; he sleeps in the room down there. They change every week. Some masters try to catch you. You get a demerit even if you whisper."

Again Dawson Minor strolled to the window, his hands in his pockets, whistling. (Students received two demerits for whistling indoors, four for putting their hands in their pockets.) He said slowly and chillingly: "Did you ever hear of people that walk in their sleep? I walk in my sleep. When I was at the Kuling School I walked in my sleep a lot."

Smith Sextus who had listened to this talk with growing resentment declared belligerently, "You didn't go to the Kuling School."

"Yes, I did. A business man in Nanking had a kid who had fits. He paid my father to send me to the Kuling School with him to watch him when he was sick. I went there two years."

The school for boys at Kuling was a very different institution from ours at Chefoo. It was situated at a fashionable summer resort in the hills far from the coast. The cost of board and tuition was said to be *ten* times higher than ours. The majority of the students were American, drawn from the homes of diplomats, oil men, and import-export men. Most of the students were being prepared for entrance into American universities. Religious exercises were limited to one hour on Sunday. Athletic games were properly coached to resemble struggles to the death. Very little was known about it at Chefoo. It was thought to be worldly, godless, and invested with glamour.

Smith Sextus returned to the attack with one more sneer. "Why would you want to go into the city at night?"

Dawson Minor was at his best under challenge. A great actor. He turned, took his time, and replied coolly, "Why, to make money, of course."

A Tennessee wildcat.

All the boys—to a varying extent—waged an unremitting war against the masters, and vice versa. Because we were all, in both camps, of English or Scottish stock, the contest turned on the burning issues of FAIR PLAY,—the gift to civilization of our race. But fair play is not as self-evident a code of behavior as it is generally believed to be. Justice, Honor, and Conscience may be implanted by God in every human being, but they are certainly interpreted, shaped and trimmed differently by environment, social class, private interest, and individual condition. Adolescents develop a fanatical idea of what is "fair." Adults, whom experience has taught that this ideal is at best an exhausting accommodation, have the authority to impose their convenient interpretations on the young. In short ALL ADULTS CHEAT. The result is that all adolescents brood over their wrongs, arm themselves for resistance, and seize every opportunity for retaliatory "foul play." Foul play is permissible to victims of foul play. Most boys are able to estimate quickly how far another boy has progressed in his accommodation to the unfairness of adults—including one's parents. It was soon obvious to us that Dawson Minor was a seasoned veteran in that unremitting war.

In the limited time that was accorded us for desultory conversation the American boys tended to associate together. Dawson Minor let the conversation flow about him unheeding. We Americans were deeply engaged in the matter as to where we were to go to college "in the states." It was all settled that Wilder Major and Wilder Tertius were to go to Oberlin College; others were to go to Berea, to Claremont; Dawson Major was to attend the college and divinity school from which his father had graduated; Harry Luce and I were to go to Yale.

For several weeks Dawson Minor behaved with the circumspection proper in a new boy. Because of those deficiencies I have mentioned he was put back into the lowest forms in certain subjects. He was brilliant in English composition and spelling, in "Bible," and "athletics," in arithmetic (he even mastered quickly those tormenting problems in pounds, shillings, and pence); yet he calculated to a nicety the degree of dullness that became his situation. He avoided association with his important older brother. He made a favorable impression. He afforded happy opportunities for the masters to score off him. In Room 7 he proved to be a fairly companionable roommate. He took no undue advantage of his seniority. During the limited free time accorded to us we generally found him lying on his bed studying ("boning up on") Latin and Greek. He took little part in our excited talk about games or food or the unfairness of masters or the cost and quality of the products at the school's candy store or "tuck shop." We were puppies; he was a huge, indifferent, unsmiling mastiff. We were never able to forget for long, however, that first alarming conversation. From time to time, with apparent casualness, he asked us about our homes, our proficiency in Chinese, what we planned to do when we left Chefoo. We knew well that everything he said and did was related to some plan, some Grand Plan.

For several weeks I was the only one in the room who was aware that he prowled at night. Later I learned, from him, the stages in his campaign. He studied the behavior and habits of the successive masters on night duty. He satisfied himself that none of them ever turned a flashlight on the sleeping students after ten-thirty. He went downstairs several nights a week as practice runs. The next problem that faced him was that of external doors and windows. The masters and all who had charge of us had tea—that unalterable, sacred institution—at four-thirty. We had supper at six-thirty. We came in from games or recreation at five-thirty. Dawson Minor found ways of returning to the main building at five. It was then that, ever so casually, he examined the windows and shutters in the long assembly room, in the classrooms, in the piano practice room, in the tuck shop. The building was old and aged by extreme alternations of humid heat and bitter cold. It has been often said that to the impassioned will nothing is impossible. It stimulates the imagination, nourishes both audacity and patience, and sustains endurance. In the gardeners' and caretakers' shed (tents and chairs for prize-giving day, wheelchairs for invalids, old cricket bats and wickets) he found a screw-driver. He found a strong wrench that could twist eroded latches. He strolled into forbidden territory, into the Headmaster's office, the faculty's cloakroom, the ladies' sittingroom: windows, shutters, latches, and locks.

By October 15 he had found—or rendered practicable—three avenues of egress and ingress.

One night in early November he spent three hours in the native city of Chefoo. He repeated the visit a week later. Thoughtfully considered, these were notable achievements. The next step was to make money; but, first there was something else he must do.

He must tell someone about it.

Men do not climb the Himalayas or discover the source of the Nile for their own private pleasure or even for the benefit of mankind. In human life the reward conferred upon feats of daring and ingenuity is the admiration of their fellow men: its name is Glory. Dawson Minor felt a great need for an audience of at least *one*.

His eyes rested speculatively on his roommates. We were a sorry lot. We were anxiously law-abiding, meek, and indubitably "good." No adventurer would dream of confiding in Wilkins. Nor in Smith Sextus, who detested Dawson Minor. There remained Wilder Minor, but Wilder Minor was light-minded; he enjoyed everything; he thought everything was funny. There was the danger that Wilder Minor might not be impressed.

In the meantime I had contrived too—though less ambitiously—to leave the bounds of our compound and to "go to China." On several afternoons a week we were all required to take part in compulsory athletics, cricket or soccer; on Wednesday afternoons, however, we were permitted to engage in some exercise of our choosing, tennis, running, jumping, swimming in season, or "rounders." I put in a request to pursue cross-country running. This privilege was open only to older boys of proven reliability, but it was accorded to me, probably because of my father's position. I gave my solemn promise not to linger in the villages, not to fall into conversation with the "natives," not to touch the offerings on the graves,—simply to complete the three-mile course and return to the school. This was delightful. On leaving the great gate of our quadrangle one turned left, ascended the slope, passed the tennis courts, passed the high walls surrounding the Girls' School, and reached the country road that ran level under the mountain. It ran through intensively cultivated fields and past farmhouses—every farmhouse is a family village; above all, it ran among many graves. These were upright inscribed slabs, graceful *stelae*. At the base of many of them were small altars or thrones, some of them in the shape of primitive houses surrounded by offerings in bright colored paper and festooned with streamers invoking the dead. The seacoast of Shantung is almost treeless, but at the mile-and-a-half turn-around point of my course was a fine grove of sycamores and gingko trees enclosing a semicircle of noble tombs. This I called the Grove of the Ancestors. Long distance running has little resemblance to the shorter heats; it is solitary and ruminative. Already at that age I had the notion that I would be a writer. It is well known that writers require long stretches of time alone,—to think. I thought throughout the entire course, but I thought best in the Grove.

One afternoon I was resting there, sitting on the ground with my back against a tree. I was not even thinking, for I had fallen asleep. I woke abruptly to find Dawson Minor sitting opposite me.

"Oh!—Hello!!" I said.

"Hello!"

"Did you get permission for cross-country?"

"I'm supposed to be at hurdles."

This was the first of many conversations in the Grove and it was there that I first became aware of Dawson Minor's grin. In the School he seldom smiled and then only in a superior removed way. Here—particularly when he had something outrageous to say or when, as on this occasion, he knew that he was not wanted—he resorted to a broad grimace. At first it seemed to have nothing behind it except brazen impertinence. I wrote in my journal that it was like the reflection of a winter sun on a sheet of polished tin. I was to understand later that it was a mask to conceal despair. We had no liking for one another but each saw in the other someone to contend with, to explore,—like dogs of different breeds.

We sat in silence.

Presently an elderly man entered the Grove. He bowed to us gravely, his hands clasped within the sleeves of his jacket. Dawson Minor rose—as any Chinese boy would do in the presence of a senior—and saluted him with great propriety. They held a long conversation. The old man seemed to be explaining the inscription on the central monument. When he had finished, Dawson Minor folded his hands; lowered his head several times, then, raising it, declaimed in a high singsong nasal voice what must surely have been a prayer. The old man took formal leave of us and returned to his village.

"What was that, Pepper?" (By this time we had acquired nicknames. Dawson Minor had introduced from American slang the word "pep," which led to his being called "Pepper." I was called Towser.)

"Whenever any 'foreign devils' come here, the village sends someone to keep an eye on them. A few years ago some boys from the School kicked up an awful mess here."

"Was that a prayer you said?"

"Sort of."

"Who taught it to you?"

"My amah."

Silence. The grimace.

"The same amah that gave you the beads?"

"Yes."

"What was her name?"

"Go Po."

"Do you . . . do you *believe* in it?"

He shrugged his shoulders, looked about a moment and then said to me with the greatest directness, "Everything Chinese is good; everything American and English is sickening."

I rose, grunted something, shook my feet preparatory to running, and started toward the road.

"What did you say?" he asked sharply.

"Think what you like. Say what you like, Pepper. But remember this: I'm not eight years old. Don't talk to me like I was.—It's late. You'd better run back the short way by the bathhouse."

I looked back at him. The grin had disappeared from his face. He was staring at me with a sort of fierceness, struggling with himself. Finally he said, with a stammer in his excitement,

"Last . . . last night I was three hours in the city . . . and that was the third time."

"Dawson, you're crazy as a coot. Why do you do it? You'll get caught and sent home."

The joyless grin returned in strength and he dashed past me down the hill.

We exchanged few words in Room 7. Wilkins and Smith Sextus were a roomful in themselves. One morning at the washstands Wilkins whispered to me, "I think Dawson has been walking in his sleep a lot."

"Well, if I were you, I'd keep it under my hat, Beanie. If any trouble comes, you don't want to be a part of it. The less you say about it, the better off you'll be."

Fortunately, Smith Sextus slept and snored through everything.

The following Wednesday Dawson Minor was sitting in the Grove of the Ancestors when I arrived.

"Have you been making any money, Pepper?" No answer. "What is it,—opium? . . . Gambling? . . . Fortune-telling? . . . I know what it is! It's snake-oil medicine. You're going to get found out and sent home. I don't know about your father and mother, but most fathers and mothers would just about die. And we up in our room are going to get into a mess of trouble too. 'Trees' [our Headmaster Dr. MacCartney] will call us into his office and ask us a thousand questions. Maybe I'll be sent home because I didn't run and tell him that you walked in your sleep. I don't want to know anything. I don't want to tell a pack of lies."

My tirade made Pepper very happy. To him this was the first whiff of glory.

"What are you so crazy about money for?"

"If you have money, you can do anything."

I rose and shook my shoes. "Like what?" I asked.

"Like going to Harvard," he said passionately. "Like curing leprosy. Like . . . like preventing those floods. What's the matter with you? Can't you see that money can do anything?"

"You're crazy," I said. "You're crazy as a mad dog."

I started down the hill.

New Haven, 1920

IT WAS widely believed, in my time, that Yale College was attended solely by clear-eyed, clean cut, high-minded, upright, downright, forthright Christian young men; and—give a little, take a little—this was true. Our contemporaries at Harvard College held that we were none too bright, that we were obsessed by athletic victories, and that we were notably deficient in polish. My father and certain friends of his who had graduated at New Haven about thirty years before us somehow managed to believe that Yale was simultaneously the finest university in the world, a hotbed of worldliness, and a den of iniquity. (He sent my brother and myself first to Oberlin College for two years in order to armor us against the temptations that beset Yale men.) There's an element of truth in legend. We began the day with obligatory prayer and we ended it with tankards of substandard prohibition beer in our hands. Clangorous bells awoke us at seven; at eight we attended chapel where undergraduate proctors kept a strict account of the empty seats. We hurried about all day from "The French Revolution" (Wilbur Cortez Abbott) to Biology I (dissecting frogs for Professor Baitsell), from Psychology (Angier) or "The History of Philosophy" (Professor Bakewell, health permitting, or the enthralling Charlie Bennett) to "Elizabethan Literature" (Tucker Brooke), "The Age of Johnson" (C. B. Tinker) and "Tennyson and Browning" (William Lyon Phelps). We had good teachers. We strove variously to edit publications, to captain teams, to get elected to fraternities and societies, to sing in the Glee Club or the Whiffenpoofs, to act in the Dramat under Monty Woolley, to be popular, to be famous, to be "a big man at Yale." Girls, girls descended on New Haven by the hundreds for the proms, hops, and tea-dances. Letters of an assumed composure were written and the answers to them feverishly awaited. As far as I knew there were no nervous breakdowns among us—such as are so frequently reported today in the larger universities—and very few outsiders. I came very near to being an outsider—and a quite cheerful contented one. I have never had any competitive drive or any closely focused ambition. I had no faint desire to join a fraternity but somehow my brother and Harry Luce (from Shantung, China) and Robert Maynard Hutchins (of Oberlin, Ohio, my future boss at the University of Chicago) "shoe-horned" me into Alpha Delta Phi. My grades were perilously low, but Dean Jones was an old friend of my father and I graduated. I derived as much stimulation from the courses I flunked as from those I passed. I rejoiced in Chemistry I under Professor Holmes at Oberlin; I've drawn on Professor Lull's "Geology I" all my life. I attended few athletic contests, partly because I had much better things to do with my strictly limited pocket-money.

At this time the Wilders were poor, really poor. My father had received eight thousand dollars a year during his consular service in China. But his health broke down (he who had never been ill a day in his life): he spent a year traveling from hospital to hospital that specialized in tropical diseases. From the little he could spare he had made some unwise investments. He returned to New Haven to represent "Yali"—Yale's college and hospital in Changsha, China. I was now practically a missionary's son.

How could my father on that missionary's salary hope to send his two sons to Yale,—having in addition three daughters: clothes, dentist's bills, carfare, "extras" . . . ?

To the impassioned will nothing is impossible.

My father was a man of religious conviction. Like most missionary's sons I had lost my "religion" some time before. It was gone before I missed it, like a coat left in some railway station. Even in my Oberlin days I had formulated for myself the phrase: *religion is the emanation from an extinct star.*

My father was a man of religious conviction. Religion operates in different ways in different persons. It hardens some natures to pride and bigotry; it softens others to sentimentality and a refusal to confront life's sterner demands. Some it inexplicably irradiates; some it brutalizes. Religion may be as Professor Freud said, civilization's greatest illusion. If that is so, it may be thought of as resembling a sun long extinct whose rays still continue to warm, animate, and inspirit the minds of men. It instilled fear and awe in the cave-dwellers; it offered the image of an overwatching Eye; it became identified with all those dawning ideas of order and morality, of the "good" and the "bad," of rewards and penalties. For thousands of years it has played a large part in the public and private life of mankind. Truth or illusion, it is ingrained in the human mind.

There are two characteristics of men and women of religious conviction that have often been remarked. The first is their way of viewing the facts of the daily life—our humble daily life —as freighted with the greatest importance, particularly in relation to the future. Everything is under that overwatching Eye; everything is on a Grand Scale. Such men and women are seldom able to transmit to their children the conviction that illuminates them, but in that charged cell, which is family life —in that enclosed space of finely tuned acoustics—they transmit the concept of scale. Their children learn to think big, to make large demands on life, on themselves, and on others. This "scale" has not necessarily any spiritual qualifications; it's enough that it's big, big. Hence the phrase "*Beware of sharks and missionaries' children.*" The second characteristic is their tendency to invest one or more peculiarly secular interests with a religious "imperative"; so do their children, for this tendency is transmittable in family life. It is transmittable in civilizations,— even in those which have long lost any religious conviction,— so compelling was the long authority of religion on the earth. (Political systems: we are often told that the Russians embrace communism as a religion; patriotism: Americans can be heard to declare that they live in "God's country"; local affiliations: our college song at Yale ended with the stirring commitment— words and music indicated an ascending order of loyalties— "For God, for country, and for Yale.")

My father *religionized* (if I may be permitted the term) education,—our education. He not only dreamed big, he demanded complicated refinements of his dream; he made it as hard for himself as possible. We were to attend schools run for the rich and schools run for the poor. This was to ensure that we would never feel awkward among the privileged or even impressed by them, nor would we lose a sense of kinship with hard-working people. Moreover, each of us was to pass a part of our early years in foreign countries, preferably to attend schools abroad for a time. Above all, the teaching was to be first class, tending to develop (it was a favorite phrase of his) "noble Christian men and women." By God, it would be impossible to dream more extravagantly than that, on a small salary.

Circumstances favored him; luck played a part; above all old friends ("treasure more precious than gold," as the poet says) were eager to assist him. Amos and I went to the Thacher School in Southern California (we were "scholarship" boys; Mr. Thacher was a classmate of our father; every student had to have a horse of his own; students "dressed" for dinner two nights a week). Isabel went to Miss Master's School in Dobbs Ferry, New York (a "scholarship" girl among heiresses; my mother was the daughter of the Scotch Presbyterian minister there and the school's pastor). We all went to a variety of public schools; my sisters went to Northfield School, founded by Dwight L. Moody, the evangelist. My brother and I worked farms, hoeing and haying and milking, from California to Vermont, waited on tables in hotels (educative, every moment of it). Amos and I went to Oberlin College, teeming with missionaries' children; there I listened to three teachers better than any—save two—that I was to hear in Yale or Princeton's Graduate School. Father's greatest success was in getting us out of the country. By twos or threes we attended German schools in Hongkong and Shanghai (*Die Kaiser Wilhelm Schule sogar*) and the Chefoo Schools. Our mother returned to America from China with Isabel and Janet by several stages: Isabel went to schools in Florence, Vevey, and Oxford. Charlotte crossed the sea to assist our Aunt Charlotte in the running of a girls' hotel in Milan. Amos after serving in the artillery during the First World War stayed on to study at the universities of Montauban, Louvain, and Oxford. Myself—as will presently be shown—went to the American Academy in Rome for a year. Father lived long enough to see all his five children *teaching* in some school or other.

Anyway, Amos and I got to Yale. I have long suspected—but not at the time—that we were "scholarship" students, subsidized from funds accumulated in my father's Senior society for members of his descendants.

The herd instinct plays a large part in men's minds; it was largely left out of mine. The fraternities and Senior societies were attended on one night of the week. A dinner was served, for there was no shortage of servants in those days. After dinner the brothers adjourned to the windowless "chapter rooms" where initiations and rituals and solemnizing hocus-pocus took place. There was a degree of prestige in belonging to them; there was an equal satisfaction in keeping others out or in feeling superior to those who may not have wanted to get in. (There is a considerable element of fear in the herd instinct.)

In the fraternities and in the drinking clubs at the end of the day we were convivial,—that is, everyone strove to be witty. But here also the herd instinct imposed its laws and limitations. Sharp malice was frowned upon; any spirit of revolt was bad form: "Yale was all right." Ten years later Robert Maynard Hutchins (Class of 1921), Dean of the Yale Law School, was to accept the call to the presidency of the University of Chicago and there to institute reforms that have influenced the structure and procedures of higher education in America ever since. He derived his insights from living under the conditions I have described; all he had to do was to turn them upside down. He said that Yale College combined the less attractive aspects of a Kindergarten and of Sing Sing; I think it was he who said that it was dedicated to "the flattery of arrested adolescence." We dimly felt this: obligatory chapel, required classroom attendance, weekly examinations, week-end restrictions; we rather liked it. It mitigated some responsibility on our part. Whatever unrest we expressed was limited to persiflage. But the most sensitive effect of herd authority was evident in the area of sex.

In this realm we were shielded to an extent unbelievable today. In "Chaucer" we were told that certain of the *Tales* were not required reading; "questions on them will not be asked in the weekly or term-end examinations." In "Shakespeare and Marlowe" many salient passages were passed over without clarification; we were given to understand that they were interpolations by tasteless hacks. But it was not necessary for the college to be so nervous about our purity. The herd instinct took care of that also. A high moral tone was prescribed by the students themselves. In the center of the campus stood a solid edifice called Dwight Hall. It was a center of elevating "discussion groups," prayer meetings, and social service programs. The members of the *most* sought after (that is, most exclusive) Senior society were all drawn from the leaders of Dwight Hall. They were ponderous, humorless, unctuous—but they were the "big men," the biggest in college. They pretty well ran Yale, and in their free time they coached basketball teams in the city slums, they appointed one of their number to rebuke—in high brotherly fashion—any student from a good background who had fallen short of the behavior expected of a "man at New Haven." They leaned down from Olympus to say a friendly word to the outsiders. Dwight Hall ruled that there was a considerable area of a young man's life which was to be discussed seldom and then only in terms of evasive solemnity. Young men tend to be either rebels or very conformist. To us—living in a forcibly delayed maturity—sex is fascinating, of course, but also discomfiting and a little frightening. But that is what it had been to most of the citizens in the United States for over a century.

Striking evidence of this unhappy condition was afforded by our behavior in the motion-picture theaters. As all who lived in college towns in those days will remember a visit to the evening showings of the "flickers" was a nightmare. It was the custom of the undergraduates to greet any tender passage with whistles, howls, and stampings; a kiss evoked ear-splitting pandemonium. Two years later when I was teaching near Princeton University and was able occasionally to go to the theater on Nassau Street, the din was even more violent and continuous since the audience in that village consisted almost entirely of students. The students attended the pictures primarily to make the noise,—that is to say, to find a vent for their confusion and humiliation and anguish. They even started their noise early in the film—to the accompaniment of street scenes, desert vistas, ships at sea—because they knew that their torment lay ahead. The sharp point of those demonstrations was that they believed that they were giving evidence of their superiority to childish representations of romance, they were offering testimony of what they called their "sophistication."

That is what the Puritan dispensation had bequeathed to us.

Now, to be sure, there were little enclaves of sin in academic New Haven. Such matters were discussed, solemnly, solemnly, in lowered voice among one's closer friends. It was said . . . a florid redheaded woman in a local tobacconist's shop, almost old enough to be our mother, was shared by some fellows in Sheffield Scientific School (but scientists tend to be godless)

. . . right up in their rooms . . . Certain daughters of esteemed faculty members were reputed to be "fast" . . . after a tea-dance under a billiard table . . . images to set a fellow's head swimming. But more of that later.

The class that graduated in 1920 was an omnium gatherum of at least four classes. Almost all of us had missed a number of years while serving in the war. Some had gone to Canada and joined the British forces long before America was involved; some, like my brother, had volunteered in ambulance units overseas and then transferred to our combat forces. Military drill—the "R.O.T.C." Reserve Officers Training Corps—was already in operation in Oberlin College during my second and last year there. When I entered Yale in the fall of 1916 over half the student body was in uniform and soon left for further training elsewhere. I arose from private to corporal in the Coast Artillery defending Narragansett Bay.

So members of the several classes returned to New Haven in 1918, resumed their education, and graduated "as of the Class of 1920." During the decade that followed our Class gained a certain reputation and was even sometimes referred to as a "golden age." We did not so view ourselves. We thought we were pygmies in the shadow of the classes from 1913 to 1916: Archie MacLeish, Wilmarth Sheldon Lewis, Brian Hooker, Cole Porter, Monty Woolley, Charles Rumford Walker, Roger Sessions, and so many more. They had been brilliant, dashing, witty, extravagant; we were merely earnest and we were relatively poor. It was not we who turned a hose on Mademoiselle Gaby Deslys during her performance at the local Shubert Theatre or wrote that deathless drinking song "Dry as a Camel's Tonsil." Except for Stephen Vincent Benét, who had published a book of poems even while an undergraduate, we were slow to arrest attention. But we were diligent. I remember Steve and Johnny Farrar reading aloud a play in Professor Jack Crawford's house; Philip Barry reading aloud a play to a few of us at the Elizabethan Club. Harry Luce and Brit Hadden were editing the *Yale Daily News* as they would before long be editing *Time*; Walter Millis and John Carter and Bob Coates were writing stories for the *Yale Lit*, though their later careers were to be made in military and political counsel and in criticism.

Salzburg

I WAS young—in my later thirties, but my time-table has always been in retard; I had more money in my pocket than I felt was due me as "professorial lecturer" at the University of Chicago. I had had a relative failure or two during the Depression years with *The Woman of Andros* and *Heaven's My Destination*. But I was healthy, filled with curiosity, and ignorant.

What I was principally ignorant of was politics. I was thoroughly book-taught in politics from Aristotle down and I took a lively interest in presidential elections that turned on our hopes that a wise government would repair the appalling condition into which the country had fallen. In writing the book which I have designated as my second failure I had written—without knowing it—a political novel. My ignorance consisted in an inability to relate the general ideas which are called politics with the relations of the individual citizen to the agencies of government that shape his life—an area of intense struggle which is also called politics.

I was young and as happy as a cricket and I went abroad for several summers in succession. On two of these trips I visited Salzburg during its festival of music and drama.

I am not fond of music in general. I deplore grand opera. But I am so admiring of great music and of a dozen grand operas that I arrange to hear them infrequently, I might say *as seldom as possible*. Just as I choose to read *Don Quixote* once every ten years on the decades of the year of my birth. Music is a rhetoric like another—that is, a mode of expressing the emotions in a language that has undergone a long and complicated development. (Salzburg is a pilgrimage-place, for two of these rhetorics —for music and for architecture.)

So early in the spring I purchased my tickets—a pair of tickets for each performance—from a travel agent. On such and such a night I would be hearing Toscanini conduct *Fidelio*; then I would be present at Max Reinhardt's production of *Faust* with Paula Wessely as Gretchen. Then Bruno Walter's *Don Giovanni* with Dusolina Giannini, and his *Die Zauberflöte*. I would hear the Masses in churches a stone's throw from the composer's birthplace.

Both summers enjoyed beautiful weather. The rain itself fell in sunlight. The narrow streets and bridges were crowded. There were not many automobiles; a few were conspicuous: a flag on top of the hood meant royalty, as the right hubcap meant an ambassador or senator or perhaps a brash assumption of importance. Buses brought throngs from Berchtesgaden, fifteen miles away, and from Vienna. The afternoon performances of *Everyman* in the Cathedral Square seated many hundreds; there were concerts and open-air serenades. An unending queue awaited admission at the door of Mozart's birthplace. (As I was a professor and looked like a professor, I was often stopped on the street by strangers and asked in one language or another "Was he *really* born there?" One cannot be too careful.) But the tickets for the principal performances had been long sold out and prices for them on the black market had risen to extraordinary heights.

There was a feverish tension in the town not solely attributable to the presence of so many notable persons or to the expectation of masterpieces. Politics freighted the air. Hitler's rule was in the ascendant; Mussolini was reaching toward a revival of the Roman imperium; the hope of social resolution was organized into parties throughout the world. In every country in Europe politics exerted its pressure on every aspect of public and private life. Families selected their guests, publishers their authors, civil servants their office workers either by a judicious mixture of "left" and "right" or by a bold resolve to support one tendency or the other. Particularly in France, Italy, and Germany the commitments assumed daily reached agonizing proportions. They involved the disavowal of old friendships and loyalties. "Your brother will not be allowed in this house." "Godmother or no godmother, you will not speak to her in the street again." Men and women seem to feel that not only their own livelihood but the security of the world and the happiness of generations unborn depended on their selection of friends and associates.

But surely we would be spared this torment in Austria— Austria, celebrated so long for its tolerance. And surely we would be spared in Salzburg, a town pre-eminently under the sign of Art. How often we had been told that art knows no boundaries, that music tames even the savage breast. Art is educative. The masterpieces of the human spirit will save us.

After the performances the town—except for one place of entertainment—soon closed up. The visitors, exhausted by their brush with the sublime, had a supper of trout or Wienerschnitzel and cucumber salad and went to bed. For the wide-awake and the well-provisioned there remained the Cafe Mirabell, its supper rooms and its gambling tables. At that time the government permitted and participated in four gambling casinos in Austria. The gamblers—industrialists, certain mysterious men and women who were said to be spies limitlessly subsidized, nobles who had somehow pulled through the dire decades— seldom did more than glance into the supper rooms and shudder. The people in the supper rooms devoted to conversation the passion that others spent upon chance. I never saw any of the artists at the Mirabell; presumably they were supping in their rooms or at Max Reinhardt's Schloss Leopoldskron or at one or other of the hospitable villas like Stefan Zweig's that surrounded the town. By exception, however, one night Alexander ———— appeared among us. The previous night he had asked and received permission to witness a childbirth in the town's hospital. He so shrank from this experience that he deemed it necessary to view—several writers were engaged in dramatizing *The Idiot* and portions of *The Brothers Karamazov* for him and he felt that it was a Russian thing to do—it prepared him—inured him—to play Dostoievski.

Like many others I had long groped for an adequate translation of the word *Stammgast*. I was often offered another foreign word, *habitué*, which fails to suggest the solidity of the German word. An *habitué* admittedly frequents certain *milieux*: one is not a *Stammgast* at the opera or at the gaming tables or at the races. Finally I decided that a *Stammgast* is one who can be found at the same place of public refreshment every day at the same hour *unless he happens to be somewhere else*. An approximation of the meaning is merely to say a "faithful." I became a faithful at the Cafe Mirabell.

By two o'clock Ferenc Molnár had drunk a great deal of cognac as he was reported to have done every night for many years. He was, as so often, between wives, and in great need of comfort and admiration. During one of these summers he was fortunately sustained by a sort of attentive and soothing nephew he had acquired—Hans Albers, the popular singer in operetta, who had suddenly revealed himself in middle life to be a great actor and who had created the title-role in *Liliom* for the public in Berlin. In the late hours, however, Molnár, increasingly drowsy, could think and speak only in Hungarian. Thinking in a language that no one in the neighborhood can think in tends to intensify a sense of isolation. Molnár was given to weeping. Again fortunately for him, a Faithful at a nearby table, surrounded by bar friends, was another Hungarian, the fascinating Marion Mill Preminger, who from time to time would throw him a life-line. At another table Erich Maria Remarque—ever buoyant, ever young—sat in a company, all buoyant, all young. At another table an extremely popular and witty old man. No one knew anything about him, but the Faithful at the Mirabell were above the lower forms of curiosity; there was very little gossip. Rumor, however, said that Dr. Helm was an unfrocked priest who sent long reports twice a week to Moscow. He was generally seated between two beautiful young women whom we all knew as Fräulein Mitzi and Fräulein Klari. They were from Vienna where they were known to be among the faithful at the Eden-Roc. They were always welcome at Dr. Helm's table, where they could be found nightly unless they happened to be somewhere else. I was the only American among the Faithful, though I brought guests to my table, old or new friends I had met in the town. The chairs and even the tables were light and there was a constant shifting of place.

The Mirabell Cafe closed at four o'clock and from a quarter before four the waiters—eminently among the Faithful and often called on to settle merry disputes—directly presented bills and snuffed candles and removed covers. But in every such company there are always a few who once having watched until four cannot go to bed until the sun rises. This was particularly true of Ferenc Molnár, who could neither retire, nor pass the hours without more brandy, nor could he drink alone. There was one bar in Salzburg that remained open all night—at the railroad station. Hans Albers, ever attentive, ever deferential, acceded to the old man's wish to continue the congenial evening there. He begged the departing guests to accompany them.

On the night that I am recalling there had been a number of more than usually spirited discussions. Eleanora von Mendelssohn (Eleonora, by right, as god-daughter of La Duse) had maintained that music was the chief of all the arts. Dr. Helm reserved that role for architecture. Remarque, who had already begun assembling his distinguished collection of paintings, affirmed that the eye was the channel of the real. Johann Neponinck, the headwaiter, Fräulein Mitzi, the historian, and the American could not be shaken from their conviction that the word was pre-eminent.

"And what is your opinion, Fräulein Klari?" asked Dr. Helm.

Both the young women had drunk many glasses of cognac and were to drink half a dozen more that night. We all react to alcohol in a different way. Fräulein Mitzi showed no sign of inebriation. Fräulein Klari had disassociated herself from our discussion. She floated; she had become seraphic. In a gentle voice without emphasis she replied: "All the arts are childish."

The Faithful were caught short. They could not believe their ears.

"What do you mean, Fräulein Klari?" I asked.

She turned her beautiful blue-marble eyes toward me and said: "All the arts are childish. They conceal from men the things that must be done."

Suddenly politics had entered the supper room at the Cafe Mirabell. The Faithful knew at once that a prostitute from Vienna was quoting a garbled Karl Marx—a Karl Marx as delivered in clubs for the working classes—four schillings for six lectures; sign your name and address when you leave.

Dr. Helm (born in the former Austrian Empire) replied, "But my dear child, men without the vision set before them by the poets and the artists would have neither the desire nor the perseverance to do what you call the things that must be done."

Fräulein Klari did not answer. She returned to the sphere above our heads—seraphic and completely assured.

An Austrian had again poured oil upon the water. Tolerance like a gentle tide flowed in about us. Only Hans Albers passed through the phase of confusion, anger, and outrage—tolerance is not a characteristic of North Germans—but finally became subdued to the climate about him.

The conversation passed on to other subjects, but presently Dr. Helm, with the flourish of tact which is in the native blood, reintroduced the awkward subject in a playful vein: "I must confess that at times I too have felt as our charming friend does," and he placed his hand lightly on that of Fräulein Klari. "We are often told that Nero fiddled while Rome burned. I have never been confident that he fiddled *well*."

Closing time came. Hans Albers begged us to adjourn to the railway station. Five of us willingly chose to do so: Remarque, Dr. Helm, the two young women, and I. There were always a number of taxis and horse-drawn carriages awaiting at the door. (The drivers' wives had awakened them at three-thirty after a refreshing sleep.) In good weather a few tables and chairs were set up on the long platform between the tracks and Josef Struck the proprietor of the refreshment-bar (his wife replaced him at seven) welcomed us with lively enjoyment, "Lieber Meister" . . . "Herr Doktor" . . . "Verehrte Herr Remarque" . . . "Gnädige Fräulein" . . .).

The will to converse had relapsed. Molnár's eyes were open (he was inveighing against something or someone), but his head had shrunk deep into the fur collar of his overcoat. Hans Albers had continually to straighten the glass in his hand.

Dr. Helm drank only coffee. He put down his cup and said: "There is a secret joy in sitting calmly in the open air in a city one loves—an hour before dawn. In Prague, in Paris. It is at hand, but one cannot see it. There is no awkward detail to arrest your attention."

Fräulein Klari from far above, again without emphasis, said: "There is no such city. Even the blessed do not know of any city where there is no awkward detail to arrest the attention." Then suddenly she descended from the seraphic realm and addressed Erich Maria Remarque. "I was born in Salzburg. I was a shop girl here. My parents moved to Vienna. When I return here in the winter I know almost everyone I pass in the street."

There was a pause.

"You have no affection for Salzburg?" I asked.

Again she rose into the upper air; her words drifted down to us like pollen. "There is no city on earth that one can love. That city will come."

The absence of emphasis in her words prevented their disrupting our meditative contentment.

The sky lightened. A cooler breeze began to lift the corners of the tablecloth.

At a quarter before six we heard the tinkle of a bell at the end of the long station platform in the direction of the town. A priest was approaching. It was his duty to officiate at Mass for the railroad workers. In his hands he bore the Host on a patten under its veil; an acolyte preceded him, wearing a cotta none too fresh, and ringing his small silver bell. Remarque drew in his long legs to let him pass. Only two of us took notice of his office. Josef faced him and lowered his head; Fräulein Mitzi rose and genuflected.

Molnár's hotel was across the street. Hans Albers raised his voice and said:

"Franz! Franz! You must go to bed—"

Molnár opened his eyes and, like an owl, blinked at the horrid dawn. They took their departure. Remarque bowed to the ladies and gentlemen and hailed a carriage. Dr. Helm offered to take the ladies to their lodging. They thanked him in the Viennese dialect for the pleasure of the evening, but they wished to stay a little longer at the railway station. Fräulein Mitzi wished to hear Mass; Fräulein Klari was lost in thought and did not wish interruption.

We moved into the refreshment bar. Mass was being served in the baggage room that adjoined it. The crowd was so huge that the door could not be firmly closed to contain them. The workers on the line, section Salzkammergut, arrived every morning with their families. Their wives had served them coffee and rolls and *schnapps* (by dispensation: they were permitted to partake lightly before the office). The wives until the last moment held the lunch they had prepared for their husbands.

There were dozens of children, the girls with handkerchiefs or bits of lace on their heads. Papa did not depart on his daily task unattended.

The Mass came to an end. The congregation passed through the room. The workmen took leave of their large families, who returned to their homes without lingering. The last to appear were the acolyte, who hurried back to the town with his sacred furniture, and the priest, who came through the door, kissing his stole and folding it into one of the capacious pockets of his cassock.

The station policeman came in from the street. I was introduced to Father Grieshaber and the Herr Wachtmann Strohl. Steaming coffee, crowned with whipped cream, was served to all. Herr Strohl turned off the lights as though reluctantly. So there were six of us left in the station room sipping our coffee meditatively: the proprietor, the policeman, the priest, two girls from Vienna, and I.

Suddenly Fräulein Klari said: "Have I no affection for Salzburg? I hate Salzburg."

Father Grieshaber said gently: "My daughter! Moderation! Moderation!"

Klari said quietly: "With all respect to you, Father, the word is not too strong. Mozart—everybody talks about Mozart from morning to night. Mozart hated Salzburg. He hated to put foot in it, he said. No wonder. He was kicked out of the Prince-Archbishop's reception room. On the toe of Count Arcos's boot. With the Prince-Archbishop shouting at him that he was a worthless irresponsible good for nothing."

"Yes, a sad story," said the policeman.

Fräulein Klari subsided into her airy brooding.

"Herr Strunk," I asked, knowing the answer, "are there any Haffners left in Salzburg?"

"Some," he replied, lowering his eyes.

"They played the Haffner Symphony yesterday and they're playing the Haffner Serenade tomorrow."

Josef pointed to the program on the wall. He asked me, "Herr Professor, did you hear *Fidelio* tonight?"

"Yes."

"Frau Lotte Lehmann—very fine?"

"Very, Herr Strunk."

He leaned forward confidentially. "I sang with Frau Lilli Lehmann."

"Oh?"

"She did everything for Salzburg. She was the greatest of all sopranos. With her own money, with her own time, she did it all. In the town theater and in the churches. For love of her and for love of the composer all the greatest artists came and *gave* their work."

"You sang with her, Herr Strunk?"

"I was a boy. I sang in the choir at St. Michael's. She listened to us, one by one, and she picked me to sing one of the boys in *Die Zauberflöte*. They use girls now, don't they?" His hands indicated an ample bosom. "My father sang too; he sang for thirty-five years in the *Sängerverein*. He sang in the chorus of priests and he sang in the Mass. A ticket for my mother was two schillings, Herr Professor. I could have found a ticket for tomorrow night for thirty schillings." He rattled the coins in his pocket. "But a man doesn't go to *Die Zauberflöte* alone—without his mother and his mother-in-law. I would be ashamed. But sixty schillings, *gute Nacht*! We have our opera and theater here in the winter." Again he leaned over the bar and said, "My grandmother was a Haffner. Fräulein Klari has a dozen cousins who are Haffners. Isn't that so, Fräulein?"

"Herr Strunk, I never heard of a Haffner writing music."

Josef mastered his mortification. With Austrian tolerance he said, gently: "Fräulein Klari, you are not an easy person to get on with."

"Oh yes I am," she said, "when people are not talking about dead things."

The policeman had been thinking. "I cannot take my wife and mother-in-law to the operas. Every other night I have to stand at the back of the hall beside the fireman. I listen, but I can't help thinking: Everybody here paid thirty schillings. —Father Grieshaber, I ask myself, too: do rich people hear the same notes as poor people?"

The priest laughed. "Oh, my young man,—what a question!"

The policeman looked around timidly. "Is that a very stupid question?"

"What he means," said Fräulein Klari, smiling at the dawn,

"do they love in the same way, do they weep at the same things, do they say 'God' in the same way. That is not a stupid question."

Fräulein Mitzi rose in indignation. "Klari, shut your face. I'll never come on a vacation with you again. All you do is *think*— think awful things." And Fräulein Mitzi burst into tears.

Father Grieshaber turned to Fräulein Mitzi and spoke to her soothingly in the dialect. I could not understand. Then he turned to Fräulein Klari. "Fräulein Klari, say what you wish to say; say it to the end."

Fräulein Klari looked at him evenly for a moment. Then she turned back to the policeman. "Herr Torgd, ask me. I know. I have been a lady's maid in five palaces and castles. Ask me. Listen. Everybody says that the poor have cares (*Sorgen*). That's just a word. It is the rich who have cares. We have sufferings (*Leiden*). Sufferings are great; they are unbearable, but we learn to protect ourselves against them. And we can rejoice when they are lifted. My mother and father, and Herr Strunk's mother and father—do you remember the war?—what suffering. But Saturday evenings at the White Stag—what laughter! As a young girl I could not believe my eyes when I saw my parents laughing so. But cares do not come and go; they are a blanket over the rich man's house. Ask a lady's maid. Everything irritates them; nothing is ever right. My parents had small envies, small rivalries, small ambitions. But in a palace there is nothing but envy, rivalry, and ambition. Now I will answer you: your Mozart wrote about joy and suffering, but he did not *stoop* to write about cares. The thirty-schilling audience, of course, does not hear the same notes. They are so accustomed to cares that they have forgotten what it is to suffer. Now I will say something else: *Only a poor man can love.* Ask me. I know!"

Again Fräulein Mitzi rose outraged. "Shameless." She covered her ears. "Father, make her stop."

"But Christ said the same thing!" replied Father Grieshaber.

Fräulein Klari said: "Now I am finished. I hate Salzburg and all this art, art, art. All the arts are childish. They prevent men from seeing the work that must be done. Burn your concert halls and opera houses. Bring down fire from heaven on your art galleries and on your cathedrals," here she turned on me and cried, "on your Cafe Mirabells."

CHRONOLOGY

NOTE ON THE TEXTS

NOTES

Chronology

<table>
<tr><td>1897</td><td>Thornton Niven Wilder born April 17 in Madison, Wisconsin, second child of Amos Parker Wilder and Isabella Thornton Niven. (He is named after grandfather Thornton McNess Niven, Jr. [1836–1908], a Presbyterian minister who served as chaplain under General Thomas "Stonewall" Jackson during the Civil War, and great-grandfather Thornton McNess Niven [1806–1895], a Hudson Valley engineer and builder. Father, born 1862 in Calais, Maine, the grandson of a Revolutionary War veteran, graduated from Yale in 1884 and received a Ph.D. in political economy in 1892; he became a renowned public speaker, and edited and eventually owned the *Wisconsin State Journal*. Mother, born 1873 in Dobbs Ferry, New York, was the great-granddaughter of Arthur Tappan [1786–1865], cofounder with his brother Lewis of the American Antislavery Society; she did not attend college but acquired an excellent education in literature, languages, music, and art, wrote poetry, and translated from Italian and French. Parents married on December 3, 1894; their first child, Amos Niven, was born in 1895.) Thornton's twin brother dies at birth. According to family legend, infant Thornton is so frail he is carried around on a pillow.</td></tr>
<tr><td>1898</td><td>Sister Charlotte Elizabeth born.</td></tr>
<tr><td>1900</td><td>Sister Isabel born.</td></tr>
<tr><td>1905–7</td><td>Through his Yale friend William Howard Taft, then Secretary of War, Amos Wilder is appointed consul general in Hong Kong. Family arrives in China on May 7, 1906. Thornton briefly attends local German school. Returns to the United States in October 1906 with mother, brother, and sisters, living in Berkeley, California. Studies violin and piano, and sings in Episcopal church choir. Attends McKinley and Emerson public schools. Conducts home theatricals. Watches rehearsals and has walk-on parts in productions at the University of California's Greek Theater.</td></tr>
<tr><td>1909</td><td>Father is posted to Shanghai and has home leave to visit family in California.</td></tr>
</table>

1910   Sister Janet Frances born. Thornton travels to China with
            his mother and sisters Isabel and Charlotte in December.

1911–13   After briefly taking classes at a German school in Shanghai,
            is enrolled in the British-run China Inland Mission School
            450 miles away in Chefoo (Yantai), where future publisher
            Henry Luce is a fellow student. Early in 1911, because of her
            health and political instability in China, mother takes two
            youngest children to Italy and Switzerland, where they re-
            main for two years. In 1912, Thornton returns to America
            with sister Charlotte and joins brother Amos at the Thacher
            School in Ojai, California, where he co-writes and directs his
            first play, *The Russian Princess*, playing the role of the villain,
            the Grand Duke Alexis. Father refuses to allow him to play
            Lady Bracknell in school production of *The Importance of
            Being Earnest*. Mother returns to Berkeley in spring 1913,
            reuniting the Wilder children under one roof; Thornton
            transfers to Berkeley High School, where he is active in the
            dramatic and vaudeville clubs and begins writing a series of
            three-minute plays. Is an indifferent student but a voracious
            reader: reads Shakespeare, Dickens, Henry James, Scott,
            and German classics. Sees Sarah Bernhardt, Sidney Howard,
            and Sir Johnston Forbes-Robertson perform. In summer
            1913, goes to San Luis Obispo, where he spends first of sev-
            eral summers doing farm work.

1914–15   Father resigns from the Consular Service for medical rea-
            sons and relocates to New Haven, Connecticut, to as-
            sume post of General Secretary of the Yale-in-China
            program. Thornton graduates from Berkeley High School
            in June 1915. At father's insistence, enrolls in the fall at
            Oberlin College. Writes to a former teacher: "I have [my
            father's] promise in writing for one year only. Then Yale,
            and I hope Prof. [George Pierce] Baker's class for post-
            graduate at Harvard."

1916–17   Stays two years at Oberlin, where he befriends fellow stu-
            dent Robert Maynard Hutchins, studies the organ, con-
            tinues writing plays, and publishes in the *Oberlin Literary
            Magazine*; finds a mentor in English professor Charles
            H. A. Wager. During the summers, works on farms in
            Kentucky, Vermont, and Massachusetts. In September
            1917, enrolls at Yale (repeating sophomore year), where
            his contemporaries include Hutchins, Luce, Stephen Vin-
            cent Benét, Reginald Marsh, John Farrar, and Philip
            Barry. Important teachers are William Lyon Phelps and
            Chauncey Brewster Tinker.

1918–19   Wilder continues busily seeing plays, writing mostly drama, including several full-length plays, among them *The Trumpet Shall Sound*. In 1918, wins the John Hubbard Curtis Prize for his short story "'Spiritus Valet.'" Spends summer 1918 working as clerk in the War Industries Board in Washington, D.C. In September 1918, joins the Army's First Coast Artillery Corps stationed at Fort Adams, on Narragansett Bay outside Newport, Rhode Island; is discharged as a corporal and returns to Yale shortly after war's end. Reviews plays for *The Boston Transcript*, and is critical of conventional melodrama and frothy comedies; is active in Yale's Elizabethan Club. First three acts of four-act play *The Trumpet Shall Sound* are published in the *Yale Literary Magazine*.

1920   *The Trumpet Shall Sound* receives Yale's Bradford Brinton Award after its final act is published in the *Yale Literary Magazine*. Wilder graduates from Yale in June, and works on Connecticut farm during the summer. In the fall, begins an eight-month residency at the American Academy in Rome, informally studying archeology. (He later wrote: "For a while in Rome I lived among archeologists, and ever since I find myself occasionally looking at the things about me as an archeologist will look at them a thousand years hence.")

1921   Writes to his mother in April: "I have found an Italian playwright whose plays I adore, the Sicilian Luigi Pirandello. Philosophical farces, actually,—strange contorted domestic situations illustrating some metaphysical proposition. . . ." Attends the first performance in Rome of Pirandello's *Six Characters in Search of an Author*. Is introduced to modern German expressionist drama. Meets Ezra Pound. Concludes his postgraduate year abroad with a six-week stay in Paris, where he begins writing "Memoirs of a Roman Student," which becomes his first novel, *The Cabala*. Reads Proust, Flaubert, and Madame de Sévigné. In June accepts offer, arranged by his father, to teach French at the Lawrenceville School, a preparatory school for boys near Princeton, New Jersey. Meets Stark Young on the return voyage.

1922–24   Establishes himself as a successful teacher and assistant dormitory master at Lawrenceville and as a speaker in local literary circles; reads extensively in seventeenth- and eighteenth-century French literature in the Princeton library; works on drama and *The Cabala* (he submits an

early version, under the title "The Trasteverine," to the
Dial Press, which rejects it). Attends theater whenever
possible in New York, Trenton, and Philadelphia, where,
in 1923, he meets producer and director Max Reinhardt.
Publishes pieces in the magazine *S4N*, and brief excerpts
from *The Cabala* in *The Double Dealer,* a New Orleans literary journal. Continually writes plays. In 1924, makes the
first of ten stays at the MacDowell Colony in Peterbor-
ough, New Hampshire, where he meets Edwin Arlington
Robinson and other authors, painters, and composers. Requests and is granted a two-year leave from Lawrenceville.

1925   Studies for a master's degree in French literature at
            Princeton and works to complete *The Cabala*, which is
            accepted for publication by Albert & Charles Boni in No-
            vember. Covers Broadway for *Theatre Arts.*

1926   Writes to a friend in January: "I am full of plays that can't
            get written. I can't sleep. I am hateful." *The Cabala* is
            published to critical acclaim in England and America; in
            April *The New York Times* hails "the debut of a new
            American stylist" and calls it a "magnificent literary
            event." Receives MA. Starts work on *The Bridge of San
            Luis Rey* at the MacDowell Colony during the summer. In
            the fall, chaperones a young man around Europe; is in-
            troduced to Ernest Hemingway by Sylvia Beach in Paris.
            Is unable to attend December premiere of his revised ver-
            sion of *The Trumpet Shall Sound*, directed by Richard
            Boleslavsky, at the American Laboratory Theatre in New
            York, a production that is reviewed unfavorably.

1927   After living in Connecticut while working on *The Bridge
            of San Luis Rey*, returns to Lawrenceville in July as master
            of Davis House. Accepts a commission to translate novel
            Paulina 1880 by Pierre-Jean Jouve for Longmans, Green
            (the translation, never published, may not have been
            completed; the manuscript is almost certainly lost). In
            November, *The Bridge of San Luis Rey* is published by Al-
            bert & Charles Boni to immediate acclaim on both sides
            of the Atlantic. (To a friend, he later wrote: "It seems to
            me that my books are about: what is the worst thing that
            the world can do to you, and what are the last resources
            one has to oppose it. In other words: when a human
            being is made to bear more than human beings can bear
            —what then? . . . *The Bridge* asked the question whether
            the intention that lies behind love was sufficient to justify

the desperation of living.") During Christmas holiday in Miami, meets boxer Gene Tunney and producer and director Jed Harris.

1928   Meets F. Scott Fitzgerald and Edmund Wilson at Fitzgerald's house in Delaware. Writes to Fitzgerald that he enjoys teaching at Lawrenceville and will probably remain there "for ages"; "a daily routine is necessary to me: I have no writing habits, am terribly lazy and write seldom." In May, delivers the Daniel S. Lamont Memorial Lecture at Yale, his first major public lecture, on "English Letters and Letter Writers." Rents a house for his mother and sisters Isabel and Janet for an extended stay in and around London. Travels to Europe, and studies the work and techniques of European dramatists and theater companies by attending performances in Germany, Austria, and Hungary. Is awarded the Pulitzer Prize for *The Bridge of San Luis Rey*. Hikes the Alps and motors through the south of France with Tunney; begins work on novel *The Woman of Andros*. In November, *The Angel That Troubled the Water and Other Plays* is published; some of the plays are published in periodicals.

1929   Wilder returns from Europe in January and, under lecturing contract with the Lee Keedick Agency, sets out on a two-month cross-country lecture tour. His royalties and related professional fees are now the main support of his parents and two youngest sisters, and in March he buys property on Deepwood Drive in Hamden, Connecticut, to build a house for the family, referring to it later as "The House *The Bridge* Built." Sister Isabel and lawyer J. Dwight Dana assume duties of caring for his business and domestic arrangements. Wilder travels to Europe with mother; sees Tunney and Hemingway. Film (mostly silent, with a segment in sound at the end) of *The Bridge of San Luis Rey*, directed by Charles Brabin, is released.

1930–31   Accepts invitation from his close friend Robert Maynard Hutchins, now president of the University of Chicago, to serve as a part-time faculty member teaching classics and writing at the university for spring quarter of 1930; the appointment, during which he teaches no more than two quarters each year, extends through 1936. *The Woman of Andros* is published in February 1930 and becomes a best seller; in *The New Republic*, Marxist critic Michael Gold attacks it and Wilder's previous work for ignoring social issues. Develops close, lifelong friendships with Ruth

Gordon, Alexander Woollcott, and Sibyl Colefax. *The Long Christmas Dinner and Other Plays in One Act* is published in November 1931.

1932–33   Wilder is asked to translate from German and adapt *The Bride of Torozko*, a play about religious prejudice in a Hungarian town by Hungarian playwright Otto Indig, but project stumbles (play is staged on Broadway in 1934, and Wilder's version is not used). In summer 1932, begins to work intensively on novel *Heaven's My Destination*. Wilder's translation of André Obey's play *Le Viol de Lucrèce* opens late in 1932 in New York as *Lucrece*, starring Katharine Cornell and Brian Aherne and directed by Guthrie McClintic; it runs for thirty-one performances. *Lucrece* is published by Houghton Mifflin in 1933. Reads the European comedies of Nestroy, Raimund, Goldoni, and Lessing, "just to make sure," as he writes later to Ruth Gordon, "that I've expunged every lurking vestige of what Sam Behrman and George Kaufman think comedy is."

1934   Wilder goes to Hollywood to work on a film treatment of *Joan of Arc* for RKO studios, to star Katharine Hepburn and to be directed by George Cukor; film is never made. Also does writing jobs for Samuel Goldwyn, including work on *We Live Again* (film based on Tolstoy's novel *Resurrection*) and *Dark Angel*. Turns down other major film assignments (as he will later do). Back at the University of Chicago, meets Gertrude Stein, who comes to lecture in November.

1935   *Heaven's My Destination* is brought out by his new publisher, Harper & Brothers, in January. Stein's *Narration: Four Lectures* is published with an introduction by Wilder. During a leave of absence from University of Chicago, he spends six months in Europe in the summer and fall, seeing Stein, Alice B. Toklas, Franz Werfel, Max Reinhardt, Pablo Picasso, and Sigmund Freud. Upon returning to America tells reporters that he intends to "abandon" the novel in favor of writing only plays, viewing the novel's omniscient voice as "out of gear with twentieth-century life" and drama "the new vehicle to succeed the narrative form." His journal notes include ideas for ten plays, among them "M Marries N" (an early working title for *Our Town*) and *The Merchant of Yonkers*.

1936   Father dies on July 2. Wilder resigns from University of Chicago. Begins work on *Our Town*. Stein's *Geographical*

History of America, with an introduction by Wilder, is published.

1937   Completes his Lee Keedick public-lecture contract, writing his brother: "The new life's begun. Taught my last class. Delivered my last lecture. The living is wonderful, and alarming; but I've plunged jubilantly into work and play no. #1 is almost done; plays no. #2 (on the Arabian Nights) and #3 ('Our Town' . . .) all planned out, as are several more." As a favor, works on a new "acting version" of Ibsen's *A Doll's House* for Jed Harris and Ruth Gordon. Works on plays at the MacDowell Colony in June. In July, travels to Paris as the first American delegate to the Institut de Coopération Intellectuel of the League of Nations, and delivers a lecture in French; sees E. M. Forster, Orson Welles, and Coco Chanel. Visits Stein and Toklas at their home in Bilignin, and attends Salzburg Festival. Retires for the fall to seclusion in Ruschlikon, near Zurich, to complete *Our Town*. Writes Sibyl Colefax in October: "Lord! What I got myself in for. A theologico-metaphisico transcription for the *Purgotorio* with panels of American rural genre-stuff." In December, after a successful tour, his version of *A Doll's House* opens on Broadway.

1938   After one performance in Princeton and a week's run in Boston, *Our Town* opens on Broadway on February 4 to mostly favorable reviews. Later that spring, Wilder is awarded his second Pulitzer Prize. Moves to a hotel in Tucson, Arizona, to complete *The Merchant of Yonkers*. Works on *The Alcestiad*. In September, takes over the role of the Stage Manager in *Our Town* for two weeks. *The Merchant of Yonkers* opens on Broadway on December 28 to a disappointing reception.

1939   Travels in Mexico and Texas, then goes to Europe in May and stays through the end of June; sees Jean Cocteau, Ruth Draper, Gertrude Stein, and Sibyl Colefax. Returns home and plays the Stage Manager in summer-stock productions of *Our Town* in Pennsylvania and Massachusetts. Describes his enthusiasm for James Joyce's *Finnegans Wake* as his "constant new companion." Devotes fall to nonfiction, except for an adaptation for Broadway of *The Beaux' Stratagem* for producer Cheryl Crawford, which he does not finish. Completes statement on the nature of theater ("Some Thoughts on Playwriting," published in

1941) and an introduction for an edition of *Oedipus Rex* (not published until 1955). Producer Sol Lesser appeals for his help in adapting *Our Town* for the screen, a task that involves meetings and continuous collaboration via letters and telegrams over several months.

1940   Stirred by news of events in Europe and inspired by ideas in Joyce, Wilder begins working on a play called *The Ends of the Worlds* that will become *The Skin of Our Teeth*. Attends May 22 premiere in Boston of film version of *Our Town*, directed by Sam Wood and starring William Holden and Martha Scott. Acts in summer-stock productions of *Our Town*. Goes to Quebec City for several weeks to work on *The Skin of Our Teeth*.

1941   Puts aside work on play to travel in late winter and spring to Columbia, Ecuador, and Peru at behest of the State Department's Bureau of Educational and Cultural Affairs, for which he studies Spanish intensively. Reads the letters of Simón Bolívar. Teaches a double load during the summer term at the University of Chicago. Travels to England with John Dos Passos as American representatives to the International Committee of PEN; meets with H. G. Wells, Edith Evans, E. M. Forster, and Cecil Beaton. Resumes work on *The Skin of Our Teeth* late in the year.

1942   Completes *The Skin of Our Teeth*. In May 1942, is accepted into the Army Air Intelligence and declares he would take "the khaki veil with an explosive cry of relief." Before reporting for duty, goes to Hollywood to write the screenplay for Alfred Hitchcock's *Shadow of a Doubt*, based on a scenario by Gordon McDonnell. On June 26, begins six weeks of basic training in Miami, then reports to Harrisburg, Pennsylvania, for Intelligence School, and is assigned as a captain to the headquarters of the 328th Fighter Group at Hamilton Field, California, and later to Washington, D.C. After previews in New Haven, Baltimore, and Philadelphia, *The Skin of Our Teeth* opens on Broadway on November 18. The next month, in *The Saturday Review of Literature*, Joseph Campbell and Henry Morton Robinson attack the play as stolen "in conception and detail" from James Joyce's *Finnegans Wake*, a charge Wilder chooses not to answer publicly, although he writes that "the ant-like industry of pedants, collecting isolated fragments, has mistaken the nature of literary influence since the first critics arose to regard books as a branch of merchandise instead of an expression of energy."

1943   In spring, Wilder is awarded his third Pulitzer Prize. Receives promotion to major on April 15, and is shipped overseas to the intelligence section of the Twelfth Air Force in Constantine, Algeria, and later to Algiers, where he is involved in planning operations. Is promoted to lieutenant colonel on August 27, 1944, and is posted to Caserta, Italy.

1944   Spends three days in Rome, his first visit since his American Academy residency. Directs all-military production of *Our Town* in Caserta. Second film adaptation of *The Bridge of San Luis Rey*, directed by Rowland V. Lee and starring Lynn Bari, Francis Lederer, and Alla Nazimova, is released. *The Skin of Our Teeth* and *Our Town* are produced in Switzerland; the latter, again directed by Jed Harris, has its first major New York revival.

1945   Wilder goes to Belgrade in February for performance of Serbo-Croatian version of *Our Town* staged by Tito's Partisans. During the Italian campaign, continues to prepare intelligence material and interrogate prisoners. Is awarded Bronze Star. Returns to America in May and is discharged from the Air Force in September. Because of poor health, cannot accept the post of cultural attaché at U.S. Embassy in Paris. Resumes work on *The Alcestiad* but puts it aside in November to concentrate on the novel *The Ides of March*. Reads Kierkegaard and avidly follows periodical literature on the new vogue of existentialism.

1946   In January at Yale, meets Jean-Paul Sartre, who asks him to translate his play *Morts sans sépulture*. Works on *The Ides of March*. Mother dies on June 29. Wilder writes short play in honor of the Century Club's centenary and records radio broadcast of *Our Town* for Theatre Guild on September 29. Receives Order of the British Empire (O.B.E.) for wartime service.

1947   Travels to the Yucatan Pennisula at the end of January, then on to Florida in April, working on *The Ides of March*. Writes in April to his agent: "I hate being alone. And I hate writing. But I can only write when I'm alone. So these working spells combine both my antipathies." Is awarded honorary doctorate by Yale in June. Completes introduction to Gertrude Stein's *Four in America* in July, and finishes *The Ides of March* in the fall.

1948   Travels to London in January to consult about Laurence Olivier's production of *The Skin of Our Teeth*. Meets T. S.

Eliot, V. S. Pritchett, Kenneth Tynan, and Peter Ustinov. Sees Sartre in Paris in February. *The Ides of March* is published on January 16. In an interview, he says: "Modern man has taken such pride in the exploration of his mind that he has forgotten there must be some laws governing that exploration. Whether it comes under religion or ethics or mere judgment, such laws must be found and respected. Otherwise the mind leads him straight to self-destruction. So my book is Caesar's groping in the open seas of his unlimited power for the first principles which should guide him." Plays Mr. Antrobus in summer-stock productions of *The Skin of Our Teeth* in Massachusetts, Connecticut, and Pennsylvania. By this time, has embarked on his voluminous scholarship on the career of Spanish dramatist Lope de Vega (1562–1635), a passion comparable to his long devotion to *Finnegans Wake*. In November, lectures for two weeks at the University of Frankfurt on "The American Character as Mirrored in Literature," and later at universities of Heidelberg and Marburg; spends two days in Berlin meeting students during the Berlin Airlift. Continues on to Switzerland, Italy, and Spain. His translation of Sartre's *Mort sans sépulture* is produced Off Broadway as *The Victors* in December to mixed reviews.

1949   Wilder returns to Hamden. Works on a new play, *The Emporium*. Visits Ezra Pound at St. Elizabeths Hospital. Is awarded honorary degrees by New York University and Kenyon College. Delivers lecture "World Literature and the Modern Mind" on the occasion of the Goethe Bicentennial at the Aspen Festival in June, where he also translates addresses by Albert Schweitzer and José Ortega y Gasset.

1950   Travels in Europe in spring; sees Max Beerbohm, Sacheverell Sitwell, and Noel Coward. Returns to the United States to accept honorary degree and perform in *Our Town* at the College of Wooster. Plays Stage Manager in *Our Town* at the Wellesley Summer Theatre, "the twelfth company I've played it with," he writes to Laurence Olivier and Vivien Leigh, adding "I advise every playwright to get somehow somewhere *that* side of the footlights." Accepts appointment as Harvard's 1950–51 Charles Eliot Norton Professor of Poetry, a position requiring six public lectures to be published by Harvard University Press. Moves into Dunster House in September; in addition to lecturing, agrees to teach large American literature class, and accepts scores of invitations to talk and meet with students and groups in Boston area. Lectures on Thoreau, Poe, Melville, Dickinson, and Whitman in a series entitled "The American Characteristics in Classic American Literature."

1951   Collapses from exhaustion March 9 and is hospitalized for several weeks. Resumes lighter schedule. Gives the 1951 Harvard Alumni Association's Commencement Address on June 21. Calls the Harvard experience the hardest year of his life. Receives honorary degrees from Harvard and from Northwestern University in June. That fall, travels to Europe to revise his Norton lectures for publication, a project that is ultimately never completed.

1952   Throughout the year, works on various projects: the Norton lectures, *The Emporium*, *The Alcestiad*, a possible screenplay for Vittorio De Sica, and a Christmas pageant play called *The Sandusky, Ohio, Mystery Play*. In May, is awarded the Gold Medal for Fiction by the American Academy of Arts and Letters. In June, receives honorary degree from Oberlin. Spends summer at MacDowell Colony. In September, heads the American delegation to a UNESCO congress in Venice. Travels to Paris to meet with Ruth Gordon and Tyrone Guthrie, who have asked him to consider revising *The Merchant of Yonkers*. Versions of three of his Harvard lectures are published in the *Atlantic Monthly*.

1953   Returns to America and resumes work on old projects. Is featured on cover of *Time*, June 12. Returns to MacDowell Colony late summer. Continues to work on *The Emporium*; finishes revisions of *The Merchant of Yonkers*.

1954   *The Merchant of Yonkers* opens successfully as *The Matchmaker* at the Edinburgh Festival in June, directed by Tyrone Guthrie and starring Ruth Gordon. "If I do finish *The Emporium* by July I'll be a very blithe fellow, indeed, and a public nuisance in Edinburgh. Of course, if I could finish the four-year-late Harvard lectures, too, all Europe would rock," he writes to Gordon. After a well-received tour, *The Matchmaker* opens a successful run in London. Wilder goes to the Berlin Festival in September, and travels on to Hamburg, Paris, and southern France to work on *The Alcestiad*, which he describes as "a humdinger—the true extension of the *Our Town–Skin* line."

1955–56   On August 22, 1955, *The Alcestiad*, retitled *A Life in the Sun*, opens at the Edinburgh Festival, directed by Guthrie and starring Irene Worth, to generally negative reviews. Wilder begins collaboration with composer Louise Talma on an opera based on *The Alcestiad*. In November *The Matchmaker* moves on to the United States where Wilder is initially involved in production details, but he is in Europe when the play opens on December 5, 1955, on Broadway, where it runs for 486 performances, Wilder's Broadway record. Works and travels in Europe; returns to the U.S. in February 1956. In June, drives to Mexico and back; as has been his lifelong habit, travels to different cities, different continents to work and "regenerate": "What do all of these long stays abroad mean, but my eternal effort to find a time and a place when I can follow an idea through," he writes in May.

1957   Along with *The Happy Journey to Trenton and Camden*, two new one-act plays, *Bernice* (starring Ethel Waters) and *The Wreck on the Five-Twenty-Five*, are performed at Congress Hall in West Berlin in September, with Wilder in the cast. Is inducted into the prestigious German society Orden Pour le Mérite für Wissenschaften und Künste. In October, is awarded the German Book Sellers Peace Prize in Frankfurt, the first American to receive this prize, delivering an address, "Culture in a Democracy," in German to audience of two thousand guests. Is awarded honorary degree by the Goethe University (Frankfurt) and receives Austria's Medal of Honor for Science and Fine Arts. Contributes preface to *Three Plays by Thornton Wilder: Our Town, The Skin of Our Teeth, The Matchmaker*.

1958   In Washington in February, receives a medal from the Peruvian government. Works on cycle of one-act plays, "The Seven Ages of Man" and "The Seven Deadly Sins," intended to be performed on an arena stage. Works with Norman Bel Geddes on "epic film" called *The Melting Pot*, but project ends when Geddes dies in May. In August Paramount Pictures releases a film version of *The Matchmaker*, directed by Joseph Anthony and starring Shirley Booth, Anthony Perkins, and Shirley MacLaine.

1959   Travels in Europe. "It's not quite clear to me what I'm doing in Europe," he writes. "I seem to remember that I came here to work, and work went fine on the boat and then I got joined to various human communities. . . .

But, boy do I work! The lives—the life-stories that I've entered." Back in the U.S., he deals with business matters, works to finish his "Seven Deadly Sins" plays, and in August acts as the Stage Manager in *Our Town* at Williamstown, Massachusetts, his final appearance as an actor.

1960–61   Continues work on "Seven Deadly Sins," and now a new cycle on the "Seven Ages of Man." Offers to help Katharine Hepburn and Spencer Tracy fashion a movie from *The Skin of Our Teeth*, but nothing comes of the project. Helps Jerome Kilty adapt *The Ides of March* for the stage. Adapts *The Long Christmas Dinner* for use as a one-act opera libretto set by composer Paul Hindemith; in German translation, the opera premieres in Mannheim, West Germany, on December 26, 1961.

1962–64   *Plays for Bleecker Street* (comprising three one-act plays: *Someone from Assisi, Infancy*, and *Childhood*) opens Off Broadway and enjoys a successful run. In German translation, the Wilder-Talma opera based on *The Alcestiad* opens in Frankfurt on March 1, 1962, to twenty-minute ovation. Wilder presents "An Evening with Thornton Wilder" to President Kennedy's cabinet in Washington, D.C., on April 11. On May 20, 1962, departs for a long retreat in the Arizona desert; by late May is in Douglas, Arizona. Here he stays twenty months, initially in a hotel, and by the fall of 1962 in an efficiency apartment. By the end of the year has put aside work on his "Seven Deadly Sins" and "Seven Ages of Man" plays and begins working on a novel that becomes *The Eighth Day*. In March 1963, reveals this work for the first time to his family, describing his story as "*Little Women* being mulled over by Dostoevsky." Theatrical adaptation of *The Ides of March*, starring John Gielgud and Irene Worth, opens in London in June 1963 but soon closes. Wilder leaves Douglas in late November 1963 to accept the Presidential Medal of Freedom at the White House on December 6, announced the previous July by President Kennedy but conferred by President Johnson after Kennedy's assassination. *Hello, Dolly!*, a musical adaptation of *The Matchmaker*, opens on Broadway, on January 16, 1964; royalties provide Wilder financial security for the rest of his life.

1965–67   Wilder resumes extensive foreign and domestic travel, working almost exclusively on *The Eighth Day*. On May 4, 1965, Lady Bird Johnson awards him the National Book

Committee's first Medal for Literature at the White House. He completes *The Eighth Day* and reads proofs in Innsbruck, Austria, in November 1966. *The Eighth Day* is published on March 29, 1967; it is a critical and financial success, and receives the National Book Award for Fiction. In September 1967, Wilder buys second home at Katama Point on Martha's Vineyard with his sister Isabel.

1968–75   Travels often, with stops in Paris, Munich, Milan, Venice, Zurich, Cannes, Florida, New York, and Martha's Vineyard. Begins to suffer from circulatory problems; eye problems and hearing worsen. Writes to Gene Tunney in 1970: "Physical pain is the summit of aloneness, of solitude. I tried to catch glimpses of a companionship in Endurance." Toys with many writing ideas, but settles into writing a series of semi-autobiographical chapters. One of them, drawing on many affectionate visits to Newport, Rhode Island, grows into his novel *Theophilus North*, written between April 1972 and April 1973 and published in October 1973; critically praised, it becomes a best seller. To friends he writes: "The book is about the humane impulse to be useful, about compassion, and about nondemanding love." Continues to travel but is more and more confined to Hamden home. Begins work on sequel to *Theophilus North*. Spends summer of 1975 on Martha's Vineyard; is operated on in September for a cancerous prostate. Dies of an apparent heart attack at home in Hamden on December 7, 1975. Buried at Mt. Carmel Cemetery, Hamden, Connecticut.

Note on the Texts

This volume contains Thornton Wilder's novels *The Eighth Day* (1967) and *Theophilus North* (1973), and three excerpts, written in 1968 and 1969, from a previously unpublished manuscript that is a mixture of autobiography and fiction.

Wilder began working on the novel that became *The Eighth Day* toward the end of 1962, during a twenty-month stay in the desert town of Douglas, Arizona. He continued writing the novel (with the working title "Make Straight in the Desert") after leaving Douglas in November 1963 and traveling widely in North America and Europe in the years that followed. As he wrote to his sister Isabel from St. Moritz on February 17, 1964, "I work as regularly as ever I have worked in my life—yet so much of it is expansion and enrichment of what is already written." After submitting the manuscript to Harper & Row he read proofs of *The Eighth Day* in Innsbruck, Austria, in November 1966. The book was published by Harper & Row in New York on March 29, 1967, and simultaneously in London by Longmans, Green & Co. It received the National Book Award for 1968, judged by Granville Hicks, Josephine Herbst, and John Updike. The text printed here is taken from the 1967 Harper & Row edition of *The Eighth Day*.

Theophilus North emerged out of Wilder's late efforts to combine autobiography and fiction, as he had done to some extent in his first novel, *The Cabala* (1926). As early as 1967, he was working on a semi-autobiographical project that, while told in the first person and based on experiences from the first half of his life, included invented characters. As he wrote to his friend, the actor Ruth Gordon, on August 15, 1968, he was writing "episodes from my life into each of which I introduce one fictional person. Each of these stories begins and ends with extended accounts that *really* happened—then enters a catalyst who precipitates on a more significant level the essence of time and place." Wilder never completed this project (excerpts from it are included in this volume's "Autobiographical Writings" section; see below), but the autobiographical impulse was also central to *Theophilus North*: like the title character, Wilder had spent a summer in Newport as a tutor in the 1920s (in 1922, whereas the novel is set in the summer of 1926) and had taught in a boys' school in New Jersey. He also characterized the book in a 1974 letter to one of his Yale classmates as "mostly wish-fulfillment fantasy" about his twin brother who died at birth: "he lived an hour; if he had survived he'd have been named

Theophilus—second sons have been so named for generations in the Wilder line—so I wrote his memoirs." *Theophilus North* was written between April 1972 and April 1973 and published by Harper & Row in October 1973; an English edition published by Allan Lane (for which Wilder made no revisions) followed in June 1974. This volume prints the text of the 1973 Harper & Row edition of *Theophilus North*.

The three excerpts from the incomplete semi-autobiographical manuscript described above are presented in the order that it appears Wilder would have used had he finished the book. The chapters were not written in chronological order. A draft of "Chefoo, China," which was to be the first chapter, was completed in late 1968, then rewritten in early 1969. "New Haven, 1920" was written by mid-February 1969. "Salzburg" was drafted by August 1968. The texts printed here are taken from transcriptions made by Donald C. Gallup, former Curator of American Literature at the Beinecke Rare Book and Manuscript Library, Yale University, based on manuscripts among Wilder's papers there.

This volume presents the texts of the original printings chosen for inclusion here, but it does not attempt to reproduce nontextual features of their typographic design. The texts are presented without change, except for the correction of typographical errors. Spelling, punctuation, and capitalization are often expressive features and are not altered, even when inconsistent or irregular. The following is a list of typographical errors corrected, cited by page and line number: 52.36, Constance go; 75.6, The; 86.18, Women's; 110.32, money?; 115.1, María; 116.26, softly.; 124.10, You grandmother; 132.10, delight,; 140.28, ") He; 141. 34, "Then; 146.6, alcoholism; 165.38, Mr Tolland; 169.29, match,; 188.15, Lu.; 190.4, is to; 218.8, Ashley's; 251.24, perfecly; 263.7, disinguish; 266.29, Sim's; 269.31, exellent; 276.16, adopted The; 278.24, charming,; 290.36, Watts; 298.12, hundred; 298.39, Maman; 303.14, morning becomes; 307.39, month.; 315.5, creature; 318.13, Silence,; 319.30, Bay; 320.17, better?; 323.38, March from Saul."; 328.27, *Maman's*; 328.31, *Père's*; 328.31, Père; 329.22, happy.; 330.42, hallelujah?" '; 332.30, tyrannis'.; 332.39, he is.; 336.7, October,; 336.22, education.'); 336.33, Macbeth; 336.37, "Your; 342.30, cried.; 344.14–15, father's return); 346.23, The; 352.2, Ashley-Nishimura; 357.29, He said.; 359.3, finshed; 362.14, movement they; 366.30, man.; 373.22, Roger's and Félicite's; 388.33, block,; 438.18, call; 459.24, fruit,; 473.3–4, "The Curfew Shall not Ring Tonight"; 474.30, say.; 475.1, Bosworth.; 504.15, wrote: Mr.; 521.18, yours," et cetera, et cetera.; 541.19, Louis's; 600.5, sorrow. . . ?, and; 609.21, Cole an; 637.7, See.; 637.7, der; 637.12, thing.; 640.5, were reward; 661.37, Bodl!; 662.8, Beside; 705.23, "Nine Gables".

Notes

In the notes below, the reference numbers denote page and line of this volume (the line count includes headings). No note is made for material included in standard desk-reference books. Biblical quotations are keyed to the King James Version. For more biographical information than is contained in the Chronology, see Gilbert Harrison, *The Enthusiast* (New Haven, CT: Ticknor & Fields, 1983); Penelope Niven, *Thornton Wilder: A Life* (New York: HarperCollins, 2012); Linda Simon, *Thornton Wilder: His World* (Garden City, NY: Doubleday, 1979). Grateful acknowledgment is made to Penelope Niven, Robin Gibbs Wilder, and Tappan Wilder for their assistance with the Chronology.

THE EIGHTH DAY

1.1   EIGHTH DAY]   An early Christian term for Sunday, or the Lord's Day, but it also refers to the first temporal day after the Creation. In his response to papers on the novel delivered at a 1970 gathering of the Modern Language Association, Amos Niven Wilder, Wilder's older brother and a biblical scholar at Harvard, recalled that Thornton had discussed with him his idea of taking the title for the novel from Isaiah's "Make straight in the desert a highway for our God." He then goes on: "He did not ask me about the title later adopted, and probably is not aware of the fact that in the earliest church the 'eighth' day was the same as the first and connoted not the beginning of a second week but the new creation and the eternal Sabbath of the Resurrection."

13.19   "turtle mounds"]   A less familiar name for Indian middens, deposits of shells made by Native Americans. The largest, in Volusia County, Florida, is about fifty feet high. "Snake mounds," usually referred to as "serpent mounds," are mysterious constructions in serpentine shapes made by ancient Native Americans; the largest known mound is in Adams County, Ohio, in the shape of seven coils stretching eight hundred feet.

18.6–7   the devil in the old story]   The demon Asmodeus hobbles on crutches across rooftops and lifts them up to see what goes on within people's homes in *Le Diable Boiteux* (*The Devil on Two Sticks*, 1707), novel by the French writer Alain-René Lesage (1668–1747).

23.23–24   slapjack and who's-got-the-thimble]   The first is a child's card game. The second is a game in which one child goes round a circle of other children and secretly puts a thimble in one child's hands; when he has finished going round the circle, "Who's got the thimble?" is called out, and all guess who is holding the object.

23.40   muggins]   A domino game.

24.25   that Queen of Prussia]   Louise (1776–1810), renowned for her beauty and grace.

27.15   pan cobble]   Useless rock fragments.

27.16   noggers]   Pieces of the square wooden logs piled together to support the roof of a mine.

28.1   'Nita, Juanita]   Love song with words set to a traditional Spanish tune by English composer Caroline Norton (1808–1877), with the refrain "Nita! Juanita! Ask thy soul if we should part! / Nita! Juanita! Lean thou on my heart."

34.15–16   Fairest . . . Eve]   *Paradise Lost*, bk. 4, line 324.

38.16   Domrémy]   Village in northeastern France where Joan of Arc was born in 1412.

39.23   *Gott . . . Sohn!*]   German: "God protect you, my son!"

41.29–30   Robertson's *Sermons*]   Frederick William Robertson (1816–1853), known as Robertson of Brighton, a famous English preacher whose renowned sermons were eventually gathered in five volumes.

50.20   a man of faith]   Or "knight of faith," concept discussed especially in reference to Abraham in *Fear and Trembling* (1843), treatise by the Danish philosopher Søren Kierkegaard (1813–1855).

55.1   *Rostbraten*]   German: roast beef.

55.3–4   Mid pleasures and palaces!]   The opening phrase of "Home, Sweet Home" (1823), song with words by John Howard Payne (1791–1852) and music by Henry R. Bishop (1786–1855).

63.1   Nellie Melba]   Famed Australian opera soprano (1861–1931).

63.8   Madame Carvalho]   French soprano Marie Caroline Miolan-Carvalho (1827–1895).

63.9   La Piccolomini]   Italian soprano Marietta Piccolomini (1834–1899).

63.10   *recueillement*]   French: a contemplative mood.

74.37–38   sang about . . . vine]   The traditional Southern folk song "Watermelon on the Vine."

74.38–39   sang about . . . table]   Marguerite's aria "Ah, je ris de me voir si belle en ce miroir" ("Ah, I laugh to see myself so beautiful in the mirror"), known as the Jewel Song, from act 3 of *Faust* (1859), opera by French composer Charles Gounod (1818–1893).

75.1 boys in Company B were] Songs from the musical version of *The Boys of Company "B"* (1907), stage comedy by American playwright and songwriter Rida Johnson Young (1875–1926).

75.2–3 sang about Dinorah . . . moonlight] Dinorah's aria "Ombre légère qui suis mes pas" ("Nimble shadow that follows my steps"), known as the Shadow Song, from act 2 of *Dinorah* (1859), opera by German-born composer Giacomo Meyerbeer (1791–1864).

75.12 "I Know That My Redeemer Liveth"] Soprano aria from part three of *Messiah* (1742), oratorio by German-British composer George Frideric Handel (1685–1759).

75.27 Princess of Trebizond] *Saint George and the Princess of Trebizond* (1437–38) is a fresco by the Italian painter Antonio Pisano, known as Pisanello (c. 1395–c. 1455), depicting the valiant saint rescuing the princess from a dragon.

76.34–35 Do you like him . . . not 'Ebenezer.'] I.e., she hasn't decided on him. The expression "to set up one's Ebenezer" meant to "firmly make up one's mind," derived from 1 Samuel 7:12, where Samuel "took a stone . . . and called the name of it Ebenezer [stone of help], saying, Hitherto hath the Lord helped us."

78.34–35, 39–40 "*There's no news . . . Duke*] Cf. Shakespeare, *As You Like It*, I.i.98–103.

81.33 *The Mill on the Floss*] Novel (1860) by English novelist George Eliot (1819–1880).

81.33 *Eugénie Grandet*] Novel (1833) by French novelist Honoré de Balzac (1799–1850).

85.10 Madame Modjeska in *Maria Stuart*] Helena Modjeska (1840–1909), Polish actor famous for her portrayals of Shakespearean heroines, often starred in *Maria Stuart* (1800), play by the German poet and playwright Friedrich Schiller (1759–1805).

90.35–91.1 New Salem, Illinois] Town where Abraham Lincoln lived and began practicing law in 1837.

103.40 *réunions*] French: gatherings.

106.9–14 a relatively obscure scientist . . . philosopher] The German-born physicist Albert Einstein (1879–1955) and the ancient Greek philosopher Plato (c. 428–c. 348 BCE).

106.36 Enoch Arden] The long-suffering, seafaring hero of "Enoch Arden" (1864), poem by British poet Alfred, Lord Tennyson (1809–1892).

117.21 a new Württemberg] The region in southwestern Germany, whose capital is Stuttgart, renowned for its cultural and educational institutions.

118.22   Covenanter's]   A seventeenth-century Scottish Presbyterian movement, fiercely nationalistic and anti-Catholic.

126.21–24   In infinite space . . . myself]   Konstantin Levin's despairing
thoughts in Leo Tolstoy's *Anna Karenina* (1877), pt. 8, chap. 9.

127.39   the parable—the prodigal son]   Cf. Luke 15:11–32.

127.40–128.1   grasshopper . . . summer]   In Aesop's fable, the grasshopper who fiddles and is left starving when winter comes is contrasted with the
ant who has stockpiled food during the summer months.

136.40   *chicha*]   In the Andes, a fermented drink most often made from
maize.

139.14–17   Under the spreading . . . strained]   The opening of "The
Village Blacksmith" (1841), by American poet Henry Wadsworth Longfellow
(1807–1882); speech from Shakespeare, *The Merchant of Venice*, IV.i.184.

153.17   'Suevia Eterna']   Latin: Swabia forever.

176.5   vale of soul-making]   Phrase of the English poet John Keats (1795–
1821), from a letter to his brother George and sister-in-law Georgiana, begun
in February and sent in May 1819.

179.28–29   *Wo ist der verfluchte Kerl?*]   German: "Where is the damn fellow?"

183.10   Lights fools . . . death]   Cf. *Macbeth*, V.v.22–23: "And all our
yesterdays have lighted fools / The way to dusty death."

183.18   Eugene V. Debs]   American union leader (1855–1926), five-time
Socialist Party candidate for president, and often imprisoned for his political
views.

187.23   Mrs. Besant]   Annie Besant (1847–1933), English reformer, theoso-
phist, and writer.

188.14–15   "*Hab kei Gelt . . . ft.*"]   German: "I have no money. . . .
Mother. . . . Help. . . . A . . . i . . . i . . . r." / "Everything's fine,
Mr. Metzger! Sleep a little! Yes!"

193.15   cubebs]   The fruit of an aromatic plant known as "Java pepper."

195.5–6   *The Wit . . . Ingersoll*]   American Civil War veteran Robert G.
Ingersoll (1833–1899) was an orator noted for his rousing defense of freethink-
ing and agnosticism.

195.18   *Fidelio*]   Opera (1814) by German composer Ludwig van
Beethoven (1770–1827).

195.29–33   another opera . . . just]   *Die Zauberflöte* (*The Magic Flute*,
1791) by Austrian composer Wolfgang Amadeus Mozart (1756–1791).

195.38   "printer's devil"]   Slang for a young apprentice in a printing establishment.

197.32   "The Song of the Shirt."]   Poem (1843) by English poet Thomas Hood (1799–1845).

199.36   Schopenhauer's matchless essay]   "On Women" (1851), by German philosopher Arthur Schopenhauer (1788–1860).

203.5   Emma Goldman]   Russian-American anarchist (1869–1940).

207.7   murphies]   Slang for potatoes.

220.39–40   'Sometimes I feel like a motherless child']   Traditional Negro spiritual.

221.2–3   the language . . . Georgia]   I.e., Gullah, a creole English dialect spoken by descendants of Africans who have lived since the mid-eighteenth century on the Sea Islands and other coastal communities of South Carolina and Georgia.

221.7   Lotus Scripture]   Ancient text, better known as the Lotus Sutra.

225.29   Handel's 'Where'er you walk']   Aria from act two of *Semele* (1744), opera by George Frideric Handel.

225.30   '*Oh, promise me.*']   Song (1889) with music by American composer Reginald De Koven (1859–1920) and lyrics by English writer Clement Scott (1841–1904).

226.7–8   Mozart's 'Alleluia']   Exuberant finale of Mozart's sacred motet for soprano and orchestra, *Exsultate, jubilate*, K. 165 (1773).

230.34   *Letters from Turkey*]   *Turkish Embassy Letters*, written between 1716 and 1718 by Lady Mary Wortley Montagu (1689–1762) while her husband was the British ambassador to Turkey.

231.26   Friedrich Froebel]   Friedrich Wilhelm August Froebel (1782–1852), German educator and educational theorist who established the first Kindergarten in 1837.

231.26–27   Jean-Frédéric Oberlin]   German philanthropist (1740–1826) after whom the Ohio college is named.

237.40–238.3   "*Mammi! . . . tesoro*]   Italian: "Mama!" / "Yes, darling. What do you want?" / "Mama, sing!" / "Yes, my precious."

239.36   Bagehot's *Lombard Street*]   Book (1873) of financial analysis by the English author Walter Bagehot (1826–1877).

245.7–8   Beware . . . middle age]   Cf. Goethe's *Dichtung und Wahrheit* (*Poetry and Truth*, 1811–33), pt. 2, chap. 6: "Was man in der Jugend wünscht, hat man im Alter die Fülle" ("What man longs for in youth, he has in abundance in old age"). Citations of this maxim sometimes substitute "middle age" for "old age," as in James Joyce's *Ulysses* (1922), when Stephen Dedalus remarks: "There's a saying of Goethe's which Mr Magee likes to quote. Beware of what you wish for in youth because you will get it in middle life."

247.23   *Goethe und die Tiere*]   German: "Goethe and Animals."

248.32   *Turnverein*'s]   German: athletic club's.

250.36   *Der Freischütz*]   Opera (*The Freeshooter*, 1821) by German composer Carl Maria von Weber (1786–1826).

251.13–14   Heine's *Buch der Lieder*]   *Book of Songs* (1827), collection of poems by German poet Heinrich Heine (1797–1856).

252.32   *en cabochon*]   French (jeweler's term): a domed cut gemstone.

253.7   *Knix*]   German: deep curtsy, required when greeting royalty.

254.17   *Sängervereine*]   German: singing clubs.

256.17   *Bombyx mori*]   Species name (Latin: "silkworm of the mulberry tree") of a domesticated silkworm.

257.5   bertha]   Collar.

260.14–16   "Oh my beloved . . . God!"]   From "Sinners in the Hands of an Angry God," sermon preached on July 8, 1741, in Enfield, CT, by American divine Jonathan Edwards (1703–1758).

260.27–28   "*Dis, cousin Jacques! . . . non?*"]   French: "Speak up, cousin James! Will you come with us to Quebec—yes or no?"

260.31–32   persecution . . . Nantes]   The Edict of Nantes, proclaimed by Henry IV of France in 1598, gave political rights and protections to Protestants and established peace between Protestants and Catholics after decades of civil and religious conflict. After the edict's revocation by Louis XIV in 1685, the nation's Huguenot minority was terrorized.

262.9–10   our "Jukes and Kallikaks"]   *The Kallikak Family: A Study in the Heredity of Feeble-Mindedness* (1912), by American psychologist Henry H. Goddard (1866–1957), and *The Jukes: A Study of Crime, Pauperism, Disease and Heredity* (1877), by American sociologist Richard Louis Dugdale (1841–1883), were influential studies in the field of eugenics.

262.34   the "Gracchi"]   The ancient Roman brothers Tiberius Sempronius (c.163–133 BCE) and Gaius Sempronius (c. 154–121 BCE), who as tribunes were populist reformers and were therefore assassinated.

265.35–36   Trafalgar . . . Nelson]   On October 21, 1805, during the Napoleonic Wars, the British navy, commanded by Admiral Lord Nelson (1758–1805), decisively defeated the French and Spanish navies off the coast of Spain. During the engagement, Nelson was killed.

267.23   Milton's poem]   I.e., *Paradise Lost.*

267.30   "*Υ a . . . diable!*"]   French: "He has a drop of the handsome devil's own blood!"

267.34–39, 268.3   "*Maman, est-ce que nous . . . Et mouche-toi!*"]   French: "Mama, are we . . . are we . . . ?" / "What? Are we—?" / "Are we descended from . . . Him?" / "Quiet, you little fool. We are relatives of the Empress. That's enough, I should think." / "But, Mama, answer me." // "Quiet, little silly. And blow your nose!"

268.36   *romans roses*]   French: pink novels; i.e., romance novels.

269.2–3   Chevalier Bayards, Joséphines]   Pierre Terrail, Chevalier de Bayard (1473–1524), was known as the valiant and chivalrous "knight without fear and beyond reproach." Joséphine de Beauharnais (1763–1814), glamorous first wife of Napoleon, was born on Martinique.

270.2   *le petit à Beaurepaire*]   French: the little one from Beaurepaire (a town in France).

270.11   *le vert de houx*]   French: green holly, used as a coloring agent.

278.16   *grain de beauté*]   French: beauty mark.

288.23   scamooter]   Slang: a petty thief, a swindler.

290.17–18   *feuilletés* and *entrelacements*]   French: layers and interlacings.

290.36–37   Mr. Watt . . . inoculations]   Scottish inventor James Watt (1736–1819) improved the design of the steam engine, contributing to the Industrial Revolution. English scientist Edward Jenner (1749–1823), known as the "Father of Immunology," developed the smallpox vaccine.

291.15–16   great Tsar . . . serfs]   Peter the Great (1672–1725), modernizing ruler who began construction of Russia's capital, St. Petersburg, in 1703; Czar Alexander II (1818–1881), whose Emancipation Manifesto (1861) freed the Russian serfs.

296.40–297.1   the greatest . . . Negro]   Russian writer Alexander Pushkin (1799–1837) was the great-grandson, on his mother's side, of Abram Hannibal, an Abyssinian nobleman who was purchased as a slave by Peter the Great. Pushkin recounted the traditions associated with his ancestor in the novella "The Negro of Peter the Great" (1837).

303.6   *Ben-Hur*]   *Ben-Hur: A Tale of the Christ* (1880), enormously popular novel by American writer Lew Wallace (1827–1905).

304.22–23   *faute de mieux*]   French: for lack of something better.

307.12–13   The Golden . . . Poetry]   *Golden Treasury of the Best Songs and Lyrical Poems in the English Language* (first edition, 1861), widely read anthology of English poetry edited by Francis Turner Palgrave (1824–1897).

307.24   *With Clive* . . . Henty books]   English novelist George Alfred Henty (1832–1902) wrote many works of historical fiction, including *With Clive in India, or The Beginnings of an Empire* (1884) about Robert Clive, 1st Baron Clive (1725–1774), the English military officer who was largely responsible for establishing the supremacy of the East India Company. At the battle of Plassey in 1757 the British army under Clive decisively defeated the Nawab of Bengal and his French allies, confirming British dominance in Bengal and southern India.

311.37–38   *diseuses*]   French: female reciters.

312.2   *Athalie* and *Britannicus*]   Plays, respectively from 1691 and 1669, by French dramatist Jean Racine (1639–1699).

312.4–5   Molière's miser and his casket]   French playwright Jean-Baptiste Poquelin (1622–1673), known as Molière, wrote his satirical comedy *L'Avare* (*The Miser*) in 1668; its moneylender protagonist Harpagon keeps his money in a small casket buried in his garden.

314.16   *Va te coucher, chérie*]   French: "Go to bed, darling."

315.10–11   Pascal and Bossuet]   French authors Blaise Pascal (1623–1662), mathematician and philosopher, and Jacques-Bénigne Bossuet (1627–1704), theologian and orator.

317.31–32   *Dieu!* . . . *Aide-nous!*]   French: "God! God! We are poor creatures. Help us!"

323.38   *Saul*]   Oratorio (1739) by George Frideric Handel.

327.13–14   *Je t'embrasse mille fois*]   French: "I embrace you a thousand times."

328.34   *Je t'embrasse fort*]   French: "A big hug."

330.2   *ishkabibble*]   "Who cares?" (slang expression, perhaps of Yiddish origin).

331.14   Paryas]   Low-caste Hindus (i.e., pariahs).

332.29–30   As another actor said . . . *tyrannis*]   American actor John Wilkes Booth (1838–1865) shouted "Sic semper tyrannis" ("Thus always to tyrants") during his assassination of Abraham Lincoln. The Latin phrase is the Virginia state motto and is thought to have been said by Brutus at the assassination of Julius Caesar.

334.22–24   We do . . . mercy]   *The Merchant of Venice*, IV.i.200–202.

336.35–36   Cleanse . . . heart]   *Macbeth*, V.iii.44–45.

337.12   The truth will make you free]   Cf. John 8:32.

337.19   'made whole.']   John 5:6.

337.30   *Maman! Qu'est-ce que tu as?*]   French: "Mama! What's the matter?"

354.23   Aristides]   Conservative Athenian statesman and military commander (530–468 BCE), ally of Themistocles, and known as "Aristides the Just."

354.33   *Milchkaffee*]   German: coffee with milk.

361.20   *Malade Imaginaire, Tartuffe*]   Titular characters of Molière's plays from 1673 (*The Imaginary Invalid*) and 1664, respectively.

361.24   *Charbonville*]   "Coaltown" in French.

362.39   *Pilgrim's Progress*]   *The Pilgrim's Progress* (1678), an allegory by John Bunyan (1628–1688) about its protagonist Christian's journey to the Celestial City.

363.2   Lycurgus . . . Aristides]   Lycurgus (c. 800–730 BCE), legendary founder of Sparta's political system; Epaminondas (410–362 BCE), Theban military and political leader who defeated the Spartans and was renowned for his generosity and incorruptibility; Solon (c. 640–558 BCE), Greek statesman and poet, founder of Athenian democracy; Aristides, see note 354.23.

363.4–5   tyrannicides and warriors . . . Brutus]   Cassius (d. 42 BCE), Roman general who with Marcus Junius Brutus (85–42 BCE) and others conspired to assassinate Julius Caesar; Cincinnatus (519–430 BCE), Roman warrior and statesman legendary for his virtue; Horatius Cocles, Roman hero who in the sixth century BCE held back the Etruscan army of Porsenna from the wooden Sublician bridge until it could be demolished, then swam across the Tiber to safety.

369.22   'Make straight . . . God.']   See Isaiah 40.3.

369.28   stone . . . rejected]   Cf. Psalm 118:20, Luke 20:17.

369.29–30   'God moves . . . perform.']   The opening lines of "Light Shining Out of Darkness" (1774), hymn by English poet William Cowper (1731–1800).

369.36–37   the tree . . . Jesse]   Cf. Isaiah 11:1.

371.8   flaming walls of the world]   *Flammantia moenia mundi*, term used by the philosopher Titus Lucretius Carus (c. 94–c. 55 BCE) in book 1 of his didactic poem *De rerum natura* (*On the Nature of Things*) to describe the sphere that surrounds the earth.

THEOPHILUS NORTH

375.1   THEOPHILUS NORTH]   The following paragraphs are taken from an incomplete essay that Wilder intended to serve as a preface to *Theophilus North*:

Throughout a long lifetime every man acquires a certain number of generalized ideas about human experience that he feels to be peculiarly his own. They are his own not necessarily because they are original with him but because he has lived with them—applied them, modified them, tested them, rejected them then readopted them. The sign that they are not merely notions is that they have the capability of growth—observation confirms them—and of consolidation, they are like snowflakes on a window pane; they form clusters and patterns. Some he received as a child from tradition (and from among these he rejected many); some from reading; some from chance remarks overheard. Some long latent within him were clarified by crisis and distilled by reflection. Some, though considerably developed, were discarded as the result of an enlightenment.

He has given to them a name—a private and absurdly pretentious name: they are "deposits of radium."

This book is constantly informed by a number of these "clusters of energy."

Here are some of them: All men aspire to excellence. All men strive to incorporate elements of the Absolute into their lives. These efforts are doomed to failure. Every man is an archer whose arrow is aimed to the center of the target; but our arrows are leaden, their feathers are ill [ms. illegible] our eyesight is imperfect; our education has failed to distinguish the true from the false targets; the strength in our arm is insufficiently developed. All men aspire to incorporate elements of the Absolute into their lives.

To the impassioned will all things be possible. The founder of the Christian faith is reported to have said, "If you have faith [as a grain of] mustard seed, you shall say unto this mountain, be removed, and it will [remove] and [——] and it shall be open to you. And all things are possible to those who love God." That is, of course, absurd. Something must be the matter with all "the terms of reference." As I have often amused myself by saying, "Hope never changed tomorrow's weather." Yet . . . yet . . . history abounds with achievements that fill us with wonder.

All men aspire to excellence. The very crimes against the human race are derived from the "dream" of establishing an orderly existence. War itself is the "dream" of eliminating bad men and bad societies. All energy is the corruption of an aspiration to excellence. Gold is exhausted radium and lead is exhausted gold.

It is a basic condition of the human mind to wish to be free. The desire is noble and wreaks a large part of the harm in public and private life.

What does a man do with his despair?

Greek myth tells us that a direct view of Medusa's head turned a man to stone. Perseus gazed only at her reflection in his shield, cut off her head and rescued Andromeda.

Pascal said: "Neither the sun nor death permit themselves to be looked at fixedly."

At the margin of every man's consciousness is the knowledge that he must die and that the universe must have an end; i.e., the possibility that all the efforts to achieve an orderly world are doomed—that existence is an absurdity and a farce.

What does a man do with his despair, his rage, his frustration?

There is a wide variety of things he does with it.

One or other of them is pictured in each of the chapters of this book. . . .

376.1   Robert Maynard Hutchins]   American educator and author, Wilder's lifelong friend (1899–1977).

384.12–13   "Hard-hearted Hannah"]   Popular song (1924) with music by American composer Milton Ager (1893–1979) and his frequent collaborator, lyricist Jack Yellen (1892–1991), along with Bob Bigelow and Charles Bates.

388.27   As Goethe said]   In "Wanderers Nachtlied II" ("Wayfarer's Night Song II," 1780).

390.34–35   Schliemann's . . . nine cities]   German archaeologist Heinrich Schliemann (1822–1890) calculated that Homer's Troy was buried beneath present-day Hissarlik in Turkey and began excavating the site in 1871. Based on his discoveries he theorized that there were nine Troys, one built on top of another over the centuries.

391.13   Rochambeau]   Jean-Baptiste Donatien de Vimeur, comte de Rochambeau (1725–1807), French nobleman and soldier, commander of French forces sent to help the Continental Army in the American Revolutionary War.

392.1   John Louis Rudolph Agassiz]   Swiss-American naturalist and Harvard professor (1807–1873).

393.1–2   ill-fated Stanford White]   Influential American architect (1853–1906), dramatically murdered in Madison Square Garden by millionaire Harry Thaw because of his affair with Evelyn Nesbit, Thaw's wife.

397.10   Bevo]   Non-alcoholic "near-beer," produced by Anheuser-Busch brewers and popular during Prohibition.

398.11   cully]   Fellow, mate (slang).

405.17   Dr. Grenfell]   Sir Wilfred Grenfell (1865–1940), English medical missionary in Labrador and Newfoundland.

420.21–26   *Then the fair-tressed . . . Troy*]   From *Iliad*, bk. 1.

423.10   Paderewski]   Ignacy Jan Paderewski (1860–1941), Polish pianist, composer, and diplomat.

423.38–39   Palladian . . . Brenta]   In the style of influential Italian architect Andrea Palladio (1508–1580), many of whose classical-inspired villas were built near Vicenza, some near the River Brenta.

424.30   Elihu Yale]   English merchant and philanthropist (1649–1721) whose gift of books helped start the Collegiate School of Connecticut, which in 1718 changed its name in his honor to Yale College.

427.39–428.1   *The Trumpet Shall Sound*]   Four-act play written by Thornton Wilder as a Yale undergraduate, and published serially in 1919–20 in the college's undergraduate literary magazine. It was awarded Yale's Bradford Brinton Award and, as revised, was produced Off-Broadway in 1926.

436.26–27   Nita Naldi's . . . Ethel Barrymore's]   Nita Naldi (1894–1961), American silent film actor; Ethel Barrymore (1879–1959), American stage and screen star from a famous family of actors.

438.18–19   Where duty . . . there]   Cf. st. 3 of "Stand Up, Stand Up for Jesus," hymn with words (1858) written by George Duffield Jr. (1818–1888) and later set to a tune (1830) written by George James Webb (1803–1887).

440.39   *mutter-nackt*]   German: naked as a newborn (literally "mother-naked").

441.8–9   *Du bist . . . Vorwärts*]   German: "You're a good fellow! Let's go!"

442.5   Worth]   Charles Frederick Worth (1825–1895), English fashion designer and renowned couturier, founder of the House of Worth in Paris.

442.9–11   your Emperor . . . Ischl]   Franz Joseph I (1830–1916), emperor of Austria from 1848 until his death, had a summer residence at Bad Ischl, a spa town in central Austria.

447.3   *exigeants*]   French: exacting.

448.32   "The Last Rose of Summer"]   Song written by Irish composer Sir John Stevenson (1761–1833) to a poem (1805) by Irish poet Thomas Moore (1779–1852).

448.34   Madame Schumann-Heink]   Ernestine Schumann-Heink (1861–1936), Austrian-American contralto.

448.34   'The Rosary']   Sentimental song (1898) with music by American composer Ethelbert Nevin (1862–1901) and words by American poet and publisher Robert Cameron Rogers (1862–1912).

450.16   Mount Vernon]   George Washington's estate in Virginia.

451.15–16   *the Kneisel Quartet*]   Renowned American string quartet, the first full-time professional string quartet in the United States, formed in 1885 by Franz Kneisel (1865–1926), first violinist of the Boston Symphony.

453.32   *Irasci . . . essem*]   Latin: I am quick to anger, and as quickly appeased. From *Epistles*, I.xx.25, by Roman poet Quintus Horatius Flaccus (65–8 BCE).

454.34–35   my old friend Mr. Gibbon]   English historian Edward Gibbon (1737–1794), author of *The History of the Decline and Fall of the Roman Empire* (1776–88).

456.15–16   *Vous . . . France*]   French: "You speak French, sir?" / "I spent a year in France."

456.37–38   George Berkeley]   Anglo-Irish philosopher (1685–1753) noted for his writings on subjective idealism. In 1728, newly married, he set out for America, landed at Newport, and lived for four years on a plantation nearby, "Whitehall," in Middletown, Rhode Island. After his return to London, he was named Bishop of Cloyne in Ireland.

457.35–36, 39   Alfred North Whitehead . . . Gasset]   Alfred North Whitehead, English mathematician and philosopher (1861–1947); Bertrand Russell, English philosopher and social critic (1872–1970), coauthor with Whitehead of *Principia Mathematica* (1910); Henri Bergson, French philosopher (1859–1941); Benedetto Croce, Italian philosopher (1866–1952); Giovanni Gentile, Italian philosopher (1875–1944); Ludwig Wittgenstein, Austrian philosopher (1889–1951); Miguel de Unamuno, Spanish philosopher (1864–1936); José Ortega y Gasset, Spanish philosopher (1883–1955).

458.3   Pharos]   The lighthouse on the island of Pharos off the coast of Alexandria, one of the Seven Wonders of the Ancient World.

458.28   Gustavus Adolphus]   Gustav II Adolf (1594–1632), king of Sweden from 1611 until his death at the Battle of Lützen. By his military and diplomatic prowess he initiated the Golden Age of Sweden.

458.31–32   *The Analyst*]   Berkeley's *The Analyst* (1734), subtitled "A DISCOURSE Addressed to an Infidel MATHEMATICIAN [Isaac Newton]. WHEREIN It is examined whether the Object, Principles and Inferences of the modern Analysis are more distinctly conceived, or more evidently deduced, than Religious Mysteries and Points of Faith." It is the source of the quote at 459.1–4.

458.34   Leibnitz]   Gottfried Leibniz, German philosopher (1646–1716).

458.36   Edmund Halley]   English astronomer (1656–1742) who first calculated the orbit of the comet named for him.

460.8   the Browning Club]   After the death of English poet Robert Browning (1812–1889), a number of so-called Browning Societies sprang up around the world, dedicated to the appreciation of Browning's work and that of his wife, poet Elizabeth Barrett Browning (1806–1861).

460.15   George Bancroft]   American historian (1800–1891).

464.36–37   'object all sublime'] From act two of *The Mikado* (1885),
comic opera by W. S. Gilbert (1836–1911) and Arthur Sullivan (1842–1900):
"My object all sublime / I shall achieve in time— / To let the punishment fit
the crime."

472.31   Cassius Marcellus . . . Gaul"] Famous Roman marble copy of a
Hellenistic statue, made around 230 BCE (and for centuries called "The Dying
Gladiator"). The Gallic hairstyle and moustache are distinctive, but not necessarily associated with Vercingetorix, Gallic chieftain (c. 82–46 BCE), defeated
at the Battle of Alesia by the forces of Julius Caesar in 52 BCE.

473.25   Croce on . . . Vico] Croce's *The Philosophy of Giambattista Vico*
(1911). Vico (1668–1744) was an Italian philosopher.

477.14–15   Westward . . . way] From st. six of Berkeley's poem "On the
Prospect of Planting Arts and Learning in America" (1752).

481.29–30   my brother and Bob Hutchins] Thornton Wilder's older
brother, Amos Niven Wilder (1895–1993), biblical scholar and poet, and Robert Maynard Hutchins (see note 376.1).

481.35   *jeunesse dorée*] French: gilded youth.

482.1   Elizabethan Club] Social club at Yale University founded in 1911
and named after Queen Elizabeth I of England; members are elected based on
their witty conversation.

483.35–36   Richthofen] Manfred von Richthofen (1892–1918), ace German fighter pilot during World War I, popularly known as the Red Baron.

485.2–4   to say nothing . . . later war] See Chronology, 1945 entry.

485.27–29   Goethe . . . daily] See the passage from Goethe's letter to
Schiller, December 13, 1803, translated by Matthew Arnold in his essay "On
Translating Homer" (1861): "From Homer and Polygnotus I every day learn
more clearly that in our life here above ground we have, properly speaking, to
enact Hell." Arnold then remarks, "If the student must absolutely have a key-
note to the *Iliad*, let him take this of Goethe."

487.39   what New Englanders call 'near'] I.e., stingy.

489.4–5   General Pershing] American commander John J. Pershing
(1860–1948), leader of the American Expeditionary Forces in World War I.

489.23   *linguiça*] A spicy pork sausage that originated in Portugal.

491.24   drove like Jehu] I.e., recklessly, from 2 Kings 9:20: "and the
driving is like the driving of Jehu the son of Nimshi; for he driveth furiously."

495.31   American 'big three'] The Medal of Honor, the Distinguished
Service Cross, and the Distinguished Service Medal.

496.21–26   *Na ja . . . sagen*]   German: "Well yes, Major, I know you." / "And I know you, dear Colonel. You are Colonel Vanderwinkle, right?" / "Indeed. Wasn't it a pity what happened at the Saint-Charles-of-the-Mills ridge? You broke my left wing there. You were a devil, it's fair to say."

497.36   Asmodius]   More often spelled "Asmodeus," the king of demons in the Book of Tobit.

497.37   Bellerophon]   Hero of Greek mythology, famed for slaying the Chimera. See *Iliad*, bk. 4, 155–203.

499.24   Prudentius]   Aurelius Prudentius Clemens (c. 348–c. 413), Roman Christian poet.

499.25   Candidus]   St. Candidus (d. 287), Theban soldier and Christian martyr.

506.25   George Washington Greene]   American historian (1811–1883), college classmate and lifelong friend of Henry Wadsworth Longfellow.

506.26   Agassiz families . . . great son]   Alexander Agassiz (1835–1910), son of Louis Agassiz (see note 392.1), was himself a noted zoologist, oceanographer, and mine operator.

507.29   "Eureka!"]   Poe's final book, the cosmological treatise *Eureka: A Prose Poem* (1848).

509.12   Elzevirs]   A family of prominent Dutch printers and publishers in the seventeenth and eighteenth centuries.

513.29–30   "Thick . . . Vallombrosa."]   Milton, *Paradise Lost*, bk. 1, lines 302–3.

515.33–34   *Hiawatha* and *Evangeline*]   *The Song of Hiawatha* (1855) and *Evangeline: A Tale of Acadie* (1847), two famous poems by Henry Wadsworth Longfellow.

519.29   'A Psalm of Life,']   The most frequently quoted poem from Henry Wadsworth Longfellow's first collection, *Voices of the Night* (1839).

521.13   Bowditch]   Nathaniel Bowditch (1773–1838), American mathematician and astronomer credited with founding modern maritime navigation.

521.36   the Hawkshaw eye]   "Hawkshaw" was slang for a detective, derived from a character in *The Ticket-of-Leave Man* (1863), play by English dramatist Tom Taylor (1817–1880).

532.20–22   Canst thou not . . . heart?]   See note 336.35–36.

535.18–19   Héloise and Abelard]   The French theologian Pierre Abélard (1079–1142) fell in love with his pupil Héloïse, and the couple conceived a child together. At the instigation of Héloïse's uncle, Abélard was castrated. They continued their relationship via letters.

536.37   *derrière . . . cabinet*]   French: rear, go to bed, toilet.

539.16   "*Voulez-vous . . . moi?*"]   French: "Do you want to go to bed with me?"

539.17–18   '*Tuc . . . t'accompagne?*']   French: "You are alone, my sweet. Would you like me to accompany you?"

539.20   '*Tu . . . verre?*']   French: "Do you want to buy me a drink?"

539.25–26   "*Pas ce soir.*"]   French: "Not tonight."

540.19–33   "*Bonsoir . . . amie.*"]   French: "Good evening, my pet." / "Good evening, miss." / "You're alone. Would you like to amuse me a little?" / "I'm busy this evening. . . . Thanks." / [. . .] "Perhaps another time. You're charming." / "A-o-o! . . . Say then: just a half-hour, sweet. I have a pretty room with all the latest American gadgets. One can amuse himself to distraction." / [. . .] "Miss, I'm late. I really must go. But another time." / [. . .] "Good luck, sweetheart."

542.14–29   "*Bonsoir, Monseigneur . . . suivre.*"]   French: "Good evening, my Lord. You do us a great honor." / "Ah, Henri-Paul, how are you?" / "Very well, my Lord, thank you." / "And your wife. How is she?" / "Very well, my Lord. She thanks you." / "And your dear children?" / "Very well, my Lord, thank you." / "Well then! This is your son? . . . What is your name, sir? Frederick? Like your grandfather! My grandfather was a great friend of your grandfather. —Tell me, Henri-Paul, I had asked for a table for three. Would it still be possible to add a fourth? I've invited the Duc de Montmorency. Would that be alright?" / "Certainly, my Lord. The Duke has arrived and awaits you. If your Highness will kindly follow me."

543.6–7   "*Mes amis . . . monde.*"]   French: "My friends, the streets are *so* jammed; it's the end of the world."

549.31–32   "*Ah, Monsieur Nort' . . . Desmoulins*]   French: "Ah, Mr. North, what a pleasure to see you again. I am Denise Desmoulins . . ."

550.18   *Mrs. Wiggs of the Cabbage Patch*]   Best-selling novel (1901) by American writer Alice Hegan Rice (1870–1942).

551.18–22   *Emma Woodhouse . . . her*]   The opening of *Emma* (1815), novel by English writer Jane Austen (1775–1817).

552.20–21   *Daisy Miller . . . young*]   American novelist Henry James (1843–1916) lived as a teenager with his parents in Newport on two occasions. His novella *Daisy Miller* appeared in 1878; his unfinished novel *The Ivory Tower*, set in Newport, was published posthumously in 1917.

560.30–31   *Eine Kleine . . . corpus*]   Mozart's Serenade No. 13 for strings in G Major, K. 525 (1787), known as "A Little Night Music," and his motet "Ave verum corpus" ("Hail, true body [of Christ]"), K. 618 (1791), written for the feast of Corpus Christi.

567.1–2   Now go . . . banishment]   *As You Like It*, I.iii.137–38.

567.3   Ellen Terry]   English Shakespearean actor (1847–1928).

567.6–7   I am all . . . too]   *Twelfth Night*, II.iv.120–21.

567.8   Julia Marlowe]   English-born American Shakespearean actor (1865–1950).

569.3–6   PORTIA . . . that!]   *The Merchant of Venice*, VI.i.181–84.

574.7   Butterick patterns]   Tissue paper dress patterns in various sizes, first issued in 1863 by American tailor and inventor Ebenezer Butterick (1826–1903).

578.15–17   *L'alba . . . marina*]   Dante, *Purgatorio*, I.115–17: "The dawn was vanquishing the matin hour which fled before it, so that I recognized from afar the trembling of the sea" (trans. Charles S. Singleton).

578.24   Mino da Fiesole]   Italian sculptor (c. 1429–1484) celebrated for his portrait busts.

582.24–25   *Opus elegantissimum, juvenis!*]   Latin: Most elegant work, young man!

587.9–10   Antigones . . . Eteocleses]   The two daughters and two sons of Oedipus and Jocasta in Greek mythology.

587.26–27   *Grüss Gott . . . Herrn!*]   German: "Greetings, Baron!" / "Ah, Professor! Praise the Lord!"

587.31   *Schön!*]   German: wonderful!

587.36   *punkt*]   German: on the dot.

588.13–14   *Gott hilf uns . . . Wiederschaun*]   German: "God help us. You're a devil of a fellow." / "Till next time."

593.27–28   Give me . . . appetite]   *Inferno*, XIV.91–93.

594.22   *Ave atque vale!*]   Latin: "Hail and farewell!" From the last line of the elegy for his brother, "Multas per gentes," by Roman poet Gaius Valerius Catullus (c. 84–c. 54 BCE).

594.31   Magna Graecia]   Latin: Greater Greece—i.e., the extended network of Greek colonies established in the eighth and seventh centuries BCE. It included Sicily and parts of the southern Italian peninsula.

596.17–18   Mendelssohn's "Oh, That We Two Were Maying"]   Poem by Charles Kingsley (1819–1875), set to music not by German composer Felix Mendelssohn (1809–1847) but by French composer Charles Gounod (1818–1893), American composer Ethelbert Nevin (1862–1901), and English composer Alice Mary Smith (1839–1884).

596.23   Pergolesi's *Stabat Mater*] Italian composer Giovanni Battista Pergolesi (1710–1736) wrote his *Stabat Mater* ("The sorrowful mother stood") in 1736.

599.24   Knight of the Two-Headed Eagle] An honorary order of the Freemason brotherhood.

600.14   Grillparzer] Austrian dramatist and novelist Franz Grillparzer (1791–1872).

601.37–38   *Caro . . . Ben*] Song ("My dearest, believe me") by Italian composer Giuseppe Giordani (1751–1798).

605.18–19   Hell is *they*] Wilder's translation of "L'enfer, c'est les autres," phrase from the play *Huis Clos* (*No Exit*, 1944) by Jean-Paul Sartre (1905–1980), French philosopher, novelist, and playwright.

619.11–12   hymn . . . *near*] Most likely "Yield Not to Temptation" (1868), gospel hymn by Horatio Richmond Palmer (1834–1907), though it does not contain the words "Jesus is near."

622.3–4   *Le Médecin malgré lui*] Play (*The Doctor in Spite of Himself*, 1666) by Molière.

622.28–29   the famous park in Copenhagen] Dyrehaven (Deer Park), park on former royal hunting ground in Klampenborg, a northern suburb of Copenhagen.

623.18   Whittier's poem] "The Barefoot Boy" (1855), by American poet John Greenleaf Whittier (1807–1892).

625.4   Landseer] English painter Sir Edwin Landseer (1802–1873), whose specialty was paintings of animals.

627.10–12   Was it Rousseau . . . wonder?] French philosopher and writer Jean-Jacques Rousseau (1712–1778) wrote an influential novel on child development, *Émile ou de l'éducation* (1762).

628.16   *l'explication de texte*] French: explication of the text, a method of literary analysis that prefers objective "close reading" of a text's style and imagery.

635.28–29   John Drew . . . Gillette] Irish-American actor John Drew (1827–1862); English actor Cyril Maude (1862–1951); American actor William Gillette (1853–1937).

637.1–2   Stone walls . . . cage] Lines from the final stanza of "To Althea, from Prison," poem (c. 1642) by English poet Richard Lovelace (1618–1657).

638.4–5   Otis Skinner in *The Honor of the Family*] American actor Otis Skinner (1858–1942) was lauded for playing the comic villain Colonel Phillipe

Bridau (see 638.13–14) in *The Honor of The Family*, based on Balzac's novel *La Rabouilleuse* (1842) and adapted for the stage in 1903 by French dramatist Émile Fabre (1869–1955). The play opened on Broadway in 1908.

638.36   Dr. de Martel] French neurosurgeon Thierry de Martel (1875–1940), chief surgeon at the American Hospital of Paris at Neuilly, just outside the city.

639.1   novelist "Gyp"] Pseudonym of Sibylle de Riquetti-Mirabeau, comtesse de Martel de Janville (1849–1932), satiric French writer.

648.23–24   I've warmed . . . depart] From "I Strove with None" (1849), poem by English poet Walter Savage Landor (1775–1864).

652.14–16   Bach's music . . . *fällt*] Three cantatas by German composer Johann Sebastian Bach (1685–1750): "Oh God, How Much Heartache" (1725), "Hold in Remembrance Jesus Christ" (1724), and "Like Rain and Snow Falling from the Sky" (c. 1713).

653.32–33   hymn . . . *Zeit*] "God's Time is the Best Time," sacred cantata (1708) also known as the *Actus Tragicus*.

653.34–35   *Ich bin müde . . . Mann*] German: "I am tired. Thank you, young man."

655.17–18   "Then felt I . . . ken."] John Keats, "On First Looking into Chapman's Homer" (1816), lines 9–10.

660.37   Adeline Genée] Danish-English ballet dancer (1878–1970).

661.14   *Zum Wohl!*] German: To your health!

663.20–21   Be thou . . . calumny] *Hamlet*, III.i.135–36.

669.35–36   *Alciphron . . .* Berkeley] *Alciphron, or the Minute Philosopher* (1732), Berkeley's defense of religion.

672.35   pistes] French: trails.

682.21   "La Argentina"] Stage name of Antonia Mercé y Luque (1890–1936), Argentinian flamenco dancer.

692.27   *Charmes d'amour . . . peindre?*] Cf. "Charme de l'amour, qui pourrait vous peindre!" ("Charm of love, who could paint you!"), in chap. 4 of *Adolphe* (1816), novel by Swiss-French writer Benjamin Constant (1767–1830).

703.34   Busoni's] Italian composer Ferruccio Busoni (1866–1924) made many transcriptions of Bach's music, and in 1920 made an important edition of Bach's solo keyboard music.

704.5–7   *In Dir . . . sein*] Two chorale preludes for organ by Bach as transcribed for piano by Busoni: "In Thee Is Gladness" and "When We Are in Direst Need," part of Bach's incomplete *Orgelbüchlein* (*Little Organ Book*),

begun and written mostly during his Weimar period (1708–17); the latter pre-
lude was also revised shortly before Bach's death in 1750.

708.5–6   the words of Glaukos]   Cf. *Iliad*, bk. 6.

AUTOBIOGRAPHICAL WRITINGS

717.13   Heraclitus said]   The remark is in fact attributed to the pre-Socratic
Greek philosopher Protagoras of Abdera (c. 490–420 BCE).

719.24   history recently published]   John Kobler, *Luce: His Time, Life,
and Fortune* (1968). American publisher Henry Luce (1898–1967) was founder
and editor-in-chief of *Time* and *Fortune* magazines, among others.

731.28   the Wiffenpoofs]   Founded in 1909 at Yale, the oldest collegiate a
cappella singing group in America. They were named for a term introduced in
Irish-American composer Victor Herbert's opera *Little Nemo* (1908). Their
most famous member is Cole Porter.

734.22–23   *Die Kaiser Wilhelm Schule sogar*]   German: Even the Kaiser
Wilhelm School.

737.23–25   Archie MacLeish . . . Roger Sessions]   American poet Archi-
bald MacLeish (1892–1982), Yale class of 1916; American book collector and
scholar Wilmarth Sheldon Lewis (1895–1979), Yale class of 1918; American
poet and lyricist Brian Hooker (1880–1946), Yale class of 1902, best known for
his stage adaptation of Edmond Rostand's *Cyrano de Bergerac* and his work
with Czech-American composer Rudolf Friml (1879–1972); American songwriter Cole Porter (1891–1964), Yale class of 1913; American actor Monty
Woolley (1888–1963), Yale class of 1911, best known for his performance in the
play (1939) and movie (1942) of *The Man Who Came to Dinner*, by George S.
Kaufman and Moss Hart; American author and labor activist Charles Rumford
Walker (1893–1974), Yale class of 1916; American composer Roger Sessions
(1896–1985), who, after graduating from Harvard at age 18, came to Yale to
pursue graduate studies in music.

737.27–28   Mademoiselle Gaby Deslys]   Madeline Claire (1884?–1920),
French dancer and actor famous for her jewelry and her liaisons with royalty.

737.30   Stephen Vincent Benét]   American poet and story writer (1898–
1943), Yale class of 1919; his first book of poems was *Five Men and Pompey*
(1915).

737.33   Johnny Farrar]   American editor, writer, and publisher John C.
Farrar (1896–1974), Yale class of 1919, founded the publishing houses Farrar &
Rinehart and Farrar, Straus and Giroux, as well as the Bread Loaf Writers'
Conference.

737.33   Professor Jack Crawford]   American author and teacher Jack Ran-
dall Crawford (1878–1968) was a professor in the Yale English Department and
offered an early course in contemporary drama.

737.34   Philip Barry]   American dramatist (1896–1949), Yale class of 1919, whose best-known plays include *Holiday* (1928) and *The Philadelphia Story* (1939).

737.35   Harry Luce and Brit Hadden]   Luce (see note 719.24) and Briton Hadden (1898–1929), both Yale class of 1920, cofounded *Time* magazine in 1923.

737.37   Walter Millis . . . Coates]   American journalist and historical author Walter Millis (1899–1968), Yale class of 1920; American journalist, biographer and novelist John Franklin Carter (1897–1967), left Yale to work in Italy as a newspaper correspondent; American novelist and art critic Robert M. Coates (1897–1973), Yale class of 1919, was for forty years the art critic of and a contributor to *The New Yorker.*

738.21   Salzburg during its festival]   In an effort to revive European culture after World War I, an influential group of artists—including the Austrian poet, dramatist, and librettist Hugo von Hofmannsthal (1874–1929), the German composer Richard Strauss (1864–1949), and the Austrian-American stage director Max Reinhardt (1873–1943)—revived in 1920 a summer festival in Mozart's birthplace devoted to opera, chamber music, and theater.

738.35   Paula Wessely]   Austrian actor (1907–2000).

738.36   Dusolina Giannini]   Italian-American soprano (1902–1986).

739.9–10   performances of *Everyman*]   Every year since its founding, the Salzburg Festival opens with a performance in the city's Cathedral Square of *Jedermann*, Hugo von Hofmannsthal's German adaptation of the English medieval morality play, its allegory centered on the struggle of good and evil in a man's soul.

740.3   music . . . breast]   Cf. *The Mourning Bride* (1697), by the English playwright William Congreve (1670–1729): "Music hath charms to soothe a savage breast."

740.20   Stefan Zweig]   Austrian novelist, biographer, and man of letters (1881–1942).

740.21–22   Alexander ——]   The manuscript here is illegible.

741.1   Ferenc Molnár]   Hungarian-born playwright and novelist (1878–1952), who when he immigrated to America in 1940 was known as Franz Molnár. Among his best-known plays are *Liliom* (1909), *The Guardsman* (1910), and *The Swan* (1920).

741.6   Hans Albers]   German actor, singer, and film star (1891–1960).

741.15   Marion Mill Preminger]   Hungarian-American writer (1913–1972), married in 1932 to Austrian-American film director Otto Preminger (1905–1986).

741.16–17   Erich Maria Remarque]   German author (1898–1970) whose most famous work is the antiwar novel *All Quiet on the Western Front* (1929).

742.9–10   Eleonora von Mendelssohn]   German actor (1900–1951), named for Italian actor Eleonora Duse (1858–1924), known as La Dusa.

745.39   Lotte Lehmann]   German-American soprano (1888–1976) associated with the German operatic repertory.

746.2–3   Lilli Lehmann]   German operatic soprano (1848–1929).

THE LIBRARY OF AMERICA SERIES

The Library of America fosters appreciation and pride in America's literary heritage by publishing, and keeping permanently in print, authoritative editions of America's best and most significant writing. An independent nonprofit organization, it was founded in 1979 with seed funding from the National Endowment for the Humanities and the Ford Foundation.

To subscribe to the series or to order individual copies, please visit www.loa.org or call (800) 964.5778.

*This book is set in 10 point Linotron Galliard,
a face designed for photocomposition by Matthew Carter
and based on the sixteenth-century face Granjon. The paper
is acid-free lightweight opaque and meets the requirements
for permanence of the American National Standards Institute.
The binding material is Brillianta, a woven rayon cloth made
by Van Heek-Scholco Textielfabrieken, Holland. Composition by Dedicated Book Services. Printing by
Malloy Incorporated. Binding by Dekker Book-
binding. Designed by Bruce Campbell.*